**"Lycaena, return to us, even if it
must be in blood."**

Dark flame burst from the six pillars, flowing in thin streams to the air above the altar. It collected together, shaped, took form. Fire became flesh and cloth. Light and heat became wing and dress. Keles dropped to her knees, and she wept with dozens of others. "Return to us," Eshiel demanded, and Lycaena answered. Somehow, despite her death, she answered. She came. She lived.

"My goddess," Keles said, eyes wide, hands reaching, soul offered once more to the wondrous being of compassion. A touch upon her fingertips, hot and dripping with blood. In that moment, Keles knew she would never leave. What price Eshiel demanded, she would pay. What lives must be offered, let them be offered. The empire had taken their goddess. Let their soldiers be sacrificed for her return.

"It's true," she said, and wept uncontrollably. She closed her fingers and clutched her fists to her breast so she could feel the residual heat. The years of warfare and despair, of crushing doubt and self-hatred for failing to stop the Anointed One's sacrificial knives, bled away.

"You live. Goddess, you live."

Praise for
David Dalglish

Praise for The Bladed Faith

"Filled with intense action and complex characters who are easy to fall into, *The Bladed Faith* is what might happen if Final Fantasy crossed with *The Way of Shadows*! I loved it!" —Rob J. Hayes, author of *Never Die*

"David Dalglish's beautiful, grandiose and expansive *The Bladed Faith* begins at the roots of a rebellion.... This is a rebellion with soul, and one that promises to reach even greater heights as the series continues. Given Dalglish's track record, don't be surprised if he somehow manages to top the triumphant standard he sets with *The Bladed Faith*."
—*BookPage* (starred review)

"This dark adventure will hook genre fans with its detailed world building, strong characters, and gory, action-packed scenes. Readers who enjoy Mark Lawrence and Erika Johansen will appreciate Thanet's masked, sword-carrying hero and rebel team of misfits, eagerly anticipating a continuation to Dalglish's new series." —*Booklist*

"*The Bladed Faith* is an action-packed start to David Dalglish's new Vagrant Gods series. Full of sorcery, bloodshed, and a surprisingly charming found family, the story's twisty final chapters set up an ending that promises much more excitement to come." —*Paste*

"*The Bladed Faith* is gripping, violent and action-packed. It is also about colonialism, PTSD, fighting the good fight & what it truly means to put your life on the line for what's right. This is David Dalglish at his finest and the Vagrant Gods trilogy promises to be his best story that he's published so far." —*Fantasy Book Critic*

"Dalglish's plotting and pacing are top-notch.... This book is Arkane Studio's Dishonored meets D&D's divine magic."

—*Grimdark Magazine*

Praise for The Keepers

"Dalglish manages to combine familiar elements in exciting ways... that's sure to keep readers turning pages."

—*Publishers Weekly* on *Soulkeeper*

"A dark and lush epic fantasy brimming with magical creatures and terrifying evil.... Dalglish's world building is subtle and fluid, and he weaves the history, magical workings, and governance of his world within the conversations and camaraderie of his characters. Readers of George R. R. Martin and Patrick Rothfuss will find much to enjoy here." —*Booklist* on *Soulkeeper*

"*Soulkeeper* is a fast-paced, page-turning ride with a great, likeable main character in Devin Eveson. It's the definition of entertaining."

—John Gwynne, author of *Malice*

"With strong world building, imaginative monsters, and a capable system of magic, this series will please readers who enjoy dark epic fantasy with engaging characters." —*Booklist* on *Ravencaller*

"Fans will love the second installment of this dark fantasy about very human characters beset by inhuman dangers." —*Kirkus* on *Ravencaller*

By David Dalglish

VAGRANT GODS

The Bladed Faith

The Sapphire Altar

THE KEEPERS

Soulkeeper

Ravencaller

Voidbreaker

SERAPHIM

Skyborn

Fireborn

Shadowborn

SHADOWDANCE

A Dance of Cloaks

A Dance of Blades

A Dance of Mirrors

A Dance of Shadows

A Dance of Ghosts

A Dance of Chaos

Cloak and Spider (novella)

THE SAPPHIRE ALTAR

VAGRANT GODS: BOOK TWO

DAVID DALGLISH

orbitbooks.net

Copyright © 2023 by David Dalglish
Excerpt from *Vagrant Gods: Book Three* copyright © 2023 by David Dalglish
Excerpt from *The Blighted Stars* copyright © 2023 by Megan E. O'Keefe

Cover design by Lauren Panepinto
Cover illustration by Chase Stone
Cover copyright © 2023 by Hachette Book Group, Inc.
Map by Sámhlaoch Swords
Author photograph by Michele Coleman

Orbit
Hachette Book Group
1290 Avenue of the Americas
New York, NY 10104
orbitbooks.net

First Edition: January 2023

Orbit is an imprint of Hachette Book Group.
The Orbit name and logo are trademarks of Little, Brown Book Group Limited.

The publisher is not responsible for websites (or their content) that are not owned by the publisher.

The Hachette Speakers Bureau provides a wide range of authors for speaking events. To find out more, go to hachettespeakersbureau.com or email HachetteSpeakers@hbgusa.com.

Orbit books may be purchased in bulk for business, educational, or promotional use. For information, please contact your local bookseller or the Hachette Book Group Special Markets Department at special.markets@hbgusa.com.

Library of Congress Cataloging-in-Publication Data
Names: Dalglish, David, author.
Title: The sapphire altar / David Dalglish.
Description: First Edition. | New York : Orbit, 2023. | Series: Vagrant gods ; book 2
Identifiers: LCCN 2022026621 | ISBN 9780759557123 (trade paperback) | ISBN 9780759557116 (ebook)
Subjects: LCGFT: Novels.
Classification: LCC PS3604.A376 S37 2023 | DDC 813/.6—dc23
LC record available at https://lccn.loc.gov/2022026621

ISBNs: 9780759557123 (trade paperback), 9780759557116 (ebook)

Printed in the United States of America

LSC-C

Printing 1, 2022

*To Newt and Cherae, who came in and
helped exactly when and where I needed it most*

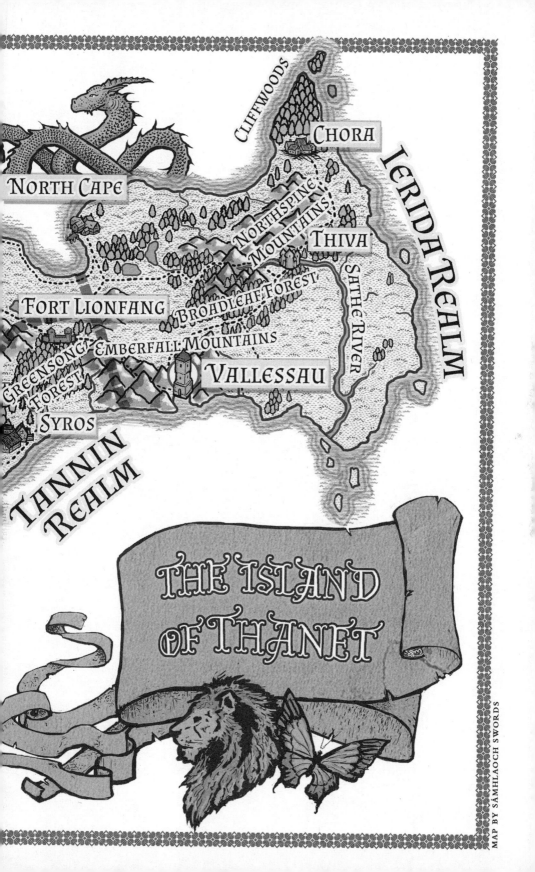

CLIFFWOODS

CHORA

NORTH CAPE

IERIDA REALM

NORTHSPINE MOUNTAINS

THIVA

FORT LIONFANG

BROADLEAF FOREST

SATHE RIVER

EMBERFALL MOUNTAINS

GREENSONG FOREST

VALLESSAU

SYROS

TANNIN REALM

THE ISLAND OF THANET

MAP BY SÁMHLAOCH SWORDS

A REMINDER, FOR THOSE WHO NEED ONE:

The Everlorn Empire invaded the island of Thanet and, to Prince Cyrus Lythan's horror, executed his parents and slaughtered the Lion god, Endarius. Two years later, they publicly execute the Butterfly goddess, Lycaena, despite attempts from the Thanese resistance to stop it. During the following chaos, Cyrus is presumed dead but in truth is rescued by a longtime family friend, the paladin Rayan Vayisa, and brought to the leader of the newly formed resistance: Thorda Ahlai. There Cyrus is made an offer: train under Thorda and become the figurehead of a new resistance. He will become the Vagrant, a skull-faced persona crafted by Thorda to hide Cyrus's identity until the time is right to reveal the believed-dead prince is alive and fighting for his throne.

For two years, Cyrus does just that, trains with Thorda and the rest of his resistance. Much of his time is spent with Stasia Ahlai, known as the Ax of Lahareed, as well as her sister, the shape-shifting god-whisperer Mari, also known as the Lioness. A late arrival is Arn Bastell, the Heretic, a former paragon who comes to Thanet at Thorda's insistence. Reluctant but still willing to fight with them is Keles Lyon, once known as the Light of Vallessau before publicly forsaking her belief in the slain Butterfly goddess to spare her life. Along with her uncle, Rayan, they become a vicious group of killers, attacking the empire at every turn in the island's capital of Vallessau. Their foes? The God-Incarnate's daughter, Sinshei vin Lucavi, her loyal paragon, Soma Ordiae, and the head of the invasion, Imperator Magus of Eldrid.

Their progress is threatened when a group of devout believers in the Vagrant, to whom Cyrus has revealed his true identity, are captured by Magus and scheduled for public hangings. They plan an ambush but are betrayed by a traitor in their organization. The innocents are hung, soldiers attack from all sides, and high atop a bell tower Cyrus faces off against Imperator Magus. During that fight, Magus gloats to Cyrus about the truth of the island—Cyrus's family has done something similar to what the empire has done. Four hundred years ago they arrived on Thanet as invaders, overthrew the ruling Orani family, slew their beloved Serpent god, Dagon, and then buried the truth of their deeds.

Unfortunately for Magus, the sacrifices of the faithful empowered the Vagrant, granting him power akin to the rituals used to empower the empire's paragons. The two duel, with Cyrus killing the Imperator before escaping with the others in the aftermath. His joy is short-lived, for Magus has confirmed a traitor in the organization: Thorda himself. The leader of the resistance wanted the sacrifices of the faithful. He wanted the lives given to the Vagrant, to craft a god of death to finally challenge the empire's God-Incarnate.

After confronting Thorda, Cyrus chooses to abandon the resistance and strike out on his own. He swears to forsake the Vagrant persona, though Thorda insists it shall not be so easy. Meanwhile, boats arrive in Vallessau's harbor, bringing the God-Incarnate's son, Galvanis, to Thanet's shores, where he looks upon the lack of faith with dismay and swears to bring the entire island to heel.

PROLOGUE

KELES

Keles stood in the center of the empty tent, her arms crossed and her hands bound behind her back. The rope dug into her skin as she slowly twisted her wrists. The rational part of her mind said to be afraid, but oddly enough, she felt no fear. She had suffered imprisonment at the hands of the Everlorn Empire. What threat were loyal followers of the slain Lycaena?

Of course, they might not be truly loyal to the Butterfly goddess. Based on their claims, they might even be insane...

The tent flaps opened behind her. She tilted her chin and turned, determined to present herself as calm and honorable despite her current predicament.

"I am Keles Lyon," she told the new arrival, "faithful servant of Thanet, and I demand that you remove my bindings."

Her authoritative tone wilted into surprise before the man towering a good foot taller than her. His head and face were clean-shaven, and twin butterfly wings tattooed in black ink curled up from his eyebrows and across his bald pate. His face was thin and bony, as if he were a few harsh days shy of starvation, and his nose crooked from being broken and not properly healing. He wore a red robe tied with a rope sash and a silver dagger tucked into it. His arms were crossed over his chest, and the loose sleeves of his robe fell back to expose his bare arms. Where there weren't tattoos on his pale skin, there were scars, deep and winding ones more fitting to a man of war than a priest.

"No," he said. His light brown eyes studied her as he paced a circle. "I don't think I will."

"Why not?" she asked. "Do you believe me a threat?"

He continued circling her, his right hand gently stroking his chin. His voice was deeper than the sea and smoother than any wine.

"There's not much left of the little girl I once saw," he said. "But war tends to strip away the vestiges of childhood. I know your face, and I remember your name, but it was not the one you used when we last met."

Keles's insides twisted. She had tried to bury that past.

"I'm not her anymore," she said.

"What did they call you?" this strange priest said, ignoring her protest. Around and around he walked, a wolf prowling a newly discovered lamb. "If I remember right, you were 'the Light of Vallessau,' were you not?"

She flinched at the title. It had been foisted upon her when she was sixteen, the heroine paladin fighting the invading forces of the empire.

"I forfeited any such claim at the forsaking ceremony," she said.

"And yet now you are here, so very far from Vallessau. Might you explain, Keles? Set my mind at ease?"

Keles met his narrowed gaze with a faint smile.

"I will confess no secrets to a man whose name I do not know. Only a fool would do so under such a disadvantage."

The priest drew his dagger.

"Are you a fool, Keles?"

"Do you think me a fool, stranger?"

At last, he smiled. It lit up his narrow face.

"I think you are many things, daughter of Vallessau, but a fool is not one of them."

He curled around her and then cut the ropes that bound her wrists. The severed pieces dropped to the dirt floor of the tent. Keles stretched her shoulders as she rubbed at the raw skin. When he returned to face her, he dipped his head in apology.

"My name is Eshiel Dymling, faithful servant of our beloved goddess, Lycaena."

Tradition would have her salute with her sword, then lay the blade flat over her left arm, but she had been disarmed upon arrival, so instead she lowered her head in greeting.

"Well met, Eshiel. I must admit, I expected a warmer welcome when I came to your little forest camp."

"We must always be watchful for imperial spies. A little silver, and an empty belly, can loosen even loyal tongues."

Now that he had ceased his circling, he faced her directly. She felt judged, but would he find her worthy, or wanting? And why did she suddenly care?

"Your wrists are freed, and our names are shared," he said. "We are as equals, so I ask you again, Light of Vallessau, why have you come to my village?"

The thought of voicing her reasons filled her with embarrassment. They were childish, delusional hopes, yet here she was, two weeks of hard travel into the northern reaches of Thanet, through the Cliff-woods, to an unremarkable little camp lost amid the trees. All for a fool's hope. All for a dream that could not be real. But oh, what a dream it was...

"Certain rumors have reached us in Vallessau," she said. She stared him dead in the eye and challenged him to lie. "I have to know. Is it true?"

Eshiel crossed the wide tent to the entrance, pushed aside the flap, and gestured for her to follow. He still held his dagger.

"Nothing I tell you would ever be enough," he said. "So come see for yourself, if you are willing to endure the blood it costs."

A shiver ran through her. Was it fear, or excitement? This handsome man, he was watching her, studying her. She would not cower. As the Light of Vallessau, she had strode the front lines of the battlefield, her blade gleaming and her shield unbreakable. She feared no spilling of blood.

Together they stepped out into the heart of the bustling camp. Her first impression when she had arrived in the waning evening hours had been of a loose collection of tents and huts built from the surrounding ash trees and then covered with linen. It was orderly and clean despite the meager standard of living. Keles had estimated maybe thirty or forty people lived there while she'd been marched into Eshiel's tent, but that estimate had been off by a wide margin.

"Stay with me," Eshiel said as the train of followers swelled. Hungry, distrusting eyes watched her, and Keles made sure to keep beside him. They walked a well-worn path through the trees to the white cliffs that gave the forest its name, all conversation about them dwindling with each passing step.

The crash of waves greeted the forest edge. Beyond were steep clifftops towering in defiance of the Crystal Sea beyond. The path they walked ended at the highest of the cliffs. Six lit torches awaited. Appointed members of the procession pulled the torches free of the earth and carried them high above their heads. Eshiel led the climb up the incline, where a half circle of tall stones, six in total, lined the narrow clifftop's edge. These pillars were wide at the bottom but slender and curved inward near the top, so they appeared like fingers of a buried giant reaching out from the ground. Moss grew along their wind-blasted gray surfaces. Walking into their center felt like walking into the presence of history. These stones were *old*. Who had placed them, and how many centuries prior?

The sacred feeling of this site was clearly shared by the others. The people accompanying Eshiel and Keles's walk fell silent. No one spoke. The only sound was the muffled shuffling of feet, the rustle of cloth, and the heavy breathing of the elderly. Even the children held their tongues, which was a miracle in and of itself. The young had certainly never shut their mouths during the sermons she'd attended at the Twin Sanctuary.

Then again, the Twin Sanctuary did not possess a massive stone slab in its heart caked in deep red stains that could only be dried blood. A man lay upon it, his hands tied behind his back in the same manner the villagers had bound Keles. His mouth was gagged and his eyes blindfolded. He had been stripped of all clothing but his undergarments. Whether he was unconscious or sleeping, she did not know, but there was at least visible movement of his bruised chest. Two men stood guard over him, clubs in hand.

Keles tried to remain calm when she spoke. To her relief, there wasn't the slightest quiver in her voice.

"Who is that man?"

Eshiel halted just shy of the half circle. The accompanying villagers fanned out to either side, and they moved with a purpose. The torchlight flickered.

"An imperial soldier we captured on patrol to Chora," Eshiel said, referring to the nearby village whose elder had guided Keles into the forest. He loosened the sash to his robe and then shed it so that he was naked from the waist up. All across his muscular body were winding tattoos, and for each tattoo there was a matching scar, some a full foot in length. Whatever had been done to this man, it had been brutal. He turned to her, no more smiles on his face or sharp banter on his tongue. His voice lowered, meant only for her.

"There is no coming back from this, Keles. If you stay, you must share in all of it until the necessary end. I will not blame you for leaving...though I will be disappointed."

The movement of the people ceased, for they had taken their places. Completing the ring, Keles realized. What had been a half circle was now full. Stone and flesh, the everlasting and the ephemeral. Torches burned in the human ring, while only moonlight lit the six weathered pillars. In the center, the prisoner upon an altar, and the man with the knife.

"Lycaena has never preached a need for blood sacrifice," Keles said, feeling the first hints of panic nibbling at her mind.

"And what need was there in a time of peace?" Eshiel asked, this time louder and for all in attendance. "On calm days, the sword stays sheathed, but let it be drawn when night falls and the burglar comes prowling."

The bound man rocked, a moan escaping his lips. He sounded drugged, which would explain his lack of struggle. Faint hope had dragged Keles here, and it died as she watched Eshiel lift the knife. This couldn't be right. This was madness. The people were indulging Eshiel's slaughter of imperial soldiers because they were frightened and angry. It was rebellion framed as ritual. It was war disguised as worship. Stars help her, there were *children* in attendance.

"On this night we give to our beloved goddess," Eshiel continued. The deep rumble of his voice was his thunder; the moonlight shining off his raised dagger, his lightning. Perhaps it was a trick of the light, but it seemed the tattoos across his face and arms glowed a faint crimson. He stood at the altar, the bound man before him, the stones behind him, and a field of stars above. There was something primal about his presence, wild and unchecked by the laws of the priesthood and the structure of faith Keles learned during her paladin training within the Heaven's Wing.

"To Thanet, we give our prayers," Eshiel instructed.

To Thanet, we give our prayers, echoed the crowd.

"To the goddess, we give our all."

To the goddess, we give our all.

Keles hated herself for it, but she repeated those words. She would remain no innocent bystander. Whatever blood flowed this night, it would coat her hands equally with the rest.

"From blood and bone, shadow and fire, from the land and the sea, we scream your rebirth," Eshiel shouted.

The rebirth comes, the people echoed.

Down came the knife, opening the man from breastbone to crotch. Whatever drugs kept him tame were no match, and the bound imperial shrieked in pain. The chants of the crowd rose in volume to match. Keles glanced aside. Nothing felt real. A small girl, no older than ten, clutched the hand of her mother, and she belted out those words at the top of her lungs.

Blood and bone. Shadow and fire. We scream rebirth.

Eshiel dove his hands into the opened chest. He sank them up to his elbows, coating them in blood and gore. His eyes closed as he began his prayer, one matched by those in attendance. Keles wondered how many times they had performed this atrocity. How many bodies did it take to create a red stain so wide and deep as the one upon that stone altar?

"Fly to us, she of wing and flower, of storm and sun," they chanted. "Give us light, give us heat, so we may sing."

Her legs turned wooden. Her feet were buried in the earth. To move, to break this spell, was impossible. Eshiel warned her, had he not? If she stayed, she must see this to its end. At least the screaming had stopped.

"Wing and flower, storm and sun," continued the chant, shorter and quicker. "Give us light and heat, we sing."

Fire shimmered along the base of the six stones. It ignited in silence, and it spread higher across the stone surface without consuming the moss. Its color shifted from a natural fire to a more ethereal mixture of blue and crimson. Keles gasped, but the others continued their chant, this revelation a normal part of their ritual.

Light, she thought as the flames burned across the stone pillars. *Heat*.

A shiver collected in the base of her neck and then shot to her arms and legs. Wind swirled around the crowd, and it smelled not of the sea, but of a blooming field of flowers. Eshiel bowed his forehead against the open rib cage. His arms sank deeper into the dead man's core. The corpse shimmered, flesh curling and peeling as if within a furnace. The wind howled. The cliff shook. Eshiel cried out, wordless, primal, and then tore his arms free.

The corpse exploded into flame, consumed with such fury not a shred of ash or bone fell upon the witnesses. Eshiel stood to his full height, bare chest heaving, tattoos rippling, and they were fire, the tattoos, they were *burning*. His head tilted back as the communal prayer ceased. Blood trickled down his face, mixing with his tears as a wave of emotion overcame him. His voice, normally deep as the ocean, suddenly trembled as he whispered.

"Lycaena, return to us, even if it must be in blood."

Dark flame burst from the six pillars, flowing in thin streams to the air above the altar. It collected together, shaped, took form. Fire became flesh and cloth. Light and heat became wing and dress. Keles dropped to her knees, and she wept with dozens of others. "Return to us," Eshiel demanded, and Lycaena answered. Somehow, despite her death, she answered. She came. She lived.

"My goddess," Keles said, eyes wide, hands reaching, soul offered once more to the wondrous being of compassion. A touch upon her fingertips, hot and dripping with blood. In that moment, Keles knew she would never leave. What price Eshiel demanded, she would pay. What lives must be offered, let them be offered. The empire had taken their goddess. Let their soldiers be sacrificed for her return.

"It's true," she said, and wept uncontrollably. She closed her fingers and clutched her fists to her breast so she could feel the residual heat. The years of warfare and despair, of crushing doubt and self-hatred for failing to stop the Anointed One's sacrificial knives, bled away.

"You live. Goddess, you live."

CHAPTER 1

VAGRANT

Cyrus slumped against the wall with head bowed, his body covered with a tattered cloak and muck-stained clothes. He hid his face from the passing soldier using the folds of his hood. He never knew which face these imperials would see. It was strange, not trusting his own face. Thinking about it made him uncomfortable.

He thought about it a lot.

"Hurry up, would you?" someone shouted from the end of the alley.

Cyrus had staked this position out the night before. Nearby was a tavern, and supremely drunk soldiers tended to come out here to piss. This meant the alley reeked, but it also meant it was largely avoided. Now the hour was dark, the city quiet, and this soldier alone but for a distant companion who sounded much too eager to return to his drinking.

It had taken several hours of waiting for a proper victim to arrive, but the one thing Cyrus had in abundance was time. He sat there, thoroughly ignored by the passing soldier. The most acknowledgment he received was a slight adjustment of gait so the soldier didn't step on him.

"Hate this backwater beer," the man grumbled in the imperial tongue. "Spend more time pissing than drinking."

Cyrus grinned beneath his hood. This soldier would accompany an invasion force to their island, and then, years of subjugation later, insult their beer? Cyrus's hands fell to the swords hidden underneath his cloak. As if he needed more justification.

"Is your stomach not well?" he asked in imperial as he stood. His clothes made not a sound from the movement. It was something he'd noticed lately. His footfalls were silent, and it was from no effort on his own part. It was the same with his clothes, the strength of his swings, and the speed at which he moved. The people believed he was Thanet's ultimate murderer, and after Thorda's heinous sacrifice, Cyrus had become exactly that.

The soldier's trousers were unbuckled and his cock in hand when he glanced over, confused why a homeless vagabond would know his native tongue. Cyrus stood there, swords still hidden. Calm. Patient. Waiting for the moment to arrive, for it always did arrive.

"Who are y—"

The Vagrant's grin. It was always the grin, seen by those Cyrus deemed his victims. Cyrus could feel it on his face. It felt too wide. Too hard. The soldier's eyes bulged, and he stumbled backward with his pants still low. Only then did Cyrus let his cloak slip and the moonlight glimmer off his swords. Did it glimmer off his crown, too? Cyrus did not know. What he was, and what his enemies saw, were not the same. Not yet.

Cyrus closed the distance between them in a dash. The soldier reached for his sword, but the weapon swayed wildly from his unbuckled belt. His fingers closed about the hilt just in time for him to die. Cyrus's longsword rammed deep into the man's belly, while his shorter, reverse-gripped blade sank directly into his throat, ending any attempt at a warning scream. Blood gushed across Cyrus's gloved hands, warm and sticky. The soldier gargled and convulsed as he died, kept standing by the steel that killed him.

Cyrus's efforts were akin to clearing a beach one grain of sand at a time, he knew that, but it still felt good to be doing *something* against the Everlorn Empire, however ultimately irrelevant. He watched the life leave the eyes of his foe. It had bothered him, for a time, witnessing the transition into death. It didn't anymore.

"Good riddance," he said, and yanked his weapons free. The body collapsed at Cyrus's feet. After a quick search, he found a half-empty coin purse containing a mixture of Everlorn currency (which Thanese businesses were forced to accept) and several original Thanese silver crowns. Cyrus pocketed the purse and then stepped away. It was time to go before he drew more attention. Cyrus turned, but he managed only two steps before his legs locked tight.

Not yet.

A hard pain struck Cyrus in the gut. He winced and gritted his teeth. No, he would not cut a bloody crown. He'd decided this when the day began. The Vagrant persona, he would forsake it. He was Cyrus Lythan, the dead prince returned. That was all he needed to be. He had to stop playacting in both roles.

Another step. His limbs shook, and he feared he would drop his swords. His stomach twisted tighter, and he felt close to vomiting. A deep, dark voice whispered in his mind, so faint it might have been his imagination. Might have, if Thorda had not blessed him with the sacrifice of forty men and women willing to believe in a savior.

Take your due.

Vertigo came next. It felt like he was holding his breath. It felt like he was attempting to stop his heart. Every natural order of the world, denied out of sheer pride. His body could not endure. His mind, stubborn as it was, cracked beneath the discomfort. He turned to the body.

A single slash. That was all it took. One long, arcing cut across the man's forehead to carve the Vagrant's crown. Relief came the instant he finished. The sickness vanished. The Vagrant had taken his due.

"Hey, Alex, you done pissing yet? I want to go home."

The friend near the entrance. Cyrus didn't wait for him to come looking. He sprinted out of the alley and into the middle of the street, a savage beast hunting amid the starlight. His swords crossed over the man's throat before he knew he was in danger. The body collapsed, and Cyrus knelt over it, a fire burning in his chest. A glance to his left, and he saw two women near the tavern entrance recoiling in horror.

They didn't scream, though, nor did they call for aid. They were women of Thanet. They knew who defended Vallessau. One of them turned away, while the other met his gaze. Her face hardened. She swiped two of her fingers across her forehead.

Cyrus didn't try to fight it this time. He cut his crown upon the dead man's head, temple to temple, and then flicked his swords clean before sheathing them. He pulled his hood lower so that it covered much of his face. Only his mouth and jaw would be visible, and he put a finger to them.

"Shhhhh."

He retreated, two soldiers a fine sacrifice made in the dead of night.

Behind him, the second woman rushed to the body, her fingers dipping into the blood so she might paint her forehead with a true crown, the Vagrant's blessing for those who had begun to believe anew in a free Thanet.

❧

One month ago, Cyrus had forsaken the Vagrant persona while storming out of Thorda Ahlai's home. What followed were long days and nights stalking the city for vulnerable soldiers, eating meager meals from street vendors, and sleeping in rented rooms paid for with coin taken from his kills. It was a paltry effort against the imperial invasion, nothing like the progress made with Thorda's team of elite behind him, but it was honest. It was straightforward. Most importantly, the victims were of his own choosing.

There would be no washing out the blood coating his gloves, so Cyrus discarded them prior to entering the Belhaven Tavern. He'd never considered himself much of a drinker, but lately he appreciated how it blurred the final nighttime hours before he slept.

Cyrus told himself he did this because kills were easier at night. It had nothing to do with how his heart raced and his blood pulsed come the arrival of the stars. That the people of Vallessau viewed the Vagrant as a creature of the night was irrelevant. A trick of the mind. A self-fulfilling prophecy.

So once his room was paid for (with significant extra to remove the tavern keeper's scowl given the extremely late hour), Cyrus found himself a corner to sit in and drink whatever the keeper considered his tavern's finest. It was the same beer the dead guard had disparaged, Cyrus realized after his first few gulps. Something about that returned a smile to his face. Heavens help him, he was giggling. He felt delusional.

Most of all, he felt afraid of that whispering voice demanding its due.

"Someone's in a good mood," said a familiar voice. Cyrus glanced up as his old friend Rayan settled into the chair opposite him. He carried a large leather bag, and it rattled with metal when he set it down. Cyrus suspected the paladin carried his weapons within, hidden to avoid the potential ire of soldiers.

"Even the homeless may find reasons to laugh," Cyrus said, pretending all was well between them. The last time he'd seen Rayan had been the day of the hangings. The reveal of Thorda's great betrayal. The question was, did Rayan know the truth of it?

"Homeless by choice, I will point out," the paladin said, and smiled. He was as handsome and finely groomed as ever, wearing freshly laundered trousers and a white shirt marked with silver buttons. Instructors at the Heaven's Wing, the former academy for teaching paladins of Lycaena, had demanded not a hair on their heads be out of place, for these champions were the embodiment of their goddess. Even with Lycaena dead and the academy burned to the ground, Rayan continued those traditions, if only out of stubborn habit.

"That hardly makes me unique," Cyrus said. "Keeping a home is hard. As for me, the men I kill tend to carry enough to buy a room and a decent meal. I can't complain."

The tavern keeper appeared with a second wood cup filled with beer. Rayan must have ordered it when he arrived. For Cyrus to not notice was unacceptable. He had to keep his wits about him, even when wallowing in alcohol. His grin slipped. Why was the paladin here? And why now?

"So how are things back...you know, with everyone?" he asked. He said it with a shrug, pretending he didn't actually care and was only making idle chat. It was a lie, of course. What he most wanted to know was whether Thorda had revealed the truth, or if he had been a coward and kept it to himself. Personally, Cyrus gave it a coin-flip chance.

"Everyone misses you," Rayan said. He sipped at the beer. "You could come back, you know. Whatever happened between you and

Thorda, we can work through it. His plan to stop the hangings, it might have failed, but it failed due to us underestimating the empire's cruelty. It is a mistake we will not make again."

Cyrus drained half his cup to hide his frustration. That answered that. Thorda, the brilliant tactician and financier of countless rebellions, his teacher and master of the blade—a damn coward.

"Why are you here?" Cyrus asked. He slammed down the cup. "Why really? It's been a long, hard month and no one came for me before. Have things truly gone so sour?"

Rayan glanced around to ensure no other ears were listening.

"Sour does not come close to describing it, Cyrus. With Heir-Incarnate Galvanis's arrival, things have turned dire. He brought with him a retinue of paragons, as well as a Humbled god by the name of Rihim. Their combined might makes even the smallest of operations dangerous. Worse, they somehow have discovered a means to root out our safe houses. Trust in Thorda and his resistance is plummeting, at least here in Vallessau. We need you, I will not lie about that, but that is not why I am here. This is no plan of Thorda's. I come to ask you for a favor."

"A favor?"

"Yes, a favor." Rayan reached across the table to playfully jab him in the shoulder. The touch left a warmth on his shoulder Cyrus tried hard to ignore. If he focused on it, he might realize just how badly he missed his friends. "Surely after all I've done for the Lythan family, you owe me at least one, wouldn't you agree?"

Another little jab to Cyrus's heart, and one he did a poor job hiding. Rayan did not know the truth of his Orani heritage. A favor? After what the Lythan family had done to the Orani bloodline, Cyrus owed him a throne.

"And what is this favor?" he asked. "It better not be coming back with you to Thorda. That's off the table, I can tell you, and I'd be disappointed in you for asking."

Instead of answering, the paladin pulled a note out from his breast pocket and slid it across the table. It was the sturdy, blocky, and precut pages used for sending messages via the Thanese courier-works, folded once across the middle. Cyrus opened it and read.

I hope all is well, and your days safe. I believe I have located where these cultists built themselves an enclave. If I am correct, it is but a few days from Chora, in the shadow of the Cliffwoods. I must admit, I feel trepidation, but also relief. I will have my answer. No more rumors. This nonsense can be put to rest by the evidence afforded to my own eyes. When I learn more, I will share. Much love to you, Uncle.

Keles

"Rumors?" Cyrus arched an eyebrow. "What rumors?"

"Rumors of the most outrageous sort," Rayan said. He crossed his arms, and he looked incredibly uncomfortable. "Ones claiming that in the far reaches of Ierida, our beloved Lycaena has returned to us."

Cyrus glanced at the note. The island was divided into four realms for governance, with Ierida being the northernmost, split by the Northspine Mountains and half-filled by the Broadleaf Forest. Beyond them were miles and miles of fields until the Cliffwoods, which marked the farthest reaches of the island. Chora must be one of the small farming villages tending those fields.

"Is that possible?" he asked.

"Thorda insists slain gods can indeed come back to earthly form, but it is a long and difficult process. They are beings of faith, and when a populace witnesses one killed, it causes irrevocable damage. More often than not it takes generations, and years of the god or goddess slowly healing and becoming whole while their worshipers maintain their faith. That's what he says, anyway."

"And what do you think?"

The paladin's face darkened.

"I think someone is taking advantage of our people's hurt for their own gain, and that someone might be willing to go to great lengths to keep the ruse going. That letter was Keles's last. I fear what happened to her, Cyrus, and I would like you to accompany me in finding her."

The thought of seeing Keles again, of her being in danger, flooded Cyrus with a mixture of emotions he had no hope of deciphering. Rayan was waiting for an answer, and so Cyrus used questions to stall.

"Why not bring Stasia? Or Mari? In her Lioness form she might even be able to smell out Keles like a bloodhound."

Rayan hesitated. He did not want to say what he was about to say, that much was clear.

"Thorda did not believe the resistance could afford the absence of either of his daughters."

"Not even for someone so dear to you as Keles," Cyrus said, finishing the unspoken thought. "That's Thorda, through and through. We are just tools to be used by someone like him."

"Is that why you left?"

Cyrus wanted to tell him how Thorda manipulated all of them to his own ends. He wanted to confess every single aspect of it, vomit out the words until the story was told. How Thorda had built a persona for Cyrus to embody, each and every detail chosen in advance. How he had Cyrus encourage the otherworldly aspects of it, which in turn fueled the rumors Thorda spent two years spreading during Cyrus's training. And how, as the final culmination of that effort, Thorda had engineered the capture and execution of forty souls faithful to the Vagrant.

Forty souls, convinced the Vagrant was the dead prince returned to life. Believing in him. Faithful. Loyal. Sacrificed, like the Seeds used to turn mere human men into the mighty paragons of the Everlorn Empire. And in return, Cyrus's strength had grown tenfold. His reflexes heightened. His gifted ring of Anyx allowing him to traverse shadow to shadow almost on a whim. Everything Thorda had promised, and nothing Cyrus had expected.

But to tell Rayan of Thorda's betrayal was to tell him the reason for that betrayal, and exactly what Cyrus was becoming. *What* the Vagrant was becoming. And he couldn't. He wouldn't. The words would not come to his lips.

"Thorda knows why I left," Cyrus said instead. "I see his cowardice has not yet abated."

"Cowardice is not something I associate with a man so ruthless," Rayan said. "But whatever happened between you two, I shall not pry further, even if all of us, including Thorda, miss you dearly."

Rayan reached into the bag he carried. Cyrus recoiled at what emerged from within. It was the crowned skull mask. The last he'd seen it, he had returned it to Thorda, split in half from the battle against Magus of Eldrid. The mask had been repaired, with such expertise not a crack marked its painted-white front. Cyrus stared at the wide, toothy grin as his insides trembled.

That mask. That crown. He feared it more than anything, and yet he felt such an intense desire to hold it, to wear it, to *become* it, that he found his hand reaching without a thought. The moment it touched his skin, the spell broke. Just a bit of carved and painted wood, that was all. The crown was plain silver. Not jagged. Not decorated. Just a round band to hold the mask to his face.

"Thorda thought you might need this," Rayan explained. "The road north will be heavily patrolled, and there is a chance we must defend ourselves."

Cyrus knew it was more than that. This was an attempt to bring him back into the fold. It was a reminder of what Thorda had created, as if Cyrus could ever forget. Perhaps it was also an apology. With Thorda, one could never tell. He was stone and ice, more familiar with a frown than a smile.

"You truly think Keles is in danger?" he asked.

"This entire island is full of desperate people. If Keles reveals their potential salvation for a lie, then yes, I fear the harm that may follow. The deceived are as likely to harm the truth bringer as they are to admit fault."

Cyrus stuffed the mask into a pocket of his trousers, glad to have it out of sight and terrified by the excitement it gave him nestled so close to his body. Mild electricity jolted through him as if from a second heart.

"Then it seems we are going north."

He grinned. Rayan recoiled in his seat, and Cyrus wondered just whose grin the paladin saw.

CHAPTER 2

SINSHEI

Sinshei hated these meetings at the council table. She hated the subservience she needed to display. And with the exception of her paragon, Soma, she hated every single person inside that room.

"Every day," her brother, the Heir-Incarnate Galvanis vin Lucavi, said with exaggerated frustration. "Every single day, I receive word of another soldier, priest, or magistrate cut down with their forehead carved open with a bloody crown."

His frown deepened, and when he crossed his arms, the chair beneath him groaned in protest. Magus had sat in that same chair during prior discussions on how to best subjugate Thanet. Comparing the two reaffirmed just how huge her brother was. The Uplifted Church preached that the Heir-Incarnate's greater size and strength, dwarfing even that of paragons, was proof of his divine right to be the next physical embodiment of the God-Incarnate. Sinshei suspected it was more complicated than that. In her memories as a little girl, she didn't remember Galvanis as quite so big, nor his face so rigid and white, as if he were carved out of marble.

"We have offered bounties, but without a name or a face we have no way to verify what few claims we receive," Sinshei said. "And with the Vagrant's apparent distaste for open combat, he picks at us like a mosquito."

She was trying to downplay the Vagrant's threat, and for one particular reason: Galvanis blamed her for the bastard's mere existence. It didn't matter that Imperator Magus and Regent Goldleaf deserved equal blame. It didn't even matter that the two were dead. Had they lived, Galvanis would have blamed her all the same. Sinshei was forever expected to accomplish miracles, and forever blamed for failing.

"Then coordinate your search efforts throughout the city," Galvanis said. "If the Vagrant were truly a mosquito, then we could end him with hardly any effort, yet that is clearly not the case. Even Rihim has struggled to engage the bastard in a fight."

Rihim was the Humbled former god that Galvanis brought with him from Gadir, a god of the hunt from the conquered nation of Antiev. He was Galvanis's trained pet, and so Rihim was given patience and understanding, two things so rarely extended Sinshei's way.

"Such citywide coordination proves difficult without a proper regent," she said. Galvanis had declared himself Imperator, but unlike Magus, he had not also taken the title of regent. Currently Magus's former Signifer, Weiss, held the role of regent-temp. It was meant as a placeholder, and even Weiss knew that. He sat quietly at the table, a little pad of yellow paper before him and a charcoal pencil in hand to scratch notes. Sinshei vastly preferred him over Gordian, and when things settled, she would try to convince Galvanis to make the position permanent.

"And a proper regent will be appointed in due time, but having had two perish within months at the hands of the Vagrant, I find myself reluctant to name a third." Galvanis made a disgusted expression, one almost comical on his pristine face and perfectly square jaw. "Truly, this man's methods make even the Skull-Amid-the-Trees seem civilized. What I would give to face him in open combat so we might end this nonsense without needless deaths."

"'The Empire's greatest threats are rarely found upon the battlefield,'" Sinshei quoted from the Pames Memoirs.

"You would speak Anointed Enfar to me?" Galvanis asked. "Then quote it correctly. 'The Empire's greatest threats are rarely found upon the battlefield, *but instead within the hearts of man.*' Those hearts are yours to win over, Anointed One. Your church is not rising to its responsibilities."

Sinshei felt a momentary echo of time hearing such a complaint. Magus had grumbled the same. With him, she had argued her priests could not adequately perform their duties when the Vagrant and his fellow insurgents were murdering them in their homes. To her brother, she would offer no such defense. Excuses meant nothing to him.

"We do the best we can," she said, relying on the one thing her brother would accept: the inherent inferiority of the local populace. "These islanders are wicked and stubborn in their hearts. It is no wonder the message of the God-Incarnate struggles to take root. We are scattering seeds across a hard, dry land."

Galvanis leaned back in his chair, and he tapped his fingers together.

"I have read everything the Deep Library of Eldrid contained of Thanet's history. They do seem a stubborn lot. That so many were displaced followers of Endarius fleeing Mirli has no doubt seeded cowardice within them as well. I sympathize with your struggles, dear sister, I truly do, but I sympathize more with our dead. This must be stopped."

"I can handle him, if given proper time and tools. Skilled and dangerous as he is, the Vagrant is but one man cloaked in rumors and lies. Anyone he speaks with becomes a weakness. Every tale-teller might know a modicum of truth to be exploited. These killings he performs now are a pittance compared to the grand overtures he first attempted when building his name. I'd wager he's weak, or in hiding. Time, my brother, all I need is time."

"Time is the one resource we grow thin on," Galvanis said. "But enough on this. As you say, the Vagrant is one man. It is a goddess that worries me now. Do you have the totality of rumors I requested?"

She did, compiled by one of her magistrates. She slid him the single curled scroll across the table.

"I first thought the rumors would originate from within Vallessau," she said as her brother's blue eyes skimmed the writing. "But unlike the Vagrant rumors, tracking the source was surprisingly easy. They're travelers from the northern realm of Ierida, all of them."

"And do you believe them?" Galvanis asked, still reading.

"The people do, and many supposed witnesses held firm their belief despite interrogation. At the least, it is worth considering."

Her brother finally finished reading the list. Her stomach tightened. The look on his face, it was strikingly unpleasant.

"The goddess Lycaena, returned," he said. "How could you fail so utterly, dear sister?"

Weiss's scratching of his pencil halted momentarily, then resumed in earnest.

Sinshei kept her face calm and passive, betraying nothing of her frustrations bubbling beneath the placid surface. Of course her brother would blame her for this. A few days after Magus's death, the most outlandish of rumors had started spreading throughout Vallessau. They claimed that the Butterfly goddess, Lycaena, had returned from death to answer the prayers of her faithful. As to where she was, none would specify beyond vague references to Ierida.

"This development has caught all of us off guard," she said. "Official reports we receive from Ierida insist that matters go smoothly."

Galvanis folded his hands together and shook his head.

"Only if you accept the reports at face value, Anointed. Tucked along the bottom they report their missing and their dead, and that number has steadily grown at unparalleled rates over the past month."

"It is not uncommon for soldiers to desert their duty, or the occasional local to attack a drunk or vulnerable man from Gadir…"

Excuses. She was making excuses. God-Incarnate help her, she tried so hard to avoid them. Her brother's eyes narrowed. His muscles tightened, and his chiseled jaw hardened into a perfect square.

"This conquest was given six years to prepare Thanet. The god Endarius died on the first day of our arrival. Two years later, Lycaena was publicly executed! Five years in total, three without their gods, and yet you failed to convert their hearts and minds to the true faith. Call this land dry and hard all you wish, but sometimes the blame of an ill crop must fall upon the farmer. For the people to maintain their faith in their slain goddess so strongly that she might return? *Unacceptable.*"

Her oldest brother was not Magus. He did not smash the table with his fists. He did not draw a weapon or physically act out his frustration beyond the raising of his voice. But it was enough. The stone trembled beneath Sinshei's feet. One of the cracks in the table deepened. Sinshei cast her gaze low, refusing to meet his eye. Only silence and respect would suffice here. All else would worsen his ire.

"Faith here in Thanet is fickle and thin," said Galvanis, at last breaking the silence. When he spoke, the scratching of Weiss's pencil resumed. "What prayers they offer my father are meager. We cannot risk a potential return of a goddess. We cannot risk the *rumors* of a potential return, not with how fragile a state I find this island in."

"Forgive me," Sinshei said, and she bowed her head in respect. "I will organize a contingent of soldiers, paragons, and priests to scour northern Ierida in search of the source of these rumors."

"No. Such a matter is far too important, and the excessive failures on this island deny me trust in others to achieve a proper conclusion. I will lead the contingent north. If one of Thanet's heathen gods has returned, her divinity will shine like a beacon to my eyes. She, and all her followers, will die to my blade."

"What of the Vagrant?" Sinshei dared ask. "You would leave Vallessau while belief here in the Vagrant festers?"

Galvanis stood and rested his hands on the table. Already damaged from when Soma struck it with his spear, it cracked further from the Heir-Incarnate's weight. His blue eyes pierced into Sinshei's as he smiled a statue's smile.

"You reveal your true fear of this 'one man cloaked in rumors and lies,'" he said. "But worry not, little sister. I shall leave Rihim here to continue his hunt. Where you fail, I trust the Humbled to succeed."

Sinshei bowed her head to hide her shiver.

"I trust your wisdom above all else. Safe travels, dear brother."

Sinshei remained seated until Galvanis exited the room, for doing otherwise would appear disrespectful. Signifer Weiss scribbled a few more lines during the wait.

"What could you possibly still be writing?" she asked him. Frustration and hurt harshened her tongue.

The scarred man glanced up, and after a moment's hesitation, he shrugged.

"See for yourself."

He slid the pad to her. The paper was rough and yellow, and it crinkled at her touch.

No potatoes here. Possible replacements? They have radishes. Cauliflower,
perhaps? With so much cheese, don't need exact. Must check spices—
I think they grow a chili similar to our yellow peppers.

She lowered the pad and stared at the man as if seeing him for the very first time.

"Is this...are you writing out a recipe?"

Signifer Weiss faintly grinned.

"I find myself on an island I do not know, in a position I did not strive for, under the direct order of the Heir-Incarnate. The last thing I desire is to be noticed. Over my years I have learned a quiet man taking notes is left to his own devices by important men, especially if those important men assume the notes are about themselves."

Sinshei arched an eyebrow.

"Did you employ this strategy in our meetings with Magus, too?"

"Not as often. Magus would listen to my advice. I do not anticipate the same from you or Galvanis."

That might be changing soon, Sinshei decided. Weiss was a quiet man, but clever, and he'd risen to his rank for good reason. She slid the notes back to him.

"Try speaking more often," she said. "You may find yourself surprised."

He rose from his chair and bowed low.

"I will consider it, Anointed One."

She let him leave first, and now alone, she pondered her plans in silence. With Galvanis departing, and Signifer Weiss only regent-temp, she would effectively have the run of the capital for the first time since landing on Thanet. The question was, what should she do with that opportunity?

Sowing doubt in Galvanis among her magistrates would be a first step. She'd have to be careful. While she'd done similar with Magus, it was one thing to speak ill of a lumbering paragon of Everlorn's Legion. It was another to whisper dark rumors of the man who would soon become God-Incarnate. She tapped her lips. Perhaps she could force all the city's soldiers into confession booths over the next few weeks. A list of sins could be useful in capturing loyalty from those in the right positions.

Mind still whirling, she exited the room. Her loyal paragon, Soma Ordiae, waited for her in the hallway, a bemused expression on his face. She idly wondered if he'd exchanged words with either Galvanis or Weiss. His blue platemail was polished to a shine, and his spear was safely clipped to his back.

"Another productive meeting?" he asked.

"For once, yes," she said. "My brother plans an excursion into Ierida to find the source of the rumors of Lycaena's return. I would know what transpires. Volunteer to go on his merry hunt. See if there is anything useful to learn, things that he would not tell me upon his return. And if Lycaena truly has resurrected, and a fight between them occurs, well..."

"Fear not, I will take what openings are available to me," Soma said. His platemail rattled as he tilted his head to one side. "Though are you certain it is wise for me to leave your side? The Vagrant and his band of miscreants still lurk about, and they will be emboldened with the Heir-Incarnate's departure. I would hate to leave Vallessau only to return to find a crown carved into your forehead."

Sinshei winced at the thought. The Vagrant had been useful in bringing down Imperator Magus, but he had also humiliated Sinshei by killing Gordian Goldleaf mere moments after his paragon ritual. Whoever he was, his potential upside was dwindling as his lingering presence continued to be unfairly blamed on her.

"I can protect myself," she said, and she shimmered a single golden blade of light above her hand. A snap of her fingers, and she dismissed it just as quickly.

"Our magistrates possess similar magics," Soma argued. "And they have died all the same. I hold much greater trust in my spear."

"Your concern for me is touching," she said, neither believing his concern nor feeling particularly touched. "But fear not, Soma. I will not be alone here in Vallessau."

Distaste flashed across Soma's face, fast enough she might have imagined it.

"You mean the Humbled."

Sinshei graced him with her brightest, fakest smile.

"Indeed I do," she said. "And with Rihim hunting, only a fool would dare grace the midnight streets."

CHAPTER 3

MARI

Barely ten people," Arn said. "Hardly worth the effort."

Mari peered around the corner at the group waiting in the opposite room. The walls were bare, with portions blackened with hints of a recent fire. They were in what had once been a brothel, before the Uplifted Church had condemned the practice, emptied the rooms at sword point, and nailed its doors shut.

"If we abandon those ten, then our next meeting will contain only five," Mari said. "Each and every soul is worth the effort, Arn. I would think a former paragon would understand that."

The giant man leaned against the wall, his arms crossed over his chest. The chainmail hidden underneath his oversized dark leather coat rattled from the movement.

"We paragons focused on killing gods and beating up heretics more than developing the faith of the populace. Priests handled the prayers and lectures. Our violence was to prove the priests spoke true when praising the God-Incarnate as almighty."

"Faith through murder," she said softly. "No wonder Everlorn rots down to its roots."

Mari scanned the ten people. She recognized two families from prior sessions. Along with them was an elderly woman she did not know, and two husbands recently arrived in Vallessau who had begun attending a few weeks prior. It was a paltry crowd compared to her earliest days as the Lioness, but she refused to let the dwindling numbers lessen her spirits.

"You assume the rot did not start from the roots," Arn said. He fiddled with one of the leather straps to his silver gauntlets. "Whatever stories we know of the first God-Incarnate Ashraleon, I suspect they are highly embellished."

Mari knew only the basics of Ashraleon. The Everlorn Empire measured time by the reign of their God-Incarnates, and right now they were in the 599th year of the Sixth Age. Soon, Lucavi's power, presence, and very identity would pass on to his chosen son and heir, Galvanis vin Lucavi. So would begin the Seventh Age. Mari hoped that Thanet would be a black eye upon the empire to mark the start of that new age.

The shutters to the window behind them opened, and in climbed Mari's sister. Stasia's twin axes were sharp at her hips, and they glinted in the moonlight that spilled into the room. She wore a black mask tied over the lower half of her face, and her eyes were brown, not red, courtesy of the magic of the word-lace around her neck. Her dark hair was tied in a short ponytail, and it clung to her skin, wet from the rain that swept in through the open window.

"I don't think any more are coming," Stasia said. "Go ahead and start. I'll keep an eye outside just in case there are stragglers."

"I'm less worried about stragglers and more about patrols," Mari said.

Stasia grinned behind her mask, but Mari detected the worry in her eyes she tried to hide.

"If it's Rihim you're paranoid about, don't be. I'll wallop him back to wherever he came from if he tries to ruin our gathering."

Mari pecked her sister on the cheek. The wet cloth was cold to her lips.

"Don't you dare try to fight him on your own or I will be very, very upset with you."

Stasia laughed, the amusement in her sister's eyes now genuine. It warmed Mari's heart.

"Fine, fine. I give my word, so go do your thing."

She climbed back out the window, leaving Mari alone with Arn. His attention returned to his gauntlets, absent-minded, fiddling with the straps, which often meant he was nervous or anxious. Mari held back a smile. The big oaf acted gruff, no doubt a necessity given his brief time as a paragon, but over the past weeks she'd decided it was entirely a front. Arn was soft-hearted, quick to laugh, and eager to be helpful. Not bad to look at, either, she sometimes admitted when spotting him walking about her father's mansion with only a loose shirt exposing a chest as broad as the horizon and arms packed with muscles. He could probably lift her with one arm if he wished to do so.

A rush of inappropriate thoughts caused her cheeks to flush. She reluctantly pushed the thoughts away. She had a duty to perform, and it required a somber mind. Yet perhaps she could have a little bit of fun...

"Turn around, please," she told Arn, and then without waiting, she lifted the hem of her dress and pulled it overhead, stripping down to her thin undershirt and leggings.

"Why?" Arn asked, looking up. His eyes immediately went to her chest, and then his face blushed a deeply satisfying shade of red. He spun to put his back to her. "Hells, woman, you could have just answered the question."

"For such an abrasive, foul-mouthed ex-paragon, you are awfully easy to embarrass."

"You're an ass, Mari."

In response, she smacked his own, just a tap with her palm that somehow deepened the color of red on his neck to rival that of strawberries.

"Hush," she said. "I have work to do."

Mari folded her dress and set it beside the doorframe. Next came her underclothes. Now fully naked, she knelt and bowed her head with her eyes closed. Slow, steady breaths helped push away the playfulness and tighten her focus. Her mind slipped deeper into the realm of the spiritual, to where the god Endarius lurked.

Your faithful await, she silently whispered.

Then let us greet them, rumbled the Lion.

The change hurt, but it was a good hurt. The power of the divine swept through her mortal flesh. The bones in her knees broke and switched angles. Gray fur sprouted across her flesh. Her teeth elongated, her senses sharpened, and claws extended from her fingertips. The sharpest pain came from her shoulder blades as two featherless wings burst out her back. They were long, thin appendages of bone, symbols of the now-undead god Endarius.

Mari shook her head side to side as if shaking off water. Bone plates pierced through her fur along her forehead, shoulders, and hips, to form armor, completing the transition. The word-lace remained clasped to her neck, and it translated her growl to Arn.

"Come, Heretic, and wear your mask."

He turned about and gestured to the fox skull tied over his face with leather cord.

"Already ahead of you," he said, and together they strode into the opposite room, where the families waited.

The mixture of adults and children stood alert and silent upon her arrival. The room was dimly lit with candles, each positioned so the light and shadows they cast could not be seen from outside. The steady downpour falling upon the rooftop was the only sound. It was comforting, and despite her appearance, Mari did her best to convey a similar comfort.

"I have come, children," she said. "Speak your prayers, for I would hear them, and answer."

One of the fathers stepped forward, holding the hands of his two children. He was a kindly man named Daven, one of several prominent fishmongers employing dozens to help gut and clean the hauls brought in to the docks.

"Come, Striya, Ulren," he told his children. "Kneel and pray, just like I taught you."

The three knelt before Mari and bowed their heads. After a moment's hesitation, the father began, his words echoed by his children. It was known as the Lion's Prayer, taught early to the young. Even if Endarius were not a part of her, she could recite it by memory.

"The Lion keep us safe in both storm and sun," it began. Endarius stirred within Mari, and she gave him full control. More prayers followed, spoken with all due reverence.

"Keep us safe so we may witness the brightest dawn," she said along with them at the end of the prayer. A deep sense of longing and loss struck Mari in her breast. "You are faithful, Fishmonger Daven, and have always been. May your children be blessed a thousandfold, and see their land be made free."

Striya and Ulren stared wide-eyed at Mari, overwhelmed by her presence. Daven better understood the meaning of such a gift, and his eyes swelled with tears.

"Thank you," he said. "Each and every night we pray for your return. We hold faith. We do. We do."

Mari closed her eyes and stepped closer. Her nose brushed against his chest, her muzzle rubbing against him. His arms wrapped about her neck.

"We miss you," he said, so softly she wondered if she was meant to hear.

The three stepped back. With their departure, she saw the two husbands by the window, whispering softly, each holding a candle. Mari glanced at Arn, who lurked by the boarded-up door. He startled as if waking from a daydream, then realized what bothered her.

"Hey, away from the window," he told the two men. "This stays in the dark."

Both profusely apologized, and they set the candles back to where they had been, their light safely cast out of sight of the midnight road. Mari turned her attention back to the next who'd come for a blessing, this time the old woman with milky white eyes, who approached carefully with rapid taps of a cane. Her dark skin was deeply wrinkled, and her face thin. Her curly white hair was pulled back into a bun, and she brushed it with her hands as she approached, as if to check it was still tight. The simple, almost instinctive act made Mari smile. The woman had to be past her eightieth year, if not ninetieth, and yet she still cared for her appearance when meeting her god.

"I heard of you, but did not come," she said. Her hands shook when she reached out, but her words were sharp. "I didn't want to believe. I had you in my heart, which is all I needed. Do you remember me, god? Do you remember the prayers I offered at your feet?"

Endarius offered up his memories, and Mari allowed them to rush over her. She was elsewhere on Thanet, amid a rolling forest filled with revelers. The Planting Festival, she somehow knew. Songs of worship marked the retreat of winter and the hard work to come in preparing the fields. Enormous fish the size of her arm cooked on metal tins above tremendous bonfires. The scent of peppered shrimp and cracked oysters filled the air.

The grass was green, the trees blooming with flowers. Joy and laughter were constant, as were the lines of believers come to request a boon or blessing from their god. The memory shifted, and Mari witnessed a much younger woman kneeling before her in a pretty yellow dress.

"I was born into darkness," this woman (Tasha, her name was Tasha) pleaded. "Please, grant me sight, if only for a moment so I may look upon your glory. Whatever you ask of me, I shall give it. Whatever cost I must pay, I will pay."

"My cost is heavy and long," Endarius told this woman dozens of years prior. "Live well. May your joy be endless and true. Succeed, and I shall consider my debt paid."

And then the Lion breathed across her face while priests chanted and revelers sang.

The memory receded, and Mari looked upon this far older version of the praying woman. She wore yellow, just as she had all those years ago.

"When did you lose your sight again?" Mari asked. "When did your faith falter?"

Tasha clasped her hands together and turned her head.

"The day Lycaena...the last things I ever saw were the knives of the Anointed One. It was hard to hope after that."

Mari padded two steps closer to the woman. Old and young versions hovered before her, memory and present, the twin images both bearing the same request. Endarius had granted it before, when beloved by the island and empowered by their prayers. Could he do so now?

Even you would doubt me? the Lion snarled within her skull. *Would that I had a better host.*

Mari accepted the rebuke. How could she deem herself capable of restoring Thanet's faith if she held none herself?

"I have not forgotten you," Mari told the old woman, Endarius once more fully in control of her tongue. "I have not forgotten your song. I demand nothing now that I did not demand then. Look upon me, Tasha. Open your eyes."

The old woman obeyed. Mari leaned closer, and she breathed warm breath across those milky eyes. Magic stirred within her, a sudden pull that left her chest aching. In years past, this act might have cost Endarius nothing, but now, in his dwindling state, he gave much of himself to foster the miracle, and yet he did so gladly. Mari breathed, and breathed, until the passage of breath became a soft growl.

The white faded from Tasha's eyes just as it had in the forest. Her deep brown irises shone bright in the candlelight.

"I never should have doubted," she said, and she flung her arms around Mari's neck. "Forgive me, O Lion, forgive me, I beg."

Mari tilted her neck so her face rubbed along the woman's side. Her four legs trembled from the effort of the healing, but she fought to keep her voice strong.

"May your joy be endless and true," she said. "Live well, in these final days granted to us."

Next came the husbands. They each wore a lone feather tied with string, a remembrance of the colorful mane Endarius bore in his living form. They were both tall, their hair long and dark.

"We're not worthy," the more handsome of the two said. He bowed low. "I pray you will still listen to our desires."

Mari dipped her head and half closed her eyes, a feline reaction to show her calm state and open heart.

"I will always listen to the prayers of the—"

Stasia crashed through the window, scattering glass, wood, and blood. She rolled along the floor and then came up to a stand with her great-ax at the ready. Wind and rain howled, unwelcome amid the quiet prayer.

"It's Rihim!" she shouted.

The Humbled blasted through the opening. He was a hulking monstrosity of muscle and fur, more humanoid than Mari, stalking on two legs instead of four. His fur was sleek and dark like a panther's. He crashed into Stasia, fighting against her ax in an attempt to claw her flesh. Their momentum collided them into the other wall, smashing wood and showering charred plaster to the ground.

The families screamed. Arn cursed beside the door. Only the two men did not panic. Before Mari could order them to flee, she spotted their long, sharpened knives. She bared her teeth. The candles at the window, they were a signal. Endarius echoed her fury within her breast.

Not lovers or practitioners at all. Spies.

They were so close, and they had surprise on their side. Mari's wings lashed inward like striking scorpion tails. She killed the first in time, but the other sank his dagger past the bone plate and deep into her shoulder. Pain flooded her. Blood poured down her leg and paw to the burnt floorboards. Mari roared, and her mind went red with Endarius's rage.

He may have cut her, but she would rip him apart. Her teeth crunched into his ribs. His blood gushed across her face and stained her bone armor. Her wings knifed across his throat, deeper, harder, sawing until his spine snapped and his head dropped. Her paws raked the body, tearing more flesh free to expose nerves, sinew, and bone. What was left of him collapsed into a mess at her feet. All her fear, confusion, and betrayal manifested in a single roar.

A semblance of her sane, coherent self returned from the overwhelming primal rage, and she looked for her sister. Stasia was trapped against the wall, pinned by the divine strength of the Humbled. The ax shook between them, barely holding those razor sharp claws at bay.

"Your reputation for strength is well-earned, Ax," Rihim said. The muscles of his arms bulged, pressing the ax harder against her chest. He leaned closer, his nose almost touching Stasia's face. His nostrils widened, and he breathed in deep. A grin split his lips, and his eyes widened. "But of course. You are not mortal. You're a goddess. Weak. Broken. Who worships you, wretch?"

Mari flew across the room, her teeth sinking into Rihim's arm. He snarled like the panther he resembled, and with frightening ease, he cast Mari aside. The distraction was enough for Stasia, though, and she cracked the Humbled across the jaw with the handle of her ax and then spun free of his grip.

"We need out!" she cried.

"Working on it," Arn bellowed. Everyone present had snuck in through the window so the doors might remain boarded up and the building inconspicuous. Arn appropriately decided they needed a much quicker and larger means of retreat, and so he crossed his arms and blasted his way through the boarded-up door like a human boulder. Planks, nails, and dust showered in all directions.

"Good enough," Stasia said, a mere step behind him. Everything was chaos. The families fled only to discover more soldiers waiting. Even worse, paragons were among their number. Arn battled one of them, a gold-armored man with similar gauntlets to his own. They rained blows on each other, rapid strikes as Arn fought for an escape route through the soldiers that the families might use.

Mari did not follow, not yet. She positioned herself between Rihim and the exit, determined to slow the Humbled while the others fled. She expected the god to immediately attack, but instead he crouched low in the middle of the former brothel. Their group had encountered him several times over the past month, but this was the first time Mari had a good look at his panther face, his fur so dark it seemed more blue than black, and the shining gold of his predator eyes. His tongue slid across the wood, licking up the spilled blood from when the spy had stabbed her shoulder. His eyes lifted. He bared his teeth.

"Miquoan," he purred. "I knew it."

Mari faked an attack, then pivoted at the last moment to follow Arn outside. Her wings slashed the throat of a soldier foolish enough to stop her. Another swung a sword, and she snapped its metal between her teeth. Two dozen soldiers surrounded them, perhaps more. They tried to seal off the building, but they had not anticipated the fury of their prey. Some wrangled the fleeing worshipers, others blocked off the street. Mari hesitated, unsure of what to do or where to go.

Stasia was never one to hesitate. She cleaved a soldier in half, kicked the pieces away, and then glanced over her shoulder, her body glistening with rain and blood.

"Scatter!" she screamed.

There was no time to argue over the order. Arn, Stasia, and Mari split in three different directions. No fighting, no organizing a defense, just a desperate flight to escape their pursuers. Two soldiers tried blocking her way with their swords and shields. She couldn't slow down or be careful, not with Rihim chasing her, and so she slammed right into them. Strength met strength, and the mortal men faltered. One struck her face with his pommel, but it hit bone and bounced off. Her paws slashed open the armor and ribs of the first, and her wings tore open the jugular of the second.

Even that delay was too much. Rihim vaulted after her, his two legs possessed of terrifying strength. She turned, saw him nearing, and braced for an impact that never came. The mangled body of a soldier collided mid-leap with the Humbled, thrown by a furious and blood-soaked Arn.

"Ax said scatter, so scatter!" he shouted.

The way clear, Mari put her back to the chaos and the screams and the trapped worshipers of Endarius. She poured every last bit of her energy into her sprint. A single word echoed in her mind, and she let it guide her. Buildings passed in a blur. She leaped from rooftop to street to rooftop, claws granting her stability against the wet surfaces. No rest. No slowing. Alarm bells sounded from every direction.

Run. Run. Run.

Minutes passed. Her lungs burned. Her paws ached. She kept high, leaping from roof to roof, yet every time she glanced over her shoulder, Rihim was there. Every jump, every turn, he was but a handful of seconds behind her. The speed of the Lioness wasn't enough, and no twists or tricks mattered.

He was chasing her. No, he was *hunting* her. The scent of her spilled blood was a potent mix of divinity and mortality any sharp nose could track. Even now, the wound in her shoulder bled. It would heal when she returned to her human form, but to do that meant becoming vulnerable.

Mari used all her strength to leap across an entire street, and then skidded to a halt atop the shingles. No choice. There was nowhere she could run that would be far enough. Claws digging into the unstable surface, she spun about and raced straight for the chasing Humbled on the opposite rooftop. If the sudden turn surprised him, he showed no sign of it. He lunged across the gap, and Mari met him with a mighty leap of her own.

Their bodies collided midair. Instinct took over. She swiped and bit as his claws raked across her flesh and caught on her bone armor. Twisting, turning, positioning the Humbled where she wanted him. She pulled her lower legs up and pushed off the Humbled. The act flung Rihim downward, while it returned Mari to the opposite rooftop.

He would climb. He would follow. Mari bought herself only seconds, but those seconds were all she needed. She backtracked, laying the scent of her passage double over the first. She had to confuse the Humbled, make him doubt. Houses passed beneath her, one after another, just enough to gain distance before Rihim returned to the rooftops.

There. A home with open windows blocked by thick curtains. She hopped down to the street, turned, and leaped on through, releasing Endarius's magic while still midair. The change hit, rapid and painful, and then she landed on the floor, naked and bruised. It was a bedroom, the bed occupied, a man and woman startled awake from the noise.

"Please," Mari pleaded, the word-lace about her neck translating her hurried Miquoan into Thanese. She knelt before them, praying the hearts of these strangers were kind. "I must hide."

The husband, an older man with hair so white it seemed to glow in the pale light, nodded and pointed to a closet, also curtained off. Mari entered without a word. She dared not move. Dared not speak.

The roof rattled upon Rihim's arrival. She heard sniffing, then a soft growl. Mari held her breath.

Think I kept running. Think I'm already a mile from here, leading you back to the start, where your nose cannot track.

Shingles cracked, and dust fell from the ceiling as Rihim resumed his chase. Mari released her held breath. Her gamble had worked. The scent of her, that mixture of Endarius's divine essence and her own human blood, was significantly different from when she was just her normal mortal self. She closed her eyes and forced her heart to calm down. With Rihim chasing her, that meant Arn and Stasia should have had an even easier time escaping. There was no reason to panic, no reason to worry. Yet.

The curtain parted. It was the woman, dressed in a gray shift, her hair bundled up in a bonnet. She looked Mari up and down, and she showed no bashfulness at Mari's nakedness.

"You're with them," she said. "With the faithful."

Mari stood tall.

"I am no friend of Everlorn," she answered.

In response, the woman slipped past Mari and reached up to a high shelf while on her tiptoes. When she stepped back, she held a thick plain dress.

"Then take this. Vallessau is no place to wander naked at night."

"Is anywhere?"

Despite her nervousness, despite the weirdness and surprise of the night, the older woman smiled.

"Nowhere a young lady like you should be. Keep safe. We shall lock the door behind you when you leave."

The dress was an odd fit, a bit too wide and much too tall, but naked insurgents hiding in closets could not afford to be choosy. Mari hurried out of their bedroom, keeping her face angled away from the couple. The less they saw of her, the better. Mari put her ear to the door, listened for a moment, and then exited out into the rain.

No sign of Rihim, nor any chasing imperial soldiers. Mari thanked any and all gods who might be listening.

You are welcome, Endarius grumbled inside her mind.

"It was your blood he tracked," Mari snipped back.

And your slowness that allowed it to be spilled.

The god had her there. She let the matter drop. Every mission had a fallback position set in advance, a meeting place should the members of Thorda's elite be forced to scatter. Mari hurried down the rain-soaked streets, her ears alert for any potential patrols. None crossed her path.

Arn was already waiting at the chosen alcove, just a random spot easily missable from the street. He saw her, and his face immediately brightened.

"You're a sight for sore eyes," he said. "Did you steal a dress?"

"Gifted, not stolen," Mari said, joining him under an awning safe from the rain. She shivered from the cold air brushing across her wet dress, one much too thin for the weather. Her long hair clung to her back and neck. "Any sign of Stasia?"

"She fled opposite me when we scattered," Arn said. "She's on her way, I'm sure of it. Just had to take a wide path around the patrols, I'd wager. No reason to panic."

"Who is panicking?"

She didn't mean to, but her rebuke came out harsh. It was true, though. Mari was as calm as one could be given the circumstances. It was Arn who fidgeted and looked ready to burst out of his own skin.

"The night's been a bit of a shitstorm," Arn said, as if that explained things. "I wouldn't blame you if you were, that's all."

Mari positioned herself at the edge of the alcove, peering around the corner so she could watch for her sister. Behind her, Arn began pacing. Whatever happiness he'd shown upon seeing her quickly faded away. He muttered to himself, and when he wasn't muttering, he was clacking the fingers of his gauntlets together. A nervous tic. Mari ignored him as best she could and watched for her sister. Stasia shouldn't be too far behind...

"Why?" Arn suddenly ranted. "Why here? Why now? Couldn't he have stayed away?"

"Someone infiltrated one of our groups," Mari said, not even looking at the ex-paragon.

There, racing down the street, was her sister. Alone. No pursuers. Relief swept through her, overwhelming in its power. Stasia's great-ax hung loose in her grip, dripping a mixture of rain and fresh blood. "It's happened before. It'll happen again."

"I don't mean the damn Humbled."

That got her attention. Mari glanced over her shoulder

"What are you blathering about?" she asked. She'd assumed he was upset at the Humbled's arrival, but now she was not so certain. What then could it be?

"The paragon with gauntlets like mine," Arn said. He thudded the back of his head against the stone wall of the alcove. "I recognized him, and I think he may have recognized me."

"Oh," Mari said. "Is that bad?"

"Very bad," Arn said, and he sighed. "His name is Dario...Dario Bastell, my older brother."

Mari didn't know what to make of such a connection, but there was no hiding how much it bothered Arn. The giant man closed his eyes, and he smashed his gauntlets into the stone wall hard enough to crack two deep divots.

"Why of all the lands of all the world are you on gods-damned Thanet?"

CHAPTER 4

VAGRANT

Rayan was friends with everyone. That was the conclusion Cyrus reached when the paladin recognized the courier directing his cart for the weekly trip north out of Vallessau. A quick conversation later, and the two rode in the back, sparing themselves miles of walking. They separated at the first village and followed the main road toward the city of Thiva. Their first week they spent camped in little clearings deemed safe by the constant parade of travelers. At one point they stayed in a surprisingly enormous tavern built in the middle of seemingly nowhere, its soft beds a welcome reprieve from the hard ground, but then it was right back to the road.

"We should reach Thiva tomorrow," Rayan said one night beneath the stars. "If we are lucky, we will bunk in far finer quarters. I bring news from Thorda to Ierida's master, Lord Mosau."

Cyrus kept his annoyance to himself. Thorda would refuse to give Rayan aid in finding his niece, but then immediately use him for his own ends when the paladin left? He should not have been surprised. They awoke early the next morning, and by midday, they arrived at the seat of the ruling family of Ierida.

Thiva was dwarfed by Vallessau in size, but it did have its charms. The city butted up against the Broadleaf Forest, and from within those trees flowed out the Sathe River, narrow and deep. The river bisected the city, but in turn, the locals had built over a dozen bridges crossing it, each one painted a different color. Unlike the homes Cyrus was used to, squat and with their foundations more often stone instead of wood, the homes here had high walls and sharp rooftops. They were painted, too, each of them a similar rustic color he presumed of a dye made with a plant nearby.

"It's like Thiva wants to be as different from Vallessau as possible," Cyrus remarked as they walked the central road. The doors were curved along the top instead of what he had considered the normal rectangle. Bright colors filled the curtains draped over windows, each with rippling or alternating patterns. The painted bridges in particular were gorgeous works of art, with little stories of heroes carved into the sides and open holes in monsters' mouths so one could push a bit of bread through to feed the waterfowl congregating underneath.

"I suppose you were never allowed to travel much," Rayan said.

"That is one way to describe imprisonment."

The paladin flinched.

"Forgive me, I do not mean to be so callous. When you were older, your father would have taken you across our magnificent island to meet the people you would rule. You will find that Vallessau is unique among Thanet, with a style and culture all its own. I suspect it being the grandest of our cities, with citizens come from all four realms, plays a part in that."

This time it was Cyrus who flinched, and he scooted around a woman carrying a wicker basket atop her head as a way to hide his discomfort. Yes, being both the political and trading capital of the island was one way to explain it.

The arrival of the Mirli people who overthrew the original Orani family and established the Lythan bloodline upon the throne was another. What styles had they brought with them across the Crystal Sea? What traditions, what clothes, stories, and tastes had come with them and then slowly spread for hundreds of years, erasing those of the first Thanese?

"I suspect you're right," he said lamely.

Though the Sathe River had largely been left to flow as it might, the lone divergence was in the city center. The river had been split in half and then widened so it formed a circular moat before merging back together on the other end. Within this little man-made island loomed Thiva's castle, though "castle" didn't fit how Cyrus thought of it. The complex was entirely made of wood, the outer wall a palisade of sharpened stakes. Beyond was the castle proper, and though its height could not compare to the larger towers of Vallessau, it was beautiful in its design.

No line was allowed to be perfectly straight. The rooftop curled, as did the banisters and supports. Windows were perfect circles. Banners hung across the walls, each painted a lovely shade of blue and then marked with swirling white lines heavier along the bottom than the top. The main pillars were decorated inversely, solid white with blue dips and swirls that seamlessly melded into the nearby walls.

The effect was as if the castle were rising up from the water, like a wave cresting against the shore. Here in Thiva, they were far from the sea, and yet the sea was still here in the heart of their city. Upon arriving, Cyrus glanced at the surrounding moat, and he saw the only stone constructions throughout the area: spikes lurking just beneath the water's surface. No boats would cross this sea.

A line of greeters, traders, and petitioners stood at the lowered drawbridge. Cyrus and Rayan took up their spot at the back and patiently waited for their turn. After a dreadfully long and dull wait, Rayan spoke to the bridge guard.

"Tell your master a man from Vallessau comes bearing a private message."

"You got a name, or a reason why I should bother Lord Mosau with your unspoken petition?" the tired guard asked.

In answer, Rayan leaned closer so no one nearby might overhear.

"My name is Airam of nowhere."

The guard pretended to be bored, but his arguing ceased immediately, and he beckoned them onward while also waving at another guard manning the main entrance.

"Jevins there will find you a place to wait for our lord," he said. "Just tell him your name, and he'll know what to do."

"Who is Airam?" Cyrus asked as they crossed the drawbridge. It groaned beneath their feet. He tried not to imagine the unseen spikes lurking underneath. Past the drawbridge was a stretch of worn earth. To either side grew a beautiful garden, the outer edge walled off by bushes of catmints and roses. Beyond was the castle, its blue doors opening at their approach.

"It's a password," Rayan said. "One given to any messenger we send from Vallessau. The guards know not to ask questions upon hearing it, and it also means no real names need be offered."

The interior was cool and pleasant, the ground tiled sandstone. A breeze blew through the circular window, and Cyrus let it tease his hair before he flopped down onto a long gray couch marked with a half dozen blue pillows.

"Appreciating a return to the finer life?" Rayan asked as he took his own seat in a padded pine chair.

"After the past month?" Cyrus laughed. "Yes, I am."

A trio of servants arrived, the oldest of them unable to hide a wince at seeing the road-weary pair lounging on the pristine furniture.

"This evening's meal is not yet ready," he said, "so my lord has asked that we prepare you two a bath, and a change of clothes if you are in need of them."

"That sounds wonderful," Rayan answered for the both of them.

The bathhouse was warm and cozily lit, and its enormous tub sized for at least a dozen to share. Cyrus scrubbed himself diligently, for he'd yet to have a chance to wash away the grime of his month away from Thorda's estate. He dipped beneath the water, ran his fingers through his hair, and then came up sputtering.

"I must admit," he told Rayan. "It's been a long time since I received such royal treatment. I'm surprised how much I miss it."

The older man groaned as he stretched out his back and sank deeper.

"I myself am not surprised in the least."

Once they were smelling nice and wearing a change of clothes, they followed the same elderly servant to the dining hall. There, before the set table, waited Lord Jase Mosau. He was a handsome man, smiling wide with bright teeth, his skin an earthy brown and his hair a shade darker than Cyrus's. He was dressed comfortably in gray trousers, a silver belt, and a high-collared shirt whose red pleasantly complemented the copper color of his eyes. He clasped his hands before him and dipped his head in greeting.

"It is a pleasure as always to meet a paladin of Lycaena." He fixed his gaze on Cyrus. "And it is an even greater pleasure to confirm the survival of our dear prince with my own eyes."

The air caught in Cyrus's lungs. He'd not thought to cover his face. The dark cloak and clothes he wore for battle were in his rucksack, as were his swords. Over the past month, his dirty long hair and the over-all disarray of his clothes did well to disguise him.

"I am surprised you recognize me after all these years," he said, searching for footing after being caught so off guard. He'd been only sixteen years old at his last public appearance.

"I was there the day you were born," Jase said. "It has been a few years, but I saw you plenty when speaking with King Cleon, may the Lion and Butterfly rest his soul. You were a quiet child, your nose often buried in a book. Your father once lamented that if he wanted your attention it was easier to write it on a scrap of paper and slide it between the pages than to call your name."

Cyrus blushed. One time he'd ridden a carriage to Syros with his parents, and after much pleading, they'd allowed him to bring a leather-bound collection of fables to read during the long, boring hours. His father consistently elbowed him, gesturing to sights outside the carriage window, such as a particular view of a valley, a flock of birds, or a cluster of bushes blooming with jasmine flowers. His father would then rattle off names of the flora and fauna like a schoolteacher.

He'd been unimpressed and annoyed by the constant bothering, but Cyrus understood now it wasn't the sights his parents wanted, but the company. To view the wondrous together, for Cyrus to appreciate what Cleon and Berniss found beautiful. Now he wished for a thousand such rides, to sit in rapt attention as his father cataloged each and every bird and flower.

Cyrus reeled from the memory, and he struggled to speak against the sudden emotion.

"I am glad there are those who still remember my father fondly," he said. The polite words of political theater were clumsy on his tongue, and he was glad they were alone.

"More than you might suspect," Jase said, and he glanced over Cyrus's shoulder to the door. "And here comes another. I believe you have met?"

An older woman dressed in military finery joined their meal, her gray hair loose and hanging to her waist. She stood at perfect attention, somehow both respectful and at ease with her hands crossed behind her back.

"Indeed we have," Kaia Makris said. She bowed deeply. "Welcome to Thiva, my prince."

Though he had met her only once, Cyrus recognized her immediately. Kaia was the reason Cyrus had revealed his face at one of Thorda's meetings, finally exposing the truth of his survival in his attempt to obey Thorda's orders to win over her support. How many of those who looked upon him at that moment had later hung due to Thorda's schemes? In seeking to win their favor, Cyrus had sealed their deaths. That the reveal, and the deaths that followed, were both of Thorda's engineering only made the ache sting worse.

"Thiva is truly beautiful, a vibrant flower amid the forest," Rayan said. "If only we could stay and enjoy your hospitality longer, but alas, we cannot. But while here..."

Rayan removed his boot and pulled out a thin scrap of paper held shut with a ring of wax. Jase took it, broke the wax, and unfurled it. His eyes squinted to read the tiny writing.

"The Coin's ambitions grow by the hour," he said, and crumpled the paper. "I suppose you do not know the message you carried?"

"I do not."

Jase gestured to the table, set and waiting.

"Sit. Eat. Your journey must have been tiring. As for the message, I would not bother you with logistics. Suffice it to say that the Coin wants soldiers to arrive in Vallessau via boats, and wants them sooner than I anticipated."

"And yet much later than most have been waiting," Kaia added.

They sat, Rayan and Cyrus on one side, Jase and Kaia on the other. The food was extravagant and, unlike Vallessau cuisine, contained more spoils of the forest than the ocean, such as fire-roasted venison and plates of quail plucked and simmered in sauces containing honey and berries. Compared to the simple rations Cyrus and Rayan carried, and the stew they ate at their first night's inn, it was a divine feast. Cyrus tore into it, proper etiquette and grace be damned. He was starving, and the meal absolutely delicious.

"Should I send a compliment to my cooks?" Jase asked.

Cyrus lifted a thumb and shook it in response. There would be no speaking, only eating. He left the speaking to Rayan and the others.

"I suspect the prince is not accustomed to such simple travel on foot," Rayan said. He winked. "He will earn his road calluses, though, for we still have far to go."

"I suspected we were but a momentary diversion," Jase said, tearing a small piece of bread from a nearby plate and dipping it in the quail's berry sauce. "For the both of you to bring a simple message is unnecessary, happy as I am to finally meet the Vagrant in person."

"I agreed to this 'momentary diversion' out of hope you might have information useful to me," Rayan said. "Rumors from the north have reached Vallessau's streets, which means they assuredly reached Thiva long before us."

"You speak of Lycaena," Kaia said, not even waiting for the paladin to finish.

Cyrus and Rayan exchanged a look, and then both nodded.

"I am blessed to command the farthest northern reaches of Ierida in Jase's name," she continued. "And I have heard much of these rumors. I dismissed them at first, but no longer. The whispers grow stronger, as do the number of those who believe them."

"Do you know where these cultists might be hiding, or who spreads such rumors?" Rayan asked.

"I have no location, but I do have a name. A priest of your goddess, before the empire came, a man by the name of Eshiel. Do you know him?"

Rayan shook his head. "I cannot say I do. But I will find him. Thank you, Miss Kaia, for your aid."

"If only we could offer more," Jase said. "These rumors bode ill, and I fear the attention they will bring to my lands. The Uplifted Church will not take kindly to their work being undone."

"I would hope the opinion of the church was not your highest priority," Rayan said, a bit of venom sliding into his voice.

"When my people suffer at their whims, I must give them all my attention and more," Jase replied. Though he tried to hide it, Cyrus sensed a bit of annoyance at the paladin's barb. "Placating their occasional inquiries is a delicate act."

"Strange, how placation often mirrors subservience."

"Do you question my loyalty, Paladin?"

"Your loyalty," Rayan said, and he pointed to Cyrus, "was to that young man and his family, and yet when Everlorn's ships arrived, you cast it aside before a single rise and fall of the sun."

The lord set down his drink. His chair groaned as he stood. Cyrus thought him merely insulted, but then he leaned forward, his fists on the table, and spoke with trembling rage. His eyes flung daggers toward Rayan.

"So easy for you to challenge my decisions," he said. "So simple to compare your life to mine, as if we might offer it up equally, but they are not equal. My responsibility was not, and has never been, to the royal family. It may seem that way in the city on the cliffs, but here in Ierida, my responsibility is to my people. I am to protect them, teach them, bless their lives, and guide these lands to safety and prosperity."

"And so you bent your knee to Everlorn," Rayan said.

Jase smashed the table with his fists.

"Do not play at fools," he seethed. "Endarius died *in the very first battle*. One of our gods, slain, and in the heart of our island. Vallessau was lost. By the time I was even informed our island was at war, the king and queen had been executed and that young man over there was held prisoner. I am not without maps and history texts, Paladin. I am not without reason. We are a gnat before a giant, and the best hope for my people to live, to survive, was to avoid being swatted by that giant's fingers. With blood and death all around me, I made the hardest decision of my life. I pray you will never be faced with one similar."

Cyrus swirled his own wine in its silver cup, disgust stirring in his belly. Not all of it was aimed at Jase.

"Every reason you speak justifies your betrayal," he said. "And every justification tells me I should not trust you now."

Kaia cleared her throat before Jase might speak.

"I was there when my lord made his decision," she said. "It was made with a heavy heart, and to spare the innocents of our realm. It was also made with a belief the empire would tire of our island and grow frustrated by the great distance between us. They would appoint a regent, one they deemed capable of keeping the populace well-behaved. Our surrender, and cooperation, was always under the hope that the Thanese way of life could survive if controlled by sympathetic governance."

Rayan crossed his arms and leaned back in his chair. He seemed remarkably calm for having a lord of the four realms be so furious with him.

"You thought you would be that regent one day," he surmised.

Jase slowly returned to his seat. The splotchy redness of his neck started to fade.

"Regent Gordian Goldleaf was an ambitious man from Gadir, and he wanted nothing to do with Thanet beyond using it as a stepping-stone to power in a more noteworthy kingdom. After Lycaena's execution, I thought the matter would be settled. An ill-advised rebellion was at an end, the god and goddess were dead, and so far as I knew, the Lythan family line had ended. Once in power, I could lessen the empire's presence and defang their church. I whispered in Gordian's ear my willingness to take the burden from him so he and his family could return to the mainland."

The lord smirked, and he took a long drink of his wine. When he set it down, he did not try to hide his disgust.

"And then Gordian made it clear to me no one of Thanese blood would ever hold the title of regent. 'I would sooner grant it to a pig' is how he phrased it. The very next day, I set Kaia to work. If the rebellion survived, I wanted to be there for its founding. It took time, but I connected with the Coin's network of spies. And then, not a year later, the strangest whispers reached my ears, whispers later confirmed by the Coin himself: Prince Cyrus had survived and would soon begin his war against the empire, albeit in disguise."

Cyrus remembered his first and only encounter with Kaia. Thorda had given him a mission to convince the vassal of the Vagrant's trustworthiness.

"I was asked to alleviate your concerns over my loyalties," he said, turning to the older woman. "Yet you knew my identity before we ever met?"

Kaia straightened, her posture proud but her gray eyes downcast.

"Forgive me," she said. "The Coin believed it best that the people learn of your survival, but he feared you would refuse to reveal yourself if ordered. I was to be an example of the doubts and concerns hampering our resistance, to see how you might respond."

"You were to bait me into revealing myself," Cyrus said simply. Venom dripped off his tongue. He almost revealed Thorda's name in return, but that would be petty. It could put Stasia and Mari in danger, a risk he would never accept. "I suppose I should stop being surprised the Coin would manipulate me so callously."

"For good or ill, the Coin uses every weapon available to him," Kaia said. "And you are a weapon, Prince Cyrus. I was meant only to sharpen you."

Another plate arrived, thick slices of fruit smothered in honey and sprinkled with crushed walnuts. Cyrus tried one, found it too sweet and sticky to his taste.

"You must understand, our defeat in a normal war was inevitable," Jase said. "I sought only for my people to endure Everlorn's wrath, change their pledge of allegiance from a throne in Vallessau to one in Eldrid, and then carry on with their lives. The God-Incarnate would announce our conquest to his bloodthirsty populace, we'd bow our heads, and then they would forget us. Condemn me as a traitor to Thanet, or call me naïve if you wish. I will accept these titles, for in bearing that shame, I ensured that the Dead Flags never flew in Ierida."

"Again and again you justify treason, while offering me little in return to justify trust," said Rayan.

"Your master, the Coin, trusts me," Jase said. "Is that not reason enough?"

Cyrus could not have laughed harder.

"No," he said. "It is not. Something changed your mind. You went from cooperating with the empire to betraying them, and I do not believe it solely because Gordian denied your plans. One man can be manipulated, killed, or removed. Yet now you participate in a war you were convinced could not be won. Why?"

The handsome lord crossed his arms and studied Cyrus. The scrutiny filled him with a need, fleeting and unwanted, to hide behind his mask. Or his true face.

"I wish I could give you a better answer," Jase began suddenly. "But the truth is, it is a belief held deeply in my gut that something is *wrong*. What it is, I cannot decipher, but I know it to be true. When it comes to coin, to trade, to construction, the empire sets down no roots. Yet when it comes to faith, they are fervent to the extreme. They kill and butcher. They want our prayers, but not our goods? Why seem so disinterested in us, and yet so focused at the same time? They give no sign they will be leaving, yet no sign they are making this their home. Most worrisome of all, nearly every man and woman brought over by their boats has been a soldier, not a tradesman or merchant."

Cyrus picked at his food. This was the first he'd heard of such suspicions. It had always made sense to him that the flood of soldiers would arrive nonstop.

"Is that so unusual?" he asked.

"I have spent many hours discretely discussing the matter with Everlorn soldiers who consider me trustworthy," Kaia explained. "As have my servants and spies. After five years of conquest, we should be awash in people from Gadir. Representatives of the grand merchant companies should be scouting our island's bounty for what would best profit them, and how to transport it across the Crystal Sea. Yes, Gordian Goldleaf arrived with his family, but he should have brought with him a whole host of minor nobles, each hoping to establish themselves upon Thanet. Every conquest is seen as a ripe opportunity to plunder, and to gain in renown. But not here. Not on Thanet."

Jase nodded appreciatively to his vassal, and then he leaned closer, fingers steepled.

"Just as confusing, no one from Thanet has been sent to Gadir. An exotic people, from an exotic island, yet no one has been coveted and brought back as lovers, trophies, wives, or servants? Instead, they embargo us even more severely than before. What is it they fear? Our faiths? Our history? Our blood? Why conquer us, if they would trap us here? Why subdue us, if they would show no interest in the bounty of our land?"

Cyrus thought over his time imprisoned in the castle with Gordian, of the conversations he'd overheard when no one noticed him lurking. Had things been different? He didn't remember anything particular being remarked, but at the same time, there had always been an impatience to what Gordian did, a sense of running out of time. Why show such haste, if he did not seek to leave the island as Jase claimed?

"Perhaps we overlook the obvious," Cyrus offered. "The God-Incarnate is jealous above all others. One world, one nation, one god. Is that not their creed?"

Jase shook his head, clearly unsatisfied with such an explanation.

"I do not know what they plan, but I know there *is* a plan. Gordian gave me every indication he wished to be gone from Thanet, but that he had no choice in remaining. Thanet must be prepared, he would say. It must be made ready. But for what? I do not know. What I do know is that I fear the Uplifted Church and the madness of its priests. I regret nothing of my surrender, prince. It has kept me in power and spared my people the hardships others endured elsewhere. Where I erred was thinking we had reached the limits of what they would take from us. If our gods and our sovereignty are not enough, then I fear what next they take with their knives."

Rayan pushed away his plate and stood. He glanced at Cyrus, his expression calm and unreadable.

"I thank you for your hospitality," he said. "Forgive me for letting my emotions get the best of me. If the Coin trusts you, then I trust you."

"You are forgiven," said Jase. "For I would never condemn a man for being protective of his prince." He clapped, and a servant appeared from around the edge of the door. "Please, see Rayan to his room."

"I think I'll join him," Cyrus said, also hurrying to his feet. The thought of being alone with Kaia and Jase intimidated him. They were both older and wiser when it came to matters of Thanet, and while Cyrus could declare himself a prince, he had few who truly served him compared to the Lord of Ierida. It made Cyrus feel like a child playing pretend.

"If you wish," Jase said, and he stood so he might bow. "Pleasant night to you, my prince. Should I not see you again before you depart, I wish you both the best of luck in tracking down these rumors of a living Lycaena. May she live, and soon grace us with her presence. I fear, however, the naked truth shall be far less beautiful, and far more cruel."

CHAPTER 5

VAGRANT

They were given a pair of guest rooms side by side, with clean beds and lit candles. Cut flowers still wet from the river sat on tables by the windows, their vases matching the swirling blue and white of the outside banners. Cyrus's belongings were waiting for him, brought by the servants during their bathing. He searched through them, confirming the presence of his swords and mask.

Especially his mask.

Why such fear? he wondered as he touched the painted wood with his fingertips. *Why such a caress?*

Cyrus jammed the mask back into the pile of clothes, tied the sack shut, and refused to dwell on it further. Moments later, after a knock on the door, he joined Rayan in the matching room. The paladin lay atop his bed, his head propped up by a pillow. A half-full glass of wine rested on the bedside table, an open bottle beside it.

"I see you're quick to make yourself comfortable," Cyrus said as he shut the door.

"Should I not?" the paladin asked with a laugh. "Some say sleeping on hard floors and depriving yourself of comforts will make you a stronger person. I say it leads to a bad back and an unwelcoming disposition."

"Is that why you were so...unwelcoming...to Jase?"

"Do not judge Jase harshly by my own distaste. I tend to disagree with most lords. Born into their privilege, they too often view themselves inherently superior to the people they are meant to guide and protect."

"My parents were born into their privilege," Cyrus said.

"A privilege given to them by my goddess, and by the mighty Lion. It is not the same."

Except it wasn't given, it was taken from the Orani. Cyrus almost admitted as much then and there, but he was tired, his skin raw from the soap, and his belly overstuffed. He wanted to sleep, yet his mind felt aflame, and so he sought friendship instead.

"Your complaints may be valid, but I don't get that feeling from Jase. He cares for those in his realm."

"And yet keeping power has been the heart of all his decisions. Oh, to help others, he insists. Consider me doubtful. Even tyrants will claim their actions are for the betterment of the masses. Judge them by their fruits, not their words."

"And so far, his fruits are a realm mostly at peace compared to the bloodshed in Vallessau."

Rayan sat up, grabbed the bottle of wine, and offered it to Cyrus.

"Are you so certain you wish to argue such matters now? If so, at least get a little drunk first. It'll make things more bearable."

Cyrus surrendered to his elder's wisdom. He took a long drink, the faint cherry flavor pleasant across his tongue. With alcohol in his veins, perhaps he would possess the courage needed to voice the fear he'd kept locked within him ever since the nightmares of burning boats.

"I just wonder, what if Jase has a point?" Cyrus asked, setting down the bottle.

"The man rambled without ceasing. Narrow matters down for me. Which of his arguments do you think most had value?"

The paladin had a grin on his face, and his tone was gentle. He was trying to alleviate the tension, and it would have worked if Cyrus's thoughts weren't so grim. Still, he appreciated the effort.

"Our war against the empire's initial invasion was one of constant failure," Cyrus said. "What if we had never fought? What if we will-ingly accepted a place in Everlorn's growing borders? If we'd simply knelt, if we'd bowed our heads…"

The words trailed off. The rest were too painful.

Rayan's hand settled on Cyrus's shoulder.

"You blame yourself," he said.

Cyrus closed his eyes, heard his mother's scream as Magus's sword fell.

"If I'd not tried to escape, then maybe they'd have lived. We would be together still."

"Do you hate me for that? For being the one who sought to rescue you?"

Cyrus shook his head. It might sound like it, but he'd never once blamed Rayan for trying to smuggle him out of the castle. How could he? Amid the burning docks and crumbling walls, such an escape made perfect sense.

"I have never," he said. "Please, Rayan, believe me when I say I have ever looked on you as a friend and protector."

The old paladin smiled.

"Good. Now listen to me, as your friend, when I tell you this. Even if you surrendered, another reason would have been given to take your parents' lives. Heed this lesson instead. If you had come with me, you would have remained free. It was your attempt to placate the empire, and give them what they wanted, that made you their prisoner."

"Is that why you hate Lord Mosau?"

The paladin sighed.

"There are many kinds of death, Cyrus, and if you live long enough you will see them all. Many fear the swift and brutal strike of a sword. I do not, for I know my goddess awaits me when the light of this world fades. It is the slower deaths I fear, and it is a slower death Jase delivers his subjects when he bows his head to the empire. A long, unending bleeding, what is good and vital draining away drop by drop into Everlorn's cup. Their faith. Their sovereignty. Their dignity. The executioner's ax remains above their necks; yet instead of falling swiftly, it sways back and forth, ever slowly, the cuts thin at first, but only at first."

Cyrus grabbed the bottle and tilted it in a toast.

"Then here is to victory, or a swift death," he said, and drained a third of it.

If Cyrus slept, it was for only a few minutes before he was startled out of his bed by frantic knocking on his door. He did not open it until he held a sword in hand. A servant waited on the other side, and he blanched at the sight of naked steel.

"Please, you must gather your things and follow me," the young man said.

"Why? What has happened?"

The servant hesitated a moment.

"The empire is here."

The empire was everywhere in Thanet, even in Thiva. Cyrus had seen their priests preaching on street corners and upon high pedestals set alongside the river. But for Jase to have them flee in the middle of the night meant someone had come to the castle, someone Jase could not refuse...

"Who?" he asked, and stepped out from his room. "Who is here?"

The door to Rayan's room opened, and the paladin stepped out with his armor and belongings bundled and on his back. His sword, however, was now buckled to his waist.

"Time is not on our side," he said. "Save your questions for later."

Cyrus glanced between him and the servant, then accepted the gentle rebuke.

"So be it."

He dressed, but not for travel as Rayan did. He donned his hood and cloak, belted his swords to his waist, and then reached for his mask. The wood felt like fire in his hand, but he did not don it. Not yet. Into his pocket, instead.

Only if I need it, he thought. *Only then.*

Faint, distant laughter mocked him.

"How will we escape unnoticed?" Cyrus asked once back out in the hall. The distant clamor of movement, of a sleeping castle coming to life, echoed throughout halls. "There is only the drawbridge."

"There are places in the garden one may hide," the servant explained. "We will wait there until I receive a signal the drawbridge is clear, and then you may cross. Now hurry, please, the runners from the outer gate bought us precious little time!"

The pair hurried after the servant, following him down hallways and to a side door exiting the castle into the green gardens outside. They hunkered down among the rows of bushes, safely hidden, but Cyrus's curiosity was too strong.

"We're to wait until the bridge out is clear, yeah?" he asked their guide.

"Indeed."

"Then I'm going to said drawbridge to have a gander at our uninvited guests."

Panic widened the servant's eyes.

"It is not safe!"

Cyrus turned and grinned at him.

"That has never stopped me before."

He crouch-walked through the garden, head bowed and hands gliding along the grass to keep himself balanced. He'd seen only a glimpse of the garden upon arriving at the castle, but he remembered the rows of rose and catmint bushes that formed a sort of barrier marking off the pathway between the drawbridge and the castle entrance. He hurried there and, through the red and purple blooms, peered at the enormous imperial retinue filling both the drawbridge and the street beyond.

Dread settled in Cyrus's heart. Among the dozens of soldiers were two paragons, each a potent foe on their own. All together they would require an army to be killed. An army, or a god. Yet Cyrus's dread came not from them, but from the man who walked at their forefront, the Heir-Incarnate, Galvanis vin Lucavi.

Cyrus had never laid eyes upon him before, and he peered over the bush as high as he dared. Bathed in the moonlight, the heir's pale skin took on a bluish tone, so smooth, so perfect, he looked less like a man and more a marble statue come to life. His long blond hair was tied into a ponytail and then draped over his shoulder, the end tied with silver thread that sparkled in the night. His golden armor was thick even for a paragon, yet he moved with the fluidity of a hunting panther.

You recognize him, don't you? What he is? What he's becoming?

"He's nothing like me," Cyrus whispered in protest, but there was no one to hear him.

You know better. You sense the divine. Stop lying to yourself, Vagrant.

It was true. Galvanis reeked of it, like a scent only Cyrus could track. Prayer and faith radiated off of the Heir-Incarnate in lucid purple waves. It crackled through his skin like lightning. He might be human, but not entirely. A transformation had already begun, one Cyrus was painfully intimate with. All this, due to the faith of the populace in his appointment granted by his father.

A shiver ran through Cyrus. If this was the power of the Heir, how grand and terrifying was the might of the God-Incarnate himself?

The blue doors opened, and Jase stepped out with his head and back already bowed. He greeted the Heir-Incarnate loudly, and when he dropped to his knees, his servants and soldiers gathered behind him did the same. Galvanis observed him a moment, said something Cyrus could not hear, and then bade the man to stand.

Rayan joined Cyrus during the commotion, crouching by his side, and together they watched the silhouette of the Heir-Incarnate vanish into the castle. His retinue followed, dozens of soldiers laughing and chatting as they flooded inside in search of food and bed.

"There are few tasks that would bring the Heir-Incarnate out from Vallessau," the paladin whispered, echoing Cyrus's thoughts.

"He's hunting Lycaena, to execute her a second time if she lives."

Rayan nodded in agreement. His face hardened, his lips curling into a worried frown. Their guide servant rushed to their side, and Cyrus needed no explanation that the rapid hooting of an owl from the gateway was the signal they waited for. Rayan stood, and he shifted his rucksack to the opposite shoulder. He glared at the closed doors of the castle, then shook his head.

"Whatever dangers Keles faced have magnified tenfold," he said. "For her sake, we must find her, Cyrus...before the empire does."

CHAPTER 6

STASIA

Stasia hesitated at the door to the makeshift forge. Her father had sequestered himself within more and more over the past month. If he left, it was to look over lists and maps with messengers while plotting insurrections all across Thanet. It seemed he had abandoned Vallessau and was focusing his efforts elsewhere. She knew that wasn't true, though. He still thought Vallessau could be saved.

He was just convinced only the missing Vagrant would save it.

Frustration gave her the strength to push open the wood door. She and her sister were busy fighting, bleeding, and nearly dying for this damn city. If only her father would notice and appreciate *that* sacrifice, instead of pining for a brat who fled the moment things turned dire.

"How go things?" she asked. Her father's back was to her as he bent over an anvil with a tiny hammer in hand. At the sound of her voice, he spun around, his body positioned between her and the anvil.

"Better, if I were not interrupted," he said. "Is something amiss?"

"Must something be amiss for me to speak with my father?"

He crossed his arms. A faint smirk tugged at the right half of his face.

"History says yes, Stasia." He turned back around, and she heard the ping of metal, a much higher pitch than the steel of his normal weapons. He opened a nearby cupboard and deposited his work into it fast enough she caught only a quick glimmer of silver bracelets. That done, he wiped his hands on his smithy apron. When he next spoke, he sounded much more at ease.

"Forgive me, I should not snap at you," he said. "I'm glad you're here, for I've a request to make, and it saves me time from hunting you down."

Stasia hesitated. The reason she came, these thoughts, these questions—she could not banish them. They were worms crawling through her skull. Yet they felt foolish, too, and she could not shake a fear her father would mock her for acknowledging them.

"Sure, what is it you need?" she asked. So much easier to let him guide the conversation, and to delay her reason for coming.

"Commander Pilus has been training soldiers in Pelion," he said. "It is a small village eighty miles southwest of here along Tannis Road, in case you are unfamiliar. Our spies confirmed that the Heir-Incarnate is heading north with a contingent of his soldiers, so it is prudent we strike while they are absent. I would have you visit our new recruits and test their mettle against your own."

"Do you think it is wise for me to leave when things are so dangerous in Vallessau?"

Her father shrugged.

"It is not my fault we are shorthanded of capable individuals. With Rayan dragging the Vagrant north, it is either you, Mari, or Arn. Of the three, I trust the Lioness and the Heretic to handle a Humbled, at least until Cyrus returns to the fold. The task of aiding Pilus therefore falls to you."

Stasia tried not to feel hurt by such a decision. Arn was a paragon, and Mari a god-whisperer. They each possessed supernatural gifts for a fight against the panther god. Stasia, meanwhile, had only her well-honed but still natural human muscles to guide her axes.

At least, she assumed them natural. Soma and Rihim claimed otherwise...

"Until Cyrus returns to the fold?" she asked. "I'm sorry, but did we all forget how and when Cyrus left?"

"He has not left!" Thorda shouted. Stasia lifted her chin and stepped closer. Her hands clenched into fists. Her frustration gave her the courage to face him eye to eye.

"Wake up, Father. He is gone, and has been for a month. Whatever happened between you and him, it won't repair on its own. Let me talk to him. We spent years training together. Maybe if you would *tell* me what happened, I could help."

"There is nothing you can do. He must accept his destiny, and he will, Stasia. He will. I hold faith."

Stasia's mood soured, and there was only one way she knew how to react—with anger.

"Of course you hold faith in him," she said. "Gods forbid you hold faith in your own daughters. We're just the hired help here in Thanet. How could we ever hope to win without a spoiled princeling to take the credit for all our hard work?"

"I thought you wanted to topple an empire, Stasia. Or do you kill solely for accolades and praise, mighty Ax of Lahareed?"

It was such a low blow she didn't know how to respond. She had not spread those stories. Over a decade prior, she had accompanied her sister in attacking a mountainside fortress to kill an ailing regent. Afterward, she had flung his corpse off the cliff and then dove after it. Her ax had cleaved it in half, showering a gathering crowd below with bone and gore. Mari caught her as she fell, her sister gifted at that time with the form of the flying Falcon Reaper. The two had flown overhead, a defiant display against the imperial occupation.

That had only been the start. Blood had flowed like rivers from both ax and talon. And yet Lahareed still fell. Its resistance broke beneath waves of steel, faith in the Falcon Reaper faded away, and years later they departed, seeking a new nation, a new battlefield. It might have spread her reputation far and wide, but for her, it was her greatest failure. She had given everything of herself, and it led to nothing. Lahareed had shown the limits of her ax.

And yet still she fought. Still she killed. Her father should know the resolve it took to continue, shouldn't he? He knew the sacrifices she offered, the lonely nights, the inability to ever lay down roots, all to fight a war for a home she barely remembered.

"Accolades," she said, voice falling low and dangerous. "You think I suffer all this for accolades?"

Thorda picked up various tools, little hammers and pliers, and began organizing them on a pegboard. It was as if he had to be doing something, anything, to keep his gaze elsewhere.

"Truthfully, I do not know why you suffer as you do," he said. "Especially for one such as me."

It wasn't much of an apology, but Stasia had learned to live with less. She took in a long breath and counted to three before letting it out. She must approach this next topic calmly, and fully under control.

"There's something I wanted to ask you before I go," she said, easing into the actual point of her questioning. "It's about the Humbled."

"Worry not about him. With Arn's help, your sister is capable of putting him down."

Putting him down, like the Humbled were a rabid dog. Though was it all that far from the truth? Beaten and broken gods, offering up their faith to the God-Incarnate in distant Eldrid. They were sickly shadows, twisted from their original purpose. They should be defending their people, not aiding their oppressors. Perhaps putting them down was absolutely the best way to view it.

"It's not killing him I'm worried about," Stasia said. "It's something he said."

"Oh?" Thorda asked. No inflection in the slightest, and barely a lift of an eyebrow. That alone made Stasia suspicious. He should have been disdainful, or incurious. Instead, he feigned nothing at all.

"The Humbled insisted that he smelled other gods on the island," she said, then hesitated. Damn it, why was she so nervous? Even now she could not voice the entire accusation, but a hint of it. "Miquoan gods."

Thorda crossed his arms and glared.

"You bother me with the delusions of a Humbled? What could that even mean, Stasia?"

There was the disdain. There was the disregard she expected. It was almost comforting.

"I don't know," she said, and started to pace around the cramped forge. It was far from the grand space her father preferred at their countryside mansion, but stuck in Vallessau, this converted room would have to do. He'd opened holes in the roof to allow the smoke out, installed the forge, and added shelves to contain his tools and ingredients. "He seemed so sure of himself."

"Of course he is sure," Thorda said. He slammed his hammer onto a shelf. "His mind has been warped by decades of torture. He likely thinks Miquoan gods lurk everywhere he goes. His hatred of us, and of the betrayal I committed against his nation, might be the very impetus used to break him. He is not to be trusted, my daughter, only eliminated."

If only it were that simple, but Rihim's claim had tossed kindling onto an already burning fire.

"He's not the first to claim I have divine blood," she said.

"What then?" Thorda asked. "What other trustworthy person has told you lies?"

A tiny bit of heat flushed into Stasia's cheeks.

"A paragon," she admitted. "One in blue armor by the name of Soma. When we fought after the hangings, he made a claim similar to Rihim's."

"And now we are putting the word of the empire's paragons over my own."

"That's not what I'm doing."

"That is exactly what you are doing. Liars and manipulators are casting doubt upon your abilities, Stasia. They seek only to confuse you."

"But why would he lie? It doesn't make any sense. Soma said I might be a god, or at least a demi-god."

Again she hesitated. Why? She didn't actually believe this nonsense... did she? No. She had to know. She had to have an answer, one given from her father's lips, or it would drive her mad. Stasia forced out the words, even if they were halted and embarrassed.

"Am... am I one?"

At that, her father laughed.

"We are descendants of Miquo, Stasia. For hundreds of years, Miquoan gods lived and walked among us, and they sired many, many children. *Of course* you have the faint blood of gods within you. Mari does, too, as well as every single Miquoan refugee you might ever meet. We are a blessed people. It was why we isolated ourselves, and bore so much hatred from the outside world."

He made it all seem so simple, so obvious, but it wasn't. If both Rihim and Soma lied, then what was the purpose? What did either gain from it?

"Even so, I feel there's something you're not telling me." Her head lowered. Her jaw tightened. "It wouldn't be the first time."

Thorda closed his eyes a moment, steeling himself for something.

"I apologize for the lack of warning," he said, abruptly changing the topic. "But I need you to leave for Pelion before nightfall. You'll be carrying a message with you, and haste is of the utmost importance. Go prepare yourself for the journey."

The sudden dismissal had Stasia on her heels.

"I'll tell Clarissa," she said. "If she hurries, we can both be out of here before the moon rises."

"Must you bring her with you?" Thorda asked, so quick it seemed he were prepared for this possibility. "Surely you can go a few days without someone to share your bed, or have you grown soft during your time on Thanet?"

Stasia's mouth dropped open. Ever since Cyrus left, she had flung herself harder into her missions. Her axes bathed in the blood of imperials nearly every night. The only pause had come from the increasingly dangerous Humbled, whose ability to hunt them was enhanced by his divine nature. Not since Lahareed had she given so much of herself to a cause, and yet he would accuse her of growing *soft*?

"Please, Father, tell me how you truly feel," she practically snarled. "Don't mince words. We're family. We can handle the truth, right? Except for the truths you keep from me, or any inconvenient facts that might interfere with your plans."

"Are you still angry over my not informing you of the Joining Laws implementation? You would have grown emotional and abandoned Cyrus's training. We both know that. Clarissa has you—"

"Has me what?" Stasia interrupted. "Caring for someone other than myself? Or maybe willing to fight and die for anyone and anything other than you and your damn war?"

"My war," he asked. "Not yours?"

So much for her protests. So much for her insisting she didn't fight for accolades. She was so angry, so frustrated, she didn't even care.

"If you think that, you're a damn old fool," she seethed. "And you insult me worse than you ever have in your life. Fuck you, old man. Fuck you, fuck your war, and fuck every single thought in your damn head. I'm getting Clarissa, and I'm going to Pelion. Make sure your note is ready for me in the study so I don't have to track you down. After all, I'd hate to interrupt you from your oh-so-very-important work."

Stasia stormed out of the forge, not wanting to hear another word from her father. She was so angry she wanted to cry, as if that wasn't damn confusing.

It was only hours later and at Clarissa's home that Stasia realized she had never received a proper answer to her question.

CHAPTER 7

KELES

To live so deep in the woods meant daily hard work, and Keles struggled to earn her place. She was no hunter. Growing up in Vallessau as a paladin prodigy, she had learned the sword and shield instead of the bow. She was no farmer, not that there was much room to grow crops amid the tightly packed ash trees of their hidden encampment. She knew little of stitching and sewing, considered herself a poor cook, and needed to be told which mushrooms and weeds were poisonous and which were edible during her first attempt at foraging with a trio of older women. Among the people of this strange village, she felt useless and unneeded.

Keles knew how to pray to her goddess, and how to kill. Yet there was no one to draw her sword against, and what use were her prayers in a village full of people whose faith surpassed her own?

"There you are," Eshiel said, carefully stepping down the uneven earth toward the stream. Keles was up to her waist in the cold water, two thicket baskets behind her. One of the women had given her lye soap to wash the pile of sweat- and blood-soaked clothes. She wrung out a man's shirt and tossed it into the basket with the others she had cleaned, then reached for a pair of trousers from the dirty pile.

"Here I am," Keles said, trying, and failing, to keep her frustration out of her voice. Eshiel was always kind to her when they spoke, seemingly built of infinite patience, but she could not shake the feeling she was disappointing him. He tested her gently, an offer for her to lead a prayer one night, a question during a lecture the next. The prodding upset her more than she let on.

Who was she, with the faith of a flickering candle, to speak next to the burning torch that was Eshiel?

"I see you have found work," he said.

"I won't claim it suits me, but at least I am helping."

"Helping, yes, but not so much as you could. I hold great hopes for you, Keles, and I must admit, they do not involve leaving the Light of Vallessau to wash dirty clothes instead of leading Lycaena's faithful."

She scrubbed the lye harder. Keles hated whenever someone brought up her time as Thanet's hero. Not that she was ashamed of her accomplishments, or thought it wrong to have fought the Everlorn Empire. No, she hated it because it forced her to remember the forsaking ceremony. Before a great crowd, she cast aside her faith in Lycaena and swore allegiance to the empire. Lies, she sometimes pretended. The truth was that, in her darkest moments, when the night was deep, her prayers to Lycaena were stale and empty.

"Do not call me that name," she said. "I forfeited it at the forsaking ceremony, remember?"

Eshiel smiled at her, but the joy was mixed with pain in his eyes.

"I did not attend. My life was meant to end at the Dead Flags, but I was rescued from one of the Uplifted Church's underground prisons. This was prior to Lycaena's execution, when the Coin was building up his forces for one last attempt to save her. Sadly, the priests had taken a bit of sport in breaking my faith in the goddess, and I was in no shape to assist. While Lycaena's faithful fought to save her life, I lay in bed, sick and bleeding. I had to learn from others of her death. By the time the Anointed One led her forsaking ceremony, I had long fled Vallessau for Ierida."

That explained the many scars. Guilt wracked her. She had anticipated similar punishments to befall her when she was captured during the failed attempt to stop Lycaena's execution, but none came. With Lycaena's death, Anointed Sinshei had spent months preaching forgiveness, acceptance, and a doctrine of "moving forward." As much as it sickened her stomach, Keles had been the Anointed's most prized possession. The Light of Vallessau, publicly casting aside her faith in the name of peace? How poignant. How powerful.

"What task would you ask of me?" she asked. The bitter memories reminded her of how far she'd fallen, and how Eshiel had helped her rise again amid the light of the reborn Lycaena. He deserved better from her. No priest or paladin had eased the pain she felt since Lycaena's execution, but here in the wilds, Eshiel had succeeded. The least she could do was listen without complaint.

"It is a matter much better suited to your skills."

Keles lowered the trousers into the water, letting the stream wash through them.

"And which skills are those?"

The man pointed to her sheathed sword, which leaned against a nearby tree.

"The blade, Keles Lyon, brought to bear against agents of Everlorn."

⟳

It was a lengthy trip out from the forest to the nearby village of Chora. Keles sat in the back of a cart, relaxing as best she could given the bumpy ride. Her sword lay beside her. It was the only hint of her past as a paladin. If Eshiel's intelligence was true, that sword would be all she needed.

Just a lone soldier, one I suspect hopes to tarry an extra day for a bit of pleasure, he had explained.

To ensure a steady flow of sacrifices, Eshiel purposefully seeded rumors that villages in the north were full of women eager for a tumble or two if given the right amount of coin. It led to many Everlorn soldiers sneaking out at night, or breaking from patrols for a few unaccounted-for hours. Keles suspected some of those women did indeed sleep with the soldiers, if only to keep them around while runners alerted Eshiel's camp. Isolated, these men were easy prey for Eshiel's people to capture and bring back into the forest.

"We're here," Navik said from up front. He was her driver leading the donkey pulling the cart. A grizzled man, his skin a shade brighter than Keles's. His hair was cut short about the ears and neck, his hands scarred from a lifetime spent in the fields. His smile was warm, even if his brown eyes were cold.

"That was quick," she lied.

"Only if you napped through it. Anyway, keep that sword of yours hidden until I locate the soldier."

"Won't he be easy enough to spot?"

Navik grinned at her over his shoulder.

"If he's got his armor and weapons on, yeah, sure. But if he's here for a spot of play? He's probably dressed like any other local. The last thing we want is to spook him with the sight of naked steel."

The village housed maybe a hundred people in total, nearly half of them children. A few kids waved at Keles as they passed, asking if she had anything to trade.

"Nothing," she had to admit. During her time as a paladin, she'd have come bearing sweets and little paintings. Winning over the children was a time-tested strategy for earning respect and a moment of discussion with their parents. Now she had only a smile to offer, but she offered it nonetheless as they followed the outer edge of the village. Navik halted the donkey along the northwest boundary and then hopped down.

"Give me a moment to ask around," he said, which was fine with Keles. She remained in the cart. Eshiel made no secret of his camp's existence. It was only the purpose of it, and what transpired on the cliffs beyond the forest, that he kept hidden. To feed and house so many people, carts regularly traveled to the nearby villages to trade and barter.

Keles touched the sword beside her. Maybe the soldier had already left. Maybe there'd be no need of her skills.

After a short exchange with an older man, Navik was pointed toward a woman sitting on the porch of her thatched-roof hut. She did not smile when Navik greeted her, but she did nod and gesture with her thumb to the door. The man bowed low, then trudged back to the cart with his hands in his pockets, as if he had been rebuked. Keles arched an eyebrow to convey her question.

"In there," Navik answered. "Sleeping."

Keles lifted her sword.

"Then let's give him a proper waking."

In return, Navik grabbed the bundled rope Keles had used as a pillow on her ride here.

"Nice and proper," he agreed.

The woman had left the porch by the time they returned to the house. The door was closed. Keles glanced at the window. The soldier would have seen their approach if he'd been watching. Yet the woman insisted he'd been sleeping. Hopefully she was right.

Keles braced to the side of the door in case she was wrong. Navik took position opposite her. With her free hand she counted down from three, then kicked the door open.

A wide-eyed man with pale skin and fiery red hair slashed the air where she should have been had she barged straight inside.

"Snakes!" he shouted in Thanese. It seemed one of the few words he knew. "Snakes, snakes, you snakes!"

He rushed her, still trying to take advantage of the surprise. Keles batted aside his second thrust, and she planted her feet in a proper stance. Her foe was frightened and frantic. She could win this easily if she kept her head. Two more blocks, and she felt more secure in her belief.

"Snake," the soldier muttered, pulling back. He had a wood shield in his other arm, and he held it before him. His gaze flicked back and forth between Keles and Navik, who lurked behind her with the rope.

Need to end this quick, she thought. The longer they fought, the more he'd panic. She batted aside another thrust, stepped close, and slammed her elbow into his face. Blood splattered as his nose crunched from the blow. His balance lost, he staggered backward. Keles closed the distance immediately, her actions guided by thousands of hours of training.

Be with me, she prayed, the first time since that horrid day the knives fell, and then swung her sword overhead. The soldier brought his shield up to bear. A proper maneuver against any other foe. Not a paladin of Lycaena.

Light should have bathed the steel of her blade, soft and gentle with a hint of blue amid the white. Not this time. Crimson flame burst along the blade, flaring for the briefest second before the sword struck shield. Feeble wood shattered. Next came flesh. The soldier screamed as the weapon sank into his chest, ending his life. His body collapsed, but the sword remained stuck, wedged deeply into his rib cage.

"Lycaena have mercy," muttered Navik. "You nearly cut the bastard in half."

Keles put a heel to the dead man's chest, braced her legs, and yanked her sword free. She stared at its gore-slick length. No fire. No light.

"I fear I have secured us a poor sacrifice," she said, trying to make light of her nerves.

Navik shrugged.

"It's not often they're alive, honestly. The dead work, too, so long as they served the empire. Help me carry him. If we load him up on the cart, we can arrive home in time for supper."

⌒♫⌒

They brought her to Eshiel's tent upon their return to the camp. The priest greeted her at the entrance, his hands clasping hers.

"Well done, well done," he said. The skin of his palms was hard, but not from calluses. From scars. She did not pull away. "Eat with me, please."

The meal was meager, a single squirrel cut and boiled for the two of them to share, along with a few greens dug out from the forest and mixed with a handful of berries. Keles sat and nibbled on the berries. She had no appetite despite the long day of tedious travel. She couldn't shake the moment her instinctive prayer had been answered and divine power blessed her sword.

"I have already heard the tale," Eshiel said as he sat opposite her. "But I would hear it again."

"I do not wish to retell it."

The joy on the tattooed man's face hardened into something more studious.

"You're troubled. Why?"

Blessed with fire, instead of light.

"The Lycaena you summon," she said, deciding to the Heldeep with caution and quiet doubts. Let it all be made open. Her time with Eshiel had revealed him to be brilliant regarding matters of faith and history. If anyone could assuage her doubts, it was him. "The being we offer our prayers to, the one we sacrifice and spill blood upon an altar to bring forth...are you so certain it is the real Lycaena?"

Eshiel leaned back in his chair and pushed away his plate. His hand brushed at his crooked nose, a tic of his she'd noticed, done whenever he was thinking heavily.

"I had thought your doubts quelled by kneeling in her presence."

Keles smirked. If only he knew the moniker she'd briefly adopted when fighting alongside her uncle.

"We court the divine, Eshiel, of that I am certain. She may even accept the name 'Lycaena.' But is it our goddess? Is it the miracle of light and wonder who asked for peace over conflict, who preached forgiveness over vengeance? Or have we bound our faith to something...different? My Lycaena demanded no blood sacrifice. This one does. That change must mean something."

Eshiel didn't argue, nor respond immediately. Instead he crossed his arms and observed her. The silence weighed heavily in the room.

"Something happened at the village, something that bothers you deeply," he said.

Keles closed her eyes, heard the scream of the soldier as her sword broke his shield like brittle plaster.

"When I fought Everlorn's soldiers, my blade was a beacon of light in a dark war. Yet today, when I called Lycaena's name, it was wreathed in crimson flame."

"The difference frightens you?"

Lycaena's form when summoned at the sacrifice flashed through her mind. A being of fire and blood, not quite corporeal, but her presence undeniable. It could not linger for long, but with each sacrifice, Eshiel insisted she grew more permanent, and that much closer to returning to Thanet in full. She felt warmth and comfort in its presence, but was it wise to trust her feelings?

"Does it *not* frighten you?" she asked. "What if the goddess we bring back to Thanet is not the one we first loved?"

Eshiel did not answer immediately. Instead he leaned forward, his hands clasped together as if to pray. He stared for a moment at his uneaten food, then glanced up.

"Did you ever attend a twice-born ceremony, Keles?"

"Only once, when I was twelve," she said. "But my paladin training covered much of the rituals, and Lycaena's lectures upon it."

"Then you should have some idea of the preparation involved," Eshiel said. "Those final weeks prior? They felt like a lifetime. I lived and dressed crossed. I prayed the Poem of Flowers each morning, and read tracts from the Heaven's Wing each night. I used pieces of my old clothes to create the ceremonial wrapping, and if you believe your stitching is poor, you should have seen my own work, and the many little blisters and drops of blood that accompanied it. All of it led to that final moment at the cliffs of the Solemn Sands."

This would be the official twice-born ceremony. Keles had been given a minor role for the one she attended, a two-sentence litany calling on the goddess to love and protect all in attendance. She had not been close enough to witness the actual blessing that took place overhanging the cliff.

"The wrapping is nailed to the edge," Eshiel continued. "And the lone opening sealed prior to the man or woman within being cast over the side. I still remember each and every prayer I offered beforehand, but most of all, I remember the orders I was given when the wrapping was sealed. 'Think on your true self,' the priest ordered. So as I hung off that cliff, swaying in the wind, I thought of the man I wished to become. And that's when I heard the flutter of my goddess's wings."

Keles's heart ached. What she would give to have been there. Young as she was now, she had been younger still when the empire arrived. She'd been given so few moments to be with Lycaena when the goddess graced the island with her presence. For years now she'd thought that hope gone completely, but then came rumors of Eshiel's camp, and the goddess reborn...

"She hovered just beyond my wrapping," Eshiel continued, "and she placed a hand against the side. You may believe Lycaena is light, but in the moment of my birth, I remember fire. Its heat bathed over me, cleansed me, perfected me. And then she spoke, not in prayer, not to a crowd. To me, and me alone. Her orders. Her command for my life. 'Become who you were born to be, tear free, and fly.'"

Eshiel paused to gather himself from the emotions of such a memory.

"And so I flew," he said with a crack in his voice. "I put my hands right into that fire, ripped open the cloth, and fell to the water below. It was cold, Keles, so cold, after being enveloped in such warmth. I swam to the shore, and there awaited my friends, my family, and with new clothes for me to wear. Twin tables piled together with food for the feast that followed. Songs. Dancing. Yet all of it paled when Lycaena graced me with one last gift."

He put his hands to his forehead, his fingers brushing the tattooed wings.

"She touched me here, right across the brow. 'Twice-born, I name you, Eshiel Dymling.' And then she took to the heavens. I still remember the notes she played on her harp. I remember the rainbow of light that lingered in her wake. It gave me succor in the years to come. It gave me hope when the Uplifted Church cut at my flesh and seared me with their hot irons."

Eshiel's face hardened as he withdrew from memory and returned to the present.

"All twice-born rituals are now condemned by the Joining Laws," he said. "To even dress crossed is to invite the church's wrath. Some have attempted the rituals without Lycaena's presence, and they lead only to heartbreak. Her statue at the Solemn Sands was smashed. The hope, the joy, the freedom I felt, is stifled and dying. I weep for every man and woman denied. I rage for the shackles brought on boats flying gray flags and bearing bloody hands in prayer."

He stood from the table and clutched the table's edge with a white-knuckle grip. His arms trembled.

"What future awaits us if Lycaena falls into the past? What happens to we who were given a new life when her power and faith fade away? It is a horror I deny with my every heartbeat, Keles. I will not allow it.

Whatever the cost, I shall pay it. Whatever the blood required, I shall spill it. Lycaena must return. Thanet must be saved. And if the Lycaena we summon is changed, then so be it, for our island has changed. We are *not* free, and we are *not* at peace. Bring fire, instead of light. We already see the horror. We need only to burn it away."

Keles felt pinned to her seat. This man, and his belief, went beyond a torch. It was a blazing sun, and she wondered what it would be like to believe so fully. Before him she felt hollow and meager. Yet to have that faith? To know the path and walk it true? She needed it. Craved it. The empire had stolen her purpose when they hacked the wings from her goddess and bled her out before a horrified crowd. And yet Eshiel promised miracles. Promised, and by the being that birthed each and every night before him, he was so close to delivering.

"Then let us burn it away," she said. "Forgive me my doubts."

Eshiel's hand settled on her shoulder. Her breath caught in her lungs.

"Doubts need never be forgiven, for they are no crime, no sin. Now come. We have a sacrifice to perform, and tonight, I would have you hold the dagger."

CHAPTER 8

ARN

It was easy enough to find some orphan boy, his face lean with hunger, to deliver a message. All it took was a bit of coin to go along with the folded scrap of paper. Arn had written it, not in Thanese or the imperial tongue of Eldrid, but in the language of his homeland. Old Vash, as it was known, long since abandoned. Dario could read it, though. The brothers had been taught it at a young age so they might learn from the old texts and histories of their castle.

Arn's message had contained only a location, a boathouse near the docks. Another hefty bribe, and the old man who owned it had ordered the two young lads working with him to take the day off. Arn paced between the door and the current boat in progress as time crawled along. Dario would come, he knew that. That his note was written in Old Vash would be enough to convince him. The question was, how would he react?

Arn shook his head, and he laughed. He was fooling himself. His brother's reaction was not in question. So why in the God-Incarnate's hell was he doing this?

The door creaked open behind him. His heart leaped. There would be no going back now. He took a breath, steeled his reserve, and turned.

And there before him stood his brother, looking not a hint older despite their time separated. Though Arn was several years younger, family friends often insisted the two could be twins. They had the same square jaws, same wide, prominent noses, and the same green eyes. "My sweet emeralds," his mother described them.

There was nothing sweet in Dario's gaze.

"Where's the fox mask?" he asked. The first words he'd heard his brother speak in years, and they stripped away any pretense or deception between them. They had exchanged brief blows during Rihim's earlier ambush. Dario now knew, not everything, but enough. That Arn lived, and was fighting the empire on the side of insurrectionists. The question was, how might he react to that knowledge?

"No need for masks here," Arn said. "Masks are for when I'm bringing my gauntlets to a fight."

Which means we aren't fighting, he implied. He didn't want a fight, not with Dario, not here, not now, not ever. What he wanted was his older brother gone from Thanet, but Arn feared there was zero chance of that happening.

Dario crossed his arms, and he fell silent. His jaw hardened. His fists shook with a steadily growing rage, like a volcano preparing for an eruption.

"So you're here," he exclaimed. "Here. Unbelievable. Damned *unbelievable!*"

Arn recognized that tone, that anger. He had lived it nearly every day of his childhood. The brothers had been known as the two princes of Vashlee. Dario was born to be Regent-King but became a paragon instead. The honor was considered even greater, and when the responsibility to rule fell to Arn, he quickly enlisted as well. He pushed himself to near delirium every day of his training to make himself a prime candidate to become a paragon just like his older brother. He'd succeeded, he'd undergone the ritual, and oh, how proud his brother had been.

That pride was now rotten and turned into a weapon. Nothing could surpass the disappointment radiating from that withering glare.

"I could say the same," Arn countered weakly. "What are you doing arriving on a caravel with the Heir-Incarnate?"

"My work in Onleda earned me the privilege of being the Heir-Incarnate's loyal escort," Dario said. "Something you'd have known if you didn't desert us afterward. At least, I thought it desertion. Now I discover it is something more. Active insurrection against the Everlorn Empire? You've never been the smartest, Arn, but I still thought better of you. It pains me to imagine the shame that would befall our family should you be discovered."

Oh, the shame would be tremendous. His little sister, Sophie, hardly ten years old last he saw her, would bear the brunt of it. She'd be fifteen now, and looking to secure a betrothal. Rumors about his betrayal would ruin any chance she had. As much as he told himself he donned his mask to hide his paragon past, it had been Sophie he first thought of when he tied it to his face.

Dario mistook his silence for guilt, and he took a step closer and offered a hand.

"It's not too late," he said. "Whatever lies you've swallowed, we can purge them. Whatever deeds you've committed, you can atone for them. Come back with me. Turn yourself in, and become a penitent."

Arn's blood chilled at the thought. Paragon penitents, as they were known, were paragons who had lost their way amid their service to the God-Incarnate. Through ritual, prayer, and sacrifice, they underwent a lifelong process to redeem themselves in the eyes of the Uplifted Church. Given how long a paragon's life could last, this meant sometimes decades of daily lashes, sunrise prayers, and midnight confessions. It also meant they were thrown into the very thickest of battles and were the first to engage in combat with heretical gods. The unspoken expectation was that the only way penitents truly atoned was to give their lives for the God-Incarnate. The lone variance was how long it took.

"Me," Arn said. "A penitent. You want to talk about family shame? Imagine the shame having a penitent son would be."

"Better than a traitor!" Dario shook his head. Though they were the same height, it felt like his older brother was still taller, still able to look down on him. "You had such promise. Do you know why I abandoned the throne to join the Legion? With you next in line to become regent, I thought that responsibility would finally get through to you. For once in your pampered little life, you'd take things seriously. Instead, you surrendered it up in an instant."

Oh, but how serious Arn had taken service in the Legion. He'd surpassed all his peers. He'd showcased faith in the church to go alongside his physical excellence, and when magistrates came calling for more paragons, they were all too pleased by the thought of having both Bastell brothers fighting side by side in the name of Everlorn.

"I gave everything to my duty as a paragon," Arn argued. "It was not my dedication that wavered. It was me seeing Everlorn for what it truly is."

Dario's contempt could not be any greater.

"What it truly is? Is that your justification for leaving?"

"I left because of the carnage when we invaded Onleda." Arn wished his heart wasn't hammering. He wished he wasn't so desperate to hear approval from his older brother. It wouldn't be coming. He knew that. He knew. But he wanted it nonetheless. "All my training, I was told of the glorious wars I would fight, and of the joy the citizens of heathen nations would show once freed from the yoke of their cruel gods. When we marched on Vulnae, I marched at the vanguard, eager to save the city's people and bring them into the God-Incarnate's loving arms."

Arn stepped closer to his brother, and he lost whatever restraint he'd shown. His frustration and regret came pouring forth from the memory of those horrific days.

"We treated the people of Onleda like cattle. Worse than cattle. Like they were an infestation to be burned out. You were there. You saw the piles of bodies, same as I did. We both heard the weeping of children. We both choked on the ash of those we claimed to save. After such a horror, how could I possibly remain a paragon?"

So far Dario hadn't argued back. Maybe that... maybe that meant he was listening? Maybe things weren't so dire as Arn believed. He pressed on, daring to feel a glimmer of hope.

"You know exactly what I speak of. You've seen the slaughter demanded of us! Whatever wisdom we've been given by the church, it doesn't hold water in the real world. It's a deceit. It's a mask to hide their real face, and it's a hateful one of blood and bone. Now that I've spoken with others, and traveled across nations, I've gained newfound wisdom the Uplifted Church would never reach on its own. We help no one,

Dario! We hurt, and we kill, all to replace one god for another! It must be stopped if we're to have peace instead of war."

"And so you murder us," Dario said softly. "You coat your hands with the blood of your former countrymen. That is the path you now walk? The path you would have *me* walk? The killing done in the name of the God-Incarnate was unjust, but the killing of the God-Incarnate's chosen is righteous?"

Arn tried to find the right words. It…it wasn't that simple, was it? That shallow?

"The empire crafted me into a killer," he said. "I can't do much, but I can use these skills for something better. I can do what is just, and right. I defend instead of conquer. I save instead of slaughter."

Dario shoved Arn back. It was a quick, callous movement, and the intent of it was a jagged spike into Arn's heart. His words were even worse.

"'It's not right,' whines the child. 'It's not just. It's not kind.' Nameless Whore take you, have you not matured after all these years? You are a *paragon*, and yet you still bear the wisdom of a spoiled little princeling, caring only for the drink in your cup and the next skirt you could chase."

Arn wished he could pretend otherwise, but it hurt to hear his brother dismiss his deeply personal choice as nothing more than the same selfish, juvenile wants he'd partaken in when younger. He had learned. He had grown stronger, and wiser. Why couldn't Dario see that?

"I killed a god," Arn said. Memories flashed through his mind, of a fox, of blood on his gauntlets, of bones broken, but no time for that. He gritted his teeth, forced himself to focus. "And you would act as if that meant nothing? That it wouldn't change me?"

Dario crossed his arms and frowned.

"Oh, I'm sure it changed you. No one exits a battlefield unchanged. But that doesn't mean the change is for the better."

"The only better change would be the death of the God-Incarnate."

He blurted it out, that ultimate blasphemy. Arn stood before his brother, feeling fully exposed. Damn all these words and debates. He was shit at them, mostly because it made no sense. How could a truth so clear, so plain and obvious, be impossible for someone as smart as Dario to understand?

His brother uncrossed his arms and laughed. It was worse than condemnation.

"Is that what this is all about? You think the ills of the world all lie on the head of one single entity, be it a god or man? How quaint. Let me guess, Arn, you believe that by slaying almighty Lucavi the war will be won, the whole continent of Gadir will be freed, and good shall finally triumph over evil?"

Heat built in Arn's neck and curled up to his ears. Gods help him, how did Dario do this to him? How did he tear him down so easily, as if everything Arn thought and believed was as sturdy as a house of straw? Dario did not relent. He gestured wildly, an orator before an audience of one.

"Think, little brother. Think on what you would accomplish. Pretend it isn't a fool's dream, and that you succeed. Hells, let us embrace it fully, this heretical wish. Say your rebellions win, one after the other. The Everlorn Empire topples, the Uplifted Church fractures, and somehow you execute the God-Incarnate himself. Tell me, in your newfound wisdom, what would happen next?"

Arn didn't like to think on that. Killing the God-Incarnate had always seemed an impossible goal, so why expend the effort? But such an answer would never work with Dario. Worse, his reluctance to answer showed he had not put much thought beyond that immediate goal.

"I won't pretend I see the future," Arn said. "I only know that after Onleda, I couldn't go on. The Everlorn Empire's conquest was unjust and had to be stopped. I know no better way to stop it than to cut off the head of the snake."

It was exactly the answer Dario expected. Expected, yet still unwanted. His disappointment was large enough to crush mountains.

"You were hurt, you were scared, and you gave yourself a noble goal to mindlessly chase. You didn't think. You felt. So I will think for you, Arn. If the God-Incarnate died tomorrow, we would not have peace. We would have war after war, at an incalculable cost. Each and every regent would find themselves ruling an individual state. If capturing the city of Vulnae was too brutal for you, imagine what frantic, scared, and adrift regents would do to maintain power over their lands. Instead of the single God–Incarnate, we would have a hundred would-be emperors slaughtering one another. But it wouldn't stop there."

Closer. Louder. His every word stomping on Arn's chest.

"The priests of the Uplifted Church would find their authority questioned with their god slain, but you've seen what other nations do when their gods are killed. You've fought alongside them. The priests would not relinquish the power they hold over Gadir. And the church has paragons at its disposal, equal to any army. So now the regents and priests are fighting, each scrambling to secure their place in the sudden upheaval of the power structure. And that is just the empire!"

Dario waved his arms, gesturing to both Thanet and the world beyond it.

"How many nations, their populaces currently subdued, would rise up like the opportunistic vermin that they are? How many old gods will return seeking vengeance, or new ones rise from the people's fractured, vengeful faith? Imagine the church, responding to the return of these forgotten faiths. Think, Arn, of the warfare as rebellions spark anew, and regents attempt to stamp them out. Think of the absolute chaos, the loss of life. Think, little brother, *think*."

Dario's exasperation was painfully familiar. In Arn's childhood, it had been brought against him after long nights of drinking. Back then, Arn had accepted the received aggravation and insult as justified. He'd been a spoiled brat. He knew it, even as he drank and frequented brothels eager to entertain such a wealthy and connected noble. But this?

"It's wrong," Arn said. "I've seen far too many horrors to believe otherwise."

His brother's face softened. His arms lowered. Arn didn't trust it for a moment. This was a practiced vulnerability. It was the helping hand Dario would offer him after beating him bloody in a sparring match.

"The empire is not perfect. Not even the Uplifted Church preaches as such, nor would they condemn me as a heretic for saying so. We are an imperfect people. But listen to me, little brother, listen well and take it to heart. This unity we have within the Everlorn Empire, it is the closest to peace humanity will ever achieve. Yes, people die. Yes, people suffer. But viewed in totality, it is less than if we let the world return to the old ways, full of spiteful warring gods and shifting territories ruled by kings, sultans, conclaves, and tribunals. One kingdom. One god. One people. How could you ever argue against such blessed simplicity?"

Arn couldn't. He wanted to. He wanted to shout to the heavens how wrong it all was, how accepting such wholesale slaughter could never be right. But he was a man who beat things with his fists. He wasn't a philosopher. He wasn't wise. Most importantly of all, he wasn't as smart as his brother. So how did he tell him he was wrong? How to convince him?

Could he even convince himself?

"What we did, it wasn't unity," he said. "It was murder. I believe that. I must."

"You must believe nothing but the truth, and so I lay it bare before you."

Dario crossed the gap between them. His hand wrapped around Arn's head, pulling them close, holding them like the brothers they were. Their foreheads touched. Arn tensed, ready for battle, and not one of physical blows.

"You condemn our murders, and so you murder us in return. But there is no righteousness in your killing. No justice. You decry the blood on your hands, and yet hope by shedding more, your soul will emerge clean at the end. Murder will save you, you think, but only the right murders. Only if the right corpses lie at your feet. Idealistic nonsense. Foolish. Naïve."

Arn pulled away, but Dario would not relent. Their divinely blessed muscles locked tight. Dario's fingers on the back of his head were metal hooks digging into his skin. There would be no escape. His brother's green eyes held him captive. They were sincere. They were pained. Arn hated every second of it.

"Come back with me. Become a penitent before it is too late to save you, both in heart and mind. When the God-Incarnate calls me to the heavens to serve in the hereafter, I would have you follow me there, like you followed me into the Legion. Don't remain behind. Don't fall to the Hell below, to burn with the Nameless Whore. It would break my heart."

At last, the fingers relented. Arn shoved him away. Space now between them, he could finally breathe again. The words, though, they lingered, echoing again and again in his mind. So full of love, and so very cruel.

Don't remain behind. Don't fall to the Hell below . . .

"You are not my keeper," Arn said. "And my soul is mine alone to guard. I do not doubt my path. I doubt yours."

Dario shook his head. His disappointment somehow grew greater than the sun and stars. Resolve steeled across his handsome face. He spoke as if he heard nothing of Arn's protestations.

"This is a hard choice, and you've devoted years to this delusion of salvation through heresy. I will give you time to dwell on my words. If you accept, I can smuggle you back into the fold. The Heir-Incarnate trusts me, and with his help, we will begin your penitence. It will be hard, Arn, but I'll be there with you every step of the way. We can save your soul together. But hear me, little brother . . ."

He clacked his gauntlets together, a rattle of metal that chilled the air. One final message before returning to the empire Arn had forsaken. A threat of love. A promise of violence.

"If I witness you on the battlefield again, your face hidden behind bones, I will not hold back. I will break you. Whatever is left, I shall drag to Eldrid. You will be redeemed. This is my sacred duty as your brother, and I will never accept failure. By my blood and fists, you will join me in the heavens."

CHAPTER 9

STASIA

Commander Pilus Arenthan was waiting for the pair at Pelion. His graying hair took well to the sunlight, and his golden complexion had darkened since Stasia last saw him, no doubt due to a lot more time spent outdoors training his soldiers. Even without armor or uniform, he looked dashing enough, and had the posture of a man accustomed to giving orders.

"Welcome," he said. "I pray the journey was not too arduous."

The pair had packed both their belongings into a single large rucksack. Stasia removed it from the top of the carriage and flung it over her shoulder, unbothered by the weight.

"Two days of bumpy seats, the smell of horses, and a night's stay at an inn with more fleas than guests," she said. "I wouldn't call it arduous, but neither do I look forward to the return trip."

"The inn wasn't all terrible," Clarissa said, and she smiled and offered Pilus her hand for a gentle kiss upon her knuckles. "That boy in charge of their bread, give him proper ingredients and I wager he could open a shop right in Vallessau."

"You may have stumbled upon a rare culinary talent," Pilus said. He smiled warmly at Clarissa. The two communicated often at meetings Thorda organized, and she was always complimentary of Pilus when brought up in conversation. "Or perhaps hunger is the best sauce."

"I think it was a bit of both," Stasia said. The trio walked deeper into the village, and she was happy to hear the rattling carriage leaving behind them. The driver had been polite enough, but she caught him praying several times, and she was fairly certain it wasn't to Lycaena or Endarius.

"Have you a gift for me?" Pilus asked as he walked alongside her. "The Coin sent a message asking me to wait for the Ax, and here you are. I presume it is something important?"

"You'll be the one to tell me that."

Stasia handed the sealed note over to the commander. Experience had taught her not to bother opening it to sate her curiosity. The first line her father wrote would always be something like "Trust not this note if the seal is broken." As much as she wanted to know her reason for coming out to Pelion, she equally loathed the tiresome possibility of explaining why said seal was broken.

Pilus drew a knife from his belt, sliced the note open, and then unfurled it. For a moment he debated reading it aloud to her, but then changed his mind just as quickly.

"Here," he said, handing it over. "I suspect this is for you as much as it is for me."

Stasia accepted the note and skimmed over her father's neat, compact handwriting.

> *Trust not these orders if my seal is broken.*
> *Act on the morrow. Ax will lead the vanguard to ensure victory.*
> *Take the fort. No survivors. Burn what cannot be looted.*
> *Retreat to Pelion when finished to await further instruction.*
>
> *—the Coin*

"Take the fort," she said, lowering the note. "As in Fort Lionfang? Have you anywhere near the numbers for such a feat?"

Pilus grinned at her.

"I see you are unfamiliar with my accomplishments," he said. "Walk with me, Ax, and look upon the army I have built."

⨕⨕

The commander explained as they walked deeper into the woods. His training grounds were a good fifty miles farther south, and several others were dotted about the region, their numbers small and mobile. A week prior, Thorda had sent orders for them to gather in the nearby forest.

"I have assumed Fort Lionfang would be my target for the past few weeks. Not merely to hold it, mind you. The current Lord of Tannin hides within instead of taking his proper seat in the city of Syros deep to the south. He is a cowardly man by the name of Acastus Agrito and prefers the safety of his soldiers over a crowded populace. Once the Coin sent his note to prepare for moving out, I was all too eager to begin our preparations."

"Preparing how?" Clarissa asked. "Have you any siege weaponry to break the fort's walls or gates?"

"Neither will be necessary. We've scouted their nightly patrols along the walls. It is a skeleton crew, if even that. I suspect they are struggling to bring adequate numbers across the Crystal Sea, and the Heir-Incarnate's arrival has only further consolidated the empire's strength in Vallessau."

Something is strange about Thanet, thought Stasia, remembering a conversation she'd had with her sister. Normally the conquered territory's regent would work with the Uplifted Church to recruit faithful converts into the military, bolstering ranks and adding a local face to the peacekeeping efforts. So why did they not do so here? Did they believe Thanet too weak in its faith in the God-Incarnate? Or perhaps Lord Agrito feared any recruits could be potential assassins and traitors?

"Ten men can hold off a hundred if the walls are high enough and their arrows plentiful," Stasia said.

"A fact I am aware of, Ax. I will not throw away any lives needlessly. My soldiers trust me, and I will repay that trust. They will receive the best training I may offer, the best gear I may outfit them in, and the wisest of my plans when it comes to battle."

"Fair enough," Stasia said, too tired and travel sore to argue. Hoping for transparency from her father was like hoping for the sun to rise in the west. Whatever his plan, she'd learn it in time, and modify it if she truly thought it asinine. This Pilus did seem the intelligent sort, but Stasia had seen more small-scale skirmishes than most anyone alive. If her father's note said she was to lead the vanguard, then she would lead it as she saw fit, and force the commander to adapt accordingly.

The brush thickened around them, the thinner trees marking the outer rim of the forest near Pelion growing wider and taller. Minutes later, she heard the first distant murmurs of conversation, pierced by the occasional shout or laugh. They must be getting close.

"I've never been to an army encampment before," Clarissa said. "Is it like a hunter's camp?"

"Somewhat," Stasia said. "A really, really big hunting camp. If experience has taught me anything, it's going to smell of smoke, sweat, and shit, and not in that order."

Pilus shifted directions, and they came upon the semblance of a footpath. They followed it into the camp, first encountering the latrine trench. Boards were laid across it to form a simple bridge, though Stasia distrusted it and instead leaped over.

"My apologies," Pilus said as Clarissa tested the boards, found them sturdy, and then hurried after. "But the wind blows the way it blows, and we dug accordingly."

Once past a few more trees, the grounds opened up, the remains of dozens of stumps marking the efforts to clear out a place to live within the forest. The sight of it gave Stasia a strange sensation of nostalgia. How many similar camps had she visited throughout her life? Men and women gathered together, laughing and chatting. Nervous energy intermixed with boredom. Some trained, some cleaned, and many others lounged about waiting for the killing orders to come. Stasia estimated two hundred soldiers in total, not bad for a force built directly underneath Lord Agrito's nose.

Clarissa stepped closer to Stasia, and she took her free hand in hers.

"I suppose you did warn me about the smell," she said softly.

Stasia shifted the rucksack of their belongings to her other shoulder.

"I've seen a lot of these camps, but for what it's worth, this one's set up better than most."

"Appreciated," Pilus said, overhearing the discussion. "If you'd follow me, please?"

He led them through the camp, a quick little jaunt past the mess tent, the training grounds, a second latrine trench, and the many rows of sleeping tents. He pointed out a well-beaten path that led to a stream for drinking, and a secondary path farther downstream for bathing.

All the while, men and women stared. Stasia's mind itched. She should be wearing her mask. Each and every one of them was seeing her face, and the brilliant make and shine of her axes alone hinted at her identity. Yet she wanted them to trust her. Her hand pressed to her word-lace. A compromise, at least. She felt a tingle, and the red of her irises faded to brown. There. At least she might have some plausible deniability should any of these soldiers be captured and tortured.

"This was once a hunting retreat we greatly enlarged," Pilus said once their little tour was over and he brought them to his yellow command tent. "There is a little cabin normally reserved for myself. It is all yours for the night, but before you settle in, there is a matter I wish to discuss involving tomorrow's mission."

Stasia crossed her arms and prepared herself for frustration. It wouldn't be the first time a commander had cold feet when it came to letting her, an outsider, lead their troops. Her mood must have shown on her face, because the older man immediately adopted a softer tone and clarified.

"I have no objection to you leading the attack," Pilus said. "But that does not mean I lack reservations. These men and women under my command are largely untested, well trained but lacking experience. In plain language, they are nervous, and nervous soldiers fight poorly and flee easily. I believe that is why the Coin has sent you."

Stasia frowned at him. This was a switch. She'd feared he would want her out of the way, but now learned she was expected to carry the morale of an entire force.

"I can bolster a line and fight as well as twenty," she said. "But I can't take a whole fort on my own if your soldiers abandon me."

"Your abilities are secondary to my concern. It's your reputation I want. My soldiers, they know of the Ax of Lahareed. It will elevate their efforts to fight alongside you. They want to believe your presence here means we are capable of accomplishing the impossible. Yet stories and rumors are fickle and unreliable. Let us leave nothing to chance. If you are to lead them tomorrow night, I believe you should secure their confidence through more than just reputation. Give them a demonstration of your skill."

All of Stasia's worries and frustrations broke away into an eager smile.

"If you believe it best I beat a few of your men senseless, then who am I to disagree?"

"Will you actually be causing injuries?" the older man asked. "That may influence who I volunteer."

And then he winked. The playfulness of it had Stasia bursting into laughter. She'd not often worked with Pilus over the years, with most of his time spent outside Vallessau where the eyes of the empire were not so sharp. He'd always seemed competent, though, and now she decided he might be a bit of a charmer, too.

"Send me your gods-damned best," she said. "I'll give your camp a show they'll remember."

Pilus pointed to a portion of cleared earth heavily trodden so not even grass endured. A rope circled the perimeter, forming the clear boundaries of a sparring ring.

"Wait there. I'll bring both challengers and a crowd."

Stasia thumped a fist to her breast, a salute she'd learned at some point over the past two decades.

"I expect a hot meal and a warm bed waiting for me afterward."

"You shall have both and more," Pilus said. He saluted, then hurried into the scattered tents, pointing and barking orders. Stasia made for the training circle. Clarissa followed at her side, a bounce in her step so lively she was almost skipping.

"Someone is excited," Stasia said.

"It's not often I get to see you and your axes in action."

"You've seen me train plenty."

"Training is not fighting, and you know it."

Stasia laughed and kissed her on the cheek.

"For your sake, I'll try to make it entertaining."

Pilus gathered up most of the camp to watch. As for her opponents, four men and one woman stood in a loose line, wood training swords held in hand. Stasia unclipped her axes and set them on the ground beside Clarissa, who blew her a kiss for good luck.

"Will these suffice?" Pilus asked, and he offered her two rounded poles. They were of the proper length, though lighter than her axes.

"I've trained with similar," she said, accepting them. "They'll do. What of your soldiers? Have you any rules for when they duel?"

"The first to drop their weapon, step out of the ring, or get knocked to their rear loses the spar. All else is fair."

"Good enough for me."

Her first opponent was wide-eyed and nervous. Stasia stood perfectly relaxed, her grin daring him to make a move. When he tried, it was with a thrust at her abdomen lacking any real strength behind it. She exploded into action, batting it aside with her left hand while her right swept low and then up, cracking against his wrist. Out went the wood sword.

"Next."

The man left blushing, made worse by the ribbing of his friends as he stepped back into the crowd. A larger man came next, his hair long and his body resembling that of a lumberjack. More muscle than necessary, it'd make him slow, but he'd end most fights with a single hit.

Most fights. Not one against her. She let him swing, a dreadfully slow wind-up that again reminded her of a lumberjack chopping a tree. She blocked the hit with both her poles, and though the impact was enough to strain her wrists, she pretended it meant nothing.

"My turn," she said.

He had strength, but no speed. Stasia struck him with her shoulder, then rolled around him, back to back, before sweeping her poles in an arc. They collided with his knees, crumpling him.

"Next."

The third man knew how to wield a sword, that was refreshing. He blocked her first blow and planted his feet well, holding fast when she tried to trip him up with a sudden burst of strength. Her next swing was a feint, and he fell for it, sword up to block. She slipped both poles underneath, striking his stomach and taking away his breath. When he doubled over, she put a boot to his chest and kicked, tumbling him out of the ring. The entirety of the fight lasted but a handful of seconds, but he'd at least made her work for it.

"Could you at least play with them a bit?" someone shouted, and others laughed. Stasia clacked her weapons together overhead, all smiles as the performance swept her up.

"Hardly my fault. I'm not even sweating. Both of you, get in here. Maybe a threesome will get the crowd going."

Laughter joined the cheers as the next two opponents entered. They whispered a plan to each other, their words lost amid the noise of the boisterous crowd, and then approached side by side. Stasia bounced atop her toes, keeping limber and ready. The woman began the attack with a shout to her teammate.

"Now!"

They charged, weapons high for downward slashes. The coordination wasn't bad, but she had faced paragons. These two paled compared to such foes. She blocked both, her arms wide, one pole for each attack. The pair of them pressed with all their might, their jaws clenched, their teeth bared, and their faces turning red as their muscles tightened. She flexed in return, her heels digging into the earth. Her weapons fell an inch, drawing them in close, making them think they would break her.

And then she slammed them away in a single mighty heave. They faltered, their balance broken, and she gave them no quarter. Her poles looped up and around, striking knees and lifting heels so they dropped. The gathered crowd erupted into applause, and Stasia beamed at their excitement.

Her enthusiasm wasn't matched by her two defeated foes.

"How in the Heldeep is she that strong?" the woman asked.

"Because she's not human," the other said as he scrambled up from his ass. "By gods, woman, we won't be needed tomorrow if you're with us."

Stasia's mood dove straight down into the dirt beneath her feet.

But of course. You are not mortal.

"We're just playing with sticks," she said, and tossed the poles to the watching soldiers. She trudged over to her belongings. "Let's make this interesting."

"Stasia?" Clarissa asked, multiple questions wrapped in that lone word.

"It's fine," she said, and faked a smile. "You wanted a show, didn't you?"

Stasia grabbed her axes and then, after a moment's debate, also tied her black mask over her face. Might as well give the camp the entire package. She returned to the center of the ring, her axes twirling in her grasp. Seeing real steel, the next opponents Pilus had lined up set aside their wood weapons and drew swords instead. The first entered the ring, and Stasia shook her head.

"No," she said. "All three of you."

They exchanged glances. Stasia cocked an eyebrow, and she emphasized her words with a point of her ax.

"Did I stutter? Next, next, and next. Let's go."

Tension returned to the air. Suddenly this wasn't a game. The crowd hushed. The three men formed a triangle about her, bare steel glinting in the sunlight. Stasia caught Pilus pushing to the front of the ring to watch, and for a moment she thought he would call off the exhibition.

His faint nod to her said otherwise.

"Tomorrow night, you will follow *my* commands," she shouted before the trio could attack. "I am the veteran of a dozen wars. I am the heart of countless resistances. I am the Ax of Lahareed, and I am here, with you, to lead. To *fight*."

Stasia slammed her axes together. The sound of steel rang throughout the dead-silent crowd, and she charged straight into the trio. They quaked before her, weapons useless, skill meaningless when confronted with her fury. The crowd roared at her savagery, but she did not see them, did not hear them, as she knocked her foes' weapons from their hands and their bodies from the ring.

Instead she heard Soma's words, mocking her again and again.

And so very good for a mere mortal.

♊

"It doesn't seem fair to send you here with so little warning and then expect you to lead an attack the very next night," Clarissa said. The pair were in the room granted them, a small but cozy cabin with thick curtains over the windows for privacy.

"I'm used to it," Stasia said, flopping onto her back, testing the bed. Packed straw with two blankets atop it. Not the best, but she'd had worse.

"Just because you're used to it doesn't mean it's right. Plus, that's a lie. I can tell it bothers you."

"Leading a fight doesn't bother me."

"Then what does?"

Stasia stared at the low ceiling. A spider had weaved a web in the corner, and she wondered if it was venomous. Wouldn't that be a hilarious way to die? Survive a hundred battles, hit the grave from a tiny spider crawling onto her while she slept. It might even be appropriate.

Clarissa touched her shoulder, jolting her out of her thoughts.

"It may hurt your dainty pride, but I am just as stubborn as you are," she said. "Talk to me. Something has bothered you since we left Vallessau."

Stasia sighed, greatly exaggerated.

"Fine," she said as Clarissa sat on the edge of the bed. "But you're going to think I'm crazy."

"Your sister transforms into a slain Lion god. I am used to crazy."

Stasia laughed, and suddenly her worries were so much less daunting.

"Fine. One of the empire's paragons first made this claim, and then the Humbled spoke similarly. They believe I have the blood of a god or goddess in me."

"You?" Clarissa asked, and she poked Stasia in the side. "A goddess? Had you hit their heads before they spoke?"

The bed had two pillows, and Stasia smacked Clarissa across the chest with one of them.

"It's not so strange as you might think. When we talk of gods and goddesses in Miquo, it's different than elsewhere. Our gods resembled men and women, and their lives were not eternal, but closer to twice that of a mortal. So it's possible somewhere along my family line there was a child sired by a god. It wouldn't mean I'm a goddess now, either. My father had a term for this comingling, but I don't remember what it was. Trust me, Clarissa, Miquo had far too many gods and goddesses. I sat through school classes dedicated just to learning their names and faces, all multiple generations of them."

"It does sound miserable."

"You're mocking me."

"I might be. If I was, you would deserve it for hitting me with a pillow."

Stasia reached, fingers curling behind Clarissa's neck, and then gently pulled her close for a kiss.

"Fair enough," she said once they separated, and then she grinned ear to ear. This smile of hers had extricated her from a thousand missteps and mistakes in the past. Based on the way it made Clarissa melt before her, it appeared to work again. Her lover leaned against her, tilting so her back was to Stasia, and then lay on the bed. Stasia's arms enveloped her, and their legs intertwined. Holding her, feeling her touch, was enough to soothe away the annoyances of the day.

Stasia closed her eyes. Night hadn't yet fallen, but their trip to Pelion was long and had started early. Sleep didn't sound like too bad an idea . . .

"Would it be so terrible if you were a god?"

It seemed sleep would not be coming after all.

"I don't know," Stasia said. "I don't *feel* like a goddess. I'm fit and radiant, don't get me wrong. I guess I could be the Nameless She. There's always rumors she's been reborn every few years."

"The who?"

"Right, you don't know her. The God-Incarnate's first wife, or as he calls her, the Nameless Whore. No one knows what she did, but supposedly he exiled her to his hell, where she is forced to torture terrible sinners like you and me for all eternity."

Clarissa turned to look over her shoulder, playfulness sparkling in her blue eyes.

"So you're saying you sympathize with a woman who tortures bad people all day?"

Stasia jabbed her in the ribs with a thumb for the audacity.

"A woman who likely did nothing wrong and has been cursed so thoroughly even her name is forbidden? I extend some sympathy, yes."

Clarissa squirmed a bit from the pressure of her thumb, then relaxed.

"You're avoiding the question," she said after a moment's peace. Stasia sighed. She had indeed been hoping the other woman would let the matter drop.

"No, it wouldn't be the worst if by some miracle I was a Miquoan goddess. But it's not the idea that upsets me, it's the . . . accusation."

"I suppose I don't understand," Clarissa admitted. "If someone was

so impressed by you they believed you divinely gifted, how is that anything other than a compliment?"

Stasia tried to put to words the awkwardness and anger that awakened within her when Rihim mocked her prowess. *Of course*, he'd said.
Those two words in particular, as if Stasia's strength were an oddity
needing explanation and not the end result of a lifetime of dedication.

"When I was twelve I demanded that Thorda put me through the
same training my blood-father endured," she began. Maybe if she just
rambled out enough words an explanation would form on its own. "It
was...difficult. So many nights I fell asleep crying, but I survived. And
for twenty, no, twenty-five years now I have woken up early for my
runs. I have practiced. I have spilled sweat and blood. If there is anyone
alive who has put in as much work as I have, who has devoted equal
hours and effort, I am yet to meet them."

Soma's amused smile hovered in her vision, and she wished she could
bury an ax through his teeth.

"For all that effort to be so easily swept aside, as if it meant nothing? As if
I didn't earn it? It galls me. There's no divine blood making me this strong.
I made me this strong. *Me.* And piss on anyone who argues otherwise."

Clarissa pulled free so she could roll over, the two lying face-to-face.
Their foreheads touched, and Clarissa absently stroked her fingers along
Stasia's jawline, down her neck, and across her shoulder. Back and forth,
as if sculpting her, or memorizing the line through her fingertips. The
motion calmed her. Yet again Stasia reminded herself the brilliant little
clerk was better than she deserved.

"Now you've made me curious," Clarissa said. Her tone was playful,
but it felt like a smoke screen. "Pretend you are a goddess, and we were
married. Is there a word in Miquoan for what that would make me, akin
to a woman becoming queen when she marries a king?"

"There is, actually." Clarissa lifted an eyebrow, and she leaned in
eagerly. Stasia milked the moment for all its worth, and then whispered
the answer. "The word you're looking for is 'insufferable.'"

The tiny woman was quick when she wanted to be. A pillow smashed
Stasia in the face, and deep down, she knew she deserved it.

CHAPTER 10

VAGRANT

Cyrus stood before the lone juniper tree and frowned at the symbol carved into the side.

"I don't recognize this," he told Rayan, who had lagged behind and was only now catching up. The road had grown steeper and rockier as they progressed north, and though the paladin never once complained, Cyrus could see the toll it was taking on him.

"What is 'this'?" Rayan asked, and he set down his rucksack. His armor was inside, and though the weight burdened him, he refused Cyrus's offers to carry it. "If I'm not fit to carry it, I'm not fit to wear it" had been his maddeningly simple argument.

"This carving," Cyrus said, and he stepped back so his friend might see. A curving horizontal line cut through the bark. About a foot below it was a crude spiral, the toughness of the bark or the dullness of the instrument resulting in said spiral being less smooth and more a series of hacks and cuts to shape it.

"Ill tidings is what it is," Rayan said. His mouth curled in disgust. "It is the mark of the Serpent. The top line is meant to be the surface of the Crystal Sea, and the curl below, Dagon sleeping away the centuries."

Cyrus stared at the spiral, eyes tracing it inward to the center, as his stomach churned.

"But why put it in so obvious a place?"

"A bold symbol to inspire boldness. Is it truly so strange?"

Magus's words upon the bell tower returned to Cyrus in an unwelcome echo.

Dagon became a villain in your stories, his true history slowly forgotten as the centuries passed . . .

"I didn't think Dagon had any worshipers left," he said.

"In Vallessau, he doesn't," Rayan said, and there was no hiding the satisfaction in his voice. "My brethren and I made sure of that. But Thanet is a big place, and there are many dark corners and crevices to hide in. Someone near here still worships the foul beast. I pray we do not stumble upon them."

The paladin glanced back at the faint smoke that blurred the sky from dozens of campfires, and to the hazy mass that was the Heir-Incarnate's retinue.

"And for their sake, I pray the priests of Everlorn do not stumble upon *them*."

They resumed their travel. To their right was a beautiful green valley with raspberry bushes cut down the middle by a small stream. On their left towered the Northspine Mountains. Travelers were few, and had been since leaving Thiva. It was as if the island knew of Galvanis's approach and hunkered down to wait out his passage.

"So why would someone still worship Dagon?" Cyrus asked, not wanting to abandon the topic just yet. The knowledge given to him by Magus of Eldrid floated unwelcome in his mind. He had heard all the stories growing up. Dagon was the deceiver. The liar, the trickster, the conniving Serpent who ruled the Heldeep and punished the evil and unrepentant. Dagon was the enemy of all that was good, and it was only by the combined strength of Lycaena and Endarius that he had been cast to the bottom of the sea.

"Why do people steal, or lie, or harm their neighbor?" Rayan asked in return.

"Usually with reason, even if an ill one, and you give me no reason at all."

The old paladin chuckled. His armor rattled as he shifted the rucksack from one shoulder to the other.

"I have spoken with a few ardent worshipers of Dagon, if you must insist. This was during my early years as a paladin. I sought them out in their prisons, for truth be told, I thought I could redeem them. The arrogance of youth, I suppose. Many were twice my age, if not more. They wanted none of my wisdom, and yet they countered with little of their own. It wasn't wisdom they offered people, though. It was certainty."

Cyrus glanced over his shoulder.

"I'm not sure I understand. Are you saying their faith was greater?"

Rayan laughed.

"Do you traffic in blasphemy now, prince? No, their faith was not greater. It was...different. I could try to instruct them in the lessons Lycaena gifted to us, but they did not want to learn. They did not want to change. Instead, they clung to not a creed or an accepted pattern of behavior but what they declared truth. Dagon lives, they would tell me. Dagon, the first god, the true god, they so firmly believed. Endarius and Lycaena were the usurpers, but Dagon would one day return to cast down those false gods of Thanet."

Cyrus clenched his jaw. They weren't wrong. Dagon had been overthrown, his royal Orani family cast down by the Mirli wealthy and nobility to establish a new bloodline. The Lythan bloodline. Dagon's worshipers had every right to be furious at the injustice their god suffered.

"That was the certainty they offered others?" he asked. His throat felt raw.

"It is much easier to focus on a single truth than to change your life entirely through a faith meant to guide and better you. These worshipers of Dagon, they need not give of their time and wealth to help others. They need not bend the knee, learn to tame their tongue, or cast aside sinful vices. Dagon is the true god to them. That alone was enough. Believe it, and you are better than the fooled. Trust Dagon lives, and know you are superior to those who cherished the Butterfly or found bravery in the Lion."

Cyrus stayed just ahead of the paladin on the road, glad to have his back to him and his inner debate hidden. Could he admit the truth? Would Rayan even believe him? It would only be natural to doubt the testimony of an Everlorn paragon. At least Rayan was a paladin of Lycaena. The truth might hurt him less. Her sin was one of neutrality, not of conquest.

"And now all three gods are dead," Rayan said. Quieter. Tired. "Perhaps fate does favor their faith. They have endured centuries without sight of their god, while we mourn the publicly executed and slain.

They worshiped in secret, while we preached alongside kings and queens. Maybe they will endure the poison that is the Uplifted Church that we in our heartbreak cannot."

Cyrus turned and smacked his friend in the chest with the back of his hand.

"Now who traffics in blasphemy?" he asked. Rayan smiled in return.

"Doubt does not fade with age, Cyrus. We only better learn to live and flourish alongside it. My heart will ever be Lycaena's, for I have seen her beauty, and I have borne witness to the miracles she granted our people. Let me fear the future in quiet among friends. It is a rare solace."

"All right then," Cyrus said, and he couldn't help himself. He felt warm inside at such a statement. "If that's what it takes for me to be a good friend, I'm here to listen."

"I'd rather you speak for a while. I worried about you during your absence. We all did. Where you were. What you were hoping to accomplish. We didn't even know why you left, or if we ourselves were to blame…"

Cyrus shook his head. The ground sloped downward, carrying them toward a distant forest, and he struggled to maintain a steady pace. So much easier to run.

"The reason was Thorda," he said. "Only Thorda, never any of you. Please, believe me, even if I am not ready to explain."

⌒⌒

The next day they broke from the mountains. Hours later, they arrived at the village of Chora, and Keles's last known location.

They jogged much of it, for the empire was on their heels.

"We have Keles's letters to guide us," Cyrus said as they entered the village. Men and women eyed the pair warily, but none yet confronted them. "What guides the empire's path?"

"I have suspicions, ones I have been unwilling to voice for fear of lifting my hopes undeserved. If Lycaena has returned, if she is whole in body and spirit, then I suspect the Heir-Incarnate senses her presence. She will be a torch, and he drawn to it like a moth."

They passed thatched-roof huts until reaching the village square. Still no man or woman stopped them, forcing Rayan to choose a nearby man pulling a cart to stop.

"Forgive me, good sir, but have you a village elder or leader I might speak with?"

The man, deeply tanned from countless hours beneath the sun, gave them a hard look.

"Who is asking?"

"A paladin of Lycaena, and his friend. We come on pilgrimage."

The mention of a paladin raised his eyebrows.

"That so? Fine. I suppose that's enough for Dolores to see you."

He left his cart and walked with them a space until he could point toward a seemingly unimportant home.

"She's in there," he said. "Be polite and knock first."

Cyrus trailed after Rayan, happy to let the charismatic paladin lead the conversation. Rayan's hand halted an inch from the door. His fist opened, and he ran fingers along the door's edge, to where a small butterfly was carved. He said nothing, only let his fingers linger, and then he finally knocked.

The door opened, and an elderly woman in a faded brown robe greeted them. The snap of her voice, however, was lively and young.

"Come in, come in, we're well used to people like you. Sit on the floor."

The pair did as Dolores asked. Goose-feather pillows awaited them, and Cyrus groaned loudly at the pleasure of taking the weight off his feet. Rayan was a bit more dignified, though he did stretch his arms and back after setting down his rucksack.

"You two creak and groan as if you're my age," the woman said as she passed between them to an even larger stack of pillows. "What brings you to my village?"

"A name, and a rumor," Rayan said. "Eshiel Dymling, a priest of Lycaena. I wish to meet with him."

"And who are you to seek him?"

In answer, Rayan drew his sword, and he offered it to her hilt-first. The hilt resembled a butterfly, and the cross guard was shaped like spread wings. To possess such a weapon risked earning the Uplifted Church's ire.

"My name is Rayan Vayisa, a loyal and true paladin of Lycaena. I was born to serve King and Queen Lythan, and in my youthful days, I walked the noble path of the Heaven's Wing."

Dolores chewed despite having nothing in her mouth.

"Well, I'll be, I thought I saw the last of you after the execution." She need not say whose execution. "And your friend?"

"My name is my own," Cyrus said. "For knowing it will put you in danger."

He tried to appear mysterious and threatening. It earned him a hearty laugh.

"I have little life left in me to endanger, but I know a rebel heart when I see one. Why is it you search for Eshiel?"

"My niece," Rayan answered. "She came here chasing rumors, and I wish to find her and confirm for myself if these rumors are true. Most important of all, I wish to warn of the Heir-Incarnate's approach."

The older woman leaned back.

"We knew Everlorn soldiers were on their way. But you say the Heir-Incarnate is with them?"

"We saw him with our own eyes back in Thiva," Cyrus chipped in. "He comes, and with him, his vanguard of soldiers and paragons."

Rayan leaned closer to the woman. He pulled the sword to his chest, and he clutched it as if it were his own child.

"I need not tell you why the Heir-Incarnate comes, or what he seeks to do. Help me. Show me the way."

Dolores silently debated for a moment, her soft brown eyes flicking back and forth between them.

"Eshiel tells us to send him only the faithful and the desperate," she said. "I'd wager you're both. Come with me. The younger boys know the path to their camp, and I'll have you meet with one."

"Thank you," Rayan said. He extended his hands, and the elder reluctantly accepted them. His fingers curled around hers, and he bent at the waist so he might press his forehead to them. "For your kindness, and your trust. Please, stay safe."

"Do not fear, paladin," the elder said. "We in the north know how to survive. When that imperial bastard comes marching through, we will be long gone. I suspect if anyone is in danger, it is you."

CHAPTER 11

KELES

Keles barged into Eshiel's tent without waiting for permission.

"What is the meaning of this?" she asked, then immediately paused. The priest was naked from the waist up, and he knelt with his back to her. Words left her. The scars, they were so many...

"I am praying," he said, his head still bowed. "I thought you familiar with the concept?"

Keles flushed, and she was glad he could not see it.

"Your faithful," she said. "I hear them talking. The *way* they're talking, and about you. They're eulogizing you while you're still alive."

"It is their right."

He was avoiding an explanation. Her insides hardened.

"They tell me another sacrifice shall take place tonight," she said. "Yet I have seen no prisoners. So who is it, Eshiel? Who?"

At last he stood. His gaze turned her way. The meager candlelight flickered off his tattooed face, and it glinted in his eyes.

"Lycaena is so close to returning, Keles. The problem is, Thanet's lack of faith wars against her essence. The doubt of the unbelievers who saw her slain poisons the faith of those who would see her live again. Our goddess graces us with her presence amid fire and blood, but it is only temporary. She is not yet whole. And so I shall make her whole."

"And what of your people? Would you abandon them? Leave them scattered and alone? Choose another, Eshiel, someone, anyone!"

The faintest smile graced his lips.

"They will not be alone."

Keles's eyes widened. At long last she knew what his great hopes for her were.

"No," she said.

"They will need someone to guide them in my absence."

"*No.*"

"A faithful servant they trust, who fought and bled for them, one who has experienced their doubts, and who even publicly cast aside her faith at her lowest moment only to return to the fold."

Damn it all, he wasn't listening, he wasn't understanding. Panic replaced her fear.

"You can't do this," she insisted. "This isn't my village, these aren't my people. Heldeep take me, I'm still younger than most of them. I can't do this, I can't lead them. What they need, what *I* need, isn't this, isn't me, it's you, it's..."

She shut her mouth. Heat built in her cheeks and neck. Goddess help her, what was she even saying? Eshiel approached her, and he gently cupped her cheek in his hand. His voice was gentle, even if his eyes were fire.

"I have lived my life to its fullest in the service of my beloved goddess. I have seen joy and redemption, and witnessed countless miracles. Our next generation would know only suffering. If I may spare them that, then there is no cost too high to pay. When the priests brought their knives to my flesh, they demanded I swear allegiance to the God-Incarnate. I refused. My life belongs to the goddess, I told them. It is hers, and hers alone. That is how my heart and mind survived. So if my goddess calls for that life now, who am I to refuse? In my darkest moments, I offered it to her. In my finest hour, she shall accept."

She leaned into his touch. For a time, she had called herself a paladin of the Butterfly goddess. Could she become that once more? What honor remained of her, after the forsaking ceremony?

"At the moment of Lycaena's death, I broke," she said. "And before all the world, I forsook her. Who am I to lead her people now? Please, Eshiel, let it be any other."

He kissed her forehead. His lips were feverish.

"You are so much stronger than you know," he told her. "Whatever your doubts, your fears, and your failings, let them wither into dust and be forgotten. Cast aside the broken and the Light of Vallessau alike. You are Keles Lyon, and you are worthy to lead, so long as you still hold love in your heart for our goddess."

"It cannot be that easy."

Eshiel smiled, and her heart ached to think it would be the last time she might ever see that smile.

"Never did I say it would be easy. To forgive and accept ourselves is the hardest task we may ever know. I hold faith in you to succeed, Keles, even if you do not. It matters not the chasm of your doubts, for tonight, we shall witness miracles."

Not a soul remained behind in the forest camp. At Eshiel's behest, Keles stood closest to the altar. He wanted the people to see her at his side, and for her to be the first to greet the newly reborn Lycaena. Eshiel climbed atop the altar and turned to face the crowd, still bare-chested so all might see the beauty of his winding tattoos and the ugliness of his scars.

"For many long seasons you have trusted me," he began. Whispers and prayers of the crowd fell silent. Even the children watched, rapt. "Through cold winters and blistering summers, you have kept at my side. You have prayed with me, trusted me, and it is because of you that we walk this joyous road. Our goddess returns! She lives, praise be!"

"Praise be!" the crowd echoed, Keles among them.

He walked back and forth on a stone surface stained crimson.

"Some of you may be afraid. You may feel the stings of doubt. Hold faith in the caressing wings. Trust the narrow path. I was a wretch in a prison cell when Lycaena put this path before me, and she shall choose another to walk in my stead. You are not alone, my children. You are never alone when you keep Lycaena's name close to your heart."

He was preparing them for her leadership. Reminding them of his prison sentence, just as she was once imprisoned. Claiming her chosen, even as she stood at the head of the crowd before the altar. Her nerves grew, and she tried to tell herself she could do this without him. She had led before, and she could lead again, especially with the goddess at her side.

Eshiel turned to the six stones between him and the edge of the cliff. Wind blew in from the sea when he lifted his arms. For a moment, insane as it was, she believed him a master of the elements. He lowered his head. His voice quieted, but in the ensuing silence, there was no need for him to shout.

"To Thanet, we give our prayers," he began.

Fires surged across the stones. The air was thick with faith. Belief dwelt in the blood and in the murmured prayers. For years, these people had worked to resurrect their beloved goddess. For years, they had worshiped atop this cliff, consecrating it, empowering it. Had Eshiel planned this from the very beginning? Did he sense the cost, even as he built his congregation?

Beneath him, the crimson stains turned slick and wet as if freshly spilled.

"To the goddess, I give my all."

Eshiel drew the dagger from his belt. Gleaming silver, freshly washed and sharpened. He fell silent and still. The prayer, though, would not be halted. The people cried out their hopes to the stars in perfect unison.

From blood and bone, shadow and fire, from the land and the sea,
we scream your rebirth.

Keles led that prayer, her voice lifted above all others. She fell into the role so easily. Had she not done so a hundred times before as the Light of Vallessau?

"Fly to us!" Eshiel screamed, piercing the call of prayer. All others fell silent. Some wept. Others trembled. "One of wing and flower, of storm and sun. Give us light, give us heat, we sing!"

Rivers of flame soared from the stones. The old blood staining the altar floated up from the stone to meet the fire. The mixture gathered, blessed by the sea winds and kissed by the moonlight. From its center spread four fluttering wings outlined with smoke and char. The blood blackened from the fire so it almost resembled her pristine flesh. Keles remembered it smooth as polished stone, but this new flesh was cracked and uneven. Incomplete.

"Lycaena, return to us," Eshiel cried.

"Return to us!" Keles echoed, and the crowd obeyed. The cries repeated, again and again, a desperate plea. *Return to us. Return to us.*

The blood-and-fire goddess extended a hand. A face appeared within the flames. For the first time in Keles's presence, the goddess spoke.

"Even if it must be in blood."

This was the moment she dreaded. Horror writhed through her. She couldn't shake the memory of when the priests had torn Lycaena's body apart with their daggers. Of the moments after. Keles had watched the Anointed One toss the slain goddess's hair to the crowd like a perverted trophy. Now she would witness another life taken by the dagger. That it was Lycaena who demanded it made it all the worse.

But Eshiel conveyed only acceptance. He gazed upon his goddess and smiled.

"Even if it must be in blood."

Eshiel turned the dagger so its sharp edge pressed to his breastbone. Lycaena's hands curled around his, enveloping his fingers, holding the dagger's hilt. Eshiel's choice, but the act done together. His blood, her guidance. Despite the wind, despite the fire, despite the crowd, his whisper reached the ears of all present.

"An act of faith. An offer of love."

Together, goddess and priest slammed the dagger deep to the hilt. Keles screamed. Eshiel didn't.

They ripped the dagger from his stern to his belly. Blood and innards erupted.

This time Eshiel screamed.

"Return to us," the frightened crowd murmured, a protest to the horror. Tears swelled in Keles's eyes, but she wiped them away. They would look to her. They would need her. Her heart was numb, her mind a blank white canvas, but she forced out words.

"Return to us," she said, and stood tall. "To Lycaena, we pray. To Lycaena, we give our all."

To Lycaena, this vision of swirling fire and spilled blood. Keles thought the goddess would consume Eshiel's body completely, or set him upon the altar, but instead she cradled Eshiel like a child to her bosom. Her wings fluttered, wider and wider, the shadow stretching as if to claim the horizon.

"From your very first prayer, I loved you," Lycaena said. "From the very first drop of spilled blood, I needed you."

And then the goddess closed her eyes and began her own prayer.

An act of faith. Keles had doubted, but had she not always? Ever questioning her role and her abilities. Even when they championed her as the Light of Vallessau, she had felt like an impostor pretending at what others expected of her. But Eshiel had not doubted. The knives of the priests never broke him. The goddess's execution did not shake him. Out here in the woods, beyond sight of church and city, he had reclaimed his faith.

As Keles watched, that faith claimed him in turn.

The goddess bowed her head. Her wings wrapped about their bodies, enclosing them in their billowing wisps of shadow. The sea winds whipped through them, carrying pink and crimson petals birthed from nowhere. The wind teased the hem of a dress made of flame.

"My dearest child," she spoke. The sound of her words filled Keles with an irrefutable need to bow. "I will not traverse this path without you. You are my champion. You are my anointed. You are my beloved, and I command you to live."

Her fire seared across his flesh, closing the wound. Her blood flowed into his body, replacing that which was lost. Her wings cupped him, hovering him in the air as he writhed. Her fingers brushed the tattoos across his face. They blazed with light. They burned with fire. Eshiel gasped, and so Lycaena released him. He collapsed to unsteady legs, then dropped to his hands and knees with his head bowed and limbs trembling.

"Rise," she commanded as all around, the crowd wept upon their knees.

"I would kneel," he rasped, as if his lungs were still learning to work again.

Lycaena cupped his chin with her fingers and lifted his gaze to meet her own.

"You have spent your life kneeling. I would have you walk with your head amidst the stars. Let none look down upon you. Eshiel thrice-born,

I name you. Upon Thanet, there are none more loyal, and none more beloved in my eyes."

"Thrice-born," he sputtered. "I am unworthy, my goddess. I am unworthy, but if you speak it, then I must accept."

Keles had viewed Eshiel as a bastion of faith, as someone whose strength she envied and whose confidence made a mockery of her persistent doubts. Now she saw a different side. He stood as commanded, but his shoulders sagged. His head bowed. He leaned into her embrace, and she accepted him readily. Shadow held him steady. Fire kissed his head, but he was not burned. Blood held him close, but it did not stain. He wept. They were the tears of years of struggle. They were hidden doubts never allowed to be made visible. Keles wept with him. If only she were brave enough to join him. If only Lycaena could gaze upon her with that same boundless love and acceptance.

The people behind her erupted into song.

Give us light, give us heat, we sing.

"I'm sorry," Keles whispered, letting their chorus drown out her confession. "My fear. My sorrow. Take it from me, my goddess. Please, take it. I want it no longer."

Something burned within her, hot and overwhelming. It felt like hope. It felt like relief. This wondrous being could set the path for Keles to walk, so she need not ponder it anymore. She need not fear. She need not doubt. She must only obey, and the world itself would make way.

Eshiel stepped back, already stronger. He kept one hand extended, holding Lycaena's, and then addressed his faithful. Power shimmered in his tattoos. When he raised his free hand toward the sky, fire burst off it in waves.

"I walk a narrow road toward a free Thanet," he told those in attendance. "Who here shall walk it with me?"

Men, women, and children lifted their hands and voices. They cried out their dedication. They professed their love. It became a wave, a tsunami, an overwhelming aura of faith and emotion. Keles was right there in the middle of it all, arms high, tears flowing, smiling with the relief,

smiling with the understanding that a deep, broken part of her world
had finally been made whole.

The Lycaena of her childhood, the goddess of her heartfelt prayers,
lived once more. Let her identity as a paladin be restored. Let her walk
with sword gleaming and shield emblazoned at Eshiel's side, to fight for
a deity deserving every sliver of her passion.

"What monster is this?"

The protest pierced the song. Frightened men and women parted. A
mixture of elation and dread filled Keles upon seeing her uncle stride
forth from the forest at the bottom of the incline, his sword drawn and
his shield at the ready. The look on his face was pure horror.

"It is no monster," Keles shouted. "Lycaena has returned to us."

He pointed his sword.

"You would call this abomination 'Lycaena'?"

"I do! I know it to be true!"

"Only because it has you in its thrall, child."

"You're wrong!" She brought her loving gaze back to the reborn
goddess. Her form was different, true, but she was still the goddess she
had served, the goddess she prayed to for comfort in her darkest hours.
In those eyes, she saw fury, yes, but she also saw love. She saw protectiveness in the way she clutched Eshiel's hand. If given a chance, Keles
could convince Rayan of that. Once he accepted the new form, once he
acknowledged that Lycaena must dress herself in battlements of war for
the coming age, then he would believe.

And then a new voice spoke, one that filled her with dread. Her uncle
was not alone.

"There is no truth upon that bloody altar."

No, it couldn't be, not here, not now. Keles turned. He crouched
atop a heavy tree branch like a raptor. His cloak blew in the awakening
wind. The moonlight reflected off a grinning skull mask, so bright it
shone like a beacon.

Cyrus, the Vagrant Prince, had come to pay his due to the goddess of
fire and blood.

CHAPTER 12

VAGRANT

Cyrus's joy in seeing Keles was tempered by the horror of the burning goddess dripping with blackened blood. Power radiated off her in waves like a living maelstrom. It set his skin to crawling. It pulsed shivers through him. Deep within, a dark voice screamed in purest rage. This being was dangerous. This goddess was death come to Thanet on fiery wings.

"Who are you to interrupt this sacred rite?" Eshiel asked. He stood before the monster he had summoned through untold slaughter upon his altar. His tattoos burned with flame. "Who are you to pass judgment upon our island's goddess?"

Rayan opened his mouth to speak, but Cyrus did not let him. Every fiber of his being rebelled against the creation before him. She was blood and shadow given form and then clothed in a dress of fire. She was destruction and sacrifice made manifest. To give her the same name as the wondrous and beautiful goddess who had shared a stage with Cyrus before her death? Sacrilege.

"I am Thanet's Vagrant, killer of paragons and slayer of both Regent Goldleaf and Imperator Magus of Eldrid. I am her protector, her guardian. I am the shadow that will banish all false gods from my island, even ones you would spin out of nightmares."

He thought this re-creation of Lycaena would protest, or argue, but so far she remained silent.

"False gods?" Eshiel asked. "Who are you, hidden behind mask and crown, to speak of false gods?"

Because I know them all too well, Cyrus thought.

"Please, Vagrant, you must listen," Keles shouted. Cyrus winced. She was so desperate, so frightened. What had happened to the woman who proudly declared her faith in Lycaena ended? Who was so certain the Butterfly would not return to Thanet's blue skies? "It's her. I know it, this is her."

"My heart never belonged to the goddess," Cyrus said. He looked to Rayan, and despite his own thoughts, he vowed to accept the decision of someone wiser. "Though I see an abomination, I will trust the one whose faith never faltered. Tell me, Paladin, what do you see?"

Rayan pointed with his sword. The crowd between him and the ritual altar parted in fear of the coming battle, pushing to the sides of the clifftop or skirting toward the tree line.

"I know the face of the goddess to whom I pray," he said. Faint bluish light glowed from his drawn blade, the polar opposite to the fire and blood that embraced the thing atop the cliff. "I know the voice of the beloved that has protected me since birth."

Lycaena tilted her head as if confused. For the first time, she spoke. Her voice moved with the power of creation. It twisted Cyrus's insides and sent shivers racing through his blood from its sheer wrongness.

"Rayan," she said. "Dearest one. Will you not embrace me?"

The paladin's approach never slowed. His sword rose higher, as did his shield. The man prepared for battle.

"I know the love that once graced our island," he said. "But you? I know you not."

Cyrus vaulted from the branch to the ground without the slightest noise to his landing. He drew his blades, keenly aware of the symbol of the Butterfly carved into his left hand's hilt. Rayan and Cyrus had not discussed a plan of action, for neither had truly believed Lycaena might be returned, let alone that she would appear in such a form. Could they challenge a goddess and her followers?

Did they even have a choice?

Eshiel clapped his hands together. Fragments of light shimmered off his shoulder blades like sparks escaping the heart of a forge. For the briefest moment, they resembled a folded pair of wings.

"Your doubt is not our condemnation, but your own," he said. "Strike at us if you wish. I will spare you the altar, but not the grave."

Rayan charged, unintimidated by the priest, and none dared interfere. Cyrus sprinted in his shadow, but his own path would not be so easy. Keles stepped in his way, her sword swinging for his chest. To his shock, dark flame wreathed its steel. He skidded to a halt with swords up to block, and grunted at the strength of the hit when their weapons connected.

"You can still accept her," Keles said. "You don't have to fight."

Another swing. Cyrus parried it sideways with his off-hand, rotated as he stepped closer, and then slammed her with his shoulder. She staggered backward, and he pleaded with her during the momentary reprieve.

"This isn't you. You're enthralled. Can you not sense it?"

Even now he felt the pull on his soul. This Lycaena wasn't just a creation of faith, but a swirling vortex demanding it from all in her presence. She was a bottomless hole. She was a consuming fire, and all of them would burn.

"It is the truth I feel that guides me now, Vagrant, and it says you must flee."

She assaulted him again, wild strikes lacking precision or tactic. He held firm, blocking them with both blades while watching for a chance to disarm her. It was so unlike the calm and calculating woman he knew. She was being driven by fear and panic, and it only reinforced his belief. Lycaena had done something to her, changed something within her. This devotion, it wasn't real. It couldn't be.

He watched Rayan's fight when able. Eshiel had prevented Rayan from reaching the reborn goddess. Though he wielded no weapon, he was more than an equal match for the paladin. Fire swept from his hands in streams, blazing and ferocious. Rayan either dodged or blocked with his shield, his every step closer a struggle against the torrent.

A swing from Keles forced his attention back her way. She lacked armor but made up for it in the raw power of her sword. When he blocked, the rattle traveled up to his teeth. If his weapons were not

Ahlai-made, he wondered if they would have shattered. Or perhaps their strength was blessed by the Vagrant, a curiosity he could not afford to dwell on as that burning blade looped and swung. No swings were meant to be lethal, or even go unblocked. She was trying to batter him away, scare him off like he was a coyote attacking a herd.

"You never knew true faith," she said, still trying to convince him. "Only worship, and only if laid at your feet."

"I don't need to know faith. I know who you are, and who is upon that cliff. If it's Lycaena, it's only a shade of her, warped, cruel, and unworthy of you. Let it die!"

Keles's eyes widened with rage, and she chopped an overhead blow with the hilt clutched in both hands. Cyrus parried it aside, winced at the uncomfortable heat, and then kicked at her wrists. She did not drop the blade, but she screamed as her arms wrenched awkwardly. Cyrus's planned follow-up died as Lycaena's voice washed over him, feeling like the crawling touch of a thousand maggots.

"Step aside, faithful one."

Keles jabbed her elbow toward his face during his distraction. His feet twirled, pulling him away, and in the brief opening he looked to the clifftop.

Eshiel and Rayan's battle, for all appearances, had ended in a stalemate. Upon her order, the priest retreated so his goddess might float toward Rayan with her arms lifted. The flame of her dress flowed upward, crawled across the churning blood of her arms to her ashen fingers, and then shaped into a jagged sword clutched tightly in one hand. Rayan lifted his shield, unafraid.

"Enough of this," Cyrus said, and he tried to sidestep past Keles. She shifted to block his way, her sword still lifted.

"No."

"He'll die!"

"He won't. He'll see the truth, Vagrant, he will, if only you would let him!"

The truth? The only truth Cyrus saw was his friend facing off against a being of blood and fire. Could he be wrong? Was the real Lycaena buried somewhere deep inside that being summoned by the altar?

"You are not my goddess," Rayan told the reborn Lycaena. "I will not be moved."

"Because you are blind," she said as she so calmly swung. Rayan met it with his shield, and though he did not cry out, Cyrus saw the shock of the impact nearly topple him.

"Fooled," she said.

Another hit, this one strong enough to buckle his right knee. He stood immediately and lifted his battered shield in challenge.

"Deceived."

At the last minute he sidestepped another strike, surprising her with his sudden movement. The swing narrowly missed, while his own cut across her abdomen. The faint light upon his blade dimmed, and though the steel pierced the shimmer of blood that was her skin, it spilled only a faint cloud of ash to the ground. Keles cried out, and her sword lowered, her attention no longer on Cyrus.

"Uncle, stop!"

Lycaena swept a hand at him, and blood flung from her fingertips like ropes that grew in length as they flew. They latched about Rayan's legs and then clung to the ground, holding him in place. With no other choice, he raised his shield and braced for the coming blow.

"I would mend you, in heart and soul, but you are beholden to that which is lost," she said. Her sword rose, this time held in both hands. "Fear not. In the endless fields beyond, I shall have all eternity to open your eyes."

Cyrus slammed into Rayan's side, dug in his heels, and shoved. The bloody tendrils tore, and now free, the paladin tumbled down the incline toward the forest. His friend safe, Cyrus spun to face the goddess. She loomed over him, and now so close, he felt an intense desire to kneel. Her height was twice his own, her burning dress wondrous and terrifying, her blood-soaked face and flesh of deepest nightmares. The blade meant for Rayan swung for his own head, and he crossed his swords to meet it.

He was becoming a god in his own right, he told himself. He was blessed by sacrifice no different than what fed this monster. People prayed to him, perhaps haltingly, perhaps not knowing it was even prayer, but that faith powered him. He could face this foe. He could stand strong.

And then Lycaena's sword hit his, and he knew himself for a fool.

His knees buckled. His arms shook. The muscles in his back spasmed with pain. The heat was so great, he feared his painted mask would catch flame. He pushed, and struggled, and at last gasped for air at a sudden reprieve.

"You live on stolen faith," she said, and lifted her sword for a second blow. "For my people, for my children, I shall reclaim it."

It did not matter if it was cowardice. Cyrus could not survive a second blow. He backflipped away, descending halfway down the incline. Her sword sundered empty earth. He landed unsteadily beside Rayan and fell briefly to one knee.

"She's strong," he told his friend.

"I am aware."

Cyrus glanced over his shoulder. Keles approached from one direction, the goddess the other.

"Do we flee?" he asked.

Rayan was given no chance to answer. Frightened shouts along with a march of feet and rustle of branches rose up behind them. Cyrus glanced over his shoulder, then let out a curse. A terrible night was only growing worse.

The empire had arrived.

CHAPTER 13

VAGRANT

So this is the desperation of the conquered," Galvanis vin Lucavi said as he emerged from the forest at the bottom of the incline. Two paragons flanked his sides as he approached the clifftop, one wearing golden plate, the other a deep blue. The Heir-Incarnate confidently strode toward the seething mass of divine rage that was the reborn Lycaena. His armor shone in the moonlight, cast with an orange hue from the goddess's fire. The hilt of his enormous sword was carved of gold and ivory, its tips jeweled with rubies. He carried it in one hand, though given its size and weight, most men would lift it with two, if they could lift it at all.

"Your people went unwatched in these wild lands," he said, and pointed the blade to Lycaena. "And so to these wild lands you brought forth living blasphemy."

Soldiers followed in his wake, and they spread out to form an impenetrable line of steel blocking any retreat by the worshipers. Cyrus kept still and watched carefully. Too many different factions. Too many deadly combatants. To escape with their lives would require the utmost care.

Eshiel stood at his goddess's side, bare-chested, hands clenched into fists. Fire leaked between his fingers. His tattoos glowed with renewed vigor. If he was frightened by the newcomers, that fear did not touch his voice.

"New shades and old conquerors come speaking of blasphemy," he said. "Let you all burn for your disbelief."

Lycaena's dress of flame wrapped about his shoulders to cover his chest as she rose to her full height. Her star-filled eyes sparked with divine rage. They were a pair to conquer a nation, a faith to sweep away mountains. For one brief moment, Cyrus felt the desire to believe. The responsibility to cast off the empire could belong to another. The prayers, they could turn from the Vagrant to she whom Thanet had first cherished.

Would you be a coward? Would you deny the path Endarius asked you to walk?

The moment passed, and Cyrus looked once more upon a monster. The blood that made up the surface of Lycaena's flesh hardened into armor. The embers that were her eyes split wide. She lifted dark hands, opened her lips, and sang three words as if they were the most beautiful song.

"Grant me sacrifice."

The command rumbled the earth and set the leaves in the forest to shiver as if swept by a storm. Eshiel pointed to the Heir-Incarnate, and his challenge bellowed out to the stars.

"Come to me, son of a god most foul. I am Eshiel thrice-born, and I shall scatter your bones and ash across the sea."

The two flanking paragons led the charge, followed by Galvanis, who walked calmly behind. The soldiers kept back, for they held no place in this battle amongst gods and priests, paladins and paragons. The one in golden armor wielded a great mace with both hands, its spherical head spiked, its tips painted white. He lifted it high above his head while he shouted to his fellow paragon.

"You've enough gods to your name, Soma," he called. "Leave this bitch to me."

Soma fell back a step, and now alone, the mace-wielder sprinted faster, faster, and then leaped across the remaining space to add strength to his blow.

Lycaena met him midair with her blade. Their weapons connected with a flash of sparks and a deafening groan of steel. The paragon grunted, all his muscle and weight unable to move the goddess an inch. He landed awkwardly, his weapon tilting, his wrists bending. Her dress grew along the bottom, the edges elongating while narrowing into two spears. They thrust into the paragon's sides like twin pincers of a scorpion, finding openings at the creases between the chestplate and belt. The chainmail beneath shredded like grass.

"Sacrifice," she called, the two spears lifting him up. His mace gave way, and with three blades she ripped him apart. Gore and armor collapsed to her feet. Some worshipers screamed. Many others cheered.

Soma's attack fared better, but only barely. His spear whipped and spun with masterful precision, yet it was clear to Cyrus he was avoiding any direct challenge of that sword. Twice his spear struck Lycaena's side, parting the fire of her dress to scrape along the blood that made up her skin. When he tried for a third, she howled with unchecked fury. Where he cut hardened into crystal and burst outward in the form of spikes. Soma twisted so his armor bore the brunt of the hit. The blood-spikes broke, unable to pierce the plate, but the impact was enough to send the paragon flying through the air. Where he landed, Cyrus did not see, for he was too focused on watching the Heir-Incarnate's approach.

"Enough," the enormous man shouted. "Your battle is with me, goddess!"

Lycaena pointed her sword, her challenge apparent. Galvanis met it with a smile on his face. He was *eager* for this.

"Like the Vagrant, you are mortal flesh uplifted beyond all natural law," she said. Her sword rose, the center blazing so brightly it passed from yellow into eye-searing white. "The lands and sea will sing at your death."

Cyrus watched, torn between awe and horror at the sight of those two weapons connecting. No mortal could resist such a blow. Rock cracked beneath Galvanis's feet as the force to crush buildings flowed through his body and out to the cliff. Sparks flashed off his sword. His arms shook, but somehow he held. A second strike followed, this one sideways. He shifted the angle of his weapon, and when they connected, it sounded like thunder. Strong as he might be, the ground beneath Galvanis betrayed him. Rocks slid, his stance sliding with them.

Unreal, Cyrus thought. The Heir-Incarnate had survived two blows when a single one had nearly brought Cyrus low, but survival was far from victory. If Lycaena was to fall, it would require his help. The problem was Keles. She watched the battle alongside him, and when he moved, her sword snapped through the air, its tip dripping flame that fell like raindrops. Trodden grass blackened into ash at the touch.

"Please, leave," she said, her voice lowering. "You don't have to do this."

He nodded toward her burning blade.

"Will you kill me if I don't?"

She was given no time to answer. Rayan stepped between the two, and he pushed Cyrus with his shoulder.

"Go, Vagrant," he said, and he turned back to Keles with his sword and shield at the ready. She glared at him while fighting for words.

"Uncle, please…"

It was all too much for Cyrus to grasp. He heard anger in her voice, but also hurt, betrayal, and confusion. Rayan was steadfast but somber, this battle the last in the world he desired. Who was at fault? Who was the monster here?

Cyrus looked to the being of blood, ash, and fire, and clung to his beliefs. This goddess was vile. For all of Thanet, she had to die.

"Please don't kill each other," he said, and charged up the clifftop. From the corner of his eye, he caught Rayan interrupting Keles's attempt to follow, and then no more. He could only pray their conflict did not come to bloodshed. Twice more Galvanis and Lycaena crossed blades. The cliff trembled, yet still the empire's chosen endured. After their last hit, she shoved him backward with her elbow. It caught him off guard, and he rolled, his armor clattering.

Lycaena reached down to her skirt. From the flames, she withdrew a slender spear of fire. A flick of her wrist and it flew. A split-second decision later, Cyrus dove in the way, his swords batting the spear so it harmlessly struck ground. Galvanis grunted at him as he returned to his feet.

"I know you," he said. "Set aside our differences and work with me. Together, let us bring low this terrible danger to our island."

Not exactly the friend Cyrus had hoped to make when this night started, but he was in no position to refuse. This reborn Lycaena was blazing with divine light, so bright it threatened to blind him. Could the Heir-Incarnate see it, too?

"Perhaps I should let her kill you instead?" he said. The words rumbled out of him almost of their own accord.

Galvanis smiled, not frightened, only amused.

"Who do you fear more, Vagrant, myself, or a goddess?"

Looking at that divine monster holding Keles enthralled, he knew there was no future in whatever faith she offered Thanet. Only suffering. Only death.

"It matters not what I fear. I will aid you, but only in this, and only for a promise of safety for the innocents trapped by your soldiers."

Galvanis gripped his sword in both hands and prepared for a sprint.

"There are no innocent souls here," he said. "But you have my word."

They charged in tandem, opposites in so many ways, yet matched in speed. Cyrus fell behind a step, allowing the heavily armored man to take the lead. The last paragon, the one called Soma, remained behind to watch. A curious detail, but not one he could dwell on, for the battle was at hand.

The opening moments were ones of caution. Cyrus and Galvanis each swung and struck with careful attention, for if Lycaena brought her full strength to bear it could be disastrous for either. They felt each other out, their speed, their aggressiveness, as they surrounded the goddess. Her burning blade was always in motion, pivoting back and forth between them. For a moment they kept her trapped, her back to the cliff's edge. There would be no retreat that did not end in a plummet to the ocean below.

As the seconds passed, Cyrus grew more aggressive. He cut at her dress. He sliced at her flesh, that shifting, bleeding surface that made his stomach churn. His aggression was rewarded with a sudden and furious turn his way. Her blade smashed into his swords, and this time he didn't try to resist. He flew back down the incline, rolled twice, and then sprinted straight back up.

"Thanet must be cleansed," Lycaena called, somehow still calm and defiant. Her attention focused on Galvanis, who had fallen defensive with Cyrus momentarily out of the fight. "She must be made free."

Lycaena waved an open hand Galvanis's way. The fire of her wings and dress swirled in a torrent across her arms, becoming a funnel tremendous in size. It whipped about her, growing larger and larger, trapping both her and the Heir-Incarnate within the inferno. Cyrus retreated, seeing no way to enter, no way to save him. The circle shrank, closing in, yet Galvanis was not afraid.

"By my father's hand, I cleanse this blasphemy," he said, reciting a prayer. "By my father's strength, I bring ruin to the savage."

The circle snapped shut. The flames burst around them, a thunderous roar. The ground shook, the grass blackened, yet the Heir-Incarnate of the Everlorn Empire stood tall. Golden light encircled him, creating a perfect sphere. Its surface was translucent, and it crackled with energy like lightning. Cyrus had seen the empire's magistrates create similar shields before, though not quite so strong. Lycaena recoiled, her eyes widening, as Galvanis pointed his sword her way.

"You are born of a few worshipers' wailing cries and a handful of sacrifices," he said. "My father has bled nations. Our prayers are legion."

With the fiery wall broken, Cyrus was once more free to join Galvanis's side, yet he hesitated nonetheless. Did he still fear the goddess more than the Heir-Incarnate? It was one thing to witness such strength in a goddess. It was another to see it in a mere human. Human, but not. Uplifted, as the empire's church might say. Blessed with the divine. Made into something more, be it through faith, desperation, or a desire for vengeance.

You look upon your reflection and know fear, the dark voice whispered in his mind. *I would have you see possibility.*

Cyrus dashed forward with swords drawn. He cut and slashed in echo of the Heir-Incarnate's enormous sword. He would not fear this wretched Butterfly. He would not cower before the might of the Heir. That inner voice, the word of the Vagrant, was right. If he was to become what he must, he could not fear the reflection. He could not believe the limitations of mortal flesh and bone.

With every strike, Lycaena retreated, overwhelmed by the ferocity of their combined barrage. The Crystal Sea awaited her. Cyrus cut across her dress, ducked beneath a retributive swing, and then cut twice more as he curled up and around to her back, his feet dancing on the thin stretch of rock that marked the cliff's edge. Her wings fluttered at him, a gust of air so hot it stung his eyes. Their surface hardened, becoming spiked, and a thousand warnings sounded in his mind.

No dodging. The cliff was behind him, and so he stepped off and fell to the water below. A hundred ember arrows streaked through where he'd been, and he laughed at the absurdity of it all. To think, not so long ago, he had struggled to hold his own against a single paladin of Lycaena. Now he fought an unholy version of Lycaena herself, and by all the gods and goddesses, he would *win*.

Everywhere was dark and shadowed, even the waves of the ocean below. Destination marked clearly in his mind, Cyrus curled his body, clenched his fist, and activated the magic of his Anyx ring. Instead of striking the waves, he smashed right through them as if they were air. A moment of disorientation later, he emerged from behind one of the six stone pillars. His momentum continued, flinging him directly at the goddess. His swords pierced her flesh halfway up the hilts, opening gashes along her bleeding skin to pour out shadow and ash like guts.

Lycaena screamed, as did her chosen champion.

A jet of flame forced Cyrus to dance away, then again as a second stream followed. Eshiel approached, fury in his eyes and fire swirling across his palms. Wings stretched from his bare back, the translucent flame unmistakably shaped like those of a butterfly. His tattoos looked not at all like tattoos anymore, but a burning pattern marking him as a partaker of the divine.

"Years of prayer," he said. "Of sacrifice. Of hiding, bleeding, and dying, all for this moment. Our goddess has returned, and on the very hour of her birth, on the precipice of this new hope for our island, you would slay her?"

Cyrus rolled to dodge a third burst and then bounced to his feet. He would have to trust Galvanis to hold his own against Lycaena. Eshiel would bury them in fire if left unchecked. His power grew with each passing second.

"Hope did not summon this beast," Cyrus said. "Hatred did."

"You witness the necessary."

"I see the monstrous."

Two smaller whips of flame burst from Eshiel's palms. They lashed at Cyrus from either direction, and so he charged directly between. His feet left the ground, and he spun in midair to avoid the whips that passed above and below, until he collided into Eshiel. The poor angle prevented him from striking with his swords, but his shoulder hit Eshiel in the gut, staggering him. Cyrus landed on his knees and finally swung, but the wings curled forward protectively. Though they were fire, they hardened like stone, and his swords clanged off uselessly.

Interesting, Cyrus thought with narrowed eyes before he rolled away lest he be charred alive. What were whips became arrows, and they flew from the priest's hands as if he were a living ballista. Grass charred beneath the barrage. Cyrus zipped back and forth, relying on pure speed. Avoid, avoid, seek an opening...

"Monstrous," Eshiel shouted. "You are death itself wearing a crown. Do not talk to me of monstrous."

Cyrus pivoted, then rolled away as the air seared around him from a massive burst of flame. It was as if the earth itself were erupting. Cyrus leaped up, retreated a step, and then saw his opening. His right heel dug in, killing all his momentum, and he lunged straight at Eshiel.

Panic guided his foe's actions. His wings curled forward to form a shield, but this time Cyrus was ready. His weapons crossed inward, striking at the gaps between the wings where they touched, and then he ripped outward with all his strength. They separated, granting him passage.

His knee struck Eshiel's gut. The bottom of his hilt smashed his throat. The priest coughed and sputtered, a bit of blood trickling across his lips. He swayed on unsteady legs, and Cyrus refused to relent. The same hilt shot upward, striking his forehead. Eshiel staggered, eyes crossed. The wings about his body flickered and momentarily faded. With Eshiel's defenses broken, Cyrus fell back a step, planted his feet for balance, and prepared for the killing thrust.

Keles's piercing scream halted his swords.

"Don't!"

Cyrus glanced her way, saw the pleading in her eyes, and he knew. He knew. She would never forgive him for this. Was he willing to pay such a price?

Perhaps he was, perhaps not, but his hesitation robbed him of that choice. Eshiel's fiery wings curled inward, forming a protective cocoon. Heat blasted out in waves, striking Cyrus with a physical force. He tumbled head over feet twice before righting himself. His slide halted at the side of the blue-armored paragon near the bottom of the climb.

"Incompetent fool," Soma said. He shoved Cyrus aside with a brush of his hand and then lifted his spear. "He will burn us all if left alive."

One pulse of his legs sent him flying, all his muscle and plate seemingly nothing but air. A recovered Eshiel wrapped the wings back around his body. They solidified, the fire itself slowing and coalescing until it somehow resembled sheets of shimmering ice.

Soma's spear plunged into the heart of the flame. The tip heated, glowed red, and then punched through. The frozen flame shattered into shards that flickered and burst. Heat washed over Cyrus, even from such a distance, followed by a physical shock wave that rattled his teeth. The sting in his eyes was not only from the light, but from the faint divine essence intermixed. That defense, that cocoon, was blessed by Lycaena, and somehow the paragon had broken through.

The ground, already cracked and weakened from the battle, gave up its last. Rock groaned, dirt tumbled. When Cyrus looked again, the entire left half of the clifftop had crumbled to the sea. There was no sign of Eshiel or Soma.

Keles screamed.

No words. No name. Just a scream.

It did not hurt Cyrus as much as it should have. There was no room for tears behind his skull mask. He turned to Lycaena, who seethed with fury, and whose flame could not breach the shield the God-Incarnate wrapped around his faithful son.

She is no goddess, whispered the dark voice. *End this.*

Galvanis pressed forward, the flames about him temporarily scattering. His sword slashed across Lycaena's legs. She bled only shadow and ash. No blood flowed within her, for blood was her skin, her armor. She screamed, fire leaping off her dress in the form of whips that lashed the Heir-Incarnate. He pivoted and turned, deflecting what he could and relying on his armor to protect what he could not. Even amid that fury, he scored another blow that ripped a gash across the goddess's stomach. Ash spilled out in plumes.

Cyrus sprinted up the incline, picking up speed as his cloak billowed behind him. His vision narrowed, and a coldness encased his mind. Everything that the Vagrant was, and what he represented, he let himself believe. No doubts. No hesitation. A flex of his legs, and he soared into the air, twice even the goddess's height. Moonlight glinted off his swords, their blades eager for blood.

Time itself seemed to slow. Cyrus saw the fiery tendrils bursting off her dress like the legs of a squid. They reached for him, and he twisted and turned, avoiding each and every one. The motions rotated him so at the very height of his leap he was completely upside down above her head, and he stared into her eyes. Within them he saw swirling stars and cosmoses with shapes and clusters for which he had no name.

He saw no compassion in them. No love. No warmth.

He saw fear.

Another twist, and he righted himself amid his fall. A burning tendril punched a hole in his cloak but missed his ribs by an inch. A second failed to strike his neck. Down, down he fell, swords out, hungry, vicious.

He let the Butterfly blade lead the way, the tip punching directly into her open, screaming mouth. The Endarius blade followed, stabbing her throat. Smoke and ash burst through the opened hole in her bleeding skin. His momentum continued, and he ripped and tore as he fell, opening her as if he were parting a curtain. His feet touched ground, his wrists turned, and then he slashed outward, completing the cuts by severing her knees from the rest of her collapsing body.

All he heard were screams—of worshipers, of Keles, of the goddess herself—and then for the second time in his life, Cyrus felt the explosion of power released by the goddess's death. Its intensity was a pale mimicry of the eruption that had shaken the stage and flattened hundreds in attendance to their knees years ago. It sparked his skin like static, and the force of the explosion was like a fist made of wind.

This time, it did not send him flying. This time he was a stone, immovable and strong. The last of her blood sizzled into smoke. Her ash parted to the wind. Her fire turned to embers, dim and fading. He spoke without thinking, with a voice not entirely his own.

"It is done."

CHAPTER 14

VAGRANT

Cyrus stood within the swirling, dying fire, the blood and ash at his feet the only corpse the slain goddess would leave behind. A shiver ran up and down his spine. The essence of the divine, the lingering power and faith—it flowed across his skin like a cool wind. He breathed it in with his eyes closed. The fighting had halted upon Lycaena's death, but Cyrus feared how long that peace would last.

Eyes opened, he glared at the Heir-Incarnate from behind his skull mask.

"You intrude upon Thanese affairs, imperial."

The towering man smirked, his pale skin almost glowing in the moonlight.

"And it was a good thing I did, Vagrant. Her power was greater than your own, but why shouldn't it be? She was a god, and you are not."

Is that so?

Instead Cyrus gestured to the remaining soldiers that lined the forest's edge at the bottom of the clifftop's incline. What few worshipers remained were huddled together, many of them too old or infirm to flee as the others had during the fray. With Lycaena dead, Rayan and Keles had ceased their own conflict to face the remaining threat. The pair stood protectively before the frightened worshipers, almost daring the soldiers to step forward and try to attack.

"The battle is ended," Cyrus said. "Tell your men to grant us passage."

"Before me are heretics who refused to worship the God-Incarnate, and you would ask that I allow them to escape?"

Cyrus tensed. The last thing he wanted was another battle. Galvanis's forces were numerous, whereas Cyrus and his friends numbered a mere three.

"I would ask you to keep your word, and be less monstrous than that which we just slew."

The Heir-Incarnate laughed. The sound of it was deeply unpleasant. It felt sick, and thrived only on the fears and uncertainties of those whose lives the man held in his hands. Galvanis rested his enormous sword comfortably atop his shoulder. When wind blew from the ocean, his hair did not sway, as if it were too heavy to be moved. Cyrus looked upon a man not birthed of flesh but instead carved from stone.

"You have done a good deed here, Vagrant, and so I will honor my promise. Go, all of you, and be free of the chains that bound your souls to the bloody Butterfly. Doubt me if you wish, but know you were spared a horrid fate. Lycaena's sacrifices would not have halted. Your friends? Your family? Even her faithful would one day give their lives in offering to that monstrosity. No gods of such cruel measures endure. They are but brief wildfires, consuming all and offering nothing in return. Ierida would have become a land of ash and corpses had I not intervened."

Soldiers parted, granting a path into the forest. The survivors rushed for it, flanked on either side by Keles and Rayan. Cyrus waited for them to leave and then moved to follow.

Galvanis swept his sword to block Cyrus's path. Their eyes locked.

"Consider this a warning," he said, voice low and for the Vagrant alone. "Whatever victories you knew before are irrelevant. Set aside your mask, and spare yourself the cruel fate your predecessors enjoyed. No other death awaits you. I am here now. Your war is over. And if you will not hang up your swords, well...you've seen the strength of my blade."

Cyrus matched the man's confidence with his own. He would not back down to any imperial, no matter their birth or station.

"I fear not you, nor your God-Incarnate. If gods and goddesses can die, then so may you."

Cyrus was gifted a porcelain smile.

"Run, Vagrant. Run to those who still worship you, and tell them to cast aside their faith. It will only lead them to their graves." The sword pulled back, clearing the way. Galvanis held it close, hilt turning, fingers twirling, eyes wide. Eager. "Or would you prove here and now how little you fear the empire's god?"

As much as it burned his pride, Cyrus had witnessed the Heir-Incarnate's strength when battling Lycaena. His own strength was largely expended, whereas Galvanis showed not a hint of exertion. Cyrus would not be baited, not into a battle where paragons and soldiers lurked nearby to aid.

"Not yet," he said, and then dashed down the path to the trees beyond.

⁓

The trio ran through forest, Rayan leading the way. They followed no path, their vague destination only southward and away from the cliffs. Minutes passed in aching, awful silence. Occasionally they heard movement in the darkness, of others fleeing the massacre. In time they quieted until it was only the three, and only then did Rayan pause to catch his breath.

"We need not push ourselves so hard," Cyrus said as his old friend leaned his weight against a tree trunk. Rayan removed his helmet and tucked it under one arm.

"I left most of our supplies at the forest's edge. We'll need to beg or buy more at Chora if we are to survive our return to Vallessau."

"Then let us pray the imperial soldiers did not ransack the village prior to arriving here."

Rayan winced at the thought.

"Indeed. Let us pray."

Silence followed, heavy and awkward. Keles stood separate from the pair, her back turned to them. Her arms were crossed over her chest and clutched at her sides as if she were caught with a chill. Cyrus stared, a thousand thoughts birthing and dying in his mind. What might he say to her? What comfort could he offer?

It was a monster, whispered that dark voice he was so familiar with now. *It needed to die.*

"Hey," he said, for he would never speak such thoughts aloud. "Are you all right?"

Her shoulders shook. Crying? No. Not crying. Laughing. Bitter, broken laughter.

"Am I all right?" she asked. "No, *Vagrant,* I am not all right. Eshiel is dead. Lycaena is dead. How could I possibly be all right?"

"It wasn't Lycaena," Rayan insisted. Keles whirled on him, furious despite her heartbreak.

"You don't know that," she said. "You witnessed her existence for but a moment. You saw only the sacrifice to make her. I was there. I felt it. I lived it. She was changed, yes, but she was...she..."

Her hands clenched into fists. Her jaw hardened, and what sorrow she suffered withered away.

"Eshiel and his faithful loved Lycaena with all their hearts. I did not cower before the cost, nor the blood. Neither would you have, if you had sided with us."

The paladin approached, and Cyrus tensed at the shift in mood. This argument of gods, it was beyond him, for he had rarely bowed his head in prayer to the Butterfly.

"Your desperation enthralled you to a murderous promise," Rayan said. "But the blood on that altar speaks louder than any prayer. The goddess I worship is not born of slaughter. She did not promise death to the unbelieving, nor pain to the doubtful. The blasphemous thing Eshiel summoned, it may have been a god, but it was not Lycaena. We did what must be done, to spare the island from worshiping a lie."

"And so it's better we worship the God-Incarnate instead?"

"Better we abide by the truth, and fight against the lie."

Keles laughed and scoffed in equal measure, her eyes red, her shoulders drooped and weary.

"I envy you, Uncle, I do. But be it wisdom or folly, I do not see the world as you do. When younger, I'd have trusted your decisions. I have no such trust left, for anyone. You are wrong. Lycaena is dead, and you helped kill her."

Rayan did not argue. He replaced his helmet and checked the sky to get his bearings.

"Galvanis may have promised us clemency, but I trust him not. Let us go, and put this forest as far behind us as we can before sunrise."

Keles shook her head.

"I shall return to Vallessau at my own pace. Please. Leave me be."

Rayan didn't seem surprised. Instead he offered her an embrace, and she reluctantly accepted. His arms surrounded her, and she endured it stiff as wood and gaze downcast. When they parted, Rayan waved, turned southward, and walked away.

Cyrus stood watching it all awkwardly. He struggled to find the proper words, for he did not want to leave her like this. He hated it, hated the confusion, hated the fighting, hated the way she looked at him as if he were a foe. The silence, it stretched, and stretched, raw and grating across his nerves. He'd been so excited to see her, and yet now they would part with hardly any words spoken between them?

"I'm sorry," he whispered. It wouldn't be enough, but what else was there to add?

"But you aren't," she said. "So why do you lie?"

Because he wanted to comfort her. Because he hated seeing her in pain. Because a tiny part of him was terrified he had made the wrong choice. He told her none of this. Words were no good, not on this night. His swords had spoken clearly enough.

Rayan's sharp voice barked from the distance.

"Come, Cyrus."

The spell over him broke, and he lowered his head. His presence brought no healing to his wounded friend, and so he bade her farewell.

"Stay safe," he said. "I pray I will see you soon."

It was as much a question as a departure blessing, but she gave him no answer when he retreated into the dark forest.

Or perhaps that silence was answer enough, and he merely refused to hear it.

CHAPTER 15

ESHIEL

Eshiel woke to the sound of crashing waves. He kept perfectly still while assessing his surroundings. The ground beneath him was soft and cold. Sand, from what he could guess, but not near the water. Slightly higher. His clothes were wet but drying. He lay on his back, and despite a careful series of stretches he felt no pain barring a consistent dull ache across his entire body. Nothing broken, nothing bleeding. Even more curious, his hands were not bound, but lay loose at his sides.

I survived the fall?

He shouldn't have. Eshiel remembered the blue-armored paragon slamming into him, his magic failing to halt the approach of that damn spear. Yet the spear had missed. The ground below them gave way, and then they were tumbling toward the ocean. His last memory had been of the moment he hit the water.

A sound of scraping metal pierced the fog in his mind. Someone nearby. Well, whoever it was, if they hadn't killed him while he was unconscious, it made no sense they'd kill him now. Slowly drawing in a single breath to steel his resolve, Eshiel opened his eyes and sat up.

He regretted it immediately.

"Oh shit."

He turned and vomited into the sand. His world danced in vertigo. The worst headache he'd experienced in his life assaulted him like a sleeping dragon now awakened. It throbbed within his forehead, and it pulsed out sharp lances to his eyes.

"You're awake," said a familiar voice, and in Thanese, not the imperial tongue. Eshiel risked another bout of dizziness to look for the source.

The blue-armored paragon sat near the beach, the waves washing along his heels and ankles. His spear lay across his lap. The metal scraping noise Eshiel heard came from the whetstone he used to sharpen its edges. Moonlight reflected off the paragon's armor, deepening the painted armor's shade of blue.

"Much to my surprise," Eshiel said. He winced at the knifing pain in his forehead. The simple act of speaking launched a dozen new hurts, nearly all located inside his skull. The shallow water must have broken his fall, not that water was the most gentle of landings from such a height in the first place. He didn't remember anything, just the fall, and a sudden pain that, at the time, he had been convinced was the moment of his death...

"You are experiencing what our surgeons in Eldrid would describe as a 'concussion.' It may pass in days, or endure for multiple months. Given you were unconscious for several hours, I would wager on it taking many weeks before the last of the symptoms cease."

Eshiel closed his eyes and focused on his breathing. The pain was starting to dull, a blessed relief. If his initial pain upon sitting up remained the worst of it, he could continue to function. Curiosity ate at him, and he took in his surroundings once more. The two sat on a small stretch of naked beach. Not far to his right loomed the great cliff from which he had brought back his beloved Lycaena.

Lycaena...

"Is my goddess dead?"

The scraping of the whetstone ceased.

"She is. She went out with a scream of pain and a shower of blood. I was not there to see it, but I would wager Vallessau's Vagrant scored the killing blow. If not him, then the Heir-Incarnate."

Eshiel pulled his knees to his chest. His hands balled into fists. Scattered memories of that night came to him, a moment of tremendous pride and worship ripped apart so only horror and loss remained.

Thrice-born, Lycaena had named him. And just like after his second birth, he had plummeted from the cliffs into the water. Unlike his second birth, the Butterfly had not been there to bless him. Friends and family did not await him at the shore, a great celebratory feast already roasting over a series of fire pits. Instead he awoke to a cold, empty night, his only greeting that of the damn blue-armored paragon, whose name Eshiel did not even know.

"Am I correct in assuming you dragged me from the water?"

Back to sharpening. A crash of waves, a scrape of metal. Those two sounds alternated in a strange rhythm.

"That I did."

Eshiel glanced over his shoulder. Behind them, the ground sloped steeply upward, becoming rockier until reaching a sudden, short climb. The ash trees started there, the thick forest that had been his home. One could even see their exposed roots poking out the edges. Had the imperials raided Eshiel's camp on their way to interrupt the sacrifice? And what of his followers? Had they been allowed to live, or had the Heir-Incarnate ordered them executed?

The loss of it all bore down on Eshiel, and his mind was too sick and damaged to endure it. He slumped, his palms pressing to his forehead as if he could push out the damn migraine making a wreck of the space between his ears. Everything he'd worked for, years of prayers, sacrifice, and preaching, undone in a single night. Despair stabbed at him. How could they ever win if it took such tremendous time to build, and yet only the most hideous of moments for the empire to destroy? Why must such misfortune plague Thanet? Why must he witness the death of his beloved goddess not once, but twice?

He looked up, glared through blurry vision at the nearby paragon, and asked the question most baffling to him of all.

"Why am I alive?"

Eshiel didn't mean it to sound so bitter, so . . . accusatory. He was glad to be alive, wasn't he?

Wasn't he?

"Is there an answer I can give that you would deem sufficient?" the paragon asked.

"None that would allay my fears, I suspect. You aided Thanet's conquering, you helped slay Lycaena, and you cast me off the edge of a cliff. Yet instead of completing your list of crimes, you rescued me from the water. Why? Would you hang me from the Dead Flags? Maybe drag me all the way to Vallessau so you might put on a gruesome show for the public?"

The paragon stood. His face was completely hidden behind his helmet, a round, full-cover style that was unfamiliar to the island. It had a metal visor that fell low across the front, and he lifted it. Beneath was a pale-skinned man, his hair blond, his eyes shining a color reminiscent of his armor.

"If I wanted you dead, I would have let you drown. If I wanted you delivered to Galvanis, I'd have bound your hands and feet. You're free, and you're breathing. Assume both were on purpose, and do not insult me again."

"How can I insult a man whose name I know not?"

The paragon removed his helmet entirely, freeing his long hair to fall down to his waist. It blew in the faint sea breeze. He was attractive, Eshiel had to admit, but then again, most paragons were. Something about their creation did that to them. They were meant to be the embodiment of the God-Incarnate's strength and power, a symbol of his might to the people, so of course they had to be chisel-jawed, musclebound warriors. Yet this man looked different somehow. Less handsome, and more beautiful. Perhaps it was the hair, the gentle curve of his cheeks and jaw, or those shocking blue eyes.

"Soma," he said. "My name is Soma Ordiae, Paragon of Spears. Now if you seek to insult me, you may do so correctly."

He smiled, and Eshiel realized "beautiful" did not go far enough to describe him. A sickness stirred in his stomach. He should *hate* this man, hate him with all his being, and yet he found himself liking the paragon instead. What was wrong with him? Were his convictions so easily cast aside?

"You have not answered my question, only deflected," Eshiel said. "Why spare my life?"

Soma shrugged.

"Perhaps being on Thanet is changing me. The island has its charms, does it not?"

"Another deflection." Eshiel pushed himself up to his feet. At the least, he wanted away from his pool of vomit. The acidic burn of it was starting to overwhelm even the scent of the ocean. "If you seek to convince me of your honesty, you do a poor job of it."

Soma jammed the butt of his spear into the sand deep enough for it to stand on its own. He crossed his arms, his head tilted slightly to one side as if observing Eshiel like he would a strange curiosity he just discovered at a market.

"If I were to wager a guess, it is admiration. Admiration, or pity. They are so often similar."

"Pity." Eshiel practically spit the word out. "I'd rather have your hatred than your pity."

"Even if it meant your death? Try not to pontificate, priest, even if that is what you're supposedly good at. And I pity you because you are trapped, and not of your own volition. I know of you, Eshiel twice-born, now named thrice-born. You are no secret to Ierida, and my ears, and my coin purse, were open when I visited taverns on our trek here. Your very life, tied to the gifts of Lycaena? It is a cruel position to find oneself in. Yet you did not wallow in pity. You did not cower in fear of the uncertain. The original Lycaena was strong, she was beautiful, but she was also a coward. A god or goddess can be many things, but a coward is never one of them. For that alone, she deserved her death. You, however, showed bravery, and perhaps that is why I surrendered to a moment of weakness, and allowed you to live."

The insult left Eshiel shaking. Twice murdered, and yet the paragon would besmirch his beloved's name?

"A coward?" He stepped closer to the paragon. It felt like fire burned in the tattoos across his body. The holy magic, it could come to him if he demanded it. Soma would kill him first, though, Eshiel knew that like he knew the sun would rise in the east, so instead he warred with words. "Lycaena fought against your soldiers from the moment you set foot on our island. She fought, and fought, even as your armies captured our cities and your paragons hunted her like dogs after a fox. Even when she was captured, she spoke comfort to us. She gave our paladins strength to fight. She gave us priests power to our prayers. What of that is cowardly, paragon? She may have lost her war against you, but defeat does not make one a coward."

Another tilt of the paragon's head. Eshiel hated how much he sought this invader's approval. For no reason should it matter to him, yet it did. And when Soma spoke, his voice full of disappointment and condescension, it hurt.

"You don't know, do you? I thought perhaps a priest of Lycaena would be given the truth, but alas, it falls on us to reveal your history. Your War of Tides? It was a war between the invader, Endarius, and the god Dagon. It was a war for the faith of the island, and one your brave Butterfly refused to intervene in. The war ended with the foreign Lion victorious, and the corpse of the Serpent set to sea in a burning boat. That is the truth buried by your royal family, each fanciful story, poem, and song meant to disguise it further. Yet we on Gadir remember Endarius. We conquered his former home not a decade after he fled."

Soma laughed, without mirth or amusement, just a deep bitterness.

"Lycaena and Endarius, a perfect match for each other in their cowardice. It is no wonder the empire's ships conquered this island in a mere day."

To argue over Endarius's origins seemed futile given the paragon's certainty. The ramifications flowed one after another in Eshiel's mind. What it meant if the Lion were a foreign god. What it meant for Lycaena to befriend him. What it meant for his understanding of Dagon as the trickster serpent of the sea, tormentor of the unrepentant down in the Heldeep.

"I've heard stories claiming as much, that Dagon allied with those opposed to the Lythan family," Eshiel said, if only to fill the damnable silence. "None that Dagon himself fought."

Soma grinned his pearl-white teeth.

"Oh, he was there, Eshiel. He fought against the Lion from Gadir, but he fought alone. Lycaena refused to take a side, and she demanded her followers do the same. Endarius could have been pushed from these shores, but no, she would not stain her hands with another god's blood.

She would remain neutral, the suffering of her own people be damned. That neutrality spared her life come Dagon's death, but at what cost? What future might Thanet have known if it were Dagon and not Endarius who co-ruled over the past four centuries?"

The idea of Dagon ruling alongside his beloved Lycaena was so foul, so *unnatural*, that Eshiel flinched. It didn't matter what this paragon said. For the trickster of the sea to rule on land? Surely all those stories couldn't be false, the ones of Dagon's cowardly nature, his overwhelming greed, and his inability to refuse a gamble. That they remained unchanged over hundreds of years was proof enough of the tales' validity.

Tales told by the faithful servants of Endarius and Lycaena. To worship Dagon was heresy. His unholy texts were burned, his followers chased out of Vallessau and forced to lurk in villages and forests where only a carefully chosen few might participate in their wicked rituals.

Eshiel was no fool. He condemned the empire for crimes that, if viewed a certain way, his own priesthood had committed against Dagon's followers. The difference should have been the righteous salvation offered to believers of Thanet's twin gods when compared to the dark road on which Dagon would lead men and women. But if the Heldeep were a lie, and Dagon were no different than any other deity…

It meant, in a perverse way, Eshiel and Soma were very much alike. They crushed followers of one god to anoint their own chosen one. Knowing this did not make things easier, but it did help explain why he still drew breath. Only a little bit, though, and not enough to satisfy his curiosity. Before this night ended, he would have at least that one matter answered.

"You said you either admired or pitied me, yet you explain neither, only insult my goddess."

Soma waved his hand in a dismissive fashion, as if explaining himself were a terrible burden. Eshiel wondered how much of it was an act, for there was no doubt that the paragon loved the sound of his own voice.

"You ask me to explain a moment of weakness, which is already born of emotion, not practical thought. I sympathize with your situation, Eshiel, I truly do. Your bondage to a goddess now slain is most unfortunate. Yet while that goddess was a coward, you did not follow in her footsteps. No, you did something about it, even if I disagree with the end result. You clung to your beliefs. You fought. You spilled blood, and by a miracle I have never seen elsewhere in all my years on Gadir, *you brought Lycaena back.* While she was forever defined by her cowardice, you were brave, so brave it bordered on madness. I respect that, Eshiel, even if I pity your misguided beliefs. If there were more men of your conviction, the empire's spread would have halted centuries ago. Then again, if there were more men of your conviction, we would not need the empire in the first place."

"Need?" Eshiel asked. It was madness to argue with a paragon in matters of faith, yet this one acted so unlike the others. It wasn't that he lacked their fanaticism; the man reeked of overwhelming certainty of faith. It wasn't for their emperor in Eldrid, though. That much was certain. "What need have we for your empire? What need does the world have of your conquering armies? You tear down cities, burn books, and set faithful believers to the sword, all for the crime of worshiping anything other than your wretched God-Incarnate. You are a savage beast, and the only need you know is your own hunger."

Soma ripped his spear free with a spray of sand. It whirled through the air, a flash of steel, and then halted underneath Eshiel's chin. The tip lifted, the cold metal pressing against the exposed flesh of his neck. Higher, and higher, like the lifting finger of one lover to another so their eyes might meet.

"Heed the lessons of Thanet," Soma seethed. "Of gods warring with one another regardless of the casualties. How they battled over faith and worship. These eternal beings are as jealous as any mortal man or woman. Humans will forever be caught in their middle, and there is only one solution, Eshiel. It is the inevitable fate that awaited Gadir from the very moment of its inception. This needs to be finished. The warfare, the fractured faith—let it all end. Let there be one god. Let there be one voice for truth, whatever truth that may be. If it is the God-Incarnate, then so be it. If another rises up and musters a force to challenge the might of the Everlorn Empire, then let them. I even pray they succeed, if only so we might finally have a conclusion to this everlasting farce."

Eshiel pulled his shoulders back and stood tall before the paragon. A wave of dizziness swept through him. His stomach hurt, and his forehead began to throb. He ignored all of it. His weight shifted forward, digging the spear into his throat to draw a faint line of blood.

Daring Soma to push it in deeper.

"That sounds blasphemous, coming from a paragon."

Soma smirked.

"Paragons are but pale imitations of the gods they swear their lives to serve. If the gods themselves bicker on matters, is it any surprise that we might also disagree? What other example have we to follow?"

He withdrew his spear from Eshiel's throat and locked it to his back. The tension of the moment passed, and Eshiel's body went from stone to jelly. Soma donned his helmet, and when he spoke, it was soft and muffled by the metal.

"I take my leave. As for you, Eshiel, accept this gift of mercy. It is a rare kindness I offer to a man who has earned my respect. But do not come back to Vallessau. The next time I see you, it will end in your death. Thanet shall have but one god, and it will not be Lycaena."

CHAPTER 16

STASIA

They moved through the forest like wolves, and Stasia was the leader of their pack. Though she exuded confidence, her inner thoughts were not so clean.

I wish Mari were here.

She halted at the forest's edge, her pupils wide to absorb the moonlight. Before her was Fort Lionfang, her target, her prey. It felt weird to hunt without her sister, but she would make do if she must.

Heavy trade and traffic passed through the Greensong Forest along the Tannis Road, coming north from Syros, the seat of the ruling family for the realm of Tannin. All who exited must pay a toll at the fort. Those walking might try to sneak around it, and Stasia saw several footpaths diverging from the road during her approach, but those loaded with carts and wagons had no such option. Whoever built the fort knew the danger of placing it so close to the forest, so there was a lengthy gap between the trees and the tall wooden palisades. Boulders lined either side of the dirt road, sealing in the short path. A massive ditch was dug before the fort entrance like a waterless moat. A drawbridge, now lifted for the night, allowed passage to the road that bisected the fort and led to a fork, one side heading toward Vallessau in the east and the other to Ialath in the northwest.

Stasia turned away, her back to a tree, and waited for Commander

Pilus. The older man arrived at the head of his soldiers, and she tried not to react at the sight of them. Vagrant's reputation had spread beyond Vallessau. Some soldiers wore black cloths sewn with white skulls over their faces, but most did not have such garb. Instead their foreheads were painted with a red slash, a mocking crown. Whether it was blood, or a juice from some local berry, she did not know, and in the moonlight, it hardly mattered.

"Does it seem unusually quiet?" Pilus asked upon joining her. He, too, wore a Vagrant crown, and for some reason that disappointed her.

"Are you worried one of your own may be a traitor?" she whispered back.

"I fear every possibility. I suspect we would not be the first resistance the empire seeded with spies."

Stasia glanced back around the thick pine tree. Parapets were built along the wall, lookout points for watchmen. Though the fort was in a pivotal location to control trade and travel, it was mostly built to deter bandits from robbing the dues all travelers must pay. From what she could tell, two men watched the forest, maybe three.

"They don't suspect an army," she said. "How confident are you in your numbers?"

The commander frowned at her.

"Now is not the time to doubt me, Ax."

"Until I storm those walls, yes, it is the time. It is the only time."

He laughed, softly.

"Consider yourself lucky you are not my subordinate. But we've scouted their numbers and sent others in disguise. There's only fifty or so soldiers, all from Gadir. If that were all we faced, we wouldn't need your aid."

Indeed, with Pilus's two hundred, they could easily overwhelm the fort. But it wasn't just fifty or sixty imperial soldiers. Magus of Eldrid had assigned a paragon to be Lord Agrito's bodyguard. Pilus had done his best to learn what he could of the man, not that the foreknowledge would help much. His name was Amon, he was a Paragon of Shields, and he could single-handedly hold that fort if his foes were mere human soldiers.

Stasia held back a shudder. Yes, she very much wished her sister was with her, but the Ax of Lahareed would have to be enough. No one else here had faced a paragon and lived. No one knew their strength, or their potential brutality when faced with death.

"When the drawbridge drops, make sure your men do not hesitate," she said. "Every kill will be precious. By the time Amon stirs from his sleep, we want as many of the imperial soldiers dead as possible. Numbers will be our only advantage. Do not waste it."

"My men will be ready," Pilus said.

"They better be. I've lived through plenty, commander, so if I die here, my spirit will blame you for it. And possibly the Lioness, too."

For their first time together, the older man actually did look worried.

"Would she?" he asked.

Stasia stifled a laugh. Her heart was racing, the excitement of the coming battle flooding her veins and turning her thoughts airy. Instead of answering him, she shrugged and turned to the fort. The plan was simple, and entirely dependent upon her.

Years of insurrections had granted Stasia ample opportunity to learn how to be stealthy, even if it was not her favorite tactic. In Aethenwald she'd learned how to move through fields like a hunting panther so that even the grass would not betray her motion. She summoned that training now. Her clothes were dark, her axes buckled to her hips. Head low, and practically crawling, she zipped across the open space between the forest and the fort. Not once did she see the eyes of the patrolmen turn her way.

The drawbridge, even when fully drawn, still left a small gap at the very top. If one were tall enough and strong enough, one could climb through. Stasia was both. She leaped, kicked off the wall for an extra few inches, and latched onto the side of the drawbridge. She slowly lifted herself up to peer through, searching for guards. None nearby. The past years of peace had dulled their fear. Her father had built a new resistance right under their noses, and now they would suffer at its awakening.

A twinge of bitterness simmered in her chest. The Vagrant's rise was supposed to signal an island-wide resurgence. When Cyrus abandoned them after Magus's death, groups were forced to move on their own. It wouldn't surprise Stasia if Cyrus had been meant to lead this charge, and not her. If only he'd told her what bothered him so. If only she could understand what had broken the young boy who had endured every single trial Stasia threw at him.

Enough of that. She had to keep her thoughts focused. Stasia curled over the side of the drawbridge and landed on the other side. She shouldn't dwell on what could not be changed. The famed Ax would lead the way where the Vagrant would not.

To her left was a boxed-in room containing the enormous crank for the drawbridge. A ladder beside it led up to the parapet where a sleepy, incompetent guard stood watch. Stasia crept to the ladder, listened for a moment for any signs he had been alerted. None. She withdrew one of her axes from her hip, breathed in deep, and then held it as she climbed.

The ladder creaked with the last step. The soldier turned, voice unconcerned.

"It's not midnight . . ."

Stasia jammed the razor-sharp edge of her ax into his throat. He gargled, his eyes bulging and blood pouring across his uniform. She caught him as he fell, holding him so his armor would not rattle. He thrashed with dying energy, more shock than purpose. If only the night were not so quiet. What she'd give for a nice, heavy thunderstorm to disguise their approach. Those were the tactics of Aethenwald, where the imperial soldiers had learned to fear the storms, not for the lightning, but for what they had dubbed Stasia's group, the Killing Rain.

She had to work quickly now. Once his body stilled completely, she slid back down the ladder. A lone guard missing from his post should not cause alarm, not immediately, but there was always that chance. Once back on the ground, she buckled her ax and grabbed the heavy pole of the crank. A testing flex of her arms found it stubborn. The crank was meant to be turned by two men working in tandem.

Well then. Time to see if she was as strong as two men.

Breathe in. Breathe out. This would be it. The noise of the drawbridge, the groaning of the wood and the rattle of the chains, would not go unnoticed. Her heart pounded even as her mind slowed. If only there were others here, someone she could joke with or laugh with at the impending danger. She missed her sister. She missed Cyrus. Hells, she even missed Arn and Rayan.

"Gods help me, I must be getting old," she said, surprised by her own sentimentality. Her legs tensed, her heels digging into the dirt. The muscles in her arms bulged.

Not that old, it seemed. The drawbridge lowered in spurts, and sure enough, it was horribly loud. Pilus's soldiers were already running before the drawbridge thudded against the dirt. At last, she heard a man near the easternmost corner shout in alarm. His was a thin cry to pierce the night, the only warning the sleeping soldiers would receive.

Too little, too late. Deed finished, and fort open, she grabbed her axes and sprinted deeper in.

The number of imperial soldiers stationed there had overwhelmed the initial accommodations the fort was built for, and so a dozen tents were pitched along the eastern side of the main road bisecting the fort. Stasia charged those tents, hoping to crush them before any swords or shields could be readied in defense. Panicked men burst through the flaps, all in various stages of disarray and undress. Some held weapons, others not. Some fled, some did not.

It didn't matter. Stasia tore through them, a whirling fury. Without their armor, and without their coordinated lines, these men were poorly prepared for a chaotic engagement. She smacked aside frantic thrusts lacking in power, for the soldiers were retreating, not charging. The first moments were a slaughter, made worse when Pilus's soldiers followed in her wake.

Come, wolves, she thought, a little manic, a little thrilled with the spray of blood from the chops of her axes. *Eat your fill.*

Screams grew with the panic. Smaller skirmishes broke out on the parapets, Pilus's men taking out the soldiers stationed there. The men in the tents fled for the north exit opposite the forest, and the attackers would have chased if not for Stasia hollering at them, every bit of her reputation and legend wielded like a cudgel.

"Hold here, damn you, hold and face our real foe in the redoubt."

She slammed her axes together high above her head, showering sparks amid the wet blood. Calling the fighters to her, to battle the only threat that mattered. Inside the fortifications was a tall, square redoubt, and it was within lived Lord Agrito...and his bodyguard.

The door to the redoubt burst open, and through it emerged an infuriated Amon. He held his shield, a thick slab of steel, as if it were a battering ram. He wielded his sword, a two-hander to even the strongest of mortal soldiers, in a single fist. His armor shone a muted gold in the moonlight, his face hidden behind a helmet designed so thin strips of metal formed a series of bars from forehead to chin.

"A rebellion of cowards and murderers," he bellowed. "Must I put you all down like the savages you are?"

Stasia lowered her axes and braced her legs. She had almost two hundred soldiers surrounding her, to face off against this lone paragon. It would be enough. It had to be enough.

Except this was the kind of fight the paragons had been made for.

Amon led his charge with his shield. A grinning face was painted silver across its surface, tongue long and eyes like a viper's. Blood splashed across its smile as his shield made contact. He was fast, so fast, Stasia rolled aside with hardly time to think. Bodies broke from his initial attack, bones snapping easily. He halted in the middle of the pack and swung his sword in an arc. The air whipped from its passage. Screams followed, men losing limbs and weapons.

Stasia slid to her knees, then kicked forward, leading the counterattack. Amon turned his shield her way, as if he sensed she was his greatest threat. She smashed her axes in a dual strike upon that serpent smile. Even with her Ahlai-made weapons, she could not punch through, but that wasn't the hope. Other soldiers rushed in, made brave by her attack. They would be as ants to him, but even the largest prey could fall to enough bites.

Stasia kept near his front, her every swing either above or beside his enormous shield. If she could keep the paragon focused on her, and keep his weapon oriented toward her attacks, then the other soldiers might find an opening along his flank. Already she saw them hacking at his armor and thrusting for its creases. Though the paragon might be a walking stack of divine platemail and muscle, he could bleed, and he could fall.

But gods help them, the cost was so high.

Every swing of the paragon's jeweled sword claimed lives. He moved with a purpose. One or two steps forward, a shield thrust to make space, and then a slash with his sword. Another bash with the shield, then a turn, cutting down three men on his left flank. The bodies piled up around him, becoming an obstacle for the rest to face. Stasia dodged beneath the swings, dropping to her knees if she must, not yet willing to risk pitting her strength directly against a paragon's. That was a losing gamble, at least until Amon was weakened from a loss of blood and exhausted by the duration of the battle.

"Bury him in steel!" she shouted, trying to encourage Pilus's soldiers. "Beat the bastard down!"

More soldiers rushed in a wave, but Amon was done with them. Despite the tremendous weight of his armor, he leaped skyward, a distance far surpassing his own height. He collided with the redoubt behind him, the wood walls cracking from the impact. His legs bunched, he twisted, and then he extended them with all his muscles. The paragon plunged straight back down into the mass of soldiers. He crashed through them like a boulder flung from a catapult. Metal shrieked as the paragon's sword cut through armor. Men shrieked with it.

Stasia pushed past soldiers torn between charging and retreating. Anger overruled her panic. Focused intensity banished any fear. This paragon, this ten-times-damned monstrosity of human sacrifice and empire worship, would die. He would. He must.

"Quit leaping around like a frog and face me!" she shouted. Distance closed, she attacked his shield, took gauge of his footing, and then collided into him with her shoulder. Doing so allowed her to transform her momentum into a roll around the shield's side, toward the paragon's exposed middle. Up went her axes, as did his sword. Their weapons locked together, and to her grim amusement, she saw his eyes widen at the effort required to keep them back.

"I know you," he said. "The butcher who killed Bordova in Lahareed."

He shoved her backward, then tried to cleave her in half. The sword pounded dirt, missing her by inches as she curled away. Her heels skidded, her movement slowing as she prepared for another lunge.

But the blood of gods does flow through you, Ax of Lahareed. It is
unmistakable.

Soma's words had haunted her, but now they gave her confidence.
Maybe it was true. Maybe she needed it to be true. She faced off against
the paragon amid the bodies and the gore-slick dirt. Amon was bleeding, at least. The constant barrage of cuts and stabs had taken their toll.
The remaining soldiers held back, either frightened or convinced they
were of no help. She felt their eyes upon her, their hope, their belief that
she could succeed. A cocky smile spread behind her black mask.

"I've killed so many paragons, I've forgotten most of their names." A
ringing cry of metal marked her axes touching as she raised them before
her. "Just as one day I'll forget yours."

It was foolish to directly challenge the might of a paragon. Wisdom
said to be quicker on her toes, the arc of her axes expertly positioned to
never grant him a moment's peace. More soldiers would come to her
aid. More would die, their insignificant cuts becoming legion. A pro-
longed fight was the best way to bring down a paragon, the casualties an
acceptable cost.

Fuck it. All of it.

You are not mortal. You're a goddess.

Stasia flung herself at the paragon with all her strength. Let Amon
witness the full fury of the Ax of Lahareed. While the people of the desert capital watched, she had chopped Regent Edgar in half and rained
his innards upon those far below the mountainside estate. She had built
her reputation with blood and fearless rage. Let it be unleashed.

The next moments were a blur of steel and crimson. Amon's shield
shifted and turned, the paragon's immense strength granting it the
necessary speed. Her axes beat upon it, seeking openings, keeping the
paragon on the defensive. At such close range, the length of his sword
was awkward, and she would not let him have distance, nor would the
surrounding crowd of soldiers. They were like pack wolves, and Stasia
would have it no other way. Amon was prey, and she the savage hunter.

Stasia slammed his shield with her right ax, showering the night with
sparks, and then twirled. Up and over the shield went her left ax, forcing
Amon to sidestep. He thrust afterward, the counter masterfully done,

but Stasia was still twirling. A brawler she might be, but she also knew how to dance. The sword cut air, and then her right hand was already descending, another high hit forcing his shield up and his legs to brace.

Low and angled came her left ax beneath the opening. She hit his hip, her ax sliding down the armor. He elbowed her, and it felt like the headbutt of a bull. His sword lashed for her waist, and she vaulted on instinct, legs lifting, spine curling. Her boot caught his chin, his head snapped back, and then she landed on her knees. His blind attempt to stomp her missed. She repaid him with an ax into his heel. His howl was music to her ears.

Back up. Endure the punch he threw that cracked across her jaw and left her ears ringing. Swing. Strike. There would be time for thoughts later, for dwelling on the strength in her muscles that refused to tire, that matched a sacrifice-blessed paragon. He blocked a double chop with his sword, and they strained against each other. A feral cry howled out of her throat, and she pushed, and pushed, locking him in place. Soldiers thrust for his back and swung for his legs, never giving him a reprieve, nor did Stasia allow him one. Blood leaked from every crease in his armor. His patience faltered. His movements tired.

"Enough!" he screamed. There was fear in his voice. One last shove tumbled Stasia and her axes away, and then he spun. His sword chopped three men in half behind him, retribution for their bravery. "Roaches, all of you!"

Amon vaulted for the parapets, leaping as if the pull of the world meant nothing to him. Stasia did not think. She did not doubt. Her legs tensed, and she followed after him, a jump that raised her twice over her own height. The paragon landed, turned, and dropped his jaw in shock that she was still with him. That half second of hesitation was all she needed. Her axes swung, and though he blocked one with his sword, the other hit him at the wrist, severing his hand from his body. His shield collapsed, the tremendous weight of it sliding free of a forearm gushing blood.

For perhaps the first time in his life, Amon panicked. He swung with his sword, a wide arc meant to cut her in half at the waist. Ignoring the instinct to duck or roll away, she instead arced her own axes upward from below, smacking the blade and batting it over her head. It left him horribly exposed. He sensed it, too, but the wall of the parapet held firm behind him, denying him retreat.

Stasia did not test his armor. One ax buried into his exposed throat. The other struck the gap at his abdomen between his breastplate and his belt. Her arms flexed, her legs pushed, and she shoved her weapons in harder, harder, down to bone, to sever the spine, to collapse the paragon in a lifeless heap of metal and meat. The moment he went limp, she tore those weapons free. A great spray of blood followed, accompanied by a roar of shock and elation from those who watched.

"For Thanet!" she screamed, for she knew her role, and what the people needed to hear. She hopped down from the parapet instead of taking the ladder, ignoring how it should have hurt, or perhaps even damaged her knees. She landed amid cheering soldiers, raised swords, and a repeated chant of *Ax, Ax, Ax!* It sounded divine to her ears, already filled with the pounding drum of her own heartbeat.

"Are you watching from the windows?" she shouted at the redoubt and the faint hint of candlelight coming from its highest levels.

No one needed an order to know she would lead the charge inside. Soldiers lit torches and gave her a path. Stasia bounded through the door broken open by Amon. She ignored the imperial soldiers within who shouted panicked nonsense at her. The swarming crowd behind her could handle them. Up the stairs, floor by floor, slamming aside any foolish enough to block her way to the top. She passed a handful of panicked servants, saw old councilors cowering by windows, but they were not her target: Tannin's lord was.

The stairs ended in what appeared to be a planning room. Shelves marked one wall, half full of books and stacked scrolls. Maps marked another. A long table lay overturned between her and the three men on the opposite side, protecting a closed door. There was no doubt in her mind that the frightened man between the two knights was Acastus Agrito. Though he'd certainly been disturbed from sleep, he'd dressed in his Gadir finest, and he held a dueling blade in one hand.

"Does she lead these savages?" he asked as she stood in the doorway. He wore no word-lace, and spoke not in the official imperial tongue, but in one she vaguely recognized. Her own word-lace about her neck translated the words, and she grinned behind her mask.

"We're all savages here," she said, word-lace modifying the sounds so all would understand. Lord Agrito's eyes widened. "But I lead the ones who will find victory this night."

The two knights at his side stepped forward, their swords drawn and shields high. Their tabards were a checkered pattern of green and blue marked in the center with a white stallion.

"You face Silverguard's finest," Acastus said, switching to the imperial tongue.

That explained the tabards. Silverguard was the former capital of some nation long since swallowed by the empire, and likely where Lord Agrito had come from before departing for Thanet. Stasia crossed her axes before her. The muscles in her arms tensed. Blood dripped across her forehead. Amon's blood.

"Do I?" she asked.

The first died the moment she lashed out, his sword a pitiful defense against the might of her swing. The other retreated, hoping the table between them would cause her to stumble, but she hopped upward. She landed lightly upon her toes, balancing on it. He swung, she blocked it with the steel of her armlets, and then she vaulted onto him. Her first hit shoved aside his shield. The second crunched his ribs inward until they punctured his heart.

Acastus shouted something nonsensical and thrust for her back, thinking she wasn't looking. Thinking she might be caught so easily unaware. A shift of her hips had the tip pass harmlessly aside. A turn. A chop. His head rolled free of his body, which swayed with legs and arms suddenly locking tight. Stasia kicked the corpse aside. It landed, shit itself, and that was that. The fort was taken. Stasia half-heartedly shook her weapon, but it would take time and a clean cloth to remove so much blood.

"Damn fool," she said, pulling off her face mask. There was so much blood splashed across the front it was getting hard to breath. "I've killed paragons. As if I'd care for your pompous knights."

One last room to check. A kick of her heel easily opened the door.

Acastus's wife stood before a four-poster bed, still dressed in a simple bed robe and with her auburn hair bound. The woman didn't try to run. She didn't scream. The bodies of the soldiers, and of her decapitated husband, were plainly visible through the door.

"Make it quick," she said, lifting her chin. "If you are capable of that kindness."

Stasia buried her ax in the woman's forehead, immediately ending the life in her eyes. She dropped, her legs stiffening awkwardly and her body spinning as her lower back hit the bed frame and tilted her onto the sheets. Blood pooled across the bed. Stasia yanked the ax free, turned for the door, and then froze. A noise. The worst noise, one she wished she could pretend she did not hear. But to do so would be cowardly.

The room contained an enormous wardrobe, and Stasia slowly opened its doors. Crouched beneath the hanging robes and dresses was a small child, not even four years old.

Lord Agrito's son, born the year he and his wife came to the island.

Pilus's voice cracked across her back like a whip.

"Is that the boy?"

CHAPTER 17

STASIA

Gods and goddesses help us," lamented Stasia. "Do none of them know how to sing properly?"

Since there was no plan to keep the fort long term, Commander Pilus ordered the entirety of it burned and then the soldiers to retreat back into the woods. There they made camp and began the celebration. Fort Lionfang had been stocked well, and they broke open its stores of ale and crates of salted meat for a veritable feast. Then came laughter, and songs, oh heavens help her, the songs.

"They're happy," Clarissa said, sitting beside her. The two had claimed a spot at the edge of the camp, huddled together atop grass and leaves. "Can you blame them? We won a great victory."

Stasia's hand convulsed on its own, fingers clenching tightly before opening.

"Yeah," she said, and withheld a groan as yet another drunken lout sauntered over with a cheer already on his lips. "A great victory."

"Come, Ax!" the man said, his gait showing him already heavily intoxicated. "We're singing your praises, and yet you're hiding over here with the missus!"

"If I wanted to join your songs I'd have already joined," Stasia said.

"Aw, don't be like that." He took a drink, a drizzle of it spilling down his dark beard. "You're a hero to us, took down that paragon none of us could handle. Ain't wrong of us to want you properly thanked for it."

Stasia held back a scream. She and Clarissa had faced a steady stream of such requests from Pilus's soldiers, and even the commander himself. Why could none of them just leave her alone?

"Consider me thanked," she said, the edge in her voice as sharp as her axes. The man stood there, waiting, but when he realized no other response was coming, he shrugged.

"Sure, sure," he said, and left muttering something under his breath Stasia held no desire to hear. She scowled and turned away.

"For shit's sake, it's one battle," she grumbled. She swirled the contents of her drink in her wooden cup. "I know the war's gone poorly here but not that poorly."

Clarissa slowly ran her forefinger over the brim of her own cup, hesitating for a moment before finally making a decision.

"Is something wrong?" she asked.

"Nothing. I'm fine."

"You're clearly not. You haven't been all night."

Stasia snorted, and she tried to wave the conversation away.

"It's a headache, that's all," she said. "Happens after battle sometimes, when the body gets all loose and the excitement fades. This shitty ale isn't helping, either."

Clarissa reached out and put a hand on her shoulder.

"You don't have to keep anything from me. I know battle can be difficult."

"No," Stasia said. "You don't."

She could take no more of this. She tossed aside her cup, spilling its contents across the dirt. With songs pounding unwelcome within her skull, she stormed out of the camp and into the forest. She needed space, and distance. No fires, no celebration, and no gods-damned songs. She walked and walked, until stopping at no particular spot and resting her back against a tree. Her gaze locked on the branches above, blotting out the clouded sky. She didn't look at Clarissa when she arrived.

"Tell me."

"It's not something you want to hear."

Clarissa stood before her, and when Stasia still refused to look, the smaller woman reached up and looped her hands around the back of Stasia's neck and pulled, forcing her gaze downward.

"Tell me," she said. "If you're struggling, I want to struggle with you. If you're upset, I want to be upset with you. If you love me, you will share it with me, no matter how dark or horrible."

Stasia saw the iron resolve in her blue eyes, mixed with a dwindling anger. There was strength in her, so much more than Stasia ever gave her credit for. At least that deserved some measure of honesty.

"You don't know who I am," Stasia said. "*What* I am. You want to know, I understand that, but if you did, if you truly did, you would not be here with me. You would leave, and you would be right to do so."

Clarissa slapped her, hard, right across the cheek. Her hand shook as she pointed a finger. In her shock, Stasia only stood there, mouth hanging open.

"Don't you dare claim I don't know *you*, and then pretend you know *me* so well in return. I decide who I love, and who I stay with. If there is more to you I do not know, stop being frightened of it and *tell me*."

Stubborn pride joined with a sting of humiliation to draw the truth out of her. Fine, if Clarissa wanted to know who Stasia was, to truly know, then let her see every last wretched, horrifying part of her. Not only Stasia Ahlai, but the legacy of the savage Ax of Lahareed.

"No survivors," Stasia said. "Those were my father's orders when we attacked the fort. That meant everyone, not just the soldiers, or Lord Agrito. The servants. The workers. Acastus's wife, I cracked her skull open on her bed. They weren't alone, though. Acastus...he had a son."

Stasia stared down at her hands.

"It was a kindness. That's what I told myself. He was Lord Agrito's son, and after all his father had done to these people, Pilus's soldiers would never let him live. They'd torture him, humiliate him, and one day publicly execute him. And if I didn't do it, then Pilus would. So I took him into my lap and whispered for him to be calm. I told him he would sleep soon. Sleep, and be safe."

A dim horror settled over Stasia's mind like frost. Reliving the moment felt like stepping into the boots of a stranger. Someone else surely did the deed, but no, it had been her. She had summoned the resolve from a lifetime of war, of bloody fields, burning trees, the crows, the slaughter of gods, the mutilation of her Miquoan homeland.

"Just a moment," she whispered. "I told him it would be but a moment. And then I put my hand around his throat."

No future remained for the boy on Thanet. She had done what was best. The kindest fate, she had told herself, told it again and again as her hand tightened, closing off the boy's windpipe.

So easy, to make a fist.

So easy, even when it broke her.

"I'm sorry," Clarissa said, and she leaned against Stasia in an embrace. "That had to have been awful, but you were put in a horrible position. You didn't want that. You didn't choose to kill a child."

"You really think this is the first time?" Stasia asked. She shoved Clarissa away, shocked by the bite she heard in her own voice. "You do, don't you?"

Hurt flashed across Clarissa's pale face, then vanished behind a calm visage. She was hiding it, hiding all her pain, and it made Stasia angrier. Hadn't Clarissa asked for this? Didn't she want to know, and claim to be unafraid? Then let her hear it. Let her hear all of it.

"Do you know how I became known as the Ax of Lahareed?" Stasia asked. "In full view of the city, I murdered the empire's regent, but that was just the start. My sister and I, we'd failed before, but this time I was determined to win. I would free Lahareed through sheer force of will. I hunted. I killed. I *slaughtered*. It didn't matter who they were, or their rank, so long as they served the empire. There is a reason my alias echoed across Everlorn. If I could hurt their priests and commanders, I hurt them, Clarissa. I murdered their friends, their families, their wives, and yes, their children. I was terror incarnate, and never before or since have my hands been so stained with blood."

That first year was but a blur in Stasia's mind. She remembered little of it, even when she tried, which was not often. The memories were like broken shards of glass, and no effort could make them whole. Her body trembled, for she might not remember the start, but she remembered the end. Their humiliating flight out of Lahareed, after the last of their resistance was captured or disbanded, had forever turned the proud title the people gave her into one of searing shame.

Words screamed out of her mouth, giving no damn to any who might overhear back at the camp.

"I gave them everything, sacrificed my humanity for their war, and still, *still* it ended in failure. The days passed into weeks, weeks into months, months into years. The scattered resistance groups fell. Two language centers were built for every one we burned. Everlorn's priests gave their sermons, and through blade and coin, they filled their churches. My father declared it hopeless, and so we moved on. Another nation. Another war."

Every single one of her thirty-seven years dragged at her like weights tied to her limbs with fraying rope. Her many campaigns flashed through her mind, each demanding they be accounted for. Lahareed. Aethenwald. The Killing Rain. Her hand, upon the throat of a child.

"I have been fighting this war since I was sixteen, Clarissa. For over two decades, I have walked with the broken and the desperate. I have shed blood in the name of the defeated and slain. Whatever crimes you can imagine, I have committed them. Whatever sins the goddess you worship believes in, I am guilty of them. I am not innocent. I am not good. Look upon the conquered fort, Clarissa, imagine the body of a child burning within it, and know *that* is who I am."

Clarissa's eyes were watching her but saw nothing. She'd withdrawn into herself, shocked and troubled while trying to absorb the enormity of Stasia's truth. It was everything Stasia had expected, and she tried to keep the bitterness out of her voice when she spoke next.

"I understand if it is too much. If you want to leave, and never see me again, I will not blame you. Do what you must. Our memories together, they'll always be special to me, I promise."

The silence that followed ached. Stasia waited for the condemnation she knew approached. This was not the first time she had lost a lover. Throughout her years, Stasia had learned the enormity of her bloodshed was too much for anyone to bear. This would be no different.

After a time, the smaller woman took Stasia's hands into hers.

"Does it hurt?"

"What?"

"When you think on all you've done, does it still hurt?"

Stasia's hands clenched into fists, crushing Clarissa's fingers. Crushing memories. For all her defiant words, she knew the honest truth. When the cruel deed was done, she had wept unseen tears over the body of the child.

"Yes," she whispered. "It still does."

Clarissa stood on her tiptoes so their lips might touch. It was a phantom kiss, the softest of connections before she pulled away. The taste of her beloved's tears lingered.

"Then you are still human. And that part of you shall have my love."

Her body settled against Stasia's, another gentle embrace. Stasia stood, shocked still, her arms locked at her sides.

"I have to believe we can become better," Clarissa continued. "Who you are, who you truly are, is not what these wars have made you. There is a kindness underneath, and even if I have to dig my hands raw, I will find it, claim it as my own, and keep it forever safe in my heart."

"I don't…" Stasia said, trying to argue (but why was she arguing, why did she even want to argue?). "I don't understand. How? How could you? I told you. I told you everything. Don't you get it? I'm not worth it."

"Don't say that." Clarissa pulled free and glared. She was crying, and she was furious. "You are the one thing I cling to, the one thing in this whole damned world that makes me happy. I will not regret this. I will not regret *you*, so please, for my sake, stop trying to convince yourself otherwise."

Stasia's tired mind could not withstand that love, that anger. Her thoughts looped and cracked.

Take the fort. No survivors.

She didn't deserve this.

Did anyone?

A hand. A fist. A hand, but now trembling.

"I love you," she said.

Clarissa pulled her close. She felt taller now, or maybe Stasia felt smaller, hunched, broken.

"Then never stop."

They embraced, quiet, each supporting the other, as far behind them soldiers drank and sang to celebrate a great victory for the island of Thanet.

CHAPTER 18

MARI

Mari raced through the dark streets as fast as her four legs could carry her. Her father's elite were scattered in three directions for three simultaneous strikes. His instructions had been firm and clear.

Should the Humbled appear, do not fight. Flee until you are safe. We are not yet ready to take down one such as him.

Arn had chaffed at the suggestion, but Mari knew it was true. The Ahlai family had encountered a few Humbled across their years of battle, and always they were savage, terrifying opponents. Outnumbering him and overwhelming him would be their best hope, but so far Rihim was always accompanied by paragons.

Mari ran a loop around her destination, taking mark of the patrols and their locations, before diverting her path. She trusted the darkness of her fur and the speed of her passage to keep her safe. After all these years, Vallessau finally felt like home. She knew its secret ways, its shortcuts, and the soldiers' paths. Once secure, she prowled the alleyway to her target.

Mari kept to the shadows, in pure dark sheltered even from the moonlight, and eyed the squat building. It had been repurposed into a language school a few weeks ago, meant to teach Eldrid's tongue to the populace. Their group had debated burning it down, but Mari wanted something more visceral. The schools were always guarded. She would write a message upon its walls with the soldiers' blood. With their entrails, she would ruin every book and every lesson within.

Only there were no guards. Mari's ears perked up, and she crouched even lower. Why would there be no guards? Had they been alerted? But how? She'd delayed coming here until the very last moment. Someone would have had to follow her the entire time, tracked her looping path, and put together where she headed, but that meant...

The noise wasn't much, just a slight groan of wood, but to Mari's sharp ears it was enough. She tensed, her gaze tilting upward, and then fear locked her still.

Rihim leered down at her from the building's apex. His sharp teeth glowed like white fireflies. The Humbled vaulted overhead, and despite his weight and size, he landed silently before the school. His gold eyes shimmered, and she failed to read the emotion within them. Was it anger or excitement that gave them such vibrancy?

"Where is your sister?" Rihim asked.

"I could ask the same of your paragons," Mari retorted.

"So we are alone, you and I. Show me your strength, Lioness. I will be your judge."

Mari snarled. Judge? She sought no judgment, certainly not from a wretched Humbled of the empire. Her ears pulled back, and she crouched in preparation for a lunge. She had never fought a being quite like Rihim, clawed and feline, even if he was more humanlike than the Lioness she now became. It didn't matter. Endarius was within her, a vicious hunter, and he had stalked fields alongside the greatest of lions. She knew the interplay of claw and tooth. What mattered now was who would be stronger, and who would be faster.

They stared, eyes locked, each waiting for the other to make the first move. A line stretched between them, taut and red. They both sensed it. Saw it. Smelled it. Thorda would have her flee, but this was a chance to kill Rihim without his paragon protectors, and she would not lose that now.

They reacted as one, the decision mutually made. Mari pounced in a great release of her tensed muscles. Her jagged wings swept wide, to strike simultaneously with her front paws. Rihim met her headlong, his two legs blasting him upward with overwhelming strength. The distance between them closed in less than a heartbeat. Mari bit, her wings cut, and his claws swung.

Gods help her, he was so fast.

The bone plate across her forehead protected her from his initial cut, but his other paw raked across her side, spilling blood. Her wings curled behind him, their timing misjudged. Her teeth sank into his chest, but her angle was awkward, and his muscle so firm and his fur so thick it mimicked armor. And then his weight was upon her. They tumbled, bruising each other, drawing rivulets of blood as they nipped and turned in a search for something deeper, seeking a wound brutal enough to cripple.

Rihim's greatest advantage was his height. Once his feet were firmly planted, and he loomed above her, she tried to dart away. Speed must be her advantage, she'd decided, but he knew it, too. His left paw tripped her, and when she fell, his teeth sank across her spine. She screamed as she squirmed. Flesh ripped as she tore free. Two quick leaps gained her some space, and then she turned to face him.

The first exchange was over, and it was Mari who bled the deepest. His tongue extended, licking the blood from his teeth and mouth.

"Weak," he said.

"You would call me weak?" Mari asked. "You, who bow to the God-Incarnate?"

"You know nothing!"

The Humbled's rage grew, yet it never took control of him. He dashed at her, and she retreated a step while knifing with her wings. Her left missed, but the right clipped his shoulder, tearing a shallow wound across his deep blue fur. The pain caused him to rotate his body on instinct, shifting the angle of his approach. She curled toward his back as he landed with his arms swinging with such speed they were but a blur. He hit only air, for Mari retreated while gifting him two more shallow cuts with her wings.

Nothing, Rihim might claim, but Mari knew how the Humbled were made. They were weak gods, viewed as pliable by the God-Incarnate. The empire imprisoned these gods, tortured them until they broke and acknowledged the God-Incarnate as worthy of worship. As for why they didn't fade away like many other forgotten deities? There were rumors for that, too, of sequestered prison camps where worshipers were allowed to pray to the Humbled, their heathen practices safely surrounded by spikes and wire so as to not "infect" the rest of Everlorn.

"How could you turn your heart to Lucavi?" she roared at him. The word-lace about her neck flared with light, as if struggling to accurately convey the anger in her words. Her feet pounded the hard ground as she circled him. "How could you worship such a monster? He who brought nothing but death and suffering to your land, to your people!"

"It was not Lucavi who betrayed us!"

Mari thought she saw an opening and went for it. Her jagged wings sliced for his abdomen. The Humbled swiped them aside with a slash of his claws. When she followed up with a bite, he sidestepped, jammed his elbow into her ribs to push off, and then retreated.

"No, it was you!" she said, chasing after him with words even as she panted and recovered her strength. "You who betrayed your faithful, and would repay their faith with slavery."

Mari thought she knew the limits of Rihim's power, of his fury. She was wrong. He crossed the distance between them with a single leap. She could not retreat, and so she met him charge for charge. Their bodies collided, and she gasped at his strength.

"Betray?" he roared. His claws raked the bone plates of her shoulders. She snapped at him, he retreated, and in that brief respite she vaulted up from the street to the nearby roof. The shingles rattled, the wood supports groaned, but the weight held. "Betray? An Ahlai daughter, daring to speak the word 'betray'?"

Mari's fur stood on end. Her every limb locked in place.

Ahlai?

Her name. He knew her family name. Meanwhile a smile pulled at Rihim's feline lips.

"Did you think you could stay hidden from me, Miquoan? I recognize the scent of your family's blood. How could I ever forget it?"

Mari had not known the nation Rihim hailed from, but now she did, and it chilled her to the marrow. To recognize both her gift as a god-whisperer and her family? Antiev. He had to be one of the minor gods of Antiev. Miquo's neighbor and rival. The land her father betrayed.

There would be no arguing with him, not when he spoke with such conviction. She must use that knowledge as her own weapon.

"Then you know our homeland was claimed just like yours was," she argued. "Yet we fight back. Even if it is hopeless. Even if it seems impossible. We fight, we burn, and we destroy, until some measure of justice reaches this world."

"Justice." Rihim laughed. "Is that your truth?"

"It is the only truth I know."

Rihim bashed the steel bindings about his wrists together.

"The only truth is in the honesty of these manacles. I was a hunter, little Ahlai. I embodied strength, dominance, and the cycle of predator and prey. Who else should I kneel before, when in all of Gadir, there is no one stronger than the God-Incarnate of Everlorn?"

Was that his excuse? Was that how Rihim maintained belief in himself and yet justified turning over that faith to the God-Incarnate? A wretched ruler in Eldrid, praised by nations, and worshiped by scattered and broken gods. Powerful and mighty, and lifted up by the most horrible atrocities. She would not let such a claim go unchallenged.

"A mighty hunter you claim to be, yet I see only an obedient deer lowering its head to the hunter's spear."

Finally he acted out of rage instead of thought. He soared through the air, snarling, his claws out and eager. The speed of him, the strength, shocked even her. They slammed together, biting, clawing, but she realized too late his intention. His thick paw closed about the lower portion of her wing. Mari twisted, biting at him, drawing blood, but it wasn't enough. He bent the wing back, back, back, until the bone snapped. Mari screamed. Her teeth closed for his wrist, yet a backhand thundered across her face. She rolled from the blow, agony spiking higher as her broken wing jutted at an awkward angle from striking the ground.

"Let Miquo's gods be equally crushed," Rihim snarled as he stalked her. "Let you and your sister be humbled as I was."

Mari staggered to her feet. Blood dripped from her nose. Her wing trembled from the pain.

"We are no gods to be humbled!"

Rihim hesitated a moment. She watched a mixture of confusion and elation paralyze him, and then he laughed. He laughed.

"You don't know," he purred. "Of course you don't. Your father is ever the liar. More betrayal. More deception. Even to his own kin."

Silence him! the voice of Endarius bellowed in her mind. Within her pain, her fear, Mari could not resist the order. She leaped at Rihim, her front paws extended, her teeth bared, her lone good wing knifing for his side. The Humbled stood tall and defiant. They collided in a roll of muscle, claw, and fang, and she was not the victor.

For every rake of her claws, he gave her two in return. When their fangs sank into each other, it was she who bled fiercest. They were both otherworldly beings, but Mari's form was impure, tainted, made of human bone and flesh changed to accommodate the divine. She was slower. He was stronger. She could not win, not hindered with a broken wing.

Mari raked his chest with her hind legs, then attempted to flee. He caught her side, his claws digging in to give him purchase, and then flung her back to the ground. His heel bashed her ribs, denying her attempt to stand. Mari snarled even as his right hand closed about her jaw, holding her head in place. His other hand rose, the black claws colored red with her blood, for one last lethal strike. His gold eyes sparkled with pleasure. His bared teeth were ever grinning.

And then he hesitated. For the first time in their entire fight, she saw him doubt. But why?

"Death-talker," he spoke. "Your gifts could be useful."

Mari broke from his grasp. Her body left a bleeding trail as she retreated. Her wing quivered, tucked tightly to her side.

"My gifts are not for your empire," she said, wishing her snarl was anywhere near as intimidating as it should have been. Some of her ribs had to be broken, it hurt so much to breathe. If he attacked, she would not be able to fight him off.

Rihim flexed and unflexed his claws as he forced himself to stand at his full, towering height.

"I will not kill you here, daughter of Ahlai. Go to your father. Ask him for the truth. Ask him who he is, *what* he is. Find out the lies you have been told. See how tainted your supposed crusade truly is. And once you learn, once you see with clear eyes..."

He slammed his manacles together, showering the ground with sparks.

"Come to me when you are finished. I would claim my payment for sparing your life and leading you to the truth."

Payment? What payment could he want that she could offer? She didn't know, nor did she want to know.

"Go," he told her, and so she obeyed.

Mari turned and fled. She ran down quiet streets and past dark homes. She ran until she was certain she was alone and then ducked into a little alcove where not even the moonlight shone. There she relinquished Endarius's form. She screamed as her body reverted. She sobbed as the pain struck her anew.

Naked upon cold stone, she shuddered and gasped on her hands and knees. Blood trickled from her nose. Her ribs pulsed with pain, the bones aching but thankfully not broken. A glance over her shoulder revealed a deep bruise across her back, her skin nearly black from the residual damage of her broken wing.

Endarius's contempt lingered about her like a stench. She closed her heart to it. Mari did not need the Lion. She wanted no voices in her mind, no divine presences, no gods or Humbled or priests or anything but clear, blessed silence.

Yet she could not have it. The words of the hunting god stung her like arrows.

Find out the lies you have been told.

"Father," she whispered to the night. "What have you kept from us?"

Twenty-five years, they had waged war for Miquo.

Twenty-five years, they had murdered in the name of Thorda Ahlai.

If I am to be judged...

Mari pushed to her feet, and she wrapped her arms across her chest and shivered. She would need to become the Lioness to flee home, but doing so would allow Rihim to track her. Knowing so frightened her. Being frightened angered her. All of it paled compared to what her father might be hiding.

"You can't have lied to us," she pleaded. "Not for so long. Not to us."

An hour later she mustered the strength to call upon Endarius. Though the bone of her wing was not broken upon the change, it was still tender and clung rigid to her body instead of obeying her commands. That was fine. There would be no further battle. Her path, her need, was of a different nature.

Mari bounded for home. Her fears were unfounded, she told herself. The Humbled had to be wrong.

Twenty-five years of lying to his daughters. It couldn't be true.

Rihim's claims dragged up memories of her father's words, words that threatened to break her. Words spoken the night before Cyrus left and the bodies hung and the ambush failed.

If I am to be judged, let it be by gods wiser than I.

Her paws pounded across the stone. Her home, too far, and yet she arrived much too soon.

Do not hate me, Mari, he had said.

Her heart was not ready. Her doubts would allow no delay.

Why would I ever hate you?

Tonight, she feared she would learn that answer, and it would break her, and in the breaking, leave a far deeper bruise upon her flesh than the one Rihim gave her.

CHAPTER 19

VAGRANT

Cyrus slumped before the fire and bathed in the warmth of the flames. They camped a few hundred yards off the southward road, far enough away to be safe from prying eyes once their fire was extinguished. From what they could gather, they were only two miles ahead of the imperial contingent on its return to Vallessau. The last thing either wanted was trouble with forward scouts.

"Shame we don't have time to hunt for a real dinner," Rayan said as he came dragging a log he'd found somewhere in the forest nearby. Half was covered with dirt and wet leaves, but he positioned it so he might sit upon the dry half.

"Missing a home-cooked meal?" Cyrus asked, pretending all was fine. And it was fine, wasn't it? They'd slain the false Lycaena. They'd rescued Keles from the clutches of the fanatics.

Not that she'd seemed all that keen on being rescued...

"The squirrels here grow fat and lazy," Rayan explained. He pulled off a boot, then the other. "Years prior my wife and I shared one fire-roasted and seasoned with lemon and pepper. It was like a gift from Lycaena herself."

Cyrus winced at the mention of the goddess. He tried not to think about the fight. The betrayal in Keles's eyes. The hope he robbed from her. It haunted him.

You are wrong. Lycaena is dead, and you helped kill her.

"What if we erred?" he blurted out. "In what we did."

Rayan rubbed at a sore spot on his calf. He kept his voice calm and his eyes low.

"Keles insisted the same. Do you share her feelings? You, who dealt the killing blow?"

Cyrus drummed his fingers against his knees, and he struggled to make sense of his own thoughts.

"Even being near that goddess, that version of her, it felt...wrong, somehow. I don't know why. I can't explain it, but it felt nothing like when I once saw Lycaena in all her beauty. None of that changes the hurt on Keles's face. You heard the belief and the anguish of those who summoned her. Maybe it wasn't Lycaena, but it was still a goddess, and still brought to help the people of Thanet. What if...what if we needed her? What if I had aided her in killing the Heir-Incarnate instead?"

Rayan groaned as he stretched out his legs, setting them close to the fire to warm his toes. Arms crossed, he eyed Cyrus with a gaze that convinced him the paladin understood far more than he was letting on.

"Their goddess was created out of sacrifice, born of pain, and birthed of a need to make others suffer. The Lycaena I worship is one of beauty, of love, and of forgiveness. That monster, you saw its form. It was fire and ash. It was a god made for murder. It would not give. It would only take, and take, and leave us a hollow and wretched people."

A god made for murder. Cyrus's face flushed and his insides burned. Rayan's condemnation might have been for the reborn Lycaena, but Cyrus could not help but feel that same condemnation settle like weights upon his own shoulders. The pain had him lashing out before he even realized what he was saying.

"And so I echo Keles's words, and you echo those of the Heir-Incarnate. Who should we trust?"

"Heroes and villains alike may speak truth, Cyrus. It is those who lie you must distrust. And as sad as it makes me to say it, you yourself are lying to me, and have been this entire trip."

The surprise robbed Cyrus of words. He stared at the paladin, debating what to admit and what to hide. Rayan's face hardened, and he shook his head as he tossed another log onto the fire.

"I may be getting on in years, but my senses are still sharp, and my eyesight fine as ever. Something has troubled you deeply during our journey, and it started long before we set foot outside Vallessau. I tire of your cryptic comments, your guilty pauses, and your unfinished sentences. The battle against Lycaena has given me an incomplete picture, one whose missing pieces I would have you fill. Will you tell me, or will you force me to pry the truth out of you?"

A sudden and horrible spike of panic struck Cyrus's chest, coupled with a desire to don his mask. It felt like when Thorda first dragged him to public balls and meetings to show off the Vagrant. To feel that way in the presence of a dear friend like Rayan angered him, but that did not remove the feelings from his breast. He balled his hands into fists. He would not don his mask. He would not.

"What are you hoping to hear, Paladin?"

Rayan tossed a stick onto the fire.

"I witnessed your fight against Lycaena. The training we gave you does not explain what you accomplished. Let us start with what you are, before you tell me how you became it."

"The stories are more connected than you think."

The older man chuckled.

"I suspect they are one and the same story, young prince, but tell it as you feel best."

Cyrus had imagined telling this story a thousand times over. While he lay in dark alleys waiting for soldiers to ambush, or while he slept in flea-ridden beds of seedy taverns, the rooms paid for in bloodstained imperial coins. Sometimes it was to Stasia, sometimes to Keles, to Mari, Rayan, or even the entire gathered group. He rehearsed the performance, imagining how good it would feel to bellow out his righteous indignation at all Thorda Ahlai had done to him. The years-long plot, the secrecy, the letters to Magus and the great betrayal of those who had trusted the Coin to bring freedom to Thanet.

When he did tell the story to Rayan, it went nothing like those rehearsed imaginings. He told it haltingly, his sentences short, his voice cold and distant. He started with what Magus had informed him, that there was a traitor in the resistance who gave up the location of the forty individuals to be captured, as well as when the rescue attempt would be made. He then labeled Thorda the traitor.

"And that is why I left," he admitted. "I could not continue to work with Thorda. Not with my trust in him broken. Not after what he had done to me."

Cyrus did not explain what all this was meant to accomplish. Rayan was a clever man. He had been to Gordian's paragon ritual. He had witnessed the battle against the false Lycaena. Let him put the pieces together. It felt...safer, doing that, than to confess what was happening to him.

Confessing would make it real, somehow. Real in a way his mind still refused to acknowledge.

And so you lie.

"The stories of what the Vagrant is, and what he can do," Rayan said. He started slowly, like a man walking on thin ice. Too strong, and he might fall through. "They weren't solely to add to your mystique. They were to shape who you were to become. *What* you were to become."

"A killer who can slay any foe," Cyrus agreed. "The grinning skull lurking in the shadows, faster than the wind and stronger than any paragon. Their prince. Their savior."

Say it. Say it, you coward.

He looked up. He met the paladin's eye.

"Their new god."

"A false god," Rayan immediately corrected. "No different than the hollow re-creation of Lycaena we put down."

Put down, like she was a rabid dog, and not a magnificent, terrifying being of blood and fire. Cyrus's throat constricted. More and more, he wondered if she was truly false. Perhaps she had been the real Lycaena, only...changed. Made different by her own worshipers, who had witnessed their island conquered and their culture shredded. Gods were meant to guide their followers, but more and more, Cyrus wondered if followers gave shape and meaning to their gods.

There are no lions on Thanet, after all.

"False or real, it doesn't matter," he said, for he would not speak those thoughts to the paladin. "I'm stronger now. You've seen it with your own eyes. And what I did to Lycaena, I don't think that's my limit. I don't know if I *have* a limit. The people's faith in me, it's growing stronger. They believe I can free Thanet. And because they think it, believe it..."

He left the rest of the thought unsaid. To name it would make it sound insane. One man against the army of an empire was impossible.

But he wasn't just one man.

Nor was he just a man.

"At least now I know why you stormed out after the hangings," Rayan said, and Cyrus was thankful for the change of subject. He was desperate to know his friend's opinion on the matter. The past month had been one of isolated confusion, a self-devouring turmoil that Cyrus had long since given up understanding. He was too close to everything. One could not judge the length of a shore when beneath its waters.

"Was I wrong?" he asked. "To leave, I mean? To be so angry with what Master Ahlai did?"

"What would you have me say? We are all desperate, even Thorda. We are hurt, and lost, and in pain. Are forty lives too many to justify what you have become? I understand the hurt of betrayal. I weep for the dead, but they died for Thanet, and for Thanet's prince. It was a sacrifice they were willing to make, even if in a manner they did not anticipate."

Rayan ran a hand over his head, smoothing out errant strands of hair despite not a single one daring to be out of place.

"You were justified in leaving after that deception. Yet as much as it pains me to admit it, a part of me believes Thorda was also justified in the path he took. How do I object? The proof is before me. I watched you slay a god with your swords. If the Vagrant can kill one god, well... perhaps he can kill another. Forty lives and a lie, to defeat an empire that has killed thousands of us. There is no balancing those scales."

"You're right," Cyrus said. "There is no balancing them. Not unless I myself kill thousands."

"Could you?" Rayan asked. He was serious, too. Painfully, terrifyingly serious. "Could the Vagrant kill thousands? An entire army? The God-Incarnate himself?"

"I don't know."

It was not the answer whispered in his mind by that cold voice that had haunted him since the hangings.

Yes, it whispered. Not eager. Not excited. Confident. Certain. *You can. You will.*

Meanwhile Rayan crossed his arms and leaned closer to the fire. Its faint glow washed over him. He was troubled.

"Now you hide things from me," Cyrus said, and he tried to pretend they were having a perfectly normal conversation, just two friends in the woods. Not two slayers of a goddess, one a paladin who should be king and the other an infantile god. "What bothers you?"

Rayan took a moment to gather himself.

"Even if I believe the results justified, it does not change the part I played in this. From the moment of my birth, I was to serve your family and keep you safe. Yet I brought you to Thorda. I witnessed the training he forced upon you, and his willingness to risk your life and mind in his pursuit of turning you into... I could have stopped it. Perhaps I should have. I will leave that decision to you, Cyrus, and not blame you if you find me equally guilty."

"*Blame* you?" Cyrus hated this, hated every single word Rayan offered in ignorance of his own heritage. Rayan owed Cyrus nothing, *nothing*, and yet his shoulders sagged beneath a weight he'd been forced to bear. A weight the Lythan family had created. "No, I could never blame you, but you don't know that yet. You don't know what I know. When I fought Magus, he told me the history of our island, the parts of it the priests of Endarius would hide."

"What would outsiders from Gadir know of our history?" Rayan asked.

"Too much," Cyrus said, "for Endarius himself came from Gadir."

The paladin hid his reaction well, but his cheek quivered the tiniest bit. Like he'd been stabbed but refused to admit any pain.

"Explain," he said. "And I will judge for myself if the vile paragon spoke true."

Cyrus started with the history Magus had unveiled. It was remarkably simple, despite how much it upended the stories Cyrus had known since his childhood. Dagon lost the War of Tides. Endarius won. The Sapphire Serpent became the foul trickster of the Heldeep, while the Lion ruled alongside the Butterfly. If the war had ended differently, would a vicious lion be what punished the wicked at the bottom of the sea?

"This casts Endarius in a much more sinister light," Rayan said when the story finished. He remained remarkably calm, but then again, as a paladin of Lycaena he had spent a lifetime discussing religion with the faithful and faithless alike. He had kept his own faith after witnessing his goddess's execution. What did a little heretical tale compare to that? "And one could argue it paints Lycaena as a coward, as well. A useful tale, if meant to shake our faith in both gods. Magus could have lied, surely you know that."

Cyrus braced himself for what he knew he had to admit next.

"Magus also told me what happened to the previous ruling family that Dagon anointed. They were forced into servitude for the Lythan family, an act meant to humiliate and break the few survivors. It lasted for hundreds of years, passed down mother to daughter and father to son. The entire bloodline. The entire *Orani* bloodline."

There it was, the secret eating away at him the entire trip out from Vallessau. He couldn't look Rayan in the eye. He stared into the fire. He sat on the wet grass and thought it a better throne than the one his family had stolen when they arrived on Thanet. Seconds drifted away. The air was thicker than the Crystal Sea.

"Did Cleon know?" Rayan asked. "No. He couldn't have known. We were friends, confidants. Your father was a good man, a *great* man. He would have told me. To know that, and say nothing, to be that cruel... or did he think it a kindness?"

That his family was capable of such cruelty frightened Cyrus. He had grown up convinced he was the descendant of a long line of unifiers, noble men and women who put the needs of Thanet above their own. Instead, they had come as conquerors and enslaved what few members of the royal family had survived the War of Tides.

"I don't know," Cyrus said. "The true history of the War of Tides has been suppressed by both gods for centuries. Perhaps I would have been told when I came of age. Perhaps when I took the throne. Perhaps never at all."

Silence followed, brief but agonizing.

"My grandfather told me a story, once," Rayan said softly, breaking the silence. "When deeply drunk, he insisted we were descendants of kings. I never believed it. I have been in enough taverns to hear countless similar claims, of forgotten relatives, confused midwives swapping babies, and secret trysts with commoners. For it to be real...what does that mean of the Lion? Of the Butterfly?"

Finally Cyrus was willing to meet the older man's eye. He felt brittle inside. Let the paladin heap ashes and scorn upon his head. Revoke the crown Cyrus had believed was his since the moment he first learned to walk. Take away the burdens and the responsibility, and leave him only with the guilt. His hands clutched his sword hilts. A guilty, broken thing. That he could be. He could do it well. Had practiced day in and day out over the past month.

A guilty, broken thing could be so very, very good at killing.

"I will amend this," he vowed. "I don't know how, but I will. I'll find a way. I won't let this be a part of my legacy."

A change swept over Rayan. His confusion and doubt peeled away. When he stood, anger and defiance chiseled his features to stone. Cyrus felt frightened and small before him. The hardness in the paladin's voice could shatter steel.

"But it is your legacy, Cyrus Lythan. It will forever be, no matter how hard you deny it. You inherited it the moment you were born destined for a throne."

Rayan was a stranger to him then, and Cyrus feared he was a stranger to the paladin. His chest ached. His father had been beheaded while he watched. Thorda had revealed himself a ruthless betrayer. Here stood the last of his idols, the heroic man who had rescued him after Lycaena's execution, and Cyrus feared he would lose him, too.

"What then of me?" he asked. "What of the Vagrant? May I still call you friend, or have I lost that right?"

The hardness receded. Not gone, not completely. It felt like claws retracting, or a sword sliding into its sheath.

"My shield is not yours, Cyrus, nor is it the Vagrant's. I do not wage this war to return you to your throne. I fight to save the island I love. I fight to protect those who refuse to offer their prayers to the vile God-Incarnate. When peace is come, and Thanet free, let us then decide who is worthy to lead our people."

"Worthy," Cyrus said. "It won't be me, I know it. Not to be king. Not to be a god."

Rayan put a hand on Cyrus's shoulder and squeezed it tightly.

"Let us not worry about it now. Tonight, you are not god, king, or usurper. Tonight, I am content to call you friend."

The words made the gentlest arrow to pierce his heart. Cyrus wiped at his eyes and wondered how he could ever be so lucky.

"Such kind words from a man who, if not for my family, would be king."

Rayan laughed at that, soft and warm, and it shed years of weariness from his face.

"You forget the Vayisa family tree, and of my mother's marriage. Based on our rules of ascension, I would not be king. Keles would be queen."

The idea had never occurred to Cyrus. But he remembered the heartbreak in Keles's eyes when the false Lycaena screamed her last. She had witnessed the death of her goddess not once, but twice. Keles was the descendant of a family whose chosen god had died and whose name had been smeared and turned into a curse. Gods and goddesses, dying before her, failing her, and here he was, the thief of a throne, becoming something uncomfortably close to a god himself.

"Perhaps, for the safety of my own neck, we let you be the one to inform her of that," Cyrus said, and he smiled. Smiled, for it was better than crying, better than drowning in guilt. Rayan smiled back, already proving he was a better man, and a kinder man, than Cyrus would ever deserve.

Deep in his pocket, the grinning mask blazed hot against his side like fire.

CHAPTER 20

KELES

Keles sat alone, an empty wood bowl before her. She wiped up the last of the soup with her fingers, surprised by her hunger. It seemed even a dour mood did not dampen her stomach after a long day of travel. A man had tried to sit in the chair opposite her, but she'd sent him running with a glare. A glare, and a flash of the sword strapped to her hip. Keles was in no mood for drunken suitors.

She leaned back in her chair, closed her eyes, and tried to imagine darkness. So much better than the images that haunted her every step. The road back to Vallessau was long, and though she was no stranger to sleeping under the stars, her stomach had protested at the sight of the roadside inn. The allure of a freshly cooked meal and a warm bed was more than she could resist.

The murmur of conversation washed over her, scattered pieces of lives oblivious to her own troubles. A half-hearted song sung by the innkeeper. The laughter of a trio of men in the opposite corner. Not enough. Imagine darkness instead of last night's events. Not Lycaena bleeding out, her body opened from neck to stern by Cyrus. Not her horrid death scream, the second Keles had heard in her lifetime. Not Eshiel, vanishing amid the collapsing cliff.

Should have stayed with Rayan, she thought with a heavy sigh of frustration. The choice hadn't seemed possible at the time. She'd been so angry, so heartbroken, in the aftermath of the chaos. Had it been fair to blame the pair? She didn't know. With the Heir-Incarnate's arrival, along with his retinue of paragons, Lycaena's death might have been guaranteed. But that didn't change who held the blade.

Cyrus, a man she considered a friend, a man with whom she'd shared her own doubts and difficulties as the Light of Vallessau, had killed Lycaena with his own two hands. Could that be forgiven? Should it ever be forgiven?

That wasn't Lycaena, he'd told her as justification for his crimes. Did he think that made it better? If he was correct, then her own actions, and those of Eshiel, the prayers and the blood sacrifice...what were they even for?

The door opened, as did her eyes. For a brief moment she hoped it would be Cyrus and her uncle. They'd been ahead of her, so it made no sense that she'd passed them somehow without noticing, but she found herself desiring it nonetheless. Was she lonelier than she thought? Or just that desperate for any company beyond the haunting memories of the prior night?

It wasn't Rayan. It wasn't Cyrus. Instead, a frighteningly familiar paragon in deep blue armor entered the inn. The din of conversation quieted, and all eyes turned to the door.

"Come for a warm meal?" the innkeeper asked, and he must deal with imperials on the daily, for he was the only one who seemed unbothered. "If so, it won't cost you a single crown."

"A warm meal, and a seat to sit in while eating it," the paragon requested.

"But of course. Plop yourself down anywhere you like and I'll bring you a bowl."

Keles stared at her table as if the long crack worn into its uneven surface was the most important thing in the world. Her hair was tied back, and she casually removed its band so it might fall forward to hide some of her face. She'd not had a chance to change her clothes. Might he recognize her?

Damn it, he was walking right toward her. His armor rattled with his every step, and the floorboards groaned. She watched him from the edges of her vision as he took a seat at the table directly in front of hers.

His back was to her so he might face the door. The chair protested as he settled into it, and he had to remove his spear first from the little hooks attached to his back.

Keles stared at the spear, polished to a fine shine. No blood on it. Had he cleaned it after murdering Eshiel? Or had the rocks and the sea done the deed for him? She had no name for this man, but she hated him more than she thought possible. Whether or not Lycaena was the "real" Lycaena, whatever that even meant, Eshiel had deserved a better fate, as did those who trusted him. The price might have been high, but the priest had brought hope to the people of Thanet.

What hope did this monster bring? What future would he give to their island beyond one of a bent knee and a tongue praising worship to a distant god none would ever meet?

"Thank you," the paragon said upon receiving his bowl from the innkeeper.

"May you find it appetizing," the portly man said in return, and then paused to softly chat with a few other patrons before returning to the kitchen. Slowly the conversation resumed at its normal volume, albeit in a slightly less exuberant tone.

Keles thought to wait out the paragon to finish his meal and perhaps go to his room. The nervousness building in her belly screamed otherwise. This man was exceedingly dangerous, and her meager sword at her side would mean nothing to him. Swallowing down her nerves, she stood. Given the position of his table, there was no way to avoid him, so she calmly walked past on the way toward the stairs. She was no one, in no hurry, and fearing nothing. She told herself those things, as if it would make them true.

The paragon's hand shot out at her passing. His fingers closed about her wrist, the edges of his armor digging into her skin.

"You need not leave on my account," he said, and smiled up at her with eyes bluer than the sea. "Only travelers with secrets should fear the presence of a paragon."

Did he recognize her? She didn't know. That smile, it revealed nothing. His eyes, they sparkled with amusement, but was it at her fear, her awkwardness, or her desperation to escape?

"I'm not leaving," she said. She flashed a sickly-sweet smile in return. "Only retiring early to bed, for I must rise early as well. Good night to you, paragon."

His grip remained. His smile widened.

"Pleasant nights, young one," he said. "Dream of me, would you?"

Keles suppressed a shudder.

"One may hope."

The paragon let go of her hand, and his attention returned to his soup. Keles made for the stairs, and no amount of self-control could keep her from hurrying. The innkeeper wished her good night as she climbed the stairs. A kind man, and she wished she could have spent some time chatting with him by the fire as the night wore on. That was no longer an option.

Keles needed out, and she needed out ten minutes ago.

The door to her room was locked, and she opened it with the key the innkeeper gave her. Once inside, she slammed it shut, locked it, and then tossed the key upon the bed. Beside it was her traveling pack with her belongings and change of clothes. She grabbed it and turned to the window.

A tight fit, but she could manage. She undid the latch keeping it closed and then heaved it open. A moment of wisdom broke through her fear, and she glanced out to ensure no one nearby watched. Not far away, she saw a muddy pen with pigs and goats, but it was currently untended. Good. The last thing she wanted was a witness. The paragon had not recognized her immediately, but he might make the connection as the night wore on.

First went the pack, landing with a dull thud. Next she hung from the windowsill and lowered herself before letting go. Her knees ached from the landing, and her teeth rattled. She'd endure. Keles grabbed her pack and slung it over her shoulders. It seemed she'd be sleeping out under the stars after all.

Keles positioned the pack's weight across her back so it was balanced and then hurried along. The sun was low, but the sky was clear. She could travel a good ten to twenty miles in the starlight and then set up camp off road. Hopefully she'd wake early with the sun, while the paragon slept the morning away in his comfortable bed. Anything to help grow the distance. She rushed for the road, trailing around the side of the inn while doing so.

The paragon waited at the front, his arms crossed, his mouth curled into a faint grin.

"Hello, Keles," he said. The shock of hearing her name locked her body still, and that half second was all the paragon needed. The last thing she saw before darkness took her was the blue shine of his gauntlet as his fist swung for her forehead.

⌒⌒

When Keles awoke she lay on her side with her hands bound tightly behind her back. Her head ached as if a spike were driven into her forehead. For a brief moment she feared she'd vomit, but thankfully it passed. As her stomach settled, and the fog over her mind cleared, she remembered the attack, remembered the fist, and pulled at her bindings while looking about.

Mere feet away, sitting beside a crackling fire, was the strange paragon. She halted her struggle. There'd be no escaping him, not while he watched her from his seat upon the soft grass.

"I have developed a habit of greeting the recently unconscious," he said. "I must be getting soft."

"I would hardly call your fist 'soft,'" she said. Speaking ignited a thousand pains in her head, especially at the swollen bruise across her forehead where he had struck her. She closed her eyes and focused on her breathing while waiting for the stings to pass. If they did pass. They hurt so terribly, and spiked so viciously, she briefly wondered if this was the rest of her life.

But less than a few seconds later the pain dwindled back down to a bearable level.

"Wounded and bound, yet still making jokes," the paragon said. "I see why so many were fond of you, Keles Lyon. As for myself, my name is Soma Ordiae, Paragon of Spears."

Goddess help her, she was in such deep shit. If only she had traveled home with Rayan and Cyrus. If only she had not stopped for a fresh meal and a warm bed at the inn. If only she had never come to Ierida and met Eshiel at all.

Remembering Eshiel, and his tumble off the cliff, reawakened brand-new hurts. And this damn paragon was responsible for that, too.

"What do you want with me?" she asked coldly.

"Ah, how familiar the question." Soma crossed the distance between them and reached for her back. She thought he might release her bonds, but instead he hoisted her up by the neck. She clenched her jaw, determined not to cry out in pain. Was this it? Would he snap her neck right then and there? It made no sense, but perhaps the cruel bastard wanted her awake when he did it. Maybe he wanted to watch the life leave her eyes, and then do who knows what sick and perverted things to her corpse afterward...

And then he set her down beside the fire.

"I want nothing from you, foolish woman," he said as he sat opposite her. "For that implies you have something you can give me. I'm far more interested in who you are, what you represent, and who you might become. Forgive my rather impolite means of persuasion, but you had the look of someone about to run, and I'd rather not bother myself with a chase."

"You knocked me out with a fist," she said. "If that is 'impolite,' I would hate to see you being rude."

"Yes," he said, and he smiled at her. The way the firelight shone across his face, the way it sparkled in his blue eyes, chilled her to the bone. His smile was like the bared teeth of a starving wolf. His gaze was a hawk spying a rabbit. She meant nothing to this man, *nothing*, and to have his interest felt like the worst outcome imaginable. "You would indeed hate it, very much so."

She stared at the stars to recover her nerves. Lycaena help her, his eyes were like sapphire needles digging into her flesh.

"Then let us be polite instead," she said. "You bind my hands and speak in riddles. I would talk openly instead."

"Yes, yes, talk. You paladins love to talk." Soma grabbed his spear and held it over the fire. It was only now she noticed he had pierced a cleaned rabbit through the middle, and he slowly twirled it over the fire. The sizzling meat awakened hunger in Keles she thought impossible given her cramps and her pounding headache. "You talk of duty, talk of honor, on and on, of compassion and righteousness and all sorts of things that humanity loves to believe make them better than they really are."

"Then what does make us better?" she asked, deciding to play along. As much as it frightened her, remaining "interesting" to this deranged paragon was her best chance at survival.

"Blood," Soma said. He ripped a leg off the rabbit and then stood. She could not see what he did when he walked behind her, but suddenly the bindings around her wrists went slack as the knot was undone.

"Run and you die," he said casually, and returned to his seat. A flick of his wrist, and the rabbit leg arced through the air. She caught it, and winced at the grease that splashed across her hands and shirt.

"I'll keep it in mind."

She ate the rabbit leg. Her mind raced in the ensuing silence. Unarmed and unarmored, she had no chance of killing an imperial paragon. At best, she might sneak away, but she suspected her bindings would return come time to sleep. As confident as he appeared, Soma would not be so foolish. The other option was to play along and hope that she might escape from wherever he planned to take her.

It would also help to know why he cared about her in the first place. Did he know she had fought alongside Cyrus and the rest during the hangings? If so, she was already dead. If not, then asking questions regarding such matters might give it away.

"You have not revealed how you know my name," she said when finished eating. That seemed the safest way to broach the subject. "Nor why you would find me so interesting."

"I was there at the forsaking ceremony," he said. "You were one of the more remarkable confessions. Who could forget the Light of Vallessau falling to her knees and lifting her hands in worship of the God-Incarnate? It's enough to bring a tear to the eye."

Except he didn't sound amused, or like he was mocking her. He sounded...displeased.

"Why would a paragon be upset by my repentance?" she asked.

Soma stared at her a moment, his head tilted slightly. Again a tremble trickled down her entire spine. Who *was* this paragon?

"You truly don't know who you are, do you?" he asked.

"Keles Lyon," she said, deciding to answer with the obvious. He shook his head, his displeasure growing.

"As I explained already, it is blood that defines us. As for your blood, you bear the responsibilities and burdens of the Orani."

"Orani?" she asked. It was her great-grandmother's name, one she'd heard only in passing. "I don't understand. Do you speak of our sacred duty to protect the throne?"

Soma laughed. It was worse than his stares.

"Protect it? You were meant to do far more than protect it. What a grim joke, that an empire on Gadir knows the history of Thanet better than the Thanese themselves. Though I suppose we have no reasons to lie or disguise the truth, whereas the Lythan family had all the reasons in the world."

Keles had not the slightest clue what Soma was going on about. So far as she knew, the empire had maintained no contact with Thanet for hundreds of years, ever since they announced a complete and total ban on any trade with the island after the influx of refugees led to the War of Tides.

"You're mistaken," she said. "Whatever you think I am, you are surely wrong. I was only a paladin of Lycaena, and I sought out rumors of her return in Ierida to condemn those who would spread lies. Your Heir-Incarnate did the same. You have no reason to detain me, and offer me none in explanation."

It was a gamble, but she believed the paragon would fall for such bait. Under no circumstances did she think he would let her go. What he might do, though, was admit the real reason he had captured her.

"I saw your reaction on that cliff when you feared Eshiel would fall to the Vagrant's blades," he said. "You know who he is. Who he really is, underneath that mask."

Keles refused to twitch or blink. It felt like wasted effort. This wasn't a guess on his part. He was absolutely certain of it. All his bluster about bloodlines was a deflection. It seemed she did have something he wanted: a name.

"I know him only by his reputation," she said, deciding to at least pretend at innocence. "As does everyone in Vallessau."

"Oh, you know him," Soma said. He stood and scattered the fire with his boot. Darkness fell across them. Lit by the moonlight, the paragon appeared a wholly new beast. His blue armor sparkled. His face, already handsome, drank in the shadows, highlighting the harshness of his cheeks and the paleness of his skin. His dirty blond hair shone like the midnight sands of the beach. He approached her, and shivers crawled along the back of her neck.

"But you know him as others do not. You were angry at his arrival. No, beyond that, you were *betrayed* by it. That is a familiarity that goes beyond rumors and casual acquaintances. You know each other. Love each other, hate each other, or perhaps even both, it does not matter to me. What does matter is that I am given a chance to speak with the Vagrant, and take true measure of the man behind the mask."

Keles had vastly underestimated the depth of shit she was now in. She bit her lower lip, now convinced her only hope for survival was to escape before arriving at wherever he took her. If she ever arrived.

It seemed Soma had similar thoughts. He tore the lengthy rope he'd bound her hands with in half, snapping it easily with his bare strength. He bound her ankles, tying them so rapidly she could barely follow the movement of his fingers. Next he grabbed her wrists, holding them tightly together with a single hand. The other hand looped the rope about. She didn't watch it being tied. She couldn't, not with how close he was, and how fierce his stare.

"You're coming with me to Vallessau, little Orani girl. You will learn. Who you are. Who you are descended from. How you were betrayed."

He knelt. His head tilted as if he was going to kiss her. His warm breath teased her skin, but he did not draw any nearer. He smelled of salt and the sea. His eyes were bluer than the ocean depths, and they held her prisoner. For one brief moment she wanted him to force the kiss. She wanted his touch, his acceptance, wanted it so terribly it shocked her with chills.

And then he withdrew. The moment passed, and deep revulsion filled its absence. He smiled down at her with savage amusement.

"But I shall let Sinshei tell you the rest. After all, when it comes to the matter of faith on Thanet, who else is more responsible than your Anointed One?"

CHAPTER 21

MARI

Thorda's new forge wasn't much, just a slender anvil propped up on bricks so it was at a comfortable height when he sat before it on a wood stool. A fire burned in the corner, much hotter than necessary so that it made the house feel sweltering in the springtime weather. This forge was better suited to smaller projects, particularly jewelry, and he was working on a pair of silver bracelets when Mari stepped inside and shut the door behind her.

"How goes things?" she asked while rubbing her shoulder. The bruise ached something fierce where the wing-bone had broken. She'd changed clothes upon returning home. Her heart had hammered in her chest the entire time she dressed. The Humbled's words would not cease. Her doubts would not relent.

"Well enough," he said, answering without turning toward her.

It was almost comical watching her father tap and tinker away on the slender bracelets with that enormous hammer of his. Surely there were other, better tools suited for the job, but her father was a stubborn one. If he could make use of his favorite hammer, then he did, suitability be damned. Mari stood quietly and watched, her right hand clutching her left arm. She didn't have to do this. She could walk away. Not all questions needed answers.

Go to your father. Ask him for the truth. Ask him who he is, what *he is.*

"Rihim spoke of you," she said, breaking the steady tapping of metal. "He knows who you are, and that you're here."

Her father lowered the bracelets, but he kept the hammer in hand. His posture straightened.

"Rihim?"

"The Humbled of Antiev. He knows you betrayed his homeland, but that's not all he knows. He said to ask you for the truth."

Thorda slowly turned on his stool. His hammer rested in his lap. Though he feigned calmness, she saw how tightly he gripped the handle. His knuckles were white. His arms quivered.

"You already know of my sins against our neighbors. I told you when you were old enough to understand."

"But did you, though?" Mari asked. "Did you tell me everything?" Wherever this bravery was coming from, she didn't know. It certainly didn't feel like her normal self to challenge her father. Who was this person who crossed the room with her hands bunched into fists and her jaw trembling?

"Why does the Humbled speak of Miquoan gods on Thanet?"

Thorda slid off the stool. Though he stood, he seemed shorter now, more hunched. His eyes, red like fire, like blood, held her captive. What emotions hid within them? Was it compassion? Or anger? She prided herself on understanding and empathizing with the feelings of others, but her father was always the one man she could never read.

"I never thought I would be the one to reveal this to you, Mari," he said. There was a rumble to his voice, and a rare weariness. "I thought, in time, you would see the truth for yourself. Miquo was a land of minor gods, and I have told you of many. Our pantheon was numerous, a multitude we guarded jealously so that even our neighbors in Antiev did not know them all. With faith spread so broadly, these gods were also weaker. More human, we liked to believe. Shorter lives. More focused purposes. We worshiped a god of the wind, a goddess of the rain, and twin gods of the moon and stars. We paid homage to the god of strife. We swore honor to the goddess of trade come every market opening. Gods of all sorts, each deserving honor and prayer regardless of the importance of their divine aspect. Music, marriage, birds, childbirth..."

He hesitated.

"Even a god of the forge."

Mari looked at her father, truly looked at him, for what felt like the very first time. She saw the faint wrinkles across his leathery face. His red eyes, vibrant as any youth's. The white streaks throughout his long brown hair. Streaks that had been there even when she was a child. It was a face she knew well. Too well. It was a face that filled her oldest memories. A face that had never changed.

"How old are you?" she asked. "How old are you really?"

Her father softly sighed.

"One hundred and ninety-two."

Mari wanted to deny it, but how could she? Everywhere they went, he ensured a fire burned. His crafting skills were legendary, as evidenced by Cyrus's and Stasia's weapons. He formed relationships with the surviving gods of invaded nations with remarkable speed for a foreigner. Remarks, once meaning nothing, came to her from throughout her life. Had he tried to hide this from her, or had she been blind to the obvious?

"What prayers empower you?" she asked. "Miquo has been captured for decades, and the priests, they were so thorough, so cruel."

In answer, Thorda lifted his hammer and showed her the Ahlai family symbol, the letter "A" in the Miquoan alphabet with a downward slash below it and the top of the letter extending as if it were the point of a sword.

"All across Gadir, tens of thousands of people wield weapons bearing my mark. They have faith those weapons will hold strong. They believe in the craftsmanship. The price they paid was a sacrifice, one they believe will ensure their safety come battle. It is worship, shallow and selfish, but worship nonetheless. It is enough to keep me alive. One day it will be enough for Stasia, should she choose to inherit this blessing."

Mari's mind was a top spinning wildly off balance. Of their two fathers, and their shared surrogate mother, Stasia had been of Thorda's blood, while Mari's was of their deceased father, Rhodes. She had always known the difference, and believed it responsible for their disparate treatment. Knowing now of Thorda's divinity, her understanding of those differences changed drastically, and not for the better.

"Inherit?" she asked. Her face flushed as her anger blossomed. "So Stasia, she could become a god herself? Why didn't you tell her? Or even give that power to her, so she could wield it against the empire? Instead you lied. You left us in the dark!"

"It is in the dark you are safest!"

Her father's outburst had her retreating a step. He placed his hammer atop the anvil, removed his gloves, and then flung them to the ground.

"Stasia will inherit this power in time. I am weak and dying, Mari. It is why I do not accompany you on your battles. If we were beneath the leaves of the godwoods, I would have already given your sister my blessing. But while we wage war in nation after conquered nation, I fear her knowing the truth. If we were discovered, or caught..." He shuddered. "As she is now, the Everlorn Empire would merely hang her from the Dead Flags. But if she were a god, however minor? They would seek to humble her. I will not allow that fate. I will not have her suffer decades of torture until her mind is broken and her faith twisted to serve that wretched deity in Eldrid. Should we be caught, I must be the one to suffer, as is just. As is *right*."

A terrible image flashed through Mari's mind. She saw Stasia flanked by priests of the Uplifted Church, rune-marked manacles clasped about her wrists. The image was so vile it filled her with a sudden, frightful urge to vomit. Little better was imagining her father in those same manacles.

"And could you resist it?" she asked.

"Long enough to die," Thorda answered. "But Stasia is young. The priests, they would have so much more time to work their will. If you have spoken with a Humbled, then you know the cruelty they inflict. The tangled words, and the warping of faith and belief until they become meaningless. I can endure you two risking your lives for my war. I cannot bear the thought of you risking your souls."

"Your war?" she asked. "*Our* war. As it has always been."

"Is it, though?" Thorda closed his eyes and looked away. "What do you even remember of our home, Mari? What love do you hold for a land you left when you were a mere eight years old? Whatever blood you spill, it belongs upon my hands, not yours."

Mari felt dizzy. The room was simultaneously too small and yet cavernously huge. Her father was a god. Her sister would become a goddess. The war against the empire shifted in her mind, every hard truth suddenly loosened like sand.

Her sister, a goddess. Her sister, born of Thorda's blood. Not her.

"Stasia, if she's your divine heir, is that why...?"

Mari hesitated. Could she truly voice this question? This unspoken fear had lingered every single day of her life. It had poked at her when she watched Thorda train Stasia how to fight. It had mocked her when he taught Stasia to work the smith, and when he anointed her heroine of yet another resistance. Not Mari. Not she who embodied slain gods and goddesses, whose purpose was to rekindle faith and to remain nameless behind the divine. All that mattered was who she became, not who she was.

That hurt, that bitterness, gave her the strength to blurt out the words. She met her father's eye as she spoke them, so he might look upon her face and see a lifetime of hurt within each and every syllable.

"Is that why you've always loved Stasia more?"

Mari thought he would be angry with her. She thought her claim of partiality regarding his love would be too strong an insult to his pride. What she did not expect was to see her hurt mirrored upon his own hardened brow.

"Mari," he said, and he stepped closer. "My sweet, dear Mari. You don't know. Damn me for this, for I never told you why you are a god-whisperer."

Her shoulders hunched, and her head dipped as she shrank before him. Would it always be this way? Would she always feel so young and childish in his shadow?

"You told me it was a gift from our pantheon, a rare blessing given to the children of Miquo."

Thorda took her hands in his, and he lifted both to his lips so he might kiss her fingers.

"From the very first second you were born, I prayed over you. I neither slept nor ate. I was at your side during your feedings, your fits, and your dreamless sleeps. For weeks, you were all my thoughts, all my prayers, all I lived for. If we are beings of faith, then I put a piece

of my faith in you, that you would be a light in my life, and the life of
your father, Rhodes. That is why you are a god-whisperer. That gift
was my intercession. You may not be of my blood, but you bear a part
of me nonetheless. You are my daughter, my truest, cherished, most
wonderful daughter. Never doubt my love, not for you, nor for Stasia.
Condemn my actions, Mari. Hate me for the choices I have made, and
the destruction my pride has wrought upon this world. But not that.
Never that."

Such naked emotion was unbecoming of her father. This vulnerability
should have made her love him more, but instead it kindled further anger.
If he were capable of such a confession, then why now? Why, after decades
of hardship and travel, and a lifetime of war, did he only now allow her to
see it? As if there weren't a thousand nights in her past when she had cried
alone. A thousand moments of grieving friends and lovers left behind in
broken homes and overflowing graveyards as the Ahlai family traveled from
one conquered land to the next. Sacrifices made, and in the name of what?
She had thought a better world, for everyone. But the blood spilled by her
father's weapons... it was worship, given unknown to the Ahlai name.

Did he even desire peace?

"I want to trust you," she said. "I do. Maybe one day, I will again."

Mari fled the little workshop and his too-hot fire (a fire, everywhere
he went a fire, how had she been so blind?) and moved with no destination in mind. Away. Out. Alone. Her insides churned with confusion,
hurt, anger, and betrayal. For Rihim to be right, it galled her further.
Everything he represented was an abomination, yet it had been he who
spoke the truth, and her beloved father who whispered deceit.

Her steps took her to the front door. Perhaps she meant to escape the
confines, but she would accomplish no such thing. The door was open,
and two young men employed by the carriage service were busy carrying belongings inside. Stasia stood in the entryway, tall and beautiful as
ever despite the ragged toll of the lengthy ride. Clarissa stood beside her,
their hands interlinked, the most intimacy they would risk in the presence of strangers. Mari felt jealous. She felt heartbroken.

"Hey, Mari," Stasia said, a grin lighting up her face. "We're back, and
we kicked Agrito's ass."

A lifetime of performance took over. Mari smiled, all pretended excitement and joy.

"That's wonderful, I'm so happy!" She closed the distance between them, her arms wrapping around the waist of her much taller sister. Stasia rocked backward an inch from the contact, then gently returned the hug.

"You all right, sis?"

Mari's bubbly laughter was false, but it was an easy falsehood. This was the role she had played for decades, to wear the faces of others so they might know comfort. The selfless one, the compassionate daughter, the giver of strength to those in need. Why should things change now? So she smiled. She bounced up and down as if flames licked her feet. She lied.

"I've never been better."

CHAPTER 22

VAGRANT

The pair halted before the door. Cyrus didn't know the home, but it was familiar nonetheless. At this point, he recognized Thorda Ahlai's preferences. A large mansion, tucked away in some obscure section of the city. It had a decent amount of fenced-in land, too, especially for the tightly packed city on the cliffs. Given the smoke billowing to the sky, Cyrus suspected he'd even built himself a small forge.

"You don't have to do this," Rayan said.

"I said I would."

"And you've had many long days of travel to reconsider that decision. This must be done with your whole heart, Cyrus. The betrayal Thorda committed, it wounded you, and some wounds do not heal easily."

"Some don't heal at all," Cyrus said, and he pushed open the door. "We keep on fighting anyway."

Thorda was waiting for him. He stood near the fireplace in the entry parlor, a poker in hand. His arms were crossed over his chest. Had he overheard their conversation outside?

"You are back," he said.

Cyrus froze in the doorway. A thousand memories came and went. Countless hours of training together. Of Thorda explaining stances and positions, shouting out their names, and teaching him to transition between them so those individual poses became a deadly, fluid dance.

Of quiet nights beside the fireplace. The promise offered him that first
night free of the Usurper King's influence.

I want a god of death the empire one day fears. Is that you?

"I am," Cyrus said, voicing none of that. How could he? What words
might suffice? Did he even want anything from his former master? Not
an apology. None would be forthcoming, nor would he demand it.
There would be no regret or second thoughts from Master Ahlai. So
what then?

"I would speak with the group," Cyrus said.

The man was a block of ice carved into human form. Not a hint of
emotion dared convey itself upon his face.

"You have no words for me, or for yourself, after this past month?"

"I have plenty of words, for everyone."

Thorda's face might be a mask, but there was no hiding the displeasure in his voice. The older man departed for the interior of his home.

"So be it."

Rayan set aside his traveler's pack and groaned with pleasure at the
removal of the weight. He had kept quiet during the tense exchange,
and now seemed eager to dispel the lingering awkwardness.

"It's nice to be off my feet," he said, removing his coat and then sliding into a luxurious chair. "You're fine company on the road, Cyrus,
but you still do not compare to a nice, padded piece of furniture."

The door burst open before he might respond.

"Cyrus!"

Mari practically ran into his arms, and he laughed as her weight barreled into his.

"It's good to see you again, Mari."

"You, too, you big dummy. You're not going to run off on us again,
are you?"

He gave her a squeeze, then stepped apart.

"I hope not."

Arn and Stasia were next, though their greetings were more
tempered.

"Welcome back, kid," was all the older Ahlai sister said. Arn less
"hugged" and more "smacked lovingly in the shoulder."

"You gave us a scare," the former paragon said with a grin.

"It wasn't my intention," Cyrus said, rubbing his arm. "And damn, are you trying to give me a bruise?"

"I'd wager you deserved it, if I was."

They took their seats, or in Arn's case, leaned against the wall. This was everyone, everyone but Keles. It would be better to have her there, to hear the truth of what Thorda had labored to create.

She already knows what you are.

He shivered. Yes, she knew. She saw his fight against the resurrected Lycaena. She was intelligent enough to piece together matters for at least a partial understanding. That made her absence hurt all the worse. Where was she now? Camping in the forest? Retreating to some distant village? Would she ever return to Vallessau, so he might explain himself?

Cyrus pushed the thoughts aside. He couldn't be distracted, not while all eyes were upon him. He shifted his weight from foot to foot in the center of the room, and he dimly realized he should be nervous. He'd been sick to his stomach with every visit to those awful balls and meetings Thorda dragged him to over the past year. Yet this was different for some reason. He looked to the various members of Thorda's elite, all watching him quietly and giving him the time and silence to speak.

Of course this was different. They were his friends. His family. Cyrus felt a tremble in his chest. He'd missed them, each and every one, and he'd had no clue just how deeply until back in their presence.

That comfort soured in his belly. One man was responsible for his departure. One man, and one betrayal. The man who had sent forty Thanese faithful dropping to their deaths. The man who had called him "son."

"I once promised I would not return here," Cyrus said, struggling to find a way to broach such a complicated topic. "I suppose today I break that promise. I've missed all of you terribly, but I won't come back without offering an explanation. My absence was not without reason, and I cannot in good conscience fight alongside you until everything is known."

Cyrus told the tale as best he remembered it, sparing no detail. He opened with Magus's arrival in the bell tower once the forty were hanged. He shared the same words, the accusations of a traitor amid their group who had alerted the Imperator of the plan. And then Cyrus turned to Thorda.

"I would have them hear it from your own lips," he said. "That is my price. Speak the name of our betrayer."

Thorda sat in his little chair by his fireplace, his hands crossed over his lap. Cyrus thought he might be angry, or bitter, but he appeared remarkably calm. When all eyes turned his way, he merely shrugged.

"It was I," he said.

The shock rippled through his friends. They shared a look, a communal question of "why?"

"The purpose, though," Cyrus said, attempting to answer that exact question. He tried to find the right words, a way to explain the absurd. "His goal, throughout all of this, was to turn me into a god that might replace Lycaena and Endarius. I would be Thanet's final hope. I would be a murderer, unstoppable, unbeatable, without remorse or pity. A new god. The true Vagrant Prince, for whom the rumors paved the way since the day my training began."

Silence filled the room. Hard stares pierced the tension. Would they believe him? Could they? No one spoke for an unbearable time, yet Cyrus refused to continue. He needed them to dwell on this fact. He needed them to understand exactly what had happened, and why he turned his back on their resistance.

In the end, it was Stasia who broke the silence.

"Did it work?" she asked softly.

Cyrus chuckled. There they were, the anxious nerves he'd grown so accustomed to feeling. It was one thing to speak the truth to his friends. It was another to reveal the change overcoming him, especially when he hadn't yet reconciled it with himself. Did he want this? Fear this? Hate it? The power was useful, perhaps necessary. But what of the cost? And was he even worthy to accept it?

Rayan had witnessed him in battle against Lycaena, but the others had not. If they were to believe such an absurd claim, they would need to see with their own eyes. So he turned his bare face to each and every one and then lowered his gaze. His eyes closed.

The Vagrant must have allies, he thought. *And for that, they must see the truth.*

A cool chill blew across Cyrus's body despite the closed door and warm fire. His face went numb. His vision darkened. He looked up.

"Yes," he said. "It did."

He needed no mirror to know the grinning skull had appeared on his face. The shocked and startled gasps of those in his company were enough. It lasted but a moment, and then the numbness vanished. This visage was one he could maintain for only a few seconds, and it was even harder when outside the thrill of combat.

"I can confirm what you have witnessed is no mere trick," Rayan said after a pause. He leaned forward, his shoulders hunched and his hands clasped together. "In the far north of Ierida, we battled a gruesome mockery of the goddess Lycaena. In that battle, I witnessed Cyrus move in ways that I would normally deem impossible. His prowess and strength impressed even the Heir-Incarnate."

"The Heir-Incarnate?" Arn asked. "It sounds like you had some fun up north."

He was trying to break the tension with his cocky grin. It wouldn't work. Cyrus and Thorda were two fires burning toward each other, consuming the very air.

"Maybe I'll tell you the story sometime," Cyrus said. He returned his attention to Thorda. "But it was in fighting Lycaena I saw the desperation of my people. I saw the despair that would ruin them, and drive them to false gods of blood and sacrifice. So let them turn to me instead. I will be the god they need, if it spares our island a cruel mockery of the faith we once practiced. Better the Butterfly still wrapped in beauty than the bloody moth. Better my name whispered in reverence, than foul prayers to the God-Incarnate."

As if you loathe it, whispered that dark voice in his mind he long wished to silence.

"This is the path set before me," he continued, pretending to not have heard. "I may have walked its first steps without knowing, but my eyes are open now. Call it blasphemous, call it madness, or call it necessary. I don't care. I have this power, and I will use it to save my people.

It is in that, and that alone, I still share something in common with our leader."

At last, Master Ahlai stood. He pulled at the sleeves of his robes, gathering himself. Nervous? No, Cyrus decided, not nervous. This man didn't know the meaning of the word. His conviction had carried him for decades. If a sliver of doubt had existed within him, it'd have long ago traveled to his heart to put an end to his series of failed rebellions.

"I have always done what I believed must be done," Thorda said. "I will offer no apologies, nor excuses, for neither are deserved. With the Vagrant, we have ourselves the weapon we need. Victory, the first real victory against the Everlorn Empire in decades, is within our grasp. I understand some of you may not agree. I will not argue with you. The door is there. If you feel my actions crossed a line, then leave through it and do not return."

His gaze swept from person to person, Rayan to Arn, Stasia to Mari. None stood. None left. How much blood was spilled between the four, Cyrus wondered? Could any of them condemn Thorda for the deaths of innocents when each man and woman in that room was a murderer famous throughout the empire? Cyrus's hands weren't innocent, either. So much blood. Perhaps it was foolish to think there might even be a noble path leading to the end.

"We all have our sins," Arn said, answering the unspoken question. "I won't condemn anyone here for their own."

"If Cyrus is willing to put it aside, then so am I," Stasia said. She glared at her father. "Though I'd be saying differently if you'd not saved Clarissa from that noose."

"Or Keles," Rayan added.

Mari stared down at her hands. She did not speak, but neither did she get up to leave.

"Very well," Thorda said, accepting the silence as her answer. "Cyrus's return is most fortuitous, for it will mark the start of our own escalation. With Lord Agrito dead, the Tannin Realm will be in chaos, and the Heir-Incarnate's attention forced upon it. He will divert soldiers and spies out from Vallessau, and so we will do the opposite. I have coordinated efforts from both commander Pilus and Lord Mosau to smuggle soldiers from their training grounds right here, into the heart of the capital."

"You would hide an army underneath the empire's very nose?" Cyrus asked.

"Hardly an army, but it will be a killing force," Thorda said. "Our war shall soon begin in earnest, now that we have our prince to lead it."

Over a month passed, and yet nothing had changed. His former master barely even had to alter his plans. Had his protest been for nothing? What point did those weeks living under bridges and in shabby lodges even serve? Cyrus felt foolish and bitter, young and stupid, too naïve and yet burdened with an army and a purpose.

"You presume much," he said. "I demand no apology, and I offer you no forgiveness, but that does not mean my return comes without requirements. What I want is a promise, Thorda, one given in full witness to this group. No more lies. No more deception. You will speak only the truth to each and every one of us. Without that, I walk back out the door, and I will save my island without cooperating with your teams or acknowledging your plans ever again."

Thorda's lips curled inward as if he tasted something sour. He glanced once, to Stasia.

"I swear it," Thorda said. "No deceptions, only the truth."

Mari startled from her chair. She stood there awkwardly, her neck and face flushing red. If she meant to say something, she changed her mind and instead crossed the room to wrap her arms around Cyrus. The embrace was far more calm and controlled than her first greeting.

"It really is good to see you again. I missed you dearly."

She withdrew. Despite the crowd, she turned to her father and addressed him as if they were alone.

"You once asked me to never hate you," she said. Her whole body shook with her words. Witnessing such hurt was heartbreaking. "It's getting harder and harder, Father."

She left without waiting for a response. Not that one would be forthcoming. Thorda's tanned skin had turned ashen, but his features were still hard as stone. His ire shifted Cyrus's way.

"I pray your promise was worth it," he said. "The truth cuts harsher than any story, and it need not always be brought to the light."

"Do not blame me for the cost of your own decisions," Cyrus shot back.

"I pay every cost, and accept every blame. I must. What cost are you willing to pay, Vagrant? What blame will you allow to fall on your selfish shoulders? Or did you think Thanet, and your friends here, would fare perfectly well during your absence?"

There was the anger and frustration Cyrus had anticipated. It had only lain dormant, waiting for his promise to return to the group. Waiting until Thorda need not fear chasing Cyrus away a second time. He grinned at the older man, and he might have summoned his second face, the face of the Vagrant, if he thought it would affect him in the slightest.

"You would try to guilt me?" he asked the man he once foolishly thought could be a father. "Not now, and not ever, Thorda. There's enough weight upon my shoulders. I need no guilt from your own bloody hands."

CHAPTER 23

STASIA

Stasia traversed Vallessau with her head down and her hands deep in the pockets of her light coat. Cyrus had stormed out after the meeting, and after some prodding by her father, she'd gone after him. On the one hand, Cyrus might need some time alone. On the other, he'd had a full month of being alone. Her gut said he needed company, not solitude and moping.

It hadn't even been a difficult guess. She found him atop the bell tower overlooking the scene of the hangings a long month ago. The execution platform had burned to ash, as had multiple nearby buildings. No attempts had been made to rebuild.

Stasia sat beside him, her legs dangling off the side, and elbowed his ribs.

"Here you go," she said, handing over three stones. They were perfectly spherical, and a deep gray color reminiscent of soot. "My father calls them smoke stones. Throw one to the ground and it'll explode in smoke and ash. Great for making timely escapes." She cleared her throat. "He made them for you. I suspect it is his way of attempting to apologize."

Cyrus accepted the stones, pocketed them, and then resumed staring. Stasia grunted. So it'd be like that, would it? He'd always been a quiet kid since she met him, happier to vanish into a room to read than laugh and joke with friends. But of course, he'd not actually had friends, had he? Just her, Mari, and Thorda. No one his age. No one who knew a regular life, one free of war and killing. To think that he'd not just endured, but thrived...

"Mari said to come by her room when you get back," Stasia continued, pretending all was fine. "She said she needs your measurements."

"Is she to sew me new clothes?"

"Perhaps? You do smell pretty foul."

He chuckled, a bit of his seriousness cracking, but it didn't last. The young prince appeared determined to brood. Silence returned, but it would not defeat Stasia.

"How long ago was it, two years ago?" she asked, her tone light, as if they were casually chatting on one of their morning runs. "No, three years, that's it, three years since we started your training. I'll admit, I thought it was a bit of a lost cause. You were such a skinny little kid, but damn if you didn't have a mountain full of heart."

"Did you know?" Cyrus asked, curt and accusing. One question, yet there were dozens within, like threads linked together into a single rope. Did she know about her father's plans? Did she know he would kill innocent believers? Did she know he would try to turn him into a god?

"No," she said. "He kept me in the dark, just like you. You were to be a symbol, and I was to train you so you didn't get killed. That was all I knew. I didn't need to know more, and so I wasn't told."

Cyrus wouldn't look at her, his gaze locked on the burned remnants of the hanging platform. It seemed like he believed her. It probably helped that a bit of Stasia's own frustrations leaked out with her words. Her entire life was filled with similar moments, such as when Thorda hadn't mentioned the riots in Vallessau after the partial implementation of the Joining Laws. The truth, if inconvenient, was best left unspoken to keep things as her father desired. Even from family.

"Such lofty ambitions," Cyrus said, and he laughed. "Hey, Cyrus, don't get killed so everyone else can do the hard work. Is that all it takes to become a god in Miquo? You must have had a very crowded pantheon, indeed."

"We did, before the God-Incarnate slaughtered them all."

Stasia was glad to see Cyrus wince. He might be hurting on the inside, but to insult her home like that felt...petty.

"Sorry," he said. "It's hard to get out of my head sometimes. Even with all I've endured, others have suffered worse."

Stasia picked up a pebble dislodged from the stone bricks and chucked it off the side.

"Others, but not many," she said, thinking of how his parents had been beheaded while he watched. She put a hand on his shoulder. He trembled at her touch. "I understand the guilt you feel, I do, so I want you to know that I ask this with full sincerity—is it truly so terrible, what you are becoming?"

He glared at her, angered at the question exactly as she'd feared he'd be.

"How could you ask that?"

"Because you've been given power, Cyrus. Power at a cost, yes, but all power comes at a cost. We fight a near unwinnable war. Clawing our way to victory won't be pretty, and it won't come without blood on our hands. Thorda is a conniving bastard, you won't get any arguments from me on that, but there's no changing what's been done, only deciding how we move forward."

"So pragmatic."

Stasia shrugged.

"I wasn't given much choice on how else to live, wouldn't you agree?"

Cyrus fell silent. He was struggling to understand, and she wanted to feel sympathy for him, maybe even pity. She couldn't muster either. No matter how hard Cyrus tried, he would not understand her life. Not completely. Yes, he had undergone tragedy and suffering, but his three years of isolation while his country was taken from him did not compare to Stasia's two decades of warfare. He had not made new friends and lovers, fought with them, and bled for them, only to watch them die. He had not wept over their graves, and then been forced to *move on*. Another battlefield, another doomed war, another culture broken and shattered and reshaped with only its most smooth and harmless remnants allowed to endure in the shadow of the God-Incarnate.

Twenty-five years, she thought. *Twenty-five gods-damned years. It's a won-der I haven't taken a knife to my own throat.*

Cyrus could not see her pain, but he could feel its presence, could sense its weight. It made him rethink his initial outburst, and after a time, he tried again. This time it felt honest, and Stasia was thankful for that.

"I feel like I have no idea what it means to be a god anymore," he admitted. "Gods were...they were Lycaena, and Endarius. They were these eternal, wondrous beings beyond my understanding, who loved us and cherished us for some unfathomable reason. They were the makers of the world. They were the divine pair who would carry us into the eternal lands beyond, and allow us to live among them without hunger, pain, and strife."

He touched his face. Still wearing gloves, she noted, and had so ever since he'd returned from his self-imposed exile on the streets of Valles-sau. Was there a reason for that? Did he fear his own touch?

"Of all people, how can *I* become a god?" he asked. "And if some-one like me can become one, what does that say about the gods we do worship? And the gods all across Gadir? Or even the God-Incarnate himself? To think this is possible, or justified, feels like an insult to them all."

"Then insult them, Cyrus. They're divine beings. They can handle whatever it is you're becoming. I'm more worried about *you* breaking under the strain, not the pride of some lousy gods across the sea or the absolute cock-weasel that is the God-Incarnate."

He laughed, and it looked like a thousand pounds had slid off his shoulders.

"I feel like I'm losing my mind any time I believe this is happening, and I'm the one it's happening to. Yet you're not all that surprised."

"Miquo's gods were different, remember?" she said. "It's...easier, for me. My father has told me stories of them, but even the dozen or so gods I know the names of are but a fraction of the eighty we worshiped. Our gods would age and give up their mortal shells to take their rightful place in the stars. Their power, their wisdom, and their faith would be passed down to another."

Stasia shrugged.

"The people chosen would sometimes be children, sometimes elderly, but they were always human. Always mortal. And then they would become divine. So for you to become the same, it's not that strange to me. The source of the power is. There is no god whose gifts you inherit. It is a new faith, infantile and wild. It's one born out of fear and desperation, and I suppose in this analogy, my father is the wet nurse."

"Or the one who impregnated Thanet so it might birth me."

He grinned at her, fully aware how disturbing the joke was to her. She socked him in the shoulder.

"Bastard," she said. "Here I am trying to be serious with you."

"That was your first mistake."

He rubbed where she'd hit him with exaggerated pain, and his smile was so genuine it transported her back to their countryside mansion. Despite the brutal training regimen forced upon him, he'd still been safely sheltered away from the world for several years. It'd allowed him to be a vulnerable young man, in a way he hadn't when locked within the castle walls as Regent Goldleaf's political prisoner.

"I'm all right with being needed," Cyrus said. "I do not feel right being worshiped. Is it possible to deny it? Can a god exist without worship?"

"You view worship as subservience, a belief the Uplifted Church has worked hard to reinforce. We Miquoans viewed it as a form of love, and no, Cyrus, I do not believe an unloved god can continue for long." Stasia grimaced and leaned forward, her chin resting atop her fists. "Ugh, I'm starting to sound like some sort of Miquoan priestess."

"Are you sure you're not one?"

"I'm just someone who has spent a lot of time in different nations among different gods. Everywhere you go, it's unique, even if it doesn't seem like it at first glance. The way people worship, the way they offer themselves, and the expectations for what they may receive in return. It's only in the Everlorn Empire that all is the same. Heads bowed, eyes low, perfect obedience to the damn God-Incarnate on his throne in Eldrid."

"That's what they want here, isn't it?"

That was certainly the assumption, but Stasia had been having doubts ever since Mari mentioned it a month back. The way the empire treated Thanet went against centuries of established order. It was sloppy, rushed, and superficial even for their church. It didn't feel like they were setting down roots, and that fact worried Stasia far more than she was willing to let on. Such matters, however, were not a discussion she wanted to have with Cyrus in his current state.

"I don't care what they want here," she said instead. "I want them gone, for all our sakes. That's what my axes are for."

Cyrus nodded. Silence fell over them, but this one felt good. It was companionship, even amid the quiet. Stasia allowed herself to admit that yes, she did miss the kid. Even if he was sometimes a brat. Given the betrayal he suffered, his leaving was more than justified. She'd certainly thrown fits for far pettier reasons when she was his age.

"I'm scared," Cyrus said, breaking the silence. His words barely rose above a whisper, for this was a confession. "I know what I have to do, and it's so much."

Stasia grabbed the young man's shoulder and squeezed it.

"Everlorn's greatest luxury to its people isn't gold or wine or perfume. It's ignorance. They never partake in the invasions. They never see the bodies or smell the stench of death on the wind. They don't know Seeds give their lives to empower their paragons, and they never witness the horrors those paragons unleash. Instead they see a heathen sovereignty brought low, its gods broken and its traditions stamped out, all lost in the glorious name of salvation."

Memories of Miquo's invasion paraded through her mind, adding a layer of bitterness to her tongue.

"But people like us? We're not allowed ignorance. And as much as it hurts, I wouldn't want it even if I could have it. Let me see the naked cruelty of this world. At least then I can try to do something about it."

"And if what we do is wrong?" Cyrus asked. "I killed the reborn Lycaena, but while I saw a monster, Keles saw a goddess. How do I know for certain the blood I shed belongs only to the cruel? What if my decisions are wrong, and the lives I take unjustified?"

"Justified," Stasia said. She closed her eyes, and though she tried not to, her hands clenched and unclenched all the same. "You can't play that game, Cyrus. We're fighting a war, one we did not start. We'll never do it clean. We'll never make perfect decisions, nor escape with our souls blameless. If you try to pick away at each death, if you try to ensure you are somehow still innocent..."

Stasia clenched her jaw. She felt a small, phantom body in her arms go still.

"I swore to never feel guilt for what I've done. Decades, I've fought, Cyrus. Decades. If I dwelt on it, if I allowed myself to feel doubt or regret..." She breathed out, nice and slow, composing herself. "It would ruin me, and I won't let it. I won't. Everlorn has taken so much from me, but I won't give it that. I will keep my life. I will still know peace and joy, and live with my spirit unbroken. No amount of blood on my hands will change that."

Cyrus scratched at his chin, falling silent as he dwelt on her words. Stasia didn't mind. It gave her a chance to collect herself and push unpleasant memories deep down into a dark abyss of her mind she swore never to revisit.

"I want to live that same way," he said. "But I'm not sure I know how."

"Yeah, well, I've had years of practice, remember?"

She nudged him with her elbow. A new smile bloomed on his face, another reminder of how kind, and how handsome, young Cyrus could be when not overly burdened.

"Fair enough," he said. "Hey, can you pretend to be a Miquoan priestess for a little bit longer so I can ask you another question?"

"I'll give it try, though I assure you, I am woefully underqualified. So what's your question?"

He took in a deep breath, then let it out.

"Did you ever love a god or goddess?"

"Physically or spiritually? I must admit, I'd be curious to know what a goddess could do with her hands."

His turn to elbow her in the side. "I thought we were trying to be serious."

"My curiosity over divine sex is *perfectly serious*, thank you."

Yet he didn't laugh. He stared at her, one eyebrow lifted, and waited for an answer. His patience was certainly higher than when she first started training him.

"You're going to make me talk about everything I'm uncomfortable with, aren't you? Fine. No, Cyrus, I did not worship any particular god in Miquo. My father made sure I participated in all the festivals, and I showed proper veneration for the pantheon, but that's all it was to me when I was that young, just a big pantheon with too many names. Prayer always felt wrong. Maybe because my heart wasn't in it, I don't know. And after Miquo fell, well…"

The names of nations passed through her mind like a parade, each with its own successes and failures.

"Sometimes, instead of being faithless, I wish I was like Mari," she said. "Each and every god she's whispered, she loves. And I want to feel the way she does, but I can't. After watching so many gods die, I cannot hold faith in any of them. And when the populace's faith wanes, I watch what it does to her. The pain of the fading, of it leaving her, it's deep and cruel and I never want to feel that way myself."

Cyrus frowned, worry creeping at his features.

"So Endarius's blessing might leave Mari?"

"If the people's faith in the Lion becomes too weak, yes. Faith and prayer, it lingers about Thanet like a mist. It cannot gather in Endarius's physical form anymore, for it has been broken, and so Endarius channels that faith into Mari. That's why she can become the Lioness, just as she became the Falcon Reaper of Lahareed. But it can run dry. The god or goddess fades. Not forgotten, but no longer trusted. The people lack belief. They lack confidence. They know only despair."

It was terrible, every time. The way Mari shivered in her room, her face pale, her eyes bloodshot, and her body covered in cold sweat. Stasia had once been shown a room of men and women suffering through poppy tears' withdrawal after the Everlorn Empire cut off the city's supply as punishment. The resemblance between them and Mari's incidents was uncanny. Caretakers did their best to alleviate the symptoms, but little worked beyond time and rest. Some recovered. Some died.

So far, Mari had not died.

So far.

"What about you?" she asked. "You keep prying into my past, but what of yours? Did you ever worship Lycaena or Endarius?"

Cyrus shrugged. He picked at the cloth of his trousers as he casually swung his legs back and forth over the drop off the tower.

"Depends on whose definition of worship we use. I didn't love them. I prayed to them when I was told, and when I did, it was rote recitation. I...I just expected them to always be there. To protect me, should I need protection."

Stasia stood, and she ruffled Cyrus's hair. He'd grown it out while living on the streets. It looked good on him, not that she'd tell him that. He was becoming a god. The last thing he needed was more compliments.

"Then maybe that's the god you'll become. Someone who will always be there, to protect those who need protecting. There are worse gods across Gadir, and ones far more selfish with their blessings."

She winked at him.

"I wouldn't love you, and I sure as shit wouldn't worship you, but I'd be fine with calling you a friend, maybe even my little brother. How does that sound?"

Her father's betrayal seemed a million miles away when Cyrus smiled up at her.

"I think it sounds better than I deserve," he said. "And everything I could ever possibly want."

CHAPTER 24

RAYAN

Rayan hesitated outside Mari's room. She'd been visibly upset during the meeting, but he feared waiting any longer. Waiting would allow the doubt rotting his insides to fester further. He knocked twice, then cleared his throat.

"Mari?" he asked. "It's me."

He heard footsteps on the other side, then the door opened. Mari's eyes were red, her face flushed. There was no hiding her residual anger.

"If you're here to cheer me up, I assure you I'm fine," she said, and she certainly sounded fine. A well-played act, one he might have believed if not for the evidence before him.

"I appreciate your kind assumptions as to my motivations," Rayan said. "But I am here to ask for help only you may provide as a god-whisperer."

The change came over her instantly. All emotion drained from her face. Her spine straightened. Her eyes sparkled with the faintest crimson light.

"Come in," she said, and stepped aside.

Mari's room was small and tidy. He spotted a stack of three tomes atop her bedside table, their leather covers highlighted with golden images of the winged Lion. They were outlawed texts detailing Endarius's beliefs. Even with the Lion dwelling within her, she sought to understand him better. Rayan approached it, and he brushed his fingertips over the gold.

You overthrew my family, he thought. *Should I hate you, Endarius? Condemn your believers, and cast them out as we did to Dagon's? What vengeance might I deliver that would not have me mirror your own crimes?*

"I suspect I know who you wish for me to whisper," Mari said, drawing him from his thoughts. "But I would hear you speak it nonetheless."

Rayan fought back a fresh wave of shame. He had never asked Mari to allow Lycaena to speak through her. Even when doubt clawed at him, he held firm. It felt like a betrayal of everything he represented to need that reassurance. Who was he to tell the people of Thanet to believe, if he himself harbored doubts strong enough to need confirmation from a foreigner? Yet this could not wait. Keles's haunting stare would not leave him.

When Rayan first met Mari, she had explained to him Lycaena's precarious condition. They'd gathered in the woods to the south of the city, safe from eavesdroppers, and begun planning their attempts to rescue the faith of the city in the two gods, Endarius and Lycaena.

Think of faith as water, and your goddess as a giant bucket, she'd begun. At Rayan's raised eyebrow, she'd laughed and wagged her finger at him. *Metaphor, Rayan, it is only a metaphor; don't start accusing me of blasphemy. But when Lycaena was slain, that bucket was smashed. The faith in her, though, remains. Even when dried beneath the sun, the water rises to the sky, to return once more as rain. Our hope is to prevent Thanet from becoming a desert.*

But can she return? he'd asked.

Gods and goddesses are defined by their faith. The people of Thanet saw her slain. It will take great faith, and many years, for them to deny their own eyes and ears and believe her returned. Even Lycaena herself felt the sting of death as her throat was cut. Some gods can overcome the memory. Most do not.

A shiver ran through him at the memory.

And what happens to those who falter?

Mari had answered with practiced gentleness, for she had delivered these dire predictions countless times, and it still hurt to hear.

Slain gods are ever pulled toward the afterlives they are to shepherd. It is a powerful call, one few resist. They pass on to the unknown, to be with their faithful believers. Their power here, in the living world, fades away.

The idea of losing Lycaena forever, of her being separate from the physical world, her prayers without power, her paladins and priests without magic, had horrified Rayan, and he was hardly the only one to feel it. Eshiel had shared that horror, and so Eshiel resorted to the oldest and most powerful form of faith. He had drawn the dagger and spilled blood upon an altar. Had he succeeded in re-creating the physical, as Keles believed? Or had he created a monster?

"The Lycaena summoned by Eshiel," he explained to Mari. "The goddess I declared false and helped murder. I must know if it was truly her. I must hear from her lips if I betrayed her."

Mari put her hand on his shoulder.

"And what if it was?" she asked. "Would you have still let her live in such a form? Would you have abided the sacrifices and bloodletting in her name?"

Rayan patted her slender fingers.

"I cannot change the acts of the past, but if I learn, if I understand, I can let them guide my future steps. If you would grant me this gift, Mari, I will not crumble before any truth revealed."

"Very well. Sit with me. My room will suffice for this."

Rayan sat across from her on the crimson carpet. She smoothed out her dress, her attention low and away from him.

"This will not be like with Endarius," she explained. "There is room within me for only one deity. Instead, the Lion shall shift aside for a time and allow the Butterfly to grant me her voice. Know that whatever you say and do, she shall hear and know. Attempt no deception. It is dangerous to lie to a god. If you doubt your own conviction, admit it plain."

"I understand. Is there anything you need of me?"

Mari shook her head. Her hands crossed before her, and her eyes closed.

"I have lived here for many years," she said, her voice dropping to a whisper. "I have walked among her believers, and they are strong still, Rayan, so very strong. I know her prayers. I have seen her wings. But if you would help, then pray to her in your heart. Call out to her, and trust that she shall answer."

Pray to her, Mari said, as if it were so easy. Rayan's throat tightened. He had given no prayers to his goddess since the battle upon the cliff.

He had feared the silence. He had feared an answer. Shame for that cowardice pushed him here, to Mari, to settle the matter once and for all.

Rayan closed his eyes and bowed his head. He kept his prayer short
and honest, a chant he might repeat when Mari began her whispering.

"Be with me, my goddess. Let me walk in your light."

His prayer looped in the silence, and with each repetition he felt his
nerves ease. Mari knelt lower, her face hidden behind cascading waves of
her long hair. Her fingers slipped to the carpet, and they dug into the fabric.

"Lycaena, hear my prayer," she whispered. "Hear it, goddess of
Thanet, and answer. I would speak, if you are willing."

Rayan felt it immediately. The air warmed. His skin prickled as if
brushed with a chill wind. A rushing sound, like gusting wind, filled his
ears despite the stillness of the room. He dared open his eyes, and was
shocked to see Mari staring at him. Her eyes…they were not human.

They were fire.

"You are afraid," she said. "Why are you afraid?"

Before the empire's boats came with their paragons and priests,
Lycaena had lived among them, taking to the skies so the sun might
shine upon her incomparable beauty. Rayan had spoken with her,
learned from her, and felt her hands lovingly touch his face when he
had been anointed a paladin. That ended three years ago. Three years of
silence, and now he heard her addressing him once more. Never could
he have guessed it would strike him so deeply, that mixture of loss and
ache in hearing her familiar voice.

Do not lie to a goddess, Mari had insisted, and so Rayan confessed
the shameful truth.

"Because I fear what you will tell me," he said. "And I fear what you
have become."

Mari leaned closer. That fire, it swirled with light, as if her irises were
a rainbow.

"You speak of Eshiel's creation."

Rayan remembered bracing himself to receive the blow from that savage deity. Her burning blade had crashed down upon his sword, yet he had
held strong. If he could endure that, then he could endure this. He must.

"Was it you?" he asked. "The being that tried to strike me down with her flame. The monster that Cyrus slew. Tell me, Lycaena, please, tell me. Was it you?"

Mari closed her eyes and tilted her head back as if in thought. When she spoke, her hair fluttered in a nonexistent wind.

"It was and it was not. If I am a flame, what Eshiel summoned was my shadow. I felt her, when she was born. I felt her like a piece of me was ripped from my chest, or a limb torn from my body. My rage. My sorrow. My desperation."

Rayan's brittle composure snapped, and tears began to flow.

"So it wasn't you?" he asked. "You were not the one who lifted her sword against me?"

There was no hiding the pain that crossed Mari's face.

"To absolve myself would be cowardice. Eshiel loved me true, and though I ached with the taking, I saw through reborn eyes and walked with flesh made real. His sacrifices stirred the worst in me, and I allowed them to be made manifest, so great was my desire to return to you. Yet I am...grateful for what you and the Vagrant did. In all my years, I never called for blood sacrifice, and you have witnessed why."

"I don't understand," Rayan said. "If our prayers, our sacrifices, can change you, or draw out different parts of you...then is my faith not built upon shifting sands? When I pray to you, my goddess, who exactly do I pray to, if you may change?"

Mari's hand brushed his face, the loving act made surreal by the heat coming off her fingertips.

"I am what I am, paladin. I will not question the faith that made me, nor the truth of my love for my children."

Rayan clenched his jaw. Something else gnawed at him, and he realized he'd been afraid to even give it voice. Yet here she was before him, promising him love. Calling him her child.

He had to know.

He had to, no matter the pain.

"Why?" he asked. He met the gaze of those fiery orbs. "My family. The Orani. Why did you never tell me?"

Mari leaned back as if she had been stabbed in the chest. Her gaze shifted, unable to meet his eye.

"What was there to gain in the telling, but to cause you harm?" Rayan shook his head.

"For good or ill, I now carry that knowledge, yet it was given by the tongue of an imperial paragon. I would hear it from you, my goddess. The full truth of it, regardless of what *harm* that truth may inflict."

The heat he had felt on his skin turned to ice. Lycaena had proudly told him the truth of her part in Eshiel's creation, but this, this is what caused her to withdraw? When she next spoke, her voice was soft and distant.

"When Endarius arrived on Thanet, he demanded we treat him as an equal. Dagon, in his pride, refused to grant him any land, or any power. War followed, dreadful and terrible. I desired peace but knew not how to achieve it. Instead of lifting my hand against my fellow deities, I blamed Dagon for his stubbornness. If he wished for war, then let him and his followers wage war. And so they did, as I watched."

Anger burned bright enough in Rayan's chest to char away any other emotion.

"My family was overthrown, and all you did was *watch*?"

Mari rose up, her hands clenched into fists as she loomed before Rayan. The fire in her eyes surged.

"Would you hate me now, Rayan Vayisa? Would you condemn me for decisions I myself have regretted for four centuries? From the moment you were born I have cherished you, heard your prayers, and given you my blessing. I am eternal, and so is my guilt, and my shame. No passage of years shall excise either, but if you must, then toss further coals upon my head, tear at my wings, and scream at me your anger. For your sake, I will endure."

Rayan looked to his shaking hands. He remembered her touch at his graduation from the Heaven's Wing. He remembered the moths swirling from Alliya's corpse. He remembered the rage of Eshiel's goddess calling him a blind fool. It was too much. His faith in her had guided his steps since the moment he was a child. He was too old to cast aside that trust now. No matter the past, he loved Lycaena. The shape of it changed, but he could not deny its presence.

"No," he said. "I will not hate you, for you have never demanded that hate of me. Speak your piece, my goddess. I will listen."

Mari paused for a long moment, and he wished he could read meaning in the hesitation.

"Dagon was cast down, defeated at the shores of Gallos Bay," she said when continuing. "The survivors of your family who did not die in battle were captured, and Endarius declared them deserving death. Their execution was to mark the end of the War of Tides and the anointing of the Lythan family. And I stepped in at last. I begged for your family's survival, for the war was done. Enough blood was shed. Let them be free."

She shook her head.

"But the Lion..."

Mari's head whipped forward hard enough Rayan feared for her spine. She collapsed onto her hands and knees. Sweat poured off her face and neck as she shivered. Her pale skin turned blotchy and red.

"Mari?" Rayan asked. "Mari, are you all right?"

The room darkened, and the scent of grass reached his nose. The floor shook as if from the steps of a great weight. Dread swelled in Rayan's breast, made worse when a new voice thundered out from Mari's lips.

"Come you now to condemn me?" seethed the Lion. "And you, foreign whisperer, would you betray He whom you sought power and blessing from to wage your war?"

"You were not invited," Mari said, her own voice breaking through.

"You sought my rage, and my vengeance, and now you have it, Miquoan."

Rayan had never worshiped Endarius, though neither had he thought ill of the majestic god. He and Lycaena were twin pillars of Thanet, eternal wisdom and guidance for the island's children. Seeing his ire directed at Mari infuriated him, for yes, Rayan would now condemn the Lion for his actions.

"You overthrew my family's kingdom," he said, stealing back Endarius's attention. "You arrived with soldiers and paladins with eyes upon our throne, no different than Everlorn."

Mari snarled, and for the briefest moment, Rayan saw a ghostly image of feathered wings rise from her back.

"What do you demand of me, Paladin? Shame? Regret? I give you nothing. Dagon was a mighty foe, but he was beaten. To let his royalty linger was a danger. To let his priests preach his wisdom, akin to allowing vines to spread and choke the garden we wished to build. I did what was best for my faithful, as I have always done."

Mari glared down at Rayan, her eyes no longer fire, but instead shimmering rainbows with dark, feline irises.

"*Mercy*, pleaded Lycaena, and so I gave it. You would serve those whom you thought to rule over. As the years passed, and we ground the memory of your reign to dust, again the Butterfly comes to me. *Mercy*, she pleads again, and so I unshackled your family. Where you might have known death, you knew honor and privilege. Condemn me, man of the Orani bloodline, but know your words are hollow, for your sires should have known only the grave, and you, been born not at all."

Wind billowed, and again sounded a distant roar. Mari's skin was rippling and paling. Her fingers were turning into claws. Rayan faced it and spoke what once was blasphemy, but he knew now was more than truth.

"You are a savage Lion," he said. "And no better than the beast with whom you share a namesake."

Mari's trembling heightened in intensity. She bared her teeth, and they were sharp and feline. Her fists pounded the floor. When she next spoke, it was her voice, and no other's.

"God and goddess of this island, you two may be, but I am master of my own flesh," she declared. "And I say *enough*!"

The world surrendered to her cry. A shock wave rolled out from her, like a rippling shift in reality itself. The fire left her eyes. The scent of grass vanished. All was quiet. The heat and the wind, they faded away to a simple, tidy room. In their absence, Rayan felt tired and hollow. He had no energy left for rage against the Lion, nor the heart for sorrow at the truths hidden by the Butterfly.

"Mari?" he asked, reaching out for her. She trembled still, but it was slower, and she no longer was hunched over as if in pain.

"I'm fine," she said, brushing aside his concern. She gave him a faint smile. "It happens. Sometimes one must put a god in their place. But what of you? Have you the answers you sought when you came to me?"

Rayan slumped back to his knees.

"I do not know," he answered truthfully. "Forever I have looked to Lycaena for guidance, but my goddess seems as lost and heartbroken as I have been since her sacrifice. And now our twin protectors...they bicker. They disagree. And for them to have lied, and deceived?" He shook his head. "Miquo may see gods as fallible, but not here. That was never our teaching. Perhaps that is why their deaths have broken us so completely."

Mari cupped his face in her hands. Despite everything, there was no hint of doubt or confusion to her actions. Her strength put his to shame. Though he might be a paladin, the wisdom Mari had gathered through her lifetime as a god-whisperer humbled him.

"We may be children, but they are *our* gods," she said. "The manifestations of *our* faith. It gives us power, if we are strong enough to endure it. The love Lycaena represents, it is real, Rayan. It is real, and needed, and I pray you never lose it. The world is made uglier with the breaking of every divine miracle. Let us cling to wonder, and plead for beauty. That hope is eternal, just like they are. Hold faith with me, paladin. Hold faith, and one day, I promise you, Thanet shall see Lycaena's wings fly her skies once more."

Rayan smiled, and he took her hands in his. Foolishness had kept him fearful of her talents. Even those who must stand strong needed their moments of vulnerability. If only he had learned this sooner instead of succumbing to his pride. If only he could teach it to the young like Cyrus and Keles, who themselves teetered at the edge of an abyss.

"Is that beautiful future still within our grasp?" he asked. He stood and lifted her with him. "Then let me live and die for that beauty, if it will ease the ache of others. I will walk that path, and I will not walk it alone."

CHAPTER 25

SINSHEI

As far as prisons went, Sinshei made sure Keles lived in a comfortable one. The windowless room had been reserved for guests, and it had been easy enough to add outside latches to the door. The bed was padded, the room stocked with candles and flint, and there was even a half-filled bookshelf. Sinshei had browsed the titles beforehand and removed any that might contain complimentary accounts of the Lythan family line.

"Has she made any attempt to escape?" Sinshei asked the two guards stationed at the door. It had been four days since Soma returned with her in tow, and only two since she confirmed Keles's identity through research.

"No, Anointed One. A model prisoner."

Sinshei's orders to her guards had been clear. No beatings, no untoward comments, not even a finger to be lifted against Keles unless she tried to escape. Once Soma had told her who Keles was, who she *truly* was, Sinshei knew that every single aspect of this plan must be perfect. Keles's hatred of the empire would be enormous and justified. But perhaps, just perhaps, there might be someone else she hated more.

"Open it, and then leave us be. I will have no one listening in."

The soldiers removed the latches, then bowed low. Sinshei entered. The door softly shut behind her. A prayer was on her lips, the power of her divine father at her fingertips just in case Keles did something fool-ish. Thankfully the young woman remained atop the bed, her knees curled to her chest. She glared at Sinshei and did not hide it. Her clothes were plain and white, given to her the day she arrived in Vallessau. The blood of the false Lycaena had been on her old outfit, and Sinshei ordered it immediately burned. As for her armor, it had been stashed in one of the castle's many vaults.

"Hello, Keles," Sinshei said. She glanced around for something to sit upon, found nothing. Though the room was well furnished, it was small, and she stood in its middle not far from the bed. A plate of food lay half-eaten nearby. If Keles had read any of the curated books, none lay about.

"If you're here to preach the love and glory of the God-Incarnate, leave now," Keles said. "It would be a waste of both our time."

"I am not here to preach. I am here to tell a story."

Keles closed her eyes and leaned her head against the wall.

"So it's worse. Parables meant for children. Lycaena save me."

"From what I heard, it was you who needed saving from Lycaena."

That earned her another glare. Sinshei kept her face perfectly pas-sive, though she was smiling on the inside. There. That was the fire she remembered. They had met only once before, Sinshei visiting an imprisoned Keles to offer her redemption at the forsaking ceremony. She had pretended Keles was no different from any other prisoner, but in truth, she had reveled in the accomplishment when the young woman knelt before a crowd and professed her faith in the God-Incarnate.

"What did the people call you during your doomed war?" Sinshei asked, feigning ignorance. "The Jewel of Vallessau?"

"The Light," Keles corrected.

"Yes, of course, the Light of Vallessau. It was a touching moment, watching you repent of your faith in your slain, heretical deity at the ceremony. I must admit, I am disappointed to hear you sought out a replacement. Did you not learn what happens when people indulge their selfish desires instead of accepting the wisdom of Eldrid?"

"I thought you said you weren't here to preach?"

The young woman's tongue was as sharp as the sword she once

wielded. Sinshei liked Keles, she truly did. It wouldn't stop her from breaking the woman, but it would make the final rebuilding, and the victory of a fully redeemed soul, that much more rewarding.

"You are correct, Miss Lyon. So let me tell you a story of a small, relatively insignificant nation known as Mirli. This nation was isolated in the northwestern corner of Gadir, cold and wet and heavily reliant on its fleet of fishing boats. Their people watched the Everlorn Empire's growth with dread. They feared the day we would arrive at their borders, to the point it was all they obsessed over."

"You speak as if their fears were unfounded," Keles interrupted.

"Would you argue, or would you hear my story? I thought you uninterested in any verbal sparring."

Keles slumped further against the wall and looked away, which was answer enough.

"The ruling family of Mirli swore to their people that they would defend the mountain pass leading into their country, but it would require great sacrifice. Every last spare coin was taxed from the populace. Their army swelled in number, mostly made up of volunteers, though with such social pressures applied to young men and women in poverty, one can certainly cast doubt over such 'voluntary' recruitment. And then, with all the wealth and military power collected into the hands of the ruling elite . . . they sailed away."

Keles wasn't looking at her, but Sinshei could tell she had the young woman's attention. How much did she know? How much did she guess? If only she could have gotten to her before she had become the Light of Vallessau. There was so much mental blight to be undone.

Sinshei let the silence linger. It fell heavy over the pair in the small room. It wasn't awkward to Sinshei, but it would be to her prisoner. Curiosity, solitude, confusion, fear, forbidden knowledge . . . it was all so much to tempt a bright mind. Too much. She need not challenge Keles's beliefs. She need only offer wisdom. She need only tell a story.

"What does this have to do with me?" Keles finally asked. It was her way of asking for more without admitting it. Perhaps she didn't even believe it herself, but Sinshei knew. Her eyes widened slightly, the only hint she would give of the smile she sealed away.

"Because the Mirli royal family sailed across the Crystal Sea, far, far away, to a little island they'd established trade with decades prior. They came to port in a place so distant from Gadir they thought they would be safe from our empire's reach. And so the royal Lythan family came to Thanet. They came with ships, and soldiers, and a lie of peace. These people, these cowards who left Mirli stripped of wealth, food, and an entire generation of healthy young men, came to Thanet as conquerors. And they brought their god with them."

Keles shifted atop the bed. All her efforts were focused on avoiding eye contact with Sinshei. More lingering silence. Let the thoughts fester, the doubts grow.

"Have you nothing to say?" Sinshei asked after a time.

"Why should I? All you offer are lies."

"They are not lies, Keles. Lies are smooth and seductive, meant to cover and hide that which must be hidden. I speak the truth, for it tears open that which hurts most. Endarius the Lion came to Thanet, and our spies followed. We watched as Dagon and Lycaena attempted to coexist peacefully with him, yet they also refused to have this foreign deity treated as an equal in both faith and politics. So began the inevitable war, Dagon and Endarius each seeking to anoint their chosen family upon the throne while Lycaena, timid peacemaker that she was, remained neutral. This was the War of Tides, as you branded it in your poems and histories. Only then did God-Incarnate Lucavi order the complete blockade of all Thanese trade. We would not have your bickering gods inflict their strife upon Gadir."

"You speak as if Dagon were a deity no different than Lycaena," Keles said. "That isn't possible. He is a trickster, a deviant, the foul demon banished to the Heldeep."

There was no lie in the compassion Sinshei conveyed when she spoke.

"The Lion god emerged victorious, while Dagon was burned and his ashes scattered to the sea. There was no foul trickster. There is no Heldeep. There are only the lies you have been told by Endarius's priests to erase the memory of Thanet's proper god and establish the new divine rule. Dagon's chosen ruling family was deposed so one properly subservient to Endarius might be put in their place."

This was it, the most vital truth. Sinshei had spent the previous day scouring through years and years of castle records. The stewards had only meant to track the hiring, removal, and death of servants, but in doing so, they conveyed far more information than intended. It had given Sinshei confirmation of what Soma suspected. She drew herself to her full height and added the proper venom to her condemnations.

"The Mirli were cowards, and their rulers cruel," she said. "The Lythan family did not execute the previous royalty. How could they, when they claimed their war was about the divine battle between gods, and not an excuse to steal the throne? Which meant other solutions, other humiliations for Dagon's chosen, the Orani."

The way Keles flinched as if stabbed showed she recognized that name, for it had been her great-grandmother's. But Sinshei was not done stabbing. She twisted the knife.

"The few surviving Orani were forced into servitude for the Lythan family line. Slavery, we might have called it on Gadir, but here it was dressed up with flowery words. Repentance. Forced humility. Imprisonment in the name of peace. As hundreds of years passed, it was warped and twisted into something else. Honor. Duty. Family pride. As for the Orani family's faith? Lycaena may have betrayed Dagon through inaction, but at least she was still true to Thanet, and so it pivoted from the Serpent to the Butterfly."

Keles was trying to ignore her. Her eyes were closed, and no doubt a terrible maelstrom swirled within her mind. Perhaps she had already reached the conclusion Sinshei built toward, perhaps not, but it would be spoken aloud either way.

"Thanet grants power through royal bloodlines, correct? Then if not for the Lythan family's usurpation of the throne, the Orani family would have continued to reign. In the eyes of some Thanese, they should still reign, even after all these hundreds of years. Don't you understand, Keles? You and yours were never meant to be servants. You were not chosen as bodyguards and spiritual guides. You were meant to rule. You were meant to be Queen Ke—"

"Get out," Keles snapped. Her entire body shook like the rattle at the tail of a snake. "I will hear no more."

Keles was in terrible pain, and desperate to deny the truths Sinshei heaped upon her like burning coals. Right now, doubt would be her only weapon. If Keles could convince herself that Sinshei lied, then she might salvage some sort of faith in her island's god and goddess. Sinshei directly attacked that doubt. Her final message would be of confidence. No doubt would be allowed, not here, not in a land ruled by the Everlorn Empire.

"There are vaults below the castle that only the royal family are meant to access," she said. "There are libraries in the Twin Sanctuary with scrolls only the most loyal to Endarius and Lycaena are allowed to read. I have scoured them. Thanet's history is a sad but predictable little story. I can give you the proof you need, if you require it, but I don't think you do. I see it in your eyes."

There would be no more conversation. Keles had withdrawn into herself as if wounded upon a battlefield. *Let her bleed*, Sinshei thought. When the Anointed One returned, she would find a paler, weaker version of the Light of Vallessau. One who might be more open to hearing Sinshei's wisdom.

Sinshei exited the room to find Soma waiting for her in the hallway just outside. She arched an eyebrow as she shut the door.

"I pray you were not eavesdropping?" she said.

"Given that I brought Keles to you, is it not fair I know how her conversion progresses?"

An instinctive reprimand almost escaped her lips, but Sinshei held it back. She must always walk a fine line with Soma. He was vital to her plans—far more so than any other paragon—but he also was subservient, and must remember his place.

"If you sought that knowledge, then simply ask," she said. "Sneakiness and deceit are not your strongest talents, Soma. Directness is, and I would have allowed it. Instead I am displeased, and my trust in you lessened."

The paragon spread his hands to either side and dipped his head in contrition.

"My curiosity got the best of me, Anointed One, and so I apologize. I pray you do not remain angry with me for long, and if it soothes your anger, know that the door clouded much of the conversation. Do you believe the young Orani girl open to your temptations?"

"I do not offer temptations," Sinshei snapped. "I offer her the truth."

"The truth will always seem a temptation to those who have lived a lie."

"Are you a philosopher now?"

He laughed.

"Not everything involves stabbing people with the sharpened point of my spear, Anointed One. If you believe me so simple, then I must admit I am offended. You also did not answer my question. How closed is the girl's heart?"

Sinshei crossed her arms behind her back, her fingers softly stroking the tight braids of her hair, which hung down to her ankles. It was a habit she'd tried and failed to break since becoming an Anointed.

"She's confused and wounded. Her faith has been greatly damaged by the false goddess the cult master Eshiel summoned, as well as that monster's subsequent defeat. Yes, Soma, she is open, but I must first give her time. I have lit a fire of doubt within her, and now it must spread and burn. Until then..."

She withdrew a rolled scroll tied shut with a bit of string from her dress pocket. Soma accepted it with a slight tilt of his head.

"Retrieve Keles's armor from the vault and bring both it and these instructions to one of our smiths."

"Instructions? Have you a plan in mind?"

"I do, and you will be a part of it. Answer me truthfully. If I gave you all my available resources, could you locate devoted followers of the slain Thanese god, Dagon? I doubt they will be plentiful, but surely a few still linger about the island."

Soma crossed his arms. His blue eyes dug into her, searching for answers she refused to surrender.

"I could, though that begs the question, *why* you would have me do so?"

"You need not know, paragon, but if you are so deeply curious, read my instructions before you deliver them to the smith. I suspect you are clever enough to ascertain their purpose."

The paragon removed his spear from his back, twirled it twice, and then bowed low.

"I am ever at your service," he said. He smiled just before leaving, and whether it was pleasure, or mockery, she did not know. A little flame of worry kindled in her stomach.

Soma's confidence stretched far into arrogance, and there was a smugness to him that implied he understood more than anyone else. She knew his ambitions. She knew the promises she had offered. As God-Incarnate, she would need a husband, and multiple heirs. He could provide both, and in return for his loyalty, he would live amid untold riches and power. Yet despite those temptations, everything he did on Thanet seemed to be for his own amusement, and nothing more.

Sinshei pinched her lip.

Soma Ordiae was useful, but it might be time to consider a way to succeed without him.

CHAPTER 26

ESHIEL

P urpose?" the guard asked. Eshiel glared at the man. His accent was thick, his hair a fiery red uncommon to the island. He clutched his census book as if it were a magical tome granting him unlimited power. To those outside the walls of Vallessau, it might even be true.

"Retribution," he said, assuming the Gadir man would not recognize the Thanese word. He tried stepping past and through the towering gate that was the only entrance through the western wall sealing in the city. There were dozens of men and women traveling with Eshiel, a collection of traders, survivors, homeless, hungry, and desperate. All were checked for contraband. With the implementation of the Joining Laws, that meant any tracts or religious symbols showing reverence for anyone or anything beyond the God-Incarnate and his Uplifted Church.

The soldier barred Eshiel's way, and his free hand drifted to his sword hilt in a clear message.

"I asked purpose." He pointed to Eshiel's face. "Forever paint. Reason?"

Eshiel swallowed down bile. He had bartered his fine red robes for simple brown trousers and a loose gray shirt. As for his tattoos, he'd smeared dirt and mud across his face the day before so it'd be dry and cracked by the time he arrived. It seemed that would not be enough.

"Visiting friends," Eshiel said. "They live here along the coast."

He came with few belongings, quickly searched. Just let him through, damn it...

The soldier scratched at his red beard.

"Face paint. Butterfly. I asking reason. Answer."

Eshiel couldn't decide if it would be better or worse if the gate guard had one of those word-laces the church granted its higher-ranking members. It was hard to charm a man who barely understood your words, but on the other hand, it was easier to lie to one.

"The tattoos?" he asked, stalling. Those near him were starting to stare. More worrisome were the other guards helping with the checks. They were glancing Eshiel's way, and one of them might be more knowledgeable about Lycaena's priests.

"Yes. Explain."

It galled Eshiel, but he saw no other way. He bowed low and clasped his hands in prayer, his palms flat and fingers up, exactly as they were shown upon Everlorn's flag.

"Penance," he said, shortening his own sentences. "I come to church for penance."

The guard was not yet convinced.

"And face?"

"Forever paint. I've come to ask the church to remove it."

Though he still seemed wary, the guard shrugged and gestured for Eshiel to enter. Eshiel brought few belongings and a handful of coins. What trouble could he possibly make?

"Visit church quick. Your face? It bad." He gave a sick smile. "Could make you a flag."

Eshiel's insides coiled.

"Understood."

The first things he encountered on the streets of Vallessau were the beggars. They lined the initial street, some loud, most not. Cups and bowls lay before them, the majority bare. Eshiel dipped his hand into his pocket, gathering what currency he had and then dropping a single coin, regardless of value, into each bowl he passed.

While most smiled or thanked him with dull, defeated voices, an elderly man with milky eyes reached for Eshiel's wrist.

"'Grant me wings, O goddess, to lift my eyes heavenward,'" he quoted. "'Decorate not my grave, for I behold a sky of beauty.'"

Eshiel's throat tightened. It was the quote that had inspired the butterfly wings tattooed across his face and head.

"'It is there, not here, I fly,'" Eshiel said, finishing the quote.

The old man released his hands and settled back into his chosen spot along the gate entrance road. He said nothing else, and when Eshiel reached into his pocket to hunt for more coin, the man retracted his bowl. Eshiel stood there, confused and uncertain.

What led you here? he wondered. The man's clothes were hopelessly dirty. They might have been expensive once, or they might have never been more than hastily stitched rags. What family did this man love and lose across the decades? That quote, that funeral prayer, for whom had he prayed it? His parents? His spouse? His children? Before him was a story, long and unique, that Eshiel would never hear. He would not learn what losses this man suffered, what humiliations afflicted him, so that he must join a hundred others lining the streets of a conquered city.

Eshiel carried on, and his heart ached. He offered a prayer to Lycaena, hating the damnable whispers of doubt that insisted she would not hear, and would not act.

Be with him, he prayed. *Grant him comfort, goddess, please. Grant him the peace I could never give.*

Eshiel walked without purpose or destination. Vallessau had never been his home during his time as a priest. His temple had been in North Cape, and there he had lived a quiet life, administering prayers over the sick and wounded with the power granted to him by his goddess. Those healing days were long past. What prayers he offered now brought fire instead.

Yet both the Vagrant and the Heir-Incarnate lived in Vallessau, and so Eshiel traveled here despite Soma's warning. "Retribution," he had told the gate guard, and it had been no lie. Thanet had suffered much, and yet the empire was not finished. If more could be taken, it would be taken, even the very names of the god and goddess who birthed the land and guided their chosen people through the eras.

"The hour is nigh!" cried an Uplifted priest. He stood on the corner, his hands raised to the heavens and sweat dripping down his brow. A handful of people gathered to listen, while the rest averted their eyes as they passed. "You were children raised in ignorance, and for that, your sins may be forgiven. But you walk in ignorance no longer! The word of Everlorn has reached your shores. You know the truth of the God-Incarnate, the one, the first, the last. Yet still you cling to your sins! Still you cling to the old ways that would lead you astray!"

Eshiel had heard countless variations of this from the priests who jailed him and cut his skin with their knives. There was a special kind of joy that lit their eyes each and every time. To speak love and salvation while inflicting misery fed their souls in a wretched way, and they loved the feast. Eshiel had preached to his congregation that pride and vanity were twin serpents with teeth so fine you would not feel the bite. Before he had been captured, he had thought the priests of the Uplifted Church were decent men deeply poisoned by such serpents. His time in the prison had corrected that belief. Instead they were the worst of humanity, indulged to the point of rot.

Pleasure, in inflicting pain on those who were different, inferior, sinful, and wrong.

Pleasure, in loving someone believed unworthy of that love.

Word and knife, prayer and punishment, elevating the giver and justifying the taking. Blood spilled to ensure a salvation demanded only when the boats arrived carrying the clasped red hands. The deepest hate, claimed to be the purest love. The priests loudly boasted their life of sacrifice even as they walked cloaked in privilege and with hearts bloated from unending indulgence.

We do what we must to save you from yourself, they had whispered as they cut what would become a new line of scars. *You suffer only from your ignorance, Eshiel Dymling. You suffer from your pride, from your stubbornness. Bend the knee and pray, that is all we ask. Offer your heart, and ask for salvation from our mighty God-Incarnate. And if you refuse, well...what are we to do with a thing so in love with its own sin it would refuse salvation?*

Eshiel Dymling, they called him. Never twice-born. They would not acknowledge that of him, nor the gift given by his goddess. No, in his darkest moments, when the dripping blood was thick and his cell reeked of shit and piss, they would whisper fears he had never once considered before the Uplifted came with their Joining Laws.

What you are is wrong.

"Do you not see the beauty in our God's promise?" the Uplifted priest continued. Eshiel put his back to him and walked away. The words followed, haunting. "We ask nothing. No animal sacrifice. No cost. No tithe. Your heart alone, you must offer, denying none and accepting all. Turn from your sins, repent, and be made whole."

Denying none, they claimed, while denying any who dared live and breathe differently than their damn God-Incarnate. Eshiel bit his tongue and walked. Just walked. To argue would earn the priest's ire, and until he knew his own purpose in Vallessau, he could not justify such a risk.

Though Eshiel's eyes were trained to look for the religious, they were not the only startling sights to someone newly come to Vallessau after years of Everlorn's occupation. Not a single sign or street post was in Thanese. Many homes were empty, their shutters broken and their walls overrun with weeds. The beggars, though, they were far more numerous, as were scrawny children running wild, their fingers slipping into any unwatched pockets. Combined with the stone buildings' more blocky styles as compared to the more flowing style common in Ierida, it was enough to make Eshiel feel like he walked a foreign city...and not the capital of Thanet.

A soldier in dark imperial garb approached ahead, and Eshiel faced away, hoping not to be noticed. It was all instinctual, done without thought or hesitance, and realizing it made Eshiel's already poor mood worsen. An unwelcome question escaped his lips, spoken only to himself.

"What are you doing here, Eshiel?"

He couldn't shake the lingering belief he was a fool. A dreamer. A deluded, desperate man clinging to the hope that a past could endure. As if he had not witnessed the power of the empire with his own eyes. His beloved Lycaena, slain yet again. All those years of his life, working to save Thanet from a dismal future, had come crashing down in a single, horrendous night.

How could he try again? How could he spend the effort, expend the sweat, and spill the blood that another such miracle required? How did one maintain faith before such overwhelming defeat? To attend the Uplifted Church was required of all Thanese. To preach the word of Lycaena meant death. There would be no equality, no fairness to the battlefield. Even if it took a thousand years, the God-Incarnate would one day win, and those beautiful days when the Lion and the Butterfly flew the skies of Thanet would be a forgotten memory.

Or worse, a blasphemy to be vociferously condemned.

Walking without destination. Living without purpose. No, that wasn't him. That was not who Eshiel would ever be so long as his lungs drew breath. His eyes were downcast, his gaze to the filthy cobblestones somehow covered with a familiar stain. Blood. The words of the beggar man came to him, the reason for his wings, so he lifted his eyes to the blue sky.

And there he saw the flags.

It had been years since Eshiel witnessed the high poles and the bodies swinging from ropes tied about their necks. They'd stopped temporarily after Lycaena's death and the forsaking ceremony. They'd stopped, so the empire could tell the people things were better now. They could say the brutality and bloodshed were the fault of those who resisted, those who rebelled, the deserved punishment of those holding on to the past.

Then Magus of Eldrid had taken over in the wake of Regent Gold-leaf's execution, and he had unleashed his wrath upon the island. The stories had reached Eshiel in the north, carried on the lips of those who came to his village seeking safety and succor. But Eshiel had not seen them with his own eyes. Now he did. He looked on them, and he remembered his horror and rage on the first day they'd flown the Dead Flags.

Abuse marked their crimes. Those still worshiping Lycaena were stripped bare above the waist and a butterfly carved into their chests. The same went for the Lion, or the rare worshiper of Dagon. Outlawed lovers had their hands nailed together. Those who plotted rebellion had their own weapons shoved down their open throats. Each corpse, a message and a warning. Sin meant suffering. Supposedly these acts would be eternally inflicted upon the faithless by the Nameless Whore in the hell the God-Incarnate prepared. The church, ever eager, did its best to make that promise real even in life.

Eshiel glanced around. No soldiers. No one protecting the display. Had the people of Vallessau been so beaten into the ground that they would not dare touch the Dead Flags?

He walked amid the hanging bodies, his jaw clenched tightly shut to focus against the stench. He would not cover his face, nor would he look away. Let him bear witness to their supposed crimes. A young woman, her mouth open and her tongue pierced by a thin metal pin so it would not retract. She must have argued heresy to a priest. An older man with the flesh peeled off his left arm. Had there been a Lion tattoo there, one more heartfelt and beautiful than the outline the priests carved across his chest?

The twenty-five corpses swayed in the faint sea breeze. The wood groaned where the ropes were nailed to the tops of the poles. The sound of it scraped along Eshiel's mind. This couldn't continue. This couldn't be accepted. How could such gruesome displays not ignite riot and chaos each and every single night?

Eshiel had no knife. He had lost his silver one at the final ceremony, when he had accepted the title of thrice-born. So feeling a little mad, and so very broken, he climbed the nearest pole so he might reach the knot.

"Tear them down," he shouted at a man skirting wide around the display. "Help me tear them down!"

No one looked his way. No one acknowledged his screaming. He climbed higher, his legs hugging the wood. He had climbed the trees of Broadleaf Forest as a child, and this was disturbingly similar. Higher, higher, until he grabbed the knot that had been tied about the thick iron nail. Eshiel clawed at it, pulling at each part of the cord. Nothing, no give, no loosening. He tried anyway, even as his fingernails cracked and his skin scraped bloody on the rough fibers.

"What are you doing?" a single passerby asked. The older man glanced up and down the street, fearful. "You'll only join them."

Eshiel ignored him. If he couldn't untie the rope at the pole, perhaps he could undo it around the body's neck. He slid down a few feet, his thighs burning, and then reached out. By the time he managed to grab hold, a soldier finally noted his efforts.

"Down!" the soldier shouted at him as he came running, his spear in hand. "Down now!"

Eshiel couldn't resist even if he wanted. His pawing at the noose around the neck failed to accomplish anything, and his grip on the pole was too loose. He slipped, started to fall, and so he grabbed at the corpse. Clothing tore, and his frantic pawing did nothing to stop his fall.

The ground welcomed him with a hard blow to his feet. He immediately dropped to his knees, and he choked down a pained cry.

"Stay there!" ordered the lone soldier arriving at the Dead Flags. Eshiel knelt before him, his hands open and fingers curled. They were slick with the blood and gore of the hanging corpse above. His knees and shins smeared the waste that dripped and pooled from the twenty-five. The horror was too much to be made real. The smell was an aberration, the wetness, a lie.

"Are you mad?" the soldier asked. Eshiel looked up at him, and by the startled reaction, he finally noted the tattoos across his face and head. The soldier spat. "Heathen. You will fly next."

Eshiel grinned. He felt feverish and mad. Heat pooled in his fingertips.

"Fly?" he asked. "Where will I fly? To the heavens? To the sky? How will you kill me when I do?"

The soldier's spear flipped to point directly at Eshiel's throat. As for how much Thanese he understood, Eshiel could only guess, but he understood some.

"Kill you now," he said. "Body fly after."

Eshiel's hands clenched into fists. The heat grew. Despite the trembling in his limbs, he was not afraid. He cared not for the spear. It wasn't fear that shook his body. It was rage.

"No," he said, even as the spear plunged. "You will not."

The spear shattered against a shield of flame. It burned in the air before him, curling on either side, a pair of wings to give Lycaena's beloved priest protection. Eshiel slowly stood as the soldier's eyes widened with panic. He reached for a dagger clipped to his waist. Eshiel grabbed his throat before he could draw it.

"Do you feel it?" he asked. The tattoos on his body flared yellow upon his flesh. Like fire. Like hot irons. The soldier locked in place. His mouth opened and closed but he could not form words. He expelled only smoke. The fire was growing from within. "I bet you do. For the first time, you truly do. Deep down is where it starts. Before you ever see the fire, it has already burned for so very long."

At last crimson flame swirled around Eshiel's hand, the final mark of an execution. The soldier dropped from his grasp, smoke billowing out of his eyes, mouth, and nostrils. His clothing caught fire next.

"There is still belief here," Eshiel told the dying soldier. The crimson flame bathed his hand but did not burn. The same could not be said for the fire that wreathed the soldier like a cloak. "It runs deep in Vallessau. Twice dead, Lycaena may be, but I am thrice-born. The anger is here. The rage. The pain, helpless and furious in equal measure."

The man's screams stopped, for there were no lungs left to scream. Flesh peeled and charred. From within the smoke, he saw the first hint of a skull and teeth.

"Lycaena lives," he told the bones. "In me. In her faithful. She needs no body. She needs only us."

He turned his rage to the ropes holding the dead. A slash of his hand, and a blade of flame cut through them. Every last one of the twenty-five collapsed. They were swollen and mutilated flesh, empty of the beloved souls that once inhabited them, and so Eshiel cleansed away the hate that had been carved into them. He burned them to bone, the fire spreading, a deep crimson that flowed like a river. Not just the corpses now, but the stained blood that had gathered for years beneath them on the cobblestones.

Eshiel wept within the inferno. This...cauterization, it was necessary if Thanet were to heal. So long he'd fought and killed to bring Lycaena back, but why? Why did he need her before him? Why did he so selfishly crave her presence? So she would comfort him? So she would prove the world was unchanged and things could return to how they had always been? Or had he hoped she would fight the war she once lost, and save Thanet from its suffering?

No. Such victories would be had, but only by those willing to walk in her shadow. The frightened and the doubtful claimed Lycaena had failed Thanet and her people. Eshiel saw it true, in the twenty-five bodies hanging untouched by a people willing to turn a blind eye to the cruelty and suffering so long as it allowed them to live their own lives. *They* had failed Lycaena. Let them fail her no more.

The fire. The fury. It would be faith enough.

"There will be a time for beauty," Eshiel whispered in the ensuing silence. "There will be a time for remembrance and love. But it is not now."

Eshiel lifted his right arm to the heavens. He opened his hand, palm upward, and then curled his fingers as if grasping the sun, or offering an unseen gift. Taking and yet giving, both as a promise. Before him were the Dead Flags, now broken, their nooses emptied and their ropes cut. His tears fell without ceasing, and he let these new images define the final days of his life. The war that must be raged. The truth Lycaena's followers must embrace if they were to survive.

A burning hand, a severed rope, and the blue sky.

CHAPTER 27

ARN

I'm fine," Arn said, trying and failing to slam the mansion door shut behind him. Stasia wedged herself in the way with her shoulder. The others in the den looked up, baffled.

"You're clearly not gods-damned fine," she shouted back.

"What in the Heldeep is going on?" Cyrus asked. He had removed his mask and cloak, but his swords were still buckled to his hips, and Arn saw him reach for their hilts. The boy's distrust was a pinprick against Arn's already bruised pride, and he refused to meet anyone's eye. Shame burned his cheeks red. Stasia, meanwhile, would not hold back.

"This pig's ass," she said, jamming her finger his direction. "*Abandoned* me. Right in the middle of our attack."

"It was time to go," he said, a pitiful explanation.

"Our target was still alive!"

"I said it was a bad time. We were sniffed out. Now fuck off and leave me be."

Arn stomped to his room, shut the door, kicked it once for good measure, and then sat on the bed. He pulled his charm out from his pocket and held it to his lips. There was no scent left, but he could imagine it. A scent of the forest. Of leaves, and earth, and the bitter breath of a fox. It used to calm him. It didn't now.

A knock on the door stirred him from his meditation.

"Arn?" Mari asked from the other side. He debated, then shrugged unseen.

"It's unlocked," he grumbled.

Mari slipped inside. She had not accompanied their assassination attempt, instead running a merry chase around the city as the Lioness to distract the Humbled, Rihim. She'd been the first to arrive home, and she'd changed into a comfortable robe and tied her long hair back into two little buns.

"Stasia said you panicked and ran," she said, her arms crossed over her chest.

"I smelled a trap and called off the attack," Arn said. "It's not my fault your sister disagreed."

Arn wasn't even sure if he was lying. Yes, he thought it might have been a trap, but normally he'd have rushed right into said trap to punish the cocky bastards for making the attempt. But then he'd seen a flash of metal, and it looked so similar to gauntlets...

Mari sat beside him on the bed.

"She said you looked afraid. That doesn't sound like you, but I also don't think she's wrong." Mari slid closer to him. "What are you afraid of? *Who* are you afraid of? Is it...is it your brother?"

Arn twirled the charm in his fingers, gazing at the curling red and white fur he had long ago memorized.

"The last time I saw him..." he started, then fell silent.

"Is that when you obtained that charm?"

To even admit as much left him feeling vulnerable, but at this point, he couldn't make himself care.

"Yeah," he said. "It was."

Her hand settled over his. Her touch sparked fire across his skin, and he looked up to meet her gaze. Her eyes were so big, her expression so comforting and earnest. Her irises, unique to the people of the Miquoan forests, captivated him. They'd been coveted for years after the nation's fall, the people brought as prized husbands, wives, and servants into Eldrid. Yet none compared to Mari's. He could fall forever into that shade of red.

"Tell me," she said, and he knew he could never refuse her.

"It's not an easy story to tell."

"Then tell only what you must."

Arn drew back his shoulders and let out a long sigh. Despite the nerves it ignited in his belly, he turned his wrist so he might take her hands in his. Her dainty little fingers looked like nothing in his giant fists, but it was she who held strong, and he who trembled. She did not refuse or pull away, and so he began.

"My final day as a paragon was also my first ever campaign, an invasion of the nation of Onleda. It was the night we laid siege to their capital, Vulnae. The night their gods died."

✑

The city of Vulnae burned. Arn stood at the head of an imperial troop contingent, twelve men armed with swords, shields, and torches, together marching unchecked into the conquered city. They should have sung glory in their victory, yet it was fear he saw in their eyes. He did not blame them. The invasion of Onleda had been nothing short of a living hell.

"Orders?" asked one.

Three bodies lay at Arn's feet. A man, his wife, and their child. They'd flung themselves to the ground and begged for mercy, swearing to serve the God-Incarnate faithfully. In return, Arn's soldiers had cut them down. Phantom memories of their faces hovered in his vision, refusing to fade away.

"You know what to do," Arn answered. "Burn it all."

Those carrying torches stepped past the bodies and into the home, searching for curtains, furniture, and clothes to use as kindling. Arn cast a glance to the bodies, then swallowed down a shiver. Once the home was lit, he easily lifted the three corpses and tossed them through the open door. No grave, no funeral, but at least their bodies would be given the dignity of a pyre instead of rotting in the open.

The next four houses were blessedly empty. In went the torches. Out came the soldiers, fires growing in their wake. Pillars of smoke billowed into the air, merging with the efforts of several dozen other similar squads to block out the stars. No natural light for Vulnae's cleansing. Only the red haze of purifying fire.

That block finished, they approached a slender bridge over one of the city's many waterways into the next district. Blurry shadows moved about in the distance. Civilians fleeing for their lives, no doubt. What little defense Onleda could offer had been stationed at the outer walls, and they had crumpled with ease. Just like every other heretical nation on Gadir, without their gods, they were nothing.

Arn stopped halfway across the bridge. Before him was a stone statue so enormous Arn needed to crane his neck to see the top. The people of Vulnae had positioned it in the middle of one waterway and even incorporated its flow into the statue's design. It resembled an enormous eagle diving into the water, its front foot pushing against the current so the waterway flowed to either side of it. While the legs were bare stone, the wings were layered with bronze that shone red in the firelight. The top of the statue betrayed the godly nature of the statue's inspiration. Four human arms sprouted from the eagle's chest, each muscular and clenching an object bearing spiritual meaning to the people of Onleda. The head was carved to resemble an eagle's mask worn over a human face. That mask was a lie. The god did not have a human face. Arn knew, for he had been there when the god was slain.

"Something wrong, paragon?" one of the men asked.

"Just redecorating," Arn said as he landed on the square pedestal holding the statue aloft from the ten-foot canals. He clacked his armored fists together and fought back a shiver.

"How many of my friends did you murder?" he asked the statue of Lorka, Onleda's god of sky and stars. "How many good men and women died to your talons?"

Onleda's invasion had started with remarkably little resistance, to the point that many questioned if her people had fled in advance of the Everlorn Empire's arrival. But they had not fled, only prepared an ambush in the miles of muddy fields that surrounded the capital of Vulnae. It was on those fields, in the dead of night, that the three gods of Onleda descended upon the imperial army.

Arn's fist bashed the eagle's back leg, which provided support to the monstrous statue. Ordinary steel might have bent against the stone, but he wore the finest gauntlets the empire could provide, their metal strengthened with thousands of hours of prayer by faithful acolytes. Arn's bones would break before those gauntlets did. He gritted his teeth, pulled back his fist, and punched it with his other hand. The stone cracked.

Archers had hidden in the fields, practically buried beneath the mud. The Onleda arrows had fallen like rain upon the imperial troops, but that was just to confuse and frighten them. The gods were the true threat, and Arn had never before seen such savagery. Like those of most nations, the gods resembled animals native to the area. Puthora had struck first, a snake over twenty feet long whose upper body was a woman garbed in shining silver armor. She had slithered through the mud with ease, slicing off limbs with twin swords. She crushed soldiers in her coiled body, smashing even paragons underneath her onyx scales. Nothing slowed her. Nothing stopped her.

Puthora was only the beginning. The goddess Velgyn protected the archers, and when imperial soldiers rushed to stop their arrows, she emerged from the mud with a deep howl. She resembled a fox, but she was the size of a bull and instead of one tail she possessed three, one aflame, one coated in frost, and one crackling with lightning. Velgyn swayed those three tails side to side as she stared down the charging soldiers, then opened her mouth to howl while holding one of the three tails aloft. The matching element burst forth in a tremendous spray. Lightning tore through their ranks. Fire charred dozens of soldiers. Most horrifying had been the frost. It had coated the men and women, locking them within icy prisons while still alive. Arn had tried to free a fellow paragon from one such prison. All he succeeded in doing was snapping off two of his friend's limbs. He couldn't scream, not with his mouth encased, but he'd seen the horror in his eyes in those long moments before he died.

Lorka was the cruelest of them all. Tumultuous winds surrounded his body when he dove from the night sky. His hunting shriek was so loud, so piercing, the stars themselves quivered. Those stars somehow fell, pulled by divine magic wielded by the ancient god. They seemed tiny until they struck the land with the force of ballista missiles. Arn had nearly lost an arm to one. The man standing beside him during the initial assault had not been so lucky. A shard of light punched a hole through his chest with such force his ribs and guts exploded out his back like a champagne bottle loosing its cork. Then came the winds, lifting soldiers off their feet like leaves in a storm. Whatever victim Lorka's talons grabbed, be it soldier, magistrate, or paragon, they died a swift death with their bodies crushed and ripped in half by the eagle god's jaws.

Arn had never seen a god so huge or so deadly. As large as the statue was, it failed to convey Lorka's raw power. No wonder the Everlorn Empire had been hesitant to invade Onleda despite its vital location at the southern tip of the Sonle River. Initial estimates put imperial casualties at over ten thousand. Arn had a feeling that number would grow in the coming days. Counting had been a nightmare. The muddy fields had swallowed bodies whole.

"You tore men apart like they were robin eggs," Arn said. "You soaked the land with our blood."

The crack in the statue deepened. Arn pounded away, wishing that with every hit of his fist, a memory would die. But the memories refused to fade. They shone brightly, every bone, every intestine. They rang clearly, those wailing screams of dying men and women.

"You deserve this," he seethed, not caring if the soldiers watching could hear. "This fire, this slaughter, every...last...bit!"

The statue collapsed, but unlike the real Lorka, it did not howl in pain. It did not thrash, and cry, and seethe in fury as a half dozen paragons pierced its body with swords and spears. Arn stood before the wreckage, and away from the soldiers, the magistrates, and the paragons, he wept. It felt childish and wrong, but he could not help himself. Who was he, to shed tears amid such carnage? Everywhere was death. Suffering filled the air as deep as the smoke.

"In Everlorn I hold faith," he whispered. "In the God-Incarnate of our nation, I pray. Give me strength, give me guidance, I beg."

The prayer offered no comfort. How could it? This fire, was it not the hope they offered so many? The required cost, to ensure conversion?

Priests of the Uplifted Church insisted the people would rejoice in being freed from their oppressive gods and embrace the God-Incarnate with open arms. Instead they fought, and they fought, until the order was given. In punishment for Onleda's resistance, and the savagery of their gods, the entire city of Vulnae would burn.

Arn wiped his face clean and then leaped back to his soldiers. He just had to survive the day, that's all. Tend to his duty. Onward they marched, across a bridge to a new section of Vulnae that needed purging. They were not alone. Another squad trudged their way, setting fire to the rows of bushes and flowerbeds before the stone homes. Arn tensed upon seeing their leader. It wasn't any mere paragon, but his brother, Dario Bastell. He'd removed his helmet, and his dark hair, tied back into a ponytail, was speckled with ash.

"How goes things?" Dario asked. Arn looked to his own men, saw them gawking and standing about, and quickly snapped for them to get to work. They rushed toward the nearest homes, torches ready, and only then did Arn respond.

"Truthfully? I will be glad to see it come to an end. The Nameless Whore couldn't conjure a worse night."

Dario nodded, and it seemed he understood, or at least feigned it convincingly.

"The first conquest is always the hardest," he said. "It will get easier for you, I promise."

"Easier?" Arn gestured about him to the overwhelming carnage. He had been promised endless victories when training as a paragon. The conquering of capitals was supposedly a joyous affair, to be met with parades and cheers at the overthrowing of brutal, bloodthirsty animal gods that lacked the majesty, the *humanity*, of the God-Incarnate. Nothing could have been further from the truth. "How could *this* ever get easier? And why would I ever want it to?"

Dario stepped near, and his voice lowered.

"You skirt the edges of blasphemy, dear brother." His arm wrapped about his neck, pulling them close enough their foreheads touched. His brother's deep voice rumbled in a whisper. "When these doubts plague you, I want you to remember our battle outside the gates. Remember the horror, the savagery, of the heathen gods. They are *monsters*. Remember their terror, their power, and never forget it. This duty we perform is difficult, but it is the price we must pay. Gadir is made better with the deaths of Puthora, Velgyn, and Lorka. Yes, that includes these people we save. Yes, even those who die this night, and burn upon a pyre. Their souls are spared. Their eternities, now made free. We give them to the God-Incarnate, and in his bosom, they will know true peace in the ever after."

An image came unbidden to Arn, one of stars falling, of winds sweeping full contingents into the air. Fields of corpses surrounded Vulnae in all directions. That was freedom? That was peace? But his brother was looking at him, judgment in his eyes, and Arn knew he could not reveal such weakness in his mind. Monsters, his brother insisted, remember they are monsters, and so he did his best to believe.

"Let no one weep for the passing of false and heretical gods," he said, one of the many creeds drilled into him to become a paragon. If only they could give him the comfort they had offered during his years of training.

"Let us instead sing praises to the salvation of children come at last to the savior," Dario finished. He smiled and patted Arn on the shoulder. "Good work, dear brother. We'll make a praefect out of you yet."

The two separated, each taking a different street. Arn marched without seeing, gave orders without hearing. The world was becoming loose and unreal to him as the carnage continued. At least the deepening smoke hid the stars; every time he looked, he swore he saw them threatening to come crashing down. And why wouldn't they? Hadn't the empire slain Onleda's god of the stars? Arn didn't know what truly made up those celestial bodies. Perhaps they would fall and obliterate every last soldier of the Everlorn Empire. Perhaps the soldiers even deserved it.

Movement at the corner of his eye, a flash of color that defied explanation. The past few blocks had shown no signs of survivors, just empty buildings as the people of Vulnae fled the spreading destruction. Arn turned and caught a glimpse of a tail slipping through the door of a square building at the far end of a narrow road.

"Couldn't be," he said. Arn glanced up and down the street, but his soldiers were busy doing their jobs. Fine with him. Surely his eyes deceived him anyway. He approached the building, which so far had escaped the flames of the larger homes on either side of it. Arn pressed against the wooden door, found it locked. Ramming it with his shoulder fixed that. When he entered, he guessed the squat little cube of a building was a temple or shrine of some sort. Each and every wall was covered with painted scrolls. The floor was soft beneath his boots and made of dried, interwoven strands of tall grass. Arn walked to its center, his gauntlets tightening into fists.

While Puthora and Lorka had been slain in the muddy fields, most reports agreed that Velgyn, while injured, had survived.

Arn saw that the reports were true. She was most certainly injured, and in ways beyond the physical. She was smaller now, as small as a real fox if it were possible for one to grow three tails. The goddess bared her fangs at him, the fur on her neck rising up in fury. Arn clanged his gauntlets together, and he clung to his brother's words.

Remember their terror, their power, and never forget.

Velgyn was small now, but only because she was weak and wounded. He stepped closer, remembering the soldiers she'd imprisoned in ice. He remembered the screams of the men and women with their flesh charred away to expose the bone underneath. Yes, Velgyn was a ruthless monster, a false god commanding the faith and loyalty of her people. Arn would save them, save them all.

"Accept this with dignity," he said as he stepped closer. The fox deity limped backward a step, unable to put any pressure on her front left paw. "The sooner you die, the sooner the people of Onleda can move on without you."

The room was quiet, the tension thick as blood, so that the soft sob he heard stood out all the clearer. Arn tilted his head to one side, curious. It came from what appeared to be a patch of wall covered by a long banner decorated with the squiggly nonsense of the language native to Onleda.

"Hiding secrets, are we?" he asked, and stepped toward the wall.

"Enough!" Velgyn shouted. Her voice was deep, and much more befitting her larger, previous form. "Your quarrel is with me, and me alone."

He ripped the banner down. His knuckles rapped the wood and found it strangely loose. A single blow crumpled the false wall.

"Let them go!"

The fox goddess leaped upon him, her tails lashing his armor, her teeth biting for his neck. Arn brought an arm up in defense, and he choked down a scream as her teeth crunched the metal of his left gauntlet hard enough to cut his skin. Still, it was only superficial, a bit of pain and blood. He could endure both.

That same could not be said for the goddess when he lifted her high into the air and then bashed her to the floor. Velgyn's injured leg snapped in half. Blood splattered from her little black nose. Arn kicked before she could roll away, and he heard the sound of ribs cracking as she flew. The wall stopped her, and the pained "yip" she released was entirely animal in nature.

"I expected better," Arn said, pulling at his damaged gauntlet so the metal wouldn't bite him so. He turned back to the false wall to see what the fox goddess was so determined to protect.

Within, crouched in the dark and squinting against the sudden influx of light, were three small children.

The wounded Velgyn staggered back to three of her feet. Her front paw hovered in the air, bone hanging loose within the skin.

"Leave them," she said. "Kill me if you must, but let them live. What gain have you from their suffering? Are you truly so monstrous?"

Arn stood shaking before the hidden entrance. His gaze shifted back and forth, from the wounded goddess to the cowering children. He had his soldiers, his torches, and his orders. It wasn't about the suffering, he told himself. It was about redeeming the souls of a nation. That was the empire's divine purpose, the justification for a thousand-year campaign to bind all of Gadir under a single, unified banner. Velgyn, she was a monster, a danger to her people, a savage heathen deity deserving death.

A monster, risking her life for three children. Small and weak, baring her teeth while holding aloft a broken paw. Not fleeing. Not abandoning them.

Arn tried to muster every answer he'd been taught, but he realized then and there that he believed none of them. Each answer was a lie. None could withstand the truth of this burning city choked with ashes.

"You don't get to ask that question," Dario said from the doorway. His brother entered the temple. There was no sign of his squadron. "Only a fool argues with a monster over the definition of a monster."

"I have this," Arn said, more defensively than he expected.

"Do you? Because I wonder."

The three children dashed for the temple door, and at their flight, Velgyn lunged unevenly for Arn's throat, struggling to find speed given her wounded leg. Arn caught the weakened goddess and held her in his hands. He endured the stings of her tails, their fire and frost a far cry from their earlier savagery. She squirmed as his platemail gauntlets closed. She yipped and howled as his fingers sank into her flesh.

"Stop," he whispered. Her teeth scraped across his gauntlets. "Please, stop, please." Lightning arced across his body. Frost built along his gauntlets. She kept fighting. Kept struggling, and all the gods and goddesses help him, he focused on her instead of the sounds he heard from the doorway. The cries of the children attempting to flee past Dario. Their pain. Their dying.

Their silence.

Velgyn's struggling ceased, and she met his eye. At last, he saw defeat. He saw sorrow. He saw beauty.

"In all things a season," she said. "Bring forth the winter."

He crushed her body in his grasp. Her bones broke. Her fur tore. His vision filled with blood and bone until the horrid deed was done. Arn held her by one of her tails, blood dripping down his hands and armor to stain the temple's reed floor.

"A mighty kill," Dario said behind him. "You have made our family proud, and on your very first campaign, no less! Think of what we may accomplish in the years to come!" He extended his hand. "Come, let us parade the corpse before our troops. They could use the boost to their morale."

"Yes," Arn said. His voice was dead in his ears. "I suppose we should."

But he couldn't move. His feet were locked in place. Dario seemed to understand, and he reached for the body.

"Give her to me," he said. "I will do it if you need time to recover."

His brother's hand closed about the body and pulled. Arn didn't let go. He heard the goddess's accusation echoing in his ears.

Are you truly so monstrous?

Dario pulled. Arn held firm.

"Let go, brother." His fingers tightened about the tail. "I said let go!"

The body ripped, the bone snapping, so that Arn held only the broken tip of the tail. Arn stared down at it, his mind locked and broken. He looked up. He saw his brother's face, and the body of the goddess. Saw the three dead children at the doorway. Dario said nothing with his lips, but his expression spoke a million words. The expectations for Arn to embrace his vaunted deed. The need to bury his guilt and shock. The pride of his family. The image of his brother, a rising star sure to become a paragon praefect, and the shadow Arn would cast behind him.

Dario left him there, alone, twirling the little fox tail between numb fingers.

"Monsters," Arn whispered.

He stepped out from the temple and viewed the great salvation he helped bring to Vulnae. He saw the piles of bodies. He smelled the burning of wood, meat, and hair. Ash blocked out the stars that had been so beloved to their slain Lorka. From every direction, he heard screams. Some of pain. Some of fear. Arn clutched the tail, and he tried to summon a verse or scripture to bring him comfort. None came. He felt hollow. The world went flat before him, not real, not real, it couldn't be real. Not this much death. Not this much destruction.

Think of what we may accomplish in the years to come!

Arn ran. He didn't dare ponder where. He couldn't give voice to the heretical thoughts blasting through his skull. He ran and ran, past soldiers, past fires, past corpses piled so high the roaring flames were yet to grant them their kiss. He ran to the city walls, and he climbed them with his gauntlets pounding handholds into the bricks. He ran to the muddy fields beyond that swallowed him up to his knees. His boots kicked stones and corpses.

He ran and ran, and not once looked back.

✑

Arn shook away the memory lest he be lost in it. He'd spent far too many nights dwelling on that horrible moment. Best not to add another.

"So that was when you decided to abandon the empire?" Mari prodded after a long silence. She had remained quiet throughout the retelling, listening intently to every detail. Arn appreciated her solemnness.

"The heathen gods were supposed to be terrifying, remorseless beasts enthralling their worshipers. When we fought outside Vulnae, it was easy enough to believe that. They were terrifying in their power, and surely Gadir was better for their death. But I never saw a god at peace. I never attended their prayers and rituals. So to see Velgyn small and wounded, giving up her life to save a few children? Save them from us. We, the saviors. We, the bringers of salvation, burning down their homes and slaughtering their parents, their siblings, slaughtering, burning…"

It took Arn a moment to gather himself. He wanted, no, he needed Mari to understand. No bumbling his words, not here. Vulnae's sacrifice had shocked him to his core, the final blow to an already crumbling foundation.

"You have to understand, in the Everlorn Empire, loyalty and sacrifice always flow upward. Converted nations give tributes to Everlorn. The people pray for the safety of our soldiers, who give their lives without hesitation for their commanders, who in turn obey our paragons. Citizens willingly sacrifice their very lives to empower us paragons, and we would gladly cut our own throats if it meant glory and honor for our God-Incarnate. Yet here was a goddess willing to die for mere children. I tried to imagine a paragon doing the same, let alone an Anointed or the God-Incarnate himself. I knew the answer, and it is never."

He lifted his hands and clenched them into fists.

"Ten men and women died to give me the strength I wield. They bled out with smiles on their faces. They cut their throats with a song on their lips. An honor, they declared it. A privilege. Fuck me. Monsters, we called the gods of Onleda. Monsters, as if that's not what we all are. As if that's not what I've been since the moment I became a paragon. And Dario? My brother? He's the only one who knows, who truly knows, how horrible I am. The one who saw me kill that beautiful, wounded goddess."

Arn clenched the little charm and fought back a wave of tears. He was stronger than that. A former paragon of the empire and a champion of a hundred battles. He was rarely one to cry, and guilt and shadowy memories would not break him now.

"For a long while I hid in the foulest grottos of conquered Onleda. I avoided every priest and soldier, because truth be told, I was terrified they would recognize me and tell my brother. He was looking for me, I was sure of it. I fled after a year, scurrying my way across Gadir, helping out where I could. Eventually I made my way back to Onleda, and by then, your father had set up a resistance movement from afar by funneling in his wealth. They were trying to restore faith in Velgyn, and I . . . well. That was my responsibility, was it not? I still had my strength, so at least I could try to make amends. It took a bit of convincing, but eventually they trusted my abandonment of the empire to be real and not an attempt to infiltrate their organization. I fought alongside them for another year before Thorda heard of my recruitment. Once he did, he demanded Onleda's rebellion send me to Thanet. Months later I was on a boat, sailing across the Crystal Sea. And now I'm here."

Arn fell silent. He'd been talking for an hour now. His throat was raw, and his emotions rawer. The little charm twirled in his fingers. That little tuft of fur and bone capped with bronze had saved him on so many dark, lonely nights. It had been his reminder of when he glimpsed a world where the strong helped the weak, and the gods would give their lives to protect their worshipers.

Mari slid even closer so that her knee was touching his. Her voice deepened, and the air around them thickened.

"I can help you, Arn, but only if you want it."

"Help with what?"

Mari removed the buns in her hair, and now loose, the waves fell across her face, hiding her from his sight.

"Our homeland of Miquo viewed gods differently than most of Gadir," she said, her gaze still locked firmly on her hands resting in her lap. "Instead of a few powerful, eternal gods, we worshiped dozens in a grand pantheon. They weren't eternal, either." She hesitated, a flash of hurt he did not understand before she continued. "They lived, bore children, died, and passed on their gifts to chosen heirs. But just because they died, we did not forget them, nor cease our worship. And for this, our bloodlines were blessed with the rare occurrences of a god-whisperer."

"Like you," Arn said.

"Yes, like me. But the gift means more than just turning into a big scary cat. That wasn't its purpose, not at first, not before Miquo was invaded. We were meant to speak with the dead gods of our pantheon. We were to share in their past existence and to ensure their knowledge and guidance survived long after their mortal bodies perished."

Her hand settled softly upon his arm. At last she looked to him. There was no worry in her eyes, no reluctance. Only compassion to set his insides aflame.

"Arn...would you like to speak with Velgyn?"

That flame turned to frost. His hands shook.

"I fear to," he said.

"I'll be with you."

Arn brushed the charm's fur across his calloused fingers.

"She died in Vulnae, thousands of miles from here. Are you sure it is even possible?"

Mari squeezed his hand. Her smile grew ever so slightly. He felt a child again, sitting before a teacher so much wiser and learned in the ways of gods and faiths.

"Prayer knows no distance."

Arn had spent many years running from his brother, but the current fear in his breast was a thousand times worse at imagining such a confrontation.

"I can't," he said. "Please, Mari, spare me such a torment. You think you offer me comfort, but I crushed the fox goddess between my gauntlets. I felt her bones break. She will not offer me absolution, only condemnation."

"You don't know that."

"And neither do you."

Mari took the charm from his hands and held it before her. Eyes closed, she breathed in as if inhaling its essence.

"Whoever you were then, it isn't who you are now. Know the offer remains however much time it takes. I hold faith it will not be so long as you believe."

Arn bunched his fists, shame swelling like burning coals in his neck and face. His eyes grew wet, and he clenched his jaw tight to fight the feeling off.

"You expect much from this coward," he said.

"You're not a coward," she said, sliding off the bed. Her free hand cupped his face, a loving touch he did not deserve. He leaned into it with eyes closed, and his need to weep increased tenfold. Gods help him, she was so kind, so beautiful. "Only wounded. When your heart is ready to cease its bleeding, come to me. We'll do it together."

Before she left, she pressed the little foxtail charm into his hands. She made him hold the proof of his most vile deed. She forced him to cling to the memory that had broken him. A memento of when he started his path toward becoming something new. A betrayer. A criminal.

A heretic.

CHAPTER 28

SINSHEI

Sinshei ordered a chair brought to Keles's bedroom before she returned. She sat in the center of the room, her hands folded in her lap, and observed the imprisoned Orani heir. Keles was sullen, her gaze averted, and what random glances Sinshei did receive were furious glares.

She's so young, and yet her heart is scarred and old, Sinshei thought. A familiar sight, if she was honest with herself, for she had been to many recently conquered nations. Youths forced into battle, their world around them crumbling, their gods dying, their beliefs challenged to their core as they witnessed death and bloodshed on a scale that would break even the hardest of minds. Keles had endured the prisons and narrowly avoided hanging on the Dead Flags due to the forsaking ceremony. Now she had witnessed the rebirth and subsequent death of a false shadow of her beloved Lycaena. Most people would break from less. Keles, so far, had not.

That would change.

"What do you want from me?" Keles asked, seizing the conversation before Sinshei might start. The young woman sat on the edge of the bed, a slight improvement over hunching in the corner. Her brown eyes looked up, meeting Sinshei's. Challenging her. Despite the word-lace she wore around her throat rendering it unnecessary, Sinshei answered in native Thanese.

"Soma told me of the battle against the false Lycaena, and in great detail. Most curious was your intimacy with the Vagrant. Soma insists that you know who he is, who he *truly* is beneath the mask and cloak. He is a thorn in the side of peace, a torch setting fires of rebellion that will consume all and aid no one. You can tell me who he is and how to find him."

"I will not give him up to you," she said. That she did not deny this knowledge was a huge tell. The emphasis she put on the "you" at the end told Sinshei even more. This matter was deeply personal.

Someone close to her, she thought. *Family? A friend?*

But something else was there, something she had not anticipated. Anger. Whoever the Vagrant was, Keles bore a deep fury toward him, and Sinshei could only guess as to the reason. Someone dear, but someone who had hurt her. Someone she could betray, but only if the betrayal was committed by her own hands, and not the empire's. Sinshei struggled to keep her smile hidden beneath a veneer of calm.

Perfect.

"Thanet is still lacking a proper regent," Sinshei said. The task was set. It was time to reveal the reward. "And given the difficulties we have faced, and the great distance between here and Gadir, we need a strong ruler whom the people trust. Perhaps one they would even love. That could be you, Keles. We will spread the truth of your island's past, at least in regard to your bloodline. We will show them the sins of the Lythan family and declare you the returned Orani queen, our regent in all but name."

She could see the desire the young woman fought to hide. It warred against her pride, perhaps honor, or a sense of loyalty to the island over any agreement with their conquerors. It was close, though, so very close. Keles was a hundred times broken, her faith twice shattered. When captured by Soma, she no doubt expected death, and yet now she was offered a throne. A false throne, perhaps, but a throne nonetheless.

Sinshei leaned closer. Her voice softened, as if with understanding. As if she somehow knew exactly who the Vagrant was, and why he was so closely connected to the troubled woman.

"You don't need to give me a name, Keles. You need only bring me proof of his death."

"I could…" She hesitated. "Even if I agreed, I could never defeat him in battle. Surely Soma told you *that* as well."

No hiding this smile. Sinshei rose from her chair, and she offered Keles a delicate hand.

"I know," she said. "Come with me."

⌘

The pair rode a carriage south out of Vallessau. Keles wore no bindings, a gesture of trust toward the woman Sinshei would make an ally. No conversation was held between them. It felt like they rode toward an execution, and in many ways, it was one. The sun had begun to set, painting red and yellow streaks across the sky. The island was beautiful, Sinshei had to admit. One could spend many happy years wandering the beaches, the tall mountains, and the rolling fields deeper within the heart of Thanet. She might have, if she had come not as an Anointed. For a time, the empire had sent missionaries to pave the way for the armies that would follow. God-Incarnate Lucavi had ended that practice within his first year. First conquest, then conversion. He was an impatient deity when it came to the ever-hungry borders of his empire.

The road roughened, and they descended from the higher rocky fields back toward the beach. Once they exited, Sinshei bade the driver to return to the city. There would be no witnesses for this ceremony except those Sinshei invited. One was Soma, who waited at the beach with an enormous chest at his feet. Within was the work she had requested of their smiths, performed admirably given the time constraints. Behind him, standing in a circle, were ten followers of Dagon.

Keles broke her silence at the sand's edge. It seemed she was nervous to come closer to the smiling paragon.

"Why are we here?" she asked, and gestured to the waiting crowd. "Why are *they* here?"

"Among the paragons, there is a special designation," Sinshei explained. "A paragon penitent. They are paragons who have gone astray in their faith but seek to return to the fold. I would have you become one such penitent, Keles, only the power will not come from any faith in the God-Incarnate in Eldrid. It will come from those who are loyal still to the god Dagon, and who recognize you as possessing his divine blessing."

"What you're offering is blasphemous to the Uplifted Church," Keles said, and she was not wrong. "Why would you allow this?"

Sinshei turned to Soma, not yet ready to answer such a question.

"Go to them, and make sure their hearts are ready," she ordered.

"As you wish," Soma said, and he dipped his head low.

Sinshei pulled her braided hair over her right shoulder so it hung down to her knees. Silently, she debated as she watched him go. Keles shuffled beside her, nervous and agitated. They were alone on this beach, just the two of them. She was asking so much of young Keles. Something must be offered in return. A sliver of honesty. A secret pain Sinshei had never shared with others.

"My mother's name was Valshei," Sinshei said. "She was a concubine in service of the God-Incarnate, taken from Aethenwald upon its conquering as a momentary infatuation. I was born in Eldrid and heard only stories of Aethenwald. My mother, she would tell them as she braided my hair, painting beautiful pictures of the deep oak woods, the looping cities full of shadow, and their rivers so deep only the strongest divers could hold their breath to reach the bottom. A beautiful land, full of strange customs. 'Never cut your hair,' my mother told me. 'Let it grow until it reaches the floor, and drag it behind you as a train to your gown if you must. Bear the weight. Never cut it.' It was important to her, so I listened. And then one day, we returned to Aethenwald."

Sinshei paused to collect the memories. She did not think of her mother often. The images were distant, and tinted with hurt. To dwell on them might make her vulnerable. Even worse, they might lead her to heresy.

A smirk crossed her face.

Too late for that.

"Aethenwald was considered an easy victory, but it was due to clever manipulation of our ambassadors. The Aethenean people thought they would have a level of autonomy upon joining the empire. More than a few royals were eager to give up their cloying, sentimental gods if it meant power concentrated in their tri-throne rule instead of split with their priests. When we broke their thrones and appointed a regent, the riots began. Treasonous poems and songs filled taverns. It was a black eye upon many in Eldrid's court, particularly those who thought a less militaristic absorption of other nations was possible. And so I traveled to Aethenwald, but not with my mother. I rode there with my brother, Galvanis vin Lucavi."

Sinshei paused for a breath. The scent of the ocean teased her throat, and she relished the feeling. It fought away the distant panic. That carriage ride had taken a month, which had felt like forever to her ten-year-old self. Galvanis, twenty years old and beaming with the confidence and glory of one recently declared Heir-Incarnate, had decided he would use that month to properly instruct her on matters of court and faith. He would tell her things the Uplifted Church thought inappropriate for children to understand. He would list the great many heresies her mother had supposedly committed with her tongue and flesh.

She remembered insisting her mother would never do such things. She swore to her older brother that Valshei was just, and true, and faithful to the God-Incarnate. Galvanis had only laughed and called her a naïve child.

"When I arrived in Aethenwald's capital," she continued, "I noted the different styles of dress, the thicker cloth to match the often stormy weather. They were visions from my bedtime stories, and it was exciting to see them real and yet...disheartening, without the luster of my childhood imagination. Stranger still, each and every man and woman was completely shorn of hair. At first I thought...I thought that was why my mother had insisted I never cut my hair. It was a sign to the God-Incarnate of our loyalty. If Aethenwald's people kept themselves shaved, we would do the opposite. My brother, he must have noticed my expression, and the way I was staring."

Of course he had noticed. He always did. He watched her like a hunting hawk. She was so often a disappointment to him, yet it never prevented him from acting *invested* in her. Whatever successes she achieved, he would smile and treat them as if they were his own. He never needed to voice that opinion. The look in his eye would be enough.

"My dearest Galvanis then told me a story of Aethenean culture. Each man and woman, from the moment of their birth, did not cut their hair. It is only upon marriage that the two lovers, on the day of their wedding, have their hair decorated, braided into each other's, and then cut. A 'coupling braid,' it is called. That braid is then set in a place of honor within the household, be it a fireplace, a doorway, or a window visible from the street. It symbolizes the love and unity between the two, and thereafter, cut or trimmed hair is seen as a mark of adulthood, of maturity."

Sinshei remembered the way Galvanis had shared this fact, the inflection in his voice. Like it had been cute, in the same way children playing pretend were cute. There was no respect for the act, only amusement. It was the exact opposite of how her mother had told her stories of her home.

"I asked him if that was why everyone was shaved. My brother, he laughed. He laughed. 'No,' he told me. 'They are shaved because I ordered them shaved. They are now married to the God-Incarnate in their hearts, each and every last one of them.' And then we exited the carriage, finally arrived to the reason we had come all that way. He never told me. A month in a carriage, bored and alone, and he never let me know my mother was in an accompanying carriage. Bound. Imprisoned. Condemned."

It had been years since she cried for her mother, and never in the presence of others. Tears were dangerous. Sorrow expressed for a heretic? Even more so. But here on this foreign shore, she let Keles see every ember of the fire that awakened within her. It was hotter than she anticipated.

"They tied my mother to a pole amidst a pyre made of a thousand cut braids. Before that crowd, Galvanis cut my mother's hair with a jagged razor and then lit it with a torch. Then he stood at my side, took my hand, and held it while we watched. Ten years old, I watched her burn. I never said a word. Neither did Galvanis, not until it was over, and her screams had ceased. Then he finally spoke."

The words had stuck with her forever, haunting her, flooding her nightmares with demons that chased with bleeding gums and smelled of burnt hair.

" 'I'm proud of you.' "

The waves crashed along the shore, the only noise to fill the silence. Sinshei stared at the men and women gathered at the beach, but she did not see them. She saw a crowd standing, shocked still as the pyre burned. At least the smell of salt was on the wind. Far better that. Far better.

"My brother, Galvanis vin Lucavi, is set to become the new God-Incarnate of the Everlorn Empire. For six hundred years, he shall reign. Unless he is stopped. Unless *I* stop him." Sinshei's mind returned to the present. No more tears. No more aching sorrow for a childhood that ended upon a pyre. "I know the Everlorn Empire is not perfect. I know there is a sickness within the Uplifted Church, allowed to fester and rot over a millennium. Others know it, too, and there are many of us in Eldrid seeking change. I could be the one to change it, Keles. It would not happen in a day, but I would have more than a day. I would have six hundred years."

"You speak as if I should care for the workings of your empire," Keles said softly.

"There are millions of imperial lives I could make better, but even if you do not care for them, I know you care for your people here on your island. I shall give Thanet back to you. I will have no need of it. For the first time in the three-thousand-year history of the Everlorn Empire, I will turn our eyes inward instead of outward. All I ask is for you to be an ally when I require it most."

"And the Vagrant?"

"A complication that must be eliminated. A test for you to overcome. They are one and the same, but only if you are willing."

Keles looked to the ocean. Together, they listened to the waves. Sinshei could only guess at the whirlwind of emotions within the young woman, but she trusted the final answer.

"I know nothing of Dagon. He is a story to me, a trickster villain long slain. How do I put my faith in him?"

"You need not hold love in your own heart," Sinshei said, and she offered Keles her hand. "You must only trust in those who do. Your blood was chosen. Whatever lingering strength the fallen deity possesses, let it become yours."

Keles accepted the hand, and they walked to the waiting ring of followers. The youngest was perhaps forty, with most participants elderly and gray. They had dressed in loose robes that resembled one another in style, and Sinshei suspected they were handmade re-creations of the official garb worn by Dagon's faithful hundreds of years ago. She imagined them as they had once been, full of wealth and color, with vibrant blue robes sashed in gold and decorated with sapphires and seashells. Not these mismatched, hand-sewn pieces, more gray than blue. Such a perfect example of a nation holding on after the Everlorn Empire's arrival. They would dress in rags if it meant pantomiming a long-lost past.

Forfeit the elders, and instead tend the hearts and minds of the young, she thought. It was one of the Uplifted Church's axioms that guided their expansion. The elderly would stick to their old ways. It was the new generations one must mold.

The ten shuffled closer, quiet, reverent. A woman grasped Keles's wrists, and she gazed at her with milky eyes. Her hair was white and wrapped in a pale scarf. She wore a pendant around her neck decorated with stones carved and painted to resemble blue fish scales.

"Long I dreamed of this moment," she said. "Yet never did I believe it would happen in my lifetime. A return of the true blood. A loyal Orani seated on the island throne."

"The Returned Queen," an even older man said beside her. He removed a pendant from around his neck and slipped it over Keles's head. The young woman accepted it silently. "Praise be. Praise be."

Sinshei noted that others wore similar pendants and stones, all resembling the scales of the slain god of the sea. No doubt those symbols were illegal long before the empire's ships arrived on Thanese shores. Sinshei had spoken with countless men and women as a priestess, and listened to their accusations against the empire, their claims of cruelty and erasure. As if what the empire did was special. None of it, not the wars, not the conversions, not the shifting of language or even the death of gods, was unique to Everlorn. The only difference was the scale of it, and the efficiency.

"You ten know what I ask of you," she said. "You ten have agreed.

Begin your prayer, and let none show hesitance. Thanet will not be spared through cowardice and regret, only absolute faith." She turned her attention to Keles. "Shed your clothes, and kneel among them."

It wasn't so long ago she had performed this ceremony on an individual she deemed unworthy. Ten Seeds, sacrificed for a spoiled, callous bastard named Gordian Goldleaf. Though these ten were not Seeds, Sinshei reluctantly admitted they were superior. They did not grow up coddled and soft in Eldrid, glorified by their peers and told their sacrifice was the highest honor attainable by mere mortals. These ten had lived in spiritual hiding, their faith hardened through tribulations and the cumulative hatred and dismissal of an entire society.

Keles disrobed and then knelt in the sand, wearing only the pendant given to her by the elderly man. Sinshei stood over her, debating how to modify the ritual. She had deflected Keles's earlier assertion, but this was an incredibly blasphemous act they were to perform. To bless the power of a paragon upon an unbeliever, and have that power come, not from the God-Incarnate, but from one of the heretical gods . . .

The church would not just execute her. They would hang her from a pole in the heart of Eldrid. Yet instead of frightening, she found it exhilarating. The concepts of faith and divinity were ironclad in the Uplifted Church's dogma. Yet here, on the wild shores of Thanet, she was performing something new and wondrous. And truly, wasn't it still in the name of the God-Incarnate, if it meant ensuring *she* became God-Incarnate?

"Close your eyes," she ordered. For a paragon ritual, normally there would be a blood sacrifice prepared, taken from a prisoner destined for the Dead Flags. Sinshei suspected that was unnecessary. Faith, that was all that was needed, and these ten had it in abundance. She knelt before Keles, and she gently took the young woman's hands in hers.

"Keep them closed, Keles Orani. Listen only to the prayers. Open your heart to them. When the power flows to you, embrace it. You need not look. You need not witness the price being paid."

The ten faithful to Dagon began their chant. Sinshei had not given them instructions on what to pray or sing, for their faith was foreign to her. She would let them pick the hymns, for they would know which best embodied their sacrifice, no differently than how they chose their dress and their decorations. She listened for a moment, her word-lace translating the Thanese in her mind. Their chant spoke of being lost at sea, down in darkness, and then discovering a light. That light guided them to the surface to behold the splendor of the moon and stars. Though the song stated the moon was the light, it implied Dagon was who truly saved them, who lifted them up when their limbs were tired, and who breathed air into their lungs when they thought they could withstand the deep no more.

A beautiful song. Hope amid despair. Light guiding out of darkness. Common themes, universal across Gadir, yet given meanings and symbols that would connect more deeply with the people of Thanet. Sinshei appreciated it, even as she felt an ache in her breast. What songs had Aethenwald known? What symbols had spoken to them, that she might never hear?

The song approached its end, and amid that growing power, the ten prepared for the sacrifice. They each extended their left arm to their neighbor, forming a circle, while the right hand hovered just above, holding the knife.

"For the Orani Queen!"

They did not cut across their throats like imperial Seeds, but instead cut the arm of their neighbor, one long slash along the wrist so they would bleed out. It was a slower death, Sinshei noted, but it allowed them to continue speaking. To *sing*.

"For the sea and wind. For the storm and fog. For the Sapphire Serpent, we give our all."

The blood pooled beneath them, thickening upon the sand. Splashes of it washed across Sinshei's feet, but she dared not move from her spot within that circle. Keles would need Sinshei to guide the released power into her. The singing faded, weakened as the blood continued to pour. The ten repeated those three lines, coughing and whispering them as their strength waned.

No matter how thin its presence, Sinshei bore the blood of the God-Incarnate within her veins. With that gift, she could sometimes see into the realm of the spiritual. Normally it took great concentration to do so, but not tonight. Magic sparked within the air. Faith burned like fire. A blue mist rose from the dying bodies, and it shone as bright as the moon.

Sinshei turned her attention to the young woman before her. To her surprise, Keles knelt but not with her head bowed, nor with her eyes closed. Despite Sinshei's orders otherwise, Keles watched. She watched the elderly slump to their knees, their strength giving out. She watched the blood pour from their arms. Keles gave silent witness, neck stiff, head tall, unafraid of the cost of the power she would obtain.

Heat swelled within Sinshei's bosom. Keles was a heathen, a foreigner, of royal blood to a rebellious throne, and yet Sinshei was so damn *proud* of her.

"Do you hear me, slain god?" Sinshei whispered. Her arms rose. "Within this circle is your vessel. Give her your faith. Let her receive the blessing of blood and sacrifice."

Dagon answered. That blue mist poured into Keles's body. Perhaps she could see it, perhaps not, but she could most certainly feel it. Her head snapped backward. Her muscles constricted. Her jaw hung open, and if she tried to speak, no words managed to escape, just a low, pained cry. Skin tore. Bones broke. The body must be reshaped. The vessel must be made pure to accommodate the divine.

There was always a chance of death during a paragon ritual, and Keles's lack of faith in Dagon dramatically worsened those odds. But Sinshei trusted the young Orani woman to endure. She was strong. Fervent. Her broken faith might have been in Lycaena, but it could be molded again. That hurt, that pain, could turn to another. For now, let it be Dagon. In time, and with Sinshei's guidance, it could turn to the God-Incarnate.

No. It could turn to *her*.

The song ended. The shaking of the world ceased. Sinshei lowered her arms, and she stepped back, keenly aware of the drying blood that formed an interior ring within the outer circle that was the bodies of the ten sacrificed faithful. A blue glow hovered around Keles, so similar to the golden aura that had surrounded Gordian after his own transformation.

"Incredible," Soma said breathlessly, and Sinshei shared his sentiment. She leaned forward and put a loving hand atop Keles's head.

"Stand."

Keles obeyed. She was taller, though not by much. Her musculature was far more pronounced, and it rippled with her movements. She was leaner than an imperial paragon, Sinshei noted. Did views of what it meant to be strong differ in Thanese society? Would her strength be diminished, or was it as many priests suspected, that the physical muscles were only incidentally related to the actual strength gained by paragons through divine transference? Sinshei wished she could hold a dozen more such rituals to satisfy her curiosity, but alas, this would be the only one. Perhaps once the Uplifted Church bowed in worship to her, she might perform such experiments. For now, she brushed a loving hand across Keles's face and smiled.

"You did wonderfully," she said. "Now dress. Soma has a gift for you."

The paragon had already anticipated the request, and he arrived carrying the enormous chest atop his shoulder with one arm. He set it upon the sand with a heavy thunk, then kicked the top open to reveal its contents: a full suit of armor and weaponry, all of it custom-made to Sinshei's specifications.

"It is your armor now," Sinshei explained to Keles. "The armor of the penitent."

The pieces of the armor were plate, but with modifications made to accommodate the night's transformation. It was slightly larger than what Keles once wore, in anticipation of her additional muscle. The pieces were each individually adjustable and designed to interlock atop one another in layers. Once she was dressed in her undershirt and garments, Soma helped her buckle the first few pieces along the chest and waist before she slid on the leggings and gauntlets. Each of them was pitch black as a starless night, and what few bits of leather visible near the joints were dyed a pale gray.

When she was fully garbed, Soma retrieved two more gifts from the enormous chest: a sword whose hilt was wrapped in black leather, and a round metal shield, its shining surface darkened and stained like her armor. Keles wordlessly accepted them, and she tested the sword a few times to learn its weight. No doubt it felt like air, given her newfound blessing. When finished, she buckled the sword to her hip, and after a quick instruction from Soma, she attached the shield securely to her back.

Her outfit was complete but for one piece. The paragon retrieved a fully closed helmet akin to his own from the chest and then handed it to Sinshei. She held it in her left hand, and with her right, she wrapped her arm around Keles's neck as if they were dear friends. Their eyes met. Within Keles's dark irises, she saw a storm of anger, excitement, and shock. Into that cacophony, Sinshei would speak kindness and understanding.

"It is behind masks we are capable of doing what must be done," Sinshei said. "A truth I suspect the Vagrant himself understands."

She slid the helmet over the young woman's head, hiding her face but for what was visible through its thin visor. Clad in dark plate, she looked a true paragon penitent, and she exuded that familiar aura of power and danger. So far Keles had not said a single word since the ritual began. She had kept everything to herself, her every confused thought. At last, she spoke.

"I will bring you his broken mask," she said. Her voice sounded different from within the helmet. Older and deeper. "And when I lay its pieces at your feet, you will make me a queen. That is our deal. Have I your vow, Anointed One?"

"You have my vow, my trust, and my love, dearest Keles," Sinshei said, and she smiled to convince the young woman of its truth.

"I desire only the first. What will you do with the bodies?"

"I will give them to the sea," Soma answered for her. "It was one of their few demands."

Her face was hidden, so Sinshei could not tell if she considered this acceptable. At best, she was indifferent, and so she shrugged. The plate rattled from the movement.

"Where shall I find you should I need you?"

"I will ensure the castle guards know to allow your safe passage," Sinshei said. "Consider this another gift, that you will always have a home with me."

"A gift." She hesitated. Was she laughing? Glaring? Did it matter? "You are too kind, Anointed One. Too kind."

The woman turned and marched away. Sinshei lingered, wanting to give the young woman space. Besides, they had their mess to clean up. Under no circumstances would Sinshei leave behind evidence of what had transpired here. If her brother discovered her blasphemy...no, she didn't want to think about that. He wouldn't just punish her. He'd try to correct her, purify her in some way, and it made her skin crawl.

"I must confess, I have not performed a sea burial before," Sinshei said, turning her attention to Soma. "How is it done? Do you fill the stomachs with stones so they sink?"

But Soma was not paying her any attention. His gaze was locked on the retreating Keles as she walked the road to Vallessau. Something— was it love?—sparkled in his eyes.

"Imagine the fate of our invasion if a legion of her kind had greeted us when our boats pulled ashore," he said quietly. "She's powerful. Perhaps too powerful, should she turn against you."

Sinshei was surprised by Soma's emotion. Normally she viewed him as a thoroughly heartless bastard, capable only of selfish amusement or abject cruelty. To see him so enamored was...unsettling.

"I care about one thing, Soma. Could you slay Galvanis with her at your side?"

Soma studied the distant black-clad woman.

"Yes," he said. "I think I could, and I would do so gladly."

CHAPTER 29

VAGRANT

It's about time Thorda started listening to my ideas," Arn said.

"It's hardly much of an idea," Cyrus argued, the pair hiding from the moonlight in the shadow of a dilapidated shop. Up ahead, five of Pilus's soldiers who had been stationed in Vallessau pulled a handcart loaded with pots of oil. Their faces were covered with familiar black cloth. Some were sewn with a white, grinning skull upon the front; others had drawn it on with chalk. This was their third stop for the night, a language school marked for flame. Cyrus and Arn had shadowed the group from afar, taking down any patrols that might interfere. The pots would be hidden, the oil ready to burn when Thorda declared the timing right.

"It'll be so much faster having these ready for us instead of lugging them around," Arn said. "Just grab them, toss them on the walls, and light up a torch."

"Assuming they are not found."

The giant man smacked Cyrus across the shoulder.

"Such a dour man you've become. That month apart did you no favors."

Cyrus smirked behind his mask.

"I don't know. I thought it helped me clear my head."

"A clear head is overrated." He pointed down the street, toward the west. "I got this group. Make sure our last stop's clear for us, would you?"

Cyrus saluted with two fingers, vaulted up to the rooftop of the language center, and sprinted. His cloak covered him, and the moonlight was a comfort. During that monthlong stint on the streets, he'd learned the rooftops of the tightly packed homes made a fine secret road out of sight of the armored patrols. From up there he could lurk, he could watch, and he could ambush. It felt like home, in its own way.

The final target was a magistrate's extravagant, and stolen, home a half mile away if he followed the street that wound through the second-highest tier of homes carved into the Emberfall Mountains ringing the city. Cyrus spotted a single patrol, two soldiers with torches standing beneath the awning of the now-shuttered gambling hall. They were talking quietly, and they sounded bored.

Cyrus's swords gave them a few seconds of excitement before they died. After dragging their bodies off the street, he continued. The home was quiet and well lit by two high lamps positioned just outside the surrounding iron fence. Cyrus lurked on the opposite side of the street, pondering a course of action. Would it draw any attention if he snuffed out those lamps? Surely not any more than a cart of masked strangers arriving with pots of oil to hide amid the bushes.

Staring at those two lamps, he felt a shiver run through him. He was the city's killer, the crowned skull lurking in the dark and walking through shadows. His battle against Lycaena had proven him capable of feats no mortal could accomplish. What, exactly, were the limits to his power?

Cyrus dropped to the ground, checked the street to confirm he was alone, and then crossed. The neighboring homes were dark, and he prayed they remained so. His gaze focused on the lamps, and the little flames protected from the wind behind glass jars. His vision narrowed. The light swelled in his mind, the flame like the faintest kiss across his forehead.

Around the lamps, the shadows darkened. Cyrus lifted a hand. The sensation shifted, now warming his palm. Their heat passed through his glove. His chest tightened. The darkness was growing deeper, tendrils of it curling around the glass, seeking to be let in. Hotter now, upon his palm. His fingers curled. His fist clenched. A pull, deep in his chest, and then the two lamps flickered and died.

Cyrus stood in the moonlight, slowly breathing in and out to calm the sudden quickening of his heart. Such a simple trick, yet the implications set his mind to racing.

You could do so much, if only you believed. If only you made the people believe.

Footsteps fell heavy on the cobblestones behind him. Cyrus turned, suddenly embarrassed and wondering what he would say to Arn. Except it wasn't Arn. It was another.

"Vagrant," the paragon spoke, her voice muffled behind her full-face helmet. Her armor was dark as obsidian and intricately designed. It flowed about her like cloth when she drew the sword from her hip and pointed it his way. Her other hand readied her shield.

"I have no time to play with paragons," he said, though uncertain if she truly was one. She was smaller than any he'd met, and he'd not once encountered a female paragon in service to the empire. Though some paragons painted their golden armor, he had yet to see one the color of night. That she would come for him alone, without soldiers or fellow paragons?

Cyrus drew his swords and held them at the ready. This foe was different, and differences meant unpredictability. Failed predictions in combat left you dead.

"I am not here to play," she said, her voice muffled by her helmet. She drew her sword back for a thrust, her shield taking its position at the lead. Cyrus narrowed his eyes, and he lowered into a crouch. So be it. He was not averse to battling in the street.

The softest rattle of her platemail marked the start of the fight. A flex of her legs, and she shot across the space between them, her sword looping wide to gain momentum before slicing inward for his chest. Cyrus dodged aside, begrudgingly surprised at her speed. Upon landing he dug in his feet, crossed his swords, and blocked another swing. Training took over, and for a brief exchange of heartbeats they tested each other. The sound of steel hitting steel rang out as they cut and parried, teasing out the extent of their skills. It was a back-and-forth, almost natural in its feeling.

Except a back-and-forth was not what this unknown assailant desired. She closed the space between them, her shield expertly positioned to hamper his movements. He kicked at it, rolled underneath a slash meant to decapitate him, and then came up swinging. His swords scraped along her shield, and then came her retaliation, a brutal chop at his collarbone.

His left hand blocked the hit, he grimaced against the jarring pain, and then he slid to his right. Her sword followed, pushing him, and he used that to his own gain. His feet left the ground, his aim the nearby pole of the lamppost. The second his heels touched, he kicked off, soaring overhead. To his annoyance, her shield was already up and blocking, so his slash for her helmet instead bounced off the painted black metal.

Cyrus was retreating before his feet touched ground. Every act, every hit or parry, had to remain fluid. He wanted her to attack again, to take the offensive while his back was to her. This would be his trap, for growing hot in his chest was a desire to unleash his savage fury upon this dark-armored stranger.

Her sword thrust for his spine. It pierced the air near his arm as he turned, his Lycaena blade deflecting off her pauldron. The ringing metal was like an alarm sounding through the empty street. She swung for his waist; he blocked and then repaid her with a kick to the chest that sent her stumbling backward. As if insulted, she slashed back into him, sword crashing down with all her strength. His weapons crossed, stopping her. The impact traveled down his arms to inflame his elbows.

Behind his mask, he laughed. To think, he once feared to meet a paragon strength against strength. As much as he might despise Thorda's plan, or the lack of a choice given to him in partaking, Cyrus could not deny its effectiveness. Pride swelled in his chest as he shoved his foe away. Had the empire ever faced such a foe as he?

Of course they had. Thorda's beloved, the Skull-Amid-the-Trees. That man had hung from the city gates, and so could Cyrus, if he was not careful. He mentally refocused, his legs properly setting to keep himself sturdy, but the expected attack did not come. His foe lingered, and though he could not see her face, he could feel the anger rolling off her.

"It's just a game to you, isn't it?" she said.

Even braced, he was not ready for the overwhelming nature of her sudden offensive. She tore into him, always seeking to close the distance between them. Their main-hand swords danced, steel striking steel as they took turns countering. Sweat dripped down his forehead and neck as she pushed closer to him, her shield another weapon to batter his body and hamper the intricate weaving of his swords as he attempted to shift between stances. There was no denying the truth, and he felt it anew when he tried to block another blow with only his off-hand held at an improper angle. The whole fight, she had been holding back.

No longer.

The Butterfly sword flew from his grip and clattered to the cobblestones. The woman's sword continued unimpeded, its aim for his neck. He dropped his right knee, instinct taking over. His head tilted; his shoulder dipped. A tug on his hood alerted him to how close to death he had been. The sword barely clipped the fabric.

Cyrus swung wild, hoping the blow would earn him a reprieve. Instead her shield smashed both his sword and his chest. Sharp pain flooded his ribs, and then he was flying backward.

At least I got my reprieve, he thought as he rolled twice and then bounced back to his feet. He'd be sporting a few bruises after this fight, that was certain. Assuming he lived. Even knowing the danger, he had underestimated this new opponent, and it almost cost him dearly. Though it might be a trick of the moon, he swore he saw faint light rising off her armor, dark and blue as the ocean.

"Games?" he said, the Endarius blade held in both hands. His training in the two-handed fighting style was meager, but currently this strange paragon stood between him and his Lycaena short sword. "I play no games, stranger. I do only what must be done."

"And how many suffer for it?"

"If you cared for our suffering, you never would have boarded a boat to our shores."

She shook her head. Dark plate rattled as she set her shield into position for a charge.

"A damn fool, even to the last."

With the nearby lamps snuffed and the sky clouded, there were so many shadows available to Cyrus. He took a single step back, waited for his foe to charge, and then dove into the alley behind him. His fist clenched. The Anyx ring burned hot, granting doorways available only to him. He reappeared from the awning directly before the magistrate's home, his body already diving for his discarded sword.

In the half second of disorientation upon emerging from the shadows, Cyrus came to the awful realization that his foe had anticipated the maneuver. Instead of following him into the alley she had immediately turned to where his other sword lay. His eyes widened.

Oh fuck me sideways.

Her shield blasted him in the forehead. Dizziness and pain followed. His momentum came to a spine-wrenching halt, plopping him onto his stomach with an ungentle landing. He brought his sword up to block an anticipated thrust only to instead receive a swift kick to the side. It was the same injured spot on his ribs, and he groaned as pain turned his vision momentarily white.

Desperation guided his movements now. He swung for her ankles. A ringing of metal confirmed her block. His sword looped for the other side to try again, only for him to gasp as his foe proved her ruthlessness. Her foot pressed his chest, pinning him, her heel grinding down on that same tender spot. He coughed, felt something wet spray across his lips and the interior of his mask.

Blood?

Down came her sword, the fight at its end. The tip touched the edge of his throat, and it hovered there in the grip of an unsteady hand. No further. The woman hesitated. Cyrus lay there, unmoving. There was something happening here he failed to understand, and the blue light shimmering from underneath her dark armor, floating like mist from a lake, convinced him she was no normal paragon of Everlorn. She could kill him but hadn't. More was at play, and he would not force her hand needlessly.

"Your mask," she said. "Give it to me."

Her voice was rough behind the metal, but there was no hiding the overwhelming rage lacing her every syllable. Cyrus stared at that helmet, trying to see through the thin slits across the eyes.

"Why do you hate me so?" he asked.

The paragon stiffened, but she was never given the chance to answer.

Arn's fist slammed her shield. She rocked backward, her heels scraping along the cobblestones as she held firm. Two more punches followed, each aimed for her face. Her shield absorbed the blows, but the barrage had her retreating, and Heretic laughed as he chased.

"Falling to a single paragon?" he called over his shoulder. "You're getting sloppy, Vagrant."

She was ready for his next punch, her sword parrying his gauntlet at the wrist as if it were another blade. His aim shifted, and she stepped into his exposed interior with her shield leading. It connected with his other arm as he brought it up to block the hit. He grunted on impact, then flung her away with a wide swing of his arm.

That was exactly what she wanted. She flew through the air several feet and then landed lightly, her feet kicking to continue her momentum as she retreated. Cyrus couldn't blame her. Their duel had been a close one, and with Heretic's arrival, the odds were distinctly against her.

Arn didn't bother chasing. Instead he clacked his gauntlets together, then turned and offered Cyrus a hand.

"Congratulations," he said. "You went and made yourself yet another new and interesting enemy."

Cyrus accepted the offered hand and bounced to his feet.

"You recognize that paragon?" he asked, gingerly rubbing his aching chest.

Arn stared at the shadowed road the assailant had fled down. A momentary darkness passed over his jovial demeanor. "Not exactly. It's his armor that makes him unique. That's the black armor of a penitent. Those who wear it are marked for their sins against the empire and are vowed to atone for it to their dying breath."

"Her," Cyrus said. He retrieved his other sword, relieved to have it back in his grasp. "I heard her speak, and she's far smaller than any paragon we've met, besides."

Arn scoffed at him.

"There are no women paragons. Never been in my lifetime, anyway."

"I know what I heard."

Though Cyrus was frustrated, Arn just laughed and smacked him across the back. His grin spread ear to ear beneath his mask. It made Cyrus feel jealous. If only his own cheer could be so infectious.

"Chin up, Vagrant. Consider this an omen. Thanet continues to be an island of firsts! We keep on fighting, and we might accomplish a few more firsts, like slaying the God-Incarnate and tumbling down an entire damn empire!"

CHAPTER 30

RAYAN

Nervous excitement filled the air. Several days of work, put at last into motion. Rayan stood with his back to the wall in the grand study of Thorda's new home, a portrait of a juniper tree beside him. As always, he could see the door, and be ready to act should a crisis occur. The rest of the elite were scattered throughout the room, listening to Thorda describe the plan in totality.

"With Lord Agrito dead, and Lord Mosau pledged for us in Ierida, the imperial hold on the island is severely weakened," the old man said. He looked dashing in a vibrant crimson robe tied with a black sash. Rayan suspected he had dressed up for the occasion. "Which means it is time we turn our attention to the jewel of the island, and the empire's strongest foothold. If we are to wrest Vallessau from their grasp, we will need an army. Assaulting the walls with a siege is beyond our resources, but sneaking soldiers in through the docks is another matter entirely."

Rayan had assumed as much given their recent targets. Thorda had ordered them to place the many pots of oil for the planned fires all along Vallessau's upper ring. It was there the prosperous lived, and where any attack would be met with heavy resistance. It was also as far from the docks as one could be while still within the circle of mountains that surrounded the city.

"What of Tannin?" Stasia asked. She and Clarissa sat beside each other on a long couch, wineglasses in hand. It was unusual for Clarissa to attend these meetings, but he suspected her role would continue to grow given her closeness to Stasia. "We burned Fort Lionfang instead of taking it, and the whole area is now leaderless. Surely there's more we could do there."

"Which is why Commander Pilus remains there with a significant number of his soldiers, sowing chaos and picking at isolated soldiers within their cities," Thorda said. "We've severed a finger of the fist holding our island. Our efforts here in Vallessau, coupled with Lycaena's resurrection in the north, distracted Galvanis for a time, but he must respond. When he does, it will involve moving significant forces out of the city, leaving the capital vulnerable. This is why we are smuggling an army into Vallessau, to take advantage of that opening. I will arrange a signal to—"

Thorda halted as the door opened. Tension immediately replaced any excitement. Cyrus straightened in his seat. Stasia leaned away from Clarissa, muscles tightening across her back and arms. Rayan's own hand dropped for his sword, but he did not draw it.

"I pray I am not interrupting," Keles said, halting in the doorway. "Nor that I am unwelcome?"

Rayan hurried to greet her by the door, and he wished the air wasn't so thick with tension.

"You are always welcome," he said, taking her hands. She wore a thick coat over her dress, and despite the warmth within the house, she kept it on as she accepted his greeting. "I've kept you in my prayers, and it is good to see you well."

"So I have your prayers to thank?" she asked, her faint smile disguising the gentle sarcasm. Others nodded or waved, except for Cyrus, who seemed reluctant to even look her way. Thorda waited for her to be seated, then resumed his plan.

"Six boats, two from Lord Mosau, four from Pilus, will approach the harbor near midday," he said. "Their weapons and armor shall be packed into crates, and the soldiers themselves disguised as passengers or crewmen."

"None of which would pass close inspection," Cyrus said. Rayan caught him stealing a glance at Keles. "Hence the fires?"

"The fires, the assassinations, and every other bit of chaos we unleash," Thorda said. "What few soldiers remain at the docks to inspect will be easily dispatched. From there, we smuggle everyone to safe houses Clarissa has carefully prepared for us over the past month."

The tiny woman blushed at the sudden attention.

"You make it sound harder than it was," she said. "And it will be exceptionally cramped. I pray you do not make them wait long."

"Their wait will depend on Galvanis taking the bait and marching west," Thorda said. "The audacity of our combined assault should be enough. He cannot afford to appear like he is losing control of the island. Hope is our greatest weapon, and his most dangerous foe. He will try to stamp it out, I am sure of it."

A large table sat in the middle of the room, and Thorda unfurled a map of Vallessau across its surface. Rayan had seen it before, a detailed layout inked on cloth that Clarissa had swiped from the city offices. Thorda began pointing out positions while the group gathered closer. One by one he placed little colored stones to represent his elite. While many members of the resistance would light the pots of oil already scattered throughout the city, Thorda's group would hit several more high-profile, and therefore more dangerous, targets to ensure a reaction from the local troops.

"Cyrus, your assassination attempt will be here, at the magistrate's home," their leader began. Next came Rayan's target, the largest of the mansions they planned to burn. Mari was meant to use her speed to her advantage, finding where reinforcements were at their weakest and attacking on their way to the various fires. Last were Stasia and Arn, together to attack a repurposed inn that now housed soldiers along the southwest ring.

"Show up, crush some skulls, and make sure everyone's good and scared so they summon imperial soldiers," Arn said, scratching at his chin. "I think I can do that. How about you, Paladin? You good for a bit of chaos?"

"I suspect I will spend most of it in your shadow, Heretic, so yes."

Thorda stepped back, and he crossed his arms while clearing his throat. The older man had never been good with expressing emotion, and Rayan knew what followed would be the closest thing to a heartfelt confession he could give.

"These past years have been ones of building," Thorda said. "Building resistance camps across the island, small and mobile, that the empire cannot hunt down. Building rumors of the Vagrant, and a hero to save the populace. Building a core group of elite, you all in this room, to carry out the work of entire armies."

Building a god to slay paragons, thought Rayan, but wisely kept his mouth shut. Thorda clasped his hands together, and he looked to the ground.

"The time for building comes to a close," he said. "Now we strike. Stasia gave us but a taste in Tannin. Cyrus hinted at the future to come when he slew Imperator Magus. Now we reclaim. Now we set free. And it is because of you six we have reached this point. Despite my failings, despite my . . . willingness to go where others may not have gone, you have stayed with me. Trusted me. I pray that in these coming days you will see that trust repaid ten thousandfold. I thank you, my elite. My friends. My family."

"Family," Cyrus said. He stepped away from the map, and the coldness of his voice ruined whatever sentiment the older man had tried to foster. "If you say so, Master Ahlai."

Every word was layered with bitterness. Rayan saw the gulf between them, and he wondered if it would ever be bridged. Thorda did not acknowledge it, nor did he try to argue.

"Eat and sleep well," he said. "Boats come to dock, and this time, they will bring freedom instead of the praying hands of the empire."

"Eat well?" Stasia said, and she took Clarissa's hand. "If you insist. There's a cookhouse near the piers that makes some divine oysters, and I could use a proper feast. Their beer is pretty good, too."

"I'll make sure she doesn't overdo it," Clarissa said. She'd kept mostly quiet during the meeting, and Rayan sensed she still felt like an outsider to the group. Still, she'd made an effort ever since the pair returned from Fort Lionfang. Whatever had happened there changed her in some small, unseen way. "Stasia has never been the greatest at self-control."

"Drunk Stasia is the worst Stasia," Cyrus chipped in, earning himself a laugh. "Actually, no, hungover Stasia is the worst Stasia. The foul language she'd mutter on our morning runs would make sailors gasp."

Stasia purposefully put her back to them, and she waved her hands in what Rayan assumed was a rude gesture from Miquo. The tension eased. It hadn't taken long for it to feel like old times. They were a group, they had their mission, and they had all the confidence in the world.

"Well, those two can run off to the pier, but I've got plans of my own," Mari said, and she hopped up from the couch. "Servants delivered carrots all the way from Gallos Bay. I didn't even know carrots grew on Thanet! Now I can finally make some proper Miquoan soup for everyone. Arn, come with me. You have muscles, and I plan on using them. You can start with cutting the onions."

The big man tilted his head.

"Do I get a say in this?"

Mari patted his arm as she passed. "Nope."

Arn reluctantly followed, his deep voice grumbling complaints even as he vanished into the kitchen.

"Ask Cyrus, he's the fancy blade master. Why do I have to chop the damn onions..."

Rayan watched with a smile, but his smile faded when Cyrus approached Keles. He pretended not to pay attention, nor to be listening.

"Hey," Cyrus said, addressing her for the first time since her arrival. The first time since they parted in the Cliffwoods after the false Lycaena's death. "I...so it's, I just wanted to say it's good to see you. Again. I'm glad you're all right."

Keles returned his greeting with an icy smile.

"Are you so certain I am all right?"

He sputtered a moment, unable to respond. The awkwardness was enough to make Rayan's heart ache. There'd always been a spark between the pair; anyone with eyes could see it. That spark remained, but it was tainted with hurt and trauma. Would it be ruined forever? Or could it heal?

Rayan was not the only one to notice the exchange. Thorda abruptly stood from his chair and cleared his throat.

"Cyrus, if you would spare me a moment?" he said. "I would look over your swords. Even a cursory glance reveals they've been subjected to much abuse during your absence."

Cyrus appeared genuinely offended.

"I sharpened and cared for them as always. If they're damaged, it happened during our fight against Ly..." He flinched as if stepping on a nail. "Well. I guess it can't hurt to have you check."

Their departure left only Rayan and Keles in the study. He appreciated the effort, even if it was forced. His niece sat with her hands together, her body hunched forward and her gaze locked on the map. She looked no worse for wear from her excursion north. If anything, she appeared stronger, healthier... except for the eyes. None of that reached her dark brown eyes. Deep circles surrounded them, and her gaze on the map was haunted.

Rayan had prayed with the dying. He had consoled orphans of war and been the rock others leaned upon when dire times came. Though he wielded a sword and shield, his place as a paladin was as a bringer of strength. His heart and his words were his true sword and shield. He knew how to give comfort to the hurt. He knew the proper verses that granted strength, the appeals to good memories, the remembrances of better times and of deep, undying love.

He knew not what to say to his dear niece, for she knew those same words, and they gave her no comfort.

"What we did was necessary," he said softly, the only truth he was certain of.

"I don't wish to argue over this."

"Neither do I, but I cannot lay my head down to rest without seeing the betrayal in your eyes. You loved the Lycaena that priest summoned. You trusted her. And when she died, I heard you..."

He couldn't finish the words. He'd heard her scream, just as she had screamed on that horrid day Sinshei brought her knife to Lycaena's flesh. The day of his greatest failure, the day he'd have taken his own life if not for finding Cyrus.

"You won't leave this alone, will you?" she asked. She rubbed her temples with her fingers. "Fine. If you insist. What makes you so certain the Lycaena you murdered wasn't real? I was there. I heard our prayers. I saw our sacrifices. Eshiel *loved* our goddess, loved her more deeply than anyone I have ever met. If anyone could bring her back in mortal form, it would be him."

"Because I had Mari whisper Lycaena when I returned to Vallessau." Keles startled at the revelation.

"You did?" she said breathlessly. "I didn't think...what did she say?"

"It was her...but only in part. Eshiel may have loved her, but was that love his motivation? No, he did not seek love, and forgiveness, and a bearer of a joyful song. He summoned fire and blood, seeking only to destroy."

"Maybe we don't need love and forgiveness," Keles snapped. "Maybe we need blood and fire to destroy those in service of Everlorn."

Rayan crossed his arms and frowned at her as if she were still his student.

"A goddess of fire and destruction is not Lycaena, no matter what name is given to her, or what blood was sacrificed to summon her. You know that. What Eshiel created was something akin to what Cyrus is becoming, a god of our own making. A piece of Lycaena was within her, buried deep, but it would have been swallowed up by the new and terrible. They may have shared a name, but you were deceived."

"Deceived." Keles's fingernails dug into her trousers. "You're right, Rayan. I was most definitely deceived."

The hairs on Rayan's neck stood on end. The bitterness that twisted her words...did she know? But she couldn't. Cyrus had confessed the truth of the Orani to him alone on their return to Vallessau.

"Why are you here?" he asked. "If you view me with anger, and accuse us of betrayal, then why come?"

"Are you asking me to leave?"

A shout arose from the kitchen before he could answer.

"...knife nearly cut my hand in half, shoddy piece of metal. How in all of Gadir does your family have shit cutlery when your dad is a gods-damned smithing genius..."

Mari was having none of it.

"Be quiet, you big baby. Oh, and before I forget, I need to get your measurements."

"My measurements? My thumb is bleeding like a stuck pig and you want measurements?"

Rayan glanced at the door, and he smiled despite his frustration.

"Arn's in a mood, I see."

When he looked back, he saw Keles twisting her fingers through a necklace he did not recognize. Its silver chain was looped through a dozen perfectly cut sapphires interlaced with seashells. Such a necklace must cost a sizable sum. Was it a gift from Eshiel?

When she caught him looking, she immediately let it go, dropping it back beneath her shirt.

"I'm sorry, I didn't come here to fight," she quickly blurted out.

Rayan knelt so he might meet her eye to eye. He couldn't shake his guilt. If he were a wiser man, a more observant one, perhaps he might understand what scarred his niece so terribly. Somehow it involved the slain Lycaena and the chaos that followed. If only he could decipher it completely.

"I don't want to fight, either," he said. "And if it helps, I want you to know I understand. I ache with Lycaena's passing, but she still remains upon Thanet. Her presence, her spirit, her love; it lingers as strong as ever. Your doubts are fair. Your worries are true. Tell me them if it will ease your burdens. I'm listening, I promise."

Keles bowed her head. Rayan knelt in silence, letting her prepare. She was gathering herself, organizing her words into some sort of acceptable order. Was this it? Would she finally open herself to him?

"There have always been thoughts I would not allow myself to think," she began. "While growing up in the eye of the church, and during your tutelage. Certain questions that, to even acknowledge, were considered blasphemous. But it wasn't the fear of the church's condemnation that kept me silent, or kept my thoughts in check. It was the answers. Some answers are too frightening."

She leaned back. Her fingers drummed across her thighs.

"Is Lycaena truly perfect? Do I even want to know the answer, if that answer is no? So I would not ask. I would not entertain such thoughts. But Lycaena is dead. Endarius is dead. Questions, not prayers, are all I have left. And one has stuck with me ever since the goddess Eshiel summoned died at the hands of the Vagrant. Even now, I fear to speak it. To acknowledge it."

Rayan took her hands in his.

"I fear no questions," he told her.

"No, you never did," she said, and for the first time since coming back, she smiled. The smile made her heartache that much worse. "I believe you, Uncle. The Lycaena brought about by Eshiel's sacrifice and prayer was not the one we once worshiped. It was a new Lycaena, one we created. But if that is true . . . then what are the gods? If they are created by *our* faith, by *our* prayers, then what are they to us? They cannot be our creators. They cannot be perfect. What if they're just our failures? What if they're our beautiful, wondrous beacons meant to blind us from the horrors that would fill their absence?"

"Do you truly believe it a horror to live without the gods?"

"It is horror with them. The lives they save, weighed against the lives they take? Does it balance? Could it ever?"

"Not while the God-Incarnate leads his campaign across the world," Rayan said. "But it is not him who bothers you."

"No. It's us. It's Thanet. It's everything. I'm sorry, I can't . . . I can't speak of this."

Something was amiss, far beyond the crisis of faith that sometimes struck men and women after years of service. Keles was probing a wound, deep and bleeding. The blade was still embedded within her heart. It wasn't Cyrus. It wasn't Lycaena. Then what?

"I beg you, talk with me," he said. "I feel it, this hidden suffering. It consumes you. Was it Eshiel? Lycaena? Or did something happen during your travels home?"

Keles stood, and she turned away so he could not look upon her face.

"Something," she said. Her shoulders trembled as she slowly breathed in and out. "Something I cannot talk about. Forgive me, Uncle. For everything."

She started for the door. Panic flooded him. He could not shake this feeling that, if she left, he might never see her again. This wound within her, it would bleed out fully and leave her hollow.

"Wait," he said. "Will you join us tomorrow? You've helped us before, and we would welcome you again without hesitation."

Keles glanced to the map, still on the table with targets marked with little colored stones. She tried, and failed, to hide her discomfort.

"No," she said. "Forgive me, Rayan. I have somewhere I must be."

CHAPTER 31

MARI

S tay safe," Stasia said as the two embraced just outside the mansion door. Mari hugged back and flashed her sister the biggest, falsest smile. Throughout the rest of the city, members of Thorda's resistance gathered in preparation. This was it, the whole plan in motion. The boats would soon arrive and give their signal to start the fires, the assassinations, and the chaos. Mari could not deny the excitement mixed with nervousness that raced through her heart and mind.

"Don't worry about me," she said. "Nothing outruns the Lioness."

The sisters departed. Alone, and in her human body, Mari walked streets that felt like home. For four years she had lived here, fought here, bled and nearly died here. Her family had remained in Thanet longer than anywhere else in their decades of leading rebellions. She wished that could have given her comfort. Instead, with every passing home, she saw signs of the slain gods. Carved grooves across wood doorways, a mark of Endarius's blessing during the Midwinter Feast. Peeled paint that had once been butterflies. Even the abundance of flowers planted along every window and on either side of every door hinted at former worship in its particular Thanese way.

"Bloom well," she whispered as she walked. "We all need a bit of your color."

Mari had no intention of following her assigned role for the day. She knew the greatest risk they faced, and she would be the one to protect them from it. Rihim would be out hunting, and she would ensure no one else faced his wrath. Just her, alone.

Her years of ambushing soldiers had taught her so much of Vallessau's winding streets, its poorer stretches along the lower levels near the docks, and the tightly packed gardens of the wealthy along the upper ring. Ever since the Everlorn Empire's invasion, a significant amount of the populace had either fled to the distant corners of the island or perished altogether amid war, starvation, and holy purges. This left a lot of abandoned homes and properties that normally would be snagged by the waves of relocated imperial citizens. Yet Thanet was anything but normal, and so they remained empty.

It was to one such empty warehouse that she traveled. The door was locked, but several windows were broken, and Mari easily climbed up. Inside were stacks of smashed crates, their contents long since looted. She stripped naked and set her clothes in a neat pile. Once ready, she tilted her head and closed her eyes. Her skin stretched. Her bones began to break and reshape.

"Come find me," she whispered. "I'm waiting."

Once in her Lioness form, she paced a circle about the warehouse, ensuring it was empty, before returning to her clothes. Satisfied, she reverted back to her human body and then dressed in the pale blue skirt and blouse she had brought with her from the mainland. She would be human when the hunting god came, for she sought conversation, not battle. Eyes closed, she sat and waited, wishing her heart would not pound so hard within her chest.

"Do you taunt me, little Ahlai girl?"

When she opened her eyes, the panther god crouched upon one of the high windows. She'd never heard him arrive.

"How so?" Mari asked.

"I smelled the Lioness, yet I come to find you alone, weak . . . vulnerable." His glinting gold eyes narrowed as he crouched lower. "Or have you finally learned the truth?"

Mari stood. Her insides jumbled. She sounded calm when she spoke, but it was a lie compared to the turmoil within her.

"I have," she said. "I know who he is. *What* he is. And I know what he did."

Rihim leaped to the ground with a heavy thud. A shiver spiked through her at his approach.

"You say much, yet say nothing. Speak the truth. The entire truth. Your family deserves no leniency, not from me."

Though he towered over her, Mari stood tall, and she tilted her chin so she might stare at him eye to eye.

"My father is the Miquoan God of the Forge, and it was he who betrayed your nation."

"Betrayed," Rihim snarled. The word bared his fangs when he spoke it. "There are no condemnations that go far enough. Our traps, our defenses, our rigged pathways and barbed ditches—he revealed them all. A century and a half of knowledge, brought to bear against us. The weaknesses of us gods. The places of our worship. Our secret homes."

He slammed his manacles together in a shower of sparks and a screech of metal. His temper temporarily stole his tongue, and it took all of Mari's willpower to remain perfectly still.

"Thorda smuggled assassins and paragons into our lands," Rihim continued. "We were at peace, and part of that peace meant respecting each other's divinity. He went where he pleased, and with him followed murderers. What he does now, with his little resistances, is but a shadow of his first betrayal. Weeks before the Everlorn Empire's army marched against us, they struck, all at once. Paragons ambushed us where we preached. Where we lived. Where we slept."

His fur stood on end. His muscled body shook.

"My wife," he seethed. "Butchered in her bed of thorns and roses. My kin, cleaved in half in their hidden caves and high towers. Everlorn attacked a heartbroken people, their souls ripped from them before the war ever began. Our fall was inevitable."

Mari clasped her hands together to keep them from shaking. All the tactics they utilized against the empire...what would they have been like when used against Antiev? If their foes were not priests of the Uplifted Church but the clerics and shamans and speakers of the original gods? The desperation, the impossibility of their task, skewed things darker. It frightened her. Shamed her. Despite her own frustrations with her father, she felt a deep need to defend him.

"But he's made amends," she insisted. "For over twenty years we have traveled battlefield to battlefield. He's poured all his wealth into rebellions. He's trained soldiers. He's even, he...even his daughters, he's turned us into weapons. Our lives, Rihim, we've given our lives to make things right. Doesn't that mean anything? Isn't it at least one step toward redemption?"

Her argument only earned her a sneer.

"Your father was a god, yet he sacrificed other gods in the name of petty grudges. His crusade to free other nations is a hypocritical joke. If he seeks to make amends, then tell me, Mari Ahlai, did he ever bring his rebellion to Antiev? Of course not. Whatever he has done, it has always been for himself. Only Miquo matters, and he would sacrifice all the world if it meant reclaiming it. There is no righteousness in your wars. There is no hope, no future, and no peace. Only death."

"You condemn my father, and yet serve the empire that slew your wife. Your hate for Thorda may be fair, but surely there is one greater deserving of it, and it is the one to whom you pray."

Rihim would not look her in the eye when he answered.

"I have spoken with the God-Incarnate. I have knelt at his feet while the great choir sang his praises. You know much, Mari Ahlai, but you do not know of what you speak. Antiev and Miquo, we tore each other apart for centuries. Now they are united. Let that peace come, for we are not deserving of anything better."

Mari's fear melted away into pity. This mighty hunter stood before her with back now stooped. The anger he brought so freely upon her father withered and died when instructed to face the God-Incarnate.

"I came as asked," she said. "What favor would you demand of me?"

Rihim crossed his arms and hesitated. He was staring at the manacles on his wrists. Did he think she could free him from them? Did he even want to be freed?

"You are a death-talker," he said, his voice surprisingly soft and hesitant. "There is one slain god I would have you speak for. Do this, and you may consider your debt to me repaid."

Mari stepped closer to the panther god and gazed upon him. What might he have been like in his prime? How fearsome and majestic was Rihim the Hunter when prowling the godwoods? Before his fur was broken with scars, his back bent, and his wrists shackled? To have hunted with him would have been worship. To traverse beneath the canopy of leaves, so thick there were only shadows even on the brightest of days, would have been as true as any prayer. Humbled, the empire called gods like Rihim. Broken, Mari would name them. Wounded. Lost.

"Give me a name."

His glinting eyes looked to the floor.

"Amees, goddess of the forest creatures. She is…she was my wife, when we walked our lands together."

"Have you any artifacts of hers?"

He shook his head.

"Whatever possessions I had were taken from me. All I can offer is a name, and my memories."

Mari reached out, carefully watching in case he reacted harshly. When he did not, she placed a hand on either side of his face. His fur was soft, and his whiskers tickled.

"Memories of a god," she said. "It will be enough."

The connection Mari shared with Endarius, of a continuous possession that could reshape her body, was a unique and drastic pact meant to be rarely used. But to let a god speak through her? To give it a voice? That was her true purpose, and had been for all other Miquoan whisperers. They were to remember and venerate the gods who came before, and to ensure their wisdom remained for future generations. She had been so young when her father taught her that communion need not be limited to gods of Miquo. So very young when she took the form of the tundra wolf god, Fenwul, and hunted her first victims.

"Amees," she whispered. Her eyes closed. Her hands tightened around Rihim's face, her fingers digging into his fur. "Let me see you. Let me hear you."

Faint images flowed into her mind. Deep forests, so akin to her cherished Miquo. Homes wrapped in vines that emerged from the earth as if grown and not built. The clear waters of the twin rivers. Along a brook, laughing, radiant, she saw a goddess dancing in a flowing dress covered with blooming flowers. Her tan skin was the color of a deer. Her eyes sparkled the green of the godwood canopy, her auburn hair long and tangled with leaves and twigs, each one perfectly in place. Longing hit Mari square in the chest, lovely in its purity, horrible in its ache.

"Amees?" she whispered again. "Hear my prayer. Hear it, and answer. I would speak, if you are willing."

Her mind traveled across the Crystal Sea. It passed over the tall grass of the Highlands and the snowcapped peaks of the Soaring Spines. It flew over the godwoods, past the miles of blackened husks torched by imperial fires, to the land of Antiev. The goddess's name echoed a thousandfold, in a realm few mortals could ever glimpse. And there, in a small, quiet place, Mari heard her answer.

I am.

Mari opened her eyes. By Rihim's reaction, they were no longer red, but green as leaves.

"Rihim," she said with a voice not her own, in words she did not choose but merely allowed to flow off her tongue. "My calm river, my moon and my stars. Is it you? Is it truly?"

Rihim flinched as if struck, but he dared not step away. He would not break Mari's touch on his face, lest it somehow cease the spell that fell over the warehouse. Already reality was giving way to the power of the divine. It swelled within her, raw and sudden. Birds landed along the windowsills, first a few, then dozens of owls and ravens. Mice emerged from nearby holes in the walls. How long had it been since a mortal had prayed the name "Amees"? How many worshipers remained hidden in Antiev, lighting candles in closets and reciting prayers committed only to memory where no fires of priests might burn?

"It is, my beloved," Rihim said. "I...I wished to speak with you again. There's so much to tell, but I...forgive me, Amees, but it is so wonderful to hear your voice. I am at a loss for words."

Mari stroked the fur along Rihim's right ear. It felt natural. It felt like a memory. She did not see the vicious Humbled that had murdered so many of her fellow resistance soldiers. Through the eyes of the forest, she saw a mighty hunter, once proud and strong. An overwhelming sense of love ignited her body, yet a sliver of pain wedged deep into its core.

"And I miss my husband. I would have him walk with me beneath the sunless sky. I would feel his touch. I would caress his face as he wrapped me in his arms, and stay within that embrace while the years passed and the birds sang us melodies. I yearn for that more than the prayers of my worshipers and the audience of the little creatures. My dear Rihim. My precious hunter. Would that he stood before me. In you, I see only a pale resemblance. Who chains you, my husband?"

He looked to the rune-lined manacles.

"I chain myself, dearest one. I have done what I must to endure, no different than the humans and the animals."

"You are no human or animal. You are a god, yet you have abandoned the hunt."

"I still hunt! I still embody the truths that made me!"

Mari shook her head. She couldn't imagine what twisted arguments and excuses Rihim used to justify his servitude. There would be no explaining them away. No arguing with them. They were scars on his mind akin to the ones carved into his dark fur. It was the work of years by the cruel, careful hands of the church. When Amees spoke again, Mari knew the forest goddess understood it, too.

"You may believe these lies, but do not ask the same of me. I will not deign to hear them."

"Please, stop," Rihim said. "I beg of you. I wish no argument. I wish no divide. I would only hear the love in your voice. Let me offer that love in return."

The growing pain in Mari's chest was so deep it frightened her. Whatever Amees saw in Rihim, it was not the husband of her past. Her love turned spoiled and rotten.

"You ask for what I cannot give."

Rihim pulled away, breaking contact with Mari's hands, but there was no stopping this. The essence of the forest flowed around her. Vines crawled up the walls. The wood that lined the crates groaned. Mari brushed her fingers through her hair, and she felt the smooth touch of leaves. The sadness in her breast grew, and with it followed tears.

"Enough," he said. "I have given her my love, now leave me be."

But it would not be so easy as that. Mari sensed Amees's pride, she who had been more than Rihim's equal in life. There was nothing timid and weak about her. She took a single step toward the panther god, and he retreated a step in kind.

"I would hold you again, but it will not be as you are. You will never be my moon and stars as you are. More hate than honor. More rage than pride."

Rihim lunged. His hand closed around Mari's throat. His claws extended, their tips sinking into her skin to draw droplets of blood.

"I said enough!" he screamed.

Together Mari and Amees stood tall before the hunter. They spoke the words he feared to hear yet knew were true.

"I loved you, Rihim," she said with two voices. "I loved you, but this chained god, I do not know."

He threw her across the warehouse. A gentle cushion of vines caught her, Amees's parting gift as the essence faded. The birds scattered. The mice ran back into their holes. The vines withered into gray and vanished like scattered ash on an unfelt wind.

"I am Rihim!" the panther god screamed at the top of his lungs. He curled his claws toward the ceiling and bared his teeth toward imaginary foes. He raged, even as he wept. "I am the Hunter of the Twin Rivers! I am Golden Eyes, I am Antiev's beloved and final survivor. I carry the memories of the forgotten. I hold the faces of the slain. I am not chained. I am…I am…I am not…"

Rihim collapsed to his knees. His claws cut across the floorboards. He shuddered as he heaved labored breaths. Mari held her solemn vigil. She would grant Rihim that dignity. When the moment passed, and he regained control, he finally looked up at her. That he remained kneeling, hands to the floor, made him resemble all the more a wild and savage panther.

"Consider your debt repaid," he softly growled. "Begone, deathtalker. The next we meet, I shall taste your blood upon my tongue."

Mari paused at the door to the warehouse. Her hand brushed the wood, her fingers settling inside the carved grooves Endarius had blessed it with some untold years prior. The Lion had lain dormant within her to allow room for the forest goddess, but now he stirred. She let that fire warm her blood. She let his rage chase away Amees's lingering sorrow, for it was more than she should ever have to bear.

"Some gods live on after their deaths, and some die while they yet live." She glanced over her shoulder. "You are wrong, Rihim, about much and more. Find what peace awaits you. Should we meet again, it will be the Lioness who claims the final hunt."

CHAPTER 32

VAGRANT

Cyrus knelt at the window high above the magistrate's extravagant dining room. The man's midday meal was finished, and he sat at the table, an open book atop the yellow tablecloth. He flipped pages idly, clearly bored. Cyrus saw no servants. Good. No innocents need suffer, just the wretched and guilty.

Would you like some excitement? he silently asked. *I am happy to oblige.*

He drew his swords, but before attacking, he checked the harbor. Given his vantage point atop the mansion, he had a clear view of the Crystal Sea. They were distant, but he saw the six ships coming to dock. The lead ship was yet to raise the red flag meant to signal the start of the fires, but Cyrus need not wait that long. He could kill the magistrate beforehand.

His attention returned to the magistrate. He was a scrawny fellow, skin leathery, hair dark, cheekbones prominent. A severe look, perhaps a fitting one. This was not the look of comfort and compassion, but of a man starving to death amid opulence.

Another turn of a page. He was fully dedicated to his book. Cyrus crossed his arms and then smashed straight through the window. Glass shattered about him, a jagged rain to accompany his fall. The magistrate looked up, his eyes wide, a panicked cry on his lips that never had time to emerge.

Cyrus landed atop him, his swords plunging straight into that open mouth. They pierced through tongue and teeth and then rammed out the bottom of his throat. Momentum crashed the both of them through the chair to the floor. Cyrus flowed with it, and when his legs hit ground he ripped his swords free with a savage glee.

Blood splashed across the tiles in an uneven spray.

Cyrus bent down to cut a crown across the dead man's forehead. When he stood, he glanced at the book still clutched in the iron death grip of the magistrate. The title was written in the imperial tongue. *Searching for Wisdom Among the Heathens.*

"Sorry, magistrate, no wisdom here for you, just a blade."

The side door blasted open with such force the hinges broke from the wall. Cyrus spun to face it, and it was only years of training that saved his life. His swords rose before him, blocking before he even saw the attack of the dark-armored paragon. Her sword struck his off-hand, and though it pressed awkwardly to his side, it kept the steel from cutting into flesh.

A trap? he wondered. Had the man he killed even been the real magistrate? He pushed off, trying to gain separation. His foe chased, matching footstep for footstep. Their blades danced off each other's, teasing defenses, testing for openings.

She was fast, but could she match his acrobatics? He shifted again, allowing her to press him toward the table, and then leaped atop it. A turn, a flex of his legs, and he vaulted high into the air. The words of the dead actor who played the Coin echoed in his ears.

Aren't you half cat now?

His gloved hand caught the edge of the broken window, pulling him through with only a slight halt of his momentum. Cyrus rolled headfirst over the shingles and then bounced to his feet. His arms spread to regain his balance atop the slanted angle of the roof. Again he looked to the harbor, and he smiled at the sight.

A red flag flew from the mast of the lead ship. In response, smoke billowed to both the south and east, along the wealthy upper rings of mansions. Members of the resistance were setting fires. Soldiers would think Vallessau under attack, but not from the docks. Time to help the others in building a distraction. *Perhaps a nice display of corpses at one of the crossways, each with a bloody crown . . .*

His paragon foe crashed through the same broken window, her shield leading the way. The frame cracked and bent to grant her armored body passage. Upon landing she slashed at him, and he would not risk fighting her when she held height over him.

"Yet again you haunt me," Cyrus said as he backflipped away. He landed atop a spire above a window and crouched low like a lurking gargoyle. He glared, the grin of his mask fully wide, and attempted to intimidate her with his presence. "Must you seek death so eagerly?"

The dark-armored paragon leaped after him, and weighted down by plate and shield, she was far less elegant. Shingles cracked beneath her weight as she landed on the spire, her sword slashing for his waist. Cyrus blocked with both blades, not willing to risk using only one. The steel connected, then locked together, as they pressed against each other.

The roof cracked beneath them. Wood groaned. Cyrus's right heel slipped, his footing uneven, and the paragon immediately seized the opportunity. Her shield swung forward, and only a panicked turn kept it from cracking his head open. Instead it hit his shoulder, and he rolled with the blow across the uneven rooftop. He saw platemail above him, his foe leaping after with sword leading.

Couldn't delay, couldn't think. He tucked his knees close and then kicked, forcing his trajectory to shift. His shoulder struck rooftop, his body pivoted, and then he fell over the edge. He continued to roll as he dropped, waist and arms turning to right himself before landing. When his heels hit the street his teeth rattled in his skull.

Hardly dignified, he thought, then immediately dove aside. His instincts proved correct yet again. The paragon landed on the ground where he'd been with her shield leading the way. He winced, imagining what that impact would have done to his bones.

"So quick to chase," he said. His swords twirled in his hands, though he truthfully did not know if his confidence was forced or not. "Have I done something to offend you, penitent? Perhaps killed one too many of your friends?"

His foe stood, her shield and sword falling into a proper stance. Cyrus was glad his mask hid his frustration. This woman, whoever she was, wouldn't talk. She wouldn't react. How had she known of his attack? Could she track him?

A thought passed through his mind, as black as his foe's armor.

Did the empire know of their plan?

The paragon pointed her sword at him. A challenge. Cyrus crossed his own before him, their steel colliding with a satisfying ringing.

"Come then," he said. "I will not be hunted again. Let one of us die this day."

They locked into battle there in the street, a vicious exchange Cyrus would hesitate to call a dance. They did not interplay, not anymore. His foe relied on her shield to rebuke any of his attacks, and then always came the counter. Twice she let his swords through, but her armor was thick, and his swords deflected. He wore no armor and could not afford to use a similar tactic. So in he went, quick hits, prodding against her defenses in search of weaknesses, before retreating back from the inevitable counter.

A disturbing thought came to him: This battle, this foe, felt like reliving a memory. Over a year ago, he first fought Rayan in the training circle at Thorda's countryside mansion. The same feeling, like trying to carve open a boulder with a spoon. But this foe was not a paladin. This foe, she was...

She was...

Cyrus had to know, if only to deny the cruel possibility. He flung himself at the paragon with heightened savagery. He forced her onto the defensive, his speed pushed to its absolute limit. Dread pushed him faster. His thrusts kept her body turned narrow behind her shield, and he hammered its surface with his blades.

"Show me what you are!" he screamed, his voice deep and thundering, for it was not his voice at all, but that of the Vagrant. "Show me the strength you wield, paragon!"

At last she met him charge for charge. He turned his body sideways, left shoulder meeting the shield while his Endarius blade rose high to block the overhead chop. Upon their collision, he rolled sideways off the shield, his feet a blur beneath him. A low dip, an altering of his momentum, and then he exploded in a backward somersault.

His heel caught the underside of her helmet, knocking it loose. He grimaced at the pain but endured. He landed lightly on his feet. The sound of metal hitting stone rang out as the helmet fell. He did not attack, even though his foe was disoriented and vulnerable. Even if his life depended on it, he could not have moved from that spot.

"No," he said. A pitiful denial, but it was all he could think to offer. Though he had guessed, the shock overwhelmed him with all its brutal truth.

Keles Lyon stood before him, her face exposed, her lip bleeding from the kick. Her brown eyes locked onto his, and a thousand words passed between them unspoken. A soft blue glow shimmered across her skin, there and gone in an instant.

"I don't understand," he said.

"You don't need to. I have the strength to match yours, and I will use it to save my people."

There was no doubting that. The energy of the divine warped around her, so similar to that of the empire's paragons. Yet he could not believe she would undergo such a ritual, nor that more Seeds had been smuggled into Thanet without Thorda knowing.

"No," he repeated. "This cannot be. How could you worship the God-Incarnate?"

"Not the God-Incarnate," she said. "Dagon, the Serpent, he who blessed my family just as Endarius blessed yours."

"The Orani," Cyrus said, the words falling from his lips without thinking.

Her eyes widened, and she lunged at him with sword slashing.

"You *knew*?"

He retreated with every step, batting away the strikes at a steady pace. It didn't feel like she thought they would kill. She wanted the contact, the connection, the refusal of steel against steel.

"Magus told me before he died!" Cyrus said in a panic. "I thought, I hoped, maybe he'd lied, he'd distorted or..."

Every word, a failure. He was stumbling, both verbally and physically. He dropped to one knee, crossed his swords over his head, and grimaced as she struck them. Pale blue light flickered across the dark steel of Keles's sword. She pressed down harder, locking him in place.

"Then you know overthrowing us wasn't enough. Conquering us wasn't enough. You had to subjugate us. Humiliate us. Lash us with chains, first real, then invisible, until we *cherished* the servitude. We thought it an *honor*. And now, when our island is suffering, when our people are dying, it isn't enough to be king. You would be our *god*."

Cyrus pushed her back, accepted a hit from her shield, and then danced away. They faced off, each of them trembling. Cyrus's arms shook with a mixture of panic and shame. The Orani. Keles had learned of her link to the Orani, and the Lythan family's invasion. All his consternation about when and how to tell her, now pointless. He'd erred. He'd erred badly.

"I meant to tell you," he said. "I swear, the moment I learned, I wanted to."

"Yet you didn't," Keles said. She lifted her sword. "I had to hear the truth from Sinshei vin Lucavi. Do you know what that was like, Cyrus? To listen to the Anointed One lay bare our nation's horrible truths? To realize how much of my life was built on lies?"

Blue light shimmered across the razor edge.

"A kingdom overthrown, a god slain, and the faithful hunted into exile. Your family is no different than Everlorn, Cyrus. We just learned to love them as their crimes faded into the past."

Her words were needles, and they stabbed into his chest, inch by inch, sinking toward his heart. There was no fixing this. A lone prince could not apologize for four hundred years of conquest and subjugation. No deeds of his would bring back the murdered Serpent. An impulse filled him to rip the silver crown from his forehead and cast it to the street. It passed, and deep within him, he felt revulsion at ever considering the possibility.

"Whatever my failures, do not let them drag you down, too!" he shouted. "What of your faith in Lycaena? Would you turn your back on her? Would you serve her murderers?"

"I have seen my goddess die *twice*," Keles said. "What faith? Who else is worthy of my worship? The foreign Lion? The conqueror pretending at salvation? At least the God-Incarnate is no lie. His armies topple nations. His worshipers inherit the land. If only Endarius and

Lycaena had been that strong. If only all of Thanet could have been spared this...this..."

Words were failing her, just like they failed Cyrus. She lowered her blade.

"Please, Cyrus, it doesn't need to end in blood. If I help her, if I kill you, then Sinshei has promised me Thanet's throne. Give me your mask so you may yet live. I will tell her you are slain. If you lay low, and abandon this hopeless rebellion, she will come to believe me. We can end this war. Thanet will have peace."

"A throne, gifted by the empire?" Cyrus asked. The dark voice within him raged at the thought.

A gift, to return what was stolen?

Before she could answer, a flash of light stole their attention. The pair turned to the docks, and the six boats sailing toward the harbor with hundreds of loyal Thanese soldiers aboard. They should have slipped past the caravels patrolling the harbor with ease, to be inspected upon docking. Instead archers on the warships fired burning arrows in great volleys. They set flame to the sails and ropes and boards. Men dove into the water, but they would find no salvation in the ocean. More soldiers marched toward the docks to seal off any potential avenue of escape.

Cyrus watched those boats burn as something deep inside his mind hardened. All of this had been perfectly planned. There was a traitor within their number. Someone privy to the most secret meetings of Thorda's resistance. Who had known when Cyrus was to place the oil for the distraction fires, and when he would assassinate the magistrate. Someone who now served the Anointed One.

The traitorous woman watched the boats burn. He could not read her expression. She was too guarded. Too closed off.

"Do you see?" Keles said softly. "This war we fight isn't even a war. Whatever strength Thorda has granted you, it will not be enough. Abandon it. Go into hiding, and put your trust in me. At Sinshei's side, I shall free Thanet, while you would only condemn her to further suffering."

"I want to trust you," Cyrus said, though he wondered if he still meant it. "But I do not trust the daughter of the God-Incarnate. Her promises are poison. We will not be given our freedom. We must take it for ourselves."

Keles turned and put her back to him. She peered over her shoulder, almost daring him to strike at her when vulnerable. He kept still, though there was a part of him that sought vengeance, and it was so much louder and stronger than he had ever thought possible. Keles was an enemy, of him, of his friends, of all Thanet.

"Then so be it, Vagrant," she said. "I sense him, as I'm sure you do, too. The Heir-Incarnate is at the docks, watching your people burn. Go to him. Weigh your worth. Take his head, and prove me wrong. At least then you will have earned that crown you wear."

It was a fool's errand. It was suicide.

Cyrus didn't care.

Men and women were dying. Yet again, boats were burning. He could not stand idly by and still claim to be his island's protector.

"I never sought to become Thanet's god," he said, the depth of anger in his voice shocking even himself. "But I will do it if I must. Cast aside your penitent armor. Forsake the Serpent. This island belongs to the Vagrant Prince, and I shall prove it to my dying breath."

Keles's look was ice.

"That is exactly what I fear."

CHAPTER 33

ARN

"It's just an easy smash and burn," Arn repeated. "Then why's my gut twisted up like two snakes fighting?"

Stasia peered around the corner of a brick wall to observe the ocean. Her face was already covered with her panther-skull mask, and her eyes shifted to a dull brown by the magic of her unique word-lace.

"I'm no expert on your gut," she said. "How often is it correct?"

He tightened the cord to his fox mask. It never seemed to fit quite right anymore.

"My gut tends to be smarter than I am."

"No need to insult yourself like that." The woman stiffened, and the playful tone exited her voice. "There. The lead boat switched its flag. Time to go."

The pair were on the highest rung of streets and neighborhoods carved into the ring of mountains that curled about Vallessau's ports and beaches. Such a vantage point gave Arn an easy view of the water below them, and the approach of the six ships carrying soldiers from both Commander Pilus and Lord Mosau. It also allowed him to see the flurry of activity atop the five warships that encircled the port. He skidded to a halt, the squirming of his stomach hardening into a single lead stone.

"We have chaos to sow, Heretic," Stasia hissed, keeping her voice down. It was broad daylight, and though the residential district was mostly quiet, they could not afford the slightest delay. They were already conspicuous enough with their masks and weaponry.

"Hold," he said, shaking his head. The soldier bunkhouse they were meant to attack would have to wait. He recognized the formation of the soldiers on the warships.

Archers along the front. Squires with tar and flame directly behind.

"No," he said. "Damn it, not again, not again!"

Stasia grabbed his gauntlet by the wrist and pulled. Her eyes were wide with impatience.

"Get your damn head together, Heretic, we need those fires lit."

Arn ripped his arm free and then pointed.

"It won't matter. They know. They somehow gods-damned *know.*"

The six boats were meant to pass through the blockade and form the proper and ordinary line into the waiting docks, to be checked by authorities appointed by the Uplifted Church. It was the same thing Arn had undergone when he arrived on Thanet months earlier. Only the imperial blockade did not let them through.

With perfectly synchronized aim, the archers on all five warships lifted bows suddenly alight with tar and flame. The fire flew. The arrows struck sails, unlucky bodies, and treated wood. It wasn't much, hardly enough to even set a sail aflame, but then came the next volley, the next, and the next.

Stasia watched the horror unfold in silence. She need not speak to convey her rage. The tensing of her muscles, the hard clench of her jaw, and the shake of her hands was more than enough.

"Who told?" she asked when the third ship burst aflame. Her voice was colder than a desert night.

"I don't know. Did your father decide the Vagrant needed extra motivation?"

It was snide and he didn't mean it. His anger was talking. All their plans, ending in flame. Hundreds of soldiers, good men and women ready to fight for their island's freedom, were burning. Already he saw many diving into the water, but there would be no safety there. The warships were breaking formation to form a new perimeter. No need for fire now. Just arrows, and a lot of easy target practice.

Stasia unclipped her axes from her waist and turned to the bunk-house farther down the road, oil pots hidden in crates stacked on the porch of the neighboring home.

"We're about to walk into a trap," she said.

"Not about to," a horribly familiar voice said from the rooftop above them. "You're in one, little brother."

Arn didn't turn. He didn't look up. He grabbed Stasia's arm and pulled, because it was time to run. They sprinted down the street, eyes ahead, legs pounding the hard stone. Dario would chase, but if they were fast, if they were clever...

The road curved, and around that curve waited twenty soldiers set up in a line two rows deep. Spears poked out through layered shields. A trap, set wide and sprung at the exact moment the flag switch had signaled the start of the distraction fires. Someone in their group was a traitor, but he couldn't dwell on that now. No one made sense, which meant whoever it was, that truth was going to hurt. Save it for later.

"Blast through!" he shouted. The chainmail layered within his long coat would help deflect weaker blows. Strength and savagery were his greatest weapons. He leaped at the last possible second, arms up and gauntleted fists clenched. The speed caught the soldiers off guard. He saw the fear in their eyes. He saw how their spears dipped, how some muttered curses. How well these men knew the might of paragons, but never had they thought it would be turned against them.

Now they knew. He landed in a clatter of metal as his gauntlets smashed armor as if it were paper. He spun, arms out, breaking limbs with their impact. Two spears caught in his coat, and he ripped them from the grips of their wielders. He flung one through the throat of its previous owner. The other he swung in a circle, earning himself more space, and then buried it halfway up the hilt in the gut of the first man who tried to close the distance.

Stasia feigned beating a path alongside Arn, but at the last possible moment she pivoted so that she followed in Arn's wake. Her axes were a whirlwind of steel, cutting down any who tried to surround them. Knowing she was there, and trusting her to protect him, urged Arn onward. Every movement, every shift of his leg or swing of his arm, propelled him forward and left broken bones in his wake.

At last he cracked two heads together, turning the skulls beneath the helmets into jelly, and stepped through the spear wall.

"You should have brought more than twenty!" Arn laughed, but his cheer was forced. Dario was on his heels. Compared to him, these soldiers meant nothing. They ran, side by side, legs churning. Twice he glanced behind. Twice he saw his brother in the distance. Where they went, he would follow. There would be no hiding. No escape.

"We need to get to the docks and salvage something out of this mess," Stasia shouted beside him. Arn skidded to a halt, and she stumbled a half step ahead. "What are you doing?"

"Buying you time," he said, wishing he felt the confidence he faked in his voice. "Go. Save who you can. Dario is my responsibility."

Stasia leaned so she could see past him. Snap decision made, she pointed a finger at his face.

"Distract, then run," she said. "No dying. Consider that an order."

The older Ahlai sister broke into a sprint. Arn chuckled with mirth he did not feel as he clanged his gauntlets together and turned.

"As if I'd take orders from you," he said, and faced his brother. Dario Bastell slowed to a walk. If he cared to chase after Stasia, he showed no such inclination.

"Again with the disguise," Dario said, and he pointed at Arn's skull mask. "Did you think a bit of bone would prevent me from recognizing you?"

"A paragon of the empire, complaining about theatrics? I guess I shouldn't be surprised. Hypocrisy was always our greatest asset."

His brother raised his fists. A familiar hardness settled over his face. This was a look Arn remembered well from all those times during training when Dario had beaten him bloody. It was the shutting down of sympathy. It was the abandonment of any emotion that could be considered weak and unwanted.

"I have ever been true to my word," said Dario. "Can you claim the same?"

The street around them blurred in Arn's mind. The past reclaimed them. He and his brother, together in a dirt circle, bare-knuckle boxing while their mother and father cheered them on. Even back then, despite all parties insisting it was merely a game, Arn knew the consequences were real. The blood and pain, they would be real.

But what of this time?

"No claims, just me beating the piss out of you," Arn said, and swung. Dario weaved away from the first few punches, light on his feet despite his size and muscle. This would not be the brawl Arn preferred, where order and tactics fell apart and the fight came down to kicks and elbows and a stronger will to survive. This would be a skillful exchange. A game. A dance.

"I recognize that skull," Dario said, twisting so the punch meant to land square on his collarbone only grazed his shoulder. "I wasn't certain at first, but now I know. A fox skull, is it not?"

Arn answered with a trio of punches thundering into the clenched gauntlets covering his face. Metal screeched against metal, but both were Ahlai-made and blessed with countless hours of prayer by church acolytes. It would take far more to break them than a few glancing blows.

"A *fox* skull," Dario repeated with emphasis. "Is that all this is? Your abandonment, your betrayal? It's because of guilt?"

Arn's fourth punch sailed wide after a subtle dip of Dario's head, and then came the retaliation. It struck Arn square in the gut, blasting out his breath. His mouth opened and closed futilely. Panic forced movement into his arms, a punch for the jaw his brother easily blocked.

Back and forth, an exchange that Arn knew instinctively he would lose. His feet danced beneath him, but his movements were always too slow, his punches lacking the strength they needed. Dario absorbed one to the shoulder, then delivered one in kind to Arn's hip. Bruises and welts spread across their divinely blessed flesh. It was this closeness that Arn preferred over other weapons, but he regretted it now his foe was someone so personal to him. What he would give to have distance as the blows rained down upon his guarding arms. What he would sacrifice to have the separation of a blade.

Dario turned, accepted a hit to his forearms. Arn pushed, hoping to break bone, but failed. The effort left him exposed, and he flung himself sideways, but not quite fast enough. The punch clipped the side of Arn's head, just enough to split his lip from the pressure against his mask. He finally scored a decent hit in return, a punch to Dario's chest that would have made pudding of a normal human's innards. His brother retreated so Arn's follow-up missed.

"I told you what I've learned," Arn spat. Blood trickled down his chin and flecked the interior of his mask. "You were there! You saw the horrors of Vulnae!"

"You're not upset at the horrors, but the guilt you felt in partaking."

What did it matter? Why make such a distinction? He guarded his face against two hits, bit down against the pain in his arms, and then lashed out blindly. He struck empty as Dario weaved and then countered with an uppercut that smashed Arn's gut and forced out the air in an awful groan that left his throat feeling raw. His legs wobbled, then collapsed when the follow-up punch struck him directly in the chest. Arn's lungs hitched, and hitched, but he couldn't draw breath.

Dario towered over him. Stronger. Faster. This was not a fight Arn could win, and they both knew it. Instead of a physical blow, he battered him with words.

"We do what we must!" he shouted. "We are the blade that severs a gangrenous limb. We are the arrow through the eye of a wolf that stalks the sheep. It is not pretty. It is not nice. But it is *vital*."

"No," Arn said. He had to force the word out with what little air he could draw. It sounded like the croaking of a dying animal. "We are murderers."

The toe of Dario's boot bashed him in the teeth as reward.

"We are all murderers, but you slew the faithful. You committed the sins. And so you must repent."

The blows rained down upon him. A crack in the bone of his jaw. Ribs snapped. He trembled on his knees, fighting for each breath, as the next barrage smashed below his rib cage. Instinct had him lifting his hands to guard. He could not have made a worse decision.

"You are not worthy of these gauntlets," Dario seethed. "The praying hands upon their wrists deserve better."

He grabbed Arn's left hand with both of his and pulled, ripping the gauntlet free. Arn could only watch in dull horror as his brother set it down and smashed it with his heel. The Ahlai-made metal could not withstand the full strength and weight of a paragon. It shrieked and crumpled, unseen hinges and bolts warping or breaking outright.

"You are not the judge of me!" Arn screamed. He felt helpless. He felt himself a child again, protesting against punishments that never seemed fair. He, always looking up to his brother. His big brother, always looking down at him with love and disappointment intermixed in equal measure.

"Better I judge you now, than our God-Incarnate after you breathe your last." Dario closed his hand about Arn's other gauntlet. Arn pulled, fighting him. The two struggled, but only Arn showed any visible sign of it. His breathing was ragged, his body bloodied. He would not surrender this gauntlet. He would not!

"You never understood," Dario said. They were so close, both of them down on their knees. His brother's free hand cupped his face. "I have always loved you, Arn. I have always wanted the best for you. To lose you now would be my greatest failure, and I will not allow it."

Arn wrested his head away from that loving touch, for it burned his skin like acid. Dario leaned even closer. His confession would not be denied.

"I will *save* you, little brother, no matter the cost."

He pinned Arn's hand to the street as if they were wrestling, lifted his other arm, and then smashed his fist straight down upon the gauntlet. The metal crunched, and within it, so, too, did flesh and bone.

Arn screamed. He tried to pull his hand free. The mutilated metal refused to allow it. The shapes were wrong.

Another hit, fist to fist. The metal snapped in half along the knuckles. Pain shot white hot through Arn's mind, and he howled as he rolled onto his back. But Dario was not yet done. He gripped the metal with both hands and then ripped it free. Blood splattered in a great spray across the both of them. Arn stared at the wreckage that was his hand and wondered if even the incredible healing abilities of a paragon would be enough.

Dario casually tossed what remained of the gauntlet aside. His gaze shifted to the burning boats at the pier.

"This foolish rebellion on Thanet has reached its end. I am begging you, Arn. Do not go down with it. So long as you draw breath, there is still time to repent."

Arn coughed blood as he curled up to his knees and then staggered to his feet.

"I won't become a penitent," he said. All the gods help him, it hurt so much to breathe, let alone speak. "The God-Incarnate will not have me. I'd rather burn in some other god's hell than serve in his heaven."

Dario returned his gaze with eyes full of disappointment...and an emotion too damnably close to love for Arn's broken spirit to handle.

"Gadir is only the first great conquest," Dario said. "Upon our deaths, we will fight in the second. The slain gods shall have no heaven, Arn. They shall administer no hell. Everlorn will reign from eternity to eternity. In that glorious future, you will be at my side, the traitor son returned penitent and welcomed with open arms."

A deep growl rolled over Arn, and it was enough to make him tremble. He turned, his teeth gritting against the pain the movement spread throughout his body.

"Everlorn shall rot upon the land they have stolen," Mari said, calmly approaching down the center of the street. Splashes of blood painted her gray fur. Her bone wings vibrated with energy. "And I will be the death that comes for her most faithful."

Arn retreated until he stood at her side. One of her wings curled around him, bringing him closer, a macabre hen gathering in her chick.

"What are you doing here, Lioness?" he muttered.

"Protecting those I care for. Run for safety, Heretic. I shall keep this monster occupied."

Dario lowered into a combat stance, his hands up and ready. Blood, Arn's blood, dripped down the shiny metal surface of his gauntlets.

"What strange creatures you befriend, little brother," he said. "I suppose I should thank you. This day will be one of many victories after I kill the fell beast that is Thanet's Lioness."

Arn refused to budge. How could he leave Mari to face Dario alone? Even without his gauntlets, he could still help with his good hand. He could still pack a wallop.

"We outnumber you. The advantage is ours," he said, but there was no strength to his boast. Dario laughed, and his ensuing grin was all teeth.

"Then come prove it."

Mari dashed forward, her wings thrusting like swords. Dario sidestepped one, batted away the other, and then met Mari's charge with crossed arms to protect his upper body. They collided, the paragon held firm, but then she flipped off and away. It wasn't a real attack, only a feint. She landed lightly and then leaped once more. Her hind legs kicked Arn straight in the chest, staggering him away. Her claws raked the stone to halt her momentum as she roared.

"I said run, you damned fool!"

As much as it hurt him, as much as he hated the thought of being so cowardly and useless, there would be no swaying the Lioness from this course of action.

So he ran.

He ran without direction in mind.

He ran without hesitation.

He ran, but he also looked back and saw Dario battling the Lioness. They were a tangle of muscle and fur, he always trying to close the distance so he could utilize his greater strength and size to full effect. Her teeth snapped at him, and in return, he struck her so hard one of her fangs flew loose in a spray of black blood.

At the first turn, when he could watch no more, he wiped his injured hand along the corner of the nearby building. If she lived, she could track the scent of his blood to find him.

If.

No, not if. Stop it, you bastard.

Smoke billowed in tremendous waves from the docks. Arn did his best to keep it behind him as he ran. No time to think about that, what it meant, or how the others were reacting. He had to get away. Another turn. Another swipe of blood. Surely she could outrace the paragon with her four legs. She would track Arn and find him, and then they could plan their next move.

He ran until he found somewhere quiet and dark, an alleyway that curved sharply so most was hidden from the main path. He trickled one last bit of blood near the entrance and then stepped within.

And then he waited. And waited. Alone with this thoughts, and the damning words of his brother. He kept his mutilated hand clutched to his chest. More time passed. He paced. Maybe he should turn back. Maybe Mari underestimated Dario and was injured. Could she escape with only three good legs? More pacing. Though he was no longer running, his heart beat faster, not slower.

It's fine. She's fine. Dario didn't kill her.

Because if Dario did kill her, then it would be no different from Arn killing her. His brother. His failure, his broken gauntlets, and his shed blood. The foul deed might as well be his, and of the mountain of sins upon his back, that was one he could not endure. To lose someone so wondrous as Mari Ahlai, to see the Lioness broken, to never again spend time with the god-whisperer who heard his tale of Velgyn and Onleda and did not recoil, did not hate, only took his hand and offered him kindness…

"Damn it!" he screamed, and punched the wall with his unbroken hand. Fresh blood dribbled across the wood as the skin scraped off his knuckles.

"Stop screaming, lest you draw attention."

He looked up, and there was Mari, peering down at him from the rooftop with her red eyes. A hop, and she landed beside him. Arn flung his arms around her neck, unable to help himself. He could finally breathe again.

"I feared the worst," he said.

"And the worst may yet come true," she growled, the word-lace shimmering blue across her throat. Her tension eased away, and she leaned closer into him, her face tilting to press her cheek to his. "Where is my sister?"

He recovered enough to withdraw, and he leaned his weight against the wall, his bloody arm clutched to his chest. He tried not to look at his misshapen fingers. Popping them all back into place was going to hurt like mad.

"The docks," he said.

"What is she hoping to accomplish?"

"I'm not sure she hopes to accomplish anything, Mari. I think she's mad and hurt, and she's going to make the imperial soldiers suffer for it."

Mari padded closer, sniffed at his hand, and then withdrew.

"You are in no shape to fight," she said, and he could not argue the point. "Return to my father's house."

"And what of you?" he asked as she bounded out of the alley. Panic rekindled in his breast, a protectiveness that was awkward and new to him. He wanted nothing more than to be at her side and see her safe.

She turned, her teeth bared in a feline grin.

"Did you not listen?" she asked. "I protect those I care for. If Stasia's wreaking havoc at the docks, then the Lioness must join the fray."

CHAPTER 34

VAGRANT

Cyrus leaped from rooftop to rooftop, crossing dozens of feet with each flex and push of his legs. The ground could not hold him. The distant fires called to him, and he dared not pause to think, for that path led to doubt and hesitation. Amid the soldiers and paragons shone a beacon of crimson divinity, a splinter to his mind's eye. The Heir-Incarnate. His foe. His prey.

At least then you will have earned that crown you wear.

His enemies numbered in the hundreds, a massive crowd gathered at the docks. The way they laughed and cheered, it was as if they attended a festival, and the distant fires were their entertainment. The Heir-Incarnate stood in the middle of it all, flanked on either side by paragon bodyguards.

Cyrus landed atop a nearby lantern pole in a crouch, his cloak wrapping about him, his hood falling low to hide his crown.

"Galvanis!" he bellowed.

All eyes turned his way. The attention swept a shiver through him, one not entirely unpleasant. The Heir-Incarnate grinned up at him, his sword casually resting over one shoulder. His gold and silver armor gleamed in the firelight.

"Were they your friends, Vagrant?" he asked. "Your acquaintances? Or were they merely your army, come to do your bidding?"

Cyrus crouched lower. He felt like a vulture seeking a meal from a high perch, and perhaps it was true, for below him he saw only dead men.

"They were heroes of Thanet," he answered. "And they deserved a far better fate than this cruelty."

Galvanis shrugged.

"Such is war. They could have marched upon the city gates if they sought an honorable battle, but instead they tried to slip in like roaches so they might bite us while we slept."

"Roaches," Cyrus said, snarling out the word. The dark impulses within him, the thirst for a bloody crown, screamed for control. He had felt the same when battling the monstrous Lycaena. This time, he would not refuse. His vision swam with the flames of burning ships. His ears rang with the cries of dying and drowning soldiers, cries by no rights he should be able to hear given the distance between them.

But he heard them still. They were like claws scraping down his spine. They were prayers, the worst kind, the final, the desperate. He could not answer them. He could not save them. But he could avenge them.

"Come face me, Galvanis," he said. The softly spoken words should not have reached beyond a few feet, let alone among the rattle of armor and raising of weaponry, yet all heard. He saw it in the widening of the soldiers' eyes, in the doubt that caused their grips to tighten about their weapons. "I shall walk a road of corpses if I must."

The soldiers anticipated a frontal assault, and they formed a wall of steel before their leader. It was exactly what he desired. He leaped into the air, not forward, but backward and away from the teeming mass of soldiers. His destination was the narrow alley beside him, cramped and full of broken crates. His feet never touched the ground, for the darkness swallowed him up, the magic of his Anyx ring transporting him.

The docks might be well lit and swarming with soldiers, but the water was dark and full of shadows.

Cyrus's momentum from his fall went unchanged, though the direction flipped, and he broke through the ocean surface with his swords raised and water spraying in all directions. He felt the prayers of the dying behind him, felt the heat of the flames on the skin of the faithful. Time itself seemed to slow. His strength would not be broken.

Two soldiers had their backs to him. They turned at the sound of his emergence, but much too slowly. His off-hand blade jammed into one man's throat and then dragged him to the water. Cyrus's shoulder hit the other, knocking him back a pace. He twisted while stumbling, mouth open to shout. Cyrus buried a sword into his face, breaking teeth and severing his tongue on the way out the back of his skull. He ripped the blade free, sending head and helmet rolling across the docks.

Panicked soldiers rushed to form a new wall between him and the Heir-Incarnate. Cyrus met their charge with unmatched ferocity. The nearest thrust was panicked and low. Cyrus hopped, his right foot stepping on the man's wrist to pin the sword low and gain him increased leverage. A swipe, and the arm severed at the elbow. Cyrus spun as he dropped, parrying an overhead chop while cutting open the throat of the first soldier he mutilated.

More muscle and steel pushed his way. Cyrus tore into them, needing the savagery to keep his mind red with rage so he could not doubt. Blood slicked the docks. A man thrust for Cyrus's waist; he batted it aside with ease and then dropped to one knee to avoid a swipe at his face. His off-hand rose, blocked another hack at his neck, and then he lunged to a stand while spinning like a dancer. The curving end of the Endarius blade cut a diagonal slash across one soldier, his armor giving way like brittle cloth, decapitated a second, and then slammed back down to redirect a spear thrust into the boards.

The soldier refused to release his weapon, and so Cyrus continued his momentum. He leaped, his right leg cracking him across the head. Swords slashed the air below him. Blood exploded when he landed, showering his cloak as he simultaneously opened one man's throat while stabbing another through the heart. He ripped his weapons free and then laughed.

He laughed, and all heard it, and knew his pleasure, his rage.

"Stand back!" Galvanis shouted. The planks of the dock rattled beneath the weight of his every step. Soldiers fled to make a path, and even the paragon bodyguards kept their weapons sheathed. He approached, his bemused smile untouched by the carnage.

"I warned you not to come here. You could have lived in the shadow of our conquest, but instead you chose death. Such is the price of pride."

Cyrus pointed a lone blade his way.

"Come, vin Lucavi," he said. "Your father may be a god, but you are flesh and blood."

Galvanis grinned at him.

"Is that what you believe? Then you are a fool. Let me show you the strength of Everlorn. Can you withstand it, or will you wilt?"

He lifted his enormous sword overhead, clutching the hilt with both hands. It was an obvious challenge, made in full view of his soldiers. Dodging would imply cowardice, or that he was indeed weaker. Instead Cyrus stood firm. He remembered Magus of Eldrid's total shock when a mere "mortal" withstood a hit that could kill gods. Let this same fear and shock come to the Heir-Incarnate. He was the Vagrant Prince of Thanet, defender of the conquered, the grinning skull in a silver crown.

Down came the enormous blade. Its edges crackled with power. Every muscle in the Heir-Incarnate's body twisted and tightened to grant it strength. Cyrus had the briefest moment to question his decision, the faintest spark of fear. He had witnessed the inhuman gifts Galvanis wielded when striking down the monstrous Lycaena. How much greater would he be than a paragon like Magus?

And then their swords connected, and Cyrus knew he had erred. An island might be praying to the Vagrant for salvation, but an entire continent of millions bowed their heads to Eldrid. They worshiped God-Incarnate Lucavi with song and slaughter, and here stood Galvanis vin Lucavi, equal recipient of those prayers, inheritor of the throne and title of godhood.

Cyrus screamed. His arms ached. His back wrenched awkwardly. His swords held, but only just. Galvanis pushed harder, and maddeningly, he showed almost no sign of strain. Cyrus crumpled to his knees, and his teeth felt ready to crack, he clenched them so tightly as he focused on keeping that killing blow from rending his body in half.

At last, he pushed it aside and then rolled. Galvanis kicked him during the retreat. Cyrus's mind flashed white. How many ribs did he break with that almost casual flick of his boot? He came to a halt at the end of the dock. Behind him was the water, and the pillars of smoke rising from the burning boats.

"One blow?" Galvanis asked. "You would falter after one blow?"

Cyrus forced himself to breathe. He glared at Galvanis, but his rage was directed solely at himself. A single exchange against the Heir-Incarnate, and now he knelt frightened and gasping for air? What had happened to him? How had his certainty and faith crumpled so hard?

He needed out. Now. He had underestimated his foe to a terrible degree. Yet despite his need, it would not be an easy escape. Soldiers swarmed the docks and the streets beyond. The daylight robbed him of darkness. Galvanis lifted his sword for another hit, and his grin was wretched. He saw Cyrus's fear. He knew victory was his.

Cyrus rolled sideways the moment the sword swung. The blade smashed through the boards of the dock. In the half second the weapon was trapped, Cyrus sheathed his off-hand blade, reached into his pocket, and pulled out one of the smoke stones Thorda had made for him.

Hope you knew what you were doing, old man, he thought as he flung the stone at his feet. The sphere cracked open upon hitting the board, and as promised, an explosion of dark smoke billowed outward in all directions. The smell of it struck Cyrus, bitter and burnt. It left a film on the back of his throat, as if he had licked the ashes of Thorda's forge. He fought back a cough. Despite its unpleasantness, its cover was deep, and the darkness beneath it more than enough. He clenched his fist, enacted the magic of the Anyx ring, and fell.

If only there had been somewhere farther to go. Cyrus collapsed not two houses away, coughing as he breathed in fresh air. Three soldiers patrolled nearby, and they spotted him instantly at the entrance to the alley.

"Perfect," he muttered.

He stood and drew his other sword. Before either could approach, they exploded in a sudden eruption of blood and steel. Stasia pushed past the bodies, her twin axes locked together to form a great-ax. Gore soaked its steel head.

"Have you lost your mind?" Stasia asked.

"Haven't we all?" Cyrus countered. He pushed aside the pain and readied for a battle. The entirety of Galvanis's forces rushed to meet them, eager for a fight.

"It's two against an army. That goes beyond our usual madness."

The first wave of soldiers closed the distance, but they never reached the pair. Mari landed in their midst, crushing a man beneath her paws. Her wings sliced the head off one, then plunged their razor sharp points into the chest of another. Blood splashed across her fur as she turned her attention to the remaining two. A sword clanged uselessly off the bone plate of her shoulder. Her teeth closed around one man's throat, ripping out his larynx. The last turned to flee. A wing pierced his back and ruptured his innards as a reward.

"Then it's a good thing there's three of us," Mari said, licking the blood from her face. The trailing soldiers saw her and retreated so they might wait for the bulk of their forces to arrive. A welcome reprieve, if unexpected.

"Four," Rayan called from behind them. His sword rose high above his head, shining with light, as he rushed toward the docks. "Or would you begrudge an old man for his late arrival?"

"Were you ambushed as well?" Cyrus asked as the paladin joined them in a line.

"I was," he said. "They are dead now, as will be our foes."

Cyrus tried to remember his confidence when he'd assaulted the docks. Instead he remembered the mockery in the Heir-Incarnate's words, the disappointment in his eyes. One blow. He'd been unable to withstand one single blow...

"Make it quick and brutal," he said. "We must diminish their number before the paragons arrive."

"There's still time to run," Mari said.

Cyrus eyed the paragons that lurked behind the charging soldiers, their weapons ready and waiting for a moment of weakness.

"I'm not dying with a blade in my back."

Rayan stepped forward and lifted his shield.

"We will not die at all," he said. "I will be the bulwark the charge breaks upon."

Cyrus felt the energy about the paladin's shield before it ever materialized in the form of glowing silver light. Rayan lifted the shield higher, his eyes closed, his mouth whispering a prayer to his goddess. The soldiers neared, closer, closer, and then down came the shield. It struck the street with a deafening crack, and the silver light exploded outward in the form of spread wings. Soldiers cried out in fear as the wings smashed them aside like a charging bull. Metal cracked, swords snapped. The first two lines of attacking soldiers tripped, fell, or retreated.

Easy prey for the Lioness. Mari leaped over Rayan, a mighty roar accompanying her descent amid the collapsed soldiers. Wings ripped and shredded armor. Screams followed. Cyrus and Stasia dashed to join her, for in that initial chaos they were at their most advantaged. He butchered frightened foes, but the moment was brief. The next wave of charging soldiers arrived, urged onward by the son of their god.

"Bring low the foes of Everlorn!" Galvanis implored from the docks. "Carve your way to glory in the eternal lands beyond!"

It was a heartless tactic, to throw regular soldiers into the fray, but it was an effective one. With each kill, each blow, Cyrus and his friends exhausted themselves. Cyrus hacked at soldiers, his every step a retreat. Lioness lunged place to place, never staying long, and trusting her bone armor to protect her at each assault. Stasia wielded her great-ax in both hands, swinging as if she were trying to chop down an entire forest. Should any seem vulnerable, Rayan would be there, his shield at the ready to protect them.

The destruction the four unleashed, it was terrifying, it was brilliant, but it was against mere mortals. It was only a matter of time before the paragons arrived.

"For Everlorn!" shouted a paragon barreling through the imperial soldiers. He wielded a great spear, the weapon held high above his head. At last, Galvanis unleashed his elite. "For the God-Incarnate!"

The paragon leaped into the air, his spear pointed and ready to skewer. Sunlight gleamed off his pristine armor. Cyrus braced to dodge but was given no chance. A pillar of flame rose up to meet the leaping paragon. It washed over him as he fell, taking advantage of his inability to protect himself or change his trajectory. The flames shimmered with strange, rainbow light, and it charred away his flesh with such heat that when he landed his armor collapsed in a clatter. Bones and ash scattered wildly from within.

Cyrus spun on his heels, baffled. That bafflement only grew when he saw a red-robed priest leading five similarly dressed men and women with flames surging from their palms and fingertips. The priest, it couldn't be . . .

"This fight is at its end," Eshiel thrice-born shouted. "Run, all of you, unless you would join the dead. We shall give you the time you need."

Before Cyrus could ask how, the priest shifted the flames that had consumed the paragon, and his followers mimicked his gestures. The fire spread across the street, forming a blazing wall dozens of feet high to seal away the chasing army. None dared challenge its heat, not after witnessing the damage it inflicted upon the dead paragon. Cyrus sheathed his swords and dipped his head in respect.

"If we run, you best be running with us."

Eshiel chuckled.

"I had no plans on dying here today."

The entire group fled, a wall of flame protecting them from any chase. They zipped down quiet streets, through a city accustomed enough to slaughter and battle that its people knew to hide within their homes until the bloodshed was done. They ran until they reached the first main intersection, with the northern road leading to the castle, the east and west toward the curling outer-ringed districts carved into the Emberfall Mountains.

"This is where we part," Eshiel said.

The Ahlai sisters were all too eager to keep running, and Cyrus wished to join them, but Rayan did not follow. He stood before the priest, his face perfectly calm. Cyrus could only guess at the emotions running through him.

"It seems fate is not finished with you," Rayan said at last.

"Not fate," Eshiel said. "Our goddess."

"Your intervention is still appreciated," Cyrus said, attempting to break the tension. The priest turned his way. For the briefest moment,

Cyrus thought the tattoos on his flesh were fully aflame, but no, it was a trick of the light. They were ink, faded and black.

"I am no friend of yours, Vagrant. Do not consider matters settled between us."

"You have a strange way of showing it," Cyrus said.

Eshiel smirked.

"You may not be friends, but you are enemies of the empire. Perhaps in time, we may reach an understanding. For now, let us walk our own paths. Farewell, and safe travels. May Lycaena watch over you."

"And she over you," Rayan answered.

Eshiel bowed his head and then joined his followers in sprinting away. Cyrus watched him go, the pit in his stomach sinking deeper. The events of the day weighed down on him, and no matter how hard he tried, he could not banish the memory of that single, horrible moment.

The Heir-Incarnate's blade crashing against his swords, pinning him, humiliating him. Revealing the lie that was his supposed godhood.

Rayan's hand settled on Cyrus's shoulder.

"Come, my friend," he said. "There will be time to grieve when we are safe."

Cyrus patted his hand, and he feigned a smile behind his mask so perhaps the lie might also reach his voice.

"Go. I will be but a moment."

Rayan raced after the sisters. Now alone, Cyrus turned his gaze to the distant ocean. The boats had all but sunk, and only scattered boards and floating bodies proved they had ever been.

"Forgive me," he whispered to those who had trusted him, to those who had prayed for vengeance as they drowned or burned. "I will answer your prayers in time. I will. I will."

CHAPTER 35

SINSHEI

Keles trained alone in a secluded corner of the castle courtyard. Despite the warmth of the sun, and how uncomfortable it must be, she wore her penitent armor. Only her helmet was missing, allowing Sinshei to see the deep concentration on her lovely face. Her sword slashed through the air, weaving a steady pattern as she'd no doubt been trained years earlier at the Heaven's Wing.

"Most paragons stop training after their ritual," Sinshei said upon arriving at her side. "The divinity in their blood is sufficient to keep their muscles strong."

"I am not most paragons, and strength does not equate to skill."

"No, it does not."

Sinshei crossed her arms and watched the woman train. Every swing looked like she was executing an imaginary victim before her. Her frustrations were boiling over. Yesterday bothered her, but which part? The death of those she might have once called allies? Or her encounter with the Vagrant, of which Sinshei'd heard only the briefest mention when Keles returned to the castle the previous evening?

"Twice now you've battled the Vagrant," Sinshei said, deciding to address it directly. "Twice now, you've failed to return with his head."

Keles's sword thrust straight forward, hard enough that wind snapped to either side.

"From what I hear, he also escaped Galvanis after they fought at the docks. Am I to be condemned for failing at what even the Heir-Incarnate could not accomplish?"

Sinshei smiled sweetly at the young woman. She was wise beyond her years, and yet painfully ignorant of the ways of Eldrid.

"Yes," she said. "You can, and will, be condemned for such. We do not abide by laws of fairness or reason. We walk the path of the God-Incarnate and his chosen Heir. Their beliefs are our beliefs, their truths our truths."

"Hardly flattering to your empire, or your god."

"Indeed. If only there were someone hoping to change it for the better."

Keles twirled her weapon twice more and then jammed it into her sheath.

"I fought him to a standstill, but when the boats began to burn, he fled for the docks."

"And you let him?"

Keles hesitated, and she looked away before answering.

"I thought Galvanis would kill him."

Sinshei was convinced the Vagrant was someone close to Keles, someone she held a personal connection with, and this only confirmed it to her.

"And you thought that would be easier," she said. "To let my brother shed the blood instead of your own hands."

The young woman gave no reply, but that was answer enough. A pang of sympathy bloomed and died in Sinshei's breast. This was hard for her, but that didn't matter. Such attachments would only get Keles killed. Sinshei closed the space between them and placed her hands on either side of her sweat-slick face. Her fingers slid into the woman's tight braids. She held her there, firm, forcing her to meet her gaze.

"Your feet are already on the path," she said. "Guilt and uncertainty are but the twin wolves nipping at your heels. Do not doubt. Do not turn back. Eyes forward, penitent. Behind you is death, only death."

Keles's face was an impenetrable mask. Her voice lowered. "Is it possible for us to kill your brother if the Vagrant cannot?"

Sinshei pulled her closer for an embrace, her soft robes wrapping about hard steel. Her lips brushed Keles's ear, for this was a promise she would only whisper, even if Galvanis were a thousand miles away.

"Together, we will. I have my blades, Soma his spear, and you your sword and shield. It will be enough. It must, for the millions who suffer."

They separated, and for a moment Sinshei believed she had reached the woman. But despite her words, her certainty, doubt yet lingered in Keles's heart.

"Must the Vagrant die?" she asked. "He is but a nuisance. Your brother is the true threat."

"The God-Incarnate sails for Thanet, and when he arrives, I will show him an island at peace, one humbled despite the chaos that preceded it, and the lives it took. The Vagrant will never give us that peace, so let him become the trophy I offer my father to take my rightful place as his heir."

Another impulse filled her to touch the woman's cheek, but she held back. Too much, she showed far too much. She put a hand on Keles's shoulder instead.

"Faith, dear Keles. Hold faith in me, and I will reward it for six hundred years."

Sinshei left her there, praying that her encouragement would be enough. Keles was so strong, and in a way different from the many fanatics she encountered in conquered nations. She questioned. She doubted. She felt fear and uncertainty, and yet despite it all, she still believed. The faith within her was a small, fragile bird desperately seeking to take flight. Sinshei felt it so clearly, saw it with the gift of her father's blood. That faith had not taken root in Dagon despite the ritual, that much she knew. There was space for another.

For her, perhaps, when the deed was done, and Everlorn worshiped an empress. The idea warmed her insides, pleasant in more ways than one, but she reluctantly pushed the idea aside. Keles was not the only visit Sinshei had planned for the evening. Her brother's mood had been jovial ever since the burning of the insurgent soldiers, but amid all the successes was one notable failure.

"You have a way with words, my dear sister," he had told her over their victory feast. "And you connect with the broken in ways most magistrates cannot. Go to Rihim. Discover the reason for his failures."

Sinshei's path back to the castle had her pass a group of twenty men, shirtless and armed with shovels and pickaxes. They hacked away at the dirt, tearing open a wide crevice. Barely visible from her perspective was an unearthed door several feet below ground.

This castle has many secrets, she thought. She tapped the wrapped cloth sealed with string and attached to her robe's belt. One of her priests had found and delivered it to her earlier that day. *But we have a few of our own, don't we?*

Deep below the castle, in catacombs recently discovered, were prison cells hundreds of years old. The air was damp and smelled so strongly of earth it made her sick to her stomach. Sconces lit the wall opposite the cells as she walked the single hall. Every prison was empty, all but for the last at the end.

The Humbled god, Rihim, knelt on his hands and knees. His claws scraped the cold stone. His golden eyes were closed, and his ears flattened. A quiver flitted through Sinshei's chest. He seemed so primal there in the dim light. His scar-torn fur rippled with the motions of his breathing. Words, too faint for her to understand, slipped off his tongue.

"I pray I am not interrupting?" she told Magistrate Castor Bouras. He was young for a magistrate, barely into his thirties, with hair red like fire and a short beard to match. His red robe was immaculate despite their dreary location. He held a prayer book in his left hand; in his right, a bladed baton.

"We have only begun the next litany," Castor said. "You need not wait on me, for it will be at least an hour before the Humbled finishes."

Sinshei entered the prison cell, and Castor stepped aside to make way. She knew little of the magistrate, for he had come with Galvanis across the Crystal Sea. Rihim was his responsibility, she knew that much. From what she had gathered from her brother, Castor had spent the better part of a decade working on the hunting god, cutting into his flesh and bathing him with prayers.

"Yesterday was filled with excitement," she said, addressing the Humbled with her arms crossed behind her back. "Traitor soldiers died by the hundreds in their boats, the insurrection's heroes were publicly beaten and bloodied, and the Vagrant himself was broken before the might of the Heir-Incarnate."

Sinshei was hardly thrilled with that last fact. She'd have been just fine if the Vagrant chopped off her brother's head, but Rihim need not know her personal desires. What mattered was his faith, and his incompetence. She leaned closer and hardened her voice.

"And yet, amid all the chaos, not a soul witnessed you partake in the battle."

Rihim opened his eyes.

"Speak plainly, Anointed. I care not for the way you humans circle about your desires like vultures above a kill."

Sinshei fought back a smile. If only she could be so blunt with the rest of Everlorn's court.

"So be it. You are a god of the hunt, famed for your tracking, and yet when our enemies were out in the open, you were not there. Where were you, Rihim? What games are you playing when you should be obediently serving?"

"I faced off against the Lioness."

"The Lioness helped the Vagrant at the docks. Did she best you?"

Sinshei did not like the way the Humbled looked to the ground.

"In a way."

Her frown deepened. Slippery language, especially coming from a deity who moments ago bemoaned such deceit. Rihim was hiding something, but what? She knelt down, careful to wrap her long hair about her waist so it did not brush against the dirty floor, and pinched her lower lip.

"In a way?" she asked.

He glared at her.

"I tried to kill her but could not. Why do you look at me so?"

Because you're lying, she thought. *But why?*

She remembered the moment Rihim had first set foot upon Thanet. He'd said something peculiar to her, and it'd stuck in her memory. Out here upon Thanet, he insisted he smelled Miquoan gods. Given his nation's deep connection to the neighboring Miquo, Sinshei had thought him jumping at shadows. The mental state of Humbled was notoriously fragile. But if he hadn't imagined it, if he hadn't invented foes for him to hunt...

"You know her," she said. "Don't you?"

The Humbled slowly rose to his feet. He towered over her, all muscle, tooth, and claw.

"This affair does not concern you, Anointed One."

Sinshei tilted her head up to meet his glare. She would show no fear to this broken thing.

"Tell me her name, Humbled. I would do what you cannot."

"She is my prey!" he roared. His fists rose, his claws extending. "My—"

The runes on his manacles flared with light. No chains connected them, but they need not, for the magic in them was strong, and blessed by the God-Incarnate's prayers. Rihim screamed as his every muscle locked tight. Faint sparks of lightning crackled along his arms. His knees buckled. His palms caught his fall, and now that they were closer to her, she heard the true punishment of the manacles.

When Sinshei had been a young girl, she had asked to try on a similar pair of manacles to hear what it sounded like. The result had been a clear, brutal lesson that her curiosity was dangerous. The noise had sent her crumpling to the floor with her hands clutching her bleeding ears. Forming coherent thoughts had been impossible. Even now she heard it, faintly in that prison cell. For Rihim, it would be deafening. A thousand voices sang their dedication to God-Incarnate Lucavi. Three sentences, forever on a loop, and quieting only when the prisoner offered up a prayer to the one true god.

I am humbled. I am loyal. I am free.

"Praise be to Galvanis, my truth, my life, my way," Rihim prayed. Immediately the glow on the runes dulled. His muscles slackened. Sinshei offered her own prayer to her father. That faith materialized into two golden blades of light shimmering through the air. They settled upon either side of Rihim's throat. With a thought, they rose, guiding his gaze up to meet hers. He held still, refusing to even breathe lest he cut himself.

"Your prey," she whispered. "What will you do with her?"

Smoke drifted lazily upward from where the blades touched his fur. The scent of it burning twisted Sinshei's stomach, and she retracted the blades until they no longer touched his neck. At their departure, Rihim sucked in a breath.

"I would make her pay for Antiev's betrayal. I would crunch her bones between my teeth and taste her blood upon my tongue."

A twist of Sinshei's fingers, and the swords swirled to hover about her shoulders. She let them linger, their golden light brightening the prison with her faith.

"I consider that a solemn vow, Humbled. Do not break it."

She dismissed her swords with a thought and exited the cell. Castor fell in step behind her, eager promises already on his tongue.

"If you give me time, I will give you the name he keeps hidden in his heart. Rihim is a stubborn one, but I am confident in my prowess."

Sinshei pointedly looked at his baton. Sharp pieces of metal, like the ends of knives, had been bolted into the wood in a spiral pattern climbing up from the base. A brutish weapon, and the dried blood upon its ends sickened her. Magistrates were supposed to be above such tools. After all, they had their faith, and all its manifestations.

"No," she said, swallowing her distaste. Castor was close to Galvanis and not to be trusted. "I do not need a name. His heart is loyal, and his rage true."

"I do not like it when Humbled keep secrets, Anointed One."

Sinshei turned, and she pulled out the object she'd brought down into the cells with her: a mangled and blood-soaked gauntlet.

"We all have our secrets," she said, and handed him the gauntlet. "Even broken gods. His is a fire burning him alive. When he is ready, give him this. Trust me when I say, the next time he hunts, Rihim shall have his prey."

CHAPTER 36

RAYAN

Y ou know me, and you know the life I have led," Rayan told the younger man, a tailor named Izan. "I have ever cherished Lycaena and her memory."

The pair conversed in the man's home along one of the lower rings of the city, not far from the docks. Hollers and laughs in equal measure poured through the nearby door as his three children played unseen. For a time, Rayan had taught them in his secret spot in the market. Before Magus of Eldrid named himself Imperator-Regent. Before the empire started hanging children.

"That's why I'm scared to take you," Izan argued. He scratched at his crooked nose and glanced at the closed door. "Eshiel loves her, too, maybe even more than you. I don't know how you'd take it if he says something you don't like."

"I bear no ill will to any man or woman who speaks our goddess's truth."

"Yeah, that's the catch, Rayan. You're going to judge whether he's speaking truth. Don't lie to me."

A banging on the front door interrupted their conversation. Rayan's hand was on his sword before either stood from their rickety seats at the table.

"Open in the name of Everlorn," a gruff man shouted from the other side.

Izan's eyes widened.

"Remain calm," Rayan said. "Answer. Tell them your children are sick with fever."

"They don't *sound* sick with fever," Izan hissed as the banging resumed on the door.

"Leave that to me."

Rayan hurried into the other room. The two boys were spitting images of their father, with cropped brown hair and a splash of freckles across their noses. The girl was an orphan, brought in during the earliest days of the invasion. Her dark curls had completely captivated Izan's wife, Azelia.

Azelia had later hung from the Dead Flags. A priest found her butterfly pendant.

"Hush now," Rayan told the children. "There are men at the door."

The three had been sword fighting with sticks, and he suspected the rearranged dresser and bed were some sort of imaginary fortification. They were buzzing with youthful energy and covered with sweat from their raucous play, and yet at his words, they instantly calmed. The oldest boy was not even ten. The maturity in his eyes rivaled that of adults.

"Should we hide, or do we run?"

"Papa says to use the window if we hear fighting," the girl chimed in. Rayan shook his head.

"Be quiet, and do as I say. Run only if I order you to do so."

They gathered together beneath the window. One of the boys took the girl's hand, and he lifted his pretend sword-stick with the other. A valiant defense. A fearful smile. God and goddess help him, if only his spirit could be so strong. Rayan wore no armor, and he'd left his shield at home, but he always carried his sword with him. He kept it sheathed as he pressed his ear to the door. The wood was thin, and he could hear the conversation between Izan and the soldiers with ease.

"Didn't you hear the bells ringing?" one asked.

Of course they had. It was why Rayan and Izan had stayed off the streets, to avoid drawing attention to them skipping the mandatory services. His stomach tightened. Would the city patrols start checking homes? They'd not gone that far before, but perhaps they would be more aggressive after their complete victory at the docks, and the Vagrant's humiliation.

"Of course, of course I heard," Izan said. Rayan could not see him, but he could imagine him, all earnest and wide-eyed sincerity. "But my oldest, he caught some sort of fever and has been sick for days. I got to stay and take care of him, you reckon? With the wife passing, it's just me, and it does nobody good taking a sick kid into church."

Rayan pointed to the oldest boy, then put a fist to his mouth and panto-mimed coughing. The eldest immediately began hacking as if he were los-ing his lungs. Rayan winced and gestured for him to pull it back a little bit.

You're sick, not dying, he mouthed, and smiled as if it were all just a game.

"Census says you have three children, not one."

Not good. This wasn't a random check. A year after the invasion, Regent Goldleaf had organized a census by means of interviewing own-ers of all homes and properties throughout the city. Had they started tracking who attended the services as well? Rayan's attention had been too focused on Thorda's resistance. He should have kept his ears alert and spoken with those forced to attend. But with his market sermons ended, his contact with parents and their children had grown rare.

"The other two are only seven, too young to go alone," Izan said. The pleading in his voice physically hurt Rayan's heart. To be so afraid when standing in your own home? It was wrong. It was vile.

"You have neighbors, don't you?"

Heavy footsteps. A bang of the door. Soldiers had forcefully entered the home. Rayan spun on his heels.

"Bed," he whispered. The oldest crawled in and scrambled for covers so he might pretend to be ill. Rayan glanced at the other two, his mind racing. The soldiers wouldn't have locked down the entire street, not without suspecting armed resistance. Izan's house had a tiny little patch of fenced-in land. Beyond it were their neighbors' homes. Surely one would take them in . . . assuming they were not attending the services.

No, not yet. Take it calm. If they were tracking with a census, and likely working an already decided route, running might doom the entire family. Izan's room was beside theirs, separated by only a curtain. Rayan pointed to the children's other bed, then hurried through the curtain so he might hide. His teeth clenched, and he prayed the floor would not creak too hard.

Once through the curtain into the dark, cramped room, Rayan drew his sword. Weapon ready, he dropped to his knees, laid his blade flat beside him on the floor, and peered underneath the bottom of the curtain.

Two of the children were in one bed, the oldest in the other. The door opened, and armored boots thudded inside. Two soldiers, not just one. From what he could tell, Izan did not follow. The three children remained dead silent atop their beds. Rayan held his breath.

"Stinks in here," one soldier said.

Rayan's hand on his sword tightened. The other pair of boots approached the bed. Feverish, Izan had claimed, but a bare hand on the boy's forehead would prove that false. How might they react? Would they force the family out immediately to attend the remainder of the sermon? Perhaps, but if they thought Izan deceived them, Rayan doubted they would let him off so easily. He'd be reported to the Uplifted Church and suffer their punishment.

"He been like this long?" the second asked the "healthy" children on the other bed.

"Th-three days," the girl answered. A quick lie, and a good one. The boots halted by the older child's bed. Rayan tensed. If the soldiers declared the sickness false, Rayan would attack immediately. Once the pair was dead, he'd have to assault any additional soldiers in the street, make it seem like it was one of Thorda's raids instead of related to Izan's house.

No armor, no shield. If the patrols were more than just a handful of men to check homes...

Be with me, Lycaena.

He slowly rose, and the first hint of the goddess's light shimmered across the steel of his sword.

"Not a plague, is it?" the first asked.

"Doubt it. Kid's soaked with sweat. The fever's already breaking, so mark it legitimate, but with a note to check again next week."

Rayan closed his eyes and slowly exhaled. He leaned away from the curtain. A week. They had time to prepare. The boots left. Rayan exited after them to find all three children silently crying.

"The goddess loves you," he whispered to them. "The goddess keeps you safe."

The door opened. Just Izan, but the young ones flinched nonetheless.

"Gone," he said.

Rayan exited to leave the father with his children. Izan's home had curtained-off windows, and he pulled one back to glance at the street. Eight soldiers, from what he could see from this angle. They went home to home, banging on doors and peering through windows. Truth be told, they looked bored. Such an upside-down world, that what the soldiers considered a tedious chore could inspire such terror in those they questioned...

"They said they'd be back in a week," Izan said when he returned from the children's room. "We have to attend, Rayan. They'll be checking on me now. Do you...do you think Lycaena will understand? I can harden my heart well enough against what the priests say, but the children, they're so young, and still learning."

Rayan put a hand on the man's shoulder.

"You do what you must to keep your family safe," he said. "Teach your children behind closed doors, and trust they will hold strong in the world beyond."

Izan glanced down. Rayan's sword, it was still drawn. He'd not thought to put it away.

"Eshiel is like you in so many ways," he said. "Both of you are willing to fight for what is right. If you give him a chance, I think you'll find a friend."

"Right now, I could use all the friends in the world," Rayan said. "Where can I find him?"

⁖⁖⁖

A heaviness weighted the air as Rayan walked. It wasn't from the occasional street preacher praising the God-Incarnate. It wasn't the sickly-hot wind blowing in from the mountains. Rayan felt it in the whispers, saw it in the fearful gazes of those who recognized him as a paladin of Lycaena.

Yesterday's failure had scarred the city. The six burned boats were but a part. Worse was the defeat of the Vagrant. The hope of the city had openly challenged the Heir-Incarnate and lost. Cyrus might have died if not for Eshiel's intervention, and so it was to Eshiel that Rayan traveled.

He had to know if another blasphemy resembling Lycaena would be summoned in the heart of the city. Izan's directions were simple enough, but Rayan quickly realized he was in no need of them, for the path he walked was one he had trod thousands of times as a young man. He traversed the high, looping roads halfway up the cliffs until arriving at a burned and ruined husk of a building.

Rayan stared at the burnt wreckage. Most sanctuaries had been repurposed into churches for the Uplifted Church, with any references to Lycaena and Endarius torn down or painted over. This right here, though, had been the Heaven's Wing. It was here that those chosen by Lycaena would train to become either priests or paladins. They would pray a thousand prayers, read countless books, and immerse themselves in the world of the Butterfly goddess. Elite champions, defenders of the weak and downtrodden, clad in either red robes or shining plate bearing vibrant cloaks and shields resembling her majestic wings.

To let such a building stand posed too much risk. On the first day of their arrival, the empire killed the Lythan king and queen and destroyed most of the island's armada. On the second, they burned the academy to the ground.

Rayan knew he should keep walking, but nostalgia pulled him closer. He knelt before what had been the front door, and he brushed aside debris. Below a thin layer of packed ash, he found it. Carved into one of the cobblestones were two sets of initials: RV and LM. It was here, on this very spot, that he met his wife, Lara. They had both been nervous to be starting at the academy, and barely thirteen years old. Their families escorted them for a grand, boisterous farewell as they stepped inside the building that would be their home for the next five years. The two hadn't talked much beyond quick hellos, but he'd remembered her beautiful hair, the color of mahogany, and the way it curled about her face as if it were a picture frame.

They'd grown closer during sparring practice. Friendship became companionship became something more. The day before their graduation, they had sneaked out in the dark to mark upon the stone a permanent reminder of their first meeting. Rayan traced the letters with his fingertips. They'd been so young then, bursting with energy and potential.

"I miss you still," he whispered. After a pause to count, he shook his head. "Twelve years, it's been. It feels like yesterday. It feels like forever."

A failure of her heart had taken her far too soon, and with a suddenness that denied him a chance to pray over her to heal the unseen trauma. Lycaena herself had attended the funeral. His goddess had spread her wings over the pyre and lifted her scepter heavenward, guiding the ash and flames skyward.

"There are green lands beyond," the goddess had spoken, each and every word permanently etched into Rayan's mind like those letters upon the cobble. "They stretch beneath blue skies and are surrounded by a crystalline sea. There is laughter, there is love, and there is no pain, only remembrance. Today we mourn the dying, but tonight we sing the joy of the eternal."

Twelve years since her death. Goddess help him.

It was surely no coincidence Eshiel picked the building directly next to the academy to be his clandestine home. The giant warehouse, fondly referred to as "the Shed" by students, was where all manner of supplies were stored for use by the academy. It'd been emptied out by the church after the invasion, and then presumably abandoned. A perfect place to gather people together in secret. The door was unguarded, and he confidently entered.

Inside, the many empty wood shelves and racks remained. They had been rearranged to give the large building partitions, with blankets and cloth strung over their sides to grant a measure of privacy. A man armed with a knife halted him immediately.

"Might I help you, stranger?" he said, pleasant despite threatening him with a weapon.

Rayan stood to his full height and summoned his decades of service to add authority to his voice.

"I am Rayan Vayisa, paladin of Lycaena, and I seek a moment's conversation with your leader."

The young man, barely into his twenties, easily wilted.

"A paladin?" he said, and then realized exactly where they were hiding. His face paled. "We meant no offense here, you know that, right? An empty building is an empty building."

"I mourn not the building, but the people who once walked it," he said, and then gestured for the man to lead onward.

They passed bunk rooms, little more than piles of blankets and pillows in the partitioned-off areas. Rayan noticed one shelf still filled with weapons, shorter knives and clubs that never would have been there during the time of the Heaven's Wing. A small fire burned somewhere nearby. He could smell the smoke, along with a hint of bubbling broth and meat.

"How many of you are there?" he asked as the young man guided him to the opposite end of the Shed.

"Here, or in total?"

Rayan shrugged to show he would accept whichever answer the man would give him.

"Well, here, there's about thirty. We're the ones without anywhere else to go, but there's more of us throughout the city, I assure you. Lots more."

"I pray it so," Rayan said. At the back of the Shed was an office for the records keeper in charge of managing supplies back in the day. Rayan's guide knocked on the door and then slipped inside. He emerged a moment later.

"He'll see you," he said, and then hurried away. Rayan stared at the cracked door and hesitated. Memories of their duel on the cliffside returned to him, a battle fought under the careful watch of a monstrosity bearing the name of his goddess.

You have come too far to retreat in cowardice now, he thought, and entered.

The desk and shelves were cleared out from the office, and in their place was a single bed. A woman lay in it, buried in blankets. Her skin was pale and her lips quivering. Rayan, no stranger to illness, immediately recognized the signs of a woman stricken with fever. Eshiel knelt beside her, a pail at his hip full of water. He dipped a cloth into it, wrung half of it out, and then began to softly dab the woman's forehead. He glanced over his shoulder at Rayan's entrance, and though he said nothing, his face darkened. It wasn't anger. Rayan would have sensed that immediately. No, this was much more akin to regret. The priest did not like to remember that moment on the cliffside, and Rayan was a walking reminder of it.

"Welcome to my new home," the priest said. "Forgive me for not greeting you at the door, but I must attend my faithful."

"Is it dire?" he asked.

Eshiel shook his head.

"I do not suspect it so. Unpleasant, but it will burn through Colette rapidly."

It was strange, to discuss matters so calmly with someone who had brandished divine fire in an attempt to kill him. Rayan crossed his arms as he observed the sick woman.

"Have you prayed over her?" he asked.

Another shadow across the scarred man's face.

"I have," he said. "And I suspect you know the result, don't you?"

The face of elderly Alliya flashed through Rayan's mind. Her stubborn demeanor, her weary smile. The swarm of moths bursting from her rigor-locked hands.

"It lacks the blessing of before," he said. Before "what" went unspoken. Before the empire arrived. Before the Anointed One executed their goddess. "People's faith wavers, as does our own. May the goddess give me the strength to rekindle that which has burned low."

Eshiel wiped sweat from his brow, and he set the cloth in the pail. The priest whispered something to the feverish woman, kissed her brow, and then stood. He beckoned for Rayan to follow, and together they exited the converted office into the far back of the Shed. There Rayan discovered the fire they had lit, and a kettle bubbling hot above it. Smoke gathered in the high ceiling, clouding the rafters. A young man watched the kettle, but he hurried away at a word from his master.

"It is easy to blame our doubts for these failings, but in this case, I believe it wrong," Eshiel said once they were alone. "In the Heaven's Wing I studied with the lofty goal of understanding the very nature of a deity, seeking to answer a question I had struggled with ever since I was a child."

"A grand ambition," Rayan said. It was all too easy to slip into the past, where he was an educator speaking with a fellow learned man of the sanctuary. Given his goal here was to better understand Eshiel, he was quite happy for the conversation. "What question was that?"

"Though we know little of them, and the past centuries have greatly diminished their number, we know Gadir was once a land with hundreds of gods. Each had their followers, and many deities founded nations, or shared them with others. Each spoke wisdom and guidance to their believers. And so I wondered...is there a universal wisdom all preached? If not, then surely there are gods better than others, ones kinder, or stronger, or better suited to guiding our people."

A variant on this theme was a common one for Rayan's sermons, and he gave the answer he always gave.

"It is not for us to debate the nature of the divine, only worship those who would care for us in this life and the next," he said. "I suspect most gods on Gadir are the same."

"All of them?" Eshiel asked. "What of ones dedicated to death, or pain? Surely those abound, too, do they not? Or what of the God-Incarnate? Is he worthy of praise, even when he promises we disbelievers will be stolen from our beloved deities and cast into the hell he prepares for his exiled Nameless wife?"

"God-Incarnate Lucavi is a bloodthirsty fiend. Trust not his lies."

"But are they lies? What if the gods become what we, their worshipers, need them to be? Those who bowed to Endarius needed strength and guidance. We who looked to Lycaena sought wisdom and comfort in a world often lacking in both. What if, for some dark reason, Eldrid needed conquest?"

"Then they are a cruel people, deserving of their god," Rayan said.

"Cruel," Eshiel said, and he closed his eyes. "Perhaps. Yet when I needed a murderer, when I needed a being who would slaughter enemies and bring pain and suffering to those I hated..."

He'd begun to tremble. Rayan reached out and rested a hand on his arm.

"As eyes adjust to the setting of the sun, so, too, did you accept the changing form Lycaena took for you. I arrived much later and saw only darkness. Do not blame yourself."

"I *must* blame myself," Eshiel said, and he pulled his arm away. "There is no one else to whom it belongs. I told myself many things to justify the actions I took to resurrect Lycaena. But those excuses were merely that, excuses. I was angry. I was hateful, and I wanted revenge. The sacrifices gave me a divine reason to kill, and after everything the empire has done to us, killing is all I desired."

"And now?"

Eshiel lifted a tattoo-laced hand.

"My anger is not abated," he said. His voice softened. "But I have witnessed my goddess born of blood and fire. Imagine for a moment a world where you did not arrive, Rayan. If you, the Vagrant, and the Heir-Incarnate had not interrupted. If Lycaena had grown stronger with sacrifice, and been given more time to gather her followers. Imagine the future where Thanet was freed, and she held total control over the hearts of our people."

His fingers curled, and crimson flame rolled across his fist like water. It cast no light, and it did not burn his flesh.

"A goddess of blood and fire, given life through sacrifice. What happens when the empire is gone from Thanet? What happens when there is no one left to sacrifice in her name? Would those sacrifices have ended? Or would we have merely changed the crime leading to the table and the knife? Murderers and rapists, I suspect at first. Lesser criminals after. Maybe doubters. Heretics. Unbelievers."

"You would have birthed a mirror of the God-Incarnate," Rayan said, finishing the thought.

Eshiel opened his fist, banishing the flame.

"Who is to say how the wretched deity was first created? He rose to power three thousand years ago, they tell us, first given form as God-Incarnate Ashraleon. Who might he have been all those ages ago? They say the Everlorn Empire was reborn from the ashes of a failed invasion. Perhaps Eldrid's people suffered. Perhaps their other gods perished. Perhaps there had even been a scared, bitter priest with a knife and a sacrificial altar..."

When Rayan sought Eshiel out, he had feared he would receive excuses from the man, or thin justifications for his actions. Instead he heard sincere doubt, thoughtful regret, and a desire to do better. Eshiel radiated charisma, and his very flesh was a mixture of scars inflicted by the empire and tattoos proclaiming his love of Lycaena. It was no wonder he had built a strong gathering in Ierida. If he avoided the empire's attention, he would certainly build another here in Vallessau.

"What then are your plans?" Rayan asked. "It seems you have abandoned blood sacrifice, but what of the war itself?"

The priest took Rayan's hands, and he held them with a firmness that matched the iron in his voice.

"I will not stop fighting," Eshiel vowed. "I will kill, and I will burn, but let those sins fall upon *me*. Let them be done by my hands, and by those who bear my trust. Let them be done, not to resurrect our goddess, but to protect those who still cherish her memory. I will gather a new flock, one seeking to sing the glory of our goddess. We will not sacrifice to bring her back, for she need not return for us to hold faith. We will walk the path she set before us in her years among us. We will protect those who are vulnerable and keep her alive in us with our prayers. Whatever I must give, I will give it, so the generations that follow may walk a safer, kinder path."

Rayan stood. He had judged far too harshly this man he had never met. He had heard rumors of a cult, of blood sacrifice, and then Keles went silent. Upon his arrival, he saw a monster born of dark deeds. Everything had matched his initial distrust, but now he heard the doubts and fears of a priest who loved their goddess with a strength bordering on desperation. This love, it was profound, it was true.

Without a doubt, Eshiel thrice-born was a broken man. It was with broken things Lycaena did her grandest works.

"My campaign with the Vagrant continues unabated," he said. "When you feel your people are ready, seek me out. We could always use allies."

A faint glimmer sparked in Eshiel's light brown eyes.

"Do not anticipate my arrival upon your doorstep anytime soon," he said. "What the Vagrant is, and what he has done, is still uncertain to me, and it will take much for me to forgive the murder of my goddess, even if her form was...changed. But for your sake, Rayan, I shall set these grievances aside. All others of Lycaena's priests and paladins have either died or cast aside their vows. For us to be the last, and yet enemies, is much too cruel a fate."

"But we are not the last," Rayan said, shaking his head.

"Do you mean Keles Lyon?"

Rayan hesitated. How much had his niece told this man? Did he know of Thorda and his elite? What of Keles's own faith, and the lack thereof following her forsaking ceremony?

"Her heart was wounded," he said carefully, "but I hold faith it may be healed."

Eshiel smiled at him, but it was one meant to hide, and Rayan saw right through it to the sorrow underneath.

"Guard your heart," he said. "I fear if you hold on to that faith, you, too, will be wounded, and I have not the words or the prayers to put either of your broken pieces back together."

CHAPTER 37

STASIA

Stasia was on her way to a morning run along the beach when Clarissa stopped her at the mansion door.

"There's something I want to talk about," she said.

"Of course. What's the matter?"

Clarissa glanced up and down the hall.

"Not here. Somewhere private."

Stasia shrugged.

"All right, our room, then."

They returned in silence. Anxious energy rolled off Clarissa in waves, and it was horribly infectious. By the time they reached the bedroom and Stasia shut the door, her skin was crawling.

"You're making me nervous," she said as Clarissa sat on the edge of the bed. Her arms crossed over her waist.

"Please, don't be, this is, it's...Lycaena help me, I thought this would be easier."

Stasia sat beside her, their thighs touching. She took one of Clarissa's hands in hers and said nothing. Whatever was bothering her, she would speak it in time. All Stasia needed to do was be there for her until she could.

"Remember how you asked if you should carry me to the city law-house to have us married?" Clarissa suddenly asked.

Stasia certainly did. Mere moments later, imperial soldiers had initiated a sweep. The pair had fled, with Clarissa surviving an encounter with the paragon Soma only due to Mari's timely intervention.

"Of course I remember," she said. "I was too late. The Uplifted Church had already changed the laws."

"We don't need the state to approve a marriage, you know. Not for us to believe it."

"I thought we agreed we would wait until things were safer, and this war over?"

Clarissa stood. New resolve hardened her features.

"Watching what has happened, the hangings, the boats, the siege at Fort Lionfang…the world is cruel. I understand that, Stasia, I do. But I also know it can be beautiful. I know there are wonderful people in it, people who are kind and giving. And I refuse to let the cruelty dictate my life anymore. I won't wait, not for changes that may never come. I'm going to live for right now, Stasia, right here and now, with no regrets, nor my desired paths untaken. All my love. All my joy. Let it be among us always."

Stasia slowly stood. The smaller woman looked up at her with those big blue eyes more beautiful than the ocean. Her soft hands closed around Stasia's calloused own.

"I know what I want, Stasia. I think you want it, too."

Bees buzzed inside Stasia's stomach. Her heart forgot to beat.

"And what is it we both want?" she asked, playing along, refusing to voice what she knew was coming.

"No more waiting. No more hoping for better, because we don't need better. We'll have each other, and we will *make* things better, with however much time the world gives us. Even if it lasts only a day, let it be a most wondrous day."

Clarissa dropped to her knees. Her eyes sparkled.

"Will you marry me, Stasia Ahlai?"

Heat flushed throughout Stasia's face and neck. Her head was a hollow space filled with air.

"It's so sudden."

Clarissa laughed.

"We've been together four years, Stasia. That's not what I would call sudden."

Stasia stared down at this woman she loved more than all the world. She wanted to embrace her, to hold her close, and to promise she would never let anything or anyone harm her. Impossible promises. The world was too big, and the dangers too great. To accept this offer meant opening her heart. It meant being vulnerable to even greater pain.

But that was foolish, wasn't it? No marriage or vows would change how she felt. Losing Clarissa would break her regardless. She was everything to her, *everything*. So what was it she feared? To make it real? To shout to the world just how dearly she held this woman, how her smile was her light and her laugh the source of all her joy?

Say something, her mind screamed, yet paralysis kept her still. Stasia felt cumbersome, and she feared she might break a moment so fragile and tender. What words were right? The answer, could she give it?

Of course she could. Stasia considered herself brave, perhaps to the point of recklessness. So let her be brave with her heart.

"Yes," she said. Her voice hitched, overcome by tears she had no idea were building. "Yes, damn you, of course the answer is yes."

Clarissa surged back to her tiptoes, and they kissed, her hands on her waist, her sides, her back, climbing upward and pulling her tighter. Stasia would have been fine for that moment to last forever, the kiss unending, but her fiancée (gods, how weird to call her that) had other plans.

"Good," she said upon pulling away. Her face was flushed, the pale skin of her neck splotchy and red. "Now come with me so I can tell your father. We'll need to hurry if we want everything to be in place for the wedding tonight."

Stasia froze in mid-attempt to wipe the tears from her eyes and cheeks. Her mind hiccupped as she struggled to speak.

"Tonight?"

Clarissa explained everything on their carriage ride out of the city and to the south. She had been preparing for several weeks, but her tentative plans had turned urgent upon arriving home from Lord Agrito's execution. That she had accomplished so much in secret should not have surprised Stasia given how clever Clarissa could be, but she was still shocked seeing her friends when they gathered about the carriage an hour before nightfall. The men were dressed in finely fitted lavender-white suits that must have cost a small fortune. Cyrus had even trimmed his vagabond hair for the event, making him look both much younger and more handsome. As for Mari, she wore a lovely red dress that rippled and twirled with her slightest movement.

"Nothing is too good for my eldest daughter," Thorda had said upon seeing her expression. He wore the only suit fashioned differently from Thanet's style of fitted coat with long coattails down to the ankle. Instead he wore a long robe, the fabric a deep purple silk spun all the way back in Miquo. It was tied with a black sash and clipped in place with silver pins whose heads were carved like blooming flowers.

"I look ridiculous," Arn had muttered, tugging at his collar. Truth be told, he did look a little amusing, the giant muscle-bound paragon stuffed into such fine clothing, but there was something charming about the contrast, too. His hair, while always short, was freshly combed and pulled back from his face in a tiny knot. His right hand, still bandaged from the fight, was hidden by a dark leather glove.

"So what will we wear?" Stasia had asked before stepping into the carriage. Only she and Clarissa were yet to dress in finery.

"We'll change when we get there," was all Clarissa offered in explanation.

They took two carriages, and a quick discussion with Thorda at the gates had the guards allowing passage through without inspection. They followed the road along the Emberfall Mountains, curling toward the thick forest that grew beyond the city's edge. Both carriages stopped at a seemingly random spot marked only with a lone wooden post. An empty cart waited nearby, and Stasia had a feeling it had brought the supplies for their wedding.

"We couldn't go far, but we still wanted somewhere private where we could celebrate freely," Clarissa explained as everyone exited the carriages. "And it turns out, priests of the Lion held private ceremonies here not far off the road."

"How did you discover that?" Stasia asked, for sure enough, there was a hidden path through the trees. Mari, hopping out of the other carriage, was quick to answer.

"Endarius told me," she said with a wink.

A few hundred feet into the trees they emerged into a beautiful glade overlooking the sea. Six wooden tables were set up in a rectangle, and by their weathered status, they had been exposed to the elements for a long, long time. Not far was a fire pit burning healthily. Two pots hung over it, as well as a spit. Stasia's mouth watered at the thought of whatever meals the group planned, for there was a sizable stack of food and ingredients on a smaller table beside the pit.

Clarissa's mother, Adella, was already busy chopping away at one of the tables, her blond hair looped into an intricate bun. It was a comical sight, for she wore a fine blue dress coupled with an enormous apron to keep it clean while she cooked. A few of Thorda's servants worked alongside her, while nearby, a congregation of resistance leaders chatted with Pilus and Lord Mosau's vassal, Kaia Makris. On the opposite end of the clearing were a handful of Clarissa's friends, those Stasia had met on occasion, and who were trusted with the knowledge of Clarissa's role in Thanet's resistance.

A smile lit Adella's face upon seeing their arrival, and she waved them over.

"There's my girls," she called out.

"I suppose I am now," Stasia said, bending at the waist to hug the older woman. "Thanks to your daughter's persistence."

"Lycaena bless her, that stubbornness made raising her difficult, but it does have its uses," Adella said.

Clarissa's turn for a hug. Stasia's eyes roamed, taking in the sights. The glade ended at a cliff, and planted unknown years earlier was a large ring of rosebushes to form a circle just before. Stasia suspected that would be where the ceremony was held. Laughter caught her attention, and she glanced over to see Cyrus, Arn, and Rayan cracking open bottles of liquor.

"You are going to love your dresses," Adella said when Clarissa pulled away. "I helped pick them out myself."

"Then I am sure they will be beautiful," Stasia said. She glanced around the clearing, and she saw no actual building or tent that might grant her privacy. "So where do I dress?" Her eyes widened, remembering previous discussions on Thanese wedding traditions. "Wait, is this where we wrap ourselves naked in silks and blankets while the crowd throws paint on us?"

"Please try not to sound too terrified," Clarissa said. "And no, we won't be doing any of that. We've not the time or the preparations. Mari will help you with your dress, while Mother helps me with mine."

"Yes, but where?"

Her fiancée winked playfully.

"Hidden in the trees. You are a Miquoan woman, are you not?"

Stasia looked for Mari and found her ordering servants about. She had a sneaking suspicion her sister had shouldered a large amount of the responsibilities when it came to the wedding. Stasia started for her, only to have her path intercepted by her father.

"A moment before we begin," Thorda said simply.

He guided Stasia to a tree stump cut not far into the forest. A thin sheet of metal was laid atop it, its purpose, she could not guess.

"Is this when you give me some loving final words?" she asked him.

"I will give you something, yes," he said. "And it is far better than any clumsy words I might offer."

Her father reached into a pocket of his robe and pulled out two silver wedding bands. Her eyes widened at the sight. These bands...the amount of care and detail carved into them was exquisite. The Ahlai name might have been synonymous with weaponry, but her father was capable of so many more impressive feats at his forge. She took the bracelets in hand and held them up to the faint light of the setting sun.

The silver bands shifted and changed throughout their entire length, as if they were shaping themselves before the very eye. On one side, little trees emerged from the silver, the Ahlai name written so small and perfectly among their leaves. On the other side, the band curled and turned like waves rolling across the surface of the ocean. The Greene family name was carved into the recesses of the waves. The waves and trees crashed together at two central gemstones, an emerald for Miquo, a sapphire for Thanet. She knew they represented those nations for the gemstones had grooves cut into them so that when the light hit just right, the outlines of their respective nations reflected off their surfaces.

"I don't know what to say," she whispered. The sight of the silver, the shape of it...she'd seen these before. Thorda had been working on these bands when she interrupted him in his forge and he ordered her to visit Pilus at Pelion.

"It is not often I am given reason to push my craft," he said. "But the work is not yet done. Place the bands upon the plate."

They seemed finished to her, but she did not argue. Instead she put them on the metal slab atop the stump as he requested. Meanwhile her father withdrew a slender hammer from one of his pockets. He hesitated a moment with his eyes closed as he whispered what sounded like a prayer.

"Here," he said when finished, and offered her the hammer. "This is yours now, daughter. Take it, and finish what I began."

"I don't understand," she said, accepting the small hammer.

In answer, he turned the bands around. Opposite the gemstones, where the two bands came together, were two overlapping loops. Lodged into those loops was a thin silver cap that still looked loose.

"Held, but not sealed," he explained.

Stasia nodded in understanding. Her father, ever in love with symbols and rituals, had left the final hit to be hers. Strange he didn't want Clarissa here, but so be it, theirs was a family of smiths and crafters, so perhaps this harkened back to her own father's wedding.

Doing her best to give the act the weight her father desired, she struck the first bracelet, sealing the twin bands together. Would this one be hers, or Clarissa's?

"Well done," Thorda said upon inspecting it. He gestured to the second. "Finish the deed."

The hammer was electric to Stasia's touch. Something about this felt personal, felt heavy. She lifted the hammer and caught Mari watching them from the tree line, a folded dress held in her arms. Their eyes met. Stasia could not understand the hurt in her sister's gaze. She brought down the hammer, sealing the second bracelet.

"I'll hold these until you are ready," Thorda said, and he took both bracelets in hand. "I believe your sister is here to help you change."

Stasia set the hammer down on the stump and walked to the tree line.

"I cannot wait to see you in your dress," Mari said, and shifted her hold of the fabric so she could clap excitedly. Her smile seemed genuine, and her enthusiasm was infectious. Had that sorrow in her sister's eyes been a trick of the light? Or perhaps Stasia projected her own nervousness onto others...

"I only pray it fits," she said.

"Clarissa gave us your measurements. I presume she knows you well enough that her guesses will be close."

Stasia coughed and blushed.

"Yes, she does indeed. All right, let's see what my beloved picked out for me."

⁂

By the time Stasia was dressed, the moon had risen, the food was cooked, and a small crowd assembled. Based on the design of the dresses, she suspected a starlight wedding had been the plan from the start. Her and Clarissa's matching dresses were a pale shade of violet that seemed to glow in the dark, setting them apart from all others in attendance. Inset gemstones, cut so small as to be nearly imperceptible to the naked eye, sparkled when they caught the faint light, forming swirling patterns along the legs and waist.

As she had expected, Stasia and Clarissa gathered in the ring of rosebushes along the cliffside. The others formed a matching ring outside the bushes. Her father stood before them to lead the ceremony. This would be no legally sanctioned wedding, after all, not with the Uplifted Church controlling the courts in Vallessau. No priest or priestess of Lycaena was here, either, nor a speaker of any Miquoan god. Just her father, commanding everyone's attention with his firm voice normally reserved for leading his rebellions.

"We come here to mark the union of Clarissa Greene and Stasia Ahlai," he said. "Let friends and family bear witness. Let the stars gaze down in jealousy. This is a joyous moment, and we are all blessed to partake."

Thorda lifted what appeared to be a roll of green silk wrapped around a wooden pole the length of his arm. The interior side was rougher than the outside, but she caught only a glimpse of it. He had set it in the grass beside him before starting, and offered no explanation.

"I have best decided on an amalgamation of both Miquoan and Thanese traditions," her father said. He offered the end piece of silk to Clarissa. She accepted it with a mischievous grin. Around and around them it went, her father quicker on his feet than Stasia would have guessed. Six loops in total to surround them, each loop pulling Stasia and Clarissa closer together, their arms circling each other as the silk wrapped tight.

"Is this where we are doused with paint?" Stasia asked.

"No paint," Clarissa said. "Just watch."

When the circling was complete, Thorda stepped back, the end of the silk held in his right hand.

"Here upon Thanet, blessed couples come together to celebrate their rebirth," he said. His voice, often deep and somber, took on an even more serious tone. He sounded like a god of creation to Stasia, one come to offer blessed scripture to his subjects. Each syllable raised hairs on her arms and neck. Each word lifted her spirit.

"They wrap themselves in a cocoon, an act meant to honor the kind and gentle Butterfly. But it is more than mere worship to a goddess. It is a symbol of rebirth for this most holy of unions recognized and held sacred by all the gods upon all the lands of Gadir. It is a change, a becoming, emerging new and wondrous and beautiful. Would that the starlight could sparkle upon Lycaena's wings as she graced you with her presence, but we are not so blessed. I hold hope for a future where your children, or your children's children, might still exchange their vows beneath her watchful eye."

He tightened his grip on the silk.

"The Ahlai, though, we come not from Thanet, but from Miquo. We come from a land swathed in darkness beneath a towering skyscape of trees. We are a people raised in the shadows of the godswood.

Patience is in our blood. It takes a century for a scattered seed to grow high enough for its branches to join the illustrious canopy. So, too, would I ask patience from you both. Aid each other. Help each other reach for the stars. Do not expect perfection, not now, not even a decade from now, but instead embrace a mutual growth that will continue into your twilight years."

Thorda lifted the silk above his head in a bunched fist.

"Will you change?" he asked them. "Will you grow?"

"We will," Clarissa said.

"We will," Stasia echoed.

Her father bowed his head. His eyes closed. When he spoke next, it was no speech, no traditional blessing. A prayer. He whispered a prayer, the first she had ever heard from him. If he was not so close, she might not have heard it at all.

"Gods of Miquo," he prayed. "Those from ages past who may only whisper, and those who yet live hidden and scattered, I beseech you. I ask naught for myself, but for my daughter. Witness her. Embrace her. Love her, and the woman she has chosen. I ask. I beg. I pray."

He lifted his head. His voice deepened, and he spoke once more for all to hear.

"In our lost land of tree and shadow, there is no day more blessed than the autumn fall. Underneath the black branches, and beneath a burning sky of leaves, our people wed. Though we are exiled from our home, I would give you that autumn, my daughter. My child."

And then he pulled the silk that bound Stasia and Clarissa. The thin fabric broke, and on the interior side she saw her father had smeared it with the ashes of his forge. Those ashes had covered their violet dresses, but at his prayer, they lifted free and into the air as glowing embers. Light washed over the crowd as the embers swirled higher, higher, higher.

Stasia looked heavenward, enraptured. The burning ashes danced on divine winds, becoming leaves and branches, a wedding canopy there on the island cliff. They burned the many colors of the godwoods, shades of orange, red, and gold. It lasted but a moment, witnessed in hushed awe of all gathered, and then the leaves broke apart. The ashes scattered upon the wind, and in the absence of their light the brilliant stars shone all the brighter.

Tears streamed down Stasia's face. A Miquoan autumn. A falling-leaf wedding. Her father had given her one, even here at the edge of the world. Whatever magic this was, whatever blessing, she did not want to question it, or understand it. Experiencing it was enough.

Thorda cleared his throat, and the ceremony resumed as if nothing extraordinary had preceded it. He pulled out the two bracelets he had forged from a deep pocket of his robe and then gave one to each of them.

"Exchange now your bracelets, and with this exchange, acknowledge your status as beloved and married, wife to wife."

Clarissa went first. She took Stasia's hand into hers. The fine silver passed over calloused fingers and bruised knuckles. The light on the emerald and sapphire stones sparkled in the starlight, twin nations in glowing relief.

"Whatever comes, I embrace it fully," Clarissa said. Though she stammered a bit, clearly nervous, the rehearsed words flowed more steadily as she continued. "Whatever future we have, I desire it. Be it a day, a year, or an eternity, I want each and every moment of it spent with you. My world was complete the moment you stepped off your boat and into my life."

Stasia swallowed hard.

"You're going to make me cry," she whispered. Clarissa's smile widened as she fought back a laugh. The deed done, she released the bracelet and offered her own wrist. Stasia took the bracelet from her father. The silver twirled between her fingertips. She had practiced no speech, and did not consider herself a master at words. What now to say?

The bracelet slid easily over Clarissa's dainty hand to rest upon her wrist. The truth, Stasia decided. The simple, honest understanding of her heart.

"Clarissa Greene, you are the best thing to ever happen to me, and you are so much better than I deserve. I love you. I hope that will always be enough."

Thorda held his arms high and clapped twice.

"And with that, I name you newly wed, Clarissa and Stasia Ahlai, my dearest and most blessed children."

They had not discussed last names, Stasia realized much too late, but it seemed her father had made the decision for them. Thorda clapped again, and their friends and family joined in. Cheers and whistles soon followed, along with demands for a kiss. Stasia and Clarissa obliged, though each was too busy smiling to perform more than a quick, chaste exchange.

"So I'm better than you deserve?" Clarissa asked, and she clinked her marriage bracelet against Stasia's. "Then it is good you have the rest of your life to work at it. Maybe by the time we are old women, we will each be what we deserve."

"Maybe," Stasia said. She leaned down, their noses brushing, their foreheads touching so she might whisper and smile. "Do you mind if we start on that tonight?"

"First we dance, sing, and make fools of ourselves. But after?" Clarissa kissed her, just once, as their friends dispersed for the tables with waiting food and drink. "After, we shall have ourselves a night neither of us will forget."

CHAPTER 38

ARN

Arn leaned his back against the enormous pine tree and watched the ceremony in silence. He clapped when others clapped. He smiled when others looked his way. The dutiful acts expected at a wedding, he performed. The ceremony was beautiful, and he would not ruin that. All the while, he kept his unbandaged hand buried in his trouser pocket, twirling the foxtail charm between two fingers.

You're not upset at the horrors, but the guilt you felt in partaking.

Afterward, the feast began. Arn held no appetite for it, but he accepted a plate and ate alongside Cyrus. He even laughed at some terrible jokes, and told more terrible ones of his own. Fitting in was so easy, when he wanted to do so. For Stasia's sake, he would manage. Once enough time had passed, and everyone was sufficiently liquored up, he excused himself and approached the table where the Ahlai family was gathered.

"Hey, Mari?" he said, tapping her on the back.

"Yes?" she asked, glancing up and over her shoulder. The red of her eyes shone, her round face illuminated in a mixture of torchlight and moonlight. Beautiful, so beautiful, and so kind. He couldn't ask for a better friend.

"Can we talk?" he asked. "Alone?"

Not a hint of concern crossed her face. She was masterful at hiding her emotions when she desired.

"Of course," she said with a smile. She turned to the others at the table. "If you'll excuse us a moment."

Arn hurried away, glad to have his back to their stares. He didn't know what they thought. Normally he'd say he didn't care, but the heat building in his neck argued otherwise. To the north was the road, so he led them south, deeper into the trees. He walked until the sounds of laughter and music faded, and their only light came from the stars above that twinkled through the thin pines. Mari followed, calm and quiet. He envied her.

"I suppose this is far enough," he muttered, stopping in a small gap.

"Far enough for what?" Mari asked. "Though given the wedding and the wine, perhaps I should have anticipated this."

She was teasing him. The smile growing at the corners of her lips gave it away. It was almost enough to change his mind. Fuck the charm in his pocket. Fuck his brother. Fuck the guilt and the sorrow and the blood on his hands. Fuck it all, and instead just have him and Mari... well...

"Your offer," he said, closing his eyes and squeezing the charm so tightly the bronze cap dug into his skin. "I want to take you up on it."

"My offer? Oh, you mean...well, it's a bit sudden, Arn, but I'd be lying if I hadn't considered..."

He opened his eyes, and he watched the playfulness of her smile fade.

"To speak with Velgyn," he said.

The younger Ahlai sister stepped back and lowered her head. She drew in a long, single breath. Gathering herself. Preparing for something difficult. The effort layered guilt onto his already overburdened conscience. She hid it from him, though, hid it as if she had spent a lifetime in hiding. When she looked up she was calm as a midnight lake.

"Sit with me."

They sat opposite each other in the leaves and the dirt. Arn tugged at his shirt collar. It was too stiff, too nice, a lavender-white outfit given to him by Thorda to wear for the occasion. No doubt it cost extra to have it made for someone so large. Already the pale color was starting to stain green and brown from the forest leaves. An impulse to tear his jacket off filled him, and he fought it down. He was nervous, thinking stupid.

Get it together, he chastised himself. *You're a damn paragon. Act like it.*

The thought sickened him instantly. A paragon...but he wasn't supposed to be a paragon any longer. He had turned against that life, becoming the Heretic. He fought the empire. He killed their paragons. He waged war against their hate and bloodshed. It should have made him better than he was. Yet when he wanted to bolster his bravery, to talk himself up, he still relied on that past. Deep down, he took pride in what he was. These changes, were they real, if that pride still lurked in his heart?

That answer terrified him, but tonight, he would prove himself strong enough to accept it.

"Do you have the goddess's charm?" Mari asked, pulling him from his thoughts. Her hand was already outstretched for it.

"I always do," he said, withdrawing the little white-and-orange tip of a tail from his pocket. He placed it into her palm. She bowed her head and closed her eyes. The charm softly rotated between her thumb and forefinger, the little white tuft at the end brushing against her lips as if she breathed in the charm's very essence. The air thickened. The hairs on his arms and the back of his neck stood on end.

"Are you certain of this?" she asked. "Once I begin the communion, there is no stopping it. The goddess will speak."

"This was your idea, remember?" he said. His attempted smile died unseen. "Yeah. I'm as ready as I'll ever be."

Mari tilted her head, and her mouth slightly opened as if she were drinking in the moonlight. Faint whispers slipped off her tongue, too quiet for him to hear. His nervousness grew. The woods around him, they were quiet, so quiet. The wedding was a thousand miles away. The burning wreckage of Onleda's capital of Vulnae was far too near. The air thickened. Strands of Mari's hair floated in a nonexistent wind.

"Velgyn, hear my prayer," Mari whispered. "Hear it, goddess of Onleda, and answer. I would speak, if you are willing."

The silence deepened. Arn was afraid to move lest he break the trance. Whatever understanding he had of the world was suddenly revealed as a lie. There was no denying it. The stars danced. Little wisps of color sparked in the air about him, and it took him a moment to realize what they were. Flickers of fire. Sparkles of frost. Little veins of lightning.

"Mari?" Arn asked.

The woman lifted her head and opened her eyes. They were not red like the children of Miquo. They shone yellow, their pupils sharp and narrow. When she spoke, it was with a voice that had haunted the last five years of his dreams.

"Why do you weep, Arn Bastell?"

"I do not weep," he said, and it was true. His eyes were dry, but his words shook, and his hands trembled.

"You do," the voice of Velgyn said through Mari's lips. "You weep every day. I hear it, child. I feel it like a prayer. Your heart bleeds without ceasing."

Arn withered beneath that gaze. What could he say to her? What possible excuse might he give a goddess for his actions? For her murder?

"Then you know," he said at last. "You know how deeply runs my regret. You know I've never forgotten, and I've never forgiven myself. I...goddess, I've tried. I swear, I have tried to do right by it. I've tried to be better. To fight the right battles. To be someone who would defend children and not be their murderer. You know that, don't you? Wherever you are, wherever I sent you..."

Words tumbled out of him like a rockslide. He wanted them to make sense. This was a speech he'd rehearsed again and again in his darkest moments, yet none of those prepared words came to him now. How could they, when the forest around him burned? He felt no heat, but he saw those flames. The sky above filled with smoke. The ground beneath him turned muddy, and he feared to press his hands into it, lest he find the corpses of those slain in the great battle outside Vulnae's gates.

"Prayers," Velgyn said. "Yes, Arn, I hear your prayers. I know your hurt. Though what you would ask of me, I do not know. Speak it. Make it known."

Arn's pulse throbbed in his neck. His stomach heaved, an inch away from vomiting. This was it. No turning back now. Five years of guilt, come to a head. Whatever crimes he had committed in his life, let this be what defined him.

"I want nothing from you," he told Velgyn. "I only wish to make amends."

Mari tilted her head to one side. Frost speckled across her forehead. Wisps of flame sparked from the ends of her hair.

"Amends?"

Arn swung his legs underneath him until he knelt on unstable ground. No hesitation. No second thoughts. He drew a knife from his hip pocket and pressed it to his throat. He closed his eyes, unable to meet the fox-like gaze. The words of his brother taunted him. Condemned him. At least now the scales could be balanced.

"Command it, and my life is yours. My crimes, my murders, they go beyond forgiveness. I crushed the innocent with my fists. I slew the divine. Before I took your life, you asked me if I was truly so monstrous. To that I say—yes, goddess, I am. I am monstrous. I am wretched. Give the order, and my blood shall spill in your name. A pitiful sacrifice, but let it be some measure of atonement for my sins."

Arn waited for the command. The silence settled heavy upon him, but his resolve did not shake. This was right. This was just. Velgyn deserved all this from him and more. If only she would speak the word and let him erase his guilt with a slice of his knife. Let the blood flow. As ten lives ended to give him strength, let his own life be given to empower a deity he himself had slain.

"You poor, wounded child. Is this what you would offer?"

Wind blew against him, and it carried the smell of smoke and charred bodies. He pressed the knife tighter to his skin until he felt a sting. The first trickle of warm blood flowed across the knuckles of his gloved hand.

"It is all I may offer," he said. "For it is all that I have."

He waited for the word to be given. He waited for the deserved condemnation to fall. Arn had crushed Velgyn's body between his fingers. She had howled and screamed as her bones broke. It was in his hands her body went limp, when whatever divine presence occupying her earthly vessel fled. What did a few slain imperial soldiers mean to that? He was piling murders atop murders, hoping one day the mountain of dead absolved him. Damn it all. Let it end. Let the knife cut deep.

"Look at me."

Thunder boomed in the heavens. He was up to his waist in mud. Frost settled across his hand, freezing the blood he had spilled. Arn shook his head, and his eyes remained shut. He couldn't. He wouldn't. His hand trembled, and he pressed the blade harder to his skin.

"I said look at me, paragon."

Arn opened his eyes. Mari was so close, her face overwhelmed his vision. It remained human, but her hair had parted in three, one piece bathed in flame, one in frost, and one in lightning. Her gaze captivated him. Her hand settled over his own, and he braced himself. This was it. With but a push, she could punch that blade deeper, opening his throat. High above, the stars shimmered, and he feared they would fall.

Mari pulled the knife away. His fingers went limp. The weapon dropped to the mud, sank in, and was lost.

"I was no goddess of vengeance," she said, holding the gloved hand. "I preached no hate and demanded no blood sacrifice. The ever-changing seasons were my domain. You have suffered enough winter, Arn Bastell. Let spring come forth in your frozen heart. If I am to hear your prayers, let them be not of suffering, but of joy."

Mari's smile was so gentle, so full of compassion. Arn's lower lip quivered. There was no stopping it now. Something brittle inside him broke, and with it came an onslaught of tears.

"I don't deserve this," he whispered, and it was a tremendous struggle to keep his voice steady. Mari's hands pressed to either side of his face, and she softly kissed his forehead. When she whispered to him, he smelled autumn leaves and tilled soil on her breath.

"I offer you renewal, child. You need only accept it. Let the broken be made anew."

Arn had no words left. His resistance died. He collapsed, face buried in Mari's chest. He sobbed as the elements faded and the wind died, sobbed as a lifetime of guilt fought against the deceptively simple words of a murdered goddess. He knelt upon soft earth and green leaves. No smoke. No fires. Just Mari's touch. Her soothing whispers. Her arms wrapped about him, holding him close.

"It's all right," Mari said, with her own voice, her own mind. "It's all right, Arn. It's all right."

Could it be so? Was it possible?

Let the broken be made anew.

"I don't know how," he whispered amid his sobs. "I don't know how. I don't. I don't."

She stroked his hair, this Miquoan woman so much smaller than him, yet so much stronger, her presence overwhelming.

"None of us do, yet we live all the same. We walk our paths. We make our choices. You heard Velgyn's words. The man with a blade to his throat is gone. Who then remains in his place?"

"I still don't know."

Mari slowly stood, her arms sliding away from him. He knelt before her, his face wet, his lavender-white suit a mess of mud and tears. The moonlight sparkled off her dress. It cast a glow across her round face and windswept hair. She was a goddess in her own right, a beautiful midnight wonder too good for his life. Everything about her was regal, calm, and dignified. She offered the fox charm, and he silently accepted it.

"I think I do."

Mari left him there, to gather himself, to decide. Once alone, he pulled the glove off his injured hand. This hand that had held the knife. The hand his brother had crushed.

The hand, now fully healed by Velgyn's touch, left without a mark or scar.

Arn clenched it into a fist and pressed the knuckles to his lips so he might whisper a promise. Yes, he would be a new man. Whoever he was, it would resemble nothing like a paragon. It would be someone who cared for others. It would be someone worthy of the look Mari had given him during his lowest moment.

"A better man," he whispered, and let the last of his tears fall.

When he was finally recovered, and he'd done what he could to wipe the dirt from his trousers, Arn lumbered toward the wedding feast. He was in no hurry, for he worried awkward questions might be asked and assumptions made about his and Mari's absence. It was that slow walk, and his own heightened senses, that allowed him to hear a sound that broke his already fragile heart. Wine and celebration called, but they would have to wait.

Arn changed his path, veering along the forest edge away from the wedding to follow the sound. He walked until he found Mari on her knees, her head bowed and her arms tucked into her chest. He found her hidden from the world, alone and finally allowed to be her true self, without mask or falsehoods.

She was sobbing. No words. No voiced plea. Just unchecked hurt and sorrow.

For a brief moment, Arn's guilt said to leave and give her the privacy she desired. This vulnerability was not meant for his eyes. He banished the thought. If he was to be a new person, then let it start here and now. She had helped him, witnessed his suffering, and accepted the burden upon her shoulders. If he could help her, or relieve that burden, then he must try.

Arn quietly sat next to Mari in the leaves and grass. The woman who had so recently seemed tall and powerful shuddered uncontrollably. He said nothing, only raised his arm. She slid closer to him, and he wrapped her in his embrace. At that moment, he would give anything and everything to have her smile again. She was too precious. Too wonderful. Her head leaned against his chest. Her sobs abated so that she might speak.

"I always speak comfort for others," she said, and wiped her face. "You. Cyrus. Rihim. Rayan. The people of Thanet. It'd be nice if someone could speak it to me."

Arn swallowed. The right words refused to come to his awkward tongue.

"What about your sister?"

Mari laughed, and it brightened his world.

"Gods, you are terrible at this. But tonight is Stasia's special night. She doesn't need my tears."

He squeezed her shoulders gently.

"Then you're stuck with me. And as we've discovered, I am a poor man for the job."

She curled her face into his vest. Her long brown hair fell across his waist.

"You're here. It is enough."

He touched the fox charm in his pocket with his free hand, feeling the soft fur, remembering the gift this incredible woman had given him. If only he could return that kindness. If only he could grant her a sliver of the joy she gave to others.

"You don't have to go through this alone," he said. "If you ever need to, if you feel like it would help, you could talk to me. As yourself, I mean."

He meant to make her feel better, but his offer only made her tears return.

"Thank you," she said through them. "Thank you. I'll remember, I promise."

Arn held her as the distant songs of the wedding drifted through the forest, accompanied by the birds of the night and the chorus of the crickets. He held her as she wept, for reasons he was not privileged to know but blessed to be present for nonetheless. He held her as the moon dipped, her tears dried, and together they returned to the celebration, all smiles and encouragement for the married couple and their cherished friends.

CHAPTER 39

VAGRANT

After the humiliation and loss of the burning boats, and the brief reprieve with Stasia's wedding a day prior, it felt good to be doing something again. Word had reached Thorda of a procession of carriages arriving from Ierida, supposedly bearing high-ranking members of the church on a visit. Cyrus lurked upon a flat rooftop overlooking the road a quarter mile past the western gates. Three carriages in total, the first two elaborate and with their windows fully blocked with curtains, the trailing one less imposing. Cyrus guessed any guards or paragons to be in the rear, with their actual targets in the front.

Another quarter mile down the street, her feline body pressed low upon her own rooftop, waited the Lioness. Her sister would be nearby, hidden at ground level. The goal was for Cyrus to spook the trio into fleeing right into their waiting hands. Cyrus watched the carriages roll on by, and then at the third, he calmly stood, bent his knees, and leaped.

His body soared as if his muscles and bones were air. There was exhilaration in the act, a surpassing of mortal abilities to feel the wind in his hair and the snap of his cloak as he dove like a hunting falcon. He landed beside the driver of the rear carriage, his swords piercing the man's neck and back. A twist, and the body flew.

Panicked shouts greeted his arrival, but Cyrus paid them no mind. Another twist of his legs and he somersaulted to the ground. His swords flashed out, cutting reins and supports. The two horses bolted free, stranding the carriage. The leading carriages raced ahead, their drivers snapping whips and calling out for aid that would not be coming, for the Ahlai sisters would have them first.

"Let's see who you're hiding," Cyrus said as he stalked to the carriage door. All thoughts of assassination and murder ended the moment he flung it open. Jase Mosau and Kaia Makris sat opposite each other. Only Kaia was armed, and she lowered her sword in shock.

"You?"

"Me," Cyrus said, glancing between them. "Isn't this a church carriage?"

"It is," Jase said. "And if you would like an explanation, you best flee now before a nosy magistrate questions our survival against such a deadly ambush."

Cyrus glanced around. With Stasia and Mari focused on the more elaborate carriages up ahead, it would be easy for the two to pretend they were never seen as a potential target.

"Fine," he said. He rattled off quick directions to Thorda's home. "Come after dark if you wish to meet."

"I will be there before the night ends," Kaia said. "Now run along, Vagrant, before someone sees you and questions our loyalty."

❧

All were present and gathered in the study of Thorda's mansion, come to hear what news Kaia brought. All but Keles, Cyrus corrected mentally, and the thought filled the back of his throat with bile.

"I must confess, I imagined something much... different, when picturing the headquarters of the Coin's famed resistance," Kaia said upon her arrival.

"We're here, and we're listening," Cyrus said. "Is there more to ask for?"

"Legions more." She glanced out the window, as if convinced she was being watched. "I cannot stay long, or my absence may go noticed. As is, I must hope the arrival of my lord will prove enough of a distraction."

"An arrival I myself find noteworthy," Thorda said. "We heard neither message nor rumor of your lord's approach."

"Because what comes has been handled with utmost secrecy," the older woman explained. "And given the death of our soldiers we sent here to Vallessau, we trusted no messenger of our own."

Cyrus flinched at the reference. The sight of the six boats haunted him still. Nothing good would ever come from that harbor, not since the empire arrived. When Thorda spoke next, Cyrus had to bite his tongue.

"We are still investigating the source of the betrayal, but rest assured, every man and woman in this room holds my highest trust."

You must tell them, whispered the dark voice in his mind.

In time, he argued back.

Kaia debated a moment and then seemingly accepted Thorda's promise. She pulled out a tightly bound scroll from her trouser pocket.

"Our orders, which we were to burn upon reading," she said. Thorda opened it and read while the others waited. His bushy eyebrows arched, and he glanced over the top of the scroll at Kaia.

"A replacement?" he asked. "Surely I would have heard whispers."

"No rumors," Kaia said, shaking her head. "No whispers. The Uplifted Church is organizing the matter to ensure silence."

"Care to fill in the rest of us?" Stasia asked.

"In six days, the Heir-Incarnate plans to anoint Signifer Weiss as the replacement for the slain Lord Agrito," Thorda explained. "A matter that would normally involve festivals, a grand feast, and a public swearing-in ceremony, all meant to garner the populace's trust and acceptance of their new lord. None of which will happen."

"You've spooked them," Kaia said. "Regent Goldleaf was killed immediately following his paragon ritual. Magus of Eldrid died after his grotesque hangings. Now Lord Agrito and his entire family were executed in the bedroom of his own fort. It does not take much imagination to see the risks of a public ceremony for Lord Agrito's replacement. They've invited the other three lords in secret, to arrive without pomp or circumstance. The ceremony will be held on castle grounds, with sparse attendance."

"They'll be ready for us," Cyrus said, putting a damper on her excitement. "You've already confirmed their paranoia. Even with their secrecy, they will take steps to prevent an attack."

The older woman shrugged his way.

"So it might be dangerous. Has that stopped you before?"

It was a fair enough argument, and Cyrus bit down his retort. The rest of the group looked to their leader. Thorda stared at Kaia, a fist pressed to his face. His thumb twirled at his white beard.

"There is much beyond our control," he said. "I would know the exact location of the ceremony, and the time. With Lord Mosau's help, we may still organize matters to our benefit. Given the disaster at the docks, and the loss of so many soldiers, we cannot refuse such a potential victory no matter how dangerous or uncertain it may be."

That settled the matter, and it seemed most were in agreement. As for Cyrus, the shame of his loss to Galvanis burned inside his chest. A potential rematch filled him with a mixture of excitement and dread.

"Then I shall return once we learn more," Kaia said. She tilted her chin and addressed them with the full authority of her station. "I thank you, for your trust, and for all that you risk for our island's freedom."

With her departure, tension eased out of the room. A future path was set. They had a mission, and an enemy to crush. What more could they want? Quiet attention was replaced with sudden, chaotic energy. Thorda exited for his room, while Arn and Mari laughed and joked about preparing another meal, this in the fashion of Arn's homeland of Vashlee.

"This I must see," Stasia said, taking Clarissa's hand. "Arn, cooking? Preposterous."

Cyrus watched them all depart for the kitchen, his tongue burning to speak but fearing to make the move. This secret. This truth. It would ruin him if he tried to swallow it down. Someone had to know. Rayan shouted farewells to the others, claiming the night too late for his old bones. Cyrus's own decision made, he rushed the door while Rayan donned his coat.

"Mind if I come with?" Cyrus asked.

"You are always welcome," Rayan said, granting him an easy smile.

The pair walked the dark street in comfortable silence. The night sky eased Cyrus's turmoil. Strange as it seemed, it felt like the stars were watching him. Caring for him. When he looked up at one particularly bright pair, he liked to imagine one was his father and the other his mother, both gazing down with affection at what their son had become.

It would be affection, wouldn't it? Or would they recoil in horror at the godly beast Thorda Ahlai created?

Such somber thoughts kept his mouth shut. Rayan was no stranger to difficult conversations, though, and he sensed Cyrus's apprehension almost immediately. He broached it casually, as if discussing a time for tea the following day.

"If something bothers you, I am always here to listen, and to offer advice if needed."

"I know, Rayan, I know," Cyrus said, relieved to have that first step taken by another. "That's not…it's not *me* I'm worried about. It's you."

That got the paladin's attention. He glanced aside, his eyes narrowing.

"If you wish to worry me, you are successful. Speak. I am listening."

Cyrus stared at the passing cobbles beneath his feet while fighting for the right words. For all his shock and betrayal when that black helmet fell to the street, it would hit Rayan doubly hard. Part of him wished to keep the knowledge to himself. Now that Cyrus knew Keles's secret, she wouldn't dare show her face. She would assume he told everyone, and avoid any contact with her uncle.

But keeping this hidden put the rest of his friends at risk. Cyrus couldn't bear this burden on his own. Someone else had to know. Someone else had to help him understand, and no one would be better than the wise and kind-hearted paladin. Still, Cyrus could not shake the feeling he was bringing the old man a vial of poison and asking him to drink it for Cyrus's own benefit.

"It's…it's about Keles," he confessed. There. No going back now.

"What about her?" Rayan asked. He did a masterful job keeping his voice steady and his face impassive, but Cyrus could feel the worry in the air grow.

"The armored paragon I fought before the boats came, the one who ambushed me and Arn...I unmasked her. I saw her face. It was...it was Keles."

The paladin halted in the street. His body was so still it was as if he had turned to stone.

"You are certain?" he asked softly.

"There is no doubt. I even spoke with her about her betrayal. I'm sorry, Rayan. I wanted to tell you sooner, I just..." His voice trailed off, and he shrugged. "I'm sorry."

More wretched silence, and yet Rayan's questions were no better when they came.

"You believe she was the one who informed the empire of our soldiers on the boats, don't you?"

"I do."

"Did she offer explanation?"

You had to subjugate us. Humiliate us.

"Sinshei told her the truth," Cyrus said. "About her bloodline. About mine. Twice she witnessed Lycaena's death, and then the Anointed One came and gave her the one thing we could not: hope. If she brought back my mask, and convinced Sinshei of my death, then she would be rewarded with rule over Thanet as queen."

"To betray her friends, her family, and her very faith, all for a crown?" Rayan shook his head, and he resumed the walk toward his home. The movement calmed him. "No. I refuse to believe things are so simple. She's better than that. Stronger than that. Such a temptation would not have swayed her."

"Would it not, though?" Cyrus asked. "You saw her when the reborn Lycaena died. You heard her when Eshiel tumbled over the cliffside. Why would she trust us? Why would she believe we could offer anything more than heartache? She believes the only way to save Thanet is to cooperate with the empire instead of fighting it, to befriend those in power instead of opposing them."

"Have you the conviction to tell her she is wrong?"

"I tell it with every battle I fight," Cyrus said. "But I do not blame her. We're fools and dreamers, Rayan. I fear she might be the only one who sees clearly."

"To forfeit all faith is not 'seeing clearly,'" Rayan snapped. "It is a little death, and one I would not wish upon my enemies."

Cyrus tucked his hands behind him to hide their trembling. He couldn't watch the reaction to such betrayal. He couldn't speak truth to such hurt, not when his own pain overwhelmed his tongue. Despite the shock and anger he'd felt when her helmet fell, all that was left in him was regret, for when it mattered most, he had failed her.

"I tried," he said. The words tumbled out of him. "Believe me, Rayan, I tried so hard to convince her. To make her come back. I begged, I argued, but I'm too damn stupid, too damn simple. My words meant nothing. I don't have your wisdom. I don't understand matters of faith, a cruel joke given what I am becoming. All I could do was beg like a fool, beg and plead, a prince upon a stolen throne before the woman whose family was overthrown. Who am I to convince her? Who am I to tell her what's right?"

He would not cry. He would *not* cry.

"Thorda crafted me into a murderer," he said, the words pushed out through a constricted throat. "That's all I am, isn't it? All that matters is the blood I was born with and the lives that I take. It would make me a god, but before Keles, I am a lie. I cannot redeem myself through killing, and my crown is a betrayal. I have nothing. I've failed. Keles is lost. Vallessau is lost. The boats, they're burning, they're still burning..."

Rayan spun, their walk halting so he might wrap his arms about Cyrus in a hug. Cyrus leaned in, burying his face in the shirt of the taller man. For a brief moment he feared there would be no give, that a mask of bone would forever mark him, but then he felt the soft fabric against his cheek. He shuddered with his eyes closed. Felt something within him crack.

"Another person's choices are not your own failures, child," said Rayan. "We all walk our paths, however hard they may be. It is her decision that she walks, hers alone."

Child, Rayan called him. What child carried the blood of so many dead upon their hands? What child carried the hopes and dreams of an entire island upon their shoulders?

The Light of Vallessau did, once upon a time. It broke her. He feared it would break him, too.

"It doesn't feel like it's a choice," he said. "It feels like she's fallen down a cliff, and I was too slow to offer my hand."

The paladin pulled away, and he smiled despite his obvious pain.

"Do not give up hope yet. She is not lost to us. No cliff is beyond the sight of our goddess." He sighed and shook his head. "I always knew her faith was damaged, and its cracks ran deep, yet never did I think she would turn her heart to the God-Incarnate. Forgive me, Cyrus. I wish to walk the rest of the way home alone. I have much to pray over, and little time to do so before we set foot in the monster's den."

CHAPTER 40

ARN

Nope," Stasia said. "Not even close, now drink."

Arn emptied his glass and thudded it down upon the table. A belch followed, indicating his disdain at his failed guess. He and Mari sat on one side of the table, the newlyweds on the other. It had been two days since Kaia arrived with the news, and the time had passed with dreadful slowness. Cyrus was training, Rayan preaching. The four of them? They'd settled on a different sort of way to wile away the midday doldrums.

"This hardly feels fair," Mari grumbled. "A drinking game with a paragon? He could down a whole bottle before getting drunk."

"Given how bad he is at the game, he's close to finishing a bottle already," Stasia mocked. "Come now, Arn, you truly think it took me until I was twenty to bed someone?"

He pointed an accusing finger in her direction.

"You...you specifically asked me to guess when you first bedded *a woman*, mind you. I thought maybe you'd had a few awful tumbles with men in your younger years before you realized you liked the fairer sex."

Clarissa elbowed her wife in the side and let out a little giggle. She had drunk the least, yet appeared the tipsiest of them all.

"Stasia strikes me as someone who's always known what she wants."

"Not always," Mari said, and shot her sister a sly smile. "Remember Lord ang-Uri?"

For once, it was Stasia who blushed.

"All right, yes, but in my defense, I was curious, and he was very, *very* pretty."

Arn laughed and slapped the table hard enough to shake the bottles.

"I smell a story!"

"You smell only yourself," Stasia said, but the ire in her voice did not match her enormous smile. Clarissa was still leaning against her. Stasia absently stroked at her face and hair while smiling down at her.

"Have we tuckered Clarissa out already?" Mari asked. She offered her own smile, but Arn suspected it was forced, as it had been for days, not that Arn was watching her closely or anything.

All right, he was watching her very closely, but that didn't mean he was wrong. She'd shed a mask in his presence on the wedding night, and now that he knew she hid so much hurt, he saw it clearer with each and every passing day. That smile. That bounciness. It was less a disguise and more a...choice, one made in the face of her struggles. To do so must require immense strength and resolve, and he loved her for it.

A cold spike of fear flooded Arn's every limb. Oh no. Oh shit.

The door to the den opened, and Thorda's whip-sharp voice startled Arn in his seat.

"A moment if you would, Heretic."

For a single ludicrous second, Arn was convinced the man had read his mind and knew his thoughts about his daughter. His cheeks blushed, and he tried to hide it by lurching to his feet with a huff.

"Yeah, whatever you need, we're not busy here," he muttered. He caught Mari staring at him as he left, and something about her smile was far, far too amused.

Arn shook his head to clear his thoughts and followed the older man out of the den, down the hall, and toward his forge.

"Given the importance of a potential attack on the castle, I would not send you unprepared into the melee," Thorda explained as they walked.

"I feel like I'm as prepared as I can be. I have my fists, and by the time we fight, I'll have my sobriety. What more could I need?"

Thorda flung open the door and entered his forge.

"You insult me, paragon, when you fail to anticipate the potential benefits of my craftsmanship."

"And you insult me when you call me 'paragon.' I've left that life behind."

Thorda paused a moment so he might turn and dip his head.

"Duly noted, Heretic, and accept my apologies, along with this gift."

He approached one of his shelves and retrieved a wooden box from up high. Without any ceremony, he offered it to Arn. It was surprisingly heavy, but that weight made sense when Arn opened the lid. Within was a pair of gauntlets bearing the pristine Ahlai-made craftsmanship known throughout all of Gadir. The metal was polished to a gleaming shine. The leather was dark black, and soft to his touch when he lifted the pair out of the box.

"Did you need no measurements?" he asked as he moved the fingers. Metal plates were intricately layered one atop the other like scales so the joints were still protected.

"I remember every weapon I make for the empire's paragons," Thorda said. "Consider it a blessing and a curse."

Arn donned the right to get a feel and was further impressed. The leather was soft and perfectly fit. The metal clicked with each oiled movement. He felt like his hands were armored with dragon scales. His fingers pressed into a fist, then opened. No resistance. Even the place where his thumb layered over the forefinger was given a carved groove to comfortably rest within.

It was a barbaric thought, but by all the gods, Arn could not *wait* to hit someone with them.

"You put effort into this," he said. "More, I mean, than what I once wore."

There was pride in that faint smile Thorda offered him, but an equal mixture of sadness.

"I never give my all to the paragon weapons, but I gave my all to these. There will be no priests and acolytes praying over them, but I assure you these gauntlets will endure whatever you ask of them. I have also taken the liberty to add symbols more appropriate to your role as a heretic."

Arn twisted his wrists and lifted them closer to inspect. Sure enough, Thorda had replaced the original clenched praying hands of the Everlorn Empire above the knuckles. In their place were three tails, expertly carved into the metal so that they could only be seen when the light hit them just so. Little symbols hovered about the end of each tail, one wisps of flame, one little snowflakes, and one arcing bolts of lightning.

He brushed his bare fingers across the symbols, feeling the grooves.

"You talked to Mari," he said.

"It was her idea that I craft these for you."

Arn returned the gauntlets to the box.

"Then I will do all I can to prove myself worthy of such a gift."

Thorda's smile was pleased, but he turned away to hide it and then dismissed him with a wave.

"You fight alongside my family and my chosen warriors. You have already repaid this gift tenfold. If I ask anything, it is that you survive and put those gauntlets to good use for many years to come."

Arn winked as he tucked the box under one arm.

"I'll do my best."

He stepped out from the forge only to halt the second he shut the door. Mari waited in the hallway with her arms crossed and her foot tapping.

"Well?" she asked.

"They're wonderful," he said. "And I have you to thank, so thank you."

Mari clapped, and she bounced on her heels.

"I knew you'd love them," she said. "Can I see?"

He opened the box, and she leaned over, her eyes widening at the shining steel. Her fingers dipped into the box, and she brushed the fox tails with her fingertips. Her smile softened. There was weight to that symbol, and it was no longer his alone to carry. Mari had whispered with Velgyn, and communed with her lingering essence amid the forest. What did it now mean to her? Arn didn't know, but he wished he did. A silence fell over them both, and it was deep, it was solemn, it was religious.

"They're wonderful," she said, ending the moment. Her hand retreated. Their eyes met. She was so beautiful, so happy.

Arn bent down and kissed her.

Oh shit.

He withdrew just as quickly, their lips touching for less than second. His face blushed a deep red, and he retreated a step while slamming the box shut. A thousand jumbled thoughts ricocheted around in his skull, blasting away any potential words he might speak. But he had to speak, had to say something, because she was looking at him, shocked and confused and with eyes twinkling, her right hand pressed to her mouth as if horrified by his touch or perhaps only holding back a laugh.

"I didn't, I mean, it was dumb, that was dumb. I got...I'm going to go now."

Mari grabbed his wrist to keep him from fleeing. He flinched as if clutched by the jaws of the Lioness and not the little hand of a woman barely five feet tall.

"It's all right," she said. "But next time, you ask first."

Her words were a cold breeze across a burning fire. Her hand released him. The feeling of her touch lingered. She winked at him, mischievous and playful. If Arn's neck grew any redder he feared his head would pop like a smushed cherry.

"Right, sorry, just...sorry."

He fled for his room, where he could embarrass himself no further. He was only halfway there when he realized exactly what she had said. He echoed the words in his mind, wanting to hope and yet embarrassed by the intensity of that hope.

Next time?

Arn placed the box on the bed, paced his room twice, and then exited. He had done something dumb. So what? He could make amends. He could...he could...a gift! Relief filled him, mixing with excitement. Yes, he could get Mari a gift to repay her for everything she had done. He rattled off ideas in his mind as he hurried out of the mansion and toward the nearest market. Nothing romantic, no flowers, no jewelry, right? But maybe he wanted something a little romantic. Did he?

Stop it, before you get both of you hurt, the rational part of him tried to argue, but Arn brushed it aside. He reached the market, long rows of shops intermixed with stalls propped up between them and at various curves and alcoves of the long, winding thoroughfare. Arn walked it, lost in thought. He had a decent amount of coin on him, given to him by Thorda to ensure he was never wanting should a mission go wrong and he must hide for a bit. So what to spend it on? He dismissed most of the clothes, for he wanted to surprise her, not have her come be fitted. Perhaps the hats, though? But a hat wasn't personal enough. He wanted to reward her! She had saved his life at Stasia's wedding, damn it, surely she deserved something more than a pretty hat.

Shop after shop, Arn debated. What in the world could he get her that compared to whispering Velgyn, or having her father craft him such magnificent gauntlets?

"It's hopeless, is what it is," he muttered aloud, fingers pinching his lip as he eyed a seashell necklace. He'd spent an hour now, browsing, each new place less promising than the last. The shopkeeper, an older woman with two moles on her left cheek, smiled broadly at him.

"I recognize that look," she said. "A man in love, aye? Come then, you want to look at what I keep safely tucked away where the sticky fingers can't reach."

Arn apologized instead, his excitement finally starting to dwindle. He exited the shop, scratched at his face, and pondered. Gods, what was wrong with him? Was he really some lovesick teenager again? What he should do, what an adult man like Arn *should* do, was go talk to her. Make sure she was ready for something more than a quick joke and a kiss while both were filled with alcohol. Far better that than misreading everything and then humiliating himself showing up with some expensive trinket or painting.

"Right," Arn said, clapping his hands. "Mari is...she's special, Arn. We do this the right way, for once."

He turned for home but walked only three steps before slowing. The mood in the air had gone wrong. People looked nervous. Following their glances, he looked left, then right. He heard no cries of alarm, but the sight was a familiar one. The crowd was parting wordlessly, hoping to avoid the attention of the man striding through their center with his gauntlets clenched and his armor shining brightly.

"There you are," said Dario Bastell, approaching in full paragon armor. "Did you think you could escape?"

Arn spun, but his way was blocked. Rihim stood in the heart of the now-panicking crowd. His lips pulled back to reveal snarling white teeth. In his clawed hand he held Arn's broken gauntlet, still stained with dried blood. Behind him rushed over two dozen soldiers wielding spears, shields, and most worrisome of all, rope.

"So your hound tracked me at last," Arn said, slowly turning in place. "But did you bring enough to take me alive?"

Soldiers rushed from around the same corner where Dario emerged, their armor shining in the afternoon sun. Dario clacked his knuckles together, and his smile was brimming with confidence. The ringing metal sang.

"I made a promise, little brother. Today, we begin your road to penance."

CHAPTER 41

KELES

Keles stood before the door to the castle armory, counted backward from five, and then stepped inside.

"You summoned me?"

Galvanis vin Lucavi stood before racks of swords and spears, looking them over with a thoroughly displeased expression. As always, he wore his armor. She wondered if he ever took it off.

"Your Grace," he corrected. He did not turn from the weapons. "You should refer to me using the honorific Your Grace, particularly as a child of a heathen land."

Keles dipped her head and swept into a bow.

"My apologies. You summoned me, Your Grace?"

The Heir-Incarnate brushed his fingers along the edges of a row of spears. He showed no care for their sharp tips, for they could not scratch the soft skin of his fingertips. Flesh it might appear to be, but Keles knew it closer to sculpted marble.

"I have learned about you, Keles Lyon... or should I say, Keles Orani?"

Keles flinched despite her best efforts. This was bad, very bad, but she didn't yet know the extent. So far he only acknowledged her bloodline. That alone would not condemn her.

"I am not certain I understand," she said. Feign ignorance. Discover more.

"Such an intriguing prisoner could not enter my castle without my knowing," he continued. "You were brought here from afar by my sister's pet paragon, and kept sequestered for reasons unknown. It was enough to pique my curiosity. What was so special about you? And how did my sister plan to use you against me? Then you were gifted the armor of a penitent and allowed to roam freely. So I listened, and I searched, and I read. What I discovered was most entertaining."

He lifted a sword from the rack and held it aloft so he might look straight down the blade. Whatever he saw, it displeased him, and he snapped the blade in half as if it were a twig and cast both parts to join several others discarded in the far corner. The ringing of the broken steel ached in her ears.

"In two days, we will hold a ceremony to anoint Lord Agrito's replacement. I would have you there at my side."

Keles swallowed down her initial question of "why." She had to be more tactful than that. She wore the armor of the penitent. Her faith was meant to be in the empire now.

"I must ask, why am I worthy of such an honor?"

Galvanis smiled at her. Her insides fluttered. He was so beautiful, his hair like spun gold, his eyes the perfect blue of a summer sky. She told herself she should hate this man, hate everything he represented, yet it did not matter. There was a charisma to him, no doubt divinely gifted, and it washed over her in powerful waves.

"The ceremony shall be attended by many merchants and lords loyal to Everlorn, and we will celebrate it with a glorious execution. During that celebration, I would have you announce your true heritage to the gathered crowd, in preparation for a later reveal to the entire island. Imagine, the true princess of Thanet, of the family overthrown by the wicked Endarius, proclaiming her love and loyalty to the Everlorn Empire? It sends quite a message, wouldn't you agree?"

Keles did well to hide her revulsion. When she had taken power from Sinshei, and pledged her heart to Dagon, she had done so with Thanet's freedom in mind. Not just its freedom, but a return to the oldest of its ways, to before the people of Gadir had arrived with their boats and their gods. To have her heritage revealed, only for the people to then see her swear allegiance and servitude to the Everlorn Empire?

It was everything she resented. Could she do it? Even if it was a lie? If she played along with Galvanis until Sinshei struck him down, Thanet still might find its freedom, yet how could she rule Thanet as its queen after such a betrayal? Would the people ever trust her? It was the forsaking ceremony all over again, this time on a far grander scale.

"Indeed it does," she said, simple, plain words to hide the disgust squirming in her guts.

Galvanis finally turned from the weapons. The moment his attention shifted her way she fought back a shiver. There was something otherworldly about the shade of white to his skin and the perfection of his features. He didn't seem like a man but the representation of one, deemed perfect by a society far, far away from Thanet.

"I do not know what games my sister plays, but they are doomed to fail. Sinshei was born in Eldrid, and coddled there, her soul seeded with sin and blasphemies by her treasonous mother. She views herself as clever and manipulative, but it is easy to believe yourself a master of secrets when every servant and citizen must bow to your whims lest they face the headman's ax. She is a fool, and like most fools, she is blind to her shortcomings. It will lead her astray. As much as it pains my heart, I suspect it will lead to her death."

Keles stood statue-perfect, her arms crossed behind her and her jaw locked shut. She would reveal nothing. Play the perfect soldier. Pray he did not realize the power that Sinshei had put into her veins.

"Do not fear," he said. "I will not force a confession. Your loyalties are certainly complicated and confusing, as one would expect of a heathen. Let me lay a clear path before you, Keles, so you may walk in wisdom. Sinshei has plans for you, I am sure of it, but I ask that you reject them. She is a fool, spoiled and reckless. Do not die with her. There is potential in you, I see that as clear as the blue sky above. Take my hand instead. Put your trust in me, Everlorn's Heir-Incarnate. Help me tame this wretched island."

His hand brushed her cheek, pressing errant strands of hair back behind her ear. The slightest contact with his fingers was like kissing lightning. She shivered at such divine power. His blue eyes swallowed her as he leaned close.

"And when I am God-Incarnate, I will remember the names and faces of those who aided me."

Keles turned away. Was this a betrayal? Did it even matter? What did she owe any of these rulers of Everlorn? Yet Sinshei had looked upon Keles with love after the penitent ritual. It had been genuine, hadn't it?

Perhaps it had been, but she should not fool herself. What did Sinshei even understand of love, with a brother like Galvanis and a father like God-Incarnate Lucavi?

Keles would not betray her, not entirely, but she would test the waters.

"Sinshei promised me Thanet would be mine."

Galvanis leaned even closer. His cheek pressed against hers. His warm breath was a desert wind. His touch burned, but his whisper was ice.

"I can give you far more than one little island."

Except Keles wanted freedom for her home and her people. Galvanis could offer her all of Gadir, and it would mean nothing to her. He thought Keles accepted Sinshei's offer out of a desire for power, and so he offered more power in turn. How else would a future god-emperor see the world? He could not imagine she sought the crown, not to rule, but to serve.

"I remain ever loyal," she said, unsure of how else to respond.

Galvanis pulled away. At his withdrawal, a bit of the spell receded, his charm not so overwhelming as to jumble her thoughts.

"Loyal to whom, little heathen?"

The Heir-Incarnate dismissed her with a wave, not caring to hear her answer, nor judge it truth or lie.

✂

Keles carried her helmet as she walked. It was too hot to wear beneath the high spring sun. She kept her eyes straight on the path east, beyond the limits of the city to the bordering cliffs, and pretended no one knew who she was. No one would recognize her. Surely it wouldn't be the Light of Vallessau in such black armor. Not a devoted paladin of Lycaena who wore the armor of an imperial penitent.

She walked and walked, until reaching the cliff. Not far to her left was the broken pedestal where a grand butterfly had once overlooked the crystalline waters. Far below her were the Solemn Sands.

It would be a fitting place to die.

Keles let the great expanse of blue wash over her sight. She stared at the horizon line, where the distance stretched on forever. She stared until it was pulling her into it with an unseen string linked to her forehead. All she had to do was let it. Accept the pull. Would Thanet be better for it?

If she refused Galvanis, he would kill her. Quickly, if she was lucky. She doubted herself that lucky. Maybe she would hang from the Dead Flags. Or maybe Galvanis would carve the flesh from her body while condemning her sins. Either way, she would be made an example to her people. She would suffer. She would die. And it would be used as a blade against the island she wished only to protect.

"Lycaena would condemn me for this," she whispered. "What of you, Dagon? I know only tales of your wickedness. How goes your judgment should I cast myself to your waves?"

Such a joke, to be in service to an unknown god, without lessons or scriptures, attempting obedience despite no face to look upon nor stories to guide her. Ten lives, sacrificed to give her this power. Ten lives, wholly devoted to Dagon despite the passage of centuries and the work of priests and priestesses to denounce them and call them evil. Yes, even her beloved Lycaena had allowed it to happen, and considered it necessary.

What did that mean for Dagon's true personality?

What of Lycaena's?

Crashing waves. Tall cliffs. The heavy penitent armor would crush her when she landed. If she lived, its weight would sink her below the water to drown. Fitting. Better. Every choice she made was a weapon against her home. Hopeless. At least she would cause no more hurt. She wouldn't see the pain in Cyrus's eyes at her betrayal. See the blue instead. Watch the horizon. Watch the unending line.

Her foot rose.

"Isn't this a fine surprise?"

Her foot lowered. When she turned, Keles discovered a dead man walking up the path to the cliffside apex. Her mouth dropped open.

"Eshiel?" she asked. "What are you doing here?

His attire was simpler than when she last saw him, a loose gray shirt above red trousers. A bit of sweat marked his brow from the exertion. If he was alarmed at her new armor, or heard rumors of her becoming a penitent, he let neither show.

"You would ask a twice-born why he would come to the Solemn Sands? Have you forgotten your schooling already?"

Her cheeks flushed with embarrassment. That hadn't been what she meant, yet his gentle rebuke left her flustered. Her insides already felt scrambled, now made worse at his arrival. Part of her wanted to embrace him. Part of her wanted to flee in shame.

"I would ask how you yet live when I last saw you lost amid the cliff's collapse," she said as he joined her side to gaze upon the Crystal Sea.

"It seems Lycaena had more planned for my life," he said. "I survived the fall to the water, and once I had recovered, I made my way back to Vallessau."

Keles sensed that was not the full story, but she let him be.

"I'm . . . I'm glad you lived," she said.

"So am I," he said, and smiled. He closed his eyes and breathed in the salty air. "But as to your first question, sometimes I visit the Solemn Sands to remind myself of what I fight for. Amidst all the paranoia, the sneaking about, and the whispered prayers, it can be easy to lose sight of why we struggle. A better future. A remembered past."

Keles crossed her arms, but she would not join him in staring at the sea. That unending line lost its allure, and so she watched the waves crash far below. Did he know why she had come? The priest was perceptive, intelligent. Her foot had risen. Gods and goddesses help her, her foot had risen.

"Or maybe I am here because Lycaena called me here," he added. "Our priesthood was always challenged to be present for those in need. Is that you, Keles? Your armor. It's certainly no design of Thanet. Do you serve Everlorn now?"

"I do what I must," she said, praying he dropped the subject yet knowing he wouldn't.

"A pity, that they wounded you so deeply. I suspect my own failures are to blame. The bleeding and burning goddess I summoned would never have soothed the hurts you suffered."

Keles winced at her stung pride. For him to act as if her decisions were done solely through hurt, or his failure, and not her own volition? It galled her.

"My family once ruled Thanet, before Endarius arrived with an army," she said. "It could be mine again. Sinshei has promised me such. Our rebellion here is hopeless, the armies of Everlorn too vast. Should they muster even a fraction of their forces, they could surround our island with a thousand warships. They could bury our beaches in soldiers, and choke our cities with the dead. The only way to survive is to make peace with them. To befriend them."

"And with Sinshei, you think you have that friend?"

Keles did not bother to hide her exasperation.

"What choice have I left to me, Eshiel? The Vagrant's petty rebellion? A handful of skilled fighters they may be, but they are too few, and their foes too many. It's an easy dream, a seductive one, that a hero will save us. It won't happen. Heroes break before the might of entire nations. They win only in stories and parables."

Eshiel gestured toward her black platemail.

"And so you don their armor, cast aside Lycaena, and profess faith in their God-Incarnate. Is a crown worth such sacrifice?"

"Is *Lycaena* worth it?" she countered. "How do you still hold faith in a twice-slain goddess?"

"Twice-slain you call her, yet I am thrice-born. What do life and death mean to gods? Who are we to declare when they begin, or when they end?"

It was exactly the slippery, elusive argument always given Keles when she asked questions in the Heaven's Wing. When a law or belief was not clear, and she questioned its authenticity or reasoning, those supposedly wiser than her would act like her questions and doubts were evidence of her own moral failings.

"They end when their bodies are slain and our prayers silenced," Keles said. "You should know. You resurrected a lie."

"Indeed I did," said Eshiel. "And it is the same lie you now believe.

The cost is too high. When you've finished paying in blood and cast-off faith, you will look upon the remains with horror."

"I will not be judged by you," she said, a hard edge entering her voice.

"I offer no judgment. I do offer counsel, if you would have it. Or should I give you fire instead? You serve the Everlorn Empire now. You're one step shy of a paragon. By all rights, you should be my enemy."

Keles drew her sword and pointed it at his neck.

"I am no paragon," she seethed. "I serve Thanet. Everything I do, I do for Thanet!"

Eshiel closed the distance between them. He tilted his head so the tip of her blade nestled just below his jaw. Blood trickled from where the sharpened steel made contact.

"When you draw steel, be prepared to use it, Keles. I have no patience for empty threats."

"It is not empty."

He should have been afraid, or angry, or feel betrayed. Instead he grinned so faintly, so confidently.

"Do tell, how does killing me better serve Thanet? Or is every single drop of blood you spill justified so long as you tell yourself it's for a traitor's crown?"

Her exhaustion, her frustration, the momentary high of the sacrifice and the misery of battling Cyrus, had left her mind battered and bruised beyond reason. She could offer Eshiel no answer. She hated even needing to give one.

"Why did you come back to Vallessau?" she asked. "Why couldn't you stay away?"

"I returned for the same reason you don that armor, Keles. Because I thought I could make things better. Hear me, please. If you hold any regard for my faith or my wisdom, you will listen to me now. The empire would have you slay your family and friends under a promise of power they will never fulfill. You will spill blood. You will feel guilt and torment. You will carve a hole in your soul, and in return for achieving their ends, they will give you their hate and contempt disguised as compassion. It will not fill that hole. It will only dig it deeper. Reject it, Keles."

He put his hand over hers. Together, they held the same blade.

"Live again. Hope again. It is never too late."

Keles jerked her hand free and sheathed the blade. Anger raged within her. At him? At herself? Sinshei? *Hope again*, he asked, as if it were a meager thing.

"In two days, the Heir-Incarnate will hold a ceremony to anoint a new lord for Tannin," she said. She could at least offer him this before she returned to the castle. "Most soldiers and paragons will be in attendance, which will leave the roads and gates poorly guarded. Flee here while you can, Eshiel. When they finish, they will scour all of Vallessau to prepare it for the God-Incarnate's arrival. You aren't safe here."

The priest reached out, and she gave him her hand. He leaned low to kiss her knuckles. When he looked up, mischief sparkled in his eyes.

"Thank you for the warning," he said. "But I am not going anywhere."

CHAPTER 42

ARN

Who is the Vagrant?"

The multi-thonged whip lashed Arn's bare chest. The tiny pieces of glass wedged into the end knots tore his skin. He clenched his jaw and braced against the pain. It was constant now, that pain. Even his paragon nature would not heal him so quickly from the abuse the magistrate inflicted.

"Who is the Ax?"

Another hit, this to his arm. Blood trickled down his bicep. He kept his eyes closed and his tongue silent. He would talk, but not yet.

"Who is the Paladin?"

The same questions, over and over. Nothing else. The magistrate, some young bastard named Castor Bouras, threw all his youthful energy into the beating. Arn sat on the floor, his back against a stone wall. His wrists were bolted to it, and his ankles to the floor. Chains wrapped his waist. He had tested them when they first locked him in the dungeon. They were thick and had no give.

"Who is the Lioness?"

Arn had to be careful not to react to Mari's alias. Not even the hint of a smile could be allowed to cross his lips. He would never in a million years give her up, but if Castor realized she was important to him, he'd focus upon her identity exclusively in an attempt to worm his way into his mind.

Another lash, back to the chest. Blood flowed freely down his abdomen and seeped into the upper portion of his trousers. Much of it had dried, leaving it sticky and uncomfortable against his waist.

"Who is the Coin?"

There it was, the last of the questions. Arn opened his eyes, grinned at the red-haired magistrate, and gave the same answer he'd given at least a hundred times already.

"Hit me harder. I fear I'll fall asleep."

A few times he'd not even answered. He'd only loudly, exaggeratedly snored. Castor raised his arm, the lashes of his whip clacking together, but then paused. The door to the dungeon cell opened.

"Leave him, magistrate. I would have words with my brother."

Arn thudded his head against the stone. All the gods damn it, he'd rather be buggered by the God-Incarnate than suffer Dario's presence. His brother entered carrying a bucket and a rag, and a single glare sent the magistrate scurrying.

"Come to gloat?" Arn asked.

Dario set the bucket of water down beside him and then dropped to his knees. He dipped a heavy white cloth into the water, wrung it out, and then gently pressed it to Arn's forehead.

"You were always handsome, and even worse, you knew it," Dario said as he gently patted away the blood. "Soldiers claim women prefer men with scars, but your face may soon put that to the test, little brother."

Despite the dire situation, despite his pain and aches, Arn laughed.

"Fuck you, Dario, and leave. I'm in no mood for pity."

"Pity is not what brought me down here."

Dario dipped the rag back into the water, wrung it clean, and then started dabbing at Arn's chest. The shards of glass in Castor's whip did not cut deep, so the wounds were narrow and shallow, but they were so very many. Arn hissed at the contact. It felt like his entire chest were aflame.

"Not pity, eh? Then what is it? Eager to see me suffer? Or are you jealous that it was Castor doing the work and not you?"

"I see your hand healed. That's good."

Dario would not think so if he knew who had healed it. The thought almost put a smile on Arn's face. His loyal, faithful brother, complimenting the work of a heretical god? Delightful.

"Why are you really here?" he asked, even though he dreaded the answer.

"Is it not obvious? I have come to pray for you, little brother."

Arn's stomach twisted.

"I do not want your prayers."

"You will receive them nonetheless."

The bolts and manacles groaned with Arn's effort. His muscles bulged and scabs tore from the strain, but Arn did not care. His head leaned forward, closer and closer to Dario's. Their eyes met as intended. Let Dario see, let him finally *see*, the truth of his little brother.

"The God-Incarnate shall never have my faith. He doesn't deserve it, and he never will. You waste your time. Kill me, or forget me. No other future awaits."

Dario's free hand shoved Arn back against the wall. His fingers pressed against the lashes, and they dug in, and in. The scabs broke. The blood flowed free.

"Your ignorance is profound, Arn, and made worse in that you think it is wisdom. You are the fool lost in the woods who insists he will find his own path. You are a drowning man screaming to the men in boats that they are the ones in danger. You stand in fire, and no matter your protestations, my own eyes see true that you are *burning*."

Arn closed his eyes and slowly exhaled.

"You're right," he said. "I am a fool. I thought I could reach you. But if you wish to help me, then bring back Castor and his whip. At least it is honest in the pain it inflicts."

Dario clasped his hands together, palms touching and fingers upward. With Arn's blood across them, they perfectly mirrored the flag that flew across the Everlorn Empire's banners.

"Heresy is seductive, and it begs to be shared. You don't seek to save me, Arn. You seek validation for your own failure. I won't give it to you. My faith is strong, and my heart true. You are just yet to see it."

Only then did Arn realize something was between Dario's praying hands. Something small, orange, and soft. There was no hiding his reaction.

"Let go," he said.

Dario bowed his head. His voice deepened. "Highest grace in Eldrid, look upon us now in our time of need. I beg intercession, for the sins of my brother are many."

With each word, Arn felt the fire leave his skin. Ice replaced it. His stomach squirmed as if he'd swallowed snakes.

"Stop it."

"Heresy has claimed his weakened heart. Doubt has arrested the confidence that once flowed true. Lost, he is lost, and I beg that he be found."

"I said stop."

But he wouldn't. Even worse, this was no performance. This was no act. Dario meant every word.

"Please, forgive me of my own failures that led to his fall. Whatever words I should have spoken, they fell silent. Whatever guide I was to present, I failed. He walked in my steps, and his walk led to sin."

Dario crushed Velgyn's fox tail with paragon strength. The bone and fur twisted and cracked. Arn's arms and legs thrashed, but he could not strike Dario, could not silence him.

"Enough!" Arn screamed, but there would be no halt. His brother knelt lower, his face to the cold dungeon floor. Tears. Gods help them all, Dario shed actual tears.

"Please, mighty Lucavi, God of Eldrid, hear me. Save me. Save us. Open his blinded eyes. Let him see your light. Do not make me walk this path alone. Do not shoulder me with such a burden, I plead, I beg."

And then Arn felt it, the presence of the God-Incarnate. It was a morning frost settling on his wounds. It was a fire stirring behind his eyes. The touch was a feather's kiss compared to the swelling when the ten Seeds cut their throats so he might become a paragon, but he recognized it nonetheless. This time he felt no comfort, no affirmation. It was fingers curling about his flesh, hot with fever and overwhelmed with greed. Arn was not a beloved lamb gone astray. He was a fly, struggling to escape the web of a spider.

None of that compared to the golden glow that shone across Dario's skin. He was a beacon in the dungeon. Darkness fled him. Light shone from his irises. He sat up, unashamed of his tears. A smile crossed his face, and it was filled with love.

"He hears," Dario whispered. He lifted the mangled foxtail directly before Arn so he might see. So he might watch. The touch of the God-Incarnate seeped into it from the faithful paragon. The golden light melted the bronze cap. It burned the fur to ash. It turned the bone to powder. "He forgives. It's not too late, Arn. Redemption awaits you. Penitence will save you. Open your closed heart, and let it in."

Arn was not prepared for the despair that struck him seeing the last physical remnant of Velgyn fade away. If only he had left it at home, like he had his gauntlets. If only he had not followed his brother into the Legion. If only he had perished during the paragon ritual, as some men did. Lucavi's power crawled across his skin. He had been a proud paragon for years. In many ways, he was still one. Lucavi's blessing had never retreated from him. Perhaps that gave his brother hope.

But there was no hope of that, not now, not ever. There had been a time when he would have raged against the cruel act his brother committed, but that rage was what Dario wanted. Arn would not give it to him. Instead he clung to a promise, one offered after the touch of a slain goddess mended his broken hand. A better man, he vowed to become. Someone worthy of a generous heart like Mari Ahlai's, worthy of the forgiveness from a goddess like Velgyn. Let him become it, even if only in death.

"My eyes are already open," he told his brother, softly echoing those words back to him. The divine light of the God-Incarnate flared brighter, wild, angry, and all-consuming. "Before me I see a man aflame, and though he smiles, he is burning."

Dario gently cupped Arn's face in his hands, and the manacles would not allow him any protest. He endured their touch, their warmth, the smear of his own blood upon his face mixing with the ashes of Velgyn's tail.

"Time, dear brother. All I need is time. I will not let your soul end at the grave."

The cell door rattled, and with it the spell seemed to dissipate. Darkness returned. The glow about Dario's skin faded as if it had never been. Magistrate Castor stepped inside and dipped his head in apology. Someone new was with him, a bronze-skinned man Arn didn't recognize. His clothing looked expensive, though. A noble? A lord? The man's copper eyes were sharp in the torchlight, and he remained just outside of the cell, watching intently.

"The Heir-Incarnate has decreed a change in plans," Castor explained. "We need to move Arn to a new location. Might you aid me?"

Dario gently patted Arn's cheek. His smile, his damned loving smile, didn't even flinch.

"Of course," he said, and then swung a fist for Arn's temple.

CHAPTER 43

VAGRANT

A full day passed without word from Arn. Thorda had insisted on patience, and tried to pry information from his spies in the castle, to no avail. So when a servant came bearing a secret note, they all assumed the worst. The message had been simple: assemble your strongest, and prepare for Kaia's arrival come nightfall. Cyrus sat with the others in the den, nervous and frustrated. At least they might soon have answers, for good or ill. He prayed, though not knowing exactly to whom, that it was not ill.

"She's here," Mari said. She had seated herself by the window, and checked it every few minutes.

Miss Kaia had dressed herself as if she were trying to be inconspicuous but lacked experience in doing so. Plain but expensive clothes, the buckle at her waist silver and too clean, and her cloak brand-new. She pulled the hood off her head upon entering the mansion and swept the room with her eyes. Thorda lurked by the fire, Rayan in a nearby chair. Cyrus leaned against the wall, keenly feeling Arn's absence. He might have made a few jokes to try to lighten the mood, or at least provoked Stasia into doing so. Instead, the older sister sat quietly with Clarissa. They all anticipated the worst, and at last, Kaia had come to give it.

"I recognize every face," she said. "Good."

"We are here as requested," Stasia said. "Care to tell us why?"

The older woman straightened up and placed her hands behind her back as if she were a general addressing her troops.

"Plans have changed. I assume you know already about the capture of one of your strongest? The Heretic?"

"We have surmised as much," Thorda said. "So he lives?"

"For now," Kaia said, tightening the knot that kept her graying hair behind her head. "But the ceremony tomorrow has been changed. Instead, Arn will be executed in honor of the God-Incarnate's impending arrival."

"We can't let that happen," Mari said, strong enough it surprised Kaia.

"And I would not see it happen, either," she said, glancing her way. "Which is why I am here. My lord Jase visited with Arn briefly, and he knows where they are keeping him prisoner. Soldiers have also been scouring the castle for hidden pathways. I've been shown one of them, and we can use it to sneak inside while facing a minimum of guards."

"I thank you for this information," Thorda said. "Tell me of the entrance, and where Arn is being held."

"No," Kaia said, and she shook her head. "If we are to rescue the Heretic, we go tonight. After two of my lord's boats burned with loyal soldiers, we have not risked a single intermediary with this information. If we do this, we do it here and now."

Cyrus looked to their leader. One key aspect to this jailbreak worried him, and he knew the brilliant man would reach the same conclusion.

"If we break in and save Arn, we give up any chance of ambushing the ceremony," he said, making sure everyone present understood the stakes. "They will suspect a traitor within the castle. It may well even implicate Lord Jase himself."

The question then was obvious. Which was more important, saving Arn, or ambushing the Heir-Incarnate and his fellow lords during the appointment ceremony? Those present exchanged glances. Most painful of all was the look Mari gave her father. There was no pleading to it, only anger threatening to burst free at any moment.

Thorda cleared his throat, his decision made.

"There will be other opportunities to strike at this newly appointed lord of Tannin. There is only one Heretic. We go, and we bring him home."

Relief swept through the room. Cyrus had feared the mission would overrule all, as it so often did with Thorda, and he had not been alone in that fear.

"Then gather your weapons and armor," Kaia said as excitement replaced the nervousness. "And follow me."

"We ready for this?" Cyrus asked his friends. They gathered in a safe house not far from the royal castle. Weapons bristled. Armor rattled. The others nodded in the affirmative, except for Mari, who softly growled.

"Always," her word-lace translated.

Cyrus swallowed down his anxieties and concerns. Somewhere deep underneath the castle, Arn was suffering in chains. It could not be allowed. He withdrew the skull mask from his pocket and slid it over his face. It was warm to the touch, its weight comforting.

"All right," he said, and turned to Kaia. Only she held a lantern. "Lead the way."

The older woman nodded, and she drew her slender sword with her free hand.

"Make it quiet, and make it quick," she said. "We don't know when the next guard change will happen, so we must be swift."

They exited as a group into the starlit night. Kaia directed them to what had appeared to be nothing more than an unassuming home easily missable in the dark. It had been clearly vacated recently. Broken furniture was gathered into a pile on the western side and its windows boarded up. Two imperial soldiers stood guard at the front of the building, looking tired and bored. Cyrus doubted they had any idea what they protected. He instructed everyone to pause, granting Mari time to take to the rooftops. Once she was above them, he clenched his fist, enacting the magic of his Anyx ring. There were so many shadows, including the doorway behind the soldiers. A single step, and he was behind them.

Mari's fangs and Cyrus's swords did their work, silent and quick.

A quick check for keys found the proper set, and in the group went, dragging the bodies along with them. Once inside, Cyrus took measure of the place. It might have been a fine home once, but the walls were stripped bare and the wood floor torn up and mangled by axes or shovels. In the room connected to the entrance, the baseboards were removed entirely, with their remnants stacked near the door. Fresh dirt was piled up in multiple places.

The result of all this excavation was the unearthing of stone steps leading down to a once-buried door, now freed.

Where we go was never meant to be found, Cyrus thought. He followed Kaia down the steps. The door was wide and sturdy, its front braced with bronze. Even after being buried beneath the floorboards, it held up surprisingly well. A ring of stones formed an arch around it, and across its center was an unmistakable carving of Endarius. The door opened into a tunnel with a perfectly smooth stone floor and a curved ceiling. Not even Stasia would have to crouch.

"What is this?" Rayan asked, his eyes locked on the symbol of the Lion.

Cyrus shook his head and followed. He had anticipated a tunnel akin to what he used to sneak into the castle in his failed attempt to assassinate Regent Goldleaf. This, however, was entirely something else. The passage widened enough that they could walk two abreast. Kaia led the way, her lantern raised to give everyone light.

"This entrance was not meant to be a secret," Rayan said after a moment. His voice echoed.

"Then why was it buried and forgotten?" Cyrus asked.

The paladin shrugged. He had no answers.

"Keep quiet," Kaia said. She glared over her shoulder. Her cheek twitched nervously. "We do not know if guards are stationed farther inside, nor how far our voices may carry."

They walked for at least a minute, their footsteps too heavy and their movements too loud. Cyrus could not shake the feeling that this tunnel was meant to be used by a large number of people. But to where? What mystery was buried beneath the castle, one seemingly blessed by Endarius?

He glanced at Mari. Might as well ask the one who would know.

"Do you know where we go?"

The Lioness closed her eyes a moment, and then shook her head.

"A place of great shame," her word-lace translated.

"Was it a prison?"

"There are cells to hold prisoners, yes. He will tell me no more than that."

The tunnel slowly widened, and to their right, Kaia's lantern caught a sudden set of stairs cut into the wall. It was once blocked off by an iron gate, but its hinges had broken with time and it lay askew on the ground. Wherever they went, it was no normal prison, even if it was dark and underground.

"How well do you know the way?" Cyrus asked Kaia softly, fearful of how far even his whisper might travel.

"I go only where Jase told me," she said. "We are nearly there, I hope."

The tunnel's slope evened out, and it widened further. The only light came from Kaia's lantern, and so they nearly stumbled over Arn completely by the time they found him. He lay slumped against the wall, the manacles around his meaty wrists nailed to the stone. His head drooped, but his chest stirred with slow and steady breaths. Asleep, or perhaps drugged, but still alive. Relief swept through Cyrus, though it was a marginal comfort against the paranoia itching deep in his mind.

Why, exactly, was Arn held prisoner here, in the final stretch of this curious tunnel just before it opened up into darkness?

"Arn!" Mari cried out with a soft little yelp, and she quickly fell to his side to check his wounds.

"I brought you something," Stasia said as Arn stirred. She grabbed a heavy pouch at her hip and opened it to reveal Arn's gauntlets, brought at Mari's request. *Just in case he needs them*, she had explained.

"Is he wounded?" Rayan asked. "I can pray over him if it is dire."

"Pray after I cut him free," Stasia said, readying her ax. "Fair warning, this is going to be loud."

Cyrus's attention shifted, for Kaia was still walking the tunnel slowly with her lantern raised high. Except she wasn't still in the tunnel. She'd stepped through a doorway of sorts into a wide, flat space the lantern's light could not begin to illuminate. Such open space seemed ridiculous given how deep they were beneath the castle.

"Kaia?"

She turned, and the look of horror on her face was Cyrus's only warning before the enormous gates dropped, sealing them inside.

"A trap," Rayan shouted, rushing the way they came. Faint light shimmered off his drawn sword, granting them sight.

Cyrus didn't think, only reacted. He crossed the space in a heartbeat, his right hand lunging through the gaps in the enormous gate. His fingers caught Kaia's collar, and a tug slammed her to the bars. With his other hand, he drew his sword and pressed the tip against Kaia's throat.

"What have you done?" he raged.

Despite the blade, and the implied threat, she did not back down. Her returned gaze was iron.

"I do not know," she said. "For I was also deceived."

Cyrus pressed the edge tighter to her skin so that she had to tilt her head back lest it cut her skin. Still she did not break eye contact. Behind her, shadows stirred. Light grew from torches high above, from places he could not see. He heard the shuffling of movement. Voices. Torches. Beyond it all, a sickness, keen in Cyrus's mind.

"Come forth, Vagrant," cried the Heir-Incarnate. His voice bounced from wall to wall, deep and imposing like the divine being he claimed to be. Kaia's eyes widened at the sound. There was no time to debate. Cyrus made a snap decision: He believed her. Someone had lied to her, and it did not take much effort to guess who. He released her and turned to the others.

Arn was free, his manacles hacked apart by Stasia's ax, but he still looked a bit groggy and out of sorts. Rayan stood a few dozen feet away, his sword illuminating the enormous gate blocking their retreat.

"What do we do?" Cyrus asked them.

Stasia glanced about, gauging options.

"These shadows are deep," she said. "You could flee the way you came."

Again the Heir-Incarnate called out from beyond.

"I know your gifts, Vagrant. Come forth from the shadows so we might look upon Thanet's supposed savior."

Cyrus shook his head. There would be no abandoning his friends, his family. He looked to Kaia, who awaited him on the other side.

"No," he said. "I will stay, and discover the measure of this deceit."

A clench of his fist, a bit of heat upon his fingers from the ring, and he stepped through shadows to emerge in the darkness beside Kaia. Finally free, he took in his new surroundings. It was a battle arena, one staggering in its size. The ground was smoothly packed dirt. The walls surrounding him were tall, perhaps ten feet in height, their sides sanded stone so they provided not a single handhold. From side to side, Cyrus estimated it three hundred feet in length, perhaps more. Scattered in uneven intervals were more entrances into the arena, some open, some barred shut.

Above the walls were rows and rows of seats. They were wood planks set upon stones, forming benches that stretched around the entire arena. Several thousand people could comfortably watch the blood sport below, and Cyrus held no doubt it was blood sport that happened in ages past. One did not build such a wide-open space deep underground for activities acceptable to the light of day.

Though it could hold thousands, Cyrus estimated a mere hundred people shuffled inside at his arrival, coming in through various other tunnels and taking their seats to watch whatever was to follow. Some wore armor, others fine silks and furs. Along the outermost ring, soldiers hurried to light over fifty ancient braziers. A dozen archers stood ready in the stands directly behind him, and he tried not to imagine what their arrows could do to his trapped friends.

Lording over the arena were two dozen fanciful padded chairs. Cyrus recognized many faces occupying them, such as Sinshei the Anointed One and her loyal paragon, Soma, regal as ever in his blue-tinted plate. The Heir-Incarnate sat in the centermost chair, and he stood and clapped at Cyrus's appearance. The soldiers, paragons, and wealthy elite clapped along with him.

"Welcome," he said, "to the Lion's Arena."

His voice projected without any perceived effort. His command over the proceedings was absolute. He looked regal and divine in his gold armor with silvered edges. To his left sat a solemn Jase Mosau. The moment Cyrus saw the man's grim smile he knew in his gut who had betrayed them, not once, but twice. Jase, who had insisted they come tonight, or not at all. Jase, who had condemned his own soldiers to die in burning boats. Cyrus could think of a thousand ways he wished to repay such treachery, all of them bloody and brutal.

To Galvanis's right sat Keles Lyon, her face no longer hidden behind her helmet. He tried not to think of her at all.

"What game is this?" Cyrus shouted back. He shouldn't have been surprised, but his own voice was deep, matching Galvanis's. Though it lacked the Heir-Incarnate's thunder, it still rumbled through the gathered crowd.

"The most honest game," Galvanis answered. "Life and death, settled by the crossing of blades."

Cyrus heard a heavy slam behind him. A quick glance showed Arn, now fully alert, ramming his shoulder into the enormous iron grate. The metal did not give even to his divinely blessed strength. Cyrus could not imagine what monsters were originally meant to be held behind such a gate. The air was thick with energy. Fear, anticipation, and faith crackled like lightning visible to his changing eyes.

"You chose an interesting place to hold such a game," Cyrus said. "Why not challenge me fairly?"

"I did challenge you fairly at the docks. You fled, remember?"

Heat built in Cyrus's neck. He fell silent, refusing to argue the point. No good would come of it. Titters of laughter and mockery fell over him, stoking his rage.

"Endarius was a savage god," Galvanis continued. He spread his arms wide and spoke as if giving a lecture. "After Dagon's banishment, there was no more war to sate his lust, and so he created his own. For years, he watched men battle for their lives. He relished the conflict. He drank in their spilled blood and feasted upon their dead. His centuries alongside Lycaena tamed his inner beast, and he eventually sealed away these tunnels in shame. Such is the cowardice of Thanet. Deny the truth, bury the shame, and pretend at honor and pride no more real than a jester's painted face."

"Yes, let us speak of pretending," Kaia said, surprising Cyrus with her interjection. She pointed at Lord Mosau. "Beside you I see one who has lived with two faces since Everlorn cast our island in chains. You ally with traitors and cowards, Heir-Incarnate, and it casts an ill shadow."

Galvanis tilted his head, an amused smirk on his lips. Jase rose to his feet, understanding he must answer such a challenge.

"All I have done, I have done for Thanet," he said. His words were not for her, though, but for the scattered wealthy traders and nobles brought to witness the coming spectacle. "All I have done, I have done for the people who put their trust in me as their lord. This is the only path toward peace, dear Kaia. Forgive me, for if I were to deceive them, I must deceive you as well. Return to me. Approach the wall, and we shall drop a ladder so you may climb to safety."

The woman drew her sword, and she stood at Cyrus's side.

"No," she said. "I am where I am meant to be."

Cyrus did not believe Jase surprised by this, but the man feigned a great sigh and dropped his shoulders nonetheless.

"So be it," he shouted. "Even great men and women can be led astray by loyalty to the past."

"Enough posturing," Cyrus shouted, more than done with any nonsense from that particular bastard's lips. "I'm here, Galvanis, just as you desired. For what reason?"

The Heir-Incarnate returned to his chair.

"I would see the strength of the Vagrant," he said. He glanced left and right to address paragons standing alert beside his chair. "Aidan. Marcus. Prove the superiority of the Uplifted Church, and the might of our faith."

The two paragons bowed and then turned for a sloping walkway beyond Cyrus's line of sight. A gate was directly beneath the Heir-Incarnate, and it steadily rose amid a rattle of chains and turning gears. Cyrus suspected wherever the paragons headed, it would lead to that tunnel entrance. After a quick gesture for Kaia to follow, Cyrus walked to the center of the arena to await the arrival of the lumbering paragons. One held a long spear, the other an ax he wielded with both hands. The gate slammed shut behind them.

"It seems the empire cares little for fair challenges," Cyrus said.

"Two against two, is it not?" Galvanis answered.

Cyrus smirked. As if that mattered. The paragons' white armor was expertly layered, and its thickness made a mockery of Kaia's thin blade.

"Forgive me for my part in this," she said.

"You are not responsible for those who deceived you." He stepped forward and pointed a sword at the paragons. "Aidan and Marcus? Care to share who is who? I'd hate to kill you before the crowd knows who they're watching die."

The ax-wielder slammed the enormous weapon to the ancient earth of the arena. A falcon crest was painted across his chest, and little wings were molded across his helmet, as was a much larger variant upon the face of his ax.

"Aidan of Eldrid, Paragon of Axes, conqueror of Noth-Wall," he said. His grin spread. "Been looking forward to this ever since I set foot on your island, Vagrant."

Cyrus ignored him and turned to the other. His outfit was even more garish, his white plate marked with black stripes and his helmet shaped like a type of horse Cyrus did not recognize. The man held his spear high above his head and spun so he might mug for the crowd.

"Marcus Edwyth, Paragon of Spears, loyal servant of—"

Cyrus crossed the distance between them in the blink of an eye, his longer Endarius sword slashing. Marcus's reflexes, gifted by the divine sacrifice that empowered all paragons, had him twisting his head and kicking out his leg despite the surprise. The boot hit Cyrus's stomach, but not before the sword sliced across the man's open mouth. Blood splashed in a sudden gargle and cry of pain.

"And I am the Vagrant," Cyrus called to the crowd as he danced away from Aidan's frantic swing of his ax. He held the bloodstained blade high above his head. "Child of Thanet, taker of tongues, and slayer of pompous, arrogant paragons."

Marcus spat out half of his tongue and screamed, the words mutilated beyond reason but his word-lace kindly translating it for all to hear.

"Pig fucker!"

The paragons charged in tandem, their weapons ready and dirt kicking beneath their boots. The crowd roared in excitement at the pending bloodshed. Cyrus grimly hoped they might soon find bloodshed among them instead of safely watching it from afar. He focused his attention on Marcus, knowing the injured paragon would be the more dangerous of the two. His blood was up and his rage ignited. Perhaps it might even lead to a fatal mistake.

The first thrust was perfectly aimed for Cyrus's chest. Instead of dodging or parrying, he decided a show of strength was necessary. He wanted these paragons to know they could not overpower him. He wanted them to suddenly doubt their capabilities, to realize they fought against an equal foe for perhaps the very first time in their lives. His swords crossed, locking the spearhead between them. Its blade scraped forward a few more inches before all its momentum was lost.

Marcus's eyes bulged in his helmet. He pushed but could not make the weapon move.

"Did you think my reputation false?" Cyrus asked. He laughed. "You are as dumb as your tongue is short."

Marcus ripped his weapon free, twirled it above his head, and then smashed it straight down. This time Cyrus dodged. He was no fool. He might be equal in strength, but he was also outnumbered. It was far better to exhaust his foe, to frustrate him, than continually match him blow for blow. The seed of doubt was planted. Time to let it germinate.

Thrust after thrust followed, quick jabs meant to open holes in his chest or abdomen. Cyrus retreated while subtly shifting his hips. His swords guided the thrusts aside, adjusting their aim so each missed by the thinnest of margins. After the fourth attempt, he halted his retreat and instead lunged forward. His thrust for the paragon's face missed, but his short sword scraped a gash across the forearm. Nothing deep, but enough to bleed.

Marcus's frustration grew. He swung the spear like a staff in a wide arc. If it connected it might have cracked Cyrus's spine, but it struck only air. Cyrus curved his entire body, let it pass overhead, and then snapped back to a stand. His swords tapped his foe's chestplate twice. No blood drawn, just a reminder that without the massive armor, his foe might already be dead.

"I can't wait to cut that mask off and expose your true face," Marcus said through the helpful translation of his word-lace. Blood dribbled down his chin. He punctuated every sentence with another swing or thrust of his spear. "I want to watch you scream as I rip out your tongue. I'll hang you naked over Vallessau's gates for all to see, then roll your head through a ditch for our soldiers to shit and piss on."

"For having lost your tongue, you sure do talk a lot."

A renewed frenzy accompanied the next few attacks. Cyrus leaped away at every hit, his swords guiding the hunting spear tip. He would make the heavily armored man chase, make him dance. In what moments he could spare, he watched his comrade battle from the corner of his eye. Kaia was skilled, there was no doubt to that. She moved with a steady grace earned from a lifetime of military service, but what skill she possessed could not match the overwhelming strength of a paragon, nor parry aside the tremendous weight of Aidan's ax.

The woman compensated by never standing still. She dashed backward, often blindly away. Sometimes she attempted a parry out of instinct, and it always resulted in her sword being casually batted aside as if it weighed as much as the air.

"Come, hag, will you not retaliate even once?" Aidan mocked. "The crowd wants a show, yet all you do is cower and run."

Marcus's spear nearly gutted Cyrus for his distraction, and he returned his focus. His feet were a blur, his swords a flash of metal as he either dodged or parried aside the spear. Twice Marcus tried to elbow or kick him, forcing out a frantic dodge. On the second, Cyrus saw Aidan lift his ax high above his head. Before he could bring it down, Cyrus dashed over, his shoulder connecting with Kaia to push her out of the way. The ax dropped. Cyrus blocked, and he bit down a scream at the impact. His swords held, for they were Ahlai-made, but his elbows ached and his arms quivered.

A turn, a duck beneath a thrust, and then he was away from the two and at Kaia's side. The woman panted from exertion. Errant strands of hair stuck to her forehead and neck, wet with sweat. She held her sword up with both hands. The blade was clean. She'd not once scored a hit.

"He's only playing with me," she said. "Focus on your own duel."

Before he could respond, she dashed at Aidan. Her swings were easily shrugged aside, and Cyrus caught the paragon allowing several hits through just so they would bounce off his breastplate.

"Do you fight at last?" He laughed. "About time, though I hoped for something better than this."

Marcus stepped between Cyrus and the pair, his spear up and at ready.

"Leave them be, Vagrant," he said with mutilated tongue. "You're mine to deal with."

Cyrus paced side to side, watching the other battle while tensing for a potential attack. Aidan batted away two more of Kaia's thrusts, and he grinned at the crowd in a pointed display of arrogance. The people laughed and clapped, and they laughed harder when Kaia scored a thin scrape across his cheek.

"Oh, you erred now, hag," the paragon muttered. He dashed into her with such speed as to make a mockery of her previous evasions. His shoulder struck her in the chest, followed by an elbow to the abdomen. She flew to the ground and landed on her back. Whether from the paragon's blows, or the awkward landing, her stomach hitched and she struggled to draw a breath.

Aidan did not raise his ax. Instead he lifted his boot and aimed its heel for her face.

"You deserve a bug's death, not a soldier's."

Marcus was ready for Cyrus's attempt to help. His spear swung in a wide arc, attempting to cut off the pathway between them. Cyrus vaulted over it, his body curling forward, and then he landed with his own heel kicking. It hit the knee of Aidan's standing leg, twisting it sideways and robbing him of balance. The foot meant to smash in Kaia's skull instead dropped backward to catch Aidan's fall.

Cyrus dared not speak, dared not even think. Instinct fully took over as he leaped to a stand. His attention bounced between the two paragons, and he attacked them with a savagery he hoped would make Stasia proud. His blades danced, forcing the paragons to keep fully defensive. He carved grooves across their platemail. He batted dents into the handles of their weapons. This assault took everything of him, and it could not endure, not when outnumbered and out-positioned. Worse, he caught Aidan drifting toward Kaia with a sick gleam in his eye.

Damn it, you cowards, he thought. New tactic. He danced back to where Kaia lay and then spun in place, a whirlwind of steel. He parried spear thrusts and shoved aside ax hits with matching strength. The paragons closed in, punching and kicking between the swings of their weapons so he was given no quarter. He cut at them, tried to punish them for such foolishness by taking off their fingers or toes, but they were too fast, too overwhelming. He could not track them both at all times, not if he also wanted to protect Kaia. Cyrus twisted sideways, his left hand shoving a spear thrust upward, his right blocking an ax hit that should have cleaved him in half. His elbow and shoulder groaned against the weight. Even gifted with divine strength, his body was starting to break, for his opponents were equally blessed.

At least Kaia had recovered. She rolled out from beside Cyrus, lurched to her feet, and sprinted for distance.

"Scurry, hag!" Aidan called. His ax hit Cyrus's crossed swords, the ringing metal so loud it was almost deafening. "Hide like a coward while the Vagrant fights for you!"

A fist clipped Cyrus's face, his punishment for trying to watch Kaia mid-fight. He rolled with it, hit the ground with his shoulder, and then twisted his legs above him so that he vaulted backward, his momentum carrying him right back to his feet. He landed beside Kaia, who reached out to touch his shoulder with her free hand.

"I am only a burden," she said. Her voice was still weak from losing her air.

"I won't let them kill you," Cyrus said, and he meant it. "All I do, and all that I am, is meant to protect the people of Thanet. You're one of them, Kaia, like it or not."

The older woman stared at him, her every emotion guarded, her thoughts unreadable to him.

"You would have been a good king," she said. She pointed. "Those fools there, could you take them if alone?"

Cyrus glared at the two paragons busy mugging for the crowd. Rage swept through his veins like wildfire.

"Yes," he said. "I believe I could."

Kaia cast a final glance to the distant Lord Mosau. Her features hardened.

"Good. Make them pay, Vagrant, especially Jase."

And then she lifted her sword and cut her own throat. Cyrus caught her body as it crumpled, cradling her in his arms as she gagged and retched blood into her lungs. Her sword hit the ground with a thud, no longer needed. A second later the crowd roared with shock and delight. Cyrus held her as he would a child, and he watched the life fade from her gray eyes.

"Make them pay?" he whispered as he lay her body to the dirt. "With pleasure."

Cyrus looked to the paragons, then to the high-domed ceiling ringed with torches. He pulled out one of Thorda's smoke stones from his pocket and smashed it to the ground. Smoke billowed around him, coupled with a bitter, burning taste in his throat. His other fist clenched.

From shadows to shadows, he passed, until he descended from the darkened ceiling, his swords drawn, their blades pointed downward like the reaching claws of a bird of prey. His cloak rippled through the air behind him.

"Above you!" he heard the Heir-Incarnate warn, but it was far too late.

Cyrus crashed into Aidan like a meteor. His swords punched right through the platemail to bury deep into flesh. His momentum pulled the paragon downward, slamming them both to the ground. The embedded weapons dragged his body across the dirt. A howl of rage thundered out of Cyrus's throat. When he stood, he ripped his weapons free in an explosion of blood that rent the slain paragon's armor. As the crowd watched, he cut a bloody crown across the body's forehead and then pointed the crimson-coated blade at Marcus. Somehow, he knew the grinning skull of his mask stretched wider.

"You monster!" Marcus howled.

Cyrus kicked backward, his body turning fully horizontal so the spear thrust gutted only empty air. Another thrust met his landing, but he parried it harmlessly above his head. Instead of dragging the weapon back, Marcus tried to sweep Cyrus's legs out from under him with the butt of his spear. Cyrus hopped over it, then realized the ploy. The moment it was underneath him, Marcus jerked it straight upward. He thought Cyrus had nowhere to dodge, and in a way, he was right.

So Cyrus didn't dodge. He tucked his knees to his chest so that the spear struck his heels. Its force catapulted Cyrus up into the air. His arms twisted, every muscle in his body flexing to guide his movements. He passed over Marcus, upside down. Time seemed to slow for the briefest moment as their gazes connected. Cyrus's arms lashed out, upper body twirling, his swords a blur.

Cyrus landed amid a flourish of cloak and shining steel. He glanced over his shoulder, his hood falling from his face so the crowd might see his skull's full grin.

Marcus's head fell from his shoulders, cleanly severed. His body went rigid, then collapsed in a heap of armor and flesh.

The crowd cheered no longer.

"I fear you are running out of paragons," Cyrus called to Galvanis in the ensuing silence. A rush of conversation followed. This was hardly the display the Heir-Incarnate wanted; Cyrus took satisfaction in that. The question was, how might he respond?

"It is the dying animal that is most dangerous," Galvanis said after a moment's pause. "And make no mistake, Thanet and her most ardent defenders will die this night."

Cyrus tilted his head slightly so his hood would cover half of his face. Torchlight flickered off his silver crown and bone mask. These people, these loyalists to distant Gadir, would see his defiance, and they would remember it. His confidence. His slaughter of the paragons. Even against such a trap, he would shift matters to his benefit until he found a way to save his friends.

"And who will kill me?" he asked. "Is it you?"

That confidence unnerved even the Heir-Incarnate.

"I know what you are, Vagrant," he said. His voice was softer, and for the first time he spoke only to Cyrus. "I was there in Miquo. I saw the bloodshed left in the wake of the Skull-Amid-the-Trees. Faith and fanaticism grant you boons unworthy of your stature. The righteousness compelling you weighs false before the truth of Thanet. I know of your family, and of whom they overthrew."

Galvanis turned and raised his hand to the side. Toward Sinshei, suddenly stiff in her seat. To Keles in her dark armor. The booming projection of his voice returned.

"Keles Lyon Orani," he said. "Ready your sword and shield. I would have you slay this pretender to your stolen throne. Hidden from both city and stars, let us witness the death of the missing Prince Cyrus Lythan."

CHAPTER 44

VAGRANT

The gate beneath the Heir-Incarnate rose, opened by a turning of gears and wheels controlled by a soldier in a little side booth high up near the back of the arena. Cyrus stood tall and patient, glad that his mask hid his rising fear. Murmurs and shouts rolled through the crowd. The repetition of his name. His old name.

Prince Cyrus?

The rumors had been seeded for years now, a whisper by the Coin, an "unbelievable" tale repeated by Clarissa over drinks. This moment, it was long in coming, yet everything about it felt wrong. It felt like theft. The moment was meant to be his. His victorious reveal, his defiant rebellion against death itself, had been stolen from him.

He glared at the distant Lord Mosau. Keles might have revealed his identity, but he doubted that after their previous conversations. No, Jase had most certainly been the one to tell Galvanis. How long had the Heir-Incarnate known? Had it been all this time? Or only upon the lord's recent arrival to Vallessau?

It changes nothing, he told himself. The Vagrant's legend was well spread throughout Thanet. The truth of royal blood in his veins, and of his vengeance against the conquerors who took his throne, would only enhance it further. He told himself that as Keles stepped into the arena with her sword and shield drawn and ready.

"Behold the obedient woman," Galvanis shouted to the crowd. "Perhaps you know her as the Light of Vallessau, but that is not her true name."

Cyrus stood tall and pretended to be unbothered. He couldn't give credence to the Heir-Incarnate's posturing. Instead he focused on Keles. He watched the way she stiffly walked toward him. He saw the lowered position of her weapons. This plan, this spectacle, was not one she had foreseen.

"Behold the bloodline whom the Lythan family enslaved! She should have been born to a throne, but the cowards who fled the nation of Mirli betrayed her and her kin. And now the lost prince rages. Now he demands retribution for what never should have been his."

Galvanis pointed a finger at Cyrus. His voice trembled with fury.

"Hypocrite! Murderer! You have carved your bloody crown across too many of our faithful, but that crown is no more real than the one your father bore. Behold your better, who serves faithfully. The rightful heir will bend the knee, while you are a nuisance, a wretch, unwanted, unneeded. Be gone from us, Cyrus. The deserved queen serves Everlorn, in faithfulness and in obedience. You are merely a spoiled prince bathed in blood and raging against the inevitable."

He clapped his hands. The sound boomed like thunder.

"Slay the past, Keles Orani. Become the future."

Cyrus looked to the woman he had considered a dear friend. Did her anger match the Heir-Incarnate's? Did she mirror his claims of betrayal? Her sword and shield rose, and so he raised his own weapons.

"These crimes of the past, I would make them right if I could," he told her.

"Even as king, it is beyond your abilities," she said. "I did not choose this battle, Cyrus, but I will end it. Sinshei will deliver us. Not you."

Keles lunged with her sword, but it was slow, half-hearted. Cyrus deflected it aside with his off-hand and countered with a hit he knew she would block with her shield. This battle, this skirmish, it wasn't real yet. They exchanged hits, their weapons colliding in a rhythm that would sound like battle to those in attendance but in truth threatened neither of them. Not yet.

"You can't be so foolish as to trust her," Cyrus said. He parried, the dance between them growing in tempo, and then countered with a sideways slash.

"You know what I was promised," Keles said, blocking with her shield.

"It will not end with my death." He pressed harder against her shield, forcing her to expend more strength to hold him back. "There will always be another nuisance to slay. How many lives will die at your blade, all for the temptation the Anointed offers? How many faithful to Lycaena and Endarius will bleed out at your feet? She would offer you reign over an island of bones!"

That got her blood boiling. She lashed at him, alternating blows with her sword and shield. He kept light on his feet, circling her. What attacks he parried sent vibrations up his arms. She was strong, so very strong, but her paragon strength was born of ten slain. His sacrifices numbered forty at the moment of his ascendence, and so many more as the imperial occupation continued.

At last he dug in his heels and crossed swords with her. Back and forth, testing reactions, the Endarius blade striking her longsword. He kept his off-hand back, waiting at the ready.

"An island of bones is what you would deliver us!" Keles shouted. "Is that what you would set your throne upon?"

He thrust for her exposed throat, and she parried at the last moment. A shiver ran down his spine. Had he known she would deflect it in time?

Had he even cared?

"At least it would be *our* throne!" he shouted back. "Our own, taken by our own hands, not gifted back by the conquerors who stole it in the first place."

His feet were too slow. Her shield caught his chest, and he rolled with the blow to prevent it from breaking his ribs.

"Who are you to talk of stolen thrones, Cyrus?"

Back up to his feet. He bounced on his toes, his hilts itching in his hands. He glared from behind his mask.

"You have to know you're wrong," he told her. "Please. Do not do this."

Keles settled into a battle stance, her shield up, her sword at the ready. Not a single emotion dared betray itself upon her face.

"I'm sorry, Cyrus. I see no other way."

Cyrus shivered. The dark voice seethed in his mind, and that rage flooded his veins with acid.

She sees it not, for I am the other way.

That rage blanked his mind. It added speed to his movements and strength to blows that even paragons must be wary of. He blasted her shield with his swords, hammering away at it no differently than when Rayan had come to test him in Thorda's countryside mansion.

"Hold you no faith in me?" he shouted at her. Two quick thrusts positioned her sword wrong, and he followed it up with a heel to her gut. She staggered, her breath lost. "No way, you tell me? No way, you insist, to the only hope the island has left?"

The brazenness of his assault sparked her own anger, and she charged into him with her shield leading. He met it with his shoulder, used the sword in the opposite arm to block her overhead chop, and then shoved her away. Steel clashed with steel as he spun, batting away another quick thrust meant to gut him while he retreated. He came out of the spin with both swords together, a mighty blow against her shield that rocked her backward on her heels.

"Look at me!" he shouted. "Do you not see Thanet's freedom made real?"

Keles turned and spat blood from a split lip.

"I look at you and see death, Vagrant! Am I the one who is truly blind?"

Blind, she called him, while serving the Anointed One. *Death*, she named him, while fighting in the name of the empire that had hung thousands at the Dead Flags. He would hear no more. He dashed at her, sudden and vicious. A panicked chop met his charge. He reversed his grip of his off-hand, blocked the chop, and then exploded into motion. His other sword thrust in and then turned, the curved edge locking aside the shield so she could not withdraw it. His leg shot up to kick her elbow. She screamed at the pain, and reflexes loosened her grip on her weapon. A shove, and the sword bounced off his block. A twist of his feet, a slash, and he knocked the sword free from her hand entirely.

Panic had her fling her entire weight behind her shield, pushing away his longer blade. He suddenly stopped resisting and instead allowed her momentum to become his. He danced before her, twisting, all black and gray and dark cloak and shining silver. His leg swept behind her knees. His sword hit the lowest edge of the shield, breaking it out of her grasp. When she landed he kicked, rolling her onto her stomach.

No mercy. No hesitation. He closed the distance between them and towered over her. The rage that fueled him refused to relent. The roaring crowd was oil upon a fire. He saw red. He saw doubt. Fear. Surrender to imperial rule. She was everything that would destroy his island. *His island!*

"Is that it?" he asked her.

Keles did not defend herself. Instead she pulled up to her knees, her head lowered, her fingers digging grooves into the dirt. To see her so resigned to death, to not fight even to her last breath, stabbed his burning heart with ice. The murmurs of the crowd died down to nothing. All was shadowed and alone, just him, Keles, and the dark voice that whispered in the back of his mind.

She seeks your crown.

The Endarius blade rose. Behind the locked gate, Rayan cried out a wordless denial. Cyrus felt free of his own body. His movements were of another. Galvanis watched, enraptured. The crowd shrieked for blood. And yet still Keles knelt with head bowed. Waiting. His sword rose. Ready. Eager. The image shifted, changed.

Cyrus, towering over Keles.

Magus, towering over his mother.

"Do it," she whispered.

His every muscle locked tight. His hands trembled. Two minds warred over one flesh. Cyrus remembered when he tried to speak his name to the crowd when he first removed his mask. How his tongue had seized. The loss of control. The divine overwhelming the mundane. He clenched his teeth so hard he feared they might crack. Keles herself had warned him when he expressed fears the Vagrant and the prince were becoming one and the same.

Only we decide who we are. No one else.

Her voice. Her wisdom. Pleading with him to remember the Vagrant was just a mask that could be removed. But could he? After the prayers?

After the sacrifices? "You are not slave to it," she had insisted, but that was before his reflection became a grinning skull. Was this savage murderer his ultimate fate? Not so long ago, he had been unable to slay Regent Goldleaf's child. Now he stood with sword raised over the head of a dear friend. Keles would be one more body between him and his goal.

She would take your throne, warned the dark voice.

To listen would be surrender. There would be no more separation between the mask and the man.

Sickness twisted Cyrus's stomach, a thousand times stronger than when he had tried to refuse cutting a vagrant's crown upon a slain soldier. Chills racked him. His heart hammered in his chest, feeling ready to burst. He heard a distant scream, and he knew not whose voice it was. Perhaps Rayan's. Perhaps his. The willpower required, it was tremendous, it was overwhelming. He could not spare a thought to any other action. Let the dark voice rage, his master no longer.

One knee bent. Then the other. His swords dropped to the cold earth.

You are wrong, Cyrus told that voice. *It is not my throne to lose.*

No dark voice would guide him here. The powers filling him, the changes overcoming him, they were of faith and divinity, and therefore beyond his understanding. But he knew who he was, and if given the choice, who the Vagrant would become. This was the true path forged of Cyrus's own decisions and not the corpse-laden one Thorda designed.

The Vagrant would fight to save Thanet, not claim it.

"I am ever Thanet's servant," he said, his voice soft, his words only for her. It was a promise made, one that pierced to the core of his being. On his knees, he confessed his truth. "And I would never harm my queen."

Though he spoke behind a mask of bone, he prayed Keles could see his eyes, and the honesty within them. Her jaw trembled. Her head lowered. Cyrus held his breath, waiting for a response, and he received it in her broken whisper.

"I ask for one thing, Cyrus. If you cannot give it to me, then kill me now, and let Vallessau bid farewell to its broken Light."

Cyrus wanted to hold her, embrace her, and make a million promises. The hurt in her kept him still. The eyes of the crowd kept him guarded.

"What is it?" he asked softly.

Keles bit her lip. Through divine-touched eyes he saw the power of paragons shimmer across her skin, blue as the ocean deep, and then crackle with lightning. Twisting. Threatening to rebel.

"Can you free Thanet? Can you save our people?"

Cyrus retrieved his swords, sheathed them, and stood. His cloak fell across him. His hood hid his silver crown. Keles's discarded sword lay nearby, and he lifted it. Fine dark steel, most certainly Ahlai-made. He brushed a bit of dirt off its gleaming edge.

"This is the only hope I know to offer," he told her. "I will give everything for my home, and for those I love. Thanet shall be made free." He flipped the weapon, extending the hilt toward her. "And I will not do it alone."

At last she looked to him, and it was her again, the Keles who had mesmerized him at Thorda's parties. The woman with wisdom beyond her years, tempered through burdens and responsibilities placed upon far-too-young shoulders. The woman called Doubt. The Light of Vallessau.

A faint hint of a smile.

"No," she said, and accepted the blade. "You will not."

Cyrus wished to embrace her when she stood, but that was no way for him to address his queen. Instead he bowed low and with an exaggerated flourish of his cloak. None in attendance would miss the symbolism. More murmurs, confused, even worried. The crowd had been promised an execution, yet two paragons lay dead, and now Keles allied with the Vagrant.

"Pitiful," Galvanis said. He stood from his chair and grabbed his enormous sword, resting beside him. "Let us bring this spectacle to its necessary end. I have slain gods, Vagrant, ones worshiped by legions of faithful. You are their pale shadow, and my sword shall ever be the burning light."

Again the soldier with the wheels and levers turned them, reopening the far gate for a third time. Keles retrieved her shield as Galvanis vanished into whatever pathway or tunnel connected it. Amid the brief respite, Cyrus offered her his hand.

"Do you trust me?" he asked.

She sheathed her sword and took his hand.

"I do."

He pulled her close, and then with his free hand he reached into his pocket.

"Shut your eyes," he said. "And if you feel like you're falling, let yourself fall, and trust me to catch you."

"Such tender affection," Galvanis said as he emerged from the open gate. His enormous sword swung lightly in one hand. "It will spare neither of you. Even together, your strength is a pittance of mine."

Memories of his failed duel at the docks awakened fresh shame to accompany the mockery. Cyrus smirked behind his mask. He had no intention of making such a mistake again. Galvanis wanted a duel, but nothing about it would be fair. The crowd was full of soldiers and paragons, and should things turn dire, they would absolutely rush to the Heir-Incarnate's aid. More importantly, his friends, still imprisoned, would face panicked retribution.

"I suppose you're right," Cyrus called back. "So let us even the odds."

In his pocket was one last smoke stone. He drew it out and smashed it at his feet, bathing him and Keles in its darkness. Though he had always gone alone, he trusted the divine magic to adapt to his own needs. Arm in arm, Keles and Cyrus sank down into the shadows.

With so many scattered torches, there was an abundance of dark places to choose from as their exit. Tucked into the back of the arena, meant to go unnoticed by the majority of onlookers in the crowd, was the soldier manning the wheels and levers. The pair emerged behind him, and the lone man was easily dispatched. Cyrus quickly scanned the controls and then kicked. The chosen wheel whirled, ropes and pulleys turning, hidden weights shifting.

The gate locking Cyrus's friends rose. All around, soldiers, traders, and paragons panicked and reached for their weapons.

"You would see the strength of the Vagrant?" Cyrus shouted to a baffled Heir-Incarnate as Thorda's elite burst out of their prison. "They're down there with you, Galvanis. I am not alone, and never will be."

CHAPTER 45

ARN

The four burst out of their cell at a full sprint, and not a one moved to engage the Heir-Incarnate. They rushed the walls instead, climbing to reach the rows of benches above. Soldiers retreated, joining the scrambling crowd of panicked onlookers, wealthy merchants, and the occasional magistrate. Mari arrived first, and though it was a sheer ten-foot-high wall, she leaped over it with ease. Screams followed as her claws and wings ended them.

"Need a lift?" Arn shouted to Stasia as they ran.

The woman twirled her twin axes.

"Gladly."

He crooked an arm and motioned toward her. She jumped and landed lightly upon his bicep. Her feet had barely touched before he flexed his muscles, every ounce of his paragon strength catapulting her as if he were a springboard. Stasia soared over the wall, her axes held high. She looked like a predator descending upon her prey, a feeling heightened by the splash of blood that followed.

Arn reached the wall, and he turned back to Rayan.

"Paladin?" he asked.

"Hardly dignified," Rayan protested. Arn pressed his back to the wall and offered his hands.

"Piss on dignified. Get up there, old man."

The paladin's foot settled into his grip, Arn grunted at the weight, and then he pushed the man up to the seats, heavy platemail and all. That done, he spun, jumped to catch the edge of the wall with a gauntleted hand, and flung himself into the fray.

Arn let loose a deep belly laugh. Trapped and forced to watch his friends battle? That had been pure torture. This? This was chaos, and it was everything he desired. The first few moments were a slaughter. Bodies broke before him, those too stubborn or stupid to flee. The ground was slick with blood spilled by the gruesome display that was the Lioness in battle. Ax accompanied it with her own namesake weapons. She had paced like a caged animal while they were trapped, and now she unleashed all her pent-up fury on anyone foolish enough to charge at her with a blade. She chopped off limbs and bashed aside defenses. No mortal, no paragon, could match her strength.

Four soldiers battled Paladin, and so Arn diverted his attention that way. They might hold fast against a lone sword, but then Arn barreled into them like a raging bull. His first hit blasted right through a man's breastplate and made a mess of his innards. The second was a backhand across the neighboring soldier's face, hard enough to spin his head until the spine snapped. The others tried to bury their swords into Arn's chest, but Paladin was there, his gleaming sword batting away the blows.

Together, fist and blade, they thrashed the remaining survivors.

"Fine timing, Heretic," Rayan said before racing along the benches.

"Hey, stay close, would you?" Arn shouted back, only to be ignored. A trickle of worry had him searching the lower arena for the only threat he truly feared, yet it seemed the Heir-Incarnate had no desire to join the fight. Instead he had turned, entered the tunnel he'd come through, and was yet to reappear.

"You damn traitor!" a rare magistrate shouted, seemingly recognizing Arn's paragon heritage. A spear of light shimmered above the bald man's head, aimed straight for Arn's chest. A half second later it thrust, guided by the man's faith. Arn dodged left, the enormous bulk that was his body smashing a bench in half. The spear hit the ground, missing him by inches. Arn reached out to grab the shaft. An object of faith it might be, but it was as solid and real as any other spear. The priest gasped, sweat pouring down his face. His willpower granted strength to the invisible hands holding the spear, and as far as Arn was concerned, it was as mighty as a dying leaf in autumn.

With one hand, Arn kept the spear pinned. With his other, he grabbed a broken chunk of the bench.

"Never warn those you're about to kill," he said, and smashed the magistrate's head in. The man crumpled, and the spear dissolved into fading light. He tossed the wood aside, clapped his hands together, and searched for new targets. Soldiers crowded together at one of the tunnel entrances. Time for some fun. Maybe if he was lucky, he might even spot that bastard Castor in the crowd and pay him back for the scars that lined his chest.

Arn glanced at the opposite side of the arena while he ran, where Cyrus and Keles battled their foes like true terrors. They were twin reapers carving through fields of wheat. The Vagrant had claimed the lives of two paragons moments ago. What could mere soldiers do when he was paired with a penitent like Keles?

As much as Arn wished, he could not afford to watch the duo, for he had his own slaughter to partake in. Arn flung himself into the soldiers, wishing he still had Thorda's fine chainmail to keep him safe. His tattered, blood-soaked clothes would have to do. A sword struck his side, but it was panicked, the flat edge hitting him and barely scraping his skin. And then he was at the tunnel entrance. Bones crunched with his every punch. He grabbed a soldier's arm and pulled, ripping it right out of the socket. Arn saw horror dawning on the agonized man's face a moment before he caved his head in with his own arm.

Brave as the soldiers might be, that broke them. The remaining three fled for a tunnel leading back toward the surface. He heard a roar, echoed by a second, and turned to see Lioness battling the Humbled. They tore into each other, biting and clawing with savagery of which only those blessed by the divine were capable.

Mari! But he managed only a step before a new challenge halted him.

"Heretic!" boomed a familiar voice.

Arn turned. His brother approached, hands clenched into fists, knuckles pressed together. With the Heir-Incarnate's departure, the remaining paragon bodyguards were free to join the fray.

"Good to see you again," Arn said, and laughed to hide his sudden nervousness. He hoisted up his own hands and turned so the torchlight could reflect off his gauntlets. "I must thank you for ruining my old pair. The replacements are even better."

Dario shook his head as he walked the line of seats.

"I promised to save you, no matter the cost," he said. "And now I discover that cost. Dozens of lost lives, each more faithful to Everlorn than you will ever be."

Arn shrugged. It was easier to pretend he wasn't bothered than to acknowledge how soundly he'd lost his last fight against his brother.

"I suppose I will ever be the disappointment."

"No longer. You have nowhere to run. I will return you to your cell, brother. Within it, I will have years to correct your heart and mind. I have helped convert the Humbled. If gods can learn, then so can you."

Arn shivered at the thought. So far his brother had shown him but a taste of what the church used to break the Humbled. Unending prayers and sermons, with no breaks for rest or sleep. Scripture upon scripture carved into flesh. Then one day, when Arn was at his lowest, the God-Incarnate would come to tantalize him with potential freedom. All for a prayer. A single prayer, given in earnest, to serve the only true god of Thanet.

Far better a physical death than such a fate.

"You forget, I'm just as stubborn as most gods, and quite dumber," Arn said, and he grinned. "I fear I would never learn."

Dario squared up to fight, his fists raised to protect his face.

"In time, Arn. All things break in time."

"The same goes for our empire, brother."

Dario had controlled their last battle, but Arn would not repeat such a fatal mistake. Before a single punch could be thrown, he tucked low and barreled forward with his shoulder leading. He endured a savage blow to his back, the pain radiating through him as a price to be paid. His shoulder hit Dario's stomach, and he screamed as the muscles in his legs and arms surged with every last bit of their strength.

But he lifted Dario, heavens help him, he lifted him up and off his feet to carry him forward. Another blow to his back, near the shoulder, but weaker. Easy to ignore with his heart racing and his pulse pounding in his ears. He climbed two steps and then flung his brother straight down as if trying to crack a boulder on the stone's edge.

Victory would not be so easy. Dario grabbed ahold of his shoulder, and both of them fell, collapsing on top of each other. Arn rewarded him with a headbutt to the nose. All sense of respectable combat taught to them at the Bloodstone vanished. Elbows and knees slammed into each other. He punched Dario in the ribs, short and lacking power, and took a knee to his thigh in return. It was chaos, brutal and uncontrolled. This was what Arn sought, the moment in battle when he was most at home. Dario might be the better fighter, but bring him down to the dirt, and so much of his proper technique fell apart beneath raw, savage anger.

And by the gods was Arn angry. Fury fueled him where fear and uncertainty had held him back in their last duel. Velgyn's burning tail refused to fade from his mind's eye. The pair rolled down the steps, jarring hits that would leave deep bruises. Dario swung for his face as they rolled, and would have caved in his skull if not for pure dumb luck. They hit a bystander with their roll, the older man in fine silks collapsing beneath them and adding a sudden bump to their roll. The brief separation threw off Dario's aim, so he only clipped Arn's ear. Blood gushed down his face, and he feared the gauntlet had ripped it off entirely.

His feet touched ground, and he stood. Dario mirrored him, his face bruised and his lip split. Behind Dario, the man they'd trampled lay still, crushed by their combined weight of muscle and armor.

"You fight like the heathens do," Dario said, and spat a glob of blood at Arn's feet. Arn laughed in return.

"Like victors?"

"Like animals."

Dario lunged at him, his full body extended to grant his punch its maximum reach. Arn sensed immediately that every bit of his brother's strength was poured into that single blow. He could punch holes in brick walls. He could shatter a soldier's bones regardless of the thickness of their armor. It was foolish, almost suicidal to do anything other than dodge.

But Arn was tired of running from his brother. He was tired of believing himself weaker. Instead he reared back, planted his legs, and swung his fist right back.

Dario's gauntlets were the finest available to the Everlorn Empire, and likely crafted by Thorda Ahlai himself. Acolytes had prayed over their leather to strengthen them further, but Arn trusted in a stronger faith. Thorda had put his heart into Arn's gauntlets, crafted them with love and skill at the request of his daughter. Dario's might bear the praying hands of the empire, but Arn's bore the three tails of the Fox.

The moment before their fists connected, he swore he saw the faintest hint of frost build across his knuckles.

A shock wave rolled outward, rippling the air. The impact traveled all the way up Arn's arm, rattling his teeth. He felt Dario's gauntlet give way. He felt his brother's bones break as metal crumpled and cut now-exposed flesh. The punch continued, snapping the hand at the wrist. Dario screamed. Arn heard it as if in a dream. The world was startlingly sharp and unreal in its clarity.

"You damn fool," Dario hollered, and he swung wild with his other hand while keeping the injured one clutched to his chest. Arn pushed it aside, stepped in, and pounded his brother in the stomach. The gauntlet caved in the armor. The impact continued, rumbling his innards. Dario coughed, blood coming up with it. Still Arn was not done. Another hit, this to the face to make up for the damage to his ear. Arn pulled back his strength at the very last second, so he left only bruises instead of shattered bones. More hits followed, kicks and elbows without mercy. Arn beat flesh and muscle until all resistance fled.

Dario collapsed onto his back. Blood dribbled across his chest to the cold floor where it combined with the larger puddle flowing from the mess that was his right hand. Arn stood over him, his shoulders rising and falling with his every breath. The rage of battle washed over him, screaming for him to finish the job. His own brother echoed the sentiment.

"Kill me," Dario said. He stared up at him with the white of one eye now solid red with blood. "Spare me the burden of witnessing your transgressions. Your future is empty. These sins. These heresies. They will eat you alive."

It would be so easy, wouldn't it? End the life that haunted him. Dario had always been stronger, smarter, the proud rock to which Arn had been a shadow. He could smash that rock with a single blow to his heart. For once in his life, he could prove his older brother wrong through the undeniable truth of broken bones and spilled blood. He'd won, hadn't he? Proven that these heathen gods were right, and the God-Incarnate false?

Arn raised a fist. He looked past the hate in his brother's eyes and saw the disappointment. The fear. Dario cared. He still cared. And Arn would be sending him into the bosom of the God-Incarnate for all eternity.

Arn lowered his fist. Perhaps it was selfish. Perhaps it was cowardly. He'd killed countless men and women loyal to Everlorn. But not his brother. Not his brother. Arn's metal gauntlets provided poor comfort, but he knelt low and cupped Dario's head in one nonetheless. No matter the awkwardness, he let himself speak the honesty in his heart.

"No," he said. "You didn't give up on me, Dario, and so I won't give up on you. I don't have your fancy words. I don't have a mind fit for arguing. I only have what I have lived. While all of Vulnae burned, I saw a world of hope, of mercy, of forgiveness. It tore me apart. It ripped me open and made me see how ugly we are."

Arn bent closer. He felt a wave of tears coming, and he did not fight them.

"It's not too late for you to see that same world. There are true miracles that go far beyond destruction, fire, and the strength to win on the battlefield. Speak with Lioness. Meet with Velgyn. Hear their words. See what we're taking from this world, and then turn away from it."

Dario grabbed that hand and flung it away. His entire body shook with the intensity of his words.

"Your wisdom is hollow, and your grace a poison. Kill me. This will not go like you think it will."

Arn gently lowered his brother's head and then stood. Doubts shrieked like gulls throughout his mind, but what other option remained? Amid all this death and despair, he had to hope.

"I bear a thousand sins to my name," he said. "But just maybe I can do this one thing right."

Arn left his brother lying there upon the stone, and he took in the dwindling battle. Soldiers fled every which way through tunnels leading presumably to the castle or the surrounding grounds. He saw no sign of the Lioness, nor Paladin, but Ax was busy gutting soldiers and looked to be in need of some help. He clacked his gauntlets together, knocking loose bits of the cloying blood spilled across their metal.

Time to get back to the chaos.

CHAPTER 46

MARI

Instinct ruled Mari's every action. This was paradise to the Lion, a conflict of life and death in the forgotten arena of his past. She shredded flesh with wild fury. She was blood-drunk and delirious. Pleasure raced through her veins. Occasionally she would feel concern for friends, but it was rare and fleeting. This carnage, it felt righteous. Nothing would touch her, for she was the Lioness, the avatar of the Lion, and this was their home, their arena, their truth made new and wondrous and bloody.

And then she saw Sinshei hiding in the far shadows, observing the battle but not partaking. A deep growl emanated from her throat.

No mercy for the Anointed, she thought, and whether it was her belief or Endarius's, she neither knew nor cared. She descended to the ground, sprinted along the edge of the arena, and then lunged with her fore-legs extended. Her teeth bared, she shivered with excitement at the fear widening Sinshei's eyes.

The crack of a spear against her side sent Mari tumbling. She landed awkwardly on two legs, then twisted to face the paragon who barred her path to the Anointed One.

"Tsk, tsk, tsk," said Soma, and he wagged his finger at her as if she were a disobedient child. "Sinshei is off-limits."

"Do you think I fear you, paragon?" she asked, the gem of her word-lace flashing.

"Truthfully?" he asked, and tilted his head to one side. "No. But I think you fear *him*."

His words were her only warning. Her wings curled inward and braced for the sudden impact. Their bones protected her more vulnerable flesh as claws raked across her side. She and her new attacker tumbled together along the benches, smashing their aged wood into splinters. Her hind legs raked across his muscled body, forcing a separation. They skidded apart, claws out, fangs bared.

"I promised to taste your blood when next we met," Rihim snarled. "And I have ever kept my promises."

"What promises did you make your followers in Antiev?" Mari asked. "Did you promise to be a slave to their conquerors?"

The panther god lowered into a coiled stance, ready for a leap. His claws carved grooves into the weathered stone.

"No more," he said. "The hunter need hear no words from his prey."

"But which of us is the hunter, Humbled one?"

He lunged. Mari pivoted sideways while lashing with her right wing. The sharp edge cut across his forearm and shoved him off course. The Humbled crashed into the seats, but he touched the ground for barely a heartbeat before he was in the air again. He sought another exchange of blows, but Mari was not there. Her paws thudded and her chest heaved as she dashed into one of the upper tunnels through which some of the onlookers had fled. She bashed two men aside, blood splattering from their heads when they hit the wall. Nothing would stop her. Nothing would slow her.

Rihim caught up to her almost instantly, but he did not try to overtake her. They ran through the tunnel at a pace only gods could match. Rihim and Mari alternated who led, often amid tumbling, snarling exchanges. They nipped at each other's heels. They roared amid the violent race. They ran without fear, seeking distance, seeking solitude. This fight would be theirs, and theirs alone.

Starlight greeted her ahead, and she pushed onward with her wings curled tightly against her sides. She burst out into the castle courtyard and landed on soft grass. Her claws carved grooves as she pivoted about to face the tunnel exit. It bore no doors, just open space braced with wood supports. Freshly dug earth marked its recent discovery. How many years had this entrance gone unnoticed, hidden beneath the grass?

She first saw the twin orbs of golden light that were Rihim's eyes, and then the rest of him emerged in an explosion of movement and muscle. They rolled, nipping and clawing at each other, but the advantage was his, given his momentum. Mari scraped free, blood dripping from multiple wounds across her sides. She sprinted, instinct fully taking over. There was something about the chase that felt needed. It felt right.

Mari's divinely blessed claws easily sank into the bricks of the outer wall surrounding the castle grounds, so that she scaled its side with ease. A lone soldier holding a spear patrolled its top, and he turned around at the noise. He let out a baffled cry, which ended unfinished when her left wing slashed open his throat. She turned, wings up, teeth bared, for Rihim's arrival.

He didn't bother climbing the wall. The strength of his legs was enough. He vaulted into the air with his arms spread wide and his claws shining like polished obsidian. This time Mari was better prepared, and she made the Humbled pay for his direct approach. The blades of her wings tore at his face and chest. Fur peeled back at the gashes to expose finely honed muscle. The wounds bled, but not much, for though Humbled he might be, he was still a god. It would take far more to slay him.

His retaliation was swift. One strike bounced off the bone plate of her shoulder; the other sank into her side and dug in. She howled, and it was her turn for fur to rip. She twisted with teeth wide, and when he withdrew to avoid her latching onto his wrist, she dashed along the rampart. Her right wing cut a shallow groove along his chest as a parting measure.

The dark stone was a blur beneath her paws. Her breath thundered in her ears. Two more soldiers kept patrol along the wall. One fled the moment he saw her. The other foolishly swung his sword at her face. She deflected it with the bone plate across her forehead and then bodied him with her shoulder. He tumbled over the edge headfirst, to an unpleasant landing given the distance and the weight of his armor.

Even that slight delay was enough for Rihim to close the gap between them. She whimpered at the sudden pain from his claws raking her hind leg. Instead of turning she sprinted faster, refusing to acknowledge the damage. They were both blessed by divine strength. Endarius was with her. The Lion would grant the Lioness victory, but not here. She had to press what advantages she could.

Speed. Balance on uneven ground. Her wings.

The ramparts ended at barred doors leading into the castle keep, but Mari held no interest in returning to such tight conditions. Instead she leaped higher, to the rooftops. Back and forth, from pillars, statues, and balconies. Stone cracked with her every landing. Tiny bits of rubble fell dozens of feet to the ground below. She paid it no mind. Higher. She must go higher.

"Would you flee to the moon itself?" Rihim howled. She landed atop a balcony, crouched for another leap, and then went nowhere as his hand closed about her ankle. Her body crashed back down, and then Rihim was upon her. Their combined weight shattered the banister, and they hung halfway over the broken edge. She curled instantly, for the slightest hesitation meant death. Her wings closed, their jagged ends tearing into Rihim's rib cage. Her teeth sank into his arm just above the manacles, and she tasted divine blood on her tongue.

Rihim endured it all, for he had her now. His other hand closed about her throat. His claws dug in, seeking her jugular. Mari bit harder, harder, trying to snap his bones in half. Blood spilled down her face and along his arm, a mixture of hers and his. She stabbed again and again with her wings, but he endured the strikes. Any wound was acceptable if it meant finally killing her.

Darkness swam across her vision. All breathing ceased. In a panicked final attempt, she released her grip on his one arm and shifted her attention to the one about her throat. She coiled at the waist, bringing her hind legs up to scrape along the entire arm. Deep blue fur peeled away. Tendons tore. Rihim howled, and at last he let her go.

Mari didn't dare risk losing such an opening. Her head swam, her vision twisting and tilting awkwardly. She still had her plan. She leaped up to the sharply slanted rooftops of the highest portions of the castle. Higher. Higher. Up the decorative spires. Make the hunter chase her. Make him awkward and unsteady.

"What do you hope to accomplish?" Rihim asked. His landings were far less gentle than hers. Shingles cracked and bent inward at his weight. "Your fight is hopeless, Ahlai daughter. You fight with the strength of a dead god, while I am very much alive."

"You draw breath, but you do not live," Mari growled down at him. He leaped at her, and he crashed into the nearly vertical side of their current tower a half second too late. She clawed her way up the edge, to the curving point at the tower's apex, and then turned to face him.

"Must you hide like a cat in a tree?" he asked. He'd found a window and braced his weight on its open ledge. The arm she'd scraped raw hung limp at his side. Though his words were strong, she could tell he was more injured than he let on.

"I do what I must," she said. "I made my own vow, remember? It is the Lioness who will find victory."

"You will not find it atop this stone spire."

Mari closed her eyes. Her wings folded to her sides. She remembered the paintings of Endarius. She felt the brush of feathers kept by his followers, treasured keepsakes on chains and bracelets. With her form, she honored him as he had been in life, but also accepted the grim truth of him in death. It was her way, as it had always been since the very first time her father had shown her the gift of a god-whisperer.

But there were many ways to honor a god, many faces, and many forms.

"Come chase, hunter," she said, and opened her eyes. "And I will show you your folly."

Mari vaulted off the high spire toward the other, shorter spire a hundred feet away. Rihim leaped after her, his trajectory instinctively chosen so he would intersect with her fall.

Only she did not fall.

Her wings spread wide like bat wings, the thin flesh catching the wind and holding her aloft. Mari flew over the skies of Vallessau, casting her shadow upon the city as the Lion had for so many centuries. A twist of her spine and she turned, spiraling like the falcon she once resembled in her time in Lahareed. Hunting the hunter. Seeking Rihim as he fell through the air, where his size and strength would serve him little.

Mari struck him head-on. Her wings closed, their sharp ends sinking into either side of his neck. Her teeth found his abdomen, and she bit and tore into it as they careened toward the spire. Flesh made way. Ribs broke. Innards spilled.

The pair smashed through the old stone like a missile. They landed atop wood stairs, which groaned and collapsed at their weight. Dust and rubble scattered around them as they fell, tumbling and bouncing to the very bottom of the tower. Mari went limp and endured the jarring hits. The battle was over. The damage was already done.

She landed on all fours, her head low and her eyes closed. Slowly, steadily, she recovered her breath. Pain washed over her in waves, but it would pass. Her wings trembled, the skin connecting them already dissolving away like mist. What bones were broken, they would heal when she gave up the power of Endarius and returned to her mortal form.

The same could not be said for Rihim.

The panther god lay on his back, his legs twisted awkwardly beneath him. They lay so perfectly still she suspected his spine had snapped. His left arm was a mangled mess. His stomach was opened, exposing gore and intestines that spilled out before him like untangled ropes. That he breathed at all bespoke his divine nature. His golden eyes stared at her through the dust, their color already starting to fade. Blood spilled from his lips to stain the fur along his neck. His words were strained and wet.

"Amees. Whisper her. Please. I beg of you."

Mari padded closer, and she licked blood off her face. The coppery taste sent shivers through her, and she fought off the rush.

"Why?" she growled, relying on her word-lace to translate. Rihim reached for her with his good arm. His manacle rattled. Fanatic desire burned deep in his golden eyes.

"Because I...because I won't see her again. She told me. Not as I am. Not after the monster I became in these chains. Let me tell her goodbye before I suffer the hell the God-Incarnate prepares."

Mari paced a full circle around his dying body. Conflict battled within her. To show him pity. To condemn his murders. To merely walk away. This broken god deserved it all and more for the lives he took and the choices he had made.

Her pacing halted. No, it did not matter what he deserved, but what she herself was willing to offer. This was her decision. Her wings curled inward. Her bones cracked as she dismissed the power of the Lion. She did not need Endarius, not for this. Her gray fur receded. Her fangs dulled. Rihim watched as he bled, and when she knelt naked at his side, he reached for her. Mari took his enormous hand into hers and held it to her breast as she gave her answer.

"No."

Rihim's eyes widened with desperate shock. "Why? Please. I beg you. I beg you!"

She shook her head, her decision made. "You will give Amees no final words."

Whatever strength was left in his body drifted away as he slumped to the ground.

"Then I am forever damned," he said. A coughing fit took him. Blood splashed across them both. "My two last memories of her, they are of her corpse, and of her condemnation. How fitting. The empire's hell, I have no need of it. I am already there."

Mari slowly brushed her hand over his forehead, her fingers curling up and over his right ear.

"You will see her again," she said. "You will walk beneath a sunless sky across fields of grass. You will embrace in a land free of our mortal strife. The trees will grow so tall they reach the heavens. The rivers shall run without ceasing, and time flow not at all. You will hunt, and love, and smile. Amees awaits you there in that everlasting land, I promise."

The color had drained from his eyes and tongue. She gently guided his hand back to his chest. He was so weak, he could offer no resistance.

"You...don't...know that."

Mari leaned over him. His divine strength was gone. There would be no tremendous explosion like when Lycaena had been sacrificed. Rihim's followers were few and scattered, and what power he might have possessed, he relinquished much of it to the God-Incarnate through his stolen worship. It was the great price the Humbled paid to survive. Mari watched and waited. No final words, she had promised.

He would speak no goodbyes, and offer no excuses, to his beloved. She would deny him that.

The final words spoken between them, they would be *hers*.

His body convulsed. His lungs hitched. No more blood. No more breath. Silently Mari spoke a name, and the power came to her instantly. She leaned closer and cupped Rihim's face to force him to look up at her. Not a parting, as he desired, but the opposite. A greeting. An invitation.

Her eyes shone green. Twigs and leaves fell from her hair.

"Come find me," she whispered with two voices.

The Antiev God of the Hunt breathed his last. Mari released his face, leaned back onto her heels, and wept. She did not know if it was her own sorrow or Amees's that overcame her. It didn't matter, for it was real, and it was necessary. She allowed the tears to fall until her insides hollowed. Until there was room for the Lion once more.

Your mercy renders you vulnerable, Endarius warned inside her mind as her body changed, fur sprouting, muscle thickening, and bones reshaping.

"Then let me be vulnerable," she said, though it came out as a growl. "There are times for mourning, and there are times for hunting."

And what of now?

Mari wiped the tears from her face and paced two circles around Rihim's body before facing the tower doorway. Resolve hardened her heart, and she pushed her pain away.

"My friends are in danger," she said. "We hunt."

CHAPTER 47

RAYAN

The soldiers, the paragons, and the petty nobles brought over from Gadir: None of them mattered to Rayan. Light gleamed across his blood-soaked blade as he carved his way through his foes, his eye on one single man. The betrayer. The murderer of hundreds of loyal defenders of Thanet. The man's name was on his lips, a war cry, a challenge.

"Jase!"

Rayan saw him among the seats, once proudly lurking at the Heir-Incarnate's right hand but now cowering among frantic soldiers pulled in all directions. Vagrant was a murderous display of blood and gore shredding through dignitaries and their bodyguards. Keles followed in his wake, and in her dark armor, she was his perfect shadow. Arn and Stasia swept through the other side, bringing down even paragons who attempted to slow their pace.

Wood groaned beneath Rayan's feet as he sprinted across the long benches. Some men fled, others shouted and swung weapons that shattered against his shield. Faith burned bright in his chest. There would be no stopping him. There would be no delay to this needed justice. A wall of five soldiers did their best, swords and spears up to greet him while Lord Mosau cowered behind.

"Even now you flee?" Rayan bellowed, his legs churning faster. He held his shield aloft, trusting its brilliance. Rainbow light flared across its surface, blinding the men. Their swords and spears swung wild, easily dodged or parried, and then he was among them. His training took over, a momentary calm to his vicious chase. Back and forth, an alternation of attack and defense. Drive his sword through a man's chest, then pull back, his shield braced to turn aside a spear's frantic thrust. Step in, cutting open another's throat with a strike much too fast for him to parry, though he did his damnedest to try. Step out, reassessing so his shield and sword were there to block the panicked hits of his foes.

The opening and closing of a butterfly's wings, in time with the beat of his heart and the drawing of breath into his lungs. No moments of weakness. Just steady, determined movements leading to victory. He was stronger. He was more skilled. The outcome was inevitable, should he not fail, and he would not fail, not with so many relying on him. Not while his island remained conquered.

The last of the five soldiers flung aside his sword and fled when Rayan pulled back after a killing slash. Rayan let him go, his single focus on the man they protected...a man who had dropped down to the arena below and was currently dashing into the nearby tunnel.

Such cowardice, he thought. He sheathed his weapons, knelt at the smooth wall's edge below him, and then lowered to a drop. He winced upon landing. Lycaena might bless him with strength, but she would not smooth the ache in his old knees from such a fall. He clenched his jaw, ignored the pain, and turned to the tunnel. No sign of Jase.

Rayan glanced about the chaos, at his friends battling the disorganized mass of imperial faithful. He held trust they would win. He felt it in the air, in the panic of the defenders and the rage of Thorda's elite. They did not need him, and so he ran into that tunnel. He let instinct guide him. Instinct, or perhaps Lycaena's gentle hand. Sometimes he passed stairs leading upward, other times closed doors to what appeared to be jail cells. The tunnel narrowed, the lit sconces growing farther apart. Shadows lengthened, but he ignored every turn and side tunnel leading to who knew where. Only Jase mattered, and Lycaena would guide him to his prey.

The sound of battle quieted. There was only his footsteps echoing within the cold, dark stone. His footsteps...and those of someone ahead. Rayan ran faster, legs pumping, heart pounding, only to quickly skid to a halt. There, a side tunnel without a single sconce to light it. He drew his sword and shield. In such deep darkness, the light of their glow was nearly blinding.

Jase Mosau held a hand to his eyes and winced against the light.

"Did you think to hide from me?" Rayan asked as he closed the distance between them.

"From one of the madmen who would destroy our island?" Jase said. "Yes, I would hide."

Rayan paused at arm's length and pointed his sword.

"Draw your blade. I will not cut down a defenseless man. That is your sin, not mine."

The lord's hand drifted to the thin blade sheathed at his hip, but he did not draw it.

"Galvanis's fury at this debacle will be tremendous," he said. "Do you understand the suffering you have unleashed upon our people? Are you so simple as to believe our little island, our speck of dirt in the ocean, can withstand an empire whose population numbers in the *millions?*"

"The waters of the Crystal Sea are vast, now draw your sword."

"But not vast enough! Our gods are slain. The royal family is dead but for a lone child without any official backing. Abandon your pride, Rayan, and look at this war for what it truly is! Hopeless. Pointless. The sooner we bow our heads and offer the God-Incarnate the prayers he seeks, the sooner we may live our lives in peace."

Rayan's grip on his sword tightened. The light across the blade shimmered red and gold.

"You would have us debate?" he asked. "You would argue justification for the deaths of those who trusted you?"

Jase's face hardened. His eyes narrowed in the swirling light.

"Galvanis told me of Thanet's fate, of its future, and it is—"

Rayan cut him open, one side of the neck to the other, so not a single word might follow. The dying lord garbled something unintelligible through the bleeding gap in his throat. He clutched at it, as if he might stem the flow. Rayan watched, silent. Feeling nothing but grim satisfaction. Jase collapsed. He died having never drawn his sword.

"I pray whichever god takes you shows you no mercy," Rayan said. Perhaps what he had done was ignoble, but he did not care. Such traitors deserved no better, and he would not listen to a coward's drivel. Better to silence him forever. Perhaps with his tongue stilled, he would not add new sins to torment himself with in the eternal lands beyond.

Rayan lifted his sword, still needing its light. Curiosity tugged at him. Just where had Lord Mosau been running? In the distance he saw the tunnel curve, and along that curve flickered a hint of burning candle-light upon the wall. He walked it, for it wasn't far, and rounded the curve.

An enormous set of doors awaited him, lit by four sconces burning along the top. Its surface was layered with gold, the malleable metal molded so the left side was shaped like Lycaena with her wings spread. On the right, carved to stand on his hind legs with paws up, roared Endarius. Rayan touched one of the enormous handles. A shiver ran through him at the sound of creaking metal. What was this place? What secrets were hidden behind such a door far below Vallessau's castle?

Echoing footsteps turned him about. He readied his sword and shield as his throat tightened and his stomach twisted uncomfortably. He need not see the man to know who approached. The aura of divinity rolled off him in waves. It felt like a sickness approached. It felt like fire, and rot, and a starving blade.

"You found the vault," Galvanis vin Lucavi said, rounding the curve. His drawn sword rested comfortably across the back of his shoulders. There was no rage in the Heir-Incarnate's voice despite the chaos of the night. He sounded remarkably calm, perhaps even amused.

"I have no interest in whatever treasures it holds," Rayan said. It took tremendous concentration to keep his voice steady. "I would return to my friends, if you'd so kindly make way."

A smile spread across the man's too-perfect face. His skin, pale as the moon, took on the hue of the flickering sconces.

"Do not play the fool, Paladin. I expect better of you. Even if you were not guilty of a thousand sins against my empire, I would take your head for robbing me of such a useful tool as Lord Mosau."

Rayan braced his legs and tightened his muscles. He had fought paragons before and withstood their strength. This fight would be no different, he told himself. He must only survive. The others would come searching for the Heir-Incarnate. Once Cyrus and the rest arrived, they could outnumber him and bring him down. They could score a victory no nation had ever accomplished in the entire history of the Everlorn Empire.

Easy to think, hard to believe. Merely standing in the man's presence unnerved Rayan. Galvanis radiated power. He moved with such ease it was as if his hundred pounds of thick plate armor weighed nothing at all. And that sword, it should have been unwieldy at such a size, yet he lifted it with a single hand and pointed its tip with nary a tremble.

"Take the first swing. Consider it my gift."

Rayan hesitated. Every extra second brought his friends that much closer. He smiled behind the skull mask of his helmet.

"If you insist."

He lunged forward, but not with his sword. His shield hit the extended tip and then slid below it. His arm flexed, shoving the weapon upward to grant an opening for his own gleaming blade. The man's armor was thick, but Rayan's blade was blessed by his goddess, and he trusted it to cut through the steel. And cut it did, parting the metal like warm butter until it hit flesh.

Flesh that did not give. Flesh that sparked with golden light and did not bleed when Rayan slid the blade across it before withdrawing.

"Now do you understand?" Galvanis said. "You could never win."

He backhanded Rayan with his gauntlet. Even with the protection of his helmet, his vision swam and his ears rang from the blow. He staggered, then gasped as Galvanis jammed the hilt of his sword right into Rayan's gut. The lower edge of his platemail bent from the impact. Another retreating step, except there was nowhere to go. His heel brushed the wall.

With Rayan trapped, Galvanis lifted his sword with both hands, readying it for the killing blow. The wiser course was to dodge aside, even in the limited space, but Rayan had to know. He had to try. When that enormous sword came crashing down, Rayan thrust his shield up to meet it. Let strength meet strength, his faith in Lycaena clashing against the faith of Everlorn and their God-Incarnate. A song to the goddess rang in his mind. Brilliant light flared across its surface, and for one single moment he dared believe he could win.

Gold shimmered across Galvanis's enormous sword, just a flash, and then raw power blasted into his uplifted shield. It rocked through him like a thunderclap. Pain exploded in waves across the entire left half of his body. His knees buckled, and he screamed, and screamed, as his every muscle locked tight. After an eternity, the blade withdrew, granting him a single gasp of air.

This is madness, Rayan thought. *If this is the strength of the son, what then of the father?*

No time to think on that. One foe at a time. His shield held through only a gift of Lycaena herself. The same could not be said for his arm. It hung limp at his side, the pain radiating out from it making it hard to focus. His collarbone had shattered, likely his wrist and elbow, too.

"You lived," Galvanis said. "I am impressed. Gods have broken before my full might unleashed."

"You flatter me," Rayan said, and coughed blood.

Galvanis closed the gap between them with his sword pulled back for a lunge. His elbow slammed Rayan's shield aside. His shoulder bent low, its armor pinging Rayan's frantic swipe away. The forced movements of his damaged limbs flooded Rayan with pain, and he had the briefest second to appreciate the precariousness of his situation before the Heir-Incarnate thrust his blade with the speed and savagery of a biting serpent.

His platemail was no protection. It didn't even slow the blade as it sank into Rayan's stomach, pushed through the guts, and scraped along his spine. Rayan doubled over, or at least tried, but the sword held him in place. His own armaments clattered to the ground, for he lacked the strength to wield them. His each and every breath was a struggle. The Heir-Incarnate watched him, strangely silent.

"You will never win," Rayan said. He forced the words out despite the horrid agony from his abdomen. The sword drove deeper, making a mess of his innards. He tried not to imagine what it would feel like when Galvanis finally pulled the weapon free. "We will...remember. Lycaena. Endarius. We will rise up. Year after year. However long...it takes."

Galvanis closed the distance between them, the sword held steady in one hand. With his other he cupped Rayan with an embrace, as if they were dearest friends. His voice softened to a whisper.

"You poor fool," he said. "Let me usher you into your heaven with a secret. When the six hundredth year arrives, and the ceremony commences, we shall spill the blood of your faithful and the faithless alike to grant power to the transition. *I* will become God-Incarnate, and take into me that essence and faith to become perfected."

He twisted the blade, not much, just enough to ignite a tremendous new wave of agony.

"*All* the faithful. *All* the faithless. Thanet shall be sacrificed to foster this rebirth, giving purpose to your heathen island. No witnesses shall remain to remember you. Your heroes? Your god and goddess? They will fade away, their names forbidden to be whispered even by the soldiers who commit the deed. Thanet shall be forgotten, a footnote in the empire's grand history. You die for nothing. You save no one."

Rayan reached for that perfectly beautiful, perfectly terrible face. His hands were weak, and shook. Horror turned his vision white. No. This...this couldn't be what awaited them all. Massacre and bloodshed on so enormous a level could not be kept hidden.

"Word...will spread," he choked out.

"Indeed," Galvanis said. He grabbed Rayan by the throat. "Whispered tales of the stubborn island of Thanet, whose people refused to bend the knee and honor the God-Incarnate. Ignorant savages, too simple and foolish to learn...and so we put them down like animals."

He ripped the sword free. Rayan did not feel it. He did not feel anything. He merely heard a wet splatter. Pain was everywhere, and his vision faltered. The Heir-Incarnate's words floated over him.

"Do not worry, though. Your island will not remain empty. Boats from Gadir will come bearing faithful citizens of Everlorn to rebuild atop your graves. In time, we will convince their great-grandchildren that their ancestors were the first, and you were never here at all."

Rayan wished to deny him. He wished to curse the empire, the God-Incarnate, and his wretched son, but no words would come. He was on his back. He did not remember falling. Footsteps, heavy and plated. The sound of doors opening on hinges long since rusted.

"Farewell, Paladin. You were a noble foe, even if an unworthy one."

CHAPTER 48

KELES

The tunnels were dark and numerous, a veritable rat maze to anyone unfamiliar with them, yet Keles and Cyrus had no choice but to rush through in search of wherever her uncle had chased Lord Mosau. The faint blue glow of her sword was a torch, and she held the naked blade aloft as she prayed.

Please, Dagon, Lycaena, anyone, show me the way.

Cyrus ran a step ahead of her, and she wondered if he could sense her uncle when she could not. The gifts available to him, she still did not fully understand. He was becoming something more, something inhuman. But then again, so was she.

"Hold," she said, skidding to a stop at a junction. "I see something."

That something was a body. It lay a dozen feet down the turn, barely visible in the sapphire light that shone from Keles's drawn sword. His throat was cut from side to side. She recognized the man upon inspection, as did Cyrus.

"It's Jase," he said. He shook his head at the corpse. "The bastard deserved worse."

It should have encouraged her to find her uncle's target dead, but instead it only heightened her worry. She'd spotted Jase fleeing during the chaos, followed by her uncle. So if Jase was dead, where then had Rayan gone?

"Rayan must have been the one to kill him," she said. She pointed at bloodstained boot prints that continued down the tunnel. "We follow."

Her cautious steps quickly turned to a run. The path ended abruptly at a tremendous door lit with two sconces. Before them, in a pool of his own blood, lay her uncle.

"Rayan," she said, sliding to her knees. He was breathing, still breathing, that's all the mattered. She ignored the tremendous wound in his gut. She ignored the way his eyes did not focus on her properly when she tilted his neck and removed his helmet. His lips moved, struggling. His eyes focused. Recognizing her, she believed, at least until he spoke.

"Lara?" he asked, and lifted a trembling hand for her face.

"No, Uncle," she said. She swallowed down a lump in her throat. "It's me, Keles."

"Keles," he said, as if the name were a strange delight to him. He breathed in sharply, and his eyes widened. "I see."

His head lolled. Keles pulled him up, one arm clutching his hands, her other propping his back. His eyes blinked slowly. He did not speak, nor look at her.

"No," she said, letting him back down. "No, no, not yet, you can't leave me yet, please, I'm back now, I'm back."

She pressed her hands to the gaping wound in his stomach. Cyrus lingered behind her, too calm, too still.

"Keles," he said.

Keles ignored him. She bowed her head and closed her eyes. She was a paladin, a penitent, a being infused with the power of gods. She was no stranger to healing prayer. It was only to whom she prayed that had changed.

"Please, Dagon," she whispered. "If this island is yours as you claim, then protect your people. Grant me succor. Grant me healing. Mend the body. Make new this torn flesh and broken bone."

For the briefest moment she felt a stirring in her breast. It was the unmistakable presence of the divine. The tingling, burning fire flowed through her limbs. In another lifetime, it would have manifested in shining white light to pass through her fingertips. That was the gift Lycaena had granted to her, and to Rayan, and to all her priests and paladins in those glorious days before the empire arrived. Keles opened her eyes and looked upon the result of her prayer.

No light. No healing. The divine presence simmered and faded. She saw only blood and torn flesh. Rayan was still. So very still.

"Uncle?"

Eyes open, but not seeing. Mouth open, but not breathing.

"Uncle?"

Cyrus's hand was a curse settling on her shoulder.

"He's gone, Keles."

Keles tore the necklace of shells and sapphires from her neck, breaking the clasp. She tossed it to the cold stone, and she felt nothing but savage fury and heartbroken betrayal. There was no healing in Dagon's presence. Whatever the slain god was, whatever he represented, it was no salve to Thanet's wounds. It was strength, it was hate, it was the uncaring tide. Not salvation.

Cyrus knelt beside her. A thin sliver of pity pierced her anger and sorrow at seeing the way the young man's hand trembled as he lovingly brushed Rayan's eyelids closed.

"No man could have asked for a better teacher," he said softly. "No man could have wanted for a better friend. Rest well in her arms, Paladin. You're home."

Cyrus stood, and after a moment's hesitation, he retrieved the Dagon necklace Keles had cast aside. It conveniently gave him a moment to put his back to her, and to grieve where she could not see. Keles looked down to the body she cradled. This man, this mentor who had served so faithfully his entire life, was gone. When she had doubted, he held true. When she turned to others, he had kept his feet firmly planted upon what he believed to be solid ground.

And this was his reward.

Keles had never hated Lycaena before. She had trusted her goddess all her life. She had loved her even more when the knives of the church's priests cut her hair, her wings, and her flesh. The absence of her goddess left a hole deep within her breast. The fading of her presence from Thanet had filled her with despair. When Eshiel brought back his blood-and-fire incarnation, Keles had been afraid, but not angry. Not hateful.

Not like her hate now. Damn the empire, damn the paragons, damn Sinshei and Galvanis and Soma and all the others, but damn most the goddess who left them so alone and helpless. She screamed it, uncaring of who might hear. With bared teeth, clenched fists, and tears flowing, she screamed, and screamed, and screamed, demanding even gods and goddesses answer.

"Why did you abandon him?" Her damning voice echoed through the stone. "What more could you want? More faith? More loyalty? Do you not care? Do you not listen?"

She raged. She burned. She did not weep.

"Have you *ever* listened?"

Keles looked once more to the wound, and she shuddered at the grotesque sight. It should have healed. It should have closed. She unclipped her uncle's cloak and bundled it into the wound to staunch the last of the leaking blood. The red pooled across the mixture of white and gray cloth. Next she grabbed his sword and shield from where they lay beside him and rested them atop his body, as would be done in a Lycaenan funeral. Last was the helmet. She debated putting it on, but the skull mask that would hide his face made her shudder. Instead she laid it atop the cloak and sword. All this she did in silence while Cyrus watched.

"We're dying for you," she whispered. Her rage was already sputtering out, leaving her insides charred and hollow. No Lycaena. No Dagon. No gods at all. She felt human, and mortal, and empty.

"Did he die alone?" It was the question she feared to speak, and whose answer terrified her throughout sleepless nights. "Is that all that awaits us at the end?"

There would be no proper funeral. No grand crypt that a paladin of such faith and devotion deserved. All she could offer was a pyre. The flame within the sconce would have to be enough. She removed one of them and paused to shudder at the sensation coming from the other side of the doors. Beyond was the presence of the divine, only sickly and wrong. The Heir-Incarnate. It had to be.

Keles returned to the body, and she knelt with her head bowed. Funeral rites bounced around her mind, and she refuted them all. No flowery words, not here. Her eyes closed. At last she let her heart break. One fleeting moment of vulnerability for her tears to fall and her voice to tremble. She pressed her face to the bloodstained cloak, and she whispered into the cloth.

"I loved you, Lycaena. Was that not ever enough?"

Keles pressed the sconce to the center of the cloak. It caught fire, but it did not burn. It *changed.*

Color bloomed throughout the white and gray. It was reddest and deepest where the blood had pooled, but then it shifted in tones, to oranges and yellows in a crystalline pattern so reminiscent of the stained glass of the fallen Twin Sanctuary. The fire leaped to the shield, charring away anything black to expose a wondrous rainbow of color. The blade of his sword shifted red. Last was the bone portion of the helmet. The fire swept across it, turning carved bone into multicolored crystal.

Rayan's body faded into dust and ash. His armor clattered empty to the ground. A lone fire burned above the cloak, shining white with its edges transitioning through the shades of the rainbow. From within that fire floated a butterfly no larger than Keles's hand, its wings and body made of embers and flame. It looped through the air twice on its steady passage to settle upon Keles's breast. Its wings flattened. Within her mind, she heard a voice.

When they severed my wings, I wept for you. When they cut my flesh, I wept for you. When I died, my tears were not for myself, but for my children, and my faithful. I am weak. I am fading. I may one day be forgotten, but I will not forget she who loved me with all her heart. I will love you in return, Keles Lyon, even unto the breaking of the world. What light I offer, it is yours. What fire I offer, it is yours.

If you would have it.

Emotions too conflicted and complicated overwhelmed Keles. Her prior rage and hate at the goddess. The shame of her cowardice at the forsaking ceremony. How she had twice cast aside Lycaena, and instead accepted Dagon's blessing, a poisoned gift from the Anointed One.

"I'm not worthy of it," she said, the one thing she was certain of.

The butterfly's wings fluttered.

The beloved are worthy, and all are beloved.

The butterfly sank below her skin, igniting a fire in her breast. Her emptiness, that cavernous darkness, now burned with light. The ache of her body, the weight of her past, her grief and sorrow, it all remained, but it bred no despair. It gave her resolve. It gave her hope. She clenched her fists to her chest, offering back a wordless prayer of gratitude. A ringing filled her ears, a song with words she could not fathom, but then words did come, a parting that let loose the last of her tears. Rayan's voice, spoken as if he stood beside her. Though no one was there, she felt his hand on her shoulder.

Then let me live and die for that beauty, if it will ease the ache of others. I will walk that path, and I will not walk it alone.

Darkness returned to the tunnel, but this time the shadows were not so deep. Warmth spread throughout her body, melting a frost she never knew had seeped all the way deep into her bones. She looked to the empty armor before her, and it felt like a gift.

"Keles," Cyrus asked, having watched the entire exchange in silence. "Are you . . ."

"I'm fine," Keles said, and she wiped away the last of her tears. The room seemed so much smaller now, the weight on her shoulders, so much lighter. The divine moment had passed, and already it felt as if it had happened in a different age, to a different person. "Better than fine."

She attached her uncle's cloak to her pauldrons, the vibrant colors a stark contrast to the black of her armor. After a moment's hesitation, she retrieved his helmet, too. With the inhuman strength of paragons and paladins, Keles ripped the nails loose. The crystalline mask fell to her hands. She held it, this grin so similar to Cyrus's. But his was pale and white, with a mocking sneer upon those bared teeth to promise pain and death. This smile, it was beautiful, awash with color, made of colored crystal so clear it was nearly transparent. Keles tore a small section of her cloak, looped the cloth through the nail holes in the skull, and used them to tie the mask to her face.

"I feel it, as I'm sure you do, too," Cyrus said as her preparations neared their end. "Galvanis is through that door. Are you ready, Keles?"

Instead of the weapons gifted to her by the Anointed One, Keles took up her uncle's gleaming sword and shield. She felt the magic in them, the desire to be wielded by his namesake. Their weight was a comfort.

"I will not walk it alone," she whispered, and then turned to Cyrus. "Yes. I am finally ready."

Together, Vagrant and Paladin entered the vault, to end the life of the Heir-Incarnate.

CHAPTER 49

VAGRANT

Galvanis vin Lucavi knelt in prayer before a sapphire altar. His back was to Cyrus, but no thoughts of assassination came to him. He was too in awe of his surroundings.

"What...what is this?" Keles asked.

The Heir-Incarnate ended his murmured prayer and stood. He turned slowly, a smile on his immaculate face. A smile that was a lie. Rage flowed off him as tangible as a summer wind.

"The hidden sin of your wretched island," he said. "The stolen wealth of the Orani. The treasures of the slain Dagon."

Paintings were stacked along one side of the vault, portraying men and women dressed in blue and red robes. The royal family, Cyrus realized, the one his own family had overthrown. The paintings' frames were silver, and they bore faint swirls to mark Dagon's presence. On the opposite side of the vault were statues, most broken in various parts and others hopelessly cracked. Some were people. Others were of Dagon, long and slender, a few still possessed of the carved sapphires wedged tightly into the stone to represent his scales.

A chest lay half open beside the door, and Cyrus reached for one of the coins inside. The sea serpent was carved onto its face. He dropped it, the ringing silver piercing the silence as it bounced to Galvanis's feet. The altar he prayed before was enormous and extravagant, the upper portions filigreed with silver, the base painted a deep blue that had weathered the passage of time. Two figures danced with each other, their arms outstretched. Each held a torch above their heads, and somehow those torches still burned, illuminating the vault. On the left was Lycaena, her wings spread wide and her scepter lifted high. On the right was Dagon, albeit in a more human interpretation. His body was layered with scales shaped like armor, his tail curled around his left leg, and his face smooth and serpentine.

This altar marked the cooperation of the gods before Endarius arrived, overthrew the Orani family, and slew the Sapphire Serpent. In the years that followed, the priests and priestesses of both gods preached of Dagon's devious nature, his temptations and cruelties, and how he prepared the Heldeep for the unrepentant.

All lies.

"These are Thanet's gods, who warred for Thanet's throne," Cyrus said, glad for the mask to hide his discomfort. "What concern are they to Everlorn?"

Galvanis shook his head. He ran his right hand along the edge of the altar, his fingertips touching Lycaena's feet and then trailing upward along her dress to her wings. There was something strangely...loving about the act.

"Don't you see?" he asked. "Even alone amid the Crystal Sea, free of the conflicts upon Gadir, you slaughtered one another. You bickered, you fought over heirs, and for centuries Thanet's rule was split in twain, with Lycaena's devotees ruling the north and Dagon's ruling the south. Oh, your historians did not lie, the War of Tides united your island behind a single crown. But look what it took to happen."

The Heir-Incarnate unsheathed his sword. Fresh blood still marked it. Rayan's blood. Cyrus swallowed down his rage as Galvanis pressed the tip of the sword into the neck of Dagon's statue. He stared at the figure, unafraid.

"Endarius arrived with his wealth and his soldiers, and he declared himself equal to your native gods. Dagon's pride would not allow it, and he demanded that the Lion kneel. And so it came to war. Our spies wrote us that a third of your island died in the conflict, through battle, disease, and starvation."

He swung, decapitating the Dagon statue. The stone head fell to the ground and split in half upon landing. Galvanis smashed the rest with his heel. He pointed the bloody sword toward Cyrus.

"Your heretical gods are worthless," he said. "As are all other gods that walk among us. Differences lead to conflict. A need for faith and power will lead us to destroy one another, as we did long before the Everlorn Empire rose from the ashes. Open your eyes. Cast off your blindness. Look upon our world with wisdom, and see the undeniable truth. Let humanity know one god. Let us know one nation. Let us speak one tongue. That is the path toward peace, however bloody it may be."

Cyrus crossed his swords before him. His rage burned, and he held none of it back. Fire flowed from his tongue. This heir, this man seeking to be a god, was everything sick and wrong in Eldrid.

"You would destroy a world of beauty and wonder to achieve your hollow peace," he said. "You would build a gray land of ash and soot, where the faithful bend by the boot on their necks to offer shallow worship. You do not get to drown the world in blood and then call yourself peacemaker, Galvanis. The conquered deny your delusions. Tyrant, I name you. War bringer, I condemn you. May all the gods and goddesses spare us your *peace*."

Galvanis pointed his greatsword, disappointment etched into his every movement.

"You are no different, Cyrus. How many have died to your swords? How much blood have you spilled amid your supposed righteous slaughter to keep a throne that should never have been yours?"

"I do not seek peace. I seek freedom."

Galvanis ignored him, and instead turned to Keles.

"And what of you, Orani woman? We slew your conquerors when we cast down the Lythan family. I see the colors of your cloak. I recognize the crystal of your mask. Would you give your faith to the goddess who allowed your throne to be overthrown? What justification could you offer in the face of such a betrayal?"

Keles stepped before Cyrus, and she stood tall in the face of Everlorn's worshiped son.

"My faith was not chosen at my birth, nor enslaved by my blood." She lifted her sword. A rainbow of light swirled across its red steel. "I found no love in the arms of Dagon, but my goddess is with me now. Her strength is my strength. Her anger is my anger. I will do what must be done. You are a monster, Galvanis, and no amount of pretty words will hide your ugliness."

Galvanis lowered into a stance, greatsword up and angled and his knees bent.

"Noble words. Noble lies. You both seek crowns, one of gold and one of blood, so come and take mine. Show me the power of heretical gods."

Cyrus's teeth split wide in a grin. If they were to find victory here, it would be by holding nothing back. If there was ever a time, it was now, and so he sheathed the Endarius blade. Slowly, theatrically, he reached into the cowl of his hood and undid the leather knot of his mask. The painted wood fell to the floor and landed with a hard clack, exposing Cyrus's face. His *true* face.

Brown eyes that hovered within hollow black spaces. Teeth that stretched all the way to where his ears should be, but there were no ears, no skin at all, just a grinning skull. Upon his brow rested a silver crown, nailed to the bone and jutted with jagged spikes along the upper rim.

"Behold the power you seek," Cyrus said, unsheathing the Endarius blade. His teeth did not move. His words rumbled out of his throat without a tongue to speak it or lips to shape it. "I am the Vagrant Prince, and I shall have my crown."

He dashed across the vault, scattering spilled coins that littered the ground, and then leaped with a final burst of speed. His swords slashed, each angled for Galvanis's throat from opposite directions. The surprise and speed were not enough. The greatsword batted aside one hit while Galvanis's elbow tilted in the way of the other, the thick armor resisting the cut, but only barely. Cyrus landed undeterred, his feet spinning. His off-hand blade struck Galvanis's thigh, and it sank through the metal with a sharpness gifted by the prayers of Thanet's most desperate.

Cyrus ripped it free to preserve his momentum, sidestepped a downward chop meant to split him in half, and then retreated. Keles charged with her shield leading, for there would be no quarter given. Brilliant light sparked off its surface as it collided with the Heir-Incarnate's chest. Lycaena's gift flooded it with power. Galvanis rocked backward, his chestplate caving inward slightly. He kicked her in the stomach as payment for the attack. She staggered, heaving as her lungs fought for air.

Galvanis tried to seize the opportunity, a slanted cut that would have cleaved through her shoulder and hip if Cyrus hadn't flung her out of the way. He felt the air of the sword's passage, felt it tug against his cloak as it clipped the trailing cloth. He turned, missed a thrust for the man's face, and then retreated. The muscles in his legs already burned as he dashed about, avoiding swing after swing of the chasing Heir-Incarnate. Paintings scattered. Carvings toppled. The footing grew unsteady, and Cyrus feared what a single errant step might cost them.

The moment Keles recovered, Cyrus halted his retreat and dashed inward. The pair struck in unison, too perfectly synchronized for Galvanis to block them both. He let Keles's sword through, and though it pierced through his armpit, it reflected off unseen armor. It drew no blood.

"Is this all you would offer me?" Galvanis asked, and his disappointment sounded honest. "This is the supposed might that would free an island from our grasp?"

He alternated his attention with each swing of his greatsword, Keles to Cyrus, with might capable of felling trees. His speed was unreal, greater even than during their previous battle at the docks. Cyrus forfeited all thought of going on the offensive. He rolled below a swing, bunched his legs, and then vaulted up and over the following one. His swords crossed before him, and the third hit square across their combined metal. The shock of it knocked him flying across the vault, and paintings tore as he landed amid their haphazard pile.

Keles thrust her sword for the spine, drawing Galvanis's attention and likely sparing Cyrus's life. The Heir-Incarnate shot his elbow backward, batting the thrust wide, and then spun with the greatsword held with one hand. Keles met it with her shield, and she gasped at the impact. Rainbow light sparked across its surface, the goddess's magic the only reason her bones did not shatter.

The two torches held by the gods of the altar cast many shadows. A clench of his fist, and Cyrus fell into the stone as if it were water. He emerged leaping from the space directly beside the altar, his swords flashing with speed. They struck Galvanis across the back, ripping into his armor to reach the flesh beneath. Twin grooves opened, shallow and bloodless. It was as if his foe's skin were a second armor, and harder than marble.

Galvanis's fist blasted him in the face, but there was no nose to break, no lips to burst. Cyrus rolled with it as best he could to spare the strain on his neck, scored a cut across Galvanis's wrist in retribution, and then danced away to recover his bearings. Keles managed a hit across the Heir-Incarnate's shoulder, buying time. Cyrus dug his heels in, shook his head to clear his vision, and lifted his blades.

In that brief moment, cold words whispered to him in his own voice. He felt them like fingers upon his throat.

Your humanity betrays you.

Keles blocked twice with her shield, screaming in pain each time. The goddess might be with her, and her body blessed by the paragon ritual, but it was still flesh and bone. It had its limits, limits surpassed by the abominable hybrid of humanity and divinity that was the Heir-Incarnate. It was a combination Cyrus knew far too well. He dashed into the fight, diverting his foe's attention to spare Keles a third strike. Their weapons crossed, the impact traveled up to his elbows, and he choked down a pained cry. Had to keep the offensive. Had to keep swinging, to keep beating against this mountain of steel and muscle.

He won't tire, the dark voice spoke. *He won't surrender. You must be greater.*

Galvanis parried two hits with a wide sweep of his sword, then punched with his free hand. Cyrus retreated out of reach, but it was what Galvanis wanted. His greatsword swept out and wide, a blur of Ahlai-made steel. Too quick to dodge. Too strong to block with his swords.

A flare of light marked its halt before it might cut him in twain. Keles and her shield stood between them, her legs braced, her entire body shaking from the effort. Her cloak had vanished. Wings the color of fire spread out of her back, translucent and billowing like hung cloth on a springtime wind. She was beautiful, she was strong, and she was shouting Cyrus's name.

His real name.

"With me, Vagrant! Cut him down!"

He dashed past her, past the greatsword still pressed to her stubborn shield. His off-hand flipped in his grasp, the two weapons held long and plunging tip-first into the Heir-Incarnate's abdomen. They should have skewered innards, but still the flesh held strong. The weapons scraped to either side, cutting a thin groove, but it was like carving into stone. No blood. Not yet. Gordian Goldleaf had not bled in those early moments of their battle at the Solemn Sands, either, yet he had still fallen in time.

Galvanis howled, his fury grimly satisfying to Cyrus's ears. The behemoth pulled his greatsword back, lifted it high, and then sent it crashing back down, directly challenging Keles to block it a second time.

A challenge she met. Her wings spread wide, wall to wall, floor to ceiling, crimson, green, and gold. This was the power of the Butterfly goddess in the fullness of its blessing, and it would not be broken. The wings washed over Cyrus as he charged through. At their touch his mind filled with visions of other times, of other places. He saw worship on open fields, heard songs of spring sung while children ran in circles with flowers in their hair. And then the sight vanished, replaced with the marble flesh and bloodshot eyes of the savage Heir-Incarnate.

His swords tore apart armor. Metal fell free, exposing muscled flesh, inhuman in its ripples. More cuts, shallow, bloodless grooves along the chest and abdomen. Galvanis withdrew, even as it galled his pride and had him shouting wordless cries of rage. Cyrus did not relent until the hilt of Galvanis's sword struck him across the shoulder, causing him to stumble. An elbow smacked Cyrus's forehead, and then the Heir-Incarnate swung. Cyrus put both swords in the way, but it was a pitiful defense. The impact sent him flying halfway across the vault.

He landed, tumbled twice, and then rolled up to his knees despite his dizziness, which had the floor pitching and turning beneath him. Cold darkness wrapped heavier and heavier across his mind. It spoke eagerly. Determined. Certain. It demanded everything of Cyrus and offered everything in return.

You are not flesh.

Energy crackled through Cyrus. He felt the prayers of the island, the whispers and the sobs of those mourning the lost and the dead. He felt their rage, their need, and their hope, that the empire would one day be forced away. It hardened the bone of his face. It sharpened the points of his crown.

Lycaena. The Vagrant. The old gods and the new, together. It had to be enough. They would get no second chance. If only the ground would stop moving beneath him. If only his vision would straighten.

You are not blood.

"We will not live in your gray world!" Keles screamed as she slashed at the Heir-Incarnate. He blocked each and every one, unwilling to risk the damage the glowing blade might do to his divinely blessed flesh. "You will not rip the beauty from our land! You will not steal the sun from our sky!"

You are a god.

At last, Galvanis had suffered enough. He smashed aside her sword, forced her to block with her shield, and then stepped close. His free hand latched about her throat. Her wings faded. Her sword flailed, deflecting off his rib cage.

"We offer you wretches salvation," he roared, and then flung her against the wall. The sound of metal bending was horrifyingly loud. Her head snapped, and blood splattered from where it hit stone. Keles dropped to her knees and then crumpled. The cold voice screamed inside Cyrus's mind as he feared for her life.

Take your crown.

All his rage, all his desperation, came together in one last barrage. The space between them vanished. Cyrus's swords were blurs even to his own eyes. Galvanis's greatsword shifted and parried, back and forth with the thick edge at the handle, but it wasn't enough. The sound of steel on steel sang a deafening chorus, and in it, Cyrus heard victory. Attack, attack, his swords shimmering with divine power. They did not glow with light like a paladin's, but instead seethed with darkness. It curled along the blades. It lined its edges. A strength, a fury, of a faith that sought only death.

Cyrus's off-hand blade lashed out, the tip striking the Heir-Incarnate's temple. With a savage cry he ripped it across the forehead, temple to temple, and then danced away. Galvanis shrieked so loud the walls shook and the silver in the chests rattled. With a shaking hand he wiped at his forehead.

The skin had peeled back to expose bone. Blood, thick and scarlet, flowed down his pale face and stained his probing fingertips. His blue eyes widened, and in them Cyrus saw doubt for the very first time. He saw fear. Poison, to a god. Death, to a man not yet a god.

"You are mortal," Cyrus said. He lifted his sword so his foe saw the fresh blood upon it. "And you are abandoned. I am the only god who will watch you die."

Cyrus thought Galvanis would launch into one final attack, a protest against the possibility of defeat. This would be the greatest moment of danger, when the Heir-Incarnate put every last shred of his strength into a counteroffensive. Cyrus's lungs burned in his chest, and aches filled his every limb, yet he stood tall, determined to see this battle to its rightful end.

He gave the Heir-Incarnate too much credit. The man turned and fled for the vault doors, a coward's heart beneath his perfect veneer. He made it only three steps before skidding to a halt, stunned to find the passage blocked.

Sinshei vin Lucavi stood with her arms spread wide and her fingers curled. Twin swords of golden light settled upon either side of Galvanis's throat. He froze, his head tilting slightly to pull away from the shimmering edges that kissed his skin. Blood trickled down his cheeks from the cut Cyrus gave him, and it sizzled into smoke upon touching those faith-born blades.

"I have dreamed of this for years," Sinshei said softly.

"Are you so great a fool?" Galvanis asked her. "You wield weapons manifested by faith in the God-Incarnate. They cannot strike me down. I am his son. I am his *heir*."

The Anointed One smiled.

"My faith is absolute," she said. "For *I* will be the next God-Incarnate."

Her hands curled into fists. The swords crossed, passing through flesh and bone, and then exploded out the other side. Galvanis staggered on uneven feet. His sword dropped from limp fingers, and then he collapsed in a pool of his own blood. His head rolled several feet before coming to a halt. The skin hardened and cracked until it resembled aged plaster.

The floating swords vanished into dust and light. Sinshei shivered with pleasure.

"That felt better than I ever imagined."

Cyrus watched golden light arc across Sinshei's body, remaining bright despite the disappearance of the swords. Her black hair shimmered in the glow of the candles. For a brief moment, Cyrus saw her as she must see herself, majestic and beautiful, the power of life and death held firmly in her hands. Her hands, and no one else's. What god would she become? And could he, in his grinning mask promising death, dare judge her for it?

The image faded, the golden light receded, and the room became dark. Cyrus risked turning away. Keles, was she...?

The paladin stood on her own two feet, albeit unevenly. Blood matted her hair, and he did not like the dazed look in her eye. Blows to the head were dangerous, and could linger, but he could not deny his relief in seeing her standing. He rushed to her side, and it didn't matter that Sinshei was watching. He wrapped his arms around her and held her close. After a moment, she returned the embrace, careful not to press her cheek against his.

Careful not to touch the grinning skull.

"I feared the worst," he whispered.

"Then you should have been faster," she said, and when he pulled away, she was grinning lopsidedly at him. She wiped at the blood on her neck, then grimaced at the amount that covered her hand. "I'll be fine, I promise. Head wounds always bleed worse than they truly are. We have bigger concerns."

It seemed they did. Sinshei's paragon bodyguard had joined her from the tunnel, and the satisfaction on his face rivaled Sinshei's. His spear thankfully remained clipped to his back. Cyrus and Keles stood shoulder to shoulder, a united front before Sinshei and Soma. It was largely a bluff, for both had been pushed beyond their limits in the battle against Galvanis. To then take on a paragon and the Anointed One?

No, whatever Sinshei wanted, they would hear it out, if only in hopes of avoiding a battle they could not win.

"I see your loyalties have shifted," Sinshei said to Keles. Her brother's blood dripped down her face and neck. "I suppose I should have antici-pated as much. Do not consider me bitter. There is much to celebrate about tonight's outcome." She turned her attention to Cyrus. "It is *you* that gives me pause."

"It breaks my heart to know I am such an annoyance."

"Beyond measure. I do not understand you, and I cannot predict you. I did not think you one to reason with, yet I discover you are the long-dead prince. I made a promise to Keles, with her as the rightful queen. Will you challenge that, Cyrus? Or will you show us both a measure of trust and honor the deal?"

"You ask for trust after ordering Keles to take my life?" Cyrus asked.

"My brother lies dead before me, and the title of Heir-Incarnate is now mine by right. Let this be the end of our hostilities. No more assassina-tions. Let me sleep without fear of the Vagrant killing my loyal magistrates. Let the inheritance ritual progress unimpeded. Give Thanet peace."

"And in return?"

"I thought it obvious? At my command, the Everlorn Empire will retreat from your island. I will give you back your rule, for you two to divide as you see fit. Make peace with me, be my ally, and I shall give you the freedom you so desperately fight for."

"We seek to be no puppet state," Keles warned.

"And you will not be one. You will be completely free, with a prom-ise written into law that we shall forever respect your independence in repayment for the sacrifices you have made."

Cyrus caught Soma smirking, and it set doubt to squirming inside his belly.

"You could be lying," he said.

"Be reasonable, Vagrant. I offer you a tiny, inconsequential island, and in return I become goddess of an empire. Why would I lie for so little, when I have so much to gain?"

Cyrus didn't know, but neither did he trust her. He glanced at Keles, seeking her own opinion on the matter. She lowered her head and voice.

"We cannot win a war against the full might of the empire," she said. "Sinshei is the one person who can give us our freedom."

Freedom, granted by the conquerors. Cyrus loathed it with every fiber of his being...but what other choice did they have?

"I shall set aside my blades, for now," he said. "I want an end to this bloodshed, I want our gods returned, and I want you departed from our island. If you can deliver us all three, then consider us temporary allies."

Sinshei clasped her hands together and bowed low, a sign of respect he'd never seen her deliver before to anyone other than her brother.

"Turbulent times are not yet finished, but my ascension approaches. I am a woman of my word, and under my care, the Everlorn Empire shall become better than it ever was. Farewell, to the both of you. I have much to do if I am to clean up my brother's mess."

Soma lingered behind after she left. His eyes swept the vault, then settled on the broken altar. His amused expression faded into unexpected solemnity.

"There are lessons here," he said. "If you are willing to heed them."

The paragon exited into the dark corridor. Cyrus breathed out a sigh of relief. The skull faded from his face, becoming flesh in an instant. He pretended not to notice how empty it left him feeling, how naked and weak. Instead he gave Keles a tired smile.

"We did it," he said.

Keles looked past him, to the empty armor of her uncle.

"We did."

Heavy footsteps from down the hall, coupled with familiar shouts, brought a smile to Cyrus face.

"Here!" he shouted, his voice carrying. The footsteps neared. Arn was the first to find them, Stasia at his heels. They entered the vault with their eyes wide at the sight of wealth and spilled blood.

"Are you well?" the big man asked, huffing and puffing from the run.

"As can be," Cyrus said, and he accepted a quick embrace. "The Heir-Incarnate is dead."

"Dead?" Stasia asked, slowing from a jog. "Are you certain?"

Cyrus pointed at the head, earning massive cheers from the both of them.

"Pretty certain."

Mari arrived moments later, her excited grumbles translated by her word-lace.

"Thank every god and goddess you're safe!" she said, flinging her paws onto either side of Cyrus's shoulders. He hugged her back, and scratched at her head as if she were just an oversized kitten. Mari nipped at his fingers, but she was laughing, and he needed no word-lace to know that.

"So are things... are they good now?" Arn asked, pointedly glancing at Keles, who had remained silent and separate from the others. Cyrus smiled at her. He saw her eyes twinkle, a bit of her own smile hidden behind the fire-colored crystal of her mask.

"I think they might be," he said, and explained to the others what had happened within the vault, and how Sinshei had slain the Heir-Incarnate when he attempted to flee. When finished, he returned to the vault and lifted Galvanis's head by the hair. Now that it was perfectly still from death, it looked disturbingly similar to some of the statues that filled the vault.

He forced back a shiver. A plan was forming in his mind, one that felt just *right* the moment it occurred to him.

"I've an idea," he said, and turned to Mari. "We'll need to act fast, and I'll need your help in particular."

"For what?" she asked.

Cyrus glanced at the head, and then to Keles.

"To put things as they always should have been."

CHAPTER 50

ESHIEL

Eshiel stood with his nine most faithful, gathered together in a circle and wearing matching brown robes. They blocked much of the slender road leading toward the northernmost portion of the harbor, not that there was much traffic to block. The city was crackling with tension, and most people with good sense were staying home.

And then there were those like Eshiel and his faithful, with an aim to cause mischief.

"I trust you nine with my life," he told them. They were young men and women brimming with faith and laden with emotional scars from seeing their beloved Lycaena slain. Unlike the others of his faithful that Eshiel ordered to stay hidden and locked in prayer, these nine were born and raised in Vallessau. They had not seen Eshiel's failed attempts at resurrecting the Butterfly goddess, nor her subsequent death. In a way, they were pure, exactly as he needed them to be.

"We won't run." A young blond woman, Colette, touched his wrist. She peered up at him from underneath her hood. "We are with you, and with Lycaena, to the very end."

Eshiel looked to the docks, and the five caravels in the distance.

"This isn't the end," he said. "This is a rebirth. Let us emerge from the chrysalis."

Keles had been true to her word. Patrols throughout the city were practically nonexistent. The gates had but a skeleton crew to make a show of inspecting travelers. The entire imperial presence had focused upon the castle, and Eshiel would not waste such an opening. The city needed a reminder of Lycaena's true power. They must remember the goddess in all her glory, lest she fade into memory.

Only two soldiers stood at the edge of the docks, and they were clearly on edge. The moment they saw Eshiel's group they drew their weapons and started shouting in the imperial tongue.

"I'm sorry, friends, I cannot understand you," Eshiel said. His smile grew. "Perhaps there is a way I can make my intentions known?"

And then the nine had out their knives. They rushed the soldiers, who panicked at the sight and turned to flee toward a rowboat tied to the dock's edge. One vanished beneath the waves, dragged down by his armor. The other fell to dozens of stabs. A poor sacrifice, and Eshiel ordered him shoved into the water to join his comrade.

"To the beach," he ordered them. They exited the docks and followed the shoreline north until the only thing between them and the Crystal Sea was a long stretch of sand. They positioned themselves in a line, and though they were nervous, faith wafted off them as real as smoke from a candle. In return, he offered them his bravest smile.

"Remain here. Let none follow where I must go."

Eshiel cast off his robe. He wore a simple pair of trousers cinched at the waist. His chest and arms were bare, as intended. He wanted the scars inflicted upon him and the tattoos of his goddess equally visible. When he shed his garments, so, too, did the other nine. Eshiel spared a glance over his shoulder, and he beamed with dangerous pride.

Each man and woman was naked from the waist up. Their bodies were covered with tattoos painstakingly added over the past weeks. They were gifted with swirls of wings. Dashes of color, particularly vibrant reds, oranges, and yellows, were inked among them with expert hands. Like a monarch butterfly. Like fire. The color shone brightly upon their skin, refusing to be muted even by the moonlight. The nine lifted their arms and bowed their heads. They held no weapons but their prayers. They bore no armor but their own faith. As it should have been, from the very beginning.

You were always powerful, my goddess, Eshiel thought as he waded deeper into the water. Waves crashed against his waist. *But I wrapped that power in knives and sacrifices. We needed neither. Prayer. Faith. Trust. Your power remains, but it must go untainted. It must be pure. Above all, it must be* yours.

Not his. Never his. The sea crept up to his chest, and when the waves came, he closed his eyes and let the crests wash over him. Perhaps he imagined it, but he thought he could hear not just the prayers of the nine, but those of the dozens of others who had accepted his guidance. They were the ardent faithful still clinging to the old ways the empire would snuff out. Prayer, all he needed from them was their prayer. Beg to the heavens that their goddess would once again show the city the way.

The sand beneath him dipped suddenly, and he could not stand, only tread water. Eshiel took one last look at the five ships, then closed his eyes and exhaled. He sank beneath the surface. He sank below the waves.

Down into the dark, where the stars could not reach.

Down to the sand and stone of the sea.

The water buoyed him back and forth, but he pushed out more and more of his air. Even beneath Thanet's ocean, he would stand upon firm ground, the rock beyond the beach, the truth of the island that had been their home for generations.

Head light, lungs burning, and with his nose filling with salt water, he prayed a new prayer. In the far north of Thanet, with his every sacrifice, and every sermon, he had emphasized the loss of their goddess and the need for her return. Not this time. She need not return, for she was not gone. The goddess was here, with him, with *everyone.*

His arms lifted. No blood. No sacrifice, no knife. Just a single prayer as his consciousness started to fail.

I am your servant, goddess, and I demand fire.

And there, in the deep water, she gave it to him.

It burst out in waves, the power casting aside the very sea. The sand beneath his feet cracked and fused to glass. The starry sky opened like parted storm clouds, only it was the ocean above him making way. Steam billowed into a wall, its hiss deafening. Eshiel gasped in a breath of air, and he dared not waste it.

"We give you our lives!" he screamed to the heavens. His hands clenched into fists. "Give us your wings!"

The wall of water surrounded him but could not come near. A bubble of flame enveloped him, holding it at bay. His fists trembled. The final word stretched on and on, his plea, his demand, his everything into that single word. The wings of the Butterfly goddess. Make them real. Make them his.

They tore from his back. The pain meant little next to their warmth. They stretched higher, higher, lifting and fluttering like a living thing. A dozen feet, two dozen, span growing, a hollow outline of burning flame. Eshiel watched, breath held, and waited for the answer.

Nine threads soared from the praying faithful at the beach. Nine whirling funnels of flame, each shimmering a different shade of color to form a resplendent rainbow. They met at the center of the grand wings and then spread like liquid, filling their expanse with their brilliance. Tears formed and dried instantly from the heat as Eshiel's heart ached with love for his chosen nine.

Higher. Higher. Above the docks. Above the city. A burning light to rival the moon. A symbol so bright no Uplifted priest could paint it over or scrub it away. He watched it grow with his arms raised, his head back, and his mouth open. Flames flickered across his bare skin. His tattoos, they burned so hot it was as if the ink were oil, yet he felt nothing but euphoria. Crimson embers fluttered off him like ash to join the wings above.

Eshiel cast his gaze to the five ships. They were disorganized and scrambling, pulling up anchor while also releasing smaller rowboats packed with soldiers. They'd come to attack, but it was too late. There was no stopping this. These boats, swords, and soldiers were but petty toys to his goddess. The power grew. The fire blazed. It was time to relinquish control. It was time for those who served Everlorn to learn the price they must pay for their crimes.

He tilted his head to the wings. They spread hundreds of feet wide, slowly opening and closing like those of a butterfly at rest. He reached for them, his hands curling, as if he could take them into his grasp and hold them close. What he would give to feel their warmth against his chest, to burn new scars over the old. They were connected to him, invisible threads latched to his heart, ignited by his prayer.

The boats were closing in. The warships were scattering. Eshiel grabbed that invisible thread. No claiming these wings for his own. No more pretending the goddess was something he alone could resurrect.

Words came to him, and they were so perfect, so beautiful. On his brightest day, Lycaena had given him an order, and he offered it back to her, a divine echo, his purest expression of gratitude and love.

"Cut free," Eshiel screamed to the heavens. "And fly!"

The wings rose, closing near the back for one last flutter.

They opened.

The fire fell.

It fell like rain. It fell like stars. It fell in great streams of color. Where it struck, it burst with explosions of flame. The caravels were bathed in it. The little rowboats collapsed instantly. The wings fell, and fell, giving of their fire and heat until nothing but the faintest shimmer of light graced the nighttime sky. Below, only wreckage remained. Huge chunks were opened across the sides of the warships as if struck by catapulted boulders. Every exposed surface burned. Every last man and woman on board was char and bone, the destruction was so thorough, so complete.

The fire faded.

Eshiel climbed the steep shelf of the beach as the water returned to the shore. By the time it reached him, it was only up to his waist, and he waded with a smile on his face. The relief in his chest overwhelmed him. His beloved nine knelt on the sand, some with arms raised, others huddled low. Some sobbed, others sang. He pushed onward with tired legs, eager to be among them. Every muscle in his body ached, and it felt like he must sleep for a year to recover his energy.

"We did it," Colette called out to him. She knelt, her hands digging into the sand. "We prayed, and she answered."

Her smile was ear to ear, and yet she broke down into sobs. He did not blame her. Hope, true heartfelt hope, could hurt like sorrow when brought to a soul starved of it for so long. Eshiel knelt, lifted her discarded robe, and offered it to her.

"Of course she answered," he said, gently brushing a strand of blond hair from her face. "So great was our faith, we gave her no choice."

He walked among the nine, thanking them, and praying with them if they needed it. There was only so much he could do on his own, and they had come through with him in the end. Ten souls, trusting their safety and lives to their goddess. If the fire had not come, Eshiel would have drowned. The nine would have revealed themselves as heathens still obedient to their slain goddess.

But Lycaena had granted him wings, and oh, how they had burned.

"Eshiel?" a familiar voice called out. He turned. After such a savage attack upon the fleet, he had expected soldiers, yet none would be coming, not with how fresh and wet the blood was on the Vagrant's blades. With him were others whose names he knew only in secret, Heretic, Lioness, and Ax.

"I see Vallessau's strange band of heroes have come to greet me," he said. He hurried toward them with a bounce in his step. He thought nothing could make him happier, but then he saw Keles amid their number. Across her back was a long cloak bearing the colors of his goddess. The lower half of her face was hidden behind bone teeth, and while the mask seemed vaguely familiar to him, he certainly did not recognize it when composed of vibrant crystal, its recesses a fluid mixture of color. It reminded him of the stained glass that once filled the windows of the Twin Sanctuary.

"It is exceptionally good to see you alive and well," he told Keles directly. "And with your faith returned to its proper home." He scanned the rest, seeking out a familiar face. "Where is Rayan, the one you call Paladin?"

"The Heir-Incarnate took his life," Keles answered.

Eshiel bowed his head to her. The skull across her lower face; so that was where he recognized it from.

"I am sorry," he said. "He was a great man, and a true follower of Lycaena. I but struggle to walk in his shadow."

Cyrus pointed to the burning boats and the smoke rising from them to cloud the sky.

"You've cast a long shadow yourself, thrice-born." He lowered his voice. "Can you gather a crowd of your followers, quickly, while the forces in the castle are still in disarray?"

"Are you planning on making a speech?"

Cyrus glanced over his shoulder.

"This isn't for me. This is for her."

Eshiel smiled. He met Keles's gaze, and his heart stirred warmly in his chest when she smiled back.

"Why, of course," he said. "I would do anything for the Light of Vallessau."

CHAPTER 51

VAGRANT

Are you sure?"

Together, Keles and Cyrus observed the crowd from their hidden perch in a nearby dock house that overlooked the pier. In the distance, the last of the boats burned. For once, that image did not scar Cyrus. These boats, these fires, they were just. They were necessary.

Cyrus turned to Keles. She had come at his request. This whole plan of his was reckless, a gamble, perhaps truly insane. He glanced at the sack she carried, stifled a mad laugh.

"Yes," he said. "I'm sure."

Over two hundred people gathered to watch the fires or mill about with friends. Eshiel thrice-born had summoned them, the man true to his word. Cyrus smiled. He had never anticipated calling him an ally, but perhaps such unconventional plans would be what saved his island.

The people had come at Eshiel's insistence to watch the fires, but that was merely the pretense. They had been truly summoned for a coronation.

"Stay hidden until I call for you." He pulled his mask over his face and raised his hood. "We must make this perfect."

Crowned and with blades drawn, he stepped out onto the balcony. The Vagrant took over completely, and Cyrus's confidence grew. He felt he could take on the entire Everlorn Empire and win. The

God-Incarnate might be on his way to Thanet, but his time would end, and mark a new beginning with Sinshei vin Lucavi. And once Sinshei left, and the island was relinquished, Cyrus was determined a new Thanet could be built in its place. One ruled by a proper name, and who remembered the true gods.

"People of Thanet!" he bellowed. As expected, his voice was deeper when spoken from behind the mask, rumbling and threatening. "Hear me!"

The crowd turned from the fires. Cyrus's grin matched that of his mask. All his nervousness and clumsy speeches during Thorda's little political meetings were from a distant age. Despite the circumstances of its birth, and the grim nature of its purpose, Cyrus was comfortable as the Vagrant. His identity hidden, he could be anyone, and anything. Someone not himself. Someone stronger, braver, and who could lead an island against an empire.

But he would not do so alone. And he would no longer abide by Thorda's plans.

"You know me," he said, the crowd silent, their attention rapt. A few had applauded or cheered at his appearance, but not many. "Some of you even wear my face. I am Thanet's protector. I am her guardian. I am her blade. With my bloodshed, I would fulfill the task the Lythan family failed. And they did fail. They failed, for they occupied a seat that should never have been theirs."

This was it. Cyrus knew it should worry him, or at least give him second thoughts. By the night's end, his proclamation would spread throughout Vallessau, and by the end of the week, to the farthest corners of Thanet. He was casting aside his own family's legacy. He was surrendering his throne. Yet he felt nothing. No loss. No fear. He remembered the savage glee Magus of Eldrid had shown in sharing the truth, and he vowed to never let such a barb be wielded against him ever again.

"The Lythan family came here as conquerors," Cyrus continued, projecting his voice louder to counter the growing murmur of fear, denial, and confusion. "They came with swords and spears, and they slaughtered the family appointed to rule by our island's gods. Dagon was no vile serpent. He was your protector! He was the divine brother to Lycaena, and he fought against the Lythan family. For such crimes, he was executed, his family ousted, and his servants put to the sword."

Cyrus hesitated. This would be a lot, a total upending of their understanding of the gods. Yet the God-Incarnate had already shattered it once. Accepting the new, the truth, would come easier now. And among that crowd, there would be those who had heard the rumors. Those who grew up with the stories of grandparents and great-grandparents, of how the priests and paladins of Endarius twisted the past. Stories Cyrus never heard in his castle as the privileged child and heir to the throne the Lion stole for him.

"Yet I know the truth!" he bellowed. No hesitation. No chance for doubt to spread. He lifted his swords high. The light of distant fires flickered across his blades and cast a shadow upon his grinning skull. Thanet's specter of death, pure in purpose in a way no royal family had been before. They would trust him, by the end.

"The Orani family was your anointed royalty, and it is to the Orani family I bow my head. Let the throne be theirs, true-born Thanese, not invaders come from Gadir. It is to them I swear my allegiance. To Thanet's queen, I kneel. I am the silent blade, and from the shadows I shall watch, and I shall protect."

He spun and dropped to one knee.

"Keles Orani, behold your people!"

It was out of his hands now. At least half the crowd was furious. So many of the rumors Thorda had spread were of the Vagrant Prince, of the vanished and presumed dead Cyrus returning to claim his throne. Yet the Vagrant now offered up that throne. They were confused. No doubt some felt deceived. It would pass, though. Cyrus held faith.

Keles stepped onto the balcony. The woman looked beautiful and regal in her dark armor, her vibrant cloak, and her glittering mask covering the lower half of her face. She walked with weapons sheathed, her shield on her back, and the sack swinging loosely at her side. She was no stranger to crowds, and as her name spread, the recognition took hold.

The Light of Vallessau, they remembered, they whispered. Cyrus lowered his head in subservience. Within his breast, the dark voice of the Vagrant dared protest.

This is a mistake.

Cyrus chuckled.

"No," he whispered. "It is not."

Keles stood at the edge of the balcony. Cyrus peered up at her. He saw the way her hands shook and how her weight shifted from foot to foot. She was nervous, but no one would see it. No one would know. The woman pulled back her shoulders, thrust forward her chest, and projected her voice as if seeking all the city to hear her words.

"Queen, the Vagrant would call me," she began. "But I shall accept no such title while pretenders sit upon our throne. I am Keles Lyon Orani, and for centuries my family has served our island, even when it was as prisoners. I inherit a legacy of servitude, and I shall not forget it, nor abandon it, in the future to come."

She pointed to the wreckage of the imperial ships.

"Boats burn, but more sail in their wake. We must stand ready. We must hold faith. Let the empire look upon Thanet and see a thorn it will never pull from its side. Let it see a spear that shall remain embedded until the day it relinquishes its hold and flees from our shores. We feel a hint of victory on the wind, but I would summon us a storm."

Cyrus's heart swelled with pride. For all of Thorda's talk about turning the Vagrant into a symbol, he had done a poor job preparing Cyrus for the emotional side of things. The speech, the mannerisms, the command of an audience. His master hoped that blood and slaughter would make up for his deficiencies. Once Cyrus was a god, all else would follow. Yet Keles took up the role with ease, and she could rally the people without bloodshed.

He glanced at the sack Keles carried.

All right, *some* bloodshed.

"Many of you saw me at my lowest," Keles said after a pause to let the murmurs in the crowd cease. "Dragged from prison, to forsake my goddess and pledge allegiance to the God-Incarnate. Know then that I understand your despair. Know that I have walked the darkest road, have felt that doubt, and believed for a time that no hope yet remained for our home."

Keles shook her head, and she gestured to Cyrus.

"But though I doubted, hope remained. The empire may call our island conquered, but I call them fools. Our war yet rages. Our people yet fight. I make you no promises. I offer no grandiose claims. Let the truth uphold my claim. Let my actions speak with power no words may match. Look upon me, Thanet, and know my soul."

Keles reached into the sack and withdrew the severed head of Heir-Incarnate Galvanis vin Lucavi.

"A free Thanet!" she cried. "That is my purpose, and by my faith, and my sword, I shall make that dream true."

Keles threw the head to the crowd. Before it even landed, the hearts of the people were hers. The burning boats and the chaos at the castle hinted at something drastic, but few would dare believe such a victory possible. Not once, in three thousand years, had the Heir-Incarnate been killed in battle.

Until he was.

"Go to them," Cyrus told her.

Keles climbed down the scaffolding. People mobbed her, asking questions about Dagon, about the Orani, and about how she killed Galvanis. Some wanted to see how she had changed and grown since they knew her as the Light of Vallessau. Others wished to touch her armor or offer their allegiance. As a hero of the old regime, anointed by the Vagrant, and vindicated by the Heir-Incarnate's head, she walked with power and authority no crown could ever convey.

Cyrus turned to leave, but the way was blocked. Thorda Ahlai waited for him, his thick robe tied tightly at his waist with a crimson sash, his arms crossed over his chest, his face as much a mask as Cyrus's grinning skull.

"You've been making plans," he said.

"I cannot help but be a troublemaker. I suspect this time you will appreciate the results."

Thorda joined him in overlooking the crowd.

"And what is your plan?" he asked.

"I would have Keles become what you first promised me. She can be the symbol that gives people hope. She can be the name and face that others cling to in their despair. And if Sinshei keeps her word, and the empire retreats, they will believe Keles responsible. The throne will be hers to take, peaceful and bloodless in its transition."

Thorda's head tilted, and he scratched at his chin. He was thinking over the news, digesting it, seeing potential futures in a way Cyrus would never understand.

"You put much faith in a priestess of the Uplifted Church, a daughter of Lucavi, she who would become god-empress. There are many reasons for Sinshei to withdraw her offer. What then, Cyrus?"

"Then I suppose it will be good I still have my swords, and with me, a figurehead to rally Thanet around in a war of independence. In tandem, we shall be vastly more effective than I ever was alone. Keles was no stranger to your political games. I, however, still barely know how to dance."

Thorda laughed. He actually laughed, and it hurt Cyrus how much he wished for the old man to accept his plan.

"Clever," he said. "But what of you? What role do you now play?"

"Will I continue being the Vagrant, do you mean?"

The older man shrugged. "I thought my question clear enough."

Cyrus glanced over his shoulder, to the murmur of the crowd. He sank into memory, of blood and fire given form.

"I've seen the gods that death, sacrifice, and hate would create. I have no intention of becoming one. What I am now, it is enough. I need not become something further. Victory is within our grasp. We need only take it. You said godhood cannot be cast aside so easily, and in that, I believe you. Once the Vagrant Prince took the throne, he would have forever been linked and deified. But Keles?"

Cyrus shook his head.

"She can become the ruler the people need. My contributions will fade, and belief in me along with them. This mask shall not be mine forever, Thorda. It is a temporary necessity, and nothing more."

Thorda hardly appeared convinced, but he did not argue the point.

"And so to Thanet's throne we appoint one from the bloodline Dagon anointed, she who is also a paladin of Lycaena. Two of the island's gods will be honored, but what of the third? I cannot imagine Endarius shall be pleased."

Cyrus removed his mask and wiped at his forehead with his sleeve.

"If the Lion wants any followers to remember him, he better learn to accept it. The God-Incarnate would leave him with nothing. At least I give him a chance to remain one of three."

They fell silent, the pair watching Keles move through the crowd. A true paladin, she walked tall, her words carefully chosen, and she prayed with many who came seeking affirmation. Near the back, a trio of men began to sing, and it was a song Cyrus did not recognize, involving a man lost at sea.

"Faith returned, that which was lost found amid joy and hope," Thorda said. He swallowed, and a glint in his eye betrayed emotion Cyrus was surprised to discover. "I crave moments like these, but they are few and far between. The Uplifted Church is thorough, so thorough. But if it can happen here, it can happen elsewhere. Forgotten and slain gods might walk Gadir once more. Hidden prayer books brought out to the light. Old songs sung anew. Worship, and love, given by the people to the gods who cherished and nurtured them in their earliest days. How I hoped. How I dreamed."

Victory was not here, not yet, but it was so very close. They both sensed it, as did the crowd. The Vagrant was responsible for much of it. Without Master Ahlai's plans and betrayals, this fate would have eluded them. Knowing that, and accepting it, were still two very different things. He felt the space between him and Thorda closing, and his hurt at the betrayal easing away, but not completely.

"You are not forgiven," he said softly.

Thorda grabbed the railing and leaned forward.

"I never sought forgiveness."

The song grew louder, and when the first ended, one much more familiar to Cyrus began, this one proclaiming the kindness and love of the Butterfly goddess. Cyrus tapped his foot and smiled. It was hard to believe that mere hours ago, they had considered their rebellion on its final legs.

"Do not let the enthusiasm of the few here cloud your mind," Thorda said, and it seemed he was determined to banish Cyrus's confidence. The older man gestured to the celebration. "Those here came to watch the fire with bloodlust in their hearts, and the gift Keles offered them is all they needed to accept her claims. Others will not be so easily won over, particularly those who hold faith in the Lion. The Lythan family was beloved by many, and they represent a time before the empire arrived. How will you convince people to cast aside their beliefs and accept the Orani? Or that the Sapphire Serpent is no vile trickster but instead a god of the salt and sea?"

Fair questions, but Cyrus's conviction was absolute.

"It doesn't matter the difficulty, Thorda. This is the way it must be. I will not be both god and king. Everlorn is proof enough of that folly. If I must be the murderer, then let Keles ascend to a throne, the fallen hero now standing tall, the broken Light of Vallessau shining brightly once more." Cyrus tried to hold back the smugness growing in his voice. "As for convincing the people about the Serpent, thankfully we count a god-whisperer among our ranks. Mari can give voice to Dagon and speak truth to the people of the events of the past."

"Endarius will not be pleased. He may even cast my daughter aside for what he views as a betrayal. Will Mari even agree to such an idea?"

There was no hiding it anymore. Cyrus's grin stretched ear to ear.

"Where do you think your daughter is right now?"

Thorda tilted his head slightly to one side, his left eyebrow raising, and then he let out a little grunt of a laugh.

"Clever," he said. "Most clever."

CHAPTER 52

MARI

Mari knelt in the sand, the collection of artifacts clutched tightly in her fingers. Waves crashed along the shore, the foamy water breaking across her knees and soaking her legs and dress.

"I'm not so certain this will work like Cyrus hopes," Stasia said. Her sister lurked farther back on the shore, so only the occasional wave would reach her boots. Her arms were crossed, her hands resting on the handles of her axes. Was she afraid, or was that merely habit? Mari wasn't sure. She hoped it was the latter.

"There's not much to be certain of here on Thanet," Mari said. She focused her attention on the artifacts. They were little things, a shell painted blue, a bracelet with fish scales shaped into a diamond, and the largest of them, the sapphire necklace Keles had offered when Cyrus explained his plan. They were rough and sharp in her fingers, but she endured the sting. Better to focus on that pain than her own doubts.

Stasia was not the only one unhappy with the plan to summon Dagon.

You would treat with the foul serpent? Endarius growled deep in the recesses of her mind.

It was you who invaded his shores, Mari growled right back. *Now you would condemn him?*

There is no room within your mortal shell for the both of us. Dishonor me at your own peril, human.

Mari was attempting to aid the bloodline Endarius himself had over-thrown upon his arrival in Thanet, but her mind was set. Perhaps this might even teach the god a bit of humility; the stars knew he needed it. Even death had not humbled him.

"Do you have anything beyond a name?" Stasia asked from afar. Silence had stretched on between them, and it seemed to make her uncomfortable. "Maybe paintings, or a song?"

"A name and these objects of worship," Mari said. "They will be enough."

She could feel the faith flowing off them, especially the necklace. Desperate people had clutched these gemstones amid even more desperate prayers. The empire's invasion, and the death of Endarius and Lycaena, had only heightened their need for a return of the old. Dagon would save them, they no doubt believed, just as Lahareed had thought Kasthan the Falcon Reaper would save them, or Anyx would Aethenwald.

"Have I missed the fun?" a new voice asked. Mari turned her attention from the starlit ocean. Clarissa walked the footpath to the shore, her smile genuine but her hurried steps and jittery movements revealing her worry.

"It's only starting now you're here," Stasia said, and she swept her wife up into her arms for a kiss. *Her wife*, Mari emphasized in her own mind. How naturally the change took place. But of course, the pair had been together for years. They had a new word to define who they were together, but their emotions and bond had not changed.

Mari turned her attention back to the sea, and she tried not to feel bitter. Again and again, she whispered gods. Again and again, she comforted those in need. She thought of Rihim dying, and that final moment of clarity in his fading eyes as he saw the visage of his beloved Amees. Would anyone be there for her when that time came? Would anyone stroke her face, or clutch her hand, or tell her stories of a forgotten past as an unknown future awaited her come passage into the hereafter?

This self-pity is unbecoming of you.

Mari bared her teeth.

Get out of my head, Lion. I doubt you will enjoy sharing it with Dagon this night.

The presence left her. Not permanently. Nothing like when a god faded and broke its intimate connection with her. This was more of a stepping aside, of taking the lingering essence of faith and worship and lurking nearby. It was how most gods she communed with preferred to remain, embodying her heart and mind only when blood must be shed.

A wave splashed along the sand, and she dipped the artifacts low so the surf washed over them. Mari supposed Thanet's God of the Sea would approve of the connection. Or maybe she just liked the feeling of water over her hands. It was a texture to focus on, while Stasia and Clarissa whispered to each other. Maybe such a connection wasn't yet lost to her. She remembered Arn bending down to kiss her, and heat flushed her cheeks at the way he had stammered and blushed. The big man was an oaf, true, but he could be amusing sometimes…

Stalling. She was stalling. Mari sat up and closed her eyes. Instead of viewing the starlit horizon, she pictured it in her mind. The gentle motion of the waves. The water's surface, stretching on and on for thousands of miles. Let the sea wash over her. Let it take her, if it must. She would commune with the long-dead Sapphire Serpent and, in her heart, offer true and earnest prayer.

"Dagon," she whispered. "Do you hear me?"

This was not meant to be like her deep sharing with Endarius, instead akin to her brief whispering for Amees, but even this lesser goal worried her. Dagon had been dead for so long, and she had argued as much to Cyrus when he proposed the plan. Yet his counterargument had been simple and irrefutable.

Dagon gave his blessing to Keles. If he is strong enough to do that for her, then he is strong enough to speak with you.

It was true. It had to be. Keles's amulet turned cold in her hands, so cold it started to burn her skin. That was an answer in and of itself, and she endured the pain. So Dagon was listening. His objects of worship were reacting. Mari tightened her focus. The distant sea became a single blue line in her mind, and it vibrated within her thoughts.

"Dagon, let me hear you. Let me see you."

Something changed. She sensed it in the air. She felt it in the absence of waves along the beach, as if the sea itself recoiled from her. The deep, sparkling blue grew stronger in her mind. It went beyond a shade of color and became something more. An essence, a presence, a wind of faith and belief and hope and fear. Her eyes were closed, but she could see it, see it so clearly, like clouds across the entire island.

"Hear my prayer. Hear it, and answer. I would speak, if you are willing."

Faith in Dagon was so much stronger than she'd ever anticipated, especially in regions far away from Vallessau. That lingering belief, powerful in spirit and yet denied a physical form, should have rushed down into her. It should have gathered within her breast, coalescing, dragging her into the realm of the spiritual so she might speak with the god. Dozens of times, she had performed this feat. Dozens of times, sometimes embraced, sometimes refused, but the pull always worked the same.

Not this time.

Mari opened her eyes. Her limp fingers dropped the artifacts.

"I don't understand," she whispered.

Stasia noticed the change, and she came hurrying over.

"What happened?" she asked. "Did you speak with Dagon?"

"No," Mari said. She grimaced at the pain in her knees as she stood. Sand clung to her dress, and she half-heartedly wiped at it. Stasia's shoulders sagged, but she put on a brave smile.

"It's all right," her sister said. "This is hardly the first time a god's told you no on the first try. However stubborn he might be, you're even more stubborn."

Mari shook her head. As the moment of prayer receded, and the vision of blue light faded, she better understood *what* had happened, but not *why*.

"Dagon didn't reject me," she said. "He couldn't have answered even if he wished."

Clarissa followed a half step behind Stasia, and the pair linked hands.

"So Dagon is gone completely?" the smaller woman asked. "Too weak to whisper?"

Stasia must have explained the plan while they watched. Mari again shook her head. Little bubbles of laughter drifted up from her belly. She couldn't help it. They were so wrong it bordered on hilarity. Meanwhile the lurking presence of the Lion seethed with absolute fury, and she feared what he might do the next time they spoke.

"You don't understand," she said. "Dagon is not weak, or rejecting me, or anything of the sort. I can't whisper him because *he's not dead*."

Stasia rocked in the sand as if punched in the gut. Her mouth dropped open, and she glanced around the island in bewilderment. It shouldn't have been so funny, but Mari laughed harder. It was too absurd. Too perfectly mirroring her own confusion. Stasia lifted her arms, and she expressed her bafflement with a burst of deserved anger.

"If Dagon is alive, then where the fuck is he?"

CHAPTER 53

SOMA

Together, Soma and Sinshei walked the battlements high atop Vallessau's castle and looked out upon the troublesome city. They had been informed of the destruction at the harbor, but it wasn't until now that they saw it for themselves. The lingering flames were enough to detect floating wreckage in the moonlight.

"It truly is a black eye upon the face of the empire," Soma said. "Boats burned, lords killed, imperials dropping left and right like swatted flies. If the Vagrant did not accept your alliance, who knows what fate awaited you as well?"

"Would you imply I am in danger?" Sinshei asked. "I thought myself safe under your protection."

"I suspect the Heir-Incarnate thought himself equally safe, Anointed One."

"Then do not forget it was my blades that took his life, not the Vagrant's or the Penitent's."

Soma held no desire to argue the point. He took mild amusement in needling the woman and in reminding her of how precarious her actual position and authority were. Wind blew against them, warm from the sea. Soma brushed the waist-high wall of the rampart with his hand. Unlike the rest of Thanet, the castle was built solely in the style of the Mirli castles on Gadir, which in turn were influenced by its own neighboring nations. Giant stone castles, to hold off armies and siege weaponry never deployed upon the island.

Hideous, to Soma's eyes, though he suspected it felt like home to Sinshei.

"Do you believe the Vagrant trustworthy?" he asked. "If he lets matters transpire as they must, it will make the transition easier. I suspect, should he discover the truth of the required sacrifice, that will not be the case."

"Ignorance is our ally," Sinshei said.

"Still, it's impressively cold, even for you, promising Keles a crown and a throne to rule an island of corpses."

"And so we keep her in ignorance as well. Nothing matters once I claim my rightful place." She gestured to the wreckage of the five imperial warships. A smile graced her lips. "Never did I imagine how complete Galvanis's failure would be. How could my father ever doubt his incompetence now?"

"By casting the blame on you instead of your brother's corpse," Soma said. He crossed his arms and leaned against the side of the rampart. "If he considers Thanet your grand failure instead of Magus's or Galvanis's, what then?"

"He won't," Sinshei said, much harsher than she intended. She paused a moment to gather herself. "Worry not on this, for I will be the only potential heir upon this island, with months of travel separating us from the rest of my brothers and sisters. Lucavi will have no choice but to grant me his blessing come the ceremony."

Soma drummed his armored fingers against the stone.

"You speak with such confidence in the decisions gods will make. What if you are wrong? What if your father refuses to give you your rightful gift?"

Thanet's Anointed turned her back to the shore and marched for the door leading back into the castle.

"Your family is famous for killing gods," she said, brave enough to suggest so much when they were high up and with only the wind as witness. "Would you be willing to kill another if it meant becoming one of the most powerful men alive?"

Soma smirked, and he did not follow her inside.

"I thought you'd never ask."

The door shut. Alone on the rampart, Soma glanced about to make sure no bothersome eyes watched from the nearby windows, and then he leaped dozens of feet into the air. He landed lightly atop the castle's highest spire and balanced upon the tip like a dancer, his weight perfectly balanced as he gazed out across the Crystal Sea.

Soma removed his helmet and held it against his hip. The wind teased his long hair, and he closed his eyes. As good as it felt, it wasn't enough. It was still blocked, false, and so he cast the falseness aside.

Human flesh peeled away. Dirty-blond hair turned bone white. Soma stood to his full height, tilted his head, and let the moonlight fall upon his sapphire scales. At the next gust of sea breeze, he sighed deeply. There it was, the cleansing softness, the flutter of it across his cheeks, a promise of the cherishing waves that cradled Thanet. How he had missed it during his exile.

"You never appreciated the beauty of what you stole," he whispered to the night. "You wanted power, you wanted to rule, and so you took it. Is that not the way of the Lion? Is that not the way of all of Gadir?"

A smile crossed his face, pulling at his scales to reveal his teeth, sharp and numerous like those of a shark. Oh, how sublime his pleasure in burying his spear into Endarius's eye upon returning to the island. Nothing could compare. Soma had wondered, right at the end, if the god would recognize him. If he would appreciate the irony, the sweet and beautiful *justice*, of dying on that spear.

Soma pulled the spear from his back and twirled it before him. It was the same spear that had pinned him to the barge they burned his physical body upon. It was this spear that had held him still as the flames kissed his scales, the wood collapsed, and his corpse fell deep into the sea. The Lion had thought him dead, and in many ways, he had been correct. Soma's heart had ruptured. His blood had spilled along the sands.

But it was the water that first birthed him. It was the water that gave him life. His followers had kept their faith and cried out their prayers amid their grief. Years and years passed, slow and steady as the waves. By the time Soma recovered, he found his island conquered and the name "Dagon" now a curse.

And so he left for a land of gods and goddesses foreign to him, a place called Gadir by those who lived upon its endless miles of grasslands, mountains, forests, and deserts. A world so unlike Thanet, at least when it came to the animals and geography. The people, though? Oh, the people were the same. Fickle. Scared. Bowing in fear before their chosen gods, gods that dwindled in number as the God-Incarnate claimed them all.

"So long was my exile," he whispered. "But at last I am home."

Soma expanded his thoughts to the sea. His influence could only reach so far, but the water surrounding the island remained his obedient servant. It was his skin, his body, his mind. He sensed the creatures below, the fish, the crab, and the squid. Most importantly of all, he felt the slice of warships across its surface.

Despite the vast distance, Soma could see the burning golden aura of the one who commanded the largest ship. The God-Incarnate of the Everlorn Empire. The one ultimately responsible for Thanet's suffering, and for Endarius's arrival. A blight upon the mortal realm. The greatest living insult to the divine. A travesty. A crimson joke.

"Four hundred years of planning, of plotting, of waiting." He clipped the spear to his back. He cast his face once more in human flesh. "Soon come to an end."

The story continues in...

BOOK THREE OF THE VAGRANT GODS

Coming in 2024!

A NOTE FROM THE AUTHOR

Ah, so I can finally chat about what I've wanted to chat about forever. But just in case, to you people with inexplicably horrible morals who read these notes *before* the rest of the novel, I beseech you to leave now. With these notes at the end, I always try to peel back the curtain and provide a glimpse into my writing process, and that's what I'm doing once more. We're talking spoilers here. Once you're finished, my note and I will be waiting for you, I promise. So we good? Yeah? All right.

So while plotting out the bones of what would become the Vagrant Gods, I read *Velocity Weapon* by Megan E. O'Keefe. To those of you who haven't read it, there are two very big twists in it that reshape your entire understanding of the story and the events taking place. I loved it. The construction, it was so fun, so perfectly hidden in plain sight, I was inspired. It led me to wonder...could I do something like that? Could I embed a twist that deeply into the narrative? I already had Thorda training Cyrus to eventually betray him, but could I do bigger? Better? So I began evaluating the plotline, the events, and tried to find where I could add layers to it. This led to the history of Cyrus's family and how the Lythan family overthrew the Orani family upon their arrival hundreds of years ago.

Not bad, but I wasn't satisfied. All the twists would be done by the first novel. They only changed the perception of events that happened hundreds of years ago. Where is the immediate effect?

And so I did what I always do when I'm stuck on something: I called my friend Rob and rambled on the phone with him for an hour or so. I told him the basic ideas, of the Lythan family, the Orani, etc. This led to seeds of Keles's new role, which was nice. But in adding in the Orani, I also introduced an intriguing idea. When the Lythan family invaded, surely Lycaena reacted, right? Why didn't she fight back? Or what if... what if Lycaena didn't, but another god did? A god who stood by the Orani family. And so Dagon came to be. I started working through the plot, pondering ideas of how to seed Dagon's history, people who still worship him in secret, maybe even a moment when Mari whispers him and we learn more of the past. Interesting, interesting, but then somewhere in that phone call, the idea hit me:

What if Dagon is still alive?

Now, that's intriguing, but that left a single question. If Dagon was alive, where had he been all this time? Why not appear when Thanet was invaded? I can't remember for certain, but I believe Rob suggested a simple answer: He wasn't there. And that's when I knew.

Soma already existed in my rough outline at the time, unchanged in how he's portrayed at the start of *The Bladed Faith*. He was meant to be a fun wild-card character working for Sinshei, someone to do her dirty work and likely be involved in a climactic battle with one of the main characters when I needed one. But what if...what if...and then I realized. Soma would be Dagon in disguise. Soma would be the one to kill Endarius in the very first chapter, avenging a crime committed against him four hundred years ago, before there was even a whisper of his very existence.

And from that moment on, every single Soma chapter was a delight to write. I've never done quite so long a mystery before, and walking that tightrope of offering clues (the blue scales underneath his skin when Stasia wounds his face, the promise to a dying Magus that he'd topple the empire, his emotional reaction to Keles unknowingly pledging servitude to him) without giving too much away was a difficult but utterly enjoyable one. I hope I did all right. If not, please know the effort was there!

As for what Soma/Dagon has been doing on the mainland, why he hid himself as a paragon, what his plan is with Sinshei... well, that's for book three. I hope you're as excited for it as I am.

All right, time for a quick wrap-up of thank-yous. Thank you to Brit, for as always being the best editor one could hope for. Thank you to Lauren and the rest of the art department at Orbit for giving me top-tier covers most authors can only dream of. Thank you to Angela for guiding me through all the various publicity aspects for *The Bladed Faith*'s launch. Thanks, Newt, for the sensitivity read as well as helping finally name Eshiel. Thank you, Cherae, for guiding me through Rayan's development. Thanks, Rob, for enduring my way, way too long phone calls.

And last but never least, thank you, dear reader. You've once again stepped into my world and spent time with my characters, entrusting me to keep you entertained. I hope I did you well.

David Dalglish
March 30, 2022

extras

orbit

extras

meet the author

Michele Coleman

DAVID DALGLISH currently lives in Myrtle Beach with his wife, Samantha, and daughters, Morgan, Katherine, and Alyssa. He graduated from Missouri Southern State University in 2006 with a degree in mathematics and currently spends his free time tanking dungeons for his wife and daughter in *Final Fantasy XIV*.

Find out more about David Dalglish and other Orbit authors by registering for the free monthly newsletter at orbitbooks.net.

if you enjoyed
THE SAPPHIRE ALTAR

look out for

VAGRANT GODS: BOOK THREE

by

David Dalglish

The adventure continues in the third novel of USA Today
bestselling author David Dalglish's new epic fantasy trilogy....

DARIO

Dario knelt beside his bed in his quiet little room, his head bowed in prayer. It was his twelfth hour doing so. No food. No drink. No sleep. His bladder ached, and he smelled of sweat, but this was not his first time enduring such a trial. He had done similarly when his brother vanished in the wake of Vulnae's fall. In the ruins of the captured castle, before the vanquished throne, Dario had bowed with his hands resting on the empty throne's cushion and pleaded for his brother's safety. He had prayed for guidance and wisdom for the missing Arn Bastell, that he might remain upon the true path despite the fire, ash, and bones that littered the city. Conquest was hell, but the rewards were great, and the dark deeds necessary.

That first time, Dario had felt the presence of Lucavi descend upon him and speak words of comfort and wisdom to his heart and mind.

You are beloved, and I am with you always, honored son. Fear not the path your brother walks. Mind your own heart, and walk with my truth proudly cherished. My eye is ever upon the lost.

Dario had bathed the throne's cushion with his tears. The relief had overwhelmed him. Wherever Arn went, whatever doubts he felt, they would be forgiven by his god upon his return. A place of honor would be waiting for him come the final war in the eternal lands beyond.

"Please," Dario whispered all these years later. The hours broke his resolve. The silence amid his room stabbed him incessantly. "You gave me succor once, in the shadow of Onleda's conquest. Why will you not comfort me now?"

His god walked the lands of this island, occupied this very same castle, and yet suddenly Dario could hear him no longer. What did it mean? About the God-Incarnate? About himself?

Two rapid knocks on his door. Dario startled to his feet. Little jolts of pain arced through the muscles of his back at the sudden movement. He was naked from the waist up and wore only a simple pair of trousers normally reserved for underneath his armor. He ignored his desire to dress. Those knocks…Could it be? Had Lucavi himself come after hearing the earnestness of Dario's prayers? Had this been a test, one finally decided?

"Come in," he said.

It was not Lucavi, but instead his daughter, Sinshei, looking as beautiful as ever in her crimson dress. Her bound hair decorated with gold lace shimmered behind her like a cloak. She stepped inside and closed the door. Dario tried to hide his disappointment. He suspected he failed.

"How goes your hand?" Sinshei said. If she cared for his lack of clothes, she showed no outward sign.

"Healing," he said. He flexed the fingers of his bandaged hand. Its pain had been a thorn in his mind for the entirety of his prayers. The wound was a direct result of a clash between him and his heretical brother. They had directly opposed each other, fist against fist, strength against strength. The ultimate test of their convictions, Dario's faith put to proof against his brother's doubt and cowardice.

It had been Dario's hand that faltered, his bones that surrendered into pieces.

"Let me see."

Sinshei unwrapped the thin cloth. While the bruises and marks from his humiliating beating had faded from his arms and chest, the same could not be said for his hand. His skin was puffy and swollen. Deep purple bruises marked his knuckles and joints where the bones had broken. Dario had popped them back into place himself. The innate gifts of a paragon should have healed them within a night or two. That they hadn't was…troubling.

"It could be better," Sinshei said after a moment. Her dainty fingers were dwarfed by his meaty own as she gently poked and prodded. "But it could also be worse."

She rewrapped his hand, apparently satisfied with her investigation. Dario stood there awkwardly as he let her. He shouldn't be so curt with her. What if Lucavi had sent her as proxy in answer to his prayers?

"Why have you come?" he asked when she finished. "I doubt Thanet's Anointed would bother checking on a lone paragon's wounds without some additional reason."

Sinshei stepped away, and her violet eyes drilled into him. Dario knew little of the woman, but what few times he'd met her had left him deeply unimpressed. Her station and birth had insulated her from much of the world. When she prayed for others, it rang hollow. When she spoke to Thanet's people of the troubles her divine father would solve, there was no understanding there, only regurgitation. Even Arn's prayers during their training had sounded more genuine.

"Signifer Weiss has been gathering testimony from all involved in the incident that led to Galvanis's death," she said. The "incident" was the planned ambush by Cyrus Lythan and his allies, with Dario's brother as the bait. The Heir-Incarnate had vastly underestimated the Vagrant's strength, and many paragons, as well as Galvanis himself, had paid the ultimate price.

"Aye, I know," Dario said. "I've spoken with him."

"Indeed, you told him of your fight and your injury," Sinshei said. She crossed her arms. "And yet others describe what you neglected to mention. You told Weiss you fled your brother after sustaining your injuries. Others, though, tell a different tale. You did not flee Arn."

She stepped closer.

"No, he let you live. I would like to know why."

Dario looked away. Something about her gaze unnerved him. It was too curious. Too . . . hungry.

"You would question my younger brother's sentimentality? He did not have it in his heart to kill me."

"He has killed so many others. Why would he spare you? You interrogated him while we held him prisoner. Perhaps your words found a place in his heart?"

Dario couldn't help it. He laughed.

"No," he said, turning back toward her. He lifted his injured hand. "No, it was quite the opposite. His faith, in whatever it may be, has not wavered. My foolish brother instead thought he saw hope in me, that I might come to join him in his heresy. That is why he let me live."

He thought his laughter and smirk would show how ludicrous a thought that was. The last thing he wanted was the attention of a member of the church, let alone Thanet's Anointed One. That she was Lucavi's daughter made it only worse. So he stood tall and exuded every bit of the bravado and confidence that had carried him through his training in the Bloodstone to become one of Eldrid's most cherished paragons.

Sinshei stepped closer. Her hand rested against the side of his face, an act of love to some, but to Dario, an unwanted connection. That gaze, it saw too much. Perhaps she was not so oblivious as he first thought.

"You fear he is right, and that terrifies you."

"That's absurd."

"Is it? The bruises on your hand say otherwise."

He wanted her hand gone. He wanted *her* gone. Twelve hours of prayer, and this was his reward? The touch of her fingers was like ice to his warm flesh.

"Arn has nothing to offer," Dario said, deciding he must reject these doubts all the clearer. Showing weakness to the daughter of the God-Incarnate was not acceptable. "He speaks of other gods, of sins and deaths, and of the cost of our campaign across Gadir. They are childish protests, no more than that. There is no substance, only doubts and questions. He would tear down the pillars and replace them with mystery, and that, I cannot abide."

Sinshei's hand retreated.

"And yet you still wonder. Answer me, paragon, and answer true. Do you believe Lucavi's conquests to be justified?"

Damn this woman. Would she not just accept his answer? He stepped closer, daring to use his height and size to intimidate her.

"I have walked fields of battle strewn with corpses numbering in the tens of thousands," he said. "If I was one to doubt, I would have already broken. My faith is strong. My heart is true. Question me no more, Anointed One."

In response, the diminutive woman reached, as quick as a viper. Her fingers closed around his injured hand and squeezed. Pain shot through him as fingernails dug into his swollen skin. He clenched his jaw but dared not resist. To do so would show weakness.

"I question because I see the truth within you," she said. "But I know why doubt lingers within your heart. Your brother's actions, they have awakened questions, but instead of answering them, you deny them. You bury them deep. Why, Dario? If you were unafraid of the answers, why pretend them unworthy of your time? If you were so confident in Lucavi's truth, why not pit it against the lies spoken to you...unless you fear Arn spoke no lies. Unless you believe the campaigns you have waged, the bodies you have walked over, and the cities you have laid low were not worth the final reward."

She squeezed harder, with strength no one of that size should possess. It felt like his broken bones were grinding together.

"What if there is wisdom there, to be unearthed like buried gold?" she continued. "I would have it, paragon, and I would share it with you if you are so brave. Are you brave enough? Strong enough?"

These were not the words of an Anointed. No daughter of the God-Incarnate should speak so poorly of her father's campaigns of conquest and valor. He pushed his damn brother out of his thoughts and finally turned his full attention to her. What game was Sinshei playing at?

"What is it you wish of me?" he asked.

"Walk about Vallessau. See the fruits of my father's labor. When you have taken its full measure, come to me and give me your honest answer."

Some strange game was afoot, and he did not yet know the rules or the players. Best to play along until he knew, and truth be told, a walk outside the castle was alluring after twelve hours of prayer locked in his room. He dipped his head to her.

"So be it."

～

Dario walked some nameless street of Vallessau. He'd briefly checked the market nearest to the castle, found its crowd tame and its wares unappealing. There were no clothes sewn with the clasped hands of the God-Incarnate. No strangers hummed hymns familiar to him since he was a babe. His next walk took him past the docks and their many boats. No painted hands on their prows, no names based on the famous paragons of the first age.

Ringing bells distracted him. To the nearest church, then. Dario followed the foot traffic that grew as families emerged from homes. Children looked dour, and their parents not much better. Though he wore no armor, his size alone revealed him as a paragon. Fearful eyes glanced his way. At the church, a squat little square building with smashed windows, a red-robed priest greeted arrivals. Dario waited at the edge, and when the sermon began, he leaned against the outside wall of the church, listening through one of those broken windows.

It started with a song brought from Gadir, one of simple praise to the God-Incarnate for his blessing and mercy. The voices that sang along were so weak and quiet they could not overcome the clapping and stomping of feet meant to accompany it.

"Ashraleon be praised," the priest said when the song finished, exuberant and excited as he invoked the name of the very first God-Incarnate. His energy was the antithesis of those gathered. Dario didn't even have to look inside to confirm it. The lack of faith billowed out the window like smoke.

His next destination was near the docks. His hours of praying had left his stomach empty, and he ate a gifted pie (not purchased—

no merchant or baker would ever be foolish enough to demand coin from a paragon). It was filled with freshly caught fish, chopped onions, and a leafy green he didn't quite recognize but appreciated the sweetness of. He went back for a second helping, pretended not to notice the baker's annoyance, and then continued on.

From there he walked the outer road along the northern edge of the city, steadily climbing higher into the portions of the city carved into the surrounding Emberfall Mountains. On a whim, he began greeting the men and women he passed.

"Lucavi watch over you both," he told one couple. Forced smiles were his only reward.

"Yeah, same to you," said a young man with holes in both knees of his trousers.

Paragons were the pinnacle of faith in the God-Incarnate, yet these people held no admiration, only fear. Yes, they were conquered people, true, but Everlorn's priests were made for hard work. Five years should have been enough time to plant seeds and see the first sprouting. Yet if he closed his eyes, Dario could almost see the aura of faith settled over the city of Vallessau. It was weak and pale. Not shining and gold, like that which had enveloped his skin as he preached his faith to his wayward brother, Arn.

Pale and missing. Not unlike when he prayed that morning.

He opened his eyes. The street had emptied of everyone but an older woman, her hair tied under a bonnet. Her limping gait was far too slow to avoid his approach.

"You," he said, grabbing her. "Do you attend the church's sermons?"

"I attend every time the bells ring," she said. Her gaze was wary; her hands, trembling.

"Every time the bells ring," he repeated. "Then list a single scripture from the Heathen's Coda. One scripture. That's all."

Her eyes widened, started to water.

"I . . . forgive me, my memory, it isn't, it is . . ."

He grabbed her shoulder. Her bones were thin. She felt like paper within his strong grasp.

"Something easier, then," he said. "Much easier. Every child on Gadir can answer true. What is the name of our first God-Incarnate, he to whom all our sermons open with in prayer?"

The woman had no answer, and they both knew it.

"Please," she said. "My leg, it hurts on these walks. I wish to go home, that is all."

"You wish to go? Then, go!"

He shoved the woman away. Her arms flailed, and she landed hard on the street. Dario stood there fuming. Awkward, unwelcome guilt bubbled in his chest. Why should he care if she was injured? Why care at all about these people's hollow, fake faith? They would soon all be dead, sacrificed to herald the arrival of the seventh age.

But then again, if death awaited, then wouldn't their faith be all that mattered? The preparation of the eternal soul, surely its purpose ranked above all. That was why preachers shouted from the corners. That was why they forced the people into churches. This faith, given to them in their final years, had to mean something. A place in the afterlife on the side of the righteous. The war that would follow in the heavens, conquest after conquest, as the heretical gods fell, their faithful were freed, and the eternal was finally united.

And yet, for the very first time, the idea of that warfare awaiting him did not excite Dario's imagination. It exhausted him. He endured the blood and the bodies on the promise of something more. But if that something more was endless blood and bodies...

There are true miracles that go far beyond destruction, fire, and the strength to win on the battlefield.

Arn had made that insistence when refusing to take Dario's life despite emerging victorious in their clash.

What would you offer me instead? Dario wondered. *What did you see that I did not?*

"Strange to hear a paragon so invested in the faith of the people," a woman said behind him. He turned about, a cutting remark on his tongue, yet he did not speak it. The beauty of the interloper shocked him. Though she wore a plain gray wrap, the cosmetics upon her face surely cost a small fortune here on this distant island. Her lips were painted red. The coppery color of her skin was highlighted with black along her cheeks and jawline. The orange powder upon her eyelids complemented the earthy brown of her eyes. Her hair was tied in interlaced knots, so intricate and numerous it would take multiple hours to finish. It was a style he hadn't seen since... well, since his homeland of Vashlee.

"While we may be the sword wielded in the God-Incarnate's hand, we of the Legion serve the same goal as the other Pillars," Dario said. "The salvation of all Gadir."

"Yet we are not upon Gadir, are we?"

Her voice was like a fine wine, deep and sultry. Though he towered over her, she showed not the slightest hint of fear. She looked like no Thanese woman he'd seen on this island. The plain garb she wore looked comical on one so beautiful and wealthy, for Dario knew that to link the many dozens and dozens of braids together on hair as long as hers was the work of at least two servants.

The woman walked past him as if he were no longer there. She knelt beside the elderly woman, who still wept in fear from Dario's outburst. The tears slowed as this stranger embraced her. She whispered something too soft for him to hear, but its calming effect was undeniable.

"What is your name?" he asked her. Might she be some noblewoman he had not learned of? Perhaps a wealthy trader who was beloved by the commoners? She spared him a moment to answer. A smile was on her face, but it did not reach her eyes.

"I have none. What is yours, paragon?"

He grunted. So it'd be that type of game, would it?

"Dario Bastell, Paragon of Fists," he said. "Champion of Vashlee, and most dutiful servant of the God-Incarnate of Everlorn."

The woman did not seem impressed.

"Titles, roles, and power," she said. "You have it all. A fine use of it, I must say, to badger an old woman on her way to the market."

She kissed the elderly woman on the temple, then together they stood. The older woman whispered a thanks, shot a fearful glance toward Dario, and then began shuffling away. He let her. His attention was now reserved solely for this interloper. They were alone now, the road somehow vacant despite the midday traffic.

"You mock my interest in Thanet's faith," he said. "But it is of paramount importance. We hold no higher quest, and so I ask, what of you? Have you accepted the God-Incarnate's blessing into your heart and repented of your sinful ways prior to his arrival upon Thanet?"

Her shoulders pulled back and she held her head high.

"Your God-Incarnate held my devotion once. He has only himself to blame for its loss."

Dario clenched his fists. Something about her defiance unnerved him, yes, but it also angered him. This tiny woman, whom he could break in an instant, showed him not the slightest fear or respect. She disrespected his God-Incarnate. She made a mockery of his inner turmoil. No others were around to witness it, for which he was thankful. This matter could be resolved quickly and without anyone's notice.

"Then come with me to the God-Incarnate's Haven," he said, and made a great show of offering his hand. "Confess what cost you your faith to our priests, and find balm within the church for your soul."

"Did it soothe your own turmoil, paragon? Did your confessions heal your wounds, or only open them further?"

This woman's insistence at his own doubts unnerved him and angered him in equal measure. He examined her face, his mind racing for a name, but none came to him. Surely he had never met this woman before. He could not imagine forgetting one so striking.

"You speak as one with knowledge, but you are wrong," he said. "I am a paragon of Everlorn. I am our empire's inspiration for this far-flung island. You allude to turmoil and wounds that are not real. They are your imaginings, woman, and nothing more."

Still that calm hint of a smile. The orange powder about her eyes seemed to have deepened somehow, turning red, or perhaps that was a trick of the light.

"Imaginings? No, Dario Bastell, they are not imaginings. I see you. I see the truth in your heart and the cruelty of your mind. You are honor twisted; you are pride fed fat. Who you are, who you truly are, cannot inspire me, for it is a fate I would never desire."

He grinned at her, all his frustration and confusion coming together into one single, ugly expression.

"Tell me, then, stranger whom I have just met, who am I truly?"

The placid expression faded from her face, and it revealed a weight behind it that could crush mountains. Her gaze held him prisoner. Her words were condemnations he was powerless to stop.

"Before me I see a man aflame, and though he smiles, he is burning."

The exact words Arn had spoken to him while imprisoned. Rage lit anew inside Dario's breast, and he reached for this strange woman's throat. He would strangle the answers out of her if he must.

"How?" he asked. "How do you—"

He grabbed air. She was gone. He spun in a circle, searching, but he saw no sign of her. It was as if she had never been.

"Will you plague me with illusions now?" he asked the emptiness of this cursed island. His gruffness was a show put on for no one. Her words wormed through his mind, unnerving him.

Dario jammed his hands into his pockets and walked back to the castle, a plan steadily forming in his head. His brother had previously contacted him through a letter delivered by some street urchin, the words written in the ancient dialect of their homeland of Vashlee. Dario suspected he could send a similar message in kind.

"Fine, then," he said. "I'll do exactly as you said, Sinshei. I'll find out the answers to my questions. I'll take the full measure of my brother's heretical truths. But if I find Lucavi wanting or the empire of Everlorn built on shifting sands..."

He thought of the strange woman and the fierce chill of her gaze. No.

He couldn't finish that thought. Not now.

Perhaps not ever.

if you enjoyed
THE SAPPHIRE ALTAR

look out for

THE BLIGHTED STARS
The Devoured Worlds:
Book One

by

Megan E. O'Keefe

She's a revolutionary. Humanity is running out of options. Habitable planets are being destroyed as quickly as they're found, and Naira Sharp thinks she knows the reason why. The all-powerful Mercator family has been controlling the exploration of the universe for decades, and exploiting any materials they find along the way, under the guise of helping humanity's expansion. But Naira knows the truth, and she plans to bring the whole family down from the inside.

He's the heir to the dynasty. Tarquin Mercator never wanted to run a galaxy-spanning business empire. He just wanted to study geology and read books. But Tarquin's father has tasked him with monitoring the settlement of a new planet, and he doesn't really have a choice in the matter.

Disguised as Tarquin's new bodyguard, Naira plans to destroy the settlement ship before they make land. But neither of them expects to end up stranded on a dead planet. To survive and keep her secret, Naira will have to join forces with the man she's sworn to hate. And together they will uncover a plot that's bigger than both of them.

ONE

Tarquin

The Amaranth

Tarquin Mercator stood on the command bridge of the finest spaceship his father had ever built and hoped he wasn't about to make a fool of himself. Serious people crewed the console podiums all around him, wrist-deep in holos that managed systems Tarquin was reasonably certain he could *name*, but there ended the extent of his knowledge. The intricate inner workings of a state-of-the-art spaceship were hardly topics covered during his geology studies.

Despite Tarquin's lack of expertise, being Acaelus Mercator's son placed him as second-in-command. Below Acaelus, and above the remarkably more qualified mission captain, a stern woman named Paison.

That captain was looking at him now—expectant, deferential. Thin, golden pathways resembling circuitry glittered on her skin, printed into her current body to aid her as a pilot. Sweat beaded between Tarquin's shoulder blades.

"My liege," Captain Paison said, all practiced obeisance, and while he desperately wished that she was addressing his father, her light grey eyes didn't move from Tarquin. "We are approximately an hour's flight from the prearranged landing site. Would you like to release the orbital survey drone network?"

Tarquin hoped his relief didn't show. Scouting the planet for deposits of relkatite was the one job for which he felt firmly footed.

"Yes, Captain. Do we have visual on the planet?"

"Not yet, my liege." She expanded a vast holographic display from her console, revealing the cloud-draped world below. "The weather is against us, but the drone network should be able to punch through it in the next few hours."

"Hold off on landing until I can confirm our preliminary survey data. We wouldn't want to put the ship down too far from a viable mining site."

Polite chuckles all around. Tarquin forced a smile at their faux camaraderie and pulled up a holo from his own console, review-ing the data the survey drones had retrieved before the mining ships *Amaranth* and *Einkorn* had taken flight for the tedious eight-month voyage to Sixth Cradle.

Not that he'd been awake for that journey. His mind and the minds of the entire crew had been safely stored away in the ship's databases, automated systems in place to print key personnel when they drew within range of low-planet orbit. When food was so expensive, there was no point in feeding people who weren't needed to work during the trip.

Tarquin's father put a hand on his shoulder and gave him a friendly shake. "Excited to see a cradle world?"

"I can't wait," he said honestly. When he'd been a child, Tarquin's mother had taken him to Second Cradle shortly before its collapse. Those memories of that rare, Earthlike world were vague. Tarquin smiled up into eyes a slightly darker shade of hazel than his own.

At nearly 160 years old, Acaelus chose to strike an imposing fig-ure with his prints—tall, solidly built, a shock of pure white hair that hinted at his advanced age. It was difficult to look into that face and see anything but the father he'd known as a child—stern but kind. A man who'd fought to have Tarquin's mind mapped as early as possible so that he could be printed into a body that better suited him after the one he'd been born into hadn't quite fit.

Hard to see through that, to the man whose iron will and vast fortune leashed thousands to his command.

"My liege," Captain Paison said, a wary edge to her voice, "I apologize, but it appears there was an error in the system. The survey drones have been released already, or perhaps were never loaded into place."

"What?" Tarquin accessed those systems via his own console. Sure enough, the drone bays were empty. "How could that have happened?"

"I—I can't say, my liege," Paison said.

The fear in her voice soured Tarquin's stomach. Before he could assure her that it wasn't her fault, Acaelus took over.

"This is unacceptable," his father said. The crew turned as one to duck their heads to him. Acaelus's scowl cut through them all, and he pointed to an engineer. "You. Go, scour the ship for the drones and load them properly. I expect completion within the hour, and an accounting of whose failure led to this."

"Yes, my liege." The engineer tucked into a deep bow and then turned on their heel, whole body taut with nervous energy. Tarquin suspected that as soon as they were on the other side of the door, they'd break into a sprint.

"It was just a mistake," Tarquin said.

"Mercator employees do not make mistakes of this magnitude," Acaelus said, loud enough for everyone to hear. "Whoever is responsible will lose their cuffs, and if I catch anyone covering for the responsible party, they will lose theirs, too."

"That's unnecessary," Tarquin said, and immediately regretted it as his father turned his icy stare upon him. Acaelus clutched his shoulder, this time without the friendly intent, fingers digging into Tarquin's muscle.

"Leave the running of Mercator to me, my boy," he said, softly enough not to be overheard but with the same firm inflection.

Tarquin nodded, ashamed to be cowed so quickly but unable to help it. His father was a colossus, an institution unto himself, a force of nature. Tarquin was just a scholar. The running of the family wasn't his burden to carry. Acaelus released his shoulder and set to barking further orders with the brisk efficiency of long years of rule.

He gripped the edges of his console podium, staring at the bands printed around his wrists in Mercator green. Relkatite green. The cuffs meant you worked for Mercator's interests, and Mercator's alone. And while the work was grueling, it guaranteed regular meals. Medical care. Housing. Your phoenix fees paid, if your print was destroyed. The other ruling corporate families—who collectively called themselves MERIT—had their own colored cuffs. A rainbow of fealty.

Working for the families of MERIT kept people safe, in all the ways that mattered. While his father could be brusque, and at times even cruel, Acaelus did these things only out of a desire to ensure that safety.

The cuffs around Tarquin's wrists came with more than the promise of safety. Mercator's crest flowed up from those bands to wrap over the backs of his hands and twist between his fingers. The family gloves marked him as a blooded Mercator. Not a mere employee, but in the direct line of succession. Someone to be obeyed. Feared. His knuckles paled.

"Straighten up," Acaelus said.

Tarquin peeled his hands away from the console and regained his composure, slipping the aristocratic mask of indifference back on, then set to work reviewing the data the ship had collected since entering Sixth Cradle's orbit.

Alarms blared on the bridge. Tarquin jerked his head up, startled by the flashing red lights and the sharp squeal of a siren. On the largest display, the one that'd previously shown a dreamy landscape of fluffy clouds under the brush of golden morning light, the words TARGET LOCKED glared in crimson text.

That wasn't possible. There wasn't supposed to be anyone here except the *Amaranth* and its twin, the *Einkorn*. Of the five ruling corporate families, none but Mercator could even build ships capable of beating them here.

"Evade and report," Acaelus ordered.

Captain Paison flung her arms out, tossing holo screens to the copilots flanking her, and the peaceful clouds were replaced with shield reports, weapons systems, and evasion programs. There was no enemy ship that he could see. A firestorm of activity kicked off, and while Tarquin knew, logically, that they'd rolled, the ship suppressed any sensation of motion.

"It's the *Einkorn*, my liege." The captain's voice was strained from her effort.

"Who's awake over there?" Acaelus demanded.

"No one should be, my liege," the *Amaranth*'s medical officer said. Their freckled face was pale.

"Someone over there doesn't like us," the woman to Paison's right said between gritted teeth. "Conservators?"

"It's not their MO," said a broad-chested man in the grey uniform of the Human Collective Army. "But it's possible. Should I check on the security around the warpcore?"

"I iced Ex. Sharp," Acaelus said. "Without her to guide them, the Conservators are nothing but flies to be swatted. Captain, continue evasion and hail the *Einkorn*."

Tarquin cast a sideways glance at Ex. Kearns, Acaelus's current bodyguard and constant shadow. The exemplar had the face of a shovel, as broad and intimidating as the rest of him, and he didn't react to the mention of his ex-partner, Ex. Sharp. It had to sting, having the woman he'd worked side by side with turn against them all and start bombing Mercator's ships and warehouses.

The fact that Naira Sharp had been captured and her neural map locked away didn't erase the specter of the threat she posed. Her conspirators, the Conservators, were still out there, and Tarquin found Acaelus's quick dismissal of the possibility of their involvement odd.

The HCA soldier was right. They really should send someone down to check on the warpcore. Overloading the cores was the Conservators' primary method of destruction. Tarquin rallied himself to say as much, but Paison spoke first.

"My liege," she said, "the *Einkorn*'s assault may be a malfunction. The *Amaranth*'s controls aren't responding properly. I can't—"

Metal shrieked. The floor quaked. Ex. Kearns surged in front of them and shoved Tarquin dead center in the chest. The world tipped and Tarquin's feet flew out from under him. He struck the ground on his side. Something slammed into him from above, stealing his half-voiced shout.

Tarquin blinked, head buzzing, a painful throb radiating from his hips where a piece of the console podium he'd been working at seconds before had landed. Red and yellow lights strobed, warning of the damage done, but no breach alarms sounded.

Groaning, he shook his head to clear it. The impact had pitched people up against the walls. Seats and bits of console podiums scattered the ground. Across the room, Paison and another woman helped each other back to their feet.

"Son!" Acaelus dropped to his knees beside him. Tarquin was astonished to see a cut mar his father's forehead, dripping blood. "Are you all right?"

Tarquin moved experimentally, and though his side throbbed, his health pathways were already healing the damage and supplying him with painkillers. "Just bruised. What happened?"

"A direct hit." Acaelus took Tarquin's face in his hands, examining him, then looked over his shoulder and shouted, "Kearns!"

Kearns removed the piece of podium from Tarquin's side and helped him to his feet. Tarquin brushed dust off his clothes and tried to get ahold of himself while, all around him, chaos brewed. Kearns limped, his left leg dragging, and Tarquin grimaced. Exemplars were loaded with pathways keyed to combat. For one of them to show pain, the wound had to be bad.

Tarquin nudged a broken chunk of the console podium with the toe of his boot. A piece of the ceiling had come down, crushing the podiums, and it would have crushed Acaelus and Tarquin both if Kearns hadn't intervened, taking the brunt of the hit on his own legs.

A knot formed in his throat as he recognized the damage Kearns had taken on their behalf. Tarquin had never been in anything like real danger before, and he desperately missed his primary exemplar, Caldweller, but that man's neural map was still in storage. Acaelus had deemed Kearns enough to cover both of them until they reached the planet.

None of them could have accounted for this.

"My liege," Kearns said in tones that didn't invite argument, "I suggest we move to a more secure location immediately."

"Agreed," Acaelus said. "Captain, what's the damage?"

"Uhhh..." Paison squinted at one of the few consoles that'd survived the impact. "The *Einkorn*'s rail guns tore through the stabilization column. This ship won't hold together much longer."

Brittle silence followed that announcement, the roughed-up crew exchanging looks or otherwise staring at the damaged bridge like they could wind back time. Tarquin studied his father, trying to read anything in the mask Acaelus wore in crisis, and saw nothing but grim resolve wash over him. Acaelus grabbed Tarquin's arm and turned him around.

"Very well. With me, all of you, we're evacuating this ship."

Tarquin stumbled along beside his father, half in a daze. Kearns assumed smooth control of the situation, sliding into his place at the top of security's chain of command. Merc-Sec and the HCA soldiers organized under Kearns's barked orders, forming a defensive column around the rest. Paison threw a brief, longing glance at her command post before falling in with the others. Tarquin found himself in the center of a crush of people, not entirely certain how he'd gotten there.

How had they gone from looking at fluffy clouds to fleeing for their lives in less than ten minutes?

The HCA soldier next to him, the one who'd said this wasn't the Conservators' MO, caught his eye and gave him a quick, reassuring smile. Tarquin mustered up the ability to smile back and read the man's name badge—DAWD, REGAR. That meager kindness reminded him that there was more at stake than his worries. These people had put their lives in the hands of Mercator.

If they died here, they could be reprinted later, but every death increased one's chance of one's neural map cracking the next time it was printed. Neural maps were never perfect; they degraded over time. Traumatic deaths sped the process exponentially, as even the best-shielded backups were never entirely disentangled from the active map.

As if there were fine threads of connection between all backups and the living mind, and sufficient trauma could reverberate out to them all.

Some people came up screaming, and never stopped. Some got caught in time loops, unsure which moment of their lives they were really living through. Neither state was survivable.

Tarquin summoned the scraps of his courage and stood straighter. He had no business in a crisis, but the employees looked to him for assurance. His terror no doubt added to their anxiety, and that was selfish of him.

Something metal groaned in the walls, taunting his ability to hold it together. Tarquin cast an irritated glance at the complaining ship. If only ships would fall in line as easily as people.

Acaelus pulled up a holo from his forearm, but whatever he saw there was blurred by his privacy filters. The information carved a scowl into his face. He slowed and swiped his ID pathway over the door to a lab, unlocking it.

"Everyone, in here," he said.

They hesitated. Paison said, "My liege, the shuttle isn't far from here."

"I'm aware of the layout of my own ship, Captain. Get in, all of you, and wait. I've just received notice that Ex. Lockhart's print order went through. I won't allow my exemplar to awaken to a dying ship. You will go into this lab, and you will wait for my return."

That wasn't right. The secondary printing round wasn't automated; it needed to be initiated. Tarquin frowned, watching the crew shift uncomfortably. Every one of them knew Acaelus was telling a half-truth at best, but none of them were willing to say it.

There was a slim possibility that whatever was causing the other errors had triggered this, but making all these people wait while Acaelus collected one person was a waste of time.

"My liege." Paison stepped forward, squaring off her shoulders.

"I can't guarantee this ship will last that long, and we require your command keys to open the hangar airlock."

"I am aware, and you are delaying. Get in the lab."

They shuffled inside without another word, though they were all watching Acaelus warily. The terror of offending their boss was greater than the fear of being left behind to die. You could come back from death. You could never re-cuff for Mercator after being fired. The door shut, leaving Tarquin and his father alone with Kearns. Tarquin's head pounded.

"What are you doing?" he demanded in a soft hiss. "Ex. Lockhart can handle herself. We have to get these people out."

Acaelus shoved him down the hallway. "*We* need to get out. I printed Lockhart to help Kearns handle the crew, but you and I are going to cast our maps back and exit this situation, because I don't know what's happened here, and I'm not risking your map."

Tarquin dug his heels in, drawing his father to a halt. "We can't just leave. I'm not going to allow the Conservators to run us off before I have proof the mining process is safe."

"If this was the Conservators, then we'd already be dead. All the nonfamily printing bays just went active, and I *do not know* who is coming out of those bays. We have to leave. Kearns and Lockhart will handle the rest."

Tarquin rubbed his eyes in frustration. "We can't abandon the mission."

"We can, and we are. Come. This is hardly the place for an argument."

Acaelus jerked on his arm. Tarquin stumbled after him, mind reeling. Sixth Cradle was supposed to be his mission. Supposed to be the moment Tarquin stood up for his family and finally squashed all those squalid rumors Ex. Sharp had started when she'd claimed the relkatite mining process was killing worlds.

While a great deal of what his family had to do to ensure their survival was distasteful, Tarquin was absolutely certain the mining process was safe. He'd refined it himself. Mining Sixth Cradle and leaving it green and thriving was meant to be the final nail in the coffin of those accusations. The one thing he could do for his family that was *useful*.

He wouldn't run. Not this time. Not like he had when his mother had died and he'd fled to university to bury himself in his studies, instead of facing the suffering that weighed on his father's and sister's hearts.

"I'm sorry, Dad, I won't—"

"Kearns, carry him," Acaelus said.

Tarquin was thirty-five years old, second in line to the most powerful position in the universe, and Ex. Kearns scooped him up like he was little more than luggage and tossed him over his shoulder without a flash of hesitation, because Acaelus Mercator had demanded it. Kearns's shoulder dug into Tarquin's ribs, pressing a startled grunt out of him. His cheeks burned with indignity.

"I'm not a child," Tarquin snapped, surprised at the edge in his tone. He never raised his voice to his father.

"You are *my* child, and you will do as I say."

Acaelus didn't bother to look at him. Tarquin closed his eyes, letting out a slow sigh of defeat. There was no arguing with his father when he'd made up his mind. He opened his eyes, and temporarily forgot how to breathe. The door to one of the staff printing bays yawned open, and it wasn't people who emerged from that space. Not exactly.

Their faces were close to human, but something had gone off in the printing. A mouth set too far right. An ear sprouting from the side of a neck. An arm that bent the wrong way around. Half a chest cavity missing.

Misprints. Empties. An error in the printer slapping together a hodgepodge of human parts. The *Amaranth* wouldn't have tried putting a neural map into any of those bodies, but whatever had caused the malfunction had also made the ship release the prints instead of disintegrating them into their constituent parts, as was protocol for a misprint.

What was left of those faces twisted, drew into vicious snarls.

"Kearns," Tarquin hissed in a sharp whisper. His voice was alarmed enough that the exemplar turned.

Kearns pulled his sidearm and fired. The earsplitting roar of the shot in such a small space slammed into Tarquin's ears, but his pathways adjusted, keeping him from going temporarily deaf. The misprints shrieked with what throats and lungs they had, and rushed them. Kearns rolled Tarquin off his shoulder and shoved him back.

Tarquin stumbled, but his father caught him and then spun, pushing him ahead. "Run!"

Fear stripped away all his reservations and Tarquin ran, pounding down the hallways for the family's private printing bay, praying that he wouldn't find the same thing there.

Kearns's weapon roared again and again, a staccato rhythm drowning out the screams of the misprints. He looked over his shoulder to find Acaelus right behind him, Kearns farther back, his injured leg slowing him down. Tarquin faced forward and sprinted—the door to the printing bay was *just* ahead.

Kearns's gun fell silent. His father screamed.

Tarquin whirled around. Acaelus was chest-down on the ground, misprints swarming over him, their teeth and nails digging into his skin, ripping free bloody chunks. He took a step toward them, not knowing what he could possibly do, and Acaelus looked up, face set with determination as he flung out a hand.

"Go home!" he ordered.

He met his father's eyes. Acaelus pushed his tongue against the inside of his cheek, making it bulge out in warning. New terror struck Tarquin. High-ranking members of the corporate families often wore small, personal explosive devices on the interior side of a molar to use in case someone intending to crack their neural maps attacked them. Acaelus had one.

Tarquin fled. He burst through the printing bay door and slammed it shut behind him, leaning his back against it, breathing harder than he ever had in his life. The explosion was designed to be small. It whumped against the door, tickling his senses.

A gruesome way to die, but it was swift. Gentler suicide pathways had been tried, but they had a nasty habit of malfunctioning. Pathways remained frustratingly unpredictable at times.

He swallowed. The staff back on Mercator Station would reprint Acaelus the second they received notice that his tracker pathway had been destroyed and his visual feed had cut. His father would be fine. Tarquin forced himself away from the door, shaking.

One of the printing cubicles was lit red to indicate it was in use. He crossed to the map backup station and picked up the crown of electronics, running it between his hands.

Tarquin knew he wasn't what his father had wanted. He lacked the clear-eyed ruthlessness of his elder sister, Leka. He couldn't stand to watch people cower beneath the threat of his ire as Acaelus so often had to do to keep their employees in line. His singular concession to being a Mercator was that his love of geology and subsequent studies had aided the family in their hunt for relkatite.

His father never complained about Tarquin's lack of participation in family politics. Acaelus had given Tarquin everything he'd ever asked for and had only ever asked for one thing in return.

When Naira Sharp had been captured and put to trial, Tarquin had taken the stand to prove her accusations false. As a Mercator, as the foremost expert in his field of study, he had disproved all her allegations that Mercator's mining processes destroyed worlds.

It hadn't stopped the rumors. Hadn't stopped the other families of MERIT from looking askance at Mercator and asking themselves if, maybe, they wouldn't be better off without them.

They needed to mine a cradle world and leave it thriving in their wake to put the rumors to bed once and for all.

Tarquin could still give his father that proof, but he couldn't do it alone. Not with misprints infesting the halls and the potential of a saboteur on the loose. He needed an exemplar.

He set the backup crown down and crossed to the printing bay control console, checking the progress on Lockhart's print. Ninety seconds left. Enough time to compose himself. Enough time, he hoped, to get to the planet after she'd finished printing.

Tarquin had never disobeyed a direct order from his father before, and he hoped he wasn't making a colossal mistake.

orbit

Follow us:

f **/orbitbooksUS**

🐦 **/orbitbooks**

▶ **/orbitbooks**

Join our mailing list
to receive alerts on our
latest releases and deals.

orbitbooks.net

Enter our monthly
giveaway for the chance
to win some epic prizes.

orbitloot.com